I0643196

Debts and Vows

The Deirdre and Elio Duet

Vero Heath

NOTICES

All rights reserved. No part of this book may be copied, used, transmitted, or shared via any means without express authorization from the author, except for small passages and quotations used for review and marketing purposes.

This is a work of fiction. All characters, events, and incidents in this novel are fictitious and not to be construed as reality or fact.

Debts and Vows Copyright © 2024 Peace Weaver Press Inc. President Veronica Doran

Cover design by Sylvia Frost at the Book Brander Boutique

ISBN: 978-1-998452-02-6

 Created with Vellum

A Debt So Ruthless

A Dark Mafia Romance

Content Notes

This is a dark age-gap mafia romance with themes that may disturb some readers. The hero, Elio Titone, is not a good man. Nor is he a particularly reasonable man, especially when it comes to getting what he wants – namely the heroine Deirdre. If you would like content warnings, please visit my website.

Chapter 1

Elio

"What about collateral? There's the house."

"I don't care about your fucking house." I don't care about this deal at all really. O'Malley's in deep with one of the three most powerful Camorra clans in Toronto and he needs money, fast. Clearly, he thinks he can try to play one Italian crime organization against another, begging on his knees to La Cosa Nostra to bail him out when Severu Serpico's soldiers come knocking, which they will.

But the Titones aren't in the business of bailing people out. We're in the business of making money. By any means necessary. And even this sprawling gingerbread house of a Thornhill mansion behind us now isn't enough temptation. Everyone knows the Irish bastard is sinking fast.

A bead of sweat rolls down from O'Malley's temple, dampening his thinning hair. His hair still has the slightest sheen of rust, a memory of red beneath the grey. Another bead of sweat follows the first, and he swallows noticeably, his ruddy throat bobbing.

Despite the August sun beating down, I know the heat isn't why he's sweating.

He's sweating because he's come to me – the last and most ruthless resort.

And I've turned him down.

No more options, O'Malley.

I stand, doing up the button of my suit jacket. The sun drenches my black-clad shoulders and the leather of my gloves, heating my skin beneath the fabric.

Fuck. I can't wait for winter.

"Sell the house if you need money," I say. "You're not that old yet. Sell a kidney. I know someone who'll pay."

O'Malley jumps to his feet, his cushioned monstrosity of a patio chair clattering over backwards to the perfectly landscaped stone.

He starts blabbering, half angry, half desperate. Telling me about how he's good for the money. How this is just a temporary blip. How we could...

I lose track of it all. All the words. All the bullshit flying like spittle from his mouth.

That isn't like me. To lose track of anything. I haven't gotten to where I am today, helping my uncle Vincenzo turn the Titones into one of the richest and most feared crime families in the country, by tuning out the details.

I got here by paying attention. Relentlessly.

That, and a whole lot of blood.

But something else has cut into the conversation. A scattered drift of notes.

Music. Violin?

The notes grow louder. Become almost solid. Like if I squint hard enough, I can see them catching the summer light.

Ignoring O'Malley completely now, I start walking, leaving the stone patio area. My black shoes crush the springy, well-watered blades of grass as I stalk over the lawn.

I scan the broad back of the brick house, searching for the source. I can't say exactly why I need to find it. I just do. The music is somehow both sharp and sweet. It pricks at my skin. Hooks into my ribs and makes my teeth grind.

Near the top of the back wall, I find the second-floor balcony. And on that balcony...

An angel.

I blink stinging sweat from my eyes, dragging my hand through my hair and slicking it back. I don't believe in angels. Never have.

A glossy mane of red hair tumbles down a slender back, the curling ends brushing the slightly flared skirt of a yellow sundress. Two pale arms float in the air, one still, the other sawing back and forth over what has to be a violin I can't see from down here. Every time she moves, the sunlight catches on her hair, setting it ablaze, a glittering inferno. My scars burn under my gloves, the ruined skin on my neck tingling. The scent of smoke from nineteen years ago fills my nose while screams echo in my head, and I'm reminded why I can't fucking stand red hair.

But the music distracts me from the past, from pain. It's deafening, yet somehow not loud enough. So soft it makes my throat go dry. So powerful it slugs me in the temple. Leaves me reeling.

Elio Titone. Fucking *reeling.*

Instincts jerk to life inside me. Instincts that have never once led me astray. Instincts telling me to cut and run. To leave, right fucking now, and never look back.

I ignore them.

I start walking again, circling around towards the left side of the house so that I can see her face.

From below on the lawn like this, I can only just see her profile. Thank fuck that's the only glimpse I get. Because even that one sliver of her face *ruins* me.

It isn't just her physical beauty. The high, round cheekbones or the shadows cast by thick, long lashes – I've seen it all before. I've been with women more alluring, more sensually appealing than her.

It's the expression shaping those features that does me in.

7

An expression of pure, deeply human joy. Something I wasn't entirely sure actually existed until now.

Her soft lips are drawn into a sublime half-smile. Her eyes are closed, her chin balanced delicately on the violin as her long, deft fingers spirit over the strings. Her other arm pushes the bow through the air with surprising force.

"What's that song?" I mutter. I almost don't want to speak. Don't want to make a single noise. But I have to know. Her song is strangling me.

O'Malley comes to a stop beside me, huffing and puffing, having followed me across the lawn. I shoot him a brutal glance, wanting to wring his neck for breathing so fucking loudly.

He pants, bending to place his hands on his knees before straightening.

"It's Irish. *An Eala Bhàn*. Was one of her mother's favourites."

My eyes crawl up the brick to the balcony once more. The girl's smile has contracted. Her brows furrow slightly. Tension creeps into her jaw and neck as her fingers fly faster, grinding the notes out harder.

The joy in the song, in *her*, darkens. Becomes edged with pain. But even in that pain, there's beauty. Beauty I want to peel back, layer by layer. To understand.

To own.

My fingers twitch at my sides, wanting to clench into fists around something. The bow. The violin's neck. Hair the colour of fire I'd rather forget.

My next words come without thought and without hesitation.

"That's it," I say to O'Malley, my eyes glued to his daughter. "The collateral."

"What?" O'Malley asks. "The violin? It was her mother's. It's worth a fair bit now, but it's nothing like-"

"Not the violin."

If not for the music, there would be a long beat of silence before he explodes. His Irish accent, dulled by years in Canada, grows suddenly sharper.

"You want my daughter?" he sputters. "What, that the only way ye can get a woman, ye ugly piece of shit?"

My pistol finds his forehead before he can even blink. His cheeks, so red with rage a moment before, drain of all colour, turning ashen.

"Watch yourself, O'Malley," I murmur softly, already imagining the spray of blood and brains on the manicured lawn. I've killed men for less insult than this.

The music stops.

The softest tremor of sound, the call of, "Dad? Are you down there?" on the summer air has me hunching into myself, slipping the gun under my jacket. My breath shudders out of me. My guts burn with something I haven't let myself feel in years.

Shame.

There's something terrible about being a monster in front of a pure little songbird like that.

It almost makes me hate her.

"That's the deal," I hiss savagely, too quiet to be heard from the balcony above.

O'Malley scowls at me. But I can already see him cracking. Even his earlier rage didn't come from the place of a protective father but was the irritation of a man who didn't want to give up a prized possession.

"Fine," he grunts. "But it won't come to that," he adds quickly. He turns away from me, running a hand down the back of his neck. His next words are so quiet I almost miss them. But that torturous music has stopped, so I catch them despite the whisper.

"God help me."

My eyes dart up to the balcony.

But no one's there.

There's relief in that. No wide eyes watching me. No music

clawing at the scar of something that might have once been called a soul.

"God can't help you now, O'Malley," I say, keeping my voice cold and steady. I mask the disgust I feel for him, so greedy and pathetic he'd offer up his daughter, a lamb to slaughter, to save his own skin. There's repulsion, too, for my own unexpected weakness. For my wanting.

But stronger than any of that – the disgust, the loathing – is the beat of that fucking music in my blood.

And I already know without a shadow of a doubt that even if I slit my own throat and bleed to death right here on the grass...

I'll never get it out.

Chapter 2

Deirdre

New Year's Eve 1.5 years later

"You're so lucky your birthday is on New Year's. Always guaranteed an awesome party," Willow says, grabbing a flute of champagne from the table beside us. "Welcome to your twenties, Dee!"

"It's not midnight yet. Technically my birthday is tomorrow," I remind her. "And I'm not sure I would call my dad's usual New Year's Eve bash an awesome party," I add with a snort, grabbing my own glass of champagne and taking a fizzy sip.

"Bitch, how would you even know what a good party is? You never want to go out with me. I told you I'd take you clubbing for your birthday and you said no!"

I smirk and roll my eyes at her. For my best friend, "bitch" is a term of endearment. Her name may be Willow, but there's nothing willowy about her. The only things sharper than her tongue are her cheekbones and the piercing crystal green of her eyes. Tonight, her jet-black hair is tied in a high ponytail, accentuating her bare neck and the plunging neckline of her curve-hugging black dress. She's actually a year younger than me, only just turned nineteen, but no one would ever guess that I was the older one between us.

She takes another sip of champagne and then tosses her ponytail over her shoulder.

"Fine. I'll grant you that this isn't the coolest New Year's party I've ever been to. It isn't even one of your dad's best, to be honest. Weren't there a lot more people last year?"

She's right. The crowd is thin this year, mostly comprised of my dad's clients and their wives milling around our large living room, picking away at the fancy cheese and pastries the catering company brought. Willow's dad, Paddy Callahan, is among them. He runs an Irish pub, *Briar and Boar*, in downtown Toronto. My dad is his business accountant.

"For a room full of mobsters it's actually kind of boring, to be honest. And they're all at least thirty years older than us. Which wouldn't normally be a problem, except none of them are hot."

My gaze cuts back to Willow, my lips pursing. I ignore her comment about older men – that's pretty much par for the course with my best friend – instead snagging on the other thing. The thing about the mobsters.

She raises her brows questioningly at me over the rim of her champagne flute, and I blow out a sigh. I can't even argue with her because it's true. My dad's an accountant. It's easy to pretend that he runs a normal firm and that his clients are all upstanding citizens. But the reality is that he helps clean money for businesses that funnel funds to the Irish mob.

It's something I don't like to think about and that I've largely been protected from. Willow, on the other hand, doesn't give a shit. She embraces the life Paddy's a part of, taking everything in high-heeled stride. But even so, neither of us have any real standing. We aren't part of the ruling Gowan family. Our dads are at the bottom of the mafia ladder, and so are the other guests here. No one truly important to Toronto's crime scene has come tonight, and that's just fine with me. Willow's right – I don't care about parties, and I care even less about having some of the city's most lethal men in my living room.

"Sorry to disappoint you," I say with a laugh. "You can still hit up the club after this and get laid."

"Oh, you know I will, Dee. But I was more thinking about *you*."

"Me?"

"Yes! How am I supposed to act as a wing woman and get my best friend's sweet little cherry licked, sucked, and popped if there's no one here good-looking enough to qualify?"

Mr. Byrne, who runs *Byrne's Butcher Shop*, nearly chokes on a macaron beside us. Mrs. Byrne pats his back then glares at us while Willow smiles innocently back.

"Jesus, Willow," I mutter before taking a huge swig of my drink. Willow is my ride-or-die, but sometimes being around her requires vast amounts of alcohol.

"What? Someone's gotta do it properly now that Brian turned out to be a giant asshole."

I cringe at his name. The name of my very recently *ex*-boyfriend.

"Ugh, don't remind me. At least he's been gone all Christmas break. He's back in Ottawa with his family."

"Good," Willow says, nodding with satisfaction, eyes crackling. "Because if he keeps up this stalker boy routine, I'm going to have to sic Ronan on his ass."

Ronan *looks* like a dishwasher at the pub, but he's actually there as security, one of Darragh Gowan's enforcers. He's a brooding, tattooed mountain of a man, and I can't help but picture him punching Brian in the face with his meaty hammer of a fist.

I dated Brian for the first half of this school year, from September until right before December exams. He's a law student at the University of Toronto where I study music. I thought he might actually be the one I'd lose my virginity to.

Until he tried to take it before I was ready.

I clench my teeth, my stomach twisting when I remember that night in his apartment. The beer on his breath as he caged me in with his body and told me he'd waited long enough. The hunted, animal fear that made me freeze, that left me unable to move, unable to fight back, unable to say a single fucking word. It was only when he clumsily undid his belt and knocked a glass from his bedside table to the floor, stepping on the broken pieces and stumbling, that I could move again. I bolted from his apartment and completely ghosted him after that.

Only problem is that he's developed an infuriating habit of turning up everywhere I go, begging for forgiveness and promising to be better. I've found him lingering outside classrooms and exam halls and even, once, outside the small music school where I teach violin to kids. In all honesty, I'm kind of surprised he went back home for Christmas at all. I thought he'd stick around just to keep following and pressuring me, and I'm beyond grateful for the distance his absence has created.

Willow must be sensing my mood, because her expression softens.

"Hey, I'm sorry, Dee." She draws me into a perfumed hug. "I'm not trying to be insensitive. What happened with Brian was fucking shit, and if he ever crosses my path, he better fucking watch himself. I just want your first time to be good. To be on your terms." She pulls back, staring at me steadily with serious green eyes. "If you give something away, no one can take it from you."

"Something can always be taken from you," I whisper bitterly. It's a lesson I've burned into my brain for ten years, starting the day my mother died.

Willow looks like she's about to say something else, but as her mouth opens, the resounding shout of "Ten!" makes us both jump.

"Already?" I ask, looking around in shock.

"Guess so! Happy birthday, babe!" Willow clinks her glass against mine and then drains it. I do the same, losing myself in the rosy feeling of champagne's warmth spreading through my body. I need the drink – I know what comes next. It happens every New Year's Eve. A requirement of my father's. I can already see him beckoning to me from across the room, ready for me to dazzle his friends and clients by playing *Auld Lang Syne*.

I love playing, but absolutely hate performing. My father likes it, though. Likes having the talented daughter he can put on display since he no longer has the talented wife. Mom was always the performer, the star. Not me.

Willow already has another drink in her hand when I set down my glass. As the people all around us chant together, "Five, four, three!" I grab my violin and head for the centre of the room.

I'm just setting my bow to the strings when bitterly cold air hits my skin, making goosebumps prickle. Somewhere in the house, a door is open, or a window. Which doesn't make any sense, because this is January in Ontario.

The sound of fireworks split the air, but even though it's New Year's that doesn't make sense, either, because it sounds like it's coming from inside this very room. It's only when screaming breaks out, and the sound repeats and intensifies, that I realize it's gunfire.

Chapter 3

Deirdre

I crouch to the floor, hugging my violin underneath myself, the most precious thing I have. Which is probably stupid. Really, really stupid. I should drop it, protect my head, and crawl to safety. But this violin was my mother's, and I can't let it go. Swearing, my heart slamming, I keep it tucked underneath my body, the bow in my hand like a blade, and army crawl under the nearest table of abandoned food. I tuck the violin and bow against the wall, then spin on my hands and knees, trying to make sense of the scene before me.

Only there's barely a scene left. Almost everybody is gone. Relief pours through me when I see Paddy dragging Willow out of the room towards the front door. She's fighting him, though, and through the ringing in my ears I distantly hear her screaming my name. Suddenly, her eyes find mine, our gazes locking, and she fights her father harder, but he loops his thick arms around her waist and hauls her out into the winter night.

Tears stream down my face, my throat contracting. I'm so happy she's gone, that she'll be safe.

But now I'm alone.

Where's Dad?

New terror grips me. If someone came into this house to attack, who else would they be looking for but the owner of that house?

No! My dad's just an accountant. He's not an enforcer, a soldier, an assassin. He's not a boss someone would have any reason to take out. So why the hell is this happening?

And where the hell did he go?

I'm not the only one with that question. I realize I'm not truly alone. Mr. Byrne is slumped over on the hardwood floor, clutching at a profusely bleeding shoulder, while a pair of black shoes approaches him. One of the black shoes presses against Mr. Byrne's crotch, *hard*.

"Where's O'Malley?"

I can't see the man's face, only hear his voice. My blood turns to ice in my veins. So, they are looking for my father.

And what will they do when they find his daughter instead?

I can't stay here.

My pulse races so hard in my throat that I can't breathe. Lungs on fire, I glance around the room to see if there's any easy way out. So far, I only see one guy with a gun. Whoever else was firing seems to have left the room. Unless it was Mr. Byrne who was the other person shooting. I notice with a swallowed gasp he's trying to reach for a gun that's slid away on the floor.

There's no way he'll reach it like this, with that other guy's foot bearing down on him. From this angle, I can see that man's black pistol shining, perfectly aimed, in the pretty golden lights of our living room.

No, the gun is too far from Mr. Byrne.

But it's close to me. Really fucking close.

"Where's O'Malley?" repeats the voice. "Mr. Serpico wants his money."

"Serpico... Severu Serpico?" Mr. Byrne pants.

Severu Serpico... I may be shielded from most of mob life, but I know who the major players are, and Severu is the leader of one of the most violent Camorra clans in the country.

17

The shoe presses harder, and Mr. Byrne howls, the muscles of his legs jumping beneath his dress pants.

"No questions. Only answers. Where is he?"

"I... I don't know! Fucking hell, man! I don't know!"

"You Irish really don't know much, do you? Did you know O'Malley's been siphoning money away from Mad Darragh's businesses? That he got cornered and then came begging on his knees to us for funds to cover it all up? The time on his loan is up, and unless you can tell me where he is you're going to pay the interest in blood."

"Fuck. Outside! He went outside!"

Oh my God.

My world tilts, everything I thought I knew about my father, my family, my *life*, evaporating in an instant. Dad was stealing? Lying? Betraying his own clients, his own boss?

This can't be real. This has to be a mistake.

But mistake or not, there's a man with a gun hellbent on finding my father. Without another word, he leaves the room, heading for the glass French doors that lead to our backyard and stepping through them.

He's going to kill my dad.

That thought gives me enough strength to get up and get out. To fight through the fear that's frozen my limbs. Without thinking, I grab the gun and sprint across the living room, tripping over broken glass and smooshed food that's scattered all over the floor. Thank God I'm wearing shoes. For a second, I wonder if I should stop and check on Mr. Byrne, but I know I don't have time. I'm not going to watch my father die on my birthday, and if I'm going to do something, it has to be now.

What I'm going to do, I have no idea. I've never even touched a gun in my life, let alone fired one at someone. Panic rises when I see my father running across the snow, the man heading straight for him, gun raised.

"Stop! I'm armed!"

The scream rips from my throat, splitting the air. The man stops and swivels. He sees me. Sees the gun I hold in my shaking hands. And starts to fucking *laugh*.

"Drop it, *bella*," he says, advancing towards me, his own gun raised to meet mine.

My toes are numb, snow seeping through the silk of my flats. Bitter wind buffets my hair. My teeth chatter, but I don't think it's from the cold.

My fingers cramp as my brain screams at me to pull the trigger. *Now. Now! Fucking now!*

But I don't. I can't. I'm too weak, too afraid. I should have tried to shoot him when his back was turned before I saw his eyes. His eyes aren't laughing now. They're lethal. And I realize that everything I've heard about the Italian mafia not killing women and children is dead fucking wrong.

"Stop," I say, but this time it's a whisper. Not a command, but a prayer. I'm begging the man, the universe, maybe even God, to make this all stop. To go back to how things were fifteen minutes ago, when my life still made sense and I knew who I was, who my father was.

But he doesn't stop. And the fear has me again, tightening its jaws around me until I can't speak or think or breathe. I am completely immobile as he bears down on me.

But... I'm *not* immobile. Suddenly, I'm grabbed from behind and spun with such dizzying, catastrophic force that my feet leave the ground, my shoes flying off and my gun dropping down to the snow. Two shots ring out, one chasing the other. Whoever's holding me grunts and grasps me tighter against his broad chest with one arm. For a split second, I wonder if it's my father, somehow come back to save me. But no, this man is huge, far taller than my father. And there's no way Dad could have made it all the way back across the lawn by now.

I don't have time to figure it out, because before I know it, I'm slung over the man's shoulder and carried back into the house. I wriggle and kick, not knowing what else to do, but it's useless. The hand on my hip is like iron, holding me in place. I plant my hands on the man's back and crane my neck to see the other man, the one who was advancing on me, crumpled on the snow, the moonlight shining on a river of blood that streams from his head.

Did I get shot, too? I wonder in a daze, noticing that moisture is soaking the front of my dress, sticky and warm liquid coating my breasts.

The man carries me through the living room, something I only see in bits and pieces through the curtain of my hair hanging down and obscuring my vision. I don't see Mr. Byrne anymore. I wonder where he's ended up. And where my father is now.

The man takes me into the kitchen. It's bright in here, but a moment later we're plunged into darkness as he flicks his hand over the light switch on the wall. He doesn't stop walking until we're swathed in the shadows of the pantry built into the wall. Finally, he puts me down, and I can try to get my bearings on who he is and what the fuck is happening.

I've dimly pieced together that it's probably one of Darragh's men who's saved me. Word must have gotten out about the Camorra being here and the reinforcements have come. But I don't recognize the man before me, and when he tells me not to scream it's not with the kind of accent I'd expect. It's a mostly Ontario accent, but there's something else edging it. Something vaguely Italian.

Oh, God. He's one of them. One of Severu's men. Camorra.

"Don't scream," he says again just as I open my mouth to do it. He obviously senses I have no plans to obey, so he claps a huge, leather-gloved hand over my mouth, guiding me backwards until my spine hits the pantry's shelves.

"There might be more of them."

More of them? More of Severu's men?

So... he's not one of them? He did shoot that other guy, after all.

His eyes are so black they obliterate me. It's a gaze that feels like abyss. My own gaze tracks over his face, my nostrils filled with the scent of leather, blood, and the clean, luxurious spice of cologne. Dark, thick hair is slicked back from his broad forehead. One rebellious piece flops forward, curling, seeming almost boyish in stark contrast to the grim darkness of his face. There's nothing else boyish about him. About the hard, muscled frame of his body, the commanding grip of his hand on my mouth, the drowning black of those eyes. He has to be at least thirty-four or thirty-five, maybe even older, his bulk packed into a perfectly tailored suit.

As I look at him, my eyes snag on an area of skin at his jaw and neck that looks wrong. Mottled and scarred. Like he's been burned.

And with sudden, breathless fear, I know *exactly* who he is. I've heard the stories – the stories of the man with the scars who never takes off his leather gloves.

He's not one of Severu Serpico's men.

He's not Camorra at all, but Cosa Nostra. And he's not a simple henchman, but the underboss of the most ruthless Sicilian family in the country.

Holding me tightly in my own kitchen, blocking me in with his massive body and watching me with an intensity that makes me shiver, is the tyrant of Toronto. A titan of bloodshed and king of crime. Vincenzo Titone's oldest nephew and heir.

Elio Titone.

The man who rules most of Toronto, of Montreal, and everything in between. The man who almost died in a fire as a boy back in Sicily, but who instead walked right through it, defying nature and death, defying God himself even as the good Lord tried to send him straight back down to hell.

His eyes roam downwards, and his nostrils flare when they get to my chest. I follow his gaze, gasping against his glove at the sight of all the slick red marring the white satin. I felt that blood, knew it was there, but the sight of it is still shocking smeared against the fabric of the dress and my pale skin.

Elio doesn't move his hand from my mouth. Instead, he shoves his gun lengthwise between his teeth, biting down on it the way an office worker might hold a mundane object like a pen when his hands are full. With his free hand, he pulls the front of my dress so hard it rips. The satin falls downward, the dress's straps ruined, until my entire front is bared to him.

Humiliation, rage, and fear all churn together, heating my skin and making my stomach clench. His gloved hand skims over my skin, poking, prodding. Pushing on the hand across my mouth, he forces my head back so he can inspect my throat before moving lower. He slides his hand over one breast, then the other, lifting each one and examining my abdomen. When my nipples harden under the hateful, arousing pressure of the leather, I start to squirm. With a grunt, he shoves his thick thigh between my legs, halting my movements. He takes the gun from his mouth and lays it on a shelf above my head.

"Stop moving," he growls.

His movements are quick but methodical, and I soon understand what he's doing.

So, he has the same question I did, then. Wondering if I had somehow been shot. But I know by now I haven't been. His thumb glides across my navel, indicating his inspection might move even lower.

I shake my head rapidly. His gaze narrows. Then he rolls his left shoulder experimentally. His expression tightens.

It's him. He's bleeding. The other gunshot...

I don't see any blood on his front, or a hole in his suit jacket indicating an exit wound, so the bullet must still be in there somewhere. His jaw works, and he looks pissed, but not overwhelmingly so. The guy looks like he just hit a patch of bad traffic on his way to work, like this is an annoying but daily occurrence for him.

Hissing out a sigh, he taps his ear, activating an earbud I hadn't seen before.

"Update, Curse?"

I can't hear whoever replies.

"Alright. Any sign of O'Malley?"

My mouth opens under his glove at the sound of my last name. He has to be talking about my dad.

But Elio completely ignores me, listening intently to whoever's speaking to him. Infuriated at the dismissal, I open my mouth even further, then snap my jaws shut, catching the pad of his middle finger between my teeth. I know the glove must dull the impact, but I bite down hard, and even so the bastard doesn't even flinch. Just raises a dark brow at me as he replies to the other person, telling them to take the bodies and move out.

Bodies? Plural?

Elio lowers his hand, yanking his finger from between my teeth, and I know this must mean there's no one left to hear me scream.

"What bodies? Where's my dad?" I ask, my words breathy and broken. I swallow hard, then cross my arms over my chest.

"Three Camorra goons. Dead now."

"And my father? Where is he?"

"If he's got any brains he's on his way out of the country."

What?

"No. No way. He wouldn't leave me here. And Darragh Gowan's men will be here soon to help. In fact, they'll be here any second. You should go before you get another bullet in your back."

I'm rambling. I know I am. And I'm probably being stupid as hell to threaten Elio fucking Titone with bullets. But he doesn't seem to particularly care about my words. He makes an odd expression. I can't tell if it's a smirk or a grimace. The scarring along his neck and jaw makes one side of his mouth pull lower than the other.

"Mad Darragh won't be sending anyone to help your father now. Or you, for that matter. Word's started getting out about O'Malley's penchant for skimming off the top. Your father may have paid back the money he took from the Irish, but Darragh's not going to forgive a betrayal like that. And judging by Sev's men here tonight, he still owes money to the Camorra." He leans closer, his breath tingling along my ear and neck as he whispers, "He owes money to me, too."

"But... you saved me!" I stammer. Why would he let my father or me live if we really owed so much? Mercy is not something Elio Titone is known for. "You got shot protecting me!"

"I didn't save you," he mutters darkly, so close that his lips brush the shell of my ear. He pulls back so I can see the ruthless darkness of his gaze. I'm horrendously aware of the hard length of his thigh pressing against my pussy and the scant protection my arms provide over my bare, bloodied breasts.

"I'm not your hero, Deirdre O'Malley. I'm your debt collector." He gives me a wolfish, crooked smile, and it's the most terrifying thing I've ever seen. "And tonight I've come to claim what's mine."

Chapter 4

Elio

This is the closest I've ever been to Deirdre O'Malley and I'm hard as a fucking rock. Heat seeps from her cunt, warming my thigh as she pants.

"I'm not yours," she whispers raggedly.

"You are now."

Her mouth tightens, and she shakes her head over and over again, as if she can shake herself right out of this reality. I take hold of her jaw, forcing her head into stillness. Her large eyes grow even wider. There's fear there. But defiance too.

"Let me make your situation perfectly clear," I say. My pulse throbs in my bleeding shoulder and my dick. "Your father owes me a great deal of money. He had until the end of the year, *last* year now, and he hasn't fucking paid. Now, that debt is transferred to you."

She swallows, delicate throat bobbing.

"We can pay it. Sell the house-"

"Not enough," I growl.

"Not enough?" she breathes. "How is that even possible? How much does he owe you?"

"Five point two million. With interest."

Her already pale face grows whiter in the gloom. I almost want her to fight me on this. Want her to command me to go track down her piece of shit of a papà instead of trapping her when she's completely innocent in all of this.

But she doesn't. She's too fucking good. Trying to protect the man who should have protected her. *Sweet little Songbird. I am going to cage you.*

"What are you going to do to me? How... how are you going to make me pay?"

She's trembling, and the defiance in her gaze wanes, replaced with terror. Her knuckles are white as bone as she clutches her own chest, hiding herself.

I let go of her jaw and ease my thigh out from between her legs. She gasps and nearly collapses with the lack of support. When her knees buckle, I grasp her waist, pulling her upright against my body.

"I may be an ugly bastard, but believe it or not, I don't need a whore." I inhale against her hair, smelling sweet vanilla. "Besides, I don't fuck redheads."

She's quiet for a moment before she whispers, "Then what do you want from me?"

What the fuck do I want from her? It's not like I haven't imagined turning her into my whore. Imagined what her pussy tastes like, what she'd feel like wrapped around my cock, my rule about redheads be damned.

I'm not sure I can even put it into words. The ache I have for her. Something far more than physical need.

"There's something inside you I need to understand," I murmur.

Something I saw on that balcony a year and a half ago. Something I've witnessed at every single one of her violin performances since then as I sat watching alone in the very back row. "You're going to play for me until I can figure it out."

"Play for you?"

I release her waist, and she remains standing this time.

"Violin, Songbird."

26

Confusion, then understanding, crystallize in her gaze.

"You want me to... to be your own personal musician?"

"*Live-in* musician," I correct her. "Let's go."

"No. No way! I'll play for you, but I'm not living with you!"

"This is not a fucking negotiation," I grunt. *Merda*, my shoulder is really starting to throb. At least it's finally distracting me from my hard-on.

"I can't. I-"

"You're not staying here," I cut in sharply. "You will live under my roof until your debt is paid in full. That is the deal I struck with your father. If he doesn't pay, I take you. He didn't pay. Now I'm taking you."

"No," she says hoarsely. "He wouldn't-"

"He did," I inform her flatly.

For the first time, I see her large eyes fill with tears. She's actually held it together pretty well so far considering everything that's happened. But cracks are starting to show. A single tear rolls from one eye, and I halt its progress with my thumb. Before it can absorb into the leather, I raise it to my mouth and taste its sweet salt.

She watches me with horrified fascination, her shock at my action stopping her crying.

"Time to go," I tell her. It's not a good idea to stay here after Curse and I have killed three of Sev's men. There's a chance Mad Darragh will send soldiers, too, and when they don't find O'Malley they'll want Deirdre. Just like I do. Those are problems I'm going to have to deal with later. I take my gun from the top shelf, and when Deirdre sees me do it, she purses her lips and takes a shaky breath.

I don't hold the gun to her head. I don't have to. She knows she has no choice but to follow me as I lead her out of the kitchen. If she doesn't walk, I'll just carry her.

I do end up carrying her though, cradling her against my chest this time, when we reach the disaster of the living room.

"Put me down! I'll walk," she says, fighting against my hold.

"Glass," is all I say. She's got no shoes, and the floor of this room is a sharply glittering mess.

"I don't care. I'd rather slice my feet open," she hisses. I feel myself smile at that. My little Irish Songbird has a spine, that's for sure.

I clutch her closer as I stride through the room and out the front door.

"You're mine now, Songbird. And I won't let anyone damage what's mine. Not even you."

Chapter 5

Elio

Outside, I see my younger brother Accursio. Though no one calls him his full name except our aunt and uncle. To everyone else, he's Curse, the Titone family's most feared assassin, deadly as a plague. As I approach with Deirdre, he shoves the corpse of the man I shot along with two others into his black Escalade's trunk and slams it shut before turning towards us.

He knows what we've come for tonight. He knows Deirdre is mine. But when his dark eyes dip, ever so briefly, to her bare upper body in my arms, jealousy tightens in my gut.

It's an absurd feeling. Curse is my most trusted man. My only brother. He'll be my *consigliere* when I fully take over this family. I've literally walked through fire for him, and money can't buy loyalty that an act like that earns. And besides that, he's only ever wanted one girl, even though he hasn't seen her since we were kids in Sicily. But even so, even knowing all this and seeing that there's not a hint of lust in his gaze, I want to slug him just for looking at her.

I walk past him to my own black SUV, unlocking it and opening the door with Deirdre in my arms. My shoulder screams as I place her in the passenger seat. I don't miss the way she shakes, and I shrug out of my suit jacket, holding it out to her. She glares at it as if it's a venomous snake. I remember her comment about how she'd rather slice her feet open than be carried by me, and I know she's too proud, or too angry, to take anything from me now.

But it's too late for that. I already paid for the satin that sags, ruined, around her waist. Paid for the shoes lost somewhere in the snow. Paid for her whole fucking life the past year and a half, through the millions I loaned her father.

I stare down at her while she stares at the jacket, both of us unmoving, locked in a standoff.

I want to say, *fine*, and drop it. Let her be cold. Let her be proud and refuse me, even while she's naked and trembling, even while she has absolutely nothing left in this world without me. Who cares if she takes the jacket? Who cares if she's warm enough?

Apparently, I do.

Dio fucking help me. Even if you've never once helped me before.

I bend down to her, and she recoils, hunching against the leather seat. I wrap my hand around the back of her neck, forcing her forward enough so that I can slide the jacket between her spine and the seat. She's tense under my hand, already straining backwards and away from me. I let go. My sudden lack of restraint on her makes her cry out with surprise, and the back of her head bounces off the cushioned headrest. I do up the jacket's button at the front, my eyes catching on the blood smeared across her perfect pale skin. *My* blood.

Grim satisfaction is sick and hot inside me when I see the way I've marked her. The way I've stained her. Bled for her and bled on her.

I'm about to close the door on her when she reaches for me, her hand slipping between the flaps of my jacket, fingers wrapping around my wrist.

"Wait!" she cries. "My violin!"

"I'll buy you a new one."

I'll buy her a whole symphony's worth of shit if it means I can figure her out. Understand her hold on me.

But she shakes her head and looks so suddenly sad that it makes my jaw tick.

"I can't leave it. It won't take long. I know exactly where it is – under a table in the living room. *Please*," she whispers.

And then I remember, casting my mind back to that stinking hot summer day and to what O'Malley said.

It was her mother's, he told me.

And as if I've been called to battle, I straighten and turn back towards the house.

The violin belonged to her mother.

And now that I remember that fact, I can't leave it behind either. I may be a scarred piece of shit, a monster, a murderer willing to take Deirdre's very freedom away from her.

But I'm not willing to do this.

I'm too sentimental about mamma shit. My one fucking weakness.

But with Deirdre in my car, her gaze like fire on my back, I start to wonder if that's not my only weakness.

"Watch her," I grunt at Curse. I toss him my keys. "Turn on the passenger seat heater."

My brother catches my keys out of the air with a nod as I stride back towards the house to retrieve the violin. With every step, I fight to keep myself here, in the present, in the depths of Canadian winter instead of Sicilian summer. But I can't help but feel as if I'm walking back into my past. Trying to get to my own mamma this time, instead of an instrument belonging to someone else's.

But I don't find my own long-dead mamma or the violin. I find a fourth Camorra soldier creeping through the living room. I'm faster than he is, gun in my hand, and I take him out by the kneecap. He howls and collapses, blood spurting between the fingers of his left hand as he shakily raises the gun in his right.

Not interested in taking another bullet tonight, I shoot the gun right out of his hand. The gun, along with three fingers, fall to the floor.

"Motherfucker... Fucking... Fuck!" he gasps, writhing and trying to clutch at both his hand and knee at the same time.

"Tell me why you're here," I say, crouching beside him.

"Holy shit." His gaze, hazed with pain, focuses on my face. "Elio Titone? What the fuck are you doing here?"

I don't know this soldier, but he knows me. Anyone in this city with half a brain in their head knows who I am.

"Getting what I'm owed. Now answer my question."

I think he's going to lose his shit on me. Maybe even lose consciousness. The metal press of my pistol against his forehead helps bring him back.

"Fuck! Here for O'Malley. Owes Mr. Serpico big time."

"How much?"

He scrunches up his face as I push the gun more firmly against his skin.

"Don't shoot! Eight hundred G's."

I don't even blink. I'm already in this for 5.2 million, what's another eight hundred grand?

"I'm going to let you live so that you can give Sev a message." I press the gun even harder for a second, then pull it away, leaving a white circle on his forehead that quickly turns red. "Tell your boss he'll get his money. Courtesy of La Cosa Nostra."

"You... you'll pay O'Malley's debt?" he wheezes.

"It's not his debt anymore. It's hers."

I don't elaborate further. I stand and leave him bleeding on the floor. As I do so, I spot the violin and bow under a table, just where she said they would be. As I pick the items up, I make a mental note to let Deirdre know that the sum she owes has now reached a cool six million.

Chapter 6

Deirdre

The man Elio called Curse watches me with silent intensity from the driver's seat, a gun in his lap. There's something familiar in his gaze. I know Elio Titone has a younger brother, and I wonder if this is him. They have the same thick black hair, too, but otherwise they don't look much alike. If Curse weren't covered in tattoos, he'd look like a Renaissance sculpture come to life, his face chiselled like an angel's.

A fallen angel, no doubt.

When I can no longer stand staring back at him, I turn my head to the passenger window, looking at the house's front door, waiting for Elio to come through it. Heat from the seat warmer blooms along my quivering legs and my stiff back, echoing the body heat on Elio's jacket when he'd forced it around me. I should have ripped it off the second he was out of my sight. Should have let it fall to the snow, ruined it even more than the bullet and blood already did.

But some strange part of me had liked the way the jacket felt, so warm against my goosebumpy skin. And if I hadn't taken it, I'd be naked from the waist up now, with nothing but my arms to cover me. I pull the jacket a little tighter, shivering again, but this time with odd, hateful pleasure at the kiss of the jacket's silk lining sliding against my skin. Elio's scent surrounds me, the same scent from the pantry – exquisite and probably astronomically expensive cologne mixed with blood, leather, and a slightly deeper masculine musk.

Wrapped in his jacket and his scent, I see him coming through the front door. I should feel dread, but I can't help the flood of relief when I see he's found my mom's violin. He holds it by the neck in one hand, the bow in the other. They look small in the grip of his black leather gloves, almost like toys.

I've already noticed how tinted these windows are from the outside. There's no way he can see me in here, but even so, his gaze pierces right through the glass. It's like he can see right inside me, like even my deepest inner thoughts belong to him now.

As the bright moonlight cascades down his form, I observe him, trying to memorize and understand every detail, to know exactly who I'm dealing with. He's so tall – he's got to be at least 6'4 – and built like a fucking tank. His black dress shirt moulds to the hard planes and curves of his muscles. I drag my gaze up to his face and I'm certain that these two are brothers now. It's not just the hair and the eyes, but also something about the way they both carry themselves, the power that pours off of them in poisonous waves.

Elio comes around to the driver's side and Curse slides out to make room for him, the younger brother trading places with the older. Curse is a big guy too, but when Elio settles himself into the seat, the space in the SUV feels suddenly smaller. Elio takes every-thing – even all the air in here.

He says a few things to Curse, and, heart thundering, I watch him. It's the left side of his neck and jaw that are scarred, so I can't see the marred skin from here. I watch him closely while he tells his younger brother to "make sure Morelli's at the house."

I let my gaze track over his hard jaw, the rugged slashes of his cheekbones, the bold nose. He doesn't have Curse's classic good looks. I remember what he said to me in the shadows, calling himself an ugly bastard, but I don't see it. He's striking. He's not handsome in

34

a refined way, but his features are so brutal and unapologetic that I can't stop staring at his profile.

Curse heads off to his own vehicle – a vehicle with a trunk full of dead men. My stomach lurches as Elio hands me the violin and bow. I try to block everything out and take comfort in the familiar feel of the wood, the strings.

But there's no blocking Elio Titone out. Especially when he turns towards me in the car's dark interior. I tense, remembering the way he touched me in the pantry. His hands on my throat, my breasts.

But he doesn't touch. He doesn't say a single word. He just grasps the seatbelt from beside my head, then tugs it downward, fastening it across my chest and lap.

He just kidnapped me in a chaotic storm of gunfire and blood and now he's worried about making sure I'm strapped in?

He's still silent as he shifts the car out of park and starts driving. Suddenly, the seatbelt thing makes a little more sense, because Elio drives fucking *fast*. Absurdly, I wonder if he has good snow tires on as he explodes out of our driveway and down the road.

Although maybe it's not that absurd, considering what happened to Mom and me. But we weren't the ones driving fast that winter day. Not like this, not like Elio.

I decide he must have snow tires on, considering how well the vehicle is handling on the slick roads.

It's crazy just how mundane that thought is. I wonder if that's a protection mechanism. If by focusing on things like seatbelts and snow tires, I can make it all a little less real.

But it is real.

This is happening.

I'm really being abducted by one of the most brutal men in this city, this country. The life I thought I had is gone, maybe forever.

No. Not forever. Dad will find me.

He wasn't among the bodies in Curse's trunk. Hopefully I've bought him enough time to figure out a way to fix this. I still can't believe what Elio has said – that my own father sold me out. I also can't believe that he would steal from Darragh.

But if he hadn't stolen from Darragh, why didn't any of Darragh's men come to help us?

It's all too much to think about. Instead, I focus on watching the landscape so I know where Elio's taking me. A chill runs through me when I picture where I may end up. A warehouse? A prison cell? Somewhere no one can hear me scream.

But he said live-in musician...

His house.

I don't fool myself. I could still end up in a warehouse, or worse, in a heartbeat if Elio decides he's done with me.

We're heading south, into Toronto proper, leaving my Thornhill neighbourhood behind. I wonder if we're going downtown. I allow myself small glances at Elio, and I see how wet his shirt is with blood at the back.

"Your shoulder," I whisper.

He keeps his eyes on the road, though he's only driving with one leather-gloved hand on the wheel. His left hand rests limply on his thigh.

"Worried about me?"

"I'm worried you'll kill us both when you lose consciousness from blood loss," I snap before I can stop myself. I clamp my mouth shut, internally berating myself. Talking back to a Titone is not smart, and I prepare myself for the blowback.

But it doesn't come. Instead, Elio laughs, a dark, gruff chuckle.

"Too many men want me dead as it is. Don't plan on making things easier for them by doing it myself."

I stare at him in disbelief. He's been shot. He's bleeding badly from the shoulder and obviously isn't using his left hand at all right now. And yet, he seems completely unperturbed. His grip on the steering wheel is relaxed and he commands the road with ease even while driving twice the speed limit.

I lurch in my seat as he takes a sharp corner.

"You're driving too fast!" I cry, unable to hold it in.

"This is slow for me, Songbird. Consider it a courtesy since I know you're not used to this yet. Soon, you will be."

Those last words are ominous, and I try not to think too deeply about what they mean.

"Aren't you at least worried about being pulled over?" I ask.

He laughs again, a disbelieving bark of sound. It's like I just asked him if he ever worries about Santa putting him on the naughty list. Like it's something nonsensical.

I lapse into silence, unsure why I've even engaged him in conversation in the first place. I return my attention to the outside world. We pass Edward Gardens and turn onto Brindle Path, one of the most expensive streets in one of the country's most expensive cities.

I've never been in this neighbourhood, but I know exactly where we are. *Millionaire's Row.* A lush, secluded neighbourhood of sprawling mansions on gigantic lots. It doesn't even feel like we're in Toronto as we pass castle-like houses on entire acreages of their own. My house is large, but it's nothing like these ones.

We continue along the street before turning onto a long and winding driveway. Gigantic trees arch on both sides, casting shadows on the glistening drive that's like an entire road unto itself. Despite the drifts of snow on either side, the driveway is immaculately snow-free and salted, its smooth black surface reflecting moonlight like still water.

We travel so far into the trees that the main road disappears. I worry at my lower lip, feeling like I'm falling further and further into a trap. Like I'm headed for the underworld and I'll never claw my way back out.

A huge gate looms ahead, manned by a tattooed guy in a booth. Elio doesn't stop, doesn't even slow down, and I gasp, thinking we'll crash right into the wrought iron, but we don't. The gate slides sideways, the man in the booth giving a deferential nod as we drive through.

I wrench around in my seat, staring backwards as the gate closes behind us. Black bars slicing through the night and cutting me off from where I came from.

From everything I've ever known.

I turn around to face my new future as Elio stops the car and darkly mutters, "Welcome home."

Chapter 7

Deirdre

ome.

This building isn't like any home I've ever seen. Maybe on TV, or in an architecture magazine, but not in real life. It's gigantic, a massive geometric structure of glass and metal. Rectangles on top of rectangles glittering in the dense woods of the property. Dimly, I wonder how close the nearest neighbouring property is. As if he can read my very thoughts, Elio tells me that the closest house to this one belongs to his Uncle Vincenzo, head of the *famiglia*, where he lives with his wife Carlotta and daughter Valentina.

The fact he guessed what I was thinking makes me feel like I'm not even safe in my own head, and suddenly I can't stand being this close to him. I unbuckle my seatbelt and force the car door open, holding my violin and bow awkwardly in my arms, wishing I had the case. My feet hit the freezing pavement, and I'm reminded of my lack of shoes. But I refuse to be carried this time.

Elio doesn't try it. He just gets out of the car and watches me from in front of the vehicle.

He's not the only one watching me. Two mafia soldiers stand at the house's massive, metal front door.

"Going to run?" Elio asks. He perches his hip against the SUV's hood and leans sideways in a pose of easy languor, like he doesn't really care if I do. But his eyes give him away. They're intense. Ravenous. Showing me the truth of the hunter ready to strike beneath the relaxed exterior.

"No," I tell him. Where would I even run to? Into the woods without shoes where his men would track me down in no time flat? No, I have to be smarter than that. Keep myself safe, alive, until I can figure out another plan. I raise my chin and hold his stare, fighting the urge to dance back and forth from one foot to the other. My feet are so cold it hurts, but I focus on the pain. It gives me something to anchor myself.

Elio looks satisfied with my answer and straightens up. He raises his right arm in an *after you* sort of gesture. I swallow hard and walk towards the door.

The soldiers at the door aren't looking at me now but at Elio. Waiting for the slightest signal from their boss, ready for the subtlest and most silent of instructions. One of the men punches in a code and then opens the door. I kick myself for not taking note of what the numbers are.

I hesitate in the large doorway, panic inside me telling me that maybe I really should run. If I go through that door, there's no coming back, and I know it.

But Elio is at my back, his heat penetrating the jacket and oozing down my spine. I hate the way it contrasts so sharply with the pain of the cold. It turns his body into a vicious sort of comfort, something a terrible part of me wants to sink into. I take a swift step forward through the door just to get away from him.

But of course, he follows. The door closes with a quiet boom, and I jump, nearly dropping my violin. Part of me is still confused about why Elio went back to get it in the first place, and I hug it to my chest, seeking comfort in my new prison.

If this is a prison, it's a beautiful one. The entryway is massive, with natural grey stone cut in big slabs for the floor. To the left, I can see an expansive dining room with a long, live-edge wood table. To the right is a huge open-concept living and kitchen area. Straight ahead is a set of iron steps leading ominously upwards.

Elio grasps my arm and heads for the stairs.

"Where are we going?" I ask, stumbling along with him. His legs are so much longer than mine and our strides are mismatched. I wouldn't be surprised if he normally takes the stairs two at a time.

"Upstairs," he grunts, and I shoot him a sharp look from the side. No fucking shit we're going upstairs. It's what we're going to find upstairs that I want a warning about.

But there's a new tightness in Elio's jaw, his brows pinching. When I fall just a little behind, I step in wetness on the stair below him before he hauls me up to his level, and I see how much he's still bleeding. The injury is finally getting to him. It makes him seem just a little more human.

And makes me feel a twinge of guilt.

I try to beat that down. If he hadn't been at my house to *kidnap me*, he wouldn't have gotten shot.

But if he hadn't been there...

I'd probably be dead right now.

"Why did you take a bullet for me?" I ask quietly. I don't really expect him to answer, but I watch him anyway. His jaw tightens further before he schools his expression into something more neutral.

"I already told you that you're mine now, Songbird. Everything about you. That includes your life."

"Does that mean you'll eventually take it from me?" I stop walking, and Elio stops too, looking down at me from one step above, making him tower even more than he usually does. His hard gaze tracks over me in my entirety – my face and dishevelled hair, his jacket sagging at my shoulders, my bloodstained dress that now is nothing more than a skirt, my bare feet sticky with his blood.

41

"I may be a monster, but I don't kill pretty little songbirds like you."

"You keep calling me that. Why?" I've never even met the man before tonight and yet he wants me as his own personal violinist. He knows I play, but how? I'm good, but I'm not a professional filling concert halls. I have no reputation as a musician in this city. Even if I was a professional, it would take me a lifetime – *more* than a lifetime – to earn back 5.2 million plus interest. It makes no sense.

"You ask a lot of questions," he mutters. He's still holding me by the elbow, and he tugs. I take a wobbly step up to his level. I want to tell him that this is nothing. That I've got about a million more questions swirling inside me, banging on the inside of my skull to be let out. But I sense that now is not the time to ask, and I try to just be grateful that I'm still alive and unharmed.

We're so close like this that my jacket-clad chest brushes his on every ragged inhale.

"You should go to the hospital," I say. There's the fucking guilt again. Always the guilt. Guilt that's been with me since Mom's death, intensifying, getting thick and ugly, as I watch Elio bleed. I shouldn't care about what happens to him, but I do. And I hate myself for it.

He gives a soft, dark laugh. It's a quieter version of his laugh in the car, when I'd mentioned that the police might pull him over for speeding. Apparently, going to the hospital is just as outlandish as dealing with the cops in his world.

Noted.

"No need. Morelli's here. But good try."

As we continue ascending the stairs, I try to figure out what he means.

But I can't. My brain feels like sludge.

"What do you mean?" I ask, giving up on trying to guess as we reach the top of the stairs and start walking down a long hallway with hardwood floors.

"Good job trying to get me out of my own house while you're in it."

I blink. I hadn't even thought of that. That if he went to the hospital and got put under for surgery he wouldn't be with me.

"Yeah, right. You'd probably just drag me there with you," I say with a bitter sigh. My head hurts.

I keep my eyes ahead but hear the slight grin in his reply when he says, "Smart little Songbird. Smart to try to get away from me. Even smarter to know that it will never happen."

"But it will, won't it? If I pay off the debt?"

My words freeze him, and his hold on my arm halts my forward progress. He pulls me around to face him. Any trace of a grin is gone, his gaze cold and narrowed as it swallows mine.

"You got six million lying around?"

"Six?" I cry, stunned. "That's not what you told me earlier!"

"That was before I took over your father's eight hundred-thousand-dollar debt to Severu Serpico. In fact," he adds, his hold tightening on my arm, "I'll probably have to throw the Camorra an extra couple hundred grand for killing three of their men tonight so we don't start a fucking war. So, add that to your mental tally."

I swallow hard, refusing to let tears fill my eyes. I can't even sell the house on my own – it's in my father's name, and at this point I wouldn't be surprised if it's mortgaged like crazy. I could sell everything I own but it wouldn't even be a fraction of the sum. I don't even have any of my stuff with me anyway. I've got nothing but this violin and the ruined clothes on my back. No money, no phone.

Holy shit.

I shift my weight slightly to see if it's there, and it is. In the dress's pocket, a small rectangle bumping my thigh.

Dresses with pockets are freaking miracles.

It's something, at least. A connection to the outside world. But it won't solve the problem of that debt hanging over my head.

A dark thought makes my stomach turn, and I don't even want to say it, but I do anyway.

43

"There are ways for young women like me to make good money fast."

His nostrils flare.

"I told you I don't need a whore."

I bristle. "Who said that you would be the client?"

Somehow his gaze turns blacker and burns brighter at the same time. I give a small, startled cry as he forces me backwards until I'm against the wall. His hard thigh is once again between mine, forcing my legs apart. The smooth leather of his gloves finds my jaw, trapping my face so there's nowhere to look but at him.

"What part of *your life is mine* did you not understand before?" he growls. "Everything you have belongs to me now. The clothes on your back, which I've already paid for. The phone in your pocket, which won't do you any good here, by the way." His voice grows gruffer, more raw. "Every flaming hair on your pretty little head, every breath you dare to breathe, every song in your fucking soul. *All. Fucking. Mine.*"

He nudges his thigh harder against me. Heat explodes along my spine as he bends to whisper against my ear, "And that includes what's between your legs."

A hot, hateful throb goes through me. My nipples prick against his jacket while I shove against his chest with my elbows, trying to protect the violin and bow.

"I thought you said you don't fuck redheads," I hiss. It had seemed such a bizarre thing for him to have mentioned before, but I latch onto it now like it's a lifeboat.

"I don't," he grits out. "Doesn't mean I won't kill any man who tries to touch what's mine."

Another treacherous pulse between my legs makes my insides squeeze. My heart beats so fast it feels like a buzz. My breath is shallow as I wriggle in his hold, but every move I make just puts more friction between my clit and his thigh until I'm aching. Aching and ashamed and *needy*, needing *something* but I don't fucking know what.

More pressure. Maybe even pain.

Some kind of release from all of this.

And I get it – a literal release. Elio lets me go and straightens when a voice calls his name from down the hall. The man who called to him is tall and thin, with grey hair and round spectacles perched on his nose. His sleeves are rolled up, and he's drying his hands on a pristine white towel as if he's just washed them.

"Come on," Elio says. He doesn't grab my arm this time, but places a firm hand against my lower back. "Time for your first performance."

Chapter 8

Elio

"Elio," Morelli says with a nod as Deirdre and I walk into my bedroom.

"Doc," I grunt in reply. Doctor Tommaso Morelli is one of the few people who calls me by my first name instead of *boss* or *Mr. Titone*. He's earned the right. He's been sewing up my scrapes since before I got my first pube. When I was fourteen, he was the one who bandaged my burns, pumped me full of antibiotics, and got me in good enough shape to leave our home in Taormina for Canada. In the end, he came with us. It wasn't safe for any of us in Sicily anymore, and as my Uncle Vincenzo's best friend, he was tainted by his link to our family, so it wasn't safe for him, either.

Didn't work out too badly for him, though. Working for our family he earns twice what the most sought-after plastic surgeons in this city make and all he has to do is be on-call to pull out the occasional bullet or sew up a knife wound now and then. He met his wife here, too, and now they have adult twin daughters, Lucia and Giulia.

"The girl?" he asks in Italian as I settle myself on a stretcher that's been brought up from the main med room downstairs. He and

I both look at her, and I see what he sees. A young woman with a ruined dress soaked in blood.

"She's fine. It's all my blood," I reply, also in Italian. It's Morelli's preferred language of conversation. He was almost forty when he left Taormina and learning English was harder for him than it was for Curse and me.

"You know the drill," he says, snapping on a pair of latex gloves. "Shirt off."

I unbutton the garment with my right hand, trying to keep my left arm still. As I do it, I keep my eyes on Deirdre. She watches me silently from a corner of the room. There's wariness in her eyes, amplified by that little stunt I pulled in the hallway, shoving my thigh between her legs and telling her that her pussy was mine.

Must be the blood loss. I'm losing all sense of sanity, of control. But I hadn't expected her to challenge me like that. To imply she'd start whoring herself out just to be free of me.

Even now, the idea makes my teeth grind and my fists clench.

Morelli frowns at me, noticing I've stopped.

"Do you need me to cut off the shirt with the scissors?"

"No," I reply, forcing my hands to relax and undoing the last few buttons. Mostly using my right hand, I peel the destroyed garment from my body.

I don't miss the sharp inhale from across the room as I toss my shirt aside. I smirk mirthlessly at her and raise my eyebrows, daring her not to look away.

And to her credit, she doesn't. Her eyes track from my neck down the long, angry line of ropy scar tissue that mars my left shoulder and upper arm. Those burns weren't even the worst – the worst are my hands. Even I can't stand looking at my own hands. Not because of what they've done, or who they've killed. But because of who they couldn't save.

Deirdre's eyes are still moving, drifting away from the marks the fire left to newer scars. Knife wounds and bullet holes that Morelli has dutifully sutured during the past twenty years in Canada. Years spent fighting tooth and fucking nail alongside my uncle to turn the Titones into something. A *famiglia* to be feared instead of one that has to flee their homeland in the dead of night.

Morelli works quickly at my back, cleaning blood from my skin, disinfecting, and taking stock of the injury. He knows better than to offer me morphine – I never take it. I don't hide from pain. I breathe it in. Consume it, let it fill me like rage, until it's a part of me. Until it forms yet another scar. It's a penance of sorts. For being alive when she isn't.

I bite back a hiss when Morelli stars digging for the bullet in the back of my shoulder. Deirdre presses her lips into a thin, bloodless line. Her face is pale, but she doesn't turn away.

Morelli's an observant son of a bitch. Always has been. I don't know exactly what it is he sees in my gaze as I stare at Deirdre, but just as he yanks out the bullet and drops it onto a small metal tray, he flicks the back of my head and sternly tells me, "No fucking tonight. You've lost too much blood."

I snort and want to tell him I've never lost too much blood for that, but it's a moot point. I didn't bring Deirdre here to fuck her, no matter what my wayward dick thinks.

I brought her here to play for me.

"I told you it's time for your first performance," I say in English, grimacing when Morelli starts the sutures. "So start playing."

Deirdre jumps, as if she was lost in a daydream and isn't expecting to be spoken to. Morelli joins in with thickly accented English, nodding as he works, "Ah, *sì*. Beautiful music. Good for healing. Soothing."

Deirdre's music has never been soothing. Not to me. It's electrifying. When she plays it makes me feel like my heart has crawled outside my fucking body and I need to understand why.

"Play," I repeat. Shakily, she rolls up the jacket sleeves that are gaping around her arms and raises her violin, placing the bow to the strings. My fingers curl around the edge of the stretcher I'm seated on and I lean forward until the sutures tug which makes Morelli scold me.

This is the first time I've been so close to her when she plays. Thirty-four years old and I'm practically holding my breath like an excited little kid.

That held breath comes out in a sigh when she stiffly grinds out the notes of *Twinkle Twinkle Little Star*.

"Not like that," I chide her.

She narrows her gaze at me, frowning.

"It's the first song that came into my mind."

Morelli finishes up at my back, bandaging the wound with a thick roll that goes under my arm and around my shoulder. I slide off the stretcher. He mutters that I should be wearing a sling, but he knows I won't do it. He cleans up, puts his tools on top of the stretcher, then wheels it out of my room. He reminds me in Italian not to forget what he said about no fucking tonight as he goes.

I start walking and then stop in front of Deirdre, keeping some space between us.

"Play something else."

Her eyes dart around the room. She licks her lips, and that pink tongue draws my eyes like metal to a magnet.

"Play for me."

"I just... I just don't like performing!" she stammers.

"I know for a fact that that's not true," I say.

Confusion wracks her features. She doesn't know that I've attended every single one of her violin performances over the past year and a half. I don't offer her an explanation. Don't bother to explain I've seen her play more than a dozen times by now. That I know she's always stiff and nervous when she first hits the stage, but then she closes her eyes and lets the music take over. When that happens, its like the entire audience disappears, and it's only her and me in the room.

Just like now.

Play that song your mamma loved, I want to tell her. That ballad

I heard on her balcony and haven't experienced again since then. Oh, I've listened to the song – some nights I play it on a goddamn loop until it becomes a part of my heartbeat. But I haven't heard her play it since that summer day. *An Eala Bhàn*. I don't even attempt the Irish pronunciation.

I can already tell I won't get what I'm looking for tonight. Deirdre's face is pale under her smattering of freckles, and she's trembling. I see what this night has done to her, what I've done to her, and I force myself to let things lie for now.

"I'll be right back," I tell her. "Stay here. When I get back, I'll take you to your room." Just before I head for my bedroom's adjoining bathroom, I close the last bit of distance between us and drag my leather-bound fingertips along her jaw until her blue eyes meet mine. "Don't even think of trying to run, Songbird. I've got soldiers stationed all over this house."

Her eyes flash, but she nods against my fingers all the same.

Chapter 9

Deirdre

Elio disappears into a massive adjoining bathroom. He leaves the door open, and I hear the sound of water running. While he's gone, I take quick stock of what's around me. We're in a gigantic bedroom – probably his. Like the rest of the house, the room is done in natural wood and grey stone, with accents of dark iron. The bed is huge – bigger than any King I've ever seen – its frame rectangular and metal. The space is cool and clean, and would almost feel industrial if not for the warm colour of the wood and the weirdly homey touches. Homey touches like book-shelves by the bed, lined with tomes on politics and history and art and...

Music.

There's an entire shelf devoted to books on music, musicians, and theory. Some of them appear to be Italian books on opera and other traditional music, but my stomach drops when I see that most of the music shelf is taken up by books about violin. Violin masters, violin makers, books about how to play violin, from beginner to advanced.

What the actual hell is going on here?

Maybe Elio has some kind of music obsession, specifically violin,

51

and that's why he wants me. But there are far more accomplished players in Toronto he could have chosen, pro violinists he could have simply hired instead of kidnapping an amateur one at the stroke of midnight on her twentieth birthday.

Near the bookshelves the theme of music continues to dominate the space. There's a massive sound system built into the wall, and I quickly realize that there are surround sound speakers along the ceiling and in the corners of the room. There's a record player, too, and a small shelf of CDs. The CDs seem out of place to me. Elio doesn't seem like the type to engage in just slightly out-of-date technology. I feel like he'd either be playing the oldest, most expensive vintage records in existence, or else listening to music digitally. I don't get close enough to look at what albums he, for some reason, has collected in CD format. Instead, I force myself to keep looking around the room to see exactly what I'm dealing with.

There are four doors leading out of this room. One is the door we came through from the hallway. Directly across from that door is the bathroom door, which still stands open. A quick glance tells me that Elio remains out of sight, and I still hear running water. I wonder if he's taken off his gloves to do whatever he's doing, then remind myself to focus.

The other two doors, one on my right and one on my left, are closed. I assume one is a closet. Maybe the room has two closets? That seems like it would be a thing for an excessively wealthy mafia titan.

So, right now, the only sure way out is the door we came through.

But he has men everywhere. He told me that himself. I lean my head out of the room to see a man dressed in all black stationed at the top of the stairs Elio and I came up before.

Shit.

As I straighten up and turn to face the bedroom again, my phone bumps my thigh. He told me it wouldn't be of any use in here – does that mean there's no service?

I keep my eyes on the open bathroom door as I gently place down my violin and bow and slide my phone out of my pocket.

I want to weep with relief when I see that I have full bars. Along with about twenty-five unread text messages from Willow. A quick look at the last few texts confirms that at least some of what Elio told me about my father was true.

12:48am: *what the hell did your dad do???? hes on the outs with fucking everyone!!! no wonder half the usual crowd didn't show up tonight. apparently darragh is tearing toronto apart right now looking for him AND YOU!!!! WHERE THE FUCK ARE YOU???*

12:49am: *my dad is freaking out that we were at your place tonight. if he finds out im texting you i can say goodbye to my phone. if that happens ill find another way to contact you.*

12:51am: *please, please tell me youre ok*

It's 1:38am now, and there's nothing else from her, which makes me think Paddy probably did take her phone. Willow is a fighter, and there's no way she would have stopped texting me in a situation like this.

I take a shaky breath and remind myself there isn't anything she can do for me right now, anyway. It's safer for her if she stays away. Clearly, my family is now completely blacklisted by the leader of the Irish mob. Darragh Gowan doesn't forget and he definitely doesn't forgive. There's a reason he's called Mad Darragh, and it's not because he's some mad lad, life of the party sort of guy.

Dad, where the hell are you?

The idea that he can fix this, that he's even still alive, feels dimmer and dimmer. I want to weep again, but this time it isn't with relief. I swipe viciously at my eyes and then, before I can talk myself out of it, I dial 9-1-1.

I hold the phone so hard against my ear it hurts. When the operator answers, "9-1-1 emergency services, do you require ambulance, police, or fire?" her voice seems way too loud in the space. Cringing, I notice the water has stopped running in the bathroom. I turn my back, hunching forward, trying to be as quiet as possible.

"Police," I whisper, heart in my throat.

A moment later, another voice is on the line, this time a man.

"Toronto police service. What is your location?"

"I... I don't know. Brindle Path. I don't know the address."

"Ma'am, I'm going to need you to speak up, please."

He sounds bored, almost irritated with me for being too quiet.

Damn it! How am I supposed to speak up when the man who abducted me is right in the next room? *Maybe you should just listen fucking harder!*

Despite my desperate frustration, I try to make my whisper less muffled. It comes out in a shaky, shouty hiss.

"I've been abducted. I'm at a house on Brindle Path. Please, I need help!"

"Are you alone? Is anyone with you?"

My insides turn to ice when a huge gloved hand closes over mine. Elio lifts my hand, and the phone, away from my ear and holds it in front of his face, stretching my arm upward. His expression is unreadable, his voice smooth, deep, and undeniably authoritative as he says, "She's not alone. She's under the care of Elio Titone."

There's a pause on the other end. My chest hurts with the force of my heartbeat. It's so loud I almost don't hear the officer's reply.

"Mr. Titone! Honour to speak with you, Sir. There's no problem here. No problem at all. I'll disconnect the call now and I hope you have a pleasant evening."

Elio doesn't say anything else, and my throat constricts when the unmistakable sound of the dial tone punctuates the air. Disbelief mingles with fury. I can't believe I've been abandoned by the very people who are supposed to protect me. The police.

My father.

No. I refuse to believe my father's given up on me. He may have done something incredibly fucking stupid, but he's clever by nature. I have to have faith that he'll get me out of this. That he's still the man I always thought he was. *I have to.*

"I told you this wouldn't do you any good in here," Elio says. For a second, I wonder if he's going to smash my phone. Or maybe me. But instead, he just holds it out to me. I'm shocked by the lack of violence in the gesture but I understand instantly it isn't one of generosity. He's not giving me my phone back as a gift or an olive branch. He's giving it back because he's so fucking powerful it doesn't matter who I contact, who I call, who I beg for help. I'm in his world now. His domain, under his rule.

She's under the care of Elio Titone.

That's what he said. *Care.* What a crock of shit.

I stare at the screen in a daze, afraid to take it and afraid not to. I don't know what he's thinking, what he wants right now, and I'm too exhausted to try to figure it out. When I don't move, Elio leans forward and slides it into my pocket for me. His hand at my hip, so close to my groin, makes adrenaline jolt through me. His thick black hair is wet and messy, and the slick, curling tendrils brush my cheek. I shiver as a single drop of water rolls down to my jaw, then down my neck, making goosebumps rise. His breath is a heated fan over my skin as he draws away. He straightens and stares at me, his expression still unreadable. Bits of hair made rebellious by moisture curl over eyes like smouldering coal. He's basically dressed the same as before just without the ear piece and shirt – wearing black dress pants and shoes and leather gloves. The leather doesn't look wet. *So he does take them off sometimes.*

Once again, just like when he first took off his shirt for the doctor, I'm overwhelmed by the hard, masculine bulk of him. At first glance, the scars are what draw my eye. The slashes and deep marks, so many I can't even count them all. Then there's the vicious, roiling red of healed burns on his shoulder, neck, and jaw. But even with those scars, there's a brutal, unrelenting allure in his form. The flexing of hard muscle dusted with dark hair that makes my stomach tighten involuntarily.

God, I hope the next time I see him he's got a shirt on.

And that I have one on, too.

When his eyes dip downward, I'm reminded of just how exposed

I am. His jacket is huge on me, and its done-up front button sags somewhere in the vicinity of my navel, leaving a plunging view of cleavage. Drawing the sides of the jacket together sharply, I turn and grab my violin and bow.

"You said something about a room?" I ask tersely. I don't particularly want to see what cold, dark corner Elio plans to put me in, but at this point anything is better than being in a room with him.

His gaze shifts to the door near the bed. The one I assumed led into a closet.

"In there."

I start to panic at the thought that I'm going to be imprisoned in a small space. A tiny, lightless closet right beside his bed. I shake my head rapidly, stumbling backwards. Elio ignores me, striding to the door and opening it.

It's not a closet. It's not a prison cell.

It's *beautiful*.

I can't see much from here, looking through the doorway. But what I do see takes my breath away. It's a totally different vibe from the clean, almost minimalist feel of Elio's room. The hardwood floor shines, polished to a rich gleam. The large bed I see from here doesn't have a metal frame, but is one of those wooden four-poster beds I always associate with princesses in movies, piled high with heavy crimson bedding and about a dozen luxurious matching pillows with golden threads at the seams. Floor lamps on either side of the bed cast a softly shimmering glow. Elio stands beside the open door, watching me, waiting for me to go in.

There's no way to avoid it, so I walk past him into the bedroom. The rest of it is just as lovely and sumptuous as the bed. Another door stands open, giving me a view into a glittering bathroom. I turn to look at the rest...

And freeze.

Elio stands in the doorway, and flanking him all along the walls are shelf after shelf of slim books I recognize instantly as sheet music. And not just sheet music. There's a sheet music stand, extra strings, duster cloths, and box upon box upon box of rosin for my bow. It's like somebody searched the internet for *what do violinists need?* and then bought the entire list ten times over. I place down my violin and bow on a small, pretty desk and try to take it all in.

Did Elio do this?

I can't imagine him doing anything even remotely like buying these things. He probably has people to do that stuff for him. But he would have had to have given the command in the first place...

"Like it?"

His question startles me. He's leaning against the door frame, arms crossed.

"Would it even matter if I didn't?" I sigh, because I do like it, and I don't want to like anything he offers me.

Elio doesn't answer, and I raise my chin.

"It doesn't matter if I like it. I don't plan on staying here long."

His dark brows rise in mocking challenge. "Oh?"

I force my voice to remain steady, force myself to fully believe the words as I say, "My dad will find a way to get me out of this. He may owe you money, but there's no way he'd leave me here."

Elio breathes out harshly, his expression darkening.

"Stay here," he mutters as he turns and heads back into the other bedroom. As he goes, my eyes land on the bandaging at his back, covering the wound he got standing between me and the gun that would have killed me. I hold tightly to all the reasons I should hate him so that I don't start sliding into guilt again, into caring that he's hurt.

When he returns, stalking into the room like an agitated wolf, he thrusts paper at me. Confused, I take it, letting my tired eyes run over the words.

No.

It can't be.

It's a contract. A contract dictating the terms of the loan Elio gave my father. And in the space beside the question of collateral, in my father's handwriting, is my own fucking name. *Deirdre Elizabeth*

O'Malley. My father's signature is there, too, at the bottom of the document, as is a savage slash of ink that must be Elio's. Between the signatures, binding the agreement, is a red wax seal.

"Still think he's coming for you?" Elio asks. There's cruelty in his question, a dark taunting that I'm ashamed to admit actually hurts me.

"You're a monster," I whisper.

Elio just takes the paper back from me and rolls it up, aloof and business-like.

"Never said I wasn't. In fact, I'm pretty sure I already told you that I am."

I stare down at my feet through a haze of heated tears. The roll of paper prods beneath my chin until my face is tipped up to Elio's.

"Your father is the sort of bastard I am intimately familiar with," he says quietly, his eyes twin black holes. "I knew he'd never pay me back when I gave him that money. From the very beginning, I didn't consider it a loan, but an *investment*."

"Why?" I croak. I don't understand any of this. A multi-million-dollar investment into *what*?

He doesn't answer me. He just leans even closer, tucking my hair behind my ear and whispering, "Happy birthday, Songbird."

Before I can even try to figure out what sort of game he's playing with me, he's gone. The door closes softly behind him, and I can instantly see there's no way to lock it from this side.

There are locks in this house. Locks and walls and bars.

But none of them are to protect me. They're here to cage me.

And Elio is the only one with the key.

Chapter 10

Elio

There's a lock on Deirdre's door, but I don't use it for two reasons.

One: she won't get far even if she opens the door and tries to escape this house.

And two: locking her in there when there's no other way out of her room is piss-poor fire safety.

Her only exit is through my bedroom. Exactly how I wanted it. I'm in my bedroom now, stalking back and forth, shoulder pinging with pain and the back of my neck prickling with awareness that Deirdre's in the very next room. The girl I've watched for the past year and a half, whose music gets into my bloodstream like a drug, is finally here. I've planned for this evening for months.

And despite all that, it actually hasn't gone much to plan at all. There weren't supposed to be other soldiers there tonight.

Fucking O'Malley. He was supposed to fully pay off his debt to the Camorra with my money, not leave another eight hundred grand hanging like that. For an accountant, he has the worst money management skills I've ever fucking seen. And to top it all off, the original hole he needed to fill – the one that he created by stealing

59

from Darragh's businesses, the reason he's in debt to Sev in the first place – has now been discovered. Mad Darragh's after him. And probably after Deirdre. Not that he'll fucking get her now.

Sev should be easier to deal with than Darragh. Pay O'Malley's debts and then add a little extra for the men I've killed. Should be enough to avoid a war. And if Sev decides he doesn't like that, I can always try to broker a deal with one of the other Camorra clans. Unlike La Cosa Nostra, with a strict hierarchy, the Camorra is much more decentralized, with multiple powerful groups all vying for power. While the Titones are the ruling Cosa Nostra family in Toronto, there are three more or less equal Camorra clans active in Ontario. If I need to, I can pit one or both of the others against Sev.

Darragh's going to be more of a challenge. The man holds grudges like a Sicilian. I won't be able to hand him a cheque to make him go away.

Severu and Darragh. Two very rich and bloodthirsty men. Two complications I don't need right now.

I don't like complications. Typically, I just shoot them in the head. Probably not the best course of action in this case.

But despite it all, despite the problems and the obstacles and the way this night has kind of gone to shit, I have her.

And ultimately, that is all that fucking matters.

My mind is on her again, wondering what she's doing on the other side of that door. Wondering if she's still wearing my jacket. Instantly, I'm overcome with the vicious need to get that jacket back when she's done with it. I don't care that it's crusty with my drying blood. I don't care that there's a hole blown open in the back of it. That jacket touched her bare skin and I am fucking keeping it. I pull out my phone and use voice-to-text to send a message to Rosa, our head housekeeper, instructing her not to throw it out.

Or wash it. Ever again.

I'm distracted from thoughts of dry cleaning – *Cristo santo*, fucking dry cleaning, never thought I'd see the day – by Curse's voice.

"Uncle Vinny's here."

I turn to my brother who is standing in the open doorway of my bedroom. We're alike in some ways. Both over six feet tall – though he's a little leaner – and same dark hair and eyes. But he got all of our mamma Florencia's beauty. Now that he's twenty-eight, the cherubic look his face used to have is gone, replaced with high, hard angles. He's scarred now, too, just like me. But at least he never burned. I made sure of that.

My fingers stretch and curl inside my gloves as I walk to my closet and grab a black dress shirt. Uncle Vinny may be largely a figurehead these days, with most of the real power resting in my hands, but even so, I know he won't tolerate me walking into a family meeting half-dressed. He's probably already going to be up my ass about Sev's men, and I don't need the added headache of him harping on about my lack of dress and decorum.

"Where is he?"

"In your office. Aunt Carlotta and Valentina, too."

"He had to bring the women?" Do Zizi and Valentina, my aunt and cousin, really need to be there while I update Uncle Vinny on how many men we shot tonight?

Curse shrugs.

"You know how Valentina is. Now that she's eighteen she insists on being part of the family business. And Zizi insists on chaperoning even though she hates this shit."

That's an understatement. Zizi tends to wrinkle her nose and ignore the gory details of the family business. Doesn't have any problem spending the millions of dollars that very same business dumps into her bank account, though.

I start doing up the buttons and swear at the shooting pain down my left arm, the weakness in my fingers. I let my arm fall useless to my side, remembering Morelli's comment about the sling. I start doing the buttons up with only my right hand, but that shit's a lot harder one-handed than undoing them.

In an instant, Curse is in the room. For a guy almost as big as me, he doesn't make a sound. Part of what makes him such a good killer. He moves like a ghost.

He doesn't say anything, and neither do I, as he starts deftly doing up the buttons. I watch his fingers as they move quickly and precisely up the length of my shirt. Even when I don't have a bullet wound in my back, his fingers move more easily than mine. The scar tissue on my hands makes some small, repetitive movements, like writing with a pen, a pain in the ass. Luckily, I don't have any problems firing a gun.

As he does up the last button at the top, my eyes catch on the name tattooed across both sets of his knuckles, one letter per finger and thumb. F L O R E N C I A, followed by a bloom of frangipani, Sicily's flower, on his pinkie. He pats my cheek firmly as he finishes and nods, and when he turns from me I wonder what he would have been like, what *we* would have been like, if the beginning of our lives had been different. If we hadn't lost what we'd lost.

If our piece of shit papà had died that night instead of our mamma.

But they're both dead now, and there's nowhere to go but forward. Unless you want the past to rise up and drown you, you have to keep putting one foot in front of the other, over and over again, until you reach the future you want, the future you've created with sweat and gunpowder and blood.

That, or you're in the fucking ground.

I follow Curse out of the room. As I pass the door that leads to Deirdre's quarters, my inhale is a little too hard, my heartbeat just a little too quick. I shake it off and head for the stairs.

Curse and I reach the ground floor, passing several guards who nod and mutter deferential greetings as we head for my office at the back of the house. My office door is open, and I can already see Uncle Vinny, Zizi, and Valentina inside. Zizi and Uncle Vinny are seated in the large leather armchairs in front of my desk, while Valentina wanders the room, inspecting the bookcases lining the walls.

Valentina sees me first, her blonde head turning just as I enter the room.

"Elio!" she says warmly, coming around the desk to greet me. Though she's my cousin, she's more like a younger sister. Her parents raised Curse and me as their own, even going so far as to give us their last name. Or maybe they didn't really give us the name Titone. We just took back Mamma's name from before she married the man who'd be the death of her.

Valentina stops short, letting her father greet me first. Uncle Vinny rises from the chair and clasps his hands to either side of my face. I lean down to kiss him on each cheek before turning and doing the same to Zizi, then Valentina. Even though it's past two in the morning, and I don't know if they've come from a New Year's Eve party or they've just rolled out of bed for this, both Valentina and Aunt Carlotta are coiffed and poised. Their hair is perfectly in place – Valentina's natural dark blonde brightened by bleach, Zizi's dyed a deep burgundy colour. Their faces are streaked with all kinds of powdery stuff in shades of pink and bronze and black.

They both love that shit. I wouldn't be surprised if my cousin and aunt are single-handedly keeping Canada's cosmetics industry alive. I asked Valentina to help prepare Deirdre's quarters – she's the one who chose all the décor – and she filled the bathroom with about eight thousand dollar's worth of lotions and potions. It baffles me that soaps and shampoos could possibly cost that much, but I know they do, because it was all charged to my credit card.

Idly, I wonder if Deirdre is using any of the stuff in the bathroom yet. If she's naked and scrubbing herself or if she'll sit in my blood just a little bit longer.

I'm not sure which idea appeals to me more.

I don't get to dwell on it long. Now that the kissing and greetings are out of the way, my uncle gets right down to business.

"So, what the fuck happened tonight?"

Unlike Morelli, Uncle Vinny speaks English and French fluently, though with a much stronger accent than me. When we first settled in Canada, we lived in Montreal, and my uncle pushed himself to learn the languages as swiftly as possible. Zizi did the same – she watched English and French soap operas all day long for years to learn. I'm pretty sure she still watches them, actually. Just doesn't need the subtitles now.

I walk over to my desk and seat myself at the high-backed leather chair there. Zizi sits back down, as does Uncle Vinny. He's much shorter than Curse and me – we got our height from Papà, and Vincenzo is our mamma's brother.

Was our mamma's brother. Twenty years later and it still sometimes feels wrong to say *was*.

But even so, even a head shorter and sitting down in a chair, Vincenzo Titone fills the space. At fifty-five years old, he's only just started going grey at the temples, the rest of his hair coal-black like Curse's and mine. And like Mamma's. His eyes are sharp, and he's built like a bull, broad-shouldered and bulky, wearing a perfectly tailored Brunello Cucinelli suit.

"Had to go get something of mine," I reply coolly.

Uncle Vinny's forehead wrinkles.

"The money you lent that Irish accountant? What the hell's his name again?"

"Jack O'Malley."

"Well, did you get it?"

Valentina's honey-brown eyes flash to mine. She knows what I know. That I never had any real intention of recouping that money. That I went for something, *someone*, else.

"Nope," I say. My shoulder throbs. As does my head. So, like any reasonable man, I take out a bottle of whiskey from the shelf beside my desk. I almost grab Scottish whiskey, but at the last moment go for Irish in honour of my songbird. I grab two scotch glasses, fill them, and raise a brow at my uncle, but he shakes his head and grunts. Valentina reaches for one of the glasses.

"That's not an appropriate drink for a young lady," Uncle Vinny says, pinning her with a hard stare. Valentina smiles, and I want to say it's sweet, but it's not. Not really.

She grabs the drink and holds it aloft in a cheery sort of salute. "If I'm old enough to get engaged, I'm old enough to drink whiskey."

"Engaged?" I ask. It's the first I'm hearing about this. But as Valentina takes a swig from the glass, I notice the monstrosity of a ring on her finger. I'd have to be blind to miss it – that thing could be seen from outer fucking space. There's a giant pink diamond in the centre surrounded by two circles of smaller pink diamonds, all perched on a rose gold band inlaid with yet more pink diamonds. It looks less like a ring and more like a fucking cupcake to me, but what the hell do I know? Valentina loves pink, and diamonds, so maybe she likes it.

"Now that she's eighteen it's time she does her duty to *la famiglia*," Uncle Vinny says. "Marry well and help grow the Titone empire."

I watch Valentina's face carefully as Uncle Vinny speaks, trying to gauge her reactions. She looks vaguely annoyed, but not overly upset. It's not like she hasn't been groomed for this by her parents since birth, but still, I want to make sure she isn't too unhappy about her husband-to-be.

I still remember the day she was born. I was sixteen and she was a wrinkled little thing who could scream the goddamn house down. I was the third person to hold her, and as my lanky teenage arms tried to awkwardly get her into a comfortable position, she promptly shit on my chest. Staking her claim and telling subtlety to go fuck itself. I smirk at the memory.

Valentina's a force to be reckoned with, but my protective instinct towards her runs deep, and I ask, "Who's the lucky guy?"

"Dario Fabbri," Zizi says, beaming nervously, her eyes flicking back and forth between Valentina and Vinny. She's always been the peace-keeper, trying to smooth over disagreements between her powerful husband and headstrong daughter. "We'll announce it after Valentina's nineteenth birthday in the summer."

Now I know why Valentina only looks mildly annoyed by all of this. Even though she's only eighteen, she could crush a guy like Fabbri under her heel any day of the week. The guy is slimy and skinny with thinning hair and a nasal voice that drives me up the wall every time I hear it on the TV or radio. But his father owns one of the largest real estate development firms in the country, and he's been newly elected a Toronto city councillor, so from a purely business point of view, I can understand the logic of the match.

My head gives a throb of complaint at the idea of having Dario fucking Fabbri yammering on at future family events. I take a sip of my drink, and Valentina follows suit, as if to say, *you and me both*.

"*Basta!* Enough about the engagement. I want to know what happened tonight." Uncle Vinny's eyes are on me. "You didn't get the money, and now we've got three dead Camorra soldiers on our hands."

"I got what I went there for," I say with a shrug that I immediately regret as my sutures pull.

"Got what you went there for? What, a fucking bullet in your back?" Uncle Vinny presses.

"O'Malley's daughter," I say. There's no way to get around it. He'll find out sooner or later.

My uncle's dark eyebrows rise in astonishment.

"You're telling me you're on the verge of starting a war with the Camorra over some freckled fucking *puttana*?" He twists to look at Curse. "This the same girl Darragh wants?"

Curse nods from his place at the door. Red-faced, my uncle turns back to me.

"So, we're going to have Severu Serpico and the Mad fucking Irishman breathing down our necks just because you wanted some tight Irish pussy?"

I stare my uncle down, my grip hard on my drink. Too hard. I owe Uncle Vinny and Zizi everything. They could have left Curse and me to die in Sicily after my father's betrayal if they'd wanted to. But they didn't. They took us with them to Montreal, raised us as their own. Gave us a new chance in a new country, a country that we are slowly but surely bending to our will. I respect my uncle more than most men probably respect their fathers. And for the first time in my life, I want to strangle him.

I don't. Instead, I put down my drink, stand, and keep my tone smooth and deadly as I say, "Deirdre O'Malley is now mine. I will keep her here and do with her as I see fit. This is non-negotiable. If there are consequences, I will deal with them." I slow my speech so that there's no mistaking my next words. "But the one thing I will not do is let *anyone* take her from this house."

My uncle's nostrils flare, and his jaw works. He's pissed – no, *enraged* – by what I've done and the fact I'm standing against him now. But he understands that arguing with me is useless. He knows me too well, knows what kind of will I possess when I get close to what I want, and what I want is Deirdre. Besides, I'm his heir. His underboss. I'm the closest thing he has to an eldest son and Aunt Carlotta can't have any more children. He's handed over more and more power to me over the years and he knows that if I wanted to, I could upend this entire operation, start a war within our own ranks. A war that I would win.

A feminine voice breaks the tense silence that follows my words.

"She's here now?" It's Valentina asking. I nod without looking at her. From the corner of my eye, I see her leave the room. Zizi clicks her tongue anxiously, swivelling in her chair and calling Valentina back to no avail.

I turn to my desk and open one of the drawers.

"Now, if you'll excuse me," I say taking one last sip of my drink before grabbing a pen, "I have a rather large cheque to write to Severu Serpico."

"Fine," my uncle says tightly, rising to go. "You can give it to him at the gala tomorrow night. No doubt he'll show his pretty face. Let's hope he doesn't turn it into a fucking bloodbath."

I forgot about the goddamn gala. There's always something on our social calendar and it usually involves a bunch of rich bastards toasting our latest charitable donation. Events like that are a way to remind this city that the Titones can give as much as they take. I don't even know what tomorrow's gala is celebrating. Zizi and Valentina always plan these things. I just write the cheques.

"It's at the Art Gallery of Ontario. The new wing we paid for," Zizi reminds me. I decide not to comment on the fact that planning a gala for the evening of January 1st is stupid and that everyone's going to be hungover. It was probably Valentina's idea. She hates when parties or holidays end and always wants to drag things out as long as possible. New Year's Eve 2.0.

The goodbye kisses are short and perfunctory. I know these two well enough to be able to tell from their body language that Zizi's anxious as hell and Uncle Vinny is still furious. But ultimately, my uncle trusts me. He knows I take care of shit when it counts.

When they're gone, Curse approaches my desk. I sit down, grab my chequebook, and start scrawling a whole lot of zeroes after the number one.

"Didn't get a chance to tell you before. But I've got a line on O'Malley."

My pen halts. I look up at Curse.

"And?"

"And it looks like he's ditched his credit cards and his phone. But one of my contacts at Pearson Airport reported that he just used cash to buy a last-minute ticket to Bermuda. Flight leaves in," he checks his watch, "eighteen minutes." My brother looks at me. "Do you want me to get him off that plane? I can make a call."

Bermuda. Nice little island. Also a tax haven. I wonder how much money O'Malley has stashed there. Money he's using to save his own skin instead of his fucking daughter's.

I'm furious on Deirdre's behalf, livid that he could leave her here. But even though I'm angry, I'm not surprised. This story has played out in my own life, and it's one I know all too well. The image of my father running from the flames, running from his own fucking family, is so seared into my brain that I can conjure it up perfectly.

He only turned back to look at me once. Turned back to see his eldest son in the flames. He watched me punching through an eight-year-old Curse's burning door, melting my own fucking skin to save his younger son the way he should have.

He fucking *saw me.* Saw me burning and fighting for our family. Heard Mamma screaming and Curse crying. He stood in the carnage his own betrayal had created, whispered, *Dio me pardoni,* then turned and fled.

It wasn't God he should have been begging for forgiveness, but me.

He did beg me, in the end.

Not that it did him any good.

I finish writing the cheque, hating my dead father as I do it. I hate O'Malley, too, for what he's done to Deirdre. And maybe that's hypocritical, because I'm far worse a man than the greedy Irish fool. He sold Deirdre, but I'm the monster who bought her.

"Let him go," I tell Curse. I got what I wanted out of O'Malley. I have no use for any of the money he has left, and honestly? I want him as far from Deirdre as possible.

Normally, I'd just kill him. Both for trying to screw me over and for the crime of what he's done to Deirdre. I have a real fucking thing about fathers failing their families, something my papà learned the hard, bloody way. But even after showing her the contract, I get the impression that Deirdre is still holding out hope her father will come back for her. That she still loves him even though he sure as hell doesn't deserve it. If I kill him, she will grieve him, and I don't want her wasting a single second of attention or emotion on her piece of shit progenitor.

The only man who will matter in her life from this day forward is me. I will be the only one she feels anything for.

Even if that feeling is hate.

Chapter 11

Deirdre

After Elio leaves, I stand silently in the room for a long time. I'm exhausted but too tired even to move or to sit down. I stare at all the music stuff, a shrine to violin, barely seeing it.

He really does want me to play for him.

I don't understand it, but it seems to be true. He brought me here for my music. The only question now is why?

Something he said to me earlier in the night comes back to me. When we were alone in the darkness. *There's something inside of you I need to understand.* I close my eyes, trying to remember what else he's said, but this entire night is like a broken mirror in my head. Some bits and pieces are clear before cracking and leading into darkness. I can't put it all back together right now.

I sway on my feet, then force myself into movement, heading for the bathroom. It's just as gorgeous as the bedroom. It has the same natural grey stone I've seen elsewhere in the house for the floor, along with the biggest bathtub I've ever seen and a giant shower in the corner, enclosed by glass. There are a few switches on the wall, and I learn quickly that one of them is for a floor heater as warmth flows into the soles of my feet.

I catch sight of myself in the mirror and gawk.

I look like a fucking mess. Mascara rings my eyes and is smudged along my freckled cheeks. My hair is a tangled disaster, and my outfit is even worse. The top half of my dress is basically destroyed, hanging down in front of my hips and legs like an apron. My upper body is swimming in Elio's jacket, far too large for me.

For some reason, I don't rip the jacket off my body. Not at first, anyway. I let my fingers drift over the beautiful black fabric, tracing the perfect stitching. Every time I move, the silk lining drags over my nipples creating a resounding twinge between my legs.

What the fuck am I doing?

I cry out with confusion and disgust at myself, tearing the jacket down over my shoulders and letting it fall to the warm stone floor. I kick it as far away from myself as I can.

But now my reflection looks even worse. My front is streaked with dark blood. Elio's blood.

He bled for me.

Then trapped me here.

I go to the bathroom door and close it. Once again, there's no lock, and I purse my lips, weighing my options. I can stay bloody and sweaty and try to tie my dress up like a halter around my neck.

Or I can risk Elio walking in on me in the shower.

I can't get that image out of my mind. The huge man with the leather gloves striding in here like he owns the place because he *does*. His dark eyes tracking over my wet, naked body.

At least there are towels in here. If I have to, I can cover myself with something quickly. And it's not just towels in here. A quick look in the cupboards under the marble countertop tells me the room is better-stocked than a spa. Bottle upon bottle of shampoo, conditioner, moisturizing lotion, perfume. Serums and sunscreens and exfoliating acids. There's makeup, too. Face masks. Even a waxing kit.

One thing I don't see, though, is a razor.

I guess they don't want me to have anything sharp.

I survey the expansive, *expensive* array of bath products, noticing yet more bottles in the shower, and wonder if all of this was already here or if it was brought here just for me. I can't imagine that all the violin stuff was just hanging around this room – who else but me would use it? It had to have been purchased for my arrival.

I hurry over to the bathroom door, opening it and peeking out to make sure Elio hasn't returned to the room, then close it again. I put my phone on the counter, then I hurry out of my dress, leaving it in a wrinkled heap along with my panties and then hustle over to the shower.

At the last second, I change course for the bathtub. The adrenaline of the night is starting to dump out of my system, leaving my legs weak and wobbly. The last thing I need is to fall over in the shower, hit my head, and be naked and unconscious in this house.

I start running the bath, marvelling at just how huge it is. It has jets, too. I grab some body wash and shampoo and conditioner from the shower and get into the tub.

I breathe out slowly as the hot water fills the tub, running over my legs, soothing my shaking muscles. The body wash smells incredible, and I hate it. I try not to breathe in the tempting luxury of the scent as I use the suds to scrub every inch of my body until my skin is pink and sensitive. I do the same to my hair, scraping my scalp with soapy fingernails. As I work the shampoo violently against my scalp, flashes of the night go through my head. Gunfire ripping through my memories. My father running. That man with the gun getting shot in the head and stuffed into Curse's trunk.

I realize I'm gripping my hair so hard it hurts, making fists around the sudsy strands. I let go, then plunge backwards until my head is submerged in the water. And I stay there. It's a game I've played with myself ever since Mom died. Tipping back into the hot water and holding my breath for as long as I possibly can. Letting the ominous rush of the water block out everything else. Waiting, lungs burning, until the last possible moment before resurfacing. The euphoria that spikes through my body when I breathe again is like nothing else I've experienced. I feel that high everywhere – my chest, my head. Even between my legs.

The longest I ever lasted was a minute and forty-two seconds. Eyes scrunched shut, the tap still thundering fresh water into the bath, I start counting.

I only get to thirty-eight when a hand reaches into the bath, touching my shoulder.

The shock of the contact makes me inhale water. I sit up, coughing violently, eyes streaming.

"Holy hell, sorry! Sorry! Jesus, you looked fucking dead in there!"

I slap one hand across my chest and scrape soaking hair away from my face with the other. Right away, just from the voice, I know it's not Elio. I would have known even before hearing the voice. He wouldn't have grasped my shoulder that gently. He would have ripped me right out of the water.

A beautiful young woman is crouching beside the bathtub. She's my age, or maybe a little younger, her loose, dark blonde curls with ombre highlights framing her heart-shaped face. Her eyes are narrowed as they take me in – warm, golden-brown irises framed by very long, spiky black eyelashes. Her shiny pink lips are puckered in a concerned sort of frown.

"Nope," I say raggedly, my throat feeling water-logged. "Not dead."

Her face relaxes a little, a smile tugging at her lips.

"Well, good. Who's gonna use all this shit I bought if you don't?" She gestures at the shampoo and body wash at the side of the tub.

"You bought all this stuff?" As I ask the question, I scoot over to the other side of the bath, turning off the water. Then I swivel back to look at the girl who's appeared in this bathroom like some kind of fairy.

"Yup. Elio asked me to get the room ready for you. He paid for it all, of course. What do you think of this one?" She raised up the body wash that had smelled so heavenly. "It's one of my favourites."

There's something disarming about her. I have no idea who she is, and I'm naked, but she's chatting to me like we've known each other forever.

But I can't afford to be disarmed. Not here. Not now.

"Elio paid for all this? What, is it all getting added onto my debt?" I ask, voice flinty. I cross both my arms over my chest and hunch down into the water.

"Oof. Yeah. Heard about that. What is it, five mil?"

"Make that six," I grind out.

She sighs and puts her elbows on the edge of the tub, placing her delicate chin onto her interlocked fingers.

"We've all got debts," she says softly. "Prices we have to pay just to occupy our rightful place. Some of us are saddled with that shit the second we are born." Her gaze drifts down to a ring on her left hand – an engagement ring. She grimaces as she inspects it closer before flipping her hand to show me. "Ugly, isn't it?"

It's... something. I'm not sure anything with that many diamonds could be called *ugly*, but it's certainly not something I would call tasteful.

"You're engaged?"

"Yup," she says flippantly, rolling her eyes. "To the human equivalent of a skid mark."

Once again, I find myself totally disarmed by her. Beneath the perfectly applied makeup is a very young face. She looks like she could be in high school and she's *engaged*.

Despite the walls I've tried to put up, I can't help but feel a sense of kinship towards her. We're both caught in situations we clearly don't want to be in. For a split second, I honestly wonder if hers is worse. I may be subject to Elio's whims, but at least I'm not engaged to the guy.

I roll my lower lip between my teeth, deciding if I should shut down, shut her out, or if I should give into the instinct that she may be a kind of ally for me here. She clearly has free reign of this house, which means she's got at least some sort of power. Plus, as much as I don't want to admit it, I like her. Her forthright, almost blasé nature reminds me a little bit of Willow. Maybe it's stupid to trust her, but I could really use a friend in here.

"I'm Deirdre. Deirdre O'Malley," I say, giving her a tentative smile. I want to offer her my hand to shake, but its soaking wet, and I'm naked, and it just seems weird.

She clearly doesn't feel the weirdness, though. She grins at me and holds out her own hand to shake. With a wobbly laugh, I take it.

"Oh, trust me, you don't need to tell me your name. I know it. I've been working my ass off the past month getting the room perfect for you under Elio's supervision. What do you think of the bedspread? Beautiful, right?"

"Yes, it is," I say weakly. I am getting whiplash. First, I'm abducted out of my own house and told I'm massively in debt to the mafia, and now I'm finding out the luxury of that room was completely prepared just for me?

"Did you choose all the violin stuff, too?" I ask.

She shakes her head as she lets go of my hand.

"Nope. That was all Elio. He's fucking obsessed. Never seen him spend so much time researching mundane shit like what kind of cloths are best to clean a violin. God, he spent like a week on that! And don't get me started on those little boxes of waxy shit for the bow strings. Picking the brand was like choosing a name for his first-born child."

I literally can't picture a single thing she's telling me. Whether she's telling the truth or not, she clearly knows Elio well. She spends a lot of time with him and doesn't seem afraid of him. And she obviously just walked through his bedroom unaccompanied.

I wonder what her relationship to him is. A funny, ugly sort of knot forms low in my belly.

"Is he... is he your fiancé?"

Her glossy mouth falls open, and then she gives a hoot of laughter.

"Hell, no! Miss me with that incest shit!" She gives a dramatic, exaggerated sort of shiver. "Got the fucking heebie jeebies now."

"Sorry," I stammer. "I'm just trying to figure out what's going on."

"No, no. It's OK. I probably should have introduced myself first before droning on and on about Elio's newfound horniness for all things violin." She tosses her long curls behind her shoulder. "I'm Valentina Titone. Elio's cousin."

Elio's cousin...

Vincenzo Titone's daughter.

I don't know what I was expecting, but I wasn't expecting this. That the Don's only child would be crouching beside my bathtub and talking to me so casually.

So, it looks like I'm gal pals with a mafia princess now.

But despite the shock of it, I'm glad she came in here.

"Hi Valentina. I'd say it's nice to meet you, but..."

"But circumstances prevent it?" she raises a flawlessly groomed brow and smirks.

Yeah, I really do like her. Can't help it. She's cute and clever and in a way is even more trapped than I am. She makes me feel a little less alone.

She rises and turns to look out the bathroom door she left open.

"Mamma and Papà are going to be looking for me. I'd better head back down." Her brows take on a pinched look. "Are you going to be OK in here?"

I can't hold back the bitter snort at that question.

"Tell your cousin to let me go and I might be OK."

The pinched look deepens.

"Hon, if what I hear is true and both Sev and Darragh are looking for you and your father, then there's nowhere safer in this city for you than here."

I seriously doubt that, but I don't get a chance to respond. A sound outside, beyond the bedrooms in the hallway, has distracted her.

"Could you close the door?" I cry after her as she turns and hurries away, high heels clacking on the stone.

I draw my knees up to my chest and wonder if I maybe shouldn't trust Valentina too much after all. I'm *sure* she hears me as she goes.

But she leaves the door open anyway.

Chapter 12

Elio

Valentina nearly collides with me in the hallway on her way out of my bedroom. I'm not sure I like how comfortable she's gotten going into my room whenever she pleases, but it was necessary for her to be able to get Deirdre's room ready when I wasn't around.

"Wondered where you'd gotten to," I mutter. I go to move past her into my bedroom, but she plants her hands on her hips and stares at me.

"What?" I grunt.

"I met Deirdre."

"And?"

"And she's sweet."

"Hmm. Haven't experienced that side of her myself," I reply as I step past her and into my room. I'm sure Deirdre can be sweet to other people. To me she's been a bit of a viper. I've got the teeth marks in my scarred finger to prove it.

"I'm serious, Elio."

Something in Valentina's tone makes me stop and turn. My cousin is smart as hell, but she hides it well when she wants to, behind loud laughter and inane conversation. But she's not laughing now. She suddenly looks about ten years older than she really is, her face sober.

"You're serious about the fact that she's sweet? Fine, I believe you," I snap. But something prickles along the back of my neck. Dread.

"She's not cut out for this. She's not from our world."

Fucking hell, I need another drink.

"Her father's an accountant for the Irish mob. Not exactly a white picket fence family," I remind her.

I can tell by the mulish fucking set to her mouth that she's not done with this conversation.

"You know what I mean! You need to be careful with her! I just went in there and she looked fucking shell-shocked! She's gonna have PTSD or some shit."

"She'll get over it."

Valentina gives a short, brittle laugh.

"Oh, like you and Curse did? You gonna tell me your brother doesn't torture men before he kills them just to keep his demons quiet?" Her voice lowers, but doesn't soften. If anything, it sharpens, like a knife. "You gonna look me in the eye and tell me you don't still have nightmares?"

Valentina's the only woman in my family I'll let talk to me like this, but even she can tell she's gone too far. She snaps her mouth shut at my expression and crosses her arms. I take a moment to compose myself before I explode. When I speak, my voice is icy with control.

"I asked for your help with soap and girl clothes and fucking bedsheets. That's it. I don't need your advice beyond that, and if I want to hear another word out of your mouth, I will fucking ask for it."

She hesitates, but because it's Valentina who couldn't keep her trap shut even if she tried, she has to get in the last word.

"All I'm saying is, if you're not careful, you're going to have agonized over music books and strings and stands for nothing. There will be no one to use them because she'll be dead. You wanted no sharp things in the bathroom? Fine. No razors, no nail clippers, there's not even a pair of goddamn tweezers. But there are other ways to hurt yourself if you really want to do it. Other ways to make it end."

In a second, I've got her, my hands wrapping around her upper arms and squeezing.

"What the fuck are you talking about?" I've never laid a hand on Valentina like this. But what she just said about Deirdre dying has snapped something inside me. Some vital thread of control.

She glares at me for a long moment, as if considering if she should answer me.

"Valentina," I growl, her name a warning. I don't like to be kept waiting. And she knows this.

My cousin lets out a short breath then says, "When I went in there, she was in the bath. Under the water. Not moving."

My feet take steps before my brain can even tell them to. As I slam towards Deirdre's bathroom, my mind runs over and over the calculations of how long she's been alone. How long did I stand there arguing with my cousin? Two minutes? Five? Somewhere in the house I hear my uncle calling for his daughter, and Valentina leaves.

I don't stop until I reach the bathroom and I find Deirdre, not in the bath, but standing with a fluffy white towel wrapped around herself. She jumps and swears, then grabs her towel so it doesn't fall down, hugging it to herself. I stare at her long and hard, as if to make sure she's really still breathing, and she stares right back, eyes wide but defiant.

Fuck. Now that I know she's OK, I realize just how close I am to her in the room. Nothing but a couple of steps and that towel between us. Her hair is soaked, the gingery red turned to the colour of old blood by the water.

I've lost blood. My shoulder and head are aching.

And my dick doesn't care. It's already responding to her, thickening in the crotch of my pants. I had her dress half-torn off while holding her against me earlier, but somehow this is even more erotic. She's stripped of everything. Clothing, makeup, blood. All that's left is her, moisture on her clean skin, running in shimmering little rivers down her chest and legs. I lick my lips, suddenly aware of how fucking thirsty I am. How much I want to put my mouth on her skin and suck.

I don't. I turn from the room, heading back to my bedroom. I go into the closet, rummaging at the back. There's a toolkit back there somewhere, and I find it, taking out a hammer. I should probably use a drill to reduce the damage, but I'm too pissed off for precision. When Deirdre sees me with the hammer in my hand, she stumbles backward to the other end of the bathroom and away from me.

But the hammer's not for her. Turning, I aim a heavy blow at the top hinge of the door. I strike it over and over again until the metal warps and the screws sag out of the wall. Then I crouch, doing the same to the bottom hinge, until the whole door is hanging on by a thread, wobbly as a baby tooth. I toss the hammer down and seize it. I can feel my muscles straining, sutures pulling, but I don't stop until the door has come loose and I toss it, useless, to the floor.

"What are you doing?" Deirdre whispers, fear and anger warring on her face.

"Taking off this door."

"I can see that! But *why* are you doing it?"

I don't answer her. Don't tell her that the thought of her dying in my house makes me feel like there's smoke in my eyes and in my lungs. Like there's fire all around me, like I'm fourteen again and I can't fucking breathe. Instead, I just point to a small dot in the corner of the ceiling. Deirdre's gaze follows my finger and she gasps.

"Is that a camera?"

"There are cameras in every room of this house," I tell her. There are even cameras in my rooms. But the feeds to the cameras in her rooms and mine are the only ones that don't go to the main security hub of the house. They're private feeds that go directly to an app on my phone and laptop. No one else has access to them, not even Curse or Enzo, my head of security.

But she doesn't need to know that. The more eyes she thinks are on her at all times, the less stupid shit she's likely to pull.

"This is insane," she says, shaking her head. "You are insane."

I don't reply to that. I just grab my hammer and head out of the bathroom. She follows me, fury rising in her voice.

"I am absolutely not using that bathroom if there's no door! I'll just use your bathroom."

"Be my guest," I tell her, hefting the hammer when I reach the bathroom in question. "Because I'm taking that door off, too."

I end up taking down three doors and tossing them out into the hallway. Both bathroom doors and the door that separates our bedrooms from each other. Deirdre watches me the entire time, clutching her towel like it's armour. When I'm done, I take the hammer back to my closet. At the last moment, I decide to toss it, along with the other tools, into the safe. Some of those tools could do some real damage to a person, and if Deirdre doesn't hurt herself, she may decide to smash my head in with a hammer in my sleep. Since I'd prefer to keep my brains inside my skull, I lock the safe.

I stand and turn, catching sight of my Songbird in her room, no door between us. This night may not have gone completely to plan, but something about this feels right. Deirdre here now, in a room that may as well be my own without a door for separation. I turn off the light in my room which makes hers glow all the brighter. I see her standing there through the open doorway like an angel illuminated. Watching me in the darkness from her place in the light.

With her eyes on me, I start to undress. I shed my dress shirt and then move to my belt. I don't miss Deirdre's sharp intake of breath and the way her eyes dip to my fingers as they undo the buckle and peel down the zipper. I let my pants fall, fully aware of how my thickened cock has created a bulge in my underwear. Deirdre's grip tightens on her towel, her knuckles bone-white.

But she doesn't look away. She's transfixed. Like she's fucking

82

entranced. I wonder if there's something a little bit sordid inside my Songbird, because she's staring at my crotch like it's hypnotized her, and I don't think it's entirely due to fear.

I may as well finish this. I sleep naked, and I don't plan on changing that just because she's in the other room. I kick off shoes, socks, pants, then lose my underwear, letting my shaft bob free. Colour rises in Deirdre's cheeks, and fuck, I'm about to get all the way hard at this rate, just from her staring. Her gaze on my dick is like a physical touch, a shivering caress of contact. *All that violin playing probably gives her strong fingers. A tight fucking grip.*

That thought makes my dick twitch, a noticeable throb of movement. It breaks whatever spell has held her in place, and she scurries away to the light switch in her own room, turning off the overhead lights before switching off her bedside lamps. I stay where I am, listening for her, catching the sounds of her rustling through the closet that Valentina's stocked for her. When I catch a shadowy glimpse of her again, it looks like she's wearing some sort of pyjama set. Shorts and a silky top with skinny straps, her wet hair in a clump, twisting like a snake down her back.

I expect her to get into bed, but she doesn't. She retreats into the doorless bathroom, keeping the lights off, and stays there. Silence tells me she's not running water or doing much of anything else in there, and I realize she's waiting for me to move away. She's hiding from me with nothing but shadows as her shield.

It's pointless, really. You can't use darkness to hide from a monster. It's like using water to hide from a shark. While bleeding. *Profusely.*

I chuckle, my breath stirring the air. I wonder if she hears it. If the sound makes her tense up. Frightens her or infuriates her.

I move away from the door, grabbing my gun out of the pile of clothes on the floor. I shove it under my pillow, then lay my head down on top so there's no way for her to get to it without waking me. I'm a light sleeper. Have been since fourteen.

I stay awake, listening until I hear the quiet but unmistakable slip of Deirdre's body between bedsheets. She's exactly where I want her. Where I've wanted her since she was eighteen years old and I saw her making music in that sundress on a hot summer's day.

She's finally here. Snug as a bug in the bed I paid for. In the house I own. In the city I rule.

Even though my dick is aching and my shoulder's pounding, there's a satisfied smirk on my lips as I finally close my eyes.

Chapter 13

Deirdre

I wake up slowly, not wanting to become fully conscious. The blankets are so heavy and warm, cocooning me, and I snuggle down. The mattress is different. Newer and better. The pillow is different, too. So plush it's like I'm in a cloud rather than a bed.

It feels amazing.

And it feels wrong.

This isn't my bed.

My eyes fly open, and I sit up like I've been electrocuted. I hold the blankets around myself, looking at the room, remembering everything that happened last night. I swallow, my throat tight and dry, as I stare ahead through the open doorway that leads into Elio's room.

I don't see him, but it almost doesn't matter. The sight of him standing there, a shadowy figure illuminated only by the glow of light spilling from my room, is burned into my brain from last night.

My whole body flushes hot with shame. I stared at him. Like, *really* stared at him. He undressed, and I couldn't take my eyes off of him, off of the thick bulge beneath the smooth black fabric of his underwear. And then, when he took those off...

I groan, burying my head in my hands. What the fuck is

wrong with me? When his cock was out, huge and long, my heart was going absolutely ballistic. Part of it was fear, but a larger part, a part I want to run away from and deny, was wondering how hot and smooth his skin there would feel under my fingertips.

It's a completely different reaction from when I was with Brian. When I was in Brian's bedroom that night, I'd been completely repulsed by him and the situation. It was like my entire body shut down with the fear. Everything turning to ice.

Elio is a thousand times more dangerous than a guy like Brian. There's no denying the huge, masculine threat of him – the power in that muscled, scarred body. So my response to him doesn't make sense. I shouldn't have been staring at his half-hard dick, wondering what it would look like fully erect. I should have been terrified out of my wits. But I wasn't frozen, my blood cold in my veins. I felt like I was on fire.

I'm not as scared of Elio as I should be. And that is fucking dangerous.

I press the heels of my hands against my eyes and rub. My eyes feel dry and grainy, and I'm dying for something to drink.

The sound of a door opening, then a clattering, rolling sound, makes my head jerk up. I relax slightly when I see that it's not Elio, but rather a short, round woman with greying hair tied in a bun at the back of her head. She's pushing a cart on wheels, and I gawk at the feast laid out on the tray on top.

"Breakfast, breakfast!" she says in a thick Italian accent. "Food. *Caffè*."

"Hello," I say tentatively as the woman brings the cart to a stop beside the bed. There are pastries, warm slices of buttered toast, a cup of yogurt drizzled with honey, and what looks like espresso in a small cup. I could definitely go for some caffeine right now, but I've never been much of a coffee drinker.

"Do you have tea, by any chance? Irish breakfast?"

The woman looks at me like I just spat on her mother's grave.

Coffee it is. It was probably stupid for me to ask for something else, anyway. I'm not a guest here. I'm a prisoner.

I pick up the small cup and take a tentative sip, wincing at the bitterly strong flavour that coats my tongue. The woman is watching me and mutters something in Italian that sounds kind of judgmental. She sighs and plants her hands on her hips then says, "Tomorrow, *caffè macchiato*? Some milk?"

I nod and smile weakly. "Maybe with some sugar?"

She snorts and tosses her hands up in a resigned sort of gesture.

"Thank you," I say, not wanting to offend her further when clearly my taste in drinks already has. I can't afford to push away any allies, even if they work for Elio. "I'm Deirdre."

"*Sì, sì*, I know," she says as she unloads the food onto the bedside table.

"What's your name?" I ask her, though she doesn't really seem up for much conversation. I take another swig of the espresso as an expression of goodwill, hoping it will encourage her.

"Rosa. I cook for Mr. Titone. Clean. Keep the house nice." At those last words, she glares at the doorway that leads into the bathroom, noticing the chunks of plaster and flakes of paint left behind by Elio's hammer rampage. She opens the cupboard-like doors on her cart and takes out a small handheld vacuum, marching over to the mess like a soldier. For someone who's got to be at least sixty, she attacks the mess with gusto, grumbling in Italian the entire time.

Now that she's preoccupied and won't notice, I put down the espresso. Thankfully, there's also a glass of ice water, and I chug it. Rosa finishes vacuuming, then returns to her cart for a rag and a spray bottle, heading for the bathroom.

I realize at that moment I desperately have to pee. For some reason I don't think Rosa would take it well if I went in there and interrupted her cleaning process.

Which means crossing my legs and waiting. Or...

Or using his bathroom.

I said I would last night. And he told me to go ahead. Rosa didn't greet anyone on that side when she came through with the tray, so I'm sure that Elio isn't over there.

Now that I'm aware of how full my bladder is, I can't ignore it. I didn't go before bed, and between the champagne last night and the water this morning I'm bursting.

I slide out of bed, padding across the room in my bare feet. I hesitate in the doorway, but a quick glance around tells me I was right. Elio isn't here. I sigh at the lack of door on his bathroom, and swear when I see yet another camera in there, just like the one in mine. I'd hoped that his bathroom wouldn't have one, but no dice. I can't imagine someone like Elio lets other guys sit around watching him on the toilet, so I keep everything crossed that no one's actively watching this feed right now. Even so, I grab a towel from a nearby rack and wrap it around myself as I shimmy my pyjama shorts down with one hand, then perch on the toilet.

I realize too late that the towel is slightly damp. It smells like Elio's fancy cologne, along with another scent, the spice of men's soap. He obviously used this towel after his shower this morning, and now I'm wrapped in it, the same fabric that was rubbed on his naked body covering my bare legs and pussy.

I should fucking pee on it. Use it as toilet paper, I think bitterly. But I don't believe that would send much of a message to Elio considering it would probably be Rosa who has to clean it up.

Holding the towel in place with one hand, I quickly wipe then hop down, flushing the toilet then awkwardly hiking up my shorts under the towel. As I do so, I glare at the camera, not quite brave enough to flip it the bird.

I let the towel fall to the floor and then wash my hands before putting it back on the rack. When I emerge from the bathroom, Rosa is busy stripping my bed.

No, not my bed, I remind myself quickly. *Just the bed I slept in.*

Even though I have nowhere else to go, I feel like I'll be in Rosa's way if I go back in there. Instead, I wander around Elio's room, perusing the books and stopping in front of the music system with its small shelf of CDs. I wondered about those CDs last night. About why he has them. Curiosity getting the best of me, I lean forward to examine the sides of the cases. There are no labels on the sides – they're just generic, plain plastic cases. Frowning, I take one of the cases off the shelf.

And I fucking freeze.

Because I recognize this CD. I recognize the shitty, almost home-made-looking label on the front with its curly font.

Maeve's Music School

August Performance

Shaking, I take all the other CDs off the shelf, more than ten of them, and sit on the floor, shuffling through them like they're cards. They're all recordings of *Maeve's Music School* performances. The school where I teach violin.

Because I'm a teacher, not a student, I don't perform at every recital or concert. As I look at the dates on the labels, I realize that Elio only has recordings of the recitals I played at over the past year and a half.

These CDs were only available to purchase at the concerts themselves. Which means...

He was there.

At every single public music performance I've had over the past year and a half, *he was there*. Listening. Watching me. And I had no fucking idea.

I drop the CDs like they've burned me, confusion turning my stomach upside down. I wondered why he took me, why he wanted me when he could afford to hire any musician in this city. But more and more I'm starting to understand that, for some reason, it has to be me. Elio has been watching me for far longer than I could have ever comprehended.

Why? Is he a stalker?

Don't stalkers do other stuff, though? Like break into your house and move things around? Steal your panties? Shouldn't they do something other than just skulk in the shadows of your public music performances?

I have no idea what any of this means. I grab all the CDs and shove them back on the shelf, hurrying out of the room. Rosa looks like she's just finishing up, piling bedding in a basket attached to the side of the cart. As she passes me with the cart and heads out towards the hallway, I notice Elio's jacket on top of the heap. With a jolt, I wonder what's become of my ripped dress and panties on the bathroom floor. One look in the bathroom tells me they're gone, no doubt in Rosa's basket.

What was that about stalkers stealing panties?

I grit my teeth, humiliation making my skin prickle and heat. *It's fine. She's just collecting the laundry. She might throw away the ruined dress, but I'll get my underwear back.*

At least, that's what I tell myself.

Chapter 14

Elio

When Rosa pushes a cart into my office, I muse out loud, "She's not eating breakfast."

I'm talking about Deirdre. She's back in her bedroom after visiting mine. But all she's done is drink water since Rosa left, and I frown at the image of the untouched food displayed on my laptop.

Rosa answers me in Italian. "Do you want me to bring her something else? She could barely drink the coffee. She wanted tea."

"Tea?" I ask, raising my brows.

Rosa all but shudders. "I know."

I lean back in my chair, eyes still lingering on my laptop. "Add it to the shopping list. Buy it today. Whichever brands are best – buy a few different ones. No, buy them all."

Tea already tastes like hot garbage, and I have to imagine that buying cheaper or less quality brands only makes it worse.

But the beverage question doesn't answer the *why is Deirdre not eating?* question. I pull out my phone, open a search engine, and use voice-to-text to ask in English, "What do Irish girls eat for breakfast?"

The results are varied. Eggs. Beans. Something called blood pudding.

"You know how to make blood pudding?" I ask Rosa.

"*Sanguinaccio dolce?*" she asks. "The sweet one?"

"No, the Irish one." I flip my phone screen around to her. "It looks like a sausage."

She glances at the image on my screen then nods. "It looks like *sanguinaccio*. I can make it."

"Follow an Irish recipe," I tell her. "And stick a birthday candle in it when you bring it to her." I grimace, the scar tissue at the side of my jaw pulling. "Just make sure it gets blown out."

I wonder what my Songbird would wish for.

Probably to be free of me.

Rosa looks at me like I've lost my goddamn mind. And maybe I have. She knows the rules as well as anybody in this house – no candles. Ever. She's probably also not keen on the idea of straying from her Italian roots in the kitchen, and the irritation is reflected in her affronted gaze. I almost want to smirk at her boldness. Men half her age and twice her weight wouldn't dare look at me like that.

I don't know what it is about old Italian ladies. They aren't afraid of anything. You could have horns and the name SATAN stamped on your forehead and all they'd do is glare, flick *salsa di pomodoro* at you like it's holy water, and tell you to get the fuck out of their kitchen.

"Make it happen, Rosa," I say, giving her a clear dismissal. But she doesn't leave. Instead, she reaches into the basket attached to her cart and pulls something out. My jacket. The one Deirdre was wearing last night. The one I instructed Rosa not to throw away or clean.

"Put it on the desk," I say, jerking my chin to a clear spot on the shining dark wood. Rosa does so, carefully flattening the garment so it doesn't wrinkle, despite the fact there's a fucking bullet hole in the back of it. As she turns to go, I spot blood-stained white satin in the basket and rise from my chair. I'm around the desk in an instant, grabbing hold of the basket so she can't roll it away. I ignore Rosa's questioning look as I fish out Deirdre's dress, crushing the delicate fabric in my fist.

I stroll back around to my chair and sit down. Rosa takes the cue to leave and rolls her cart out of the office, closing the door behind her. I finger the fabric of Deirdre's dress, remembering what it looked like on her.

And what it looked like when I ripped it off.

Something falls to the floor, and I lean down to see what it is, ignoring the pain in my shoulder as I do so. It's yet more smooth white fabric. I lay the dress over my lap and pick it up.

Deirdre's panties.

I spread the white panties in my hands, making them take shape in the air before me, and picture Deirdre in them, her legs spread on my desk. Plump pussy lips nudging the silky lining. I wonder if she's shaved or waxed, or if there's dark red hair there, curling and damp, *soaked* –

Fuck me. It's like my cock's taken on a life of its own since I got Deirdre. No control. I'm popping boners like a teenager who's never gotten his dick wet.

I ignore the absurd urge to shove Deirdre's panties into my mouth.

Instead, I press my nose to the crotch of the tiny garment and sniff.

Madre di Dio.

A couple of flicks over the keys on my laptop and I've cut off the security feed to this room and unzipped my pants. With the amount of blood I lost last night, there's no way I should be this hard. But the way that girl smells is like fucking magic.

Or maybe like a curse.

I grip my shaft and pump it in hard, swift strokes, still holding Deirdre's panties with my other hand. The worn leather of my glove is raw-yet-smooth friction gliding up and down. I don't take my time or try to draw the act out. This isn't about sensual pleasure. It's about quick release so that I can get my fucking head on straight.

I throb and lean back against my chair, groaning when the pressure on my shoulder adds pain to the flurry of sensation inside me. The tip of my dick is wet already. I'm close.

I want to shoot my load into Deirdre's panties. Completely soak the slippery fabric, stain it with myself the way I stained her skin with my blood last night. But even more than that, I want to preserve the garment exactly as it is now. I don't want to fuck up that perfect scent.

At the last second, I grab some tissues from my desk, wadding them up against my slick tip. I glance at the laptop where the feed to Deirdre's rooms is still displayed, and my hips jerk involuntarily when I see her. She's in her bathroom in those tiny pyjama shorts and tank top, bent over at the sink, washing her face. The view of her sweetly rounded ass in those shorts is fucking glorious. The arched sway of her back as her tank top rides up is a goddamn revelation. I've never really been a back guy. I like big tits, open mouths, and wet pussy. The finer, subtler points of the female form are generally lost on me.

Not lost on me now. Because all I want to do right now is splay my black gloved hand across Deirdre's lower back. Press my thumb into one of the pretty little indents above her hipbones. Admire the artistry of her spine.

Deirdre stands and dries her face with a towel, then piles her hair on top of her head, twisting it and tying it there. Even the flex of her exposed shoulders as she ties up her hair turns me the fuck on, blood pounding through my groin as I stroke. I can see her reflection in the mirror. Her raised arms make her breasts move, the small but delicious curves bouncing each time she tightens her hairstyle. I remember what it was like to palm her breasts, and for the first time in a long time, the first time I can remember, I wish I hadn't been wearing gloves. The scars on my hands are usually pretty numb to sensation though. I wouldn't have been able to feel her too much anyway.

Unless I'd used my mouth.

That thought has me closer than ever. One last long, deep inhale of Deirdre's scent throws me over the edge. I explode, dick spasming, balls tightening. I completely drench the tissues and part of my glove.

After my breathing has somewhat returned to normal, I strip off my gloves and toss them in the trash along with the tissues, then head for the bathroom that's attached to my office. I wash and dry my hands without looking at them, because I never look at them, then fish out a new pair of leather gloves from a drawer and slide them on. These ones are stiff, not as broken-in as the pair I just tossed. The tough leather reminds me of my own scarred skin. It's taken multiple surgeries just for me to be able to use my hands mostly normally, to ease all the tightness.

When I return to my office, my gaze goes first to the laptop, where I see that Deirdre is now dressed in jeans and a white T-shirt. She's pacing the room like a caged animal. I wonder if she'll try to leave through my room. I've told the soldiers stationed all over this house that she can roam if she wants to, as long as they keep her under constant supervision and don't let her go outside. I haven't explicitly told her she can leave the room, though, and I watch her to see if she's brave enough to do it anyway.

The sound of my phone buzzing distracts me, and I pick it up. It's a text from Valentina.

Don't forget the gala. 8pm. Are you bringing Natalia with you? She's on the guest list.

Natalia Rizzo. She's not my girlfriend or my mistress but she's good for a quick fuck and she loves attending snazzy shit like Valentina's galas. I have a feeling she wants to be more to me than what she currently is, though, and that thought makes me want to put a knife through my eye. I don't particularly like her, nor her me, but we get what we need from each other. Sex. Status.

Maybe I should bring her. The rushed jerk-off session at this very desk proves I need to fuck someone. Get this out of my system. Natalia would enjoy it, too, especially after the gala. Being around all that glitz, glamour, and cold, hard cash always makes her horny.

But the thought of Natalia, with her gorgeous curves and long, bleached-blonde hair does nothing for me now. Not even the slightest hint of desire stirs through me, and I know it's not because I just came. Because when I think of someone else, someone with freckles and blue eyes and red hair, hair that I normally hate, the desire comes roaring back.

I use voice-to-text to reply, *No*. My phone has a resistive screen, so technically I can type on it wearing the gloves, but it's a pain in the ass.

Thank God, my cousin replies. Valentina gets along with Natalia about as well as I get along with her outside of the bedroom. Which is to say, she doesn't. *Are you bringing someone else?*

I'm about to reply, *No*, again when I freeze. A slow smirk unfurls on my face. Because I am bringing someone. Someone who will make the night a lot more bearable, maybe even interesting.

Deirdre, I reply. *Get here a few hours early to help her get ready. Nice dress, shoes. Jewellery. The works. Use my credit card. I want her flawless.*

She looks flawless in her fucking T-shirt and jeans, to be honest, but that's not what I'm telling Valentina. There's a long pause without response, and I know it's because she's absorbing what I just said. Absorbing the fact I want Valentina to dress Deirdre like she's one of us.

I want her to look like a fucking *principessa*.

It's the perfect opportunity. The perfect, public place to put Deirdre up on display and to let everyone in this city know she's mine. I'll give Severu his money, and even if no Irish are there, no doubt word will filter back to Darragh quickly that Deirdre belongs to Elio Titone now.

And Elio Titone keeps what's fucking his.

I'll have her at my side, dripping with diamonds and pearls, just within reach and yet completely untouchable.

Untouchable to everyone but me.

Valentina's reply flashes across my phone. *I'll be there.*

I send one last reply before sliding my phone into my pocket and letting my gaze once again land on Deirdre in her room.

Good.

Chapter 15

Deirdre

Other than Rosa coming to bring me the weirdest possible lunch I could have imagined – some kind of dark-coloured sausage with a single burning candle stuck into it – I've been alone all day. I haven't heard from Willow. Or my father. Despite the fact that he's the one who's put us in this situation, I can't help but worry about him. I wonder where he is. And I wonder if Elio knows.

But I don't get any answers, and the day ticks by into afternoon. Around 4pm, a quick knock sounds at the door that leads from Elio's room into the hallway, and then Valentina breezes in.

At least she knocked, I think with an internal sigh. And honestly, I'm glad she's here. The isolation was killing me.

Her arms are loaded with stuff. She's dragging a suitcase on wheels, along with what looks like a few garment bags slung over her shoulder. She gives me a dazzling smile and strolls through Elio's room into mine, dumping all the garment bags on the bed that Rosa made when she came in to deliver the lunch I didn't eat.

"Hellooo," Valentina says in a sing-song voice as she turns to face me, hands on her hips. She looks drop-dead gorgeous, with perfect contouring, smoky eye-shadow, fake eyelashes, and bright pink lips. Her hair looks like it's been professionally done – freshly blown-out in big, luscious waves. Her outfit seems slightly out of step with her hair and makeup. She's wearing simple black leggings and a plain black T-shirt.

"Hi," I say, confused by the sudden apparition of her. "What's all that?" I ask, jerking my chin at the stuff she's put on the bed.

"Dresses and shoes. I would have brought makeup, but I've already filled your bathroom's drawers with it."

I hear her words and absorb their meaning in a literal sense, but find myself staring at her with a complete lack of understanding. She doesn't seem bothered by my lack of response. She just bends over, lays the suitcase flat, and opens it. Inside are about ten lumps wrapped in paper. As she unwraps them, I see that these are the shoes she was talking about. Each pair looks brand-new and unimaginably expensive.

"I don't know your size, so I aimed for the middle. Most of these are between seven and eight, but I have a couple size six pairs, and even a nine somewhere in here."

"Those... those are for me?" I ask, frowning and staring down at the beautiful shoes she's unwrapping like presents. "Why?" Is this some kind of weird work uniform Elio wants? I usually wear flats when I play. Wearing heels alters your posture, and can change the quality of the performance if you're not actively aware of it.

"For the gala tonight!" Valentina straightens. "Elio didn't tell you?"

I snort at that. The guy hasn't told me anything besides the fact that he basically owns me now.

Valentina rolls her eyes. "Typical. Titone men hate opening their mouths unless they're discussing business." She turns to the bed now, unzipping the three garment bags. "There's a gala at the AGO tonight. We paid for a new wing and tonight's a private opening night. Elio wants you there."

Nerves flutter in my stomach. I squeeze my hands together and press them against my belly.

"Am I the musician playing tonight?" God, I'm completely unprepared for this! Playing for the duration of an entire gala... That's *hours*. I don't have songs picked out or rehearsed, and I don't know if there's a band I need to fit into. The thought of performing at an event of that calibre with less than a day's warning makes me feel like I'm going to throw up. Having consumed nothing but water and two sips of espresso probably isn't helping in that department, either.

But Valentina shakes her head and turns around to face me again.

"God, no!" she says, sounding shocked. She shakes her head again and hastily adds, "No offense. But I booked the band months ago."

"Oh." It comes out more like a relieved sigh than a word. "Then what will I be doing there?" Maybe they need a last-minute server or something.

Valentina taps a long, polished beige fingernail against her chin.

"You'll be there as Elio's... Honestly, I don't know. Date?"

Date.

The word skewers me, and the relief I felt a moment ago vanishes, replaced once again with nausea.

"That's not possible," I sputter.

She shrugs. "I don't know. I asked him if he was bringing anyone and he said you. He wants you all dolled up, too. I brought some dresses to try..." Her words trail off as her eyes widen. "Fuck me, you're pale. I mean, you're already pale, but I didn't know somebody living could get that white. Good thing I've got a shitload of blush and bronzer in the bathroom."

I can feel what she sees – the quick exit of blood from my face.

Valentina's eyes narrow, her thick lashes fluttering heavily.

"What have you eaten today?"

"Eaten?" I echo woozily.

She mutters something under her breath and quickly closes the distance between us. She's shorter than me but surprisingly strong as she grasps my elbow and leads me to sit on a small chair over by the desk and music stand.

"Don't tell me my cousin hasn't been feeding you," she snaps.

"No, no," I say, bending to put my head between my knees. "Rosa brought me stuff."

Not that I could bring myself to eat any of it.

"Hold on," she says. I hear her heels tapping as she moves away from me. From Elio's room, I hear her calling into the hallway. "Hey! Robbie! Tell Rosa we need snacks, would ya?"

Her voice gets louder, aimed back at me.

"You're not a vegan or something, are you? Gluten free?"

I weakly shake my head, bumping my own knees as I do so.

"OK. Good. Because if you were, you really would starve in this house. There's no escaping the meat, cheese, bread, and pasta."

Normally, those are all things I like eating. But this is not normal. Not for me.

Just as I'm getting the strength to lift my head back up without feeling like I'm going to fall off the chair, Valentina's returning with a cart like the one Rosa uses, a tray perched on top. Actually, it isn't a tray, but a charcuterie board, laden with thinly sliced meat, olives, sliced mozzarella, tomatoes drizzled with balsamic vinegar, and fresh bread. There's more olive oil and balsamic in a small dish for dipping the bread, and my mouth waters. Beside the charcuterie board is a large glass pitcher of ice water with lemons and some sort of leaves floating around in it, along with two glasses. Valentina pours a glass full, then thrusts it at me.

"Here. Drink this, then have some food."

She may be smaller than me, and I'm sure she's younger, but there's an undeniable edge of authority in her voice. But I guess that comes with the territory when you're the only daughter of a mob boss. I take the glass and have a sip. While I'm drinking the water,

Valentina busies herself loading up a small plate with all kinds of stuff from the charcuterie board. When it's done, she holds it out to me.

"Come on. You don't want to attend one of my and Mamma's events on an empty stomach. The booze flows like fucking water."

I can't imagine I'll be drinking at the event, but then again, I didn't imagine I'd be attending on Elio Titone's arm, either. *Just what am I to him? What does he want me to be?*

She's right, though. I need to keep my wits about me and maintain my strength here. I can't waste away and starve.

I start with the bread, because I feel like that will go down easy on my roiling stomach. I dip it into the olive oil and balsamic and take a bite. It's possibly the best bread I've ever had, slightly warm and fluffy, with a crunchy crust softened by the oil and vinegar.

That bite seems to have awakened my appetite, and I quickly scarf down the bread, then move onto the tomato and mozzarella salad, then the prosciutto and salami and olives. The entire time, Valentina watches me with a satisfied smirk. Even though she's so young, she's giving me total Italian grandma vibes. She clearly enjoys feeding people.

After clearing my plate, I chug some water, then wipe my mouth with the back of my hand.

"Thank you," I say, meaning it. "I didn't realize how much better I would feel after some food."

"Carbs solve everything," she says with a nod.

"Well, I wouldn't go *that* far," I say. My stomach may be full now, but I'm still stuck in this goddamn house, and now I'm apparently going to an event with Elio, which makes no sense. So, I would say that things are very much *not* solved.

"OK, you're right. But they help a little," she says. Her gaze falls to the giant pink diamond ring on her finger and lingers there for a moment before she jerks her head back up to look at me. In a voice that feels falsely cheery, she says, "Alright! You're fed! Now it's makeover time."

I should have known based on how perfect Valentina's hair and makeup look that *makeover time* is serious business for her. I'm completely unprepared for the thoroughness of her onslaught. And it does feel like an onslaught – my hair pulled tightly into rollers, eyebrows plucked, my skin smudged and sponged and powdered. She even makes me shave my legs and armpits to eliminate the one-day stubble there, instructing me firmly not to tell Elio before taking the razor away again after.

We do all the makeup and hair stuff in the bathroom. It takes a long time – Valentina is a total perfectionist. But after a few hours, she seems satisfied with the state of me.

"Now, the dresses," she says, marching back into the bedroom. I stand from where I was seated on the toilet and move to follow her. Before I leave the room, I catch sight of my own face in the mirror and halt.

A shimmering, polished woman stares back. I don't look like myself. Even my freckles are gone, hidden under foundation and bronzer. My cheekbones look sharper, my nose narrower, my lips darker and fuller, my lashes longer. I like makeup and I do wear it, but not to this extent. I've never seen myself like this.

The big curlers are still in my hair, giving my head a weird, bubbly look, but even that can't take away from the stunning effect of the makeup.

Looking so different is jarring. But strangely, it's also comforting. I can pretend it's not me, Deirdre O'Malley, but somebody else in this bathroom, in this life. This new look is like armour, a mask between Elio and me, a barrier like his leather gloves.

Feeling just a little bit stronger, I turn and catch up with Valentina.

She's standing by the bed, staring downwards. The three garment bags are open on the bed, each one containing a dress of a different colour.

"That one's mine. I have to change, too," Valentina says, pointing to a pink sequined dress. "You can try those other two on and we'll see which one is better."

I shift back and forth on my feet, eyeing the camera in the ceiling. Valentina twists to follow my gaze, then sighs.

"Yeah. You'll get used to that."

I scoff. "I doubt that."

Valentina gives me a serious look. She's clearly enjoyed her role as my snack-provider and makeup/hair artist, and she's been chatty and relaxed most of the afternoon. But now, she looks grave.

"You have to get used to it, Deirdre. This is your life now. *This is it.* It's not safe, and it's not easy, but it's what you've fucking got."

The speech seems practised. I wonder if she's said these exact words to herself.

"This isn't my life," I mutter, crossing my arms and shaking my head so hard that the rollers wobble and tug at my hair. "I have a life."

"*Had,*" Valentina corrects me. "You may still be in Toronto, but where you've come from and where you are now are two completely different worlds. The sooner you accept that, the better."

"How can you say that?" I cry. I've started feeling a sense of comradery with Valentina, but it comes crashing down. She's not here to be my friend. She's here to make sure I serve Elio in whatever fashion he chooses.

But maybe I'm wrong. Because the look she gives me isn't cold, but pained.

"I say that because it's true. Because it's a lesson I've had to learn over and over again." Once again, her eyes go to her ring, and for a second she looks like she wants to cut off her own finger.

"How old are you?" I ask her softly.

"I'll be nineteen in June," she replies, closing her hand into a fist and letting it drop.

Jesus. Only eighteen, engaged, and clearly unhappy about it.

I guess being the boss's daughter doesn't afford you as much power over your own life as I thought.

"Who's your fiancé?"

"God, I don't want to talk about him," she moans. "I'm already going to have to see him tonight." She sighs, twirling the ring on her finger, then meets my gaze steadily. "Look, this is shit. I know it is. You didn't choose to be here, and I get it. I've had eighteen years to get used to these men and you've barely had a day. It's fucking garbage. But you're strong. Just like me. I can see it in those baby blues." She smiles. "And if there's anything strong women are good at, it's surviving absolute trash heaps of situations like these."

I'm not sure I feel that strong right now. I've thrown up walls, but they're all being chipped away at. By my father, with his betrayal.

By Elio with his hammer.

But I have to be strong. I'm a survivor. Even if being a survivor has filled me with guilt for half my life.

I wonder what Mom would say if she were here.

No. If Mom were alive, I wouldn't be here at all. She never would have let this happen.

"Alright, then. What kind of dress should I wear to get through an 'absolute trash heap of a situation'?" I ask.

Valentina grins and wraps an arm around my waist, leaning in and squeezing. "That's the spirit!"

I swallow, unexpected tears threatening to ruin my makeup. This is the first time I've been touched by another woman in a long time. I try to remember the last time I hugged Willow and want to cry even more.

"Are you able to get a message to someone for me?" I ask, spinning in Valentina's grip. "My best friend Willow. She's worried about me but her dad took her phone and won't let her contact me."

"No tears! Ah! Your makeup!" Valentina says, fanning her hands over my face in a frantic motion. "Is she Irish?"

I know what she's asking with that question. She's not asking just about her family background, but asking if Willow is in the life.

"Yeah," I say. There's no point in lying. "Her dad runs a pub called *Briar and Boar* for Darragh Gowan."

"Hmm. How about a letter? I could send it for you."

"Like, mail it?" That will take days, and who knows if I'll even get a response? But Valentina nods to confirm.

"From what I understand, Darragh is just about foaming at the mouth to get his hands on your dad. Or, in his place, you. He likely already knows we have you, so it's not like any of us can just go waltzing into his territory right now. I think mailing a letter is your best bet to actually get a message to Willow without everything blowing the fuck up."

"OK. That works," I say hurriedly. I don't want Willow in danger if some of Elio's men show up at the pub. And now that I think about it, maybe a letter is perfect. If I don't put a return address on it, there's no real reason some mail for her would arouse Paddy's suspicion. She can burn it when she's done.

I don't even know what I'll write. I'm alive? I'm trapped? Save me? Forget you ever knew my name?

I promise myself I'll figure it out as Valentina tells me she'll bring me envelopes and paper. She puts a note in her phone about it and then gasps.

"Oh, shit. We're behind schedule. Time to get dressed and go!" She pins me with a look. "Seriously. Chop chop. No more worrying about the camera."

It amazes me that she doesn't worry about the camera. When she sees my look, she groans and runs to the bathroom, returning with a towel.

"Here. I'll hold this around you."

I'm grateful for her as she opens up the towel and blocks the view of the camera while I shimmy out of the jeans and T-shirt I'm wearing. "Which dress?" I ask.

She cranes her neck to look at the bed.

"We don't have time to try them both on. Go with the blue one. That's the one I really wanted to see you in."

For a second, I'm not sure what she means. One of the dresses is green, the other is black. But then I realize the black one is actually the deepest shade of blue you can get before black. Deep, inky blue silk. I reach my hand out of the towel and snatch it, then step into it.

There are no zippers or buttons to do up. It's a simple cut with two straps, a deep V-neckline, and a plunging open back. I feel the air on my exposed back and I'm about to ask Valentina if I can wear the other dress instead when she whistles.

"Holy fucking shit, Irish. That's the one. Fits you like a glove."

The word glove makes me think of Elio, and my stomach tightens. I look down at myself, at the cling of fabric at my waist and hips, the long skirt with a high slit up one side. Before I can stop the thought and tell myself I'm absolutely insane, I wonder what he'll think when he sees me.

As his date. What the fuck is happening?

Valentina flings the towel away.

"Take out your rollers while I get changed! And pick some shoes!" she says. She undresses in a frenzy, and I can't help but gawk at her confidence while I yank the curlers out of my hair.

"You really don't care about the camera?" I ask. At least she's got a strapless bra on, unlike me, so she's mostly covered.

"I'm used to it," she says, stepping into her sequined pink dress. In contrast to mine, the skirt on hers is super short. "It's the same in our house. But the security feeds for the family bedrooms don't go to the main hub."

"What does that mean?" I say, running my fingers through my hair now that all the rollers are out.

"My papà's the only one with access to the family bedroom feeds. He's a lot of things, but he's not pervy enough to watch his own daughter getting changed or taking a dump. It's mostly to make sure I'm not sneaking guys in there or something, especially now that I've got this." She flaps her left hand in the air, and I know she means her engagement ring. "It's the same here, you know. Only Elio has access to the cameras in here and in his rooms."

"He didn't mention that," I say slowly. I'm not sure how I feel about that. I knew that Elio would have access to the cameras. It's his

107

house, and he has all the power. But I didn't know he was the *only* one who'd see me in here. I can't tell if I'm comforted or not, and I don't have much time to think about it, because Valentina is urging me to get some shoes on, stat.

I grab a pair of strappy silver heels in my size and try them on. They seem to fit alright, but the heel is astronomically high. Far higher than I'm used to. A quick look at all the other shoes tells me I won't get anything lower, and I may as well just stick with what I've got.

"Zip me up?" Valentina spins, and I do up the zipper at the back of her dress. Hers is strapless. Once she's done up, she turns and fluffs my hair a bit.

"You look like a goddess. Let's go!"

Go. Go to an event. With Elio.

At least it's in a public place. Nothing bad is going to happen to me surrounded by other people. A small, stupid part of me is still holding out hope that somebody might even save me from all this.

I turn towards the door, ready to leave, when Valentina stops me with a cry.

"Oh, my God! Your underwear!"

"What?" I ask, twisting back to look at her. I have no clue what's happened to my panties from yesterday, so I'm wearing one of the pairs I found in the closet.

"The back of the dress is too low. You can see the top edge of them."

"I'll put on the other dress and-"

"No time," Valentina interrupts. "Just take them off."

My cheeks flush hot. She cannot be serious. She wants me to go out in public, to come face to face with Elio, wearing *no fucking underwear?*

But her face tells me she absolutely is serious. She's practically dancing with anxiety about the time, and as much as I hate this whole situation, I don't want to make problems for her if I can help it.

Besides, it's not like Elio hasn't seen me even more exposed. At least my dress is all in one piece this time.

"Fine," I grit out. I don't have to worry too much about the camera, because my skirt is so long it completely covers me as I wiggle out of the underwear. "Better?" I spin around.

"Perfect!" Valentina says, shoving her phone in a small gold clutch. "Now let's go!"

Chapter 16

Elio

I've just emerged from my office and am crossing the main floor of the house when I hear the clatter of high heels on the stairs. I reach the front door and turn just in time to get punched in the face.

That's what it feels like. That's what my Songbird *looks* like, coming down the stairs. So beautiful she's a blow to the fucking head.

I barely notice my cousin beside her as Deirdre descends the stairs. Her steps are quick but wobbly, and she's looking down like she's afraid she's going to fall and snap her neck. Which, considering the shoes she's wearing, is probably a valid concern. My gaze slides from her silver shoes, up the tantalizing line of her leg appearing at the slit in her dress, to her hips, her sweet little waist and tits. That dress is a goddamn dream on her, encasing her body in silk so dark blue it makes her eyes look like midnight instead of their usual midday sky.

Those deep blue eyes meet mine, and Deirdre freezes on the stairs. Valentina just keeps on going, practically sprinting even though her heels are even higher than Deirdre's.

Deirdre and I stare at each other for so long I wonder if she's planning to stay on that step all night.

"Need me to carry you again?" I ask.

She inhales sharply, her lush mouth tightening.

"No, thank you," she says, her tone clipped. "I don't need another dress ruined by your blood."

Valentina tenses beside me, no doubt fearing my anger. But I surprise them both by letting out a chuckle.

"I'm all stitched up, remember, Songbird? Good as new."

Not exactly true. My shoulder's going to be a pain in my ass for a while. But Morelli checked my stitches today and put new bandages on earlier, at least, so I won't be bleeding all over her. I stare at her cleavage, her collarbones, remembering what my blood looked like smeared there, and the crotch of my pants feels suddenly tighter.

Deirdre starts walking again, descending the last few steps. My gaze is stuck on her chest, and I frown, feeling like something's missing before I realize what it is.

"Where's her jewellery?" I ask my cousin.

Valentina smacks the palm of her hand to her forehead.

"Ah, shit. It's upstairs with the shoes."

"Go get it," I tell her, keeping my eyes on Deirdre's bare neck.

"But we're late! Mamma's already there and pissed about it. I've got about a dozen texts from her and-"

I tear my gaze from Deirdre's skin long enough to give Valentina a look that sends her running for the stairs.

"I'll be right back!" she calls. She's like a tiny fucking track athlete even in those shoes. She's running like it's her job.

I'm alone with Deirdre now. There are a few soldiers scattered around the main floor of the house, and Curse and Enzo are both outside ready to go, but in this space by the door, it's just the two of us.

Deirdre looks everywhere but at me when she finally speaks.

"So, how does this work? The jewellery, the clothes. Is this all getting added on to my debt? Because I'd rather not have it at all."

I pause, drinking in the sight of her in a dress I paid for, already imagining the tens of thousands of dollars of gemstones I'm about to wrap around her throat. A collar with *Titone* spelled out in the language of diamonds.

"I'm feeling generous. Consider it a birthday gift," I say. Her gaze snaps to me, and I don't miss the way it slides up and down my body in my black suit and black shirt. The only thing not black on me is my pocket square. A slight wrinkle appears between her eyebrows when her gaze snags there, and I wonder if she recognizes it.

I almost ask her, but Valentina is back, panting as she careens down the stairs.

"Here, quick, quick!" she says to Deirdre, holding out sparkly stuff. My cousin's frenetic impatience is grinding my nerves raw. I hold out my hand for the jewellery and tell her, "Go ahead. Curse and Enzo will take you."

Valentina dumps the shimmering gems and metal into my hand without a moment's hesitation before running for the door, pulling it open and disappearing. Deirdre flutters, looks like she'll call out something like "Wait!" But it's too late. Valentina is gone and it's just us again. Her eyes fall to my hand, where bright, clear diamonds and white gold shine in stark contrast to the black leather of my glove. Her mouth primly puckered, she reaches for my hand, but I pull it back.

"I'll do it."

"What do you mean, you'll do it? If I have to wear it, I'll put it on myself."

She reaches forward again, but once again I move my hand, curling my fingers into a fist.

"We aren't leaving until I put this stuff on you."

She doesn't understand. She doesn't understand what showing up in public wearing my finery, my diamonds, means. It will tell the entire fucking city that she's mine now. Not as a debtor, someone to torture or to kill over what she owes. Not as someone I couldn't care less about losing.

But someone possessed.

Someone protected.

"Then we won't leave at all," she snaps.

I don't say anything else. I step towards her. She steps back. We do this over and over until she collides with the wall. She's trapped by my body, and I hold up my fist between us, loosening my grip slightly until a white gold chain slithers out and dangles in the air. It swings like a pendulum, and her blue eyes track the movement.

"You'll find that things will be much easier for you if you don't disobey me," I mutter.

Her eyes flash. "Maybe I don't want this to be easy."

"What do you want this to be, then?"

Her reply is flat and grim. "Over."

A concoction of emotions I don't like and won't name floods my body. I feel like I could crush the diamonds in my fist.

"Put your fucking hair behind your ears."

She stares at me in mute defiance, and I grunt as I lift my left hand, ignoring Morelli's instructions not to use that arm as much as possible. Deirdre gasps when I grasp all her hair at the nape of her neck and tug, forcing her head back, baring her throat. Her heart beats a rapid-fire rhythm there, poetry of the body and of blood. It's a song in and of itself. I want to put my fucking tongue there.

Instead, I reach to the side with my right hand, depositing the jewellery on a small stand near the wall. From the pile, I grab one earring. It's a dangly diamond thing with a simple hook to slide through her earlobe. No back or clasp.

Deirdre can't move much with her hair bound so tightly by my fist. She breathes rapidly, staring at the earring like it's a murder weapon. Her body vibrates with what I assume is fury. She doesn't look afraid. She looks fucking pissed.

But something changes when the leather of my glove brushes the shell of her ear. She makes a sound, between a whimper and a gasp, that jolts straight to my dick. Her entire body goes taut, her breath catching as I skim a single knuckle over her earlobe. I stop looking at her ear for a second and see that her eyes are scrunched shut. Her back is arching away from the wall, and it's not because I've started pulling her hair. And...

Her nipples are hard.

I couldn't see them through the dress before, but I can see them now. The temperature hasn't changed. It's toasty fucking warm. Honestly a little too hot for my liking, now that my blood is boiling inside me.

"Sensitive, Songbird?" I mutter quietly, brushing my knuckle down her ear again experimentally. I watch her as I do it. Watch the flutter that goes through the muscles in her face, the tautness that spreads down her body. Watch the way her nipples swell and tighten further, begging me to mouth them through the slippery fabric of her dress. Her hands are plastered to the wall at her back.

"Can you just get this over with?" she breathes, her eyes still closed, as if she can't stand to look at me. Can't stand to acknowledge what she might be feeling in response to my touch.

But now I want to take my fucking time. Unlike Valentina I don't really care when we arrive at this event. I don't plan to stay long, anyway. Just long enough to give Sev his money and make sure everybody sees Deirdre at my side.

Slowly, I release my grip on her hair. I don't think she needs me to hold her there anymore, and I'm right. She's completely bound by tension, just from that slight touch at her ear. She's definitely beyond sensitive there. Which is damn good information to have. I gently take her plump earlobe between my left thumb and forefinger and guide the earring hook to the small hole there. I press it slowly in, penetrating the silky flesh, while Deirdre remains perfectly still except for her ragged breathing. Bent this close to her face, I wish I'd told Valentina to go a little easier on the makeup. I can't see her freckles now, and that bothers me.

I let go of the earring, watching the long line of diamonds dangle and bump the side of her throat. Then, I ease my fingertips under her chin, tipping her head to the other side to do the same on the other ear. Her eyes flare open, and she stares at me, gaze sparking, as I reach for the other earring.

"Like to watch when men put things inside you?" I ask, feeling her gaze on me as I slide the second earring into place.

"Wouldn't know," she hisses. "I've never let a man put something inside me."

I freeze, and so does she. Her eyes widen, her lips clamping together as if she didn't mean to say that. Now that the earring is in, I release it. My fingers skim down her throat, and she swallows.

"You're a virgin?"

My fingers keep sliding down her neck, tracing her collarbones, then brushing a knuckle between her breasts.

I can barely see the red blush beneath all her makeup, but I know it's there, because it creeps up her neck, too. I slowly rub my knuckle up and down the valley between her breasts. I can't stop staring at how much she reacts to me. How flushed her fair skin gets, just from this slightest touch.

"I don't see why that matters!" she stammers.

I don't know why it matters, either. I've never cared about virginity as a concept before. A lot of men in our world do, want their mafia brides untouched, but I couldn't care less. If anything, getting saddled with a virgin who doesn't know what she's doing seems like an easy way to guarantee a boring night in the sack.

But now...

Now, I find I do care. Care that nobody else has been inside Deirdre. If I wanted to, I could be the first man, the last man, the only man who's ever fucked her. A possessive satisfaction rises up inside me, telling me that she's mine in all ways now, even if she fights it.

"I don't even know why I said that," she groans. "Well, at least it proves that I'll be useless to you in that department if you ever decide you want me for something other than violin. Since I have no idea what I'm doing."

"You'd have an idea of what you were doing if someone taught you."

She breathes in sharply at my words. She's about to say something else, but I silence her with a feather-light but unmistakeably intentional brush of my thumb over her hardened nipple.

And then I do it again.

"What are you doing?" she whispers thickly.

I don't answer her with words, instead drawing an achingly slow, firm circle around the outer edge of her nipple. Teasing, not coming close to the sensitive bud of it again. Her breath is coming in short little pants. Fuck, I want to take her breast roughly in my hand, knead it, draw up the skirt of her dress and pin her to the wall.

I don't. Jaw tight, I keep circling, slowly, so fucking slowly, until I think Deirdre is going to come apart at the seams. She's too proud to ask me to do it, but I can see she needs it.

"Do you want me to touch you there again?" I murmur against her ear. She shudders at the cascade of my breath over her skin.

"Fuck you. Let me go," is all she says, but it's practically a whine. She may not be begging me with words, but she is with her body. Her back is arching towards me, seeking my touch.

"I think you do," I say. "Right now, I bet all you can think about is what this leather will feel like sliding across your bare skin."

She jerks beneath my touch, and I know I'm right.

It would be so easy, too. To slide the silk of the dress over, maybe even rip it like I did last night. Rub the puckering berries of her nipples between my gloved fingers. Take one and then the other in my mouth so I could feel her properly, no fabric between us. My cock pounds at the thought, my tongue lashing the backs of my teeth.

I want her to beg me to do it.

Even though I know she won't.

With an impatient growl, I give her what she needs but won't ever ask for. I press my palms to the sides of her breasts, moving my thumbs across her nipples in demanding strokes. She lets out a soft moan, then clamps her mouth shut, as if pissed off by the escape of the sound. Like that moan is a betrayal.

She doesn't want to feel what she's feeling. To react to me the way she's reacting. All I'm doing is playing with her pretty little nipples, and she's getting all twitchy and wiggly, her hips bucking forward before she stops the movement, fighting for control.

She's not just sensitive around her ears. She could come like this, is probably already fucking close. The thought inflames me, makes me forget every rule, everything I've told myself about why I've brought her here.

My lips touch her ear this time when I growl, "If I pulled your panties to the side right now, I think I'd find that virgin pussy soaking for me, Songbird."

Her hands, hands that this entire time have been plastered to the wall, not touching me or pushing me away and pretending to be neutral participants in all of this, rise between us. She plants them on my chest and shoves, eyes burning me with blue fire.

"So everything you told me before is a lie, then," she snaps, shoving again. "You do want a whore. You just want me for my body."

I drop my hands from her breasts and capture her chin in my fingers, forcing her gaze to remain on mine as I lean in and tell her, "I want everything. I want your fucking *soul*."

She tries to shake her head but can't.

"Six million dollars for a soul," she whispers, and she doesn't sound angry now, but sad.

I let her go, flexing my fingers inside my gloves and shrugging, sending lancing pain through my shoulder, and simply reply, "Small price to pay."

I would have paid millions more. There's something in her that speaks to me in a language I've half-forgotten. It's like an itch at the back of my mind that I need to locate so I can scratch it until it bleeds.

I'm about to turn towards the door and take her out of here when I see something glittering. The necklace. I pick it up.

"Turn around," I say.

She just stares at me, arms crossed over her chest as if to keep those pesky, sensitive nipples of hers in check around me. I hold up the necklace, and she merely lifts her chin and narrows her gaze.

Fine by me. I can put it on like this.

I lean close to her again, and at the last second she decides to finally listen and does turn around. Maybe she thinks this is all a little better if she doesn't actually have to look at me.

I sweep her hair forward over one shoulder, doing my best to ignore the crackling colour of it. Fucking hell, she's got a lot of it. Long and thick. It completely hid her back before, but now...

Now I can see everything.

Valentina may have gone overboard on the makeup, but I have to hand it to my cousin. She chose the perfect dress.

The back of the dress isn't even a back at all. It's a gaping plunge of silk, exposing Deirdre from shoulder blade to hip. I let the chain of the necklace dangle from my hand, letting the thin end of it drag up the curve of her spine to her neck. I can see the goosebumps as they rise. See the way Deirdre's arms tighten around her body.

I move in closer behind Deirdre, taking a moment to look at the necklace to figure out how it clasps. It has a short, wide band of diamonds with a central large stone that must go at the front. I sweep it around the front of her neck, then do up the clasp at the back. I pause to admire the effect, and the effect goes straight to my balls.

Because the necklace looks like a diamond collar, fitted tightly around her throat. And the white-gold chain dangles down Deirdre's back like a glittering leash.

I finger the chain at the back, tugging lightly, and smirk when Deirdre vaults backwards in response, stumbling in her heels until she crashes into my chest. She rights herself quickly, trying to pull away from me as fast as she can.

But I don't let go of the chain until she's in my car.

Chapter 17

Deirdre

hat is happening?

W*hat is happening?*
That's the question running through my head over and over again as I sit motionless in the front passenger seat of Elio's car. It's a different vehicle from last night's black SUV. It's still black, but it's smaller, some kind of Porsche I'm pretty sure.

What is happening? What is happening to me?

The place between my legs still feels achy and damp as I squeeze my thighs together. Elio, the arrogant violent stupid fucking *bastard*, almost made me come. Just from touching my nipples.

What is happening to me?

I shouldn't like his touch on me. No, I *don't* like it. But something in my body reacts to him in a way I can't control. And the shame of it makes everything burn hotter. Makes every touch into something toxic, nearly drugging, something I'm terrified I'll start to crave if I'm not careful.

But how the hell can I even be careful? Everywhere I go, there Elio is. He houses me. Even fucking dresses me now. My fingers rise to the diamond collar at my neck, a beautiful and terrible symbol of what's become of me.

"Why are you bringing me to this event?" I ask, tracing the intricate lines of diamonds that lead into one huge one at the centre. I've got to be wearing tens of thousands worth of dollars of gems right now. Maybe even more.

I don't expect him to answer, but he actually does.

"It's the most public and efficient way to show the other people who want you that you're mine."

The other people who want me. I guess he means Darragh and the Camorra.

I let my hand fall away from the collar and rub my temples.

"Do you know where my father is?" I ask dully. Once again, I don't expect him to reply.

And once again, he surprises me.

"Bermuda."

I whip my head towards Elio, a dizzying array of emotions flying through me. The first is relief that my father is alive and he's escaped.

The second is despair.

Because he really has left me here.

Maybe he's just hatching a plan, I tell myself, chewing on my lip. *Maybe he can't figure out how to help me here with so many people after him, so he left to figure out his next move.*

I wonder if Elio can sense the hope inside me. If he can smell it the way a dog smells blood.

"He's with Bridget. She flew out there this morning."

Bridget. The name is familiar, though it takes me a second to place it.

"Bridget, like, our cleaning lady? That Bridget?"

She only worked for us for a couple of weeks a few years ago before she was mysteriously replaced. I always wondered what became of her, but she was so young, only a few years older than me, so I figured she'd just gotten a new opportunity or maybe had college to deal with. I remember her being chatty and sweet and extremely pretty. *Why would Dad need a maid in Bermuda?*

I'm embarrassed that I don't figure it out until Elio tells me.

"She's his girlfriend. Or maybe sugar baby is a better term. Has been for years."

I feel like somebody's punched me in the stomach. I lean forward, breath practically knocked out of me as it truly sinks in. My father created this entire mess and left me to pick up the pieces without a fucking thought. Clearly, he still has money on hand if he can jet off to tropical islands. And instead of using that money to try to pay his debts and save me, he flew out the woman he's fucking instead.

How did I not know any of this?

Head spinning, I try to comb through the past few years, wondering if I've missed any signs. How dense am I that not only did I not realize what was happening with the money situation, but I didn't even clue in that Bridget stopped working for us because she became my dad's girlfriend instead? His expensive little secret?

Turns out Dad had a lot of expensive secrets.

The sense of betrayal goes deeper than just me. I feel like Dad has betrayed Mom, too. Betrayed her memory in the worst possible way. I obviously didn't expect him to be alone forever after her death, but this? Banging some college-aged girl and protecting her instead of me when shit hit the fan?

This is a nightmare.

A nightmare that Elio just keeps on making more real. Adding more and more details.

"She's got expensive taste, from what I hear," Elio says. He speaks casually, as if each word isn't shattering everything I thought I knew. "She doesn't work but lives in a fancy condo in Yorkville. Drives a Range Rover. Or, she did. I wouldn't be surprised if Sev's men have already seized the vehicle."

"Please stop," I whisper. I don't even know why I bother. My father may be greedy and a coward, but Elio is cruel, and begging him won't get me anywhere.

"The truth hurts, Songbird," he replies, proving just how right I am. How cruel he is. What he says may be the truth, but he's the one wielding it like a knife, digging it right into my heart.

"But what else is it they say?" he continues. "The truth will set you free."

I stare at his profile, dumfounded.

"Free?" I echo in disbelief. The diamond collar around my neck tingles. I want to rip it off, dangle it in front of his face and ask him, *Does this look like free to you?*

Neither of us speak for a while. There's no music on in the car, and the only sound is the bleating of my broken heart in my chest. I watch the lights of downtown Toronto pass the window like fallen stars and wonder how the rest of the world can just keep on turning, just keep on being beautiful, when mine has entirely collapsed.

When we get close to the AGO, Elio finally speaks again. A sudden, casual declaration.

"You can always put a bullet in his head. That's what I did."

My hands squeeze into fists in my lap.

"You killed your own father?" I shouldn't be surprised by that. Elio's ruthless. It's what he's known for.

He laughs, but the sound is dark and brittle.

"Trust me, he deserved it."

"Trust you?" I respond with my own bitter laugh. The laughter dies in my throat when leather brushes the back of my neck. Elio fists the chain of the beautiful collar beneath my hair.

We're at the AGO now, and he stops the car. Outside, a young valet jogs through lightly falling snow towards us.

Elio leans in at the same time he tugs the chain, forcing me sideways towards him. He speaks close to my ear, not touching it, but even so a shameful shiver runs through me, zinging in my nipples and my clit, rekindling the earlier arousal.

"You're going to have to trust me, Songbird."

His breath is the barest brush of sensation on my skin, but it explodes through me. His leather-bound knuckles rest against the top of my spine, prickling and hard and soft all at once.

"This city is a snake pit. And the only one who can keep you safe here now is me."

Chapter 18

Deirdre

The cold air feels good on my skin when I step out of the car. Elio holds the door for me, his gaze a hot contrast to the winter night. Plump snowflakes hit my shoulders and hair, and I know if I'm out here too long I'll freeze my ass off. But for now, it's heaven.

Curse appears seemingly out of nowhere, startling me as the valet drives the car away. The two brothers bracket my body, both of them keenly alert, like bodyguards, reminding me of the other dangers that still lie in wait for me.

Elio's gloved hand finds the back of the necklace again, and I buck against his touch.

"No way. You're not walking me in there like a dog," I say. Elio doesn't look at me, his gaze sweeping back and forth over the snowy street. But shockingly he releases the chain.

Only to settle his hand on my lower back. My *bare* lower back. So low his fingertips dip beneath the fabric of the dress and settle on my hip.

"Better?" he asks as we enter the art gallery.

No. It's ten times fucking worse. Because instead of just humiliation, now I'm once again feeling the electric bite of arousal. The surface of his glove is cool at first, but the longer his hand is on my skin, the more heat I feel penetrating the leather. Seeping into me. Branding me. This is insane, getting turned on solely from his hand on my back. *His* hand! The man who took me, who caged me, who claims he owns me. But though I try to fight the sensations, I can't deny them. It feels like his hand is sinking right through my spine and into my pelvis, stirring and squeezing inside with cruelly expert precision. With the mere press of his palm, the claim of his fingers, he's playing my body with a mastery I could never hope to achieve at the violin. Not in a hundred fucking years.

We head towards the entrance tables, and the brothers don't even toss a glance at the two young women collecting tickets. There's a line up of attendees waiting to hand over their tickets, and I burn with their gazes as we pass right by the line. I wonder which of the dazzling women and men in suits are part of Elio's world, and which are just regular rich people out for a night on the town. Do they know who Elio is? Do they know who I am?

Can any of them help me now?

I think about twisting and looking back at those people, waiting so patiently in line. The people following the rules while Elio ploughs right through them, dragging me along with him. I think about calling out to them, begging them to save me. But I don't, because maybe I'm a coward like my father has turned out to be.

Or maybe I'm weak in other ways. Worse ways. Because Elio's hand is still there on my back, and it's like he's bound me with that simple touch. It's like I can't speak, can't even breathe if he doesn't allow it. I let him guide me further into the building, and I want to pretend I walk numbly, like an automaton. But I'm not numb. Every nerve is ragged and raw. My whole body in turmoil. Tumultuous waves of quivering heat rise, fall, *crash*. I hate it, and hate him for making me feel it.

But even the hate doesn't ease my aching clit. My over-sensitive nipples.

I wonder if the hate makes it worse.

Though it's a nearly impossible task, I try to focus on the surroundings to take my mind off my hideous reactions to Elio. Curse is still on my other side, but I'm barely aware of him or anyone else as we walk. Elio commands everything, including my attention.

We end up in a space I don't recognize. I've been to the AGO before, but it's been a while. I know it's been under construction recently, and this must be the new wing Valentina mentioned. It's a vast, glittering space with pure glass all along one towering side, leaning inwards at the top, creating a half-pyramid effect. The space is dotted with beautiful people admiring various art installations, sculptures and other three-dimensional pieces in the centre of the space, with paintings and sketches and textiles on the inner wall. At the far end of the space, there are long tables with food as well as a bar with a bartender handing out drinks. Near the food is an area free of tables and art pieces, and a few couples are dancing to music played by a small string quartet.

"There you are!"

A familiar voice cuts through the music and the chatter. Valentina hustles over. You'd never know based on how she moves that she's wearing shoes that should be considered hazardous to human health. My own feet are already aching, my arches contorted. If I tried to run like her, I'd break an ankle.

Or my neck.

Elio doesn't move his hand as his cousin joins our group. Valentina's lashes are so long and fluttery it's impossible to miss the way her gaze dips there before bouncing right back up.

"Oh, shit, your hair! I didn't have time to spray it after you took out the rollers!"

I reach up, wondering what she's talking about, then remember the snow that fell on me which has no doubt melted and changed the style. My natural hair is a weird combination of straight and wavy at the back and curly at the sides and front. A quick brush of my fingers lets me know that little baby hairs are springing up into ringlets around my face. I try to smooth them, then stop. I shouldn't care what I look like. If my hair is presentable enough. I don't even want to be here at all.

But when I stop fussing with my hair, Valentina takes over. Even in her heels she's shorter than me, because my own shoes negate any height hers add. She stretches, frowning and smoothing, muttering about hairspray. I'm about to ask her to stop, to shy away from her touch, when something happens that makes me freeze.

It's the brutally slow and unbearably erotic movement of Elio's hand against my skin. He glides his hand in a smooth, small circle against my back, his fingers caressing my hip until I can't make a sound, can barely breathe. I squeeze my inner thighs together and close my eyes. The sensations of Valentina fiddling with my hair die away, along with everything else, until there's only Elio. Elio and the leather-smooth slide of his hand on my blistering skin.

His hand dips slightly lower, and I feel a new tension enter his grip, jarring him into sudden stillness. *Fuck.* He's realized I have no underwear on. There's no way he hasn't. His fingers are well beneath my dress now, past where the top of panties would sit on my hips, and even with the gloves he'd be able to tell there's no extra fabric down there.

We both remain still but not still, frozen but vibrating beneath the silence. Then, there's a tiny movement from him. The cricking of his index finger against my hip – oh, hell, it's basically the top of my ass, who am I kidding? I think that slight nudge of his finger is to make doubly sure what he felt was real. Or rather what he *didn't* feel, what isn't even *there* to feel.

He does it again. It feels like he's cricking that finger inside me.

I constrict around nothing.

"Jesus, you don't need to squeeze your eyes shut and screw up your face like that," Valentina admonishes. "You'd think I was pulling your hair out or something."

My eyes fly open, and the world rushes back.

Valentina's hands fall away from my hair, and she shrugs. "That'll have to be good enough for now."

Elio doesn't say anything, merely increases the pressure of his palm, and I'm suddenly propelled forward. Valentina lunges out of the way so that we don't collide as Elio steers me forward.

"Where are we going now?" I ask as we move through the room. He doesn't answer with words. He simply stops and turns to face me on the dance floor. The quartet is playing something slow and lovely, a song I don't recognize. Hand still plastered to my skin, he nudges me until I stumble closer to him, my hands rising to land on his chest. And I hate it, hate that I'm using him to steady myself, to keep my balance. I'm about to rip my hands away when Elio bends and gives a single word of command:

"Dance."

Un-fucking-believable. He expects me to dance with him? I feel like a marionette, like I'm nothing to him but a prop to perform at will. And when his hand starts doing that slow circle thing on my back again, making my insides turn viscous and poisonous and hot, I realize that if I am a marionette, he controls more of my strings that I do.

Maybe even all of them.

"Put your arms around my neck," he commands. With a soft grunt, he raises his left hand to my hip. With his shoulder injury, I wonder if the movement hurts. I hope it does. I hope the simple act of holding me hurts for the rest of his life.

And at the same moment, I hate the hurt. And the guilt.

You don't walk away banged-up but generally uninjured from the car accident that killed your mother without guilt imbedding itself in your bones like shrapnel. I didn't realize how deep that guilt went, how much it's screwed me up, until now. Because I can't even be fully satisfied that Elio's injured. I know it was only because he didn't want to let someone else damage what belongs to him, an act of pure possessiveness rather than protectiveness, but that act, that injury, twists inside me now. Makes me feel like I owe him something. Something far greater than the millions of dollars I already do.

Elio's grip tightens on me, and his tone is dark when he speaks again.

"Don't disobey me, Songbird. Not in public. Not here."

I still haven't put my arms around his neck like he told me to. I wonder what would happen if I pulled away. If I screamed and caused a scene.

Elio's earlier words come back to me in a haunting rush.

This city is a snake pit. The only one who can keep you safe here now is me.

I stare at my hands, starkly pale in contrast to the perfect black of his suit's jacket. My fingers feel frozen. I can't pull them away or move them up to his neck. Either choice feels like it will have permanent and devastating consequences. Disobeying him, extricating myself from him, and putting myself at the mercy of the other men who want me.

Or submitting to him. Admitting that I need him now.

I wonder if I do. Need him. If the only way to avoid being torn apart by prowling coyotes is to put myself at the mercy of the wolf instead.

I can feel Elio's hard stare on my face as I watch my own hands. They move like they belong to someone else. Sliding slowly, then more quickly, up to the base of his neck. He's so tall, even with my shoes, that I can't wrap my arms around his neck, so I just let my hands rest there.

Elio breathes out quietly, draws his thumb up and down the shuddering place where my spine meets my tailbone, and murmurs, "Good girl."

I don't know if it's his hands on me, or the way my nipples are pressed achingly to his front, or the dark rasp of his voice around those words, but my core pulses, and heat floods my skin.

I wonder if Elio's going to try to lead me in some kind of elaborate waltz, but he doesn't. He guides me back and forth in a circling, hypnotic sort of sway.

"But maybe not such a good girl," he suddenly says, his fingers digging even lower beneath my dress. One of his fingers brushes my ass, teasing the cleft there. "Why aren't you wearing panties?"

His question grows gruff at the end. Quiet, but rough and demanding. Humiliation churns alongside the arousal. And so does anger.

"That wasn't my choice," I whisper fiercely. "It's this dress! And Valentina was rushing me and just told me to take them off and-"

"And you did it," he growls, cutting me off. "Don't blame the dress or Valentina. Take responsibility, Songbird. Acknowledge the fact that a part of you wanted to come here with me without panties. You wanted to flaunt your bare little ass and pussy."

A shift of Elio's swaying stance drives the unmistakeable bulge of his cock against my belly. My mouth goes dry.

"That's not true," I whisper. But now I'm second-guessing myself. Why didn't I fight Valentina harder on this? Why didn't I hold my ground? Am I that much of a push-over?

Or did some subconscious part of me, a part of me I didn't even know is there, want this? Want this humiliation?

"If it's not true then tell me why you're so fucking turned on right now."

I gasp, feeling like he's blinded me. Like I've been hiding in the dark and he just threw on the floodlights. Exposing me completely, leaving me stunned and breathless and blinking. Another swaying shift nudges the top of his thigh between my legs, and a riot of aching pleasure so intense it almost feels like pain shoots up my spine.

"Does this make you feel more in control?" Elio murmurs against my hair as my clit throbs needily. "Knowing that you're making me fucking insane right now?" His hands guide my hips in a slow grind against his thigh. "You're playing a dangerous game. I don't like being taunted."

Only someone with a death wish would taunt this man.

"I didn't," I pant, wriggling in his grip, and I don't know if I'm trying to get closer or get away. "I, I..."

I'm going to come.

Dear fucking God, I can feel it. A fevered pulse, a quickening between my legs. In Elio's arms, against his leg, surrounded by other people, *in public*.

What is happening to me?

Panic claws at me, and for some stupid fucking reason I feel that panic most between my legs. It sharpens every sensation. Makes the roll of my swollen clit on Elio into a bright, ecstatic point of pressure that I couldn't pull away from if I tried now. He isn't even moving my hips for me anymore, just the slow motion of our dancing is enough to bring me closer and closer to that edge.

"Fuck, Deirdre," Elio groans quietly, voice roughened. "I should spank your sweet little ass for this."

It's a shocking image. Me, bent over a table. Or his lap. That black glove coming down over and over on my bare skin, stinging, marking, claiming. It's degrading. And – God help me, what is *wrong* with me – alluring. *Shit*. His fingertips press there now, a stark and silent warning.

"Or maybe this is punishment enough," he says. "Coming in public the way you're about to."

"Stop," I whisper, screwing my eyes shut. But I don't even know who or what I'm saying it to. To Elio. To myself. To the treacherous orgasm that's building, rising, cresting inside me. There's no stopping it now, no matter how much or whom I beg. No matter who is watching. That burgeoning sweep of sensation is taking over, surging inward and crystalizing like a knife, drawing blood before it shatters. I cling to Elio, shuddering and coming hard, knowing that without his shoulders under my hands and his fingers on my ass that I'd collapse. And maybe that's what he wants. To show me that I can't even fucking stand without him now.

But now his hands are dragging upwards to my waist, and he's creating space between us like he's about to let go.

Did he hear me say "Stop" and actually listen?

Or does he just want to see me fall?

"Take her," Elio says above my head to someone else. My pussy still squeezing with the shameful aftershocks of my orgasm, I pant raggedly and swallow, dizzily wondering what he's talking about. I curl my hands into fists and let them slide away from Elio's shoulders as he releases my waist. Luckily, my rubbery legs hold. He was speaking to Curse, I realize, as his brother nods and moves in close to my side.

My gaze digs into Elio's back as he turns and cuts through the crowd, walking away without another word. He said all those terrible things to me, held me hard against him while I came in the middle of this fancy event, and now he's *leaving*? Leaving me here with his silent, brooding brother while I'm soaked and shaking and still pulsing inside from what just happened?

My breath burns my throat, and I don't know if it's because of how hard I'm breathing or because of the fury.

Chapter 19

Elio

I saw Severu Serpico enter the room the same moment my desperate little Deirdre came against my thigh. Piss-poor fucking timing. Because I'd been about to say fuck it. Fuck Severu, fuck the money, fuck the event. I was about to drag Deirdre back to my car, toss her down in the backseat, and smack her ass for coming here with no panties.

Either that, or worship her pussy with my tongue.

Maybe both of those things.

It's a needy little cunt. I can already tell. Could tell from the way she came apart just from the slight bumping grind of our slow dance. She's needy all over, I'm discovering. Her ears. Her nipples. Her beautiful lower back.

Her clit.

I can't stop thinking about her clit, nestled between her legs, naked and so swollen beneath her dress, as I stalk across the gallery. But Severu is watching me, flanked by two of his men. He's waiting, and I have to get my head on straight to deal with business now.

I really don't like interacting with other bosses with half my body's blood in my dick. Doesn't leave enough for my brain. Sev

133

Serpico is one smart motherfucker, and there's no room for mistakes where Deirdre is concerned. I approach him in measured strides and come to a stop before him.

"Severu," I grunt in greeting.

"Elio," he responds smoothly. He swirls a small glass with golden liquid in his hand. Despite the tension simmering between us, he's perfectly composed, cordial even, looking sharp in his charcoal suit. He's older than me, in his early forties, and there are strands of grey at his temples, but I don't think that matters much. He's got the kind of face that women go nuts for. The kind that seems to only get better with age. The guy looks like he should be playing a mob boss on TV or something, like he's an actor instead of a criminal, but there's nothing fake or performed about the lethal power he carries. His eyes are a warm amber colour, but his gaze is ice cold. So observant it's almost cutting.

In half a second his gaze has gone to the too-tight crotch of my pants, then back up to my face, and I know he's already figured out what's happening.

"You're keeping the O'Malley girl."

It's not a question, but I answer anyway. So there won't be any room for doubt.

"Yes."

"Her papà owes me money."

"He owes me more."

"You and Curse killed three of my men and maimed another."

"And one of them shot me."

This surprises him. Clearly, the one soldier I left alive didn't notice my injury through the agony of his own.

I can tell Sev is weighing what he wants to say next very carefully. No doubt the fact one of his men shot me has thrown a wrench into whatever negotiating power he thought he had here. He knows as well as I do that if I had been killed that night, there would have been a fucking war and his head would probably already be on a spike somewhere in my uncle's house.

I almost wonder if he's going to apologize, but instead he asks mildly, "How are you healing?"

"Like you give a fuck," I grunt. "Here. Take this. It covers O'Malley's debt plus some extra for the soldiers. A courtesy." I take the cheque out of my suit jacket's inner pocket and hold it between us. Sev's eyes flicker over the million-dollar sum scrawled on the paper. He grasps the edge of the cheque, but I don't let go yet. I draw the cheque back towards myself, pulling his hand with it, and lean towards him.

"I don't care what you do with this money," I mutter. "Give it to the widows. Invest it. Blow it on coke." My pinching grip on the cheque grows tighter. Sev doesn't let go or pull back, meeting my dark gaze steadily with his paler one as I continue speaking. "But any claim you had on Deirdre Elizabeth O'Malley is gone now. Fucking annihilated. I don't want to see any of your men within a hundred metres of her. If I do, they'll get the same treatment as the soldiers who came to her house. And there won't be a fat cheque for you in recompense this time."

Sev cocks his head, his eyes narrowing slightly. Finally, I release the cheque. He slides it into his jacket and coolly replies, "Noted." He raises his drink as if toasting me, and light glances on scotch the same colour as his eyes. "Enjoy your new plaything. You've certainly paid enough for her."

As he turns and leaves with his two men, I suddenly think he maybe isn't as smart as I thought he was. Because if he can't tell that Deirdre is worth ten times what I've paid for her then he's a damn fool.

I scan the room for Deirdre, finding her with Curse. I'm satisfied that she's safe, but I want to get her home soon. I've staked my claim on her publicly, paid Sev off, and I don't need to waste much more time here.

I take a step, the first of many to cross the gallery floor towards her, but someone blocks my path.

"Elio," says a high, syrupy voice.

"Nat," I grunt in irritated reply. I take Natalia in with a quick glance. Long, bright blonde hair swishing around her shoulders. Tight golden dress that makes her tits and hips look fantastic. Lips so lubricated with gloss they'd slide up and down my shaft like a fucking wet dream.

And I don't feel a thing.

The seductive smile on her face hardens at my lack of reaction to her. She wants me to want her and can tell that I don't.

"What's with the ginger?" she asks. And I feel something now, alright. Rage.

"None of your concern," I warn. But she ignores the deadly edge to my voice, pouting and crossing her arms until her boobs practically reach her throat.

"I thought you didn't fuck redheads," she snaps. "Didn't you tell me that last year when I dyed my hair red? I changed it back to blonde the next week and fried my fucking ends off."

It's not just red hair I don't like. It's the colour in general, especially when it veers into orange. Too garish, too hot, and most of the time I don't want to fucking look at it. Unless it's red wine, or blood, but both of those things are too dark to be confused with fire.

Deirdre's hair looks like fire. A riot of orange-red flame tumbling down her back. I stare at her, jaw working, my fingers flexing inside my gloves. For a single, mind-numbing second, I think I smell smoke, and I wonder how fast I can cross this crowded room and grab her.

But then I breathe out between my teeth, realizing it's the scent on Natalia's hair and clothing. I'd forgotten she smokes. She knows better than to do it in front of me, but she must have had a cigarette recently, because the smell is fresh and not covered up by the cloud of hairspray and perfume around her. It sets me on edge.

"Who says I've changed my rules?"

Nat's shiny lips part in an O of affronted surprise.

"Are you shitting me, Elio? I just watched you basically fuck her right there on the dance floor. It looked like you were practically inside of her! And she's dripping with goddamn diamonds. Don't tell me that they're hers."

"You and I aren't together. Why do you give a shit who's warming my bed?" I ask.

"*Warming your bed?*" she hisses. "I've never even been allowed to step foot in your goddamn house! You only ever want me to suck your dick in your car, or in hotels!"

"They were nice hotels," I remind her flatly. The most expensive Toronto has to offer. She can't complain on that front.

"That's not the point and you know it!"

She's right. I do know it. I know exactly why she's pissed and I should have seen this coming. She's the daughter of a capo loyal to our family. But she doesn't just want to be somebody important's daughter.

She wants to be somebody important's wife.

She switches tactics, going from pissy to sultry.

"Come on, Elio," she murmurs, laying a hand on my chest. "Let me take care of you tonight. Suck you." Her tongue touches her glossy lips. "Ride you."

My cock twitches, not because of Nat, but because of the image her words create. The image of a woman's head bobbing between my spread thighs. When that woman's eyes meet mine, they're not Nat's brown ones, but blue. Burning with hate and defiance and inescapable need, all at once.

Then I imagine Deirdre riding me. Fuck, she's a virgin. So innocent she probably wouldn't even know how. Would need my hands on her hips, rocking her, guiding her, just like I guided her greedy little clit against my thigh tonight.

I look over Nat's head and find Deirdre's eyes fastened on me from across the room. All the things to look at in here – the well-dressed people, the beautiful art – and I'm the one her gaze seeks out. *Eyes on me, Songbird.*

Nat is still touching me. I grip her wrist and pull her hand from my chest.

"Get out of here and take a fucking shower," I mutter, dropping her hand. "Don't ever come before me reeking of smoke again."

Nat balks and looks at me like I've slapped her, but I ignore her reaction. There's only one woman not related to me by blood or marriage in this building I actually care about.

She watches me with wary blue eyes as I approach.

Like she cannot turn away.

Chapter 20

Deirdre

I stay, shaky and silent, with Curse as Elio threads his way through the event's attendees. After he's out of my line of sight, I find myself staring at my own shoes, unable to look up and meet anyone's gaze. How many people here know what I just did? How many of them know that I just came in my captor's arms? My cheeks are hot. So is the place between my legs.

Elio is gone for a while, and I can't stand that I do it, but eventually I can't help myself from looking for him. Maybe it's the prey needing to know where the predator is. A self-preservation instinct.

He draws my attention with magnetic power and I find him instantly. He's taller than basically everyone here, a prowling wall of a man in an all-black suit. All black except for the snowy white of his pocket square, which I once again notice looks slightly out of place.

There's something else not black on his chest, I see suddenly. A hand, resting in the area of his sternum in an intimate, possessive gesture. That hand is attached to an absolute bombshell of a woman standing almost as close to him as I was a few moments ago. My insides twist when Elio's gaze meets mine over her head.

Just how many women does he have in rotation?

I'm probably just one of many. That should be a relief. Relief that Elio's attention might not always be so fiercely pinned on me.

But... it's not. It makes me feel shitty and small and pathetic. Makes me feel even worse for reacting to him the way I do, reacting to him the way I've never reacted to any man, when for him I'm just one idiotic girl out of who knows how many.

His eyes still on mine, Elio grasps the woman's wrist and pulls her hand off of his chest. He lets it drop, says something, then cuts around the blonde woman, heading straight for me. Instinctively, I try to move backwards, but my ass hits the table, rattling glasses, which makes Curse's eyes snap to me.

"What does your brother really want?" I ask as Elio approaches, taking up so much space in my vision I know he'd blot out the sun if it were daytime.

Curse watches me silently, and I decide he probably won't answer. Maybe even he doesn't know.

But then, he says something. I'm pretty sure it's the first word I've heard him speak this entire time.

It's a short reply. One single word.

"You."

There's no time for clarification, because Elio is back. I cross my arms and look away from him.

"Sev's got his money."

I'm not sure if Elio is talking to Curse or to me. Maybe both of us.

Sev's money... A million dollars, handed over like it's nothing.

Handed over for me. Elio buying me and protecting me all at once.

But who will protect me from him?

Elio's hand once again settles on my lower back, and I nearly jump out of my skin at the contact. It's like my skin is electrified. Even the softest touch jolting through me.

"Are we leaving?" I ask tightly as he steers me through the room once more. But we aren't heading for the exit. We're walking towards another table of food.

We stop in front of it, and before me is the biggest, most beautiful cake I've ever seen. It looks like a wedding cake you'd see in a magazine. Three creamy white layers decorated with elaborate blue buttercream flowers and sugar beads that look like real pearls. My stomach grumbles, and I grimace. I wish I could turn my body into a block of ice. That I had no needs. No need to eat. No terrible need between my legs. If I could somehow disconnect myself from my own inescapable physical impulses, I could be just a little more in control.

But I can't. I'm hungry. My pussy aches. My skin crawls and tingles and burns under the firm stamp of Elio's hand.

It's odd the cake is still in one perfect piece while the rest of the food has been picked away at over the evening. It's not like the event just started, and we got here late.

Almost as if reading my thoughts, Elio slides his hand off my back and grabs a large metal cake server. Some strange impulse takes hold in me.

"Wait! Don't cut it," I burst out.

Elio quirks a dark brow at me, and I flush under his gaze.

"I feel like... I feel like we're not allowed," I say, feeling incredibly stupid as I do so. But this cake is just sitting here untouched, like it's for later or something. Like someone else is supposed to take the first piece.

Elio stares at me for a long moment. Then, he turns back to the cake, lifts the cake server, and plunges it into the top tier. He does it again, creating a huge slice, then puts that slice on a plate and holds it out to me.

"Why don't you think anyone else has cut into this, yet?" he asks. I stare at the slice of cake. Red velvet. "Just who, exactly, do you think this cake is for?"

"For... for the event. I thought Valentina was going to do something with it, or..."

My brows wrinkle inward as I notice something on the piece Elio holds out to me. Thinly piped blue frosting, a tiny slice of a letter.

141

I crane my neck to see the top of the highest tier, my eyes dragging over words I hadn't noticed before.

Happy birthday Songbird.

"It's a birthday cake," I say, stunned. It's a pointless observation. He obviously knows what it is. It's spelled out on the fluffy surface. "How does Valentina know today's my birthday?"

"She doesn't."

My throat tightens. The only one who's mentioned my birthday in the past twenty-four hours is...

Elio.

"You did this?" I turn back to him, finding him still holding the plate out to me, his eyes boring into my face. His stance, holding up the plate, makes his suit jacket gape ever so slightly. It shifts the white pocket square, revealing an edge of lace that looks oddly familiar.

My breath explodes out of me.

"Your pocket square!" I hiss, my body alight with confused embarrassment. "That's my... my..."

I can't get the words out. But I know exactly what I'm looking at now. Carefully folded and lovingly tucked into Elio's luxurious, expensive pocket is my *fucking underwear*. The panties I was wearing the night he took me.

A smirk tugs at his mouth, the scarring along the left side of his jaw making the expression crooked.

"Probably a good thing I've got an extra pair on me, considering you seem to have forgotten yours," he drawls. "Maybe I should pull them out right now, unfold them, and slide them up your legs. Although, they haven't been washed."

"*Haven't been washed,*" I echo in astonishment, shaking my head back and forth so hard it makes my brain feel like it's colliding with my skull. He's not just using my panties as his pocket square at a very fancy, very public event, but he's using my *dirty* panties. "Why... What the hell?" I stammer. "Why wouldn't you at least wash them?"

It's an absurd question. Like I'm trying to tease some sort of rationality out of completely unreasonable behaviour. Oh, yes, panties as a pocket square. That makes sense, as long as they're clean!

Not.

Elio's smirk extends to a grin.

"Now why would I do that?" he asks, his voice like silk and smoke. He takes in a deep breath through his nose, filling his chest, then lets it out with a satisfied *ahh* sound. Like he's just taken in a lungful of pristinely fresh air on a mountainside hike. "Don't need cologne when I can smell like Songbird instead."

Oh my fucking God.

I absorb his words, still shaking my head in disbelief. My disbelief only deepens when I remember the scent of his cologne on him from dancing earlier, and I realize he just made a joke.

Elio Titone, a man with more blood on his hands than a butcher, has a sense of humour.

For some reason, that's even more disconcerting than his violence.

This is too much. I'm overcome with the almost feral need to get my panties back. To lay claim to them, because they're fucking mine. My hand snaps upward to tear them out of Elio's pocket, but he's faster. He blocks me with the plate, and my hand sinks into buttercream and dense red velvet, coating my fingers in sticky softness.

"Shit," I mutter, pulling my hand back and staring at the mess.

"Lick it off."

"What? No!"

He sets down the plate then grips my wrist.

"Lick it off or I will."

I stare at him mutinously, just daring him to do it. He may be insane enough to use my underwear as a goddamn fashion accessory, but he and I are the only ones who actually know what it is. That panties pocket square was a private message just for me. But standing in the middle of a public event and licking my hand in front of everyone? No way, that's-

He sucks my pinky into his mouth.

My breath catches as hot wet suction works over my smallest finger. Elio's tongue swipes along the line of my knuckles, the strokes demanding and so sensitizing I almost forget where we are. But, oh, *God*, there are people everywhere, and it feels like the whole world is watching me vibrate under this man's mouth. The thorny shame of it pulses in my clit.

I try to tug my hand away.

Elio lets my finger out of his mouth, sucking up the length of it as he does so until it's released with a wet popping sound. But he doesn't let go of my wrist.

I yank harder. He grasps me more firmly.

"I told you what would happen," he said, his voice quiet but hardened with a dangerous edge. "I told you that if you didn't lick this sweet mess off of your fingers then I would. You need to learn that when you disobey me, there are consequences."

Why do I feel those words deep in my core? Why do my nipples harden in response?

Why do I feel anything, *anything* towards this man besides pure fucking hate?

And how do I make it all stop?

Elio moves to start sucking my next finger when I cry out, "Fine!"

The word is out before I've even realized I've said it, but there's no backing down now. Because Elio is guiding my hand towards my mouth, a look of challenge in those obsidian eyes. I lick my lips, and his gaze falls to my mouth, muscles in his jaw flexing.

I start to lick my hand.

I try to do it fast. Get this over with. My tongue laps at my sticky skin, and I swallow the sweet cake and frosting down. This is hands-down the most delicious cake I've ever eaten, and that annoys me. It annoys me that the best birthday cake I've ever received came from *him*, and that it has to be licked off my own skin with *his* fingers on my wrist and *his* eyes on my face.

I try to ignore the fact that I could have just taken the plate when he'd first offered it and eaten it with a fork. Try to ignore the fact that he actually did give me a chance to eat this stupidly amazing cake like a normal person. But nothing about this situation is normal. Not the cake. Not him. And definitely not me. Not anymore.

I'm mostly looking at my own hand, trying to get every crumb and smear of frosting as quickly as I can. But when I do flick a glance up at Elio, his face has completely changed. The look of challenge there is gone, replaced by something so intense it alarms me. His jaw is set hard, his nostrils flaring, and he almost looks angry. Angry with me for doing exactly what he told me to do.

"What?" I ask, shaken by his expression. "You're the one who told me to-"

He doesn't let me finish. Face thunderous, he pulls me by the hand and says, "Let's go."

Chapter 21

Elio

I thought her submission would be better. That it would soothe something inside me, make me feel like I was getting back on track with her somehow. That it would be what I wanted.

I should have known that it would be worse. So much fucking worse. Deirdre glaring at me and hating me and telling me *no* is one thing. Deirdre obedient, sucking frosting off her own skin because I told her to, her wet pink tongue gliding all over because I've cornered her, is practically catastrophic. It turns my insides dark and hungry and twisted. It makes me want to push her harder, until she buckles. Until she breaks. Until all she can do is exactly what I tell her to because there isn't a single fucking thought in her head that I didn't put there.

Deirdre obeying me is addictive.

I'm already addicted to her music and her scent. If I get in this any deeper, I'm fucking done for.

The cold air outside helps clear my head a little, but it doesn't last long, because then we're in my car, the space so small and confined. So fucking close, so easy to tell her to take out my cock and suck it the way she just sucked her slender fingers.

I focus on the road as I drive, gripping the steering wheel hard with one hand, knowing that Deirdre's watching me.

"Am I ever going to get my panties back?"

"No," I reply curtly. I think about the intimate white fabric tucked into my pocket and want to pull it out. Stroke it. Want to press it to my face and inhale hard, but I'm pretty sure at this point if I try that I'll veer right off the goddamn road.

"Alright, then," Deirdre says. Her tone turns cool, almost business-like. "How much are they worth? Are you buying them? Does that wipe out some of my debt?"

"I loaned your family millions of dollars. You don't think I've already paid for these?" I grunt. "They were mine the second they touched your skin."

"No," Deirdre says firmly. "I have my own job, my own bank account. I bought almost all of my own clothes with my money, not my dad's. So, I'll repeat my earlier question. How much are they worth to you?"

Fucking priceless, is what I want to say. But telling her that I'd wipe her entire seven figure debt for a sniff of her used panties is not exactly going to put me in a position of power here.

But even so, I have to admit I'm impressed by her right now. Trying to negotiate with someone like me, in a situation like this.

"Name your price," I say, turning the car onto Brindle Path.

Deirdre pauses, as if she didn't actually expect me to agree to this. I can practically hear the gears turning inside her head.

"Twenty thousand dollars."

"Done."

"Wait, what?" She sounds stunned, her coolly confident business-woman mask slipping away, and I smirk.

"Should have asked for more, Songbird."

The guard opens the gate to the house, and I drive up and put the car in park.

"Fine, then," she says as we emerge from the vehicle. "What about my rate per performance? Per song?"

The answer is the same as before. *Priceless.*

I don't speak as I open the door. I start mounting the stairs and she follows without needing to be told, which makes my cock hard.

Clearly, she's learned from the negotiations in the car, because her proposed sum this time is much higher than before.

"A million dollars per song!" she declares.

I let out a bark of a laugh at the balls of an offer like that. At that rate, her debt would be paid in less than a week. It could be paid off in a single fucking night.

"Nice try," I tell her as we reach the top of the stairs.

"Fine. A hundred thousand per song."

"Not if you're going to pull more of that *Twinkle Twinkle Little Star* shit," I reply as we enter my bedroom. We both stop walking, and she looks at me, her face determined and so damn pretty it makes my fingers twitch.

"I won't," she says firmly. "You can pick the songs. I don't care. I'll learn anything, play anything."

I hear the rest of the sentence without her having to say it out loud.

I'll do anything to get the fuck away from you.

"A hundred thousand per performance, not per song," I counter. "If the performance meets my standards."

She presses her lips together, considering.

"Define performance."

"A set, unbroken period of playing. An hour. An evening. However long I say it is."

She nods slowly.

"OK. So that's, what, about sixty performances? If I play for you every day my debt will be paid in two months."

My teeth grind. I can see how smart she is. The clever, iron will driving her to save herself. I admire it, I do.

But I also want to strangle it. Want to remind her that no matter what she does, no matter how much money exchanges hands, she's mine until I say she's not.

And I can't see myself saying that anytime soon.

Or ever.

"Not so fast," I murmur, and I both loathe and love the look of unhappy doubt that flickers over her features. "I won't be hanging around here every day and night waiting for you to play for me. You won't be earning a hundred grand a day. And maybe I should bring that contract out again and remind you of the interest rate. Forty-two percent," I explain when she cocks her head in confusion.

She blanches.

"Forty-two percent," she says in disbelief. "That's outrageous. That's-"

"That's what you get when you borrow money from fucking loan sharks," I tell her. "I'm not a bank." I take a step towards her. "I'm not your friendly neighbourhood credit union." Another step, until I'm close enough to grasp her chin and tilt her face up to mine. "And I'm certainly not a charity."

"Fine," she hisses, jerking her chin from my hand. "Then let's start. Right now."

She moves away, then returns a moment later with her violin. And without her shoes.

The straps from her shoes have left criss-crossing red lines on her fair skin, and the marks make my blood heat.

"What do you want me to play?" she asks. I can tell she's trying to assume a look of professional neutrality. But that spark of defiance in her eyes is still there.

"Something good," I say, sitting on the edge of my bed and spreading my thighs. "Something Irish."

Her slender orange eyebrows rise at that, but she recovers quickly with a nod. She lifts her violin and bow, and is about to start, when I say, "Not like that."

"Not like what?" she asks, frowning.

"Not way over there." I point downwards, to the space between my thighs. "You'll play right here."

"I... I can't do that. It's too close. I won't be able to focus. I-"

"I told you that you'd earn one hundred thousand dollars per performance if the performance meets my standards," I remind her. "I get to choose where and how and what you play. Now come here."

She shifts on her little bare feet, and I wonder if she'll disobey me, if she'll fight. But she doesn't. She comes to me, with small soft steps, and there it is again, that darkness that almost feels like rage when she obeys me. A darkness that tells me to order her to kneel, right now, so I can jam my cock down her throat.

But more than anything right now, I want to hear her play. It's why I've brought her here, after all.

Deirdre stops between my knees.

"Closer," I urge her. Her breath gets shaky, but she does it anyway, stepping forward until her hips are a mere inch from my crotch.

"Now play," I rasp.

She does.

She starts slowly, the notes almost melancholic, before everything intensifies, rising and quickening into a relentlessly, tragically beautiful rhythm. I groan, letting my eyes fall shut. This is what I wanted, what I needed. This luminous, ravenous, drugged-up feeling. The bleeding, brutal beauty that Deirdre wields with the precise yet wild artistry of an angel. I fist the bedding, tilting my head back, letting the notes fall over me like snow, like rain, like a blessing and a curse. Sacred and profane. Salvation and ruin. Celestial, ethereal, and deeply, primally human.

How the fuck does she do this?

I've listened to violin on endless repeats for the past year and a half. I'm pretty sure I've even saved this exact song to a playlist somewhere. But it's not the same. Nothing touches what Deirdre does to me, and I need to fucking know why.

I crack my eyes open, as if that will help me understand somehow. But that just throws me into chaotic, lustful turmoil, because I'm about eye-level with her breasts, and every time she moves her arms, they bounce and strain the silk of her dress.

Having her this close and hearing her play, properly play, while one breath away from her skin is too fucking much. I've wanted her for too long tonight, and my dick is paying the price. My eyes glued to her chest, my ears and brain and lungs and whatever's left of my heart flooded with her song, I undo the buckle on my belt.

The sound makes Deirdre's eyes snap open. Her playing slows, then stops altogether when I take out my throbbing shaft and start to stroke it.

"What the hell are you doing?" she breathes, her eyes huge and glued to my hand on my dick.

"Keep playing," I command her, fisting myself harder.

"I... What? While you're doing *that*? That's way too distracting!"

"Then close your eyes," I grunt. "Then maybe you won't be so affected by me and the sight of my cock."

She blushes so hard that I see it through the makeup this time.

"I'm not *affected* by you!" she exclaims.

I could tell her all the ways I know that isn't true, starting with how she fucking came on my leg at the gala tonight. But instead, I just spread my thighs wider, stroke myself faster, and tell her, "Prove it."

She swallows so hard the muscles in her throat visibly contract, and fuck, does that make me feel like I'm already close.

"Keep playing," I order. I run my thumb over my agonized tip and add darkly, "Every time you stop before I tell you to, I'll dock your pay by ten thousand dollars."

That gets her attention real quick. Jaw tight, she scrunches up her face and starts to play again.

"Good little Songbird," I groan. The music roars through my blood just like desire. Velvety sensation expands in my groin, wrapping around the base of my spine and tightening in my balls. The feeling rises, binds me tighter, when I see Deirdre's nipples hardening right before my very eyes.

She may hate me, but a part of her likes this. Likes being embarrassed, likes being shoved into these situations. Even now, I can see how she's squeezing her thighs together beneath her dress.

I lean forward and suck one of her nipples into my mouth.

The music stops, and she cries out. I release my cock, raise my hand out to the side, then bring it firmly down against her ass. She jerks forward with the force of the motion, gasping. I rub the place I spanked her, tonguing her hot little bud of a nipple through the damp silk before I pull back slightly and meet her wild gaze.

"Now you're at ninety-thousand," I inform her sternly. "*Keep playing.*"

She looks like she wants to drive her bow right through my eye. I drag the silk of the dress to the side, freeing her breast, and tease her nub with my tongue before I tell her that she's about to lose another ten thousand.

Panting, she returns her bow to the strings.

And I return my hand to my cock.

Chapter 22

Deirdre

I saw my way through the melody, barely even aware of what song I'm playing now. I'm completely relying on muscle memory to keep me going as Elio sucks my bare nipple into his mouth, teasing the screaming tip with his tongue. I can't think about what I'm doing. Can't think about any of this. I just have to get through it without falling apart.

Or stopping playing.

My ass cheek stings, sparking tingles emanating outward from where Elio's hand came down on me with a *thwack*. Those sharp, prickly tingles keep fucking spreading, all the way down, down towards my pussy, lighting up my clit. There had been more shock than pain when his hand had connected with my ass, and now any pain there was is morphing into poisonous pleasure, pulsing and burning and making me wonder what it would feel like if he did it again.

But I won't find out. Because I *will not* stop playing. Not now. Not when he's challenged me the way he has. I have to keep going, keep playing by his rules. Keep earning money to chip more and more away at the chains of debt that bind me.

So, I let my arms go, let them do what they know how to do, guiding me through the rhythm of the song when the rest of my body is tumbling headlong towards another disastrous orgasm.

I never knew my nipples were this sensitive. Elio's lips and tongue are firm and wet. Demanding and greedy. Soon, he isn't satisfied with just one breast, and he urges silk away from the other, until both are bared to him. He sucks my other nipple into his mouth, biting it gently, then harder, until I yelp. But I grit my teeth and I don't fucking stop. My notes may be getting clumsy, but I keep going. My bow is my sword and I will fight until the bitter end.

The music is loud in my ears, but even so I can hear the ragged drag of Elio's breath through his nose. The filthy wet sounds his mouth makes against my nipple. The relentless pumping of his cock. A cock that is harder than any human flesh ought to be. I could tell just by looking at it, without even touching, how engorged and unyielding his shaft is. He sucks me harder, and I'm sure that he's testing me. Trying to make me falter. To prove that I can't do this. That I'm not as immune to him as I claimed.

But I keep playing. I keep doing what I know how to do – making music. I keep going until I almost think I might win this time. His mouth is hot, hateful, delicious sin but maybe I can beat him. Maybe I can make it. Just keep going, get to the end of the song, and –

Without warning, his mouth detaches from my nipple, leaving my skin feeling cold and tender. I don't open my eyes, not letting myself get distracted even for a moment.

But because of that, I have absolutely no warning when his tongue returns to me. Not on my breast.

But on my clit.

He's dragged up one side of my skirt, splitting it wide at the slit, and his face is pressed between my legs. I flinch and muffle a moan when he circles my clit in hard, relentless circles with the tip of his tongue. Pleasure and shame shudder through me in equal measure, making my clit swollen and more sensitive than it's ever been. My legs quake, threatening to collapse, as his tongue circles and flicks.

When he groans, latches on and sucks, it feels like my entire spine has turned to viscous honey.

I don't realize I've stopped playing until a vicious *thwack!* fills the silence.

"Ah!" I cry. "Fuck!" The burn on my ass cheek is sudden and bright. Just like Elio did last time, he massages me firmly immediately after doing it, dispersing jerky waves of prickling heat over my ass and through my core. It feels like my nerves have been replaced with sparklers. Like everything is darkness until Elio's hand connects and makes white light burst into a million glinting shards.

"Eighty thousand," he rasps into the damp curls between my legs.

Shit. Shit, shit, shit!

My sense of victory is fading fast. I shakily raise my bow and violin, and then moan in complaint when he draws a slick, greedy stripe over my clit with his tongue.

"This isn't fair," I whimper.

"I'm not a fair man, Deirdre."

There's no deep, abiding sense of morality guiding Elio at his core. No good man under the demands and violence. He only speaks the languages of death and sex and money. Languages that, up until this moment, I've never known a word of.

"I... I can't-"

Thwack! Another hot smack. Another long, delirious suck on my clit. Another faltering yet inevitable step closer to climax.

"Seventy thousand."

Why is this happening? Why am I *letting* this happen? Why am I not pushing his head away, kicking and screaming and fighting? No one's ever gone down on me before, and I shouldn't let him be the first.

I shouldn't be panting and clenching, practically vibrating against his tongue. I shouldn't be waiting in wriggling anticipation for his hand to find my ass again.

I shouldn't look down at his dark head at my pussy, because fuck, that's the worst mistake I could have made. Because he looks good, and I don't want to think he looks good, but he *does*. His hair is so black and thick and curling ever so slightly at the ends. It's not cut very short; it's long enough that pieces have tumbled forward over his forehead.

He meets my gaze, looking up through his hair and lashes that are darker and thicker than I'd previously noticed. He lifts his hand, the black leather shape of it in the air like an omen.

Just that, just that simple threat, has my hips rocking forward against his face, nerves in my clit jumping with expectation. But I halt the movement, and furious pride fights against my submission.

I grit my teeth and put my bow to the strings once more.

Only, I truly don't know how long I'll last now. I don't know if Elio is trying to reward me for doing what I'm told, or trying to break me. Because his mouth is suddenly harder, hungrier, his tongue dragging backwards to circle my entrance before moving forward once more to devour my quivering clit. My arms feel like they're full of sand and it's a miracle I can lift them at all at this point. My posture is completely off – I'm hunching further and further forward, like I'm curling towards Elio, curling *around* him, my body seeking contact even though I rebel against it.

I fight to keep my arms in place. Every press and slide of my fingertips is a battle. Every grind of my bow a war.

I don't know if this war is with Elio...

Or with myself.

His tongue dips backwards again, and then jabs inside me, making my toes curl against the smooth hardwood floor. But I won't stop again. I swear I won't. I'll keep going until, until...

Until the firm, leather press of his thumb sends shockwaves through my pulsing clit. He moves his tongue inside me, almost like he's *fucking* me with it, while his thumb grinds on my clit and everything clenches and burns and constricts and I can't, I fucking *can't*.

My violin and bow sag down, and I arch forward, my spine collapsing, until my hands and instruments connect with Elio's broad, muscled back. The pressure of his thumb disappears from my clit, and I know exactly what it fucking means, because I'm trembling and ashamed and so fucking ready for the terrible, electric collision of leather on silk. Hand on flesh.

Elio waits a moment before he does it. Like maybe he's giving me one final chance to finish the song.

Or maybe he just wants the crackling anticipation of the threat to build, build, build alongside the throbbing at my core, the pleasure rising like a dark symphony inside me. I'm right there, *right there*, and I can't stop it. I can't fight it. And the worst part is that maybe I don't even want to, now. Maybe there's something dirty and broken inside me, some part of me that thinks maybe I deserve this, that I need it. That the punishment is an answer to a question I've never dared to ask. The reply to some prayer that's lived, unspoken and unacknowledged, at the very core of my soul for the past ten years.

Elio's hand finally connects, the sound of the slap ripping through the air. A ragged moan tears from my throat. Biting pain and pleasure expand from where his hand grips my flesh, undulating downwards and inwards until my pussy clamps down on his tongue, over and over again.

My hands jerk and then release, my violin and bow sliding down Elio's back until they hit the bed. I fist the back of his jacket so hard I wonder if I'll rip the expensive fabric. The sounds coming out of my mouth are a fucking abomination. I don't recognize my own voice as I moan, so horny and pathetically needy as I come from getting spanked and tongue-fucked by this man who's taken everything from me. I can't even control the grinding motion of my hips now, and I whimper in embarrassment as I ride Elio's tongue, then whimper again, louder, when he pulls it away.

"*Fuck*," he groans. He'd been bent over, hinging at the waist to access my pussy, but now he straightens up in his sitting position. My pussy clenches again at the sight of him. So huge and dangerous and purely masculine, muscled thighs spread, shoulders straining the tight confines of his suit, scarred jaw flexing. Cock standing straight up from a thatch of dark hair at its base, thick and veiny and so engorged his tip is red, almost purple. And, oh God, his *face*. His *eyes*. He's got that look again. The one he had when he watched me lick the cake off my hand at the gala. That expression of murderous darkness. Rage so ravenous I can't tell it apart from desire.

The sight of his dark leather glove curling around his swollen shaft is so dangerously erotic I can't stand it. My breath rips in and out of my lungs, and my fingers dig in to his shoulders when he strokes a glistening bead of moisture from his tip. Why am I still holding on to him?

"I didn't bring you here for this, you know," he grits out, sliding his fist up and down his cock. "I really did just bring you here to play for me. But you're so fucking disobedient. And so fucking pretty when you do obey."

His words are like a physical caress, and I can't escape them. *So fucking pretty when you obey.*

"My good, bad little Songbird," he groans. "Do you see how fucking hard you make me?"

Of course I do. It would be impossible not to. Something in me shivers with satisfaction that I'm the one who did this to him. I may not have any control over this situation, or even my own body, but at least I have some control over his.

His voice lowers an entire dangerous octave. "You're not supposed to make me so hard I can't see straight."

"Then what am I supposed to do?" I whisper. "Why did you choose me? Is it just about the debt? Because I..." I hesitate, as if I'm not supposed to ask. But it's not like he was hiding them. The CDs were right there on a shelf in the open. "I found the CDs. Recordings of all my performances from the past year and a half."

Elio breathes out, long and hot, a stirring motion over my bared breasts.

The movement of his hand slows.

"Let me tell you a story," he says. "The story of the songbird, the monster, and the man." His hand stops moving altogether. "One hot summer day, the man begged a monster for money. But the monster knew it was a bad deal. He was just in the process of turning the man down flat when he heard something."

"Heard what?"

"A song. A song that got inside him, a song he couldn't shake. He needed to find out what it was and who the hell could play like that. So, he looked up. And there was the prettiest little songbird he ever did see." His hand isn't moving now, but his hips are, grinding slowly and sensuously up into his leather fist. A new roughness enters his voice as he continues. "In that instant, the monster knew he'd lend the man the money as long as it meant that he could get that songbird for himself. He'd wait, bide his time until the term ran out. But by that point, he was already hopelessly fucking addicted."

His hips buck, fucking his fist faster. I can't tear my gaze away from the way his slick head appears then disappears into the leather.

"So the monster watched the songbird every chance he got. Took her music home, too, to try to get another hit of her, even though it wasn't anywhere near enough."

His words are so rough now, almost slurred.

"And then, one cold winter morning, the first of the new year and the day that songbird turned twenty, time ran out for the man. The monster returned. And this time-" His breath catches, making the words jagged, "the monster took the songbird for himself. And he killed anyone who got in his fucking way."

A creamy jet spurts from Elio's tip, followed by another, and another. Rope after rope of come, raining down on his pants and his glove. Some of it even reaches my naked chest, wet and glistening and staining me. As his come sinks in, so does the story he's just told me. Understanding explodes in my head like a bomb.

He didn't just take me because of my father's debt. He lent my father the money, created that debt in the first fucking place, specifically so that he could have me. I remember something he said before, something I hadn't understood. Until now.

From the very beginning, I didn't consider this a loan, but an investment.

The investment was in me.

Having me wasn't a byproduct of a deal gone bad. It was the *whole fucking point*. The only reason the deal existed in the first place.

"You weren't even going to lend my dad the money until you saw me," I say tightly, my mind spinning. "You engineered this entire situation just so you could have access to me! You created the debt just to trap me with it!"

He drags a finger through the come dripping between my breasts.

"Technically, your father created the debt," Elio says coolly. "He was so deep in the hole by that point that he had no choice but to come begging to Peter in order pay Paul. But otherwise, yes, you are correct. I would never have lent your father that money if I hadn't seen you and heard you play that day." He tucks himself back into his pants and stands, looking down at me with unrepentant eyes. "I lent him that money precisely because I knew I'd never get it back. Because I knew that I'd get you in the end."

It infuriates me how easily he admits it. That he doesn't even care enough about what I think of him to deny what he's done.

"I hate you," I whisper thickly. Tears are building at the backs of my eyes, tightening my throat.

"You're free to do so," Elio says calmly. Almost cavalierly. He swipes his finger through the come on my skin again, dragging it over to my nipple and rubbing it into the agonizingly sensitive peak as he leans down.

"Enjoy it, Deirdre. Enjoy hating me," he whispers against my ear, teasing my nipple into a taut and aching point. "Because it's one of the only freedoms you have left."

I stumble backwards and away from him, reeling.

I spin, seeing the doorless entry into the other bedroom.

There's nowhere to run. And I know the act is hopeless.

But I run anyway.

Chapter 23

Deirdre

When I wake up in the morning, I feel well-rested, and I don't like it. Don't like how incredibly comfortable this bed is. Or how deeply my body fell into slumber after last night. After...

After I came. *Twice.*

I pull the covers up over my head, as if I can hide my shame that way. What is it about Elio, and my body around him, that turns me into someone I don't recognize? Someone I don't know?

My phone buzzes on the bedside table, and I whip off the bedding, reaching for it. Maybe it's my father contacting me. Maybe everything Elio told me about him leaving, about Bridget, was just a lie meant to make me fall further into this trap, this world. To make me trust him.

But there's no word from Dad.

There is, however, a text from Brian, letting me know he's back from Christmas break in Ottawa and wants to see me. I almost laugh, bitterly, about the change in circumstances since December. I spent weeks avoiding Brian, and now I couldn't even see him if I wanted to. Something tells me that meeting up with my ex-boyfriend is absolutely not something Elio would allow. And part of me is pissed about that, not because I want to be anywhere near Brian, but because of the control.

But another part of me, a part low in my belly, tightens strangely. Almost as if I like this. Like the fact that the bars of my cage have both trapped me and protected me.

But I'm not protected, am I? Not from Elio. He's the one I need to focus on, to be most worried about. I wonder what Elio would do if I did somehow meet up with another man. I wonder what he'd do if Brian tried to get to me now.

Probably wouldn't end well for Brian.

And it scares me how that thought brings me a short slice of terrible satisfaction. Fuck, what am I turning into? Elio is not my bodyguard or my boyfriend. He's my abductor. The possessiveness he feels over me is not something to be admired. It's something I need to fight.

Or I will never find my way back to my own life again.

I mentally tally how much was reduced from my debt last night. Twenty thousand from the panties – Jesus Christ, I still can't believe I'm selling my goddamn panties to the mob now – and eighty thousand from last night. Or was it seventy? I remember him getting to eighty-thousand, I remember him saying it directly against me, the words stirring over my aching clit. But I'm pretty sure I stopped then. That's when I... I...

I *came*. For the second time. He spanked me, just hard enough to hurt, just hard enough to let me know exactly how much power he holds and, at the same time, how much he held back, and some buried, dirty part of me had actually liked it.

And the worst thing is, I don't think Elio created that dirty part.

I think it was already there and he just unearthed it. Like he already understands things inside me I don't. Like he knew exactly where to dig.

And then I remember how long he's been watching me. How

long he's been wanting me. And I wonder how much he's learned about me while I had no idea he was even there.

My phone buzzes again, and I scowl, assuming it's Brian, but it's not. It's an email to my University of Toronto email address, sent from another U of T address that I don't recognize. It's a student's email address, but I don't know the name. Frowning, I open it.

HEY!!!! It's Willow! I still don't have my phone. I'm at one of the U of T libraries with my neighbour Dylan and I'm using his school email to contact you. Figured that was better than sending a text from his phone because I can log into his email anywhere to check if you've replied, but I don't have a phone for him to forward a text to.

What is happening??? I heard about last night!!! That you showed up at some Titone event at the AGO decked out in diamonds. People are saying that Elio Titone practically fucked you right there in the middle of the floor you two were dancing so close and that he got you a big slice of cake after that. Elio fucking Titone cutting and serving someone cake!!! Absolutely unheard of. Was it birthday cake? Was the party for you??? What the fuck is going on???

I have no idea how to help you right now, but so help me God, if he's hurting you, I will. Fuck Elio and fuck Darragh (who's even more pissed off after last night, just so you know). I will steal a goddamn tank and crash through the side of wherever you're being held to save you if I have to. Just let me know what's happening. Let me know where you are.

Let me know that you're OK.

Willow

My eyes blur with tears, and I clutch my phone to my squeezing chest. It feels like the entire world's forgotten about me. Like my own life has been erased, crushed under the new reality Elio's imposed upon it. But it's not true. Willow's still out there, loving me, fighting for me. Trying to help me.

She can't, of course. And that changes the tears from ones of affectionate gratitude to ones of hopeless rage. She can't help me. It's not even safe for her to be contacting me this way, especially if

Darragh's as angry as she says he is. I'm an outcast, my father a traitor, and she absolutely cannot be caught associating with me now.

As much as I want to confide in her, to beg her to help me any way she can, I won't. She wants to protect me, but I need to protect her right now. From her father and from Darragh if he finds out she's trying to help me.

I sniff hard and angrily rub tears from my eyes with the back of my hand before I shakily type a reply. With every letter that appears on the screen, I feel like I'm pulling a door shut between us, inch by inch, until it slams and a lock clicks into place.

Willow,

Thank you so much for finding a way to contact me. It means more than you can know.

That party last night wasn't in my honour, but yes, the cake was a birthday cake for me. It may be hard to believe, but I'm safe. Elio is taking care of me.

I stop typing, chewing on my lip, hating the words I've just written and yet not entirely feeling like they're a lie, either. Elio has trapped me, but he's also showered me in luxury even my father's stolen money couldn't buy. Not that Dad spent much of it on me, I think sourly. Elio's kept me fed, clothed me in finery, ordered me the most amazing birthday cake a bakery could possibly produce, and...

Licked my clit until I came.

He also spanked me, I hiss furiously inside my own head. *He told me he owns every part of me. Is heaping more and more debt on top of me with interest rates he could slash but won't.*

I want to tell Willow everything. To spill my guts to her, let her find a way to fix this. But I can't. Because Willow actually would try to fix it, and I don't want her to be the object of Darragh's ire. Or Elio's. So I grit my teeth and keep on typing.

My dad completely fucked me over. He borrowed millions from Sev Serpico and Elio to cover up what he stole from Darragh and then he didn't pay it back. That's why New Year's went down the way it did (is Mr Byrne OK???)

Elio paid off my father's debt to the Camorra and is letting me work off the money Dad owes him. For some reason he likes the way I play violin. So I'm doing that for him and slowly paying everything back that way. It's going to take a while, so don't expect me to resurface anytime soon.

Not that I can resurface at all if Darragh still wants to get his hands on me. I swallow hard, realizing for the first time that the debt might not be the only thing standing between freedom and me. Even if I pay back every cent, even if Elio lets me go, Darragh will be waiting for me. Unless he finds my father first, but I don't want that, either. Even after everything that's happened and everything he's done, I don't want Dad getting murdered over this. I lost one parent and never truly recovered. I can't handle losing another one.

Though haven't I already lost him in a way?

I might never see my father, my only living parent, again.

I focus on finishing my message to Willow so that I don't completely fall apart.

I'm safe, I type out again. *I'm making this work. You don't need to do anything for me right now. Actually, no – the number one thing you can do for me is to keep yourself safe. Nobody will take kindly to you trying to interact with me now. The last thing I want is you getting hurt over this.*

Stay safe, Willow. I love you so much.

Dee

Just as I send the message, I hear the familiar sound of a cart being pushed into the room. My head snaps up to see Rosa bringing breakfast in – a tray laden with pastries and fresh fruit and...

"Is that a pot of tea?" I ask, almost wondering if all the unshed tears are making me see things.

"Sì, sì. Tea. The boss tell me make, so I make."

The boss...

That has to be Elio.

I stare at the small glass teapot like it's something fantastical, like a unicorn that shouldn't exist but somehow does. *Elio told her to bring me tea. Because that's what I like...*

I'm almost scared to drink it. Scared of what it means. Is this kindness? Some small comfort meant to make me happy? Or is it some kind of trap?

I decide that I don't care. I've been dying for a cup of tea since yesterday, and as soon as Rosa brings the cart to a stop beside the bed, I thank her profusely and pour myself a steaming cup.

The scent hits me, and my eyes flutter shut for a moment as I simply inhale. This must be the best scent in the whole world. It's pure, visceral comfort, and my gratitude towards Elio in this moment is so overwhelming I want to cry all over again. God, this must be Stockholm Syndrome, wanting to thank my captor for a simple cup of tea.

But I can't help it. Tea isn't just tea to me. It's family and blooming warmth and memories. It's quiet, early mornings in the kitchen before school with my mom, pouring each other cups from her beautiful vintage teapot as I filled her in on homework and teachers and boys. It's the drink she made to soothe my tender heart when the boy I adored in grade nine told everyone he'd never date someone with hair the colour of an orange highlighter. It's Christmas and Sunday afternoons and soft murmurs and laughter. I always imagined that, the morning of my wedding, Mom and I wouldn't be drinking champagne as we got ready together, but sweet, strong cups of tea.

Sometimes, when I smell it, I can almost feel her with me. She didn't have a signature perfume, my mom. This – the fragrant waft of Irish breakfast tea – was the scent of her.

If Rosa is wondering why I've pressed the heated cup to my forehead like it's some kind of holy relic to be worshipped instead of something to drink, she doesn't say it aloud. Instead, she goes marching into the bathroom, attacking every surface with spray bottles and polishing rags. Soon, the cup is too hot to keep against my skin, and I lower it, staring into the dark, reflective surface of the drink before I take a sip.

It's good tea, though not as strong as I would have liked. I like tea that's been brewed long enough to really stand up to the milk and sugar I usually add. That's how Mom always made it.

But for now, this is good enough. I add less milk and sugar than I normally would so I don't overwhelm the flavour, and, throat aching with tears, I chug it like it's water in the desert. It scalds my throat, but the heat of it feels cleansing, and I keep going until I can't anymore, taking a wet and choking breath. I pick away at the food, then scarf it down, realizing that only charcuterie and a bit of birthday cake for the past day wasn't anywhere near enough sustenance.

I pour myself more tea to wash it all down, holding my cup and scooting out of the bed as Rosa approaches, ready to strip the sheets. My face feels hot as she does it. Nothing even happened in this bed, and yet it feels like she'll somehow be able to know, like I've left some kind of stain, some mark of how fucked up I am that I submitted to Elio so easily last night.

No! It wasn't that easy. I tried to fight. I...

I don't even know what happened. All I know is that it can't happen again.

I think about that – submission, and whether that's truly what I did – for most of the day as I sit alone in my room. Elio doesn't come to me, and neither does Valentina. Rosa brings me lunch (the most amazing pesto chicken and mozzarella sandwich on fresh bread) and dinner (equally amazing braised lamb with potatoes and vegetables) but otherwise I see no one. I keep expecting Elio to show up, but it seems that what he said yesterday was true. He won't just be hanging around me all the time waiting for me to pick up my violin and play for him. I'll have to take whatever opportunities I can when they come to try to make a dent in the debt.

And I'll have to play out of his reach next time.

By 9pm the solitude is starting to grate on my nerves. And so is

167

what happened last night. The more I think about it, the more I can't deny how much more I could have done to stop him. If I'd truly wanted to, I could have pulled away. I could have pushed him, kicked him, bit him. I could have told him no.

I go over and over the interaction in Elio's room last night, hoping I've just forgotten the moment I told him to stop. But I didn't forget it. Because I never fucking said it.

And suddenly, I can't sit here like his good little prisoner anymore. I have to prove to him, and maybe even more to myself, that I'm not going to be bent to his will that easily.

I stomp into the bathroom for a shower. I choose the shower this time because I can hang towels precariously from the glass that juts out from the walls and create at least some semblance of privacy. As I toss towels up over the glass with awkward, grunting movements, I wonder if he's watching me even now. I wriggle out of my clothing inside the shower then toss it out, wondering if I should try to sell him this pair of underwear as well.

And then I wonder who the hell I have become to even consider such a thing.

As I scrub myself, I wonder if Elio knows I'm showering. If, right now, his dark eyes are glued to a screen somewhere. I wonder if he's pissed about my towel barriers.

I wonder if his dick is hard. If his leather-encased fist is gripping it, stroking it, running firmly from thick veiny shaft to smooth tip. If he's going to come just knowing that I'm naked and wet in his house.

A resounding pulse between my legs makes me even more angry than I was before. I turn the water to the coldest setting, yelping at the contrast from the warmth. I force myself to wash in that cold water until I'm shivering, then I yank down one of my hanging towels and wrap it around myself, heading for the closet. I pull on a soft cotton T-shirt (there are bras, but none of them are the correct size, so I skip that) then a pair of silk underwear and slouchy pair of sweatpants.

Fully dressed now, my hair soaking the back of my shirt, I head through my bedroom and into Elio's. I don't stop until I'm at the door.

The door the leads into the rest of the house.

I've never heard anyone lock or unlock it. I also haven't been told to stay in here, though it feels like an unspoken rule. But that's exactly why I need to break it. To prove I still have half a goddamn brain in there. To prove that there's still some spirit that will fight back inside me.

My heart careens wildly in my chest, and I'm terrified that I'm going to regret this, but I do it anyway.

I pull on the door handle and open the door.

I tense, holding my breath, half-expecting Elio to be there, just waiting for me to try something like this. But he's not. There's nobody except for a guy at the top of the stairs in a black dress shirt and black trousers. He's alert, watching me closely, but he doesn't tell me to get back inside the room. Emboldened, I hold his gaze and step forward, one foot in the room and one foot out.

He still doesn't say anything, and with a shuddering breath, I step all the way out.

I fight to keep the grin off my face. This feels like a victory, no matter how small. I've stepped out of the room. Now it's time to see just how far I can go.

I turn towards the staircase, and the guard there, and start walking. The closer I get, the more my stomach twists and my nerves jangle. It's like this guy is staying still and quiet to lull me into a false sense of security so that he can grab me and bring Elio down on my head.

But even as I pass by him, my breath strangling in my throat, he doesn't touch me. I notice that he does follow me down the stairs, but otherwise he makes no move to stop me.

Which must mean...

He's been ordered to let me walk around as I please.

This jolts me into confusion. It almost makes me stop halfway down the stairs. The fact that Elio doesn't mind if I leave the room

169

and wander around his domain. I figured this was, well... not allowed, or something.

I'm about to be grateful to him again, like I was with the tea, but I fiercely tell myself not to be. Elio is not deserving of my gratitude. I shouldn't be thankful I can walk around this house, gorgeous though it is. He's the one who's reduced me to being stuck here in the first place.

The guard from the top of the stairs continues trailing me as I wander. I pass by the front door and cringe when I remember what happened there, what must have been seen on the cameras. When Elio stroked my nipples into aroused hardness after putting in the earrings that are currently on a bedside table upstairs.

I make my way into the kitchen and gape. I'm not a master chef or anything, but I do enjoy cooking, and this is the most insane kitchen I've seen. A massive black granite island floats in the middle, matching the glittering black granite countertops that go along one long end of the open space. Even with all the black, the space doesn't feel cold. The cabinets are a warm natural wood, and there's soft lighting built in everywhere. The fridge is huge – one of those super wide double door stainless steel ones. Most of the other appliances are stainless steel, too, including a very complicated looking espresso machine. Everything is sleek and modern. Except for the stove. I'm sure it's new and seriously expensive, but it has an almost vintage look to it with shiny brass knobs and a gas range top.

I eye the guard who has now stationed himself with his arms crossed at the island I've passed. He doesn't say anything or do anything else to stop me, so I give an internal shrug and head for the fridge. I yank it open, gawking at how much stuff is in this gigantic cooling contraption. Elio did say that there were soldiers stationed all over this house, and I wonder if Rosa cooks for all of them. There's a ton of prepared food in here, containers of meat and pasta and jars of sauces, as well as a small grocery store's worth of raw ingredients – fresh herbs, cheeses, cream. I expect to see tomatoes in here but I don't, and I realize there are tomatoes in a bowl on the countertop.

That bowl of beautiful colour lends the spotless kitchen a sense of hominess that feels almost comforting, and I shove it away.

Beyond the kitchen is another jaw-dropping room I hadn't noticed before – a wine cellar. Although, it's above ground, so is it still a cellar? A wine room? I have no idea. I can tell the difference between different kinds of tea at first whiff, but I have absolutely no palette or real knowledge of wine, even though I do like drinking it.

The wine room is separated from the kitchen by a glass wall so clean it's almost invisible, and I nearly walk right into it. I recover just in time, finally finding a section of the glass that opens smoothly with a slight push. It's much cooler in here than in the rest of the house, and goosebumps form along my bare arms. My braless nipples tighten.

Crossing my arms, I head into the cool, large space. It's darker in here than in the kitchen, too, and everything feels hushed. The bottles of wine all float in curved sections of wood along the shelves, reminding me of ships in a harbour.

Right now, a glass of wine sounds absolutely perfect. I have no idea if I'm allowed to do this, but I decide I don't care. The whole point of venturing out here was to prove that I'm not crushed under Elio's thumb and I'm going to go for it. I gaze around the room, having absolutely no idea which bottle to choose, so I take one out at random. It's a red, and it looks fancy and Italian. Before I lose my nerve, I scuttle back into the kitchen with my prize.

The soldier watching me now has a crease between his brows, like I'm doing something unexpected, or maybe something his boss hasn't specifically given him instructions to handle. I smirk, picturing Elio telling the guards to let me wander around the house, but not addressing what to do if the prisoner decides to get wine drunk. Not that I'm going to get drunk. I need to keep my wits about me. But a drink to take the edge off might be just the ticket.

I already feel drunk – drunk on this tiny bit of power. I realize I'm humming as I slam open drawers and cupboards, looking for a corkscrew. I eventually find one and open the wine, leaving the corkscrew with the cork still stuck in its twirly jaws on the counter. I haven't yet discovered where the wineglasses are, but in the cupboard straight ahead of me are little coffee cups for espresso. I grab one and glug the wine into the cup. *Guess I'm doing shots,* I think as I pick up the tiny cup full of wine. I raise it to my lips and am about to take a sip when a voice slices through the quiet air.

"That how you were taught to drink wine?"

The sound of someone – a very male someone – speaking surprises me so much that I slosh some of the wine down my front. I'm pissed, but then I remember that this isn't even my shirt, so why do I care if it's stained? I turn to look at the guard, then jolt into stillness when I see the guard is gone. Elio is watching me, his hip leaning against the island, the black leather on his right hand plastered palm-down against the granite. The rest of his clothing is all black – dress shirt, pants. It matches the coal-black gleam of his thick hair and the intense darkness of his eyes.

His gaze dips to the dark red wetness staining the front of my shirt. Or maybe to my nipples, because I don't have a bra on and now I'm shivering under his gaze. God, I really need that wine after all. It will warm me. Fortify me. I raise the half-empty ceramic cup to my lips.

"Stop."

I inhale sharply at the command uttered in that deadly-soft voice, cup freezing in midair. There's an instinct inside me that wants to obey him, and it's not entirely due to fear. But that's the very same instinct I've been fighting, and I have to overcome it. Now or fucking never.

I hold his gaze and take a sip.

But you're so fucking disobedient.

The sudden crash of his words from last night makes my skin heat, or maybe it's the wine. I take another sip.

Elio doesn't say anything. He moves towards me, and I want to crowd backwards against the counter and away from him, but I force myself to hold my ground. I brace for him to touch me, but he doesn't. Instead, he plants his left hand on the counter behind me with a slight grunt then lifts his other arm to open a cupboard above my head. At the sound he makes, my eyes go to his muscled but injured shoulder, and suddenly I'm in my backyard, the new year bearing down on me with hatred and guns. I'm barefoot and terrified and cold, but he has me, *he has me*, and both our bodies shudder with the impact of the shot.

"Does it hurt?"

I shouldn't be asking. I shouldn't care. I should *want* him to hurt. I'm too tender-hearted for my own good. How many times has Willow told me that? That I need to be harder and sharper, to cut my way through this world like a knife instead of letting myself be led along. Led by people like my father and my teachers and Brian. By the hole that opened up inside me the day tires slid ten years ago.

Elio is a knife. No, he's an axe. He has both the sharp edge and the bludgeoning strength. What would it be like to have power like that? To see obstacles and carve right through them, without fear and without thought? To bend everything and everyone around you to your will?

Not me, I hiss internally as Elio lowers his arm. *I won't be bent. I will not be broken.*

"Do you care?" Elio asks. There's no sarcastic sneer, no mocking tone in his voice. It's smooth and quiet. Simple and serious. Like he actually wants to hear the answer.

Except I don't even know the answer. The injury – a very serious one at that – that he got protecting me has added yet another layer of complications on top of how I feel about everything that's happened. How I feel about him.

Instead of giving him a straight answer, I ask another question.

"Why did you do it?"

He has a large stemmed wineglass in his hand. He's holding it between us, and he's so fucking close. Still not touching me, but that arm by my hip, that hand on the counter behind me, closes me in.

The massive black wall of him looms in front of me, and my head is tipped up, and his tipped down, so we can look at each other.

"No makeup today," he murmurs. A tingle of tension kisses its way up my spine. If both his hands weren't occupied, I'm sure his leathery touch would be brushing against my cheek right now the way his gaze does.

"Do you care?" I shoot back at him, echoing his own question. I wonder if he prefers me with the mask of makeup. Polished and pretty and presentable.

"I can see your freckles better this way."

My face scorches. God, it's like I'm twelve again. Like when I bought my first foundation to cover my freckles up. Only I had no idea about how to match shades. I didn't have a mom to help me and I ended up wearing foundation as orange as my hair. At least, that's what the girls at school told me between bouts of vicious laughter.

I've come a long, long way from caring about what people think of how I look. I've grown to love my ginger hair, and now freckles are actually in fashion, go freaking figure. Every once in a while, I still catch myself wishing I had blonde hair and skin that tanned instead of burned, but that's only because I miss my mom and want to see more of her gazing back at me from the mirror, not because I necessarily want to look different.

But one sentence from Elio and I'm back there, back to being a desperate, awkward kid. Why the hell do I let him get inside me like this? Why *the fuck* do I care if he doesn't like my freckles? They're part of my face and the only reason he has to look at them in the first place is because *he took me*, because he –

"I like them."

The whirlwind of childhood humiliation and confusion instantly ceases inside me, a storm collapsing in on itself. I shake my head, making wet tendrils of hair slap against my shoulder blades, because I have nothing to say to that.

So I go back to my question. The one he didn't answer.

"Why did you do it? Why did you get shot protecting me?"

Some dark emotion shutters the back of his eyes. He pushes off from the counter, turning towards the island where I left the wine bottle. He pours wine into the wineglass with his back to me and, as casually as someone might mention the state of the weather, says, "This body ain't worth shit, Songbird. I'd put it between you and a bullet any day of the week."

I gape at him, staring at the muscled power of his black-clad back. Scarred though it is, that body is an anatomical marvel. Even someone who hates him has to acknowledge that fact. Acknowledge the power packed into that six-foot-four frame. He's so big that he should be clumsy, but he isn't. Every movement is controlled, dark grace.

This body ain't worth shit.

For the first time, I get a glimpse of something other than the hardened tyrant Elio Titone. I get a glimpse of something I recognize in the most sincerely visceral way. A sense of unworthiness that grows like a thorny, viny weed, watered by guilt and by grief. I recognize it because those same strangling vines grow deep in my belly, too. They've been there ever since my mother died and I didn't.

Something happened to him once. Something I would probably understand all too well if he would ever deign to tell me.

He won't, though. He instantly shuts down that sliver of vulnerability by coolly adding, "Besides, nobody else is allowed to hurt you."

Nobody *else.*

"But you are," I hiss. "You're allowed, is that it? You fucking like it, too. My ass learned that lesson last night."

A new stiffness enters his spine. A moment ago he'd been holding up the wineglass, swirling it, but he sets it down in a tight movement. The crisp sound of the glass hitting the granite rings out like an alarm. This time I actually do step backwards and away from him as he turns and advances on me. The granite edge of the counter digs into my lower back, but the pressure only lasts a second, because

Elio's big hands are on my waist and forcefully spinning me around. The movement forces the espresso cup from my hands, and it goes crashing to the floor, sending ceramic shards and the last sips of wine spewing across the stone tile. I gasp, flinching when leather drags at my hips, thumbs hooking into the elastic waistband of the sweatpants and yanking them down. And not just the sweatpants. The panties, too. I'm completely bared to him.

Smooth leather glides across my hip and ass then presses into the place he spanked me. I can't tell if the touch is meant to me soothing or claiming. Maybe both.

"No bruises. No redness," Elio mutters. His fingers dig into my flesh, ever so slightly, and I can feel a terrible, heart-timed pounding drum up between my legs. "I was gentle last night, Songbird. I can go harder. *Much* harder."

I let out a shameful *eep* of protest. Am I protesting his words or my own body's intense reaction to them? Even now, I can feel slick dampness gathering at the apex of my thighs.

"But I didn't go hard," he says, his voice grating slightly, ragged at the edges, "because that wasn't what you needed."

"How the hell do you know what I need?" I grit out, wriggling under the pressure of his hand.

"Because I know you," he says.

It's an absolutely absurd declaration. His ego astounds me. There's not the slightest trace of doubt in his voice. I scoff in disbelief, making an awful, bitter noise at the back of my throat, but he just moves in closer to my back, fabric of his trousers teasing against my bare skin, his breath a hot stir at my ear.

"I know you," he repeats. As if saying it a second time somehow makes it true. "Under stage lights and sunshine, I've seen you bleed your soul right out of your body."

I still, because no one's ever described my playing in such a painfully beautiful way.

"I know your birthday and your school schedule and the colour of your eyes when you're angry," he continues, and there's something relentless, *merciless*, about the way he speaks now. Like he'll separate out every molecule of my being, unravel my whole entire life.

"I know your freckles are paler now than they will be in the summer. I know your best friend is Willow and your boyfriend was Brian, and that's *was*, not *is*, because if he tried to touch you now he'd have a bullet in his brain before he could fucking blink. I know what kind of panties you're wearing, or rather not wearing, at this very moment. I know how beautiful you look drenched in my blood, that your pussy tastes like paradise, and I know you don't make music only with your violin, because when you come for me, you fucking *sing*."

He knows all of this because he's watched me, watched me even more than I'd thought. This goes beyond my public music perfor-mances. This is deeper, deadlier, more obsessive. Thinking about him watching me reminds me of the cameras everywhere, and in as emotionless of a voice as I can muster, I tell him to pull my clothing back up.

I expect him to resist, but he doesn't. He skims his leather touch down the sides of my thighs to grip my sweatpants and underwear. There's something almost worshipful about the way he does it. A reverent slide down my legs, so slow I almost let out a moan. I bite it back and try to revel in the relief of having myself covered. Elio turns back to the island, grabs the wineglass, and hands it to me.

"Here," he says smoothly, as if the previous conversation hasn't even happened. "This is the kind of glass you need for this wine. It lets the wine breathe. Opens up the flavours." His eyes shift from the drink between us to my mouth. "Try it."

"I don't want it now." I truly don't. My momentary feeling of victory, of freedom, evaporated the moment he entered the room.

One of his dark brows notches up slightly.

"You opened an eighteen-thousand-dollar bottle of wine and now you're not even going to drink it from the proper glass?"

"Eighteen... thousand..." I breathe. I stare down at the drink accusatorily, as if the wine should have somehow warned me about how expensive it was before I took it off the shelf. "Let me guess. It's added onto the sum I owe you."

He gives a shrug of his good shoulder. "That's less than a pair of panties. I could always use a new pocket square."

Is he making another joke? This man is absolutely insane. But he just keeps on going.

"You're wearing a nice shade of blue. Would go well with at least three of my suits." His voice deepens slightly. "Reminds me of your eyes."

I am wearing blue silk underwear, damn him. I can't believe what I'm about to say, but a girl has to work with what she's got. And no matter what, I swear I will survive this and get out of here. If Elio's willing to open his wallet and dump it all out for my used panties like some kind of pervert then so be it.

"Fine. But I want fifty thousand for them," I say, lifting my chin with a defiance I don't quite feel but I'm pretty sure I fake adequately enough. Elio doesn't balk at the thirty-thousand-dollar mark-up. He raises his right hand and draws it along his jaw slowly, fingers rubbing at scar tissue. He narrows his gaze thoughtfully, like he's considering a lucrative business offer. A deal with contracts and figures and complex negotiations. Something glints, then hardens in his gaze. He drops his hand.

"No."

I'm the one balking now, my confidence rattled.

"You're the one who said I should have asked for more last time!" I sputter, feeling like an idiot.

"But you didn't," Elio counters maddeningly. "And now the price has been established. Twenty grand for a pocket square doused in *parfum de Songbird*. I might consider going up to twenty-five because they're the colour of your eyes, but doubling it? They'd have to be extra special. Maybe if..."

He stops, and I'm sure the silence is bait, but I take it anyway.

"Maybe if *what?*" I snap.

"Maybe if you get them extra wet for me first."

My jaw drops.

"You've got to be kidding me."

"I don't kid when it comes to what I want," he says simply, starkly, and they're possibly the truest words he's ever spoken. "Come all over those panties, soak them for me, and you'll get your fifty grand for them."

His gaze dips sardonically to my glass.

"Have a drink if you need to steel yourself first."

I grip the stem of the wineglass so hard I'm surprised it doesn't snap. But maybe I shouldn't be surprised at all. Because I am fucking weak. So weak I take a swig and actually consider doing this.

Fifty grand for an orgasm. Yesterday, getting aroused actually lost me money, but this time it will be the opposite.

It's a good deal.

And then I want to laugh, because apparently I have standards around deals like these now. I have notions of what's a good price and what's a bad one. Fifty thousand dollars for my dignity. Fifty thousand to turn me into the whore he said he didn't even want.

Or maybe I already turned into that last night. First at the gala, then in his room.

But it's *something*. One step closer to getting me out of here. Playing violin for him hasn't turned out to be as straightforward as I was hoping. Maybe this will be easier.

"Fine," I bite out. "I'll be back."

Elio chuckles, and it freezes me.

"Oh, no. You won't be doing it alone. How will I know what I'm buying is the genuine article if I'm not actually there during the process?"

Of course he wants to be involved. I wonder if it will be like last night, with his tongue playing over my clit, but this time through the silk, and my blood simmers, sending a slow, brutal throb of heat into my groin. I take another huge sip of wine and set down the glass.

"Deal," I whisper.

Elio moves towards me. I scrunch my eyes shut and flinch at his proximity. I feel the heat of him, the almost ominous pressure of his presence, before he abruptly draws back. I squeeze open one eye, then the other, to see him at the island, leaning back against it with the wineglass in his hand. He swirls it languorously, watching me.

We stare at each other for so long that awkwardness unfurls. I lick my lips, shifting back and forth on my feet, wondering when he'll touch me. My traitorous body is already anticipating it, my insides coiling, and I think bitterly that if it's wet panties he wants, he won't be disappointed.

"Well?" Elio says, swirling his drink again and taking a sip.

"Well, what?" I huff. "Aren't you... aren't you going to..."

"Help you?" he finally asks. He takes a long, contemplative sip of the wine then says, "No, I don't think I will."

So, he wants a goddamn show then. He wants to stand there, watching me make a mess of myself, completely closed-off and unaffected. Although, maybe not all that unaffected. I risk a glance down to his crotch and see the thickened, swollen outline of his shaft through his pants.

I breathe out harshly. A mixture of relief and disappointment – disappointment that fucking *terrifies* me – floods through me. And with it comes arousal I can't run from or deny. Elio watching me, his eyes dark as the sky between stars, dark with need as toxic as my own, feels like a drug. That gaze is in my bloodstream, demanding and possessive and digging deep inside me. Digging, until he can open me up and find everything, see everything. Know everything.

I know you.

"Pants down. Panties on," he says. The command sounds stern, but I hear the way the words are laced with slight strain. A gruffness he can't keep quiet.

I should stop this. Stop this *now*. But there's fifty grand at stake, a tiny little slice of my future freedom. And there's Elio, his breath coming harder than it should, and fuck, seeing him is what truly makes me want to do this. And I try not to think about what that means, about how screwed up I must be to want this in some strange way, as I hook my thumbs into the pants and I obey.

My glance goes to the camera, like a shiny black orb of an eye on the ceiling, and I wince, wondering if anyone else will see this. If someone else is watching even now. Maybe the guard who trailed me into this room before Elio dismissed him so quietly I didn't even notice. Throat dry, I kick the sweatpants off, letting them skid over the spilled wine on the floor.

"How clear is the image quality from that camera feed?" I ask quietly.

"Crystal," Elio responds, lifting his sparkling glass in the air as if to demonstrate just how clear the image of me falling apart will be for whichever men are watching now.

I'm supposed to be touching myself, I know I am, but my fists curl together in front of my pubic bone, shame spiking through me. This feeling is different from the embarrassment Elio has made me feel, the humiliation he coaxes out of me that's so terribly erotic it takes my breath away. The thought of other men watching me right now just makes me plain anxious, maybe even afraid.

"Songbird."

There's a quietness in the way his voice wraps around the nickname that draws my gaze sharply.

His expression has changed. I've never seen his face like this. It's not... No, it's not soft. But there's *something* there. Like the physical manifestation of an ache. And I can't help but think, for one batshit crazy fraction of a second, that even with the scars, even with the cruelty and the eyes that want to tear me open, when he looks at me like that, like he's *tortured* by something, like he's in *pain*, that he's beautiful.

"I cut off the feed to the main security hub the second I sent Robbie out of this room," he says carefully. "I'm the only one here with you now."

Tears of relief and gratitude burn at the back of my eyes. It's a tiny kindness. Not even a kindness at all, really, but I latch onto it like it's a lifeboat on the stormy sea that's become my life.

"Are you lying?" I whisper.

His eyes are dead serious when he replies.

"I'm not going to let one of my men watch you do this."

Not an act of kindness, then, but one of pure possessiveness. All of me belongs to him, even my pleasure.

"But... the gala..." I can't even say it. Can't even think about how many people must have seen me shuddering so wantonly against his thigh.

"You were fully dressed then. Well, mostly," he says. "And you may not be aware of this, but you were so aroused that you came from barely moving at all. We were dancing close, yes, but that's all anyone would have seen from the outside." He pauses, then bites out, "If you think I'd let anyone else see you undressed, see you truly come undone, then you have no idea who I am."

"Oh, I know who you are, Elio," I say before sliding my fingers over the blue silk between my legs. He physically jolts, and at first I think it's because of what I'm doing with my hand. But then I realize, *no*, it happened a split second before that. *It happened when I said his name.*

It's the first time I've called him by his first name. I'm not sure why I do it, but I say it again, just as my finger circles the tight bud of my swelling clit.

"I know you, *Elio*."

He exhales and puts down the wineglass like he's scared he'll snap the stem. Just like I was, except he's strong enough to actually do it. He doesn't take his eyes from my hand between my legs as he releases the glass onto the sparkling granite of the island.

"You're a tyrant," I breathe, beginning to stroke myself. "A murderer. A monster. Greedy. Selfish. Possessive. Obsessive." I accentuate every word with a circling movement of my hand until I can't speak anymore. But just because I can't say the words doesn't mean they're not piling up in my brain. *Terrible and cruel and ruinous, but you said you'd put your body between a bullet and me, and you actually fucking did it, and what am I supposed to do with that? Just what am I supposed to do with that?*

He doesn't argue with a single thing I've said. He knows each word is true. Just like I do.

I'm cold and hot at the same time. My nipples are hard, my skin heating like I have a fever. Elio's the point of infection. I know he is. But as I sigh and feel the inevitable rush of pre-climax expanding in my body, I don't know how I'll find the cure.

I can't look at him, can't hold his gaze when I come. I cry out, then try to swallow the sound, my body crunching forward, my chin falling towards my chest. My fingers work faster, faster, then slow as I grow overly sensitive, everything constricting and pulsing inside. When I finally do flutter my eyes open, Elio is there, right in front of me. His thumb and fingers go to my jaw, and he bends slightly. Dizzily, pussy pounding, I wonder if he's about to kiss me.

He gets one breath away from my mouth before he whispers, "Make sure they're good and wet before you take them off."

"I don't need to check," I hiss. I can already tell they're soaked. But Elio isn't satisfied by that, apparently. He grips my waist and lifts me until I'm seated on the counter, then grabs my knees, forcing my legs apart. I let him do it, let him look, if only so that everything is up to par and I don't have to go through this entire insane situation all over again because he didn't get what he wanted the first time around.

Nervously, I glance at him, and my heart practically stops. The intensity on his face is astounding. It's so focused that at first glance he almost looks expressionless. But on second glance, I can see the tension ticking in his muscles, the fathomless, raging hunger that turns his eyes into burning black holes focused between my legs.

Licking my lips, I glance down, trying to see what he sees, to understand why he looks like that. My pale thighs are spread wide on the counter, my skin in stark contrast to his dark gloves. Pretty blue silk covers my pelvis, and the fabric is dark with slick wetness where it sits snugly over my entrance.

Elio inhales roughly, then draws a single finger up and down that wet area. My body responds instantly, nerves raw and ready for more of what I shouldn't want. He presses firmly, driving some of the soaking fabric ever-so-slightly inside me, and my hips buck in inevitable reaction.

"Just take them off. Just take them," I moan, the muscles of my thighs twitching as Elio strokes shallowly through silk and leather into my core.

"Not yet," he rasps. "Need more."

"But... you said..."

I'm squirming against his touch. Rubbing my clit was one thing, but this, this firm, slow, nowhere-near-deep-enough touch below, is something else entirely. Part of me wants to fling myself off the counter and away from him.

Another part wants to slide the panties to the side so he can put that finger all the way in. Would he leave the glove on while he did it?

"You said I just had to... get them wet," I pant. "I came. I did what you told me to. I-"

"One more," he says, orders, *demands*. "Give me one fucking more." His finger drives the silk a little further in, entering me deeper and tightening the fabric against my clit in the most intoxicating way.

"I... I can't. I-"

"One hundred thousand."

His voice is tight and urgent. My eyes, which had fallen closed, fly open. I find him staring at his hand on my silk-clad pussy, and something like satisfaction flares inside me when I realize he's losing control of this situation and *he knows it*. He's losing control because of his own twisted desire. Desire for me. Desire he can't keep a leash on no matter how hard he tries. He took me for my music, but he can't fight how much he wants the rest of me, too.

And it gives me an idea. A terrible, damning idea. An idea that I could regret for the rest of my god-forsaken life.

The words tumble from my mouth just as I come again, making them breathy and shaky. If it isn't for the way Elio completely turns to stone, I wouldn't even be sure if he hears them.

"How much," I pant and moan, trying not to grind desperately against his finger as I explode, "would you pay for my virginity?"

Chapter 24

Elio

Every muscle in my body seems to shut down when Deirdre's words register. I'm trying to come to terms with them. And come to terms with my own response.

Trying to come to terms with the fact that it turns out I want her any way I can have her. In every way. Even if I have to pay. Even if I have to compromise everything I thought this was, what I thought that this would be.

I want to fucking tell her I'd give her everything, *everything* for that. Money, power, jewels. A thousand and one violins. Buy her a small country. Slit my fucking neck and bleed out if she asked me to, just so I could have my cock inside her when I die.

Well, shit.

I am, without a single shadow of a doubt and in every possible, conceivable, inevitable way, absolutely, categorically, one hundred percent *fucked*.

I will lose my mind, maybe even lose everything, over this girl. I've already started losing control.

And I never, *ever* lose control.

All of this plays out in my head in the space of about half a second. Deirdre is still trembling from her second orgasm, her sweet, wet body practically begging me to do it, to take her right fucking now. My cock is out of control, straining for her, my body answering hers without a goddamn care for what my brain has to say about it.

But there's something she doesn't understand. I'd give her anything. Anything except what she really wants.

"Here's the thing," I say gruffly as she tightens and rocks in tiny movements against my still hand, aftershocks of her pleasure ringing through her like an anthem that goes straight to my dick. "It doesn't matter how much I'd pay, Songbird."

She makes a questioning sound.

"Because," I say through gritted teeth, "If I claim you that way, get your innocent blood on my cock like a brand, then I will absolutely never let you go."

Not like I'm planning to let her go anyway, but still.

"Why not?" she snaps, and there's a new anger in her voice. "It's not like there aren't other beautiful women lining up to sleep with you. You don't need to keep me here."

What the fuck is she talking about?

I mean, she's right. I hadn't lied when I told her I didn't need to pay a whore. There are always women like Natalia around, women turned on by money and violence and what I represent in this world. Women who want just a little bit of that Titone power for themselves, even if it comes in the form of sucking my dick.

Then I remember Nat coming up to me at the gala. And Deirdre's eyes burning a goddamn hole in my head from across the room. No doubt she saw us together.

And no doubt she's relieved by the prospect of me being focused on someone else. On me wanting other women so that I don't want her.

She doesn't understand.

Reasonable, considering I barely understand myself. Barely understand the hold this young, defiant, brilliant, virginal little Songbird has on me.

How much would you pay for my virginity?

Cristo santo. If I thought I still had a soul I'd fucking sell it.

That has me stepping crisply away from her. I need to create some distance, cool my head, regain some semblance of control, the control I've built my name, our entire empire, on.

"Panties," I say, moving back to our original bargain. Back to a place I feel like I can get a grip on. Something a little colder, more transactional, than contemplating sliding my dick into her tight, pulsing pussy and coming all over her insides.

A flush darkens her cheeks, and she nods, scooting forward and sliding off of the counter. My eyes are glued to her as she slides the wet silk down her pale legs. She bends at the waist, pulling them off of her feet, then uses one hand to stretch the hem of the T-shirt over her bare body as she straightens to hold them out to me.

I move to take them, but she withdraws her hand a little.

"One hundred thousand, right?"

I almost want to smile at that. Spine of fucking steel, I swear. Making sure she gets her due, as she well should.

I nod, because though I may be many terrible things, things she listed out for me herself, I am at least a man of my word.

She exhales, the hardness around her mouth softening, finally passing them over. I take them, folding them carefully, methodically, before sticking them into my pocket.

I turn away from her and grab the wine glass, drinking until it's empty, staring blankly out over the kitchen island while my dick throbs. I put down the glass as Deirdre pulls up the sweatpants that had been discarded in a soft grey heap.

A small cry of pain from behind me makes every muscle in my body snap to attention. I spin around, jaw tight, finding Deirdre leaning forward over the counter, gripping it tightly. Her right foot is off the floor, curled around her left ankle, like she's stubbed her toe, or-

I see the spilled wine and the pieces of ceramic on the floor. Sharp white shards scattered like broken teeth.

My breathing feels wrong. So does my heartbeat. It reminds me of the way I felt when I saw Sev's guy aiming his gun at her in the snow that night. Like the entire world was hurled off its axis, everything turning black at the edges.

I propel myself forward without thought. Same way I didn't think, didn't stop, didn't have a fucking care in the world for the bullet that could have gone right through my head and ended everything that night. I grab her and hoist her back up to the counter where she was sitting a moment ago.

"It's fine," she chokes out, wiggling and pulling away from me. I ignore her, finding her right ankle and closing my fingers around it in an iron grip. She bucks and shimmies until she's half lying along the counter, propped on her elbows, ass up in the air, held in place by my hand on her leg.

Keeping one hand wrapped around her ankle, I smooth the other along the inside of the high, slender arch of her foot. There it is. A sharp, nasty chunk of the cup stuck in the ball of her foot. My immediate instinct is to yank it out, but then she'll just start bleeding like crazy and I don't have the shit to deal with that right here.

I hoist her up into my arms and she yelps. It reminds me of our first night, when she told me she'd rather step on broken glass than have me carry her. But she's already stepped on something broken, and I will not be argued with. Maybe she senses that. Because she doesn't even try to fight me now. Doesn't snap at me, or try to stop me. She doesn't fully give in and hold onto me, either, instead crossing her arms in an X over her chest, fists up by her shoulders, like a corpse.

I carry her up the stairs, vaulting two at a time, until I've reached my bedroom. I set Deirdre down on my bed then mutter, "Stay here," as I stalk into the bathroom. I know there's a first aid kit in there somewhere. I find it under the sink after a minute of searching then return to the bedroom.

Only to find Deirdre gone.

"For fuck's sake."

189

I hear sounds coming from her bathroom, rummaging and clattering. First aid kit in hand, I move quickly to that room. In her bathroom, she's bent over at the waist as she shoves things around under the sink, her injured foot hovering an inch off the ground as she digs for, presumably, the very thing I've got in my hand.

"Looking for this?"

At the sound of my voice her head whips back and she gives me an accusatory look over her shoulder. Her hair, that was damp before, is drying in furious orange waves. It looks like a bonfire, tendrils flashing and flickering as she ignores me and snaps her head forward again, continuing her search in the cupboards under the counter.

I watch her, a muscle pumping in my cheek. I'm not one to get stressed easily. Usually, I'm cool, collected, weighing every option with the detached precision of a surgeon. I thought I'd be relieved to get Deirdre under my control, like something inside me that appeared one and a half years ago would somehow be satisfied and I could get back to my fucking life. But with her here, all I feel is like I'm on the verge of a goddamn stroke. I watch her, so angry and so small, babying her foot like a wounded deer. If a deer had pride and a temper that was the prettiest and most irritating thing I'd ever seen.

Deirdre's face is mostly hidden, and my gaze goes to her foot. Her *bleeding* foot. In the kitchen, the chunk of ceramic had kept it stoppered well enough, but not anymore. Dark rivulets run down the length of her toes, falling onto the stone floor in slow but steady drips.

"You're bleeding all over the floor," I tell her, striding into the bathroom and standing directly behind her.

Her reply is slightly muffled, her voice bouncing around between the bottles of crap under the sink. "I'll clean it up."

For some reason that reply annoys me.

"Rosa will do it."

She lets out a harsh breath, pulls her head out of the cupboard and straightens. She doesn't turn around to look at me, instead focusing on my reflection in the mirror ahead of us.

"I'm not going to make Rosa clean up my blood!" she snaps at my reflection.

"Why not? She's cleaned mine up plenty of times," I reply.

"Yeah, well, I'm not like you," she practically spits.

I stare at the two of us in the mirror, red and black, beauty and scars, and I am fully fucking aware of that fact. Fully aware that she is on a completely different plane of existence than me, and the fact I've dragged her here at all, dragged her kicking and screaming into my darkness, is a crime against nature and order and all things good in the world.

The worst part is, *I do not fucking care.*

"Sit down," I growl, jerking my chin over at the toilet.

"Just give me the first aid kit and go," she replies irritably.

That's not going to happen. She may think that I just want to hurt her, but the reality is that watching her blood seep out of her body is notching my blood pressure up another level every time my heart beats. I'm not going to let her slap some tiny bandage on there and call it a day.

"Sit down or I will fucking tie you down."

Her eyes flare.

"You already took off my door and now you're threatening to tie me to the toilet? Are you insane?"

"If I am, it's because you've made me that way."

She lets out a sharp, angry laugh at that, and suddenly I have a bone-deep urge to know what her real laughter sounds like.

"You're telling me you were just a normal, psychologically healthy man before I came along? Yeah, I call bullshit on that, buddy."

The casual use of the word *buddy* throws me so off-balance I'm glad she's started hopping over to the toilet all on her own without needing my help. Shaking my head stiffly, I follow her. Buddy. Fucking *buddy*. If a man called me that he'd lose a goddamn finger.

Or five.

"Sit," I reiterate, and she gives me *an are you serious?* sort of look as she hops in a circle to face me in front of the toilet.

"What do you think I'm doing over here if I'm not going to sit down?"

I shrug, forgetting to keep the movement to my good shoulder, and grimace.

"Just checking. You have a perpetual need to disobey."

She slams the toilet seat down and throws her body heavily down on it, then bursts out, "Well maybe that's because I don't want to think about what it means when I do obey!"

I blink slowly at her. She clamps her mouth shut, like she's said something she shouldn't have, redness staining her cheeks.

"Is that why you left the room and went on your little wine raid?" I ask as I kneel before her. "To prove that you haven't submitted to me?"

She doesn't answer and looks away, but I don't need her to respond to know I'm right.

"I never said you couldn't leave the room."

"It was implied!" She crosses her arms over her abdomen and hunches forward, watching me on my knees.

I realize in that moment I've never looked up at a woman like this. I've never been on my knees before anyone.

Only she could get me on my fucking knees without even having to ask.

"Implied how?" I ask, grasping her ankle and examining the wound again. Fuck me, she's a bleeder. I'm going to have to take my gloves off and use the sterile ones in the first aid kit. She may consider me an infection, and maybe I am, but there's no need to make it literal.

"Well, I don't know! I've never been held prisoner before, so forgive me for not knowing all the subtle nuances of the expectations!" she replies.

I can't exactly respond in kind, can't tell her that I've never held a prisoner before either, because that would be a flat-out lie. Although, usually when someone ends up imprisoned by the Titones, it's the final step on their journey before they end up at the bottom of Lake Ontario.

Instead of answering, I grab a bunch of towels and stuff them under her ankle, setting her foot down gently before rising and heading towards the sink. I peel off my leather gloves and suds up my hands before rinsing and drying them. I don't look at my bare skin as I walk back to her and open the first aid kit.

She looks, though. Whatever other remarks she had on the tip of her tongue stay there, her angry eyes sobering.

"Those look bad," she murmurs as I snap one tight white glove on over top of my scars, then another.

"That's because they are," I respond dryly.

"Do they hurt?"

She asked me that before, about the gunshot wound. Why does she wonder if I hurt?

"Not as much as other things," I grunt.

Not as much as the fact I haven't been able to take a full fucking breath into my lungs since I first heard you play.

Almost two years of barely breathing does things to a man. Painful things.

"You mean your shoulder," she says quietly.

Not exactly what I was referring to, but I don't bother to refute her. Because, yeah, that also hurts like a motherfucker right now.

"I'm sorry."

Now that has me pausing, glancing up at her face. She looks uncomfortable, shifting back and forth on the toilet's closed lid.

"What did you just say?" I ask carefully, not quite sure I heard her right.

Her mouth flattens before her lips part once again to speak.

"I'm sorry. I'm sorry you got shot for me."

I stare at her so long without speaking that it apparently compels her to continue.

"I just feel like... Like, yes, it was your fault you were there in the first place. Because you were coming to take me. It's not like you were at my house to sell Girl Guide cookies. But..." She sighs and runs a fluttery hand through her explosive hair. "But I'm not an idiot. I know I'd probably be dead if you hadn't shown up at that moment." Her hand falls back to her lap, and her fingers worry against each other. "I keep thinking... I keep thinking, what if I hadn't raised that gun?"

"Then your father would probably be dead, or halfway there, instead of on some beach in Bermuda fucking a twenty-four-year-old," I tell her. She flinches at my words, but they're the truth. She distracted Sev's soldier, brought the violence down on her own head, just so her piece of shit papà could get away. O'Malley isn't that old, but he also isn't fast. I doubt he would have made it otherwise.

He has no idea what kind of loyalty Deirdre is capable of. Not a damn clue how much she's worth. What he's lost by leaving her.

But I do. She'll never feel that sort of loyalty towards me, but I can see it in her all the same. Like gold glinting at the bottom of a river. Shining metal holding strong under currents and ice and the thrashing of the seasons.

"Well, fine then. Whatever. You're probably right. I snagged that guy's attention so my dad could get away. And he just went ahead and left, just like he bartered me away, because apparently I'm fucking worthless."

I stiffen.

"If you want to apologize," I say slowly, almost menacingly, "then apologize for the words that just came out of your mouth."

Her brows crash together.

"What-"

"Do not ever, *ever*, say something like that in front of me again."

"Say what?" She pauses, her brows getting even more furrowed.

I grip the broken piece of ceramic and pull it out in a swift, sharp movement that makes Deirdre gasp. I disinfect the wound, knowing it stings but doing it anyway, because this is necessary and I know that she can fucking take it. As anticipated, the blood flows much faster now, and I slam a square of plush gauze against it, holding pressure there the same way I hold Deirdre's gaze.

"I don't pay millions of dollars for things that are worthless," I tell her. "I don't take bullets for things that are worthless." I get out the white medical tape, sticking it tightly to her skin, holding the gauze in place. "What your father did speaks only to his own non-existent value as a person. Not yours."

"What am I to you?" she whispers as I lay her foot back down on the towels.

Music and fire. Heaven and hell. Absolution and ruination, all at once.

I don't say any of that as I rise and snap off the gloves. Her gaze holds the question her mouth just shaped. I look down at her and reply with a single word:

"Mine."

Chapter 25

Deirdre

Elio grabs his leather gloves from beside the sink and leaves me after that, heading into his adjoining bedroom. I stay on the toilet for a long time, staring at my firmly and very precisely wrapped foot, propped up on a cushion of towels. A cushion he put there for me.

I have no idea what is going on between us. No idea why I can't seem to hate him as singularly as before. No idea why his touch sets my blood boiling. No idea why I offered him my fucking virginity when he himself told me it would never get me out of here.

No idea why he bothered to bandage me up when he could have just as easily let me do it all myself. He could have laughed at me, mocked me, left me shaking and angry and bleeding after the humiliation of seeing me come *twice*. But he didn't. Instead, he carried me up here, sank down on his knees before me, with those fathomless eyes and those terribly scarred hands, and took care of me.

Eventually I ease up onto my feet, limping over to the sink to splash my face with water and brush my teeth. I don't see Elio in my bedroom, and I don't hear anything from his. I wonder if he's already asleep, or if he's left altogether. Maybe to

196

go see that beautiful blonde from the gala. Elio is more than six feet of pure, bloodthirsty testosterone. A guy like that probably needs to bend someone over nightly just to stay alive. And he was hard before. With me. The memory goes to my core like a heated blade.

And the thought of him sleeping with that blonde woman twists it.

OK, what the actual hell?

I do not care what other women Elio spends his time with. If anything, the more time he spends with other women, the less he'll spend with me. I should be grateful. Relieved.

Then tell me why I'm not.

Maybe I'm too angry or too traumatized to feel gratitude right now. But then again, I have felt gratitude towards him for other reasons. For telling Rosa to make me tea. For turning off the security camera in the kitchen.

So why am I not grateful for this?

I don't want to think about it. Can't think about it. The same way, just as I told him, I can't think about what it means that I sometimes obey him.

But even though I can't think about it, I suddenly can't stand that I don't know if he's here or not. I dig my fingernails into my palms, willing myself to stay here, in this room. Not to go looking for him because that would be absolutely insane.

But my feet move anyway.

Just one look, I tell myself. *I just want to see if he's still here.*

I feel like I won't be able to sleep until I know for sure. I can't remain in breathless limbo. As I limp slowly to the doorway between his room and mine, I realize I don't truly know what I want to find. If I were sane, if I were normal, I should be happy if I find he's gone. Happy that I can relax a little, that I can breathe.

But...

Shut up, Deirdre.

I don't allow that thought to come to fruition.

His room is dark, but not entirely. Light from my side spills in, illuminating emptiness.

He's gone, then.

I nod jerkily, muttering, "Good," out loud so that the word can blot out any other reaction I might have had. I turn to go back into my room when I hear it.

The sound of a shower running.

I realize that some of the light in here is coming from the doorless entryway into Elio's bathroom. I still can't believe he ripped off all the doors in here, including his own. The man is fucking certifiable.

But maybe I am too. Because now I'm walking towards the bathroom. Towards the sound. Towards him.

I stop when I reach the bathroom. It's very similar to mine, but larger, and I spot Elio immediately. Even in the grand room, his presence is undeniable. A black fucking hole taking over everything.

He hasn't heard me above the streaming of the water. He's in a shower like mine, enclosed by glass. The glass isn't steamed up enough yet to obstruct my view and, Jesus, what a view it is.

You know when you watch nature documentaries and you see some massive predator, a cougar or a python or a bear, just absolutely decimate its prey? And even while you're cringing at the violence and maybe feeling sad for the cute rabbit or soft-skinned doe, a part of you can't help but admire the perfect, savage grace of the destroyer? Can't help but respect the millions of years of evolution that led to this moment, created this monster, as its brutal body strikes again and again and again?

That's what looking at Elio's naked body is like. It's like looking into the open maw of a shark, feeling the terror of the bite to come and simultaneously thinking, *my God, your fangs are beautiful.*

He's so fucking *big.* Colossal. He absolutely fills the large rectangular shower with his bulky frame. Every inch of him is hard and broad and covered in varying quantities and thickness of dark hair. I bite the inside of my cheek when I see the bandages on his shoulder, which I now notice he's keeping out of the water, tipping his head to the side to soak his hair, turning it even blacker than usual. His long legs are splayed slightly, and a tumultuous wave of sensation rocks my insides when I notice the rhythmic contractions in the muscles of his thick thighs and ass.

I can't see his right hand.

Because he's fucking it.

I have no doubt there are countless women who'd leap into his bed if he did no more than crook one of his leather-bound fingers at them. But instead, he chose this.

Maybe all it means is that he's tired, and sore, and doesn't want to go anywhere or deal with anyone else right now. Or maybe he doesn't want to let me out of his sight that easily tonight.

Or maybe it means something else entirely. Something I shouldn't contemplate or care about.

Something that whispers, then yells when I try to shut it up. Something with words that sound a lot like *he won't fuck someone else because all he wants right now is you.*

Something stupid, is what it is. And what's even more stupid is the small but undeniable flare of sick satisfaction I get from that possibility. The possibility that I'm not the only one affected more than I want to be. I'm not the only one who's been thrown into blood-heating turmoil. I'm not the only one whose entire world seems to have shrunk down into the shape of a single, strange, and solitary person.

What am I to you?

Mine.

I'm rooted to the spot, entranced by the quickening snap of Elio's hips, the tightening of his ass, the tension rippling up and down his back as water beads and rolls. I'll probably hate myself tomorrow for this bizarre urge, but I desperately want to see him come. I want to see him shudder, explode against the wall, fall apart because of how much he wants me.

I didn't see him come last time. I was too wrapped up in the explosion of my own orgasm, the stinging on my ass and the singing in my veins. I was too distracted to notice anything else until his hot spray coated my skin, and then it was basically over.

I want to see it now.

The movement of his hips slows, then stops altogether. His hand picks up the slack, pumping in quick, hard strokes, carving his triceps out of something akin to stone. My breath catches, and it takes everything I have not to reach my hand between my own legs and stroke the place that aches there. I try to tell myself I'm just feeling the aftershocks, lingering sensitivity from the other two orgasms, but I'm not. I'm reacting to this, here, *now*. Elio's nakedness under the hot stream of the water as he strokes the cock I made swell.

He doesn't shake or shudder or tremble when he comes. Instead, everything draws tight, muscles contracting almost like he's in pain. And with his shoulder and scars, maybe he is. Maybe, with the beautiful ruin that is his body, pleasure is always entwined with suffering.

His thighs lurch, driving his hips forward as his head tips back. His hair is much straighter and longer in the water, dripping down the back of his corded neck like ink. A guttural groan rips through the air. It doesn't matter that the sound of it is slightly muted by the water that patters like rain. Because it feels like Elio has put his mouth against my soaked entrance and groaned directly inside me. I feel the sound of it, each brutal vibration tightening in my core until I'm terrified. Terrified that I could come, just from that.

Terrified that he might turn around and see me.

I can't let that happen. I stole this moment, but the second he knows I'm here, all my control will be lost. Elio's head tips forward, his shoulders rounding slightly, before he turns off the water.

The silence crashes down like something catastrophic. A calamity of non-sound after the protective din of the water. I'm sure he can hear me breathing, even from across the room.

He can probably hear my fucking heart beat.

He most certainly hears my stumbling step backwards. I see the sudden alertness in his body as I move away.

If he turns, which I'm sure he does, I don't see him do it.

Because so do I.

I run. My foot throbs with every hurried step I take.

And yet, every step hurts far less than it should. And I know it's because of disinfectant and cushiony gauze and a murderously precise tape job.

I hurt less than I should because of *Elio*.

And I have absolutely no idea what to do with that.

Chapter 26

Deirdre

I wake to the now-familiar sound of cart wheels rolling into my room, but what's unusual is the person pushing it. It's not Rosa today, but Valentina.

"Hey," she says, smiling at me as I hurry to sit up in bed. "I brought you the paper and stuff for the letter and saw Rosa with your breakfast. Figured I'd bring it all in together."

"Thank you," I say. I appreciate that she remembered my request. "I'm actually not sure if I'll need it now. Willow found a way to contact me using someone else's email address."

"Oh, nice. OK. You can keep it anyway. Just in case." She nods towards a pile of lined paper and envelopes on the cart beside the breakfast pastries. There's another pot of tea today, thank God, and I mumble another thank you at her as I pour a cup.

"Want any?" I ask, suddenly remembering my manners. I mean, I feel like I can be forgiven for forgetting my manners in a situation like this. But still. I really do appreciate her looking out for me as best she can and wanting to try to connect me with the outside world. Offering her some tea seems like the least I can do.

But she just wrinkles her nose in a slightly less judgmental version of Rosa's reaction.

"No thank you. In order to make tea even remotely palatable, I have to add insane amounts of sugar to it, and my mom is already on my ass about cutting carbs to fit into my wedding dress."

I add milk and sugar, then take a sip.

"Yikes. I'm sorry," is all I manage to mutter in reply to that little tidbit. Valentina is absolutely stunning with her curves, and I shake my head at the idea she needs to trim them down for a wedding she doesn't even seem to want.

"Yeah. You're telling me." She shrugs, then heads towards the bathroom, pulling a lipstick tube out of a large leather bag that bumps her hips with every step. "Be right back," she calls over her shoulder. I drink my tea and eat a croissant while Valentina freshens up, and a few minutes later she returns, her lips freshly painted pink. Her long hair is perfectly straight and shiny, dark golden-blonde at the roots and lighter towards the ends, and she's dressed in a denim romper with incredibly short shorts despite the fact it's January.

"What's with the first aid kit and gloves?" she asks. There's a deceptive lightness in her tone. Like she's just trying to make conversation, but is actually intensely focused on my answer. I think her interest comes from a genuine place of concern, and I force a small smile, sliding my foot out of the blankets and leaning back to heft it up in the air.

"I ran into a situation with a broken cup." My smile turns bitter. "But Elio patched me up."

It doesn't seem like Valentina is easy to shock. She's small, but I get the sense she's mighty. Not the sort of person to be trifled with or who's prone to being taken by surprise. But her eyebrows snap upwards at my words.

"*Elio* bandaged you up?" She sounds so incredulous I almost feel defensive. It's not like I would make that up. But she seems completely stunned. "And those latex gloves?"

203

"Yeah, he wore them when he was cleaning the wound and putting on the bandage."

"He... *wore them*." Everything about her expression says *does not compute*. I kind of wonder if she's just going to echo everything I say with that tone of disbelief.

"Yes," I confirm, letting my foot fall back on to the bed and leaning forward to look at her more closely. "Are you... are you OK?"

She shakes her head slowly, hair swishing with the movement.

"Yes. Damn. Sorry. I just..." She shakes her head again, more quickly this time. "I just have never heard of Elio taking his leather gloves off in front of someone else before. Except for maybe Morelli, I guess, but he's a doctor."

I press my lips together, frowning down at the red duvet and sliding my fingers over its lush surface. For some reason, Valentina's words make me feel weird.

"He must take them off in front of other people sometimes," I say, wrenching my gaze up once more. I don't know why, but I have an instinct that something about this is dangerous. It means something that Elio took his gloves off in front of me, and I don't want to confront whatever that is head-on. So instead, I try to deny it. "He's your cousin. You must have seen it happen at least once. When eating, or cooking..."

Valentina snorts a laugh.

"Cooking? Um, no. That is not what Titone men do."

I swallow, reminding myself that the Titone family isn't a normal one. They're Cosa Nostra, and at the top of the fucking top, I guess Elio can't be expected to roll up his sleeves alongside Rosa and roll out the pasta dough or fill the cannoli.

"But seriously, I've known Elio my entire life," Valentina continues. "He's more like a brother to me than a cousin. And I've never, *ever* seen him take off his gloves or even change them, even though I know he has like a hundred pairs. He even wears them in the summer. Pretty sure he sleeps in them."

I chew the inside of my cheek, processing this.

"So, it's weird that he took them off in front of me?" I say, still not sure what to do with all this information.

She laughs again, more softly this time.

"Weird doesn't even begin to cover it. But then again, everything he's done with you is out of character. He's never brought a woman here before, against her will or otherwise."

Now that surprises me. A tight gold dress, platinum blonde hair, and a manicured hand on Elio's chest flash in the back of my head before I push them away.

"Never? No girlfriends?"

She shrugs.

"He hooks up with women, sure. Never brings them here though. He's actually pretty private. Which makes the fact he put you in the room adjoining his and took off all the doors extremely out of character."

Well, great. Elio's bizarre behaviour isn't just baffling to me, but even to his own family. I truly don't know if that's comforting or alarming.

"Why does he hide those scars? Why does he bother with the gloves?" I ask.

The skin I saw was absolutely ravaged, but Elio doesn't exactly seem like the type to care that much about appearances. Plus, he's helping lead one of the most ruthless crime families in the country. Scars would only serve to show just how strong he is, what he's endured. A badge of brutal honour.

"He doesn't seem to care about hiding his other scars that much," I add. He took his shirt off in front of me the first night here, and I saw the patchwork of violence that was the skin of his chest.

Valentina makes a face.

"I think he has a complex about his hands because of the fire. I kind of can't blame him considering what happened."

My heart speeds up, and I don't understand why. I know about the fire. The one he and his brother survived in Sicily against all odds. But based on Valentina's pained grimace, there must be more to it than what I've heard from the vague local legends that cling to the Titone name like fog.

I hold my breath, wondering if she'll say any more. I want to ask, but don't trust myself to. I shouldn't care about this at all, but for some reason I do, and I'm worried that if I ask too much, or appear too eager, she'll retreat. I can't mistake myself here – she's a Titone. Her loyalty, when it really comes down to it, doesn't lie with me.

She fiddles with the strap of her bag, rolling her pink lips like she's deciding something. Then, she huffs out a breath and nods.

"Look, nobody likes talking about this shit, but I'm going to tell you because you'll never hear it from Elio even though I think you need to know. For some reason, he's attached to you, and you're the one who has to contend with all the shit he's got going on, so I figure the more you understand about him, the better."

"Thank you," I say quietly. I realize how much she's doing for me right now. That she's breaking some sort of family code of silence around this issue simply because she wants to help me navigate the deeply unfamiliar waters that make up Elio Titone. Maybe her loyalties aren't as easy to decipher as I'd first thought.

She drops her bag on the floor then settles herself on the edge of the bed, tucking one leg underneath her bum and facing me.

"So, the whole reason our family came to Canada was because of Elio and Curse's papà, Giuseppe. I don't know all the details about this part, but twenty years ago he did something major to fuck over the ruling *famiglia* in Taormina. So, one night, some soldiers came and torched their house. Giuseppe, Elio, Curse, and my aunt Florencia were all inside."

My hands are starting to shake. I grab my cup of tea and hold it tightly, staring down at the liquid as Valentina goes on.

"It took a while for Elio to wake up. No smoke detectors. By the time he knew what was happening, fire was everywhere. From his room there was a clear shot out of the house, but Curse was stuck in his own bedroom. The fire was spreading between their rooms and licking up Curse's door. The doorknob completely fucked Elio's hand when he tried to open it, and he ended up punching through the burning wood to get to Curse." She stops, and a new thickness enters her voice when she speaks again. "They were only eight and fourteen. Can you fucking imagine that? Sometimes I think I'm tough shit but then I remember this story, remember what happened to them and I just..." She blows out a shaky breath like she's about to cry.

I look up from my tea and try to give her a reassuring look.

"It's alright. You don't need to tell me any more if it's too hard."

I know better than most how much family trauma and childhood loss can break a person down. How hard it is to put those heart-killing moments into words. *Only fourteen years old...*

Valentina inhales deeply and visibly steels herself.

"No. That's only part of it and you should hear the rest."

I steel myself, too. Because this story is getting inside me, it's hurting me, and I don't want to hurt for Elio.

"So, while Elio is fighting his way through literal fire to get to Curse, he sees their dad. Elio and Curse's bedrooms were on the ground floor, and Giuseppe had a workshop down there where he worked on his bike. We think he got drunk and was asleep in there when the fire started, because he wasn't upstairs in the other bedroom with Aunt Florencia. If he'd been upstairs, the piece of shit probably would have died like he goddamn deserved to. But instead, he just watched Elio pounding on that burning door, listened to his wife screaming and his other son crying, and then he *ran*."

My breath crystallizes and then breaks, every inhale jagged and cutting. My throat contracts as I try to picture what Valentina is telling me. Picture a father watching his children in that kind of situation and choosing to cut and run.

And it almost kills me that I don't even have to imagine it, because I witnessed it myself. I watched my own father sprinting across the snow, away from our house and away from me.

"Anyway, Elio got Curse out. By that time Curse was unconscious from smoke inhalation and Elio wasn't much better off. But as soon as he got Curse out, he went right back in."

"For his mother," I finish for her in a whisper.

Valentina nods.

"At that point, I think she was still alive, just trapped. But she was upstairs and there was just no way to get to her. Elio still would have tried. Except a beam in the entryway collapsed on him, hitting his neck and shoulder and forcing him back outside. I wasn't around yet, but my parents only lived a few houses away and by that time they'd shown up. Elio was physically falling apart, and even so my dad still had to restrain him from running back inside. My dad told me once, when he'd had too much wine, that it was the only time he's ever heard Elio scream."

Her tone turns wistful. "I wish I got to meet my aunt. I don't know a lot about her. Men in this family don't talk much to begin with, but especially about the things that hurt them. But my mom has told me a bit. I do know she was beautiful. She had black hair, like my dad and like Elio and Curse. I know she loved music. Apparently she had a beautiful voice."

My mother had been beautiful, too. And though neither my mother nor I were blessed with good singing voices, we both loved music. I feel the strangest sense of kinship welling up for Florencia. For this faceless woman who'd loved some of the things my own lost mother had loved. This woman who'd created men like Curse and Elio, who'd given them life, and who'd irrevocably shaped them with her death.

"Anyway, Elio has this whole thing about the burn marks on his hands. He'll never say it out loud, but I think they make him feel weak. Remind him of what he couldn't do. Who he couldn't protect."

"He can't blame himself for that. He was only fourteen," I say. I shouldn't feel sorry for present-day Elio. But a fourteen-year-old boy fighting to save his mother when his own father had so badly failed him? Well, that Elio broke my fucking heart.

"Trust me, I know," Valentina replies. Her mouth lifts on one side in a twisting sort of smile. "But I don't think he's exactly rational about that night. Kind of like you."

Her words jar me, and for a second I think she means that I'm also not rational about the night my mother died, and I wonder how the hell she could possibly know that.

"What?" I ask sharply.

"He's not rational when it comes to you."

"Oh," I say. "I mean, yeah." I wave at the doorless doorway into his room. "I could have told you that."

"Yeah, well, it's not something I would have expected," she replies. "Like I said, it's out of character for him. He's usually so focused, so business-like. He does everything for a reason. Every move is calculated and thought-out and he doesn't let anything or anyone fuck up his plans or change his mind or make him lose control. He doesn't have to keep anyone out because he doesn't let anyone in. At least, that's what I thought, until you drop the bomb on me that he took his gloves off in front of you and put a freaking bandage on your foot and now I'm just over here, like, what? Don't get me wrong, I love him, but he can be one cold, mercenary moth-erfucker."

If that isn't the understatement of the century...

"Anyway, I have to get going. Mamma and I have a lunch date with the Morellis." She bends to grab her bag, and as she turns to go, she pauses. "Maybe keep this between us. What I told you about Elio."

"Yes. Of course," I reassure her. I appreciate her telling me all this, and I'm not going to go betraying that confidence. Besides, I can't see myself bringing this up with Elio anytime soon, anyway.

But even so, her words stay with me all day long. I can't get them out of my head. Can't get *Elio* out of my head. He morphs and oscillates, swinging wildly between the man I know and what I imagine his fourteen-year-old self to have once been.

After how last night wound up unfolding, I don't venture out of the room today. I hang out in the quiet space, picking away at the lunch and dinner Rosa brings me and staring into the void of my phone. By 9pm, Elio still hasn't come back to his room or mine. I try to be relieved at that and ignore the way his absence niggles at me.

Chapter 27

Deirdre

Elio doesn't come back the next day. Or the next. After four days of not seeing him, I'm starting to get pissed. Is this how it's going to be? Me, alone in this giant, beautiful cage of a house? I can practically feel the interest accumulating on my debt, like a little bit of weight added to my shoulders every day, and I don't even have the chance to work towards paying it off because Elio isn't fucking here.

That's the only reason I want to see him, of course. To keep chipping away at my debt and actually do what I'm supposed to – play violin for him. I don't actually want to see him. Obviously. I'm not insane.

Maybe I'm just lonely. I haven't heard from Willow since that initial email, and I have to think that Paddy's got her under major lock and key right now. I wonder what's happening with Darragh and everybody else. If they're still trying to get their hands on me, or if they've given up after Elio presented me at the gala like his personal, chained-up property.

I wonder about my father sometimes, too, even though I try not to. It's too easy to slip into pity and self-loathing and questions about why I wasn't enough. Enough to protect, enough to stay and fight for.

But maybe I really am worthless, because I apparently no longer even have Elio's interest considering he can't be bothered to show his face.

It's thoughts like these that have me fuming – stewing, literally – in a very hot bath on the fifth day of not seeing Elio. My classes are supposed to resume tomorrow, so I'm in an extra shitty mood because I'm pretty damn sure I'm not going to be allowed out of here to go. All that work to get my Bachelor of Music, down the tubes. I'm halfway through my third year, still have one more to go after this, and I can't see a way around the fact that my education has come to a screeching halt.

I slide down in the hot water until I'm submerged past my shoulders, hoping the scalding heat will burn away my emotions. It would be so much easier to be numb right now. To not feel anything at all. No anger, no disappointment, no grief. No matter what I do, though, I just can't seem to manage it. I can't let go of the hurt and the frustration. But then again, maybe that's not such a bad thing. Maybe the force of that unhappiness, the sense of injustice of it all, is keeping me going. Numbness won't keep you alive. Bone-deep anger will, though. It will keep me standing when nothing else does.

I blow out air through tight lips, sending bubbles from the surface of the bath scattering in a spray of foam. The thick layer of bubbles is the only reason I feel comfortable taking a bath in here instead of doing my usual towel-curtain-shower thing. But then again, considering Elio hasn't even bothered to come check on the prisoner he was so hellbent on keeping, I doubt he's looking at the camera feed, anyway, wherever the hell he is. So maybe the bubbles aren't even necessary.

I glare up at the camera in the ceiling, resenting it and him and everything about this. The resentment grows and grows, pushing out everything else in my chest, even the ability and the desire to breathe. I suck in a huge breath then plunge beneath the water.

My eyes scrunched shut, I let the eerie melody of the water fill my ears and start to count.

One, two, three...

I force my muscles to relax even as the anxious burn I know so well starts to build in my limbs.

Ten, eleven, twelve...

I don't feel desperate for air yet. I love this part, the part before everything gets tingly and twitchy and I really have to fight to stay down here. I love the brutal calm of it. The way my body could be just a leaf or bit of driftwood or maybe even just a part of the water itself, simple and mindless and floating.

Thirty... Thirty-five...

My lungs feel tight. It's hard to stay still.

Sixty... Seventy...

I squeeze my fingers into fists, battling to hold on just a little longer. The longer I can hold it, the more euphoric that first breath when I'm out again. My thighs press together, a needy burn pulsing in my clit. I release one of my fists, strumming back and forth over my clit, fast, fast, *fast*. It has to be fast because I won't last much longer. My spine is winding tight, my legs straightening and bending reflexively.

Eighty...

I'm close. Close to everything. Close to coming, close to needing the sweet release of breathing. My fingers tingle and twitch as I rub them over my swollen clit. Just a few more seconds... Just a little more... Just-

My orgasm rips through me at the same moment a set of huge hands seizes my shoulders and wrenches me out of the water. I gasp and cough, confusion wrapping around the white-hot, black-edged pleasure that binds my core. I pant heavily, feeling water-logged and weak-limbed, blinking rapidly and scraping hair away from my face as my pussy quakes.

I try to focus my gaze, but I don't have to work too hard to see who's here. His face is a mere inch from mine. *Elio.*

A rush of humiliation makes an aftershock throb in my clit, and I snap my teeth together to keep from moaning. I stare at Elio wordlessly, taking in the absorbing black of his eyes and the furious set of his jaw.

"What the hell are you doing here?" I ask between ragged gasps, trying to get my bearings. Elio hasn't been here for days, and he has to show up *now*?

His eyes darken, though I have no idea how that's even possible. When he speaks, his voice is like ice skating over my heated skin.

"You don't get to ask a single fucking question right now." His hands are still on my shoulders, the leather soaked, and he's bent over the bathtub. The ceramic digs into my spine as he holds me in place. "What the fuck were you thinking?"

"What was I... What? What are you talking about? I was having a bath!" I feel even hotter, and it's not just from the water. It's from his proximity. What he found me doing. His probing interrogation. A quick glance down tells me the bubble layer is still thick and opaque, so at the very least he probably didn't see me masturbating.

"A bath where you stay under the surface and don't fucking breathe?" he asks, deadly quiet. I see now how his own breathing matches mine – quick and ragged. Unsteady. Like maybe he was holding his breath too, though I don't see how that's likely.

"It's none of your business!" Why, why, *why* did he have to come back now? If he's going to leave me alone, why can't he just do it for good?

"Everything about you is my business," he snaps. I get the sense he's trying to maintain a very strained leash of control on himself and his emotions. His words are clipped and tight. "I made you my business six million dollars ago. You've been my business for fucking *years*."

That just makes me even angrier. The reminder that I'm a transaction to him. Something to put on his accounting books. I stiffen and try to yank myself out of his grip, but his fingers tighten on my shoulders. His face gets closer, and something odd flickers in his gaze. A mere moment of emotion, an emotion I don't recognize in him, and then it's gone. He shoves his hands under my arms and straightens, dragging me dripping out of the bath.

He doesn't stop until I'm out of the bath entirely. He pins me naked to the wall, one hand at my shoulder, the other on my jaw, forcing me to look at him.

"Let me go. Let me-"

"Shut up," he grunts. "Shut up and look at me, Deirdre."

The use of my name stuns me. No pet nickname, no Songbird that makes me feel like an animal he owns.

My name.

He takes advantage of the momentary silence, the way I'm caught off-guard.

"This is my house, Deirdre. This is my city. You are in *my fucking world.*" His eyes practically burn a hole through my head as he hisses out his next words. "And don't you ever, for a single fucking fraction of a second, think that you can take yourself out of it. I will not allow it. Do you hear me? *I will not let you do it.*"

His eyes drop to my mouth, and for a dazed moment I wonder if he's going to crash his lips against mine.

Then the meaning of his words sinks in, piercing through the strange haze of the moment.

"Oh my God," I whisper, shock and fury spinning out inside me. "You think I was trying to *kill myself?* You think I would throw away my own life just to get away from you?" I laugh in his face, the sound bitter and harsh. "The fucking *nerve.* Your ego is absolutely insane. You actually think I'd commit suicide just to escape from you? You think you matter that much?"

The doorless entry to the bathroom is directly behind Elio, catching my attention.

"That's why you took the doors off the rooms, isn't it?"

I remember now that Valentina had found me holding my breath in the bath that first night, and that not five minutes later, Elio had stormed in with a hammer in his hand and barely controlled violence on his face.

He doesn't answer me, but I know I'm right.

I laugh again, and his mouth and gaze tighten at the same time.

"I have news for you, Elio Titone. You may be a bigshot, you may think you're everything to me now, but you're wrong. You are a mere blip on the radar of my life. I will get out of this. I will get away from you. And I promise you that I won't need to die to do it."

I'm half bluffing, half vowing with that statement. Bluffing because Elio is already far more than a blip, no matter how much I want to deny it.

Vowing because, come hell or high water, I will find a way to regain my life.

And I absolutely *refuse* to die trying.

Chapter 28

Elio

Deirdre looks so pissed off, so offended, that I actually believe her. I try to soothe the side of me that wants to grab the sledgehammer and smash the bathtub to bits, the side of me that wants to fist her hair and tell her, "Only showers from now on." Because even though I believe her now, I don't think I'll ever forget coming home, switching on her room's feed on my phone as I head upstairs, only to see her slip below the water.

And stay there.

"What the hell were you doing?" I ask, my voice softer now. I don't mean for it to be soft. It just happens. A natural response to the relief flowing through me like cool water. I slide my hand up from her shoulder until both hands are cupping her jaw. Fuck, I missed this face.

"I... I was... You don't need to know!" she stammers.

Except I do need to know. I need to know everything. I want to know the thoughts in her head before they even take fucking shape.

I know her. I made that whole damn speech about knowing her. But this Deirdre, this woman who holds herself under hot water and doesn't emerge until she's forcibly pulled, is someone I don't recognize, and I need to know her too.

But she's clamming up. Clamping down. I can see it in the shifting of her gaze, the pursing of her lips.

And I do the only thing I can think to do in that moment. Because apparently I've lost my ever loving mind.

"Five hundred thousand."

Her eyes go wide. Miles and miles of blue under those lashes.

"What?"

"Tell me what you were really doing. Five hundred thousand for the truth."

She stares at me for a beat, the only sound our breathing in tandem.

"Are you serious?"

"One million."

If I weren't cradling her jaw in my hands I'm pretty sure it would have dropped. If past me could see me now, his jaw would be dropping, too. Taking one million off her debt, just like fucking that. Unreal.

"Fine," she says with a stiff nod against my fingers. "I was holding my breath."

I give her a flat look.

"No shit, you were holding your breath. You think I'm going to shave seven figures off your debt for that obvious little announcement?"

She looks indignant now, proud and annoyed, and it makes my dick hard. I want to crowd against her, drag it against her belly, but I hold myself back. For now.

"Tell me," I urge. My mouth is so close to hers that every inhale is her exhale and vice versa. Breathing each other in.

"I just..." Her words brush my lips, and I stiffen. "I really was just holding my breath."

"But why? Why for that long?" I'd been excruciatingly aware of every second it had taken me to get up here. She was under well over a minute. That shit isn't comfortable. Nobody holds their breath that long for no reason.

Her next words come out in a rush. "I just like the way it feels, OK? There! I swear to God, you'd better pay me what you owe because that's the truth. If you don't-"

"You *like the way it feels?*" My dick twitches. "Which part? The not being able to breathe part? Or the part when you come up for air?"

"Both," she whispers, flushing so fiercely that the redness goes down her neck, spreading over her chest, leading my gaze to her tight, round nipples.

And suddenly, I understand what she's saying.

I know exactly why she did it.

"Does it make you come?"

When she tenses, but doesn't reply, I know I have my answer. I drag my right hand down and palm the front of her throat, not exerting pressure. Just the whisper of a promise.

"It's not safe to do that by yourself."

"Safe?" she laughs the word, and I feel the vibration beneath the leather and scars. "Like anything about this situation is safe."

"How many times do I have to say it," I murmur, ever so gently massaging the front of her throat. "You're safer in here than out there."

"And who's going to keep me safe from you?"

She tips her head back slightly, some subconscious part of her wanting to give me more access to her throat. I dig my thumb into the place her heart beats and she swallows a sound.

"I'm not the one sticking your head underwater for more than a minute," I remind her.

"Yeah, well, you haven't even been here for the last five days so how would you even know, anyway?"

This time, I don't hold myself back from thrusting my hard dick against her belly. She's so fucking naked, bare against the wall, and it would be so easy to hike her upwards, settle her thighs around my waist, unzip my pants, and nudge inside.

"Did you miss me?"

"What? No! What are you talking about?" she stammers. Every word, every breath, makes the muscles of her throat contract under my hand and now all I can think about is what that throat would do with my cock hitting the back of it.

I lower my mouth to the pretty shell of her ear and tell her, "Well, I missed you." I give her throat one last, tender squeeze before I finally let her go. Her arm whips to the side, grabbing a towel from a nearby rack and wrapping it around herself so viciously I wonder if she means to tear it in half.

"Yeah, right. Like you don't have women at your beck and call twenty-four seven," she says as she walks past me into her bedroom. It's quiet, under her breath. But since I am attuned to every goddamn atom in her body, because I *own* that breath, I hear it. I follow her into her room.

"Does that bother you?"

I haven't been with another woman since bringing Deirdre here, and does my body ever feel it. But a quick, mindless fuck, which is how it usually goes for me, holds absolutely no appeal right now.

The only things that appeal are angry blue eyes and freckled skin and the face of the girl who hates me.

I almost want to hate her right back for it. For closing my usual methods of release off. For making every other woman but her unpalatable. For making me want her like this when this was supposed to be simpler, supposed to be about the music and money and nothing else.

"Oh, please," she snaps, heading for the closet. "It's a relief. Go spend your time with that blonde woman from the gala. In fact, teach *her* violin. Then maybe you'll leave me alone.

"Deirdre."

"Hell, I'll teach her for you. Subtract my teaching fees from my debt. And then-"

"Deirdre."

In the midst of her rant, she doesn't realize I've followed her into the closet. She whirls and gasps at my proximity. It's a large closet, but still much more confined than the bedroom we've just come from. The lights are off in here, and only a soft glow spills in from the adjacent room. I keep moving forward until her back hits a wall of shelves laden with clothing. It reminds me of New Year's Eve. When I had her spine to the shelves in the pantry of her father's kitchen. Something bittersweet, maybe even nostalgic, pokes in my chest when I remember that night. My shoulder thuds in time with my heart as Deirdre clutches her towel and glares at me.

"I haven't been with anyone else since before your birthday."

It's actually been longer than that, but I don't elaborate.

Something changes in the set of her mouth. I don't get much time to analyze it before she spins around, yanking down some clothing from the shelf. She flinches and drops it when I move in close against her back.

"I truly don't care," she mutters. "I have no idea why you're telling me this."

"Don't you?" I slide the long, wet clump of her hair to the side, baring the back of her neck. I hold back a groan when I see goosebumps rise on her skin. "I think you're jealous but you don't want to admit it."

The thought of Deirdre jealous, sitting at home and wondering where I am, makes something burn low in my belly. I've always found jealousy in women tedious before. An irritation I have absolutely no patience for. But in my Songbird? I fucking love it. It's not the way I should feel about a debtor, someone I've made my prisoner. I should hold all the power, here.

But clearly, I don't. Because imagining Deirdre annoyed and jealous and waiting for me, like a girlfriend, like a *wife*, makes me so hard I can't fucking think. It almost, I think, makes me happy. But I'm not sure, because it's been about twenty years since I felt truly happy, and it's not an emotion I recognize these days.

"I am not jealous. You are delusional," she breathes. Her voice has changed. Some of the anger has ebbed away, replaced with a trembling huskiness.

"Don't lie to me."

I pull the towel and let it fall in a damp heap around Deirdre's ankles. I clamp my hands around her waist before she can try to wriggle away from me. But my leather gloves are soaked, and even though it's driving me nuts, I don't want to create any space between us to go grab another pair.

Without letting myself think too hard about it – because if I do I'll stop and that's the last thing I want right now – I hold her in place with my right hand, biting off my left glove and spitting it down to the floor before repeating the action on the other side.

When my hands, my *bare hands*, settle on her skin, my dick throbs so hard I think I'm going to come in my pants like a teenager. The sound that rips from my throat is guttural, groaning and brutal. I can't remember the last time I touched someone's skin besides my own without gloves. I truly don't even know if I've done it once in the past twenty years. Doctors have examined my hands, but me removing my gloves like this to purposely touch somebody else?

It does not happen.

Sensation sparks under my palms, and I can't stop myself from digging my fingers into Deirdre's sweet little waist. The scarring has numbed a lot of feeling in my hands, and I'm almost grateful, because even this is already overwhelming and I *do not get overwhelmed.*

At least, I didn't. Before.

Back before I saw her, heard her, wanted her. Back when my life was empty and pointless and actually made sense.

None of this makes sense. I was never supposed to take off my gloves. I was never supposed to need her like *this*. Need her beyond anything I've ever known before. This isn't simple lust. I can't even say that it's just obsession, even though I know I am obsessed.

"Fuck. I missed you," I say again. I had to travel up north to Thunder Bay to straighten out some business at our warehouses there, and every day I'd spent away from here, away from her, made pressure build behind my eyes.

She doesn't reply except for making a throaty little sound when my hands come up to cup her breasts. I drop my head forward just as Deirdre tips hers back, my forehead coming to rest against hers.

Her skin against mine is like a drug. It numbs the prickling feeling I get at the base of my skull every time I take off my gloves until all that's left is need. I drag my palms across her breasts, kneading, feeling her nipples rise and press against me.

I want to feel her everywhere. I keep my left hand where it is, gliding the right one down, past the pretty flare of her hip, through the soft brush of her curls. With the state of my skin, it's usually hard for me to tell when things are wet. It's not hard now. She's so slick down there my fingers slide through her folds until the tip of my middle finger is drawn to her entrance. I press, and she practically sucks me in until I'm buried to the second knuckle.

Deirdre's been fairly still and quiet in my hold, almost pliant, until now. She jerks and shudders, her back arching as her pussy clamps down with mind-blowing tightness on my finger.

"What are you doing?" she moans.

I curve my finger, stroking inwards as I grind the hard part of my palm against her clit. Her pussy spasms in response, and I just about lose it when I think of what that pressure would feel like on my dick.

"I'm taking care of your pretty little pussy."

"No." The word is a breathy moan. "I don't mean literally, I mean... *Oh my God...*"

She's close already. I can sense it in the changing of her breathing, the swollen quivering of her cunt.

"I mean," she pants, writhing like a snake, like she's trying to get closer and get away from me all at the same time, "I mean *what are you doing*? What are you doing with me? This wasn't the agreement. This wasn't what you told me when you took me."

I almost want to laugh at myself. Laugh for thinking I could ever have her here, have her simply play for me, and leave it at that. A beautiful, untouchable performer in a cage. Something so intensely, painfully beautiful it hurts to look at her and hurts even more not to touch her.

I never thought I was a fool. But maybe I am for her. Maybe she's turned me into one.

"Fine," I breathe quietly against her ear. She's seconds away from explosion, but I pull away my hands. She starts to moan in complaint, then slams her mouth shut, tensing. "Get your violin," I tell her, before turning and striding from the room. I head for my bathroom for new gloves and a chance to cool my head. To remind myself why I brought her here. What this is supposed to be.

Even if that feels completely hollow now.

I wash my hands and face in the coldest water possible, revelling in the numbing pain of it. It's not cold enough to distract from the heat pulsing through my veins, though, and after drying my hands and pulling on new gloves I adjust my crotch. I already know I'll be jerking off later and I shake my fucking head, because just what in the teenage hell has my life turned into?

When I emerge, I find Deirdre holding her violin and bow, dressed in a pyjama set. It's probably the frumpiest outfit she could find in there, as if the shapelessness of the pale blue cotton is armour. It's almost obnoxious how she still looks like a haughty, angry queen despite the slouchy garments. I get the sudden, world-tilting sense that I'm in her domain instead of the other way around, and I do not fucking like it.

I need to remind her, remind both of us, what this is.

"Play," I grunt, seating myself on the edge of the bed. She doesn't hesitate this time. She doesn't dither or dawdle or tell me I'm too distracting. She just marches right up to me, lifts her instrument, and starts.

The song is jagged and discordant, a chaotic jumble of notes that somehow threads together into a melody I can latch onto. It's bitter and chaotic, like rage made sound. It's not her usual style, but I soak it up, because it's still her and apparently I can't do anything but drink up every little bit of her I can get.

There's a hard set to her mouth and a bright flush in her cheeks, and I wonder what has pissed her off the most. Me touching her, or me leaving her hanging a moment ago.

I wonder if she finished what I started, all alone in that closet. If she coaxed that soft pussy into coming. My dick pounds.

I close my eyes, letting myself focus on the music instead of how badly I want to see Deirdre rubbing her own clit. The notes practically puncture holes in my brain, they're so sharp and harsh. But even so, even though the song isn't slow or sweet or pretty, I still react to her playing like I always do. Like the song forms a fist around my heart.

She makes me fucking feel.

I'm not used to it. I don't know what the hell to do with it. So, I just sit there with my eyes closed and my chest hurting and I fucking take it. I take it like pain and bullets and blood, because I know what to do with violence and her music, the poetry of her perfect fucking soul, feels like an assault.

Eventually, the song comes to a sudden and silent halt. I keep my eyes closed for a long moment before cracking them open again. The flush in Deirdre's cheeks has ebbed away, leaving her pale under her freckles.

"That's not your usual style," I say.

"Yeah, well, I'm not in my usual sort of mood," she fires back. Something in her cracks, sorrow bleeding through her anger. "You're going to ruin this for me."

"Ruin what?" I ask in a careful, measured tone.

She lifts her violin up again and gestures to it with the bow.

"This! This was something I shared with my mother. Something special. And now I, I..." She sighs and looks away. "I don't know if I'll ever be able to feel the same way about it again."

Something is ticking inside my head. Like a clock. Or an artery about to pop.

Something I shared with my mother... You're going to ruin this for me.

This wasn't something I had considered before. That by taking and taking and taking from her, I'd be eroding the one thing I was trying so desperately to get a hold of. That by trying so hard to have her, to control her and to cage her, I'd be destroying something precious, something I love.

No.

Need, desire, want.

Not love.

Fuck.

When I first saw Deirdre up on that balcony, it wasn't just the quality of the sound that got its hooks into me. It was the emotion. The pure, inescapable, excruciating joy. Joy, and the way it was balanced against a poignant sort of pain.

I look at my songbird, really look at her, and I don't see a hint of joy inside her now.

"What do you need?" I rasp. "I'll give you whatever you need to perform properly. To play how you want to."

Perform properly. Yeah, sure. Because that's what I care about. That's what nearly drove me out of my fucking mind when I thought she was about to drown in the bathtub. The performance of it all.

I guess Deirdre thinks what I said is just as stupid as I do. She scoffs and shakes her head.

"What I need? What I need is freedom!"

The ticking in my head gets louder, harder, like a heartbeat.

I lift my arms and gesture to the size of the room around us, just one of many in my sprawling structure of a house.

"You can be free inside this cage."

Her eyes narrow.

"Not while you're in here with me."

My hands shoot out without me even meaning for them to. I clasp her waist and haul her into my lap. Her legs are spread, her cunt pressed to my aching shaft. She tenses, and I half wonder if she's about to clock me on the side of the head with her violin. But she and I both know my skull isn't worth damaging the instrument, not to mention the fact that I've got a hard fucking head so it probably wouldn't do any good, anyway. She lays her violin and bow down carefully on the bed just as I tighten my hold on her.

"I'm not going to be on the outside of the bars looking in, Songbird. I've been doing that since you were eighteen and I am fucking done." I pull her closer, dragging her against my hard-on. "Besides, weren't you the one who just complained about the fact I haven't been here for the past five days?"

Her eyes flare.

"That wasn't a complaint! It was... an observation."

"Yeah?" I breathe. Fucking hell, she smells so good. Feels so good. "Well, I have an observation of my own." I meet her gaze steadily. "You are a goddamn liar, Deirdre O'Malley."

Now she's even more pissed, and she starts to fight me. But she's so small.

And I'm not.

Even with my injured shoulder, it's easy to flip her until she's laying across my thighs, ass up. I wrench down the stretchy pyjama pants and panties until she's bare. I don't miss the trembling intake of breath, the anticipation that's already building in her even though she doesn't want to show it.

"Lie to me again and see what happens," I murmur, the leather of my glove and inch away from her creamy skin.

"I hate you," she whispers.

I chuckle darkly in response, but don't spank her yet, because I highly doubt that's a lie.

"You may hate me, but there's a part of you that wants me. Wants this." My fingers twitch, waiting for her to deny it, but she doesn't. "Gone silent on me, Songbird?"

"What am I supposed to say?"

I can't see her face like this, just the damp curtain of her hair.

"I'm not going to just say yes, am I?" she continues. "But if I say no, you'll spank me, and I'll like it for some fucked-up reason, and I'll just prove you right anyway. There's no good answer to that question. I'm trapped and you know it." She lets out a breath and wiggles slightly. "I shouldn't like any of this. You've broken something inside me. Made me as twisted as you."

I laugh out loud at that, because the idea that my beautiful, innocent little Songbird could be as twisted as someone like me is absurd.

"I haven't broken anything," I tell her softly. I lay my hand gently on her skin. She spasms under my touch, expecting more pressure, but I keep the touch soft. "I'm just responding to something that was already there."

"No way. I wasn't like this before," she hisses adamantly.

"You make yourself come by depriving yourself of fucking oxygen. You pleasure yourself and punish yourself at the same time. You gonna tell me you only started doing that after you met me?"

She stills, and then it's like every muscle in her body goes slack. She sags downward onto my lap, deflated by the realization that I'm right. I'm right that she likes desperation and discipline and deep discomfort. And she has for a very long time.

"When did you start doing that?" I ask her. My touch on her is still gentle. So is my voice.

I can't remember the last time I spoke to someone this softly. Maybe to Curse or Valentina when they were kids. It's been years. But I'm glad I manage it now, because maybe it's the quietness that makes her actually respond honestly.

"After my mom died."

It's a choked and tiny whisper. But it explodes in my head like artillery fire. There's smoke all around me, smoke inside me, and suddenly I can't think or feel or see. I grab Deirdre, haul her upwards and against me, clutching her to my chest like I can drag her out of the hole that I know all too well. Because it's a hole that's been hungry and dark inside me for twenty years, swallowing everything that matters. Flames dance at the edge of my vision, and I focus everything I have, everything I am, on holding her.

I can tell my eyes are wide open even though I can barely see anything. I blink, then close them, burying my nose in Deirdre's damp hair.

Her voice filters through the past, through the present, through the smoke and the flames and the pounding in my head.

"Elio? Are you hugging me?"

I don't respond, just hold her tighter. Slowly, the scent of smoke fades, and when I open my eyes, I can see again.

My voice is thick when I speak into her hair.

"When you want to feel that way, when you want to not breathe, you come to me. You don't do that alone. Not anymore."

She doesn't move or speak for a long moment. But she doesn't pull away either. Just lets me hold her even though I should have let go of her by now.

And then, in a movement so tentative and slow I might have missed it if I weren't keyed in to absolutely everything she is and everything she does, she lays her head on my shoulder.

Somehow, through sheer force of will, I remain upright and breathing while that small, simple movement makes my fucking heart stop.

Chapter 29

Deirdre

Elio Titone is hugging me. And not only am I letting him, I'm nuzzling my head against his shoulder as if this is something I want, as if he's someone I care about. As if anything about this makes sense. Something is changing between us, and it scares the hell out of me.

I need to backtrack. To get back to the place where hating him was simple and easy and safe. I need to not think about the things we share, about the things we've both lost, about what he went through when he was fourteen and what I went through when I was ten. We both have pieces missing, and I can't accept that their sharp and broken edges might just match up perfectly.

So, I try to remind myself about who he is, who I am, and what he's done. I need to remind myself that he's a tyrant who doesn't care about my feelings or my freedom. I ask the one thing of him I know he'll refuse me, and that refusal will push me away from him again, back to where I can be angry and safe.

"My classes start tomorrow. I want to go," I say. My pulse speeds up in anticipation of him saying no. I'm already feeling the thrill of the rage that will flow through me, knowing it will send me right out of his arms. Arms that feel way too warm and solid around me.

"Fine."

I freeze, shocked into stone-stillness. *Did I just hallucinate? There's absolutely no way...*

"What did you just-"

"I said that's fine."

I lift my head from his shoulder so I can stare at him. I must look as confused as I feel, because he shrugs and says, "I told you I'd give you whatever you need to perform to the best of your ability. If that means attending classes, so be it."

I want to push him on this, to question him, but I also don't want to give him a chance to change his mind. I can taste that little bit of freedom already and I won't let it disappear.

"What about my job?" I ask, wondering if he'll give me even more if I request it now. "Teaching at the music school."

Elio quirks a dark brow.

"You already have a job. One that pays infinitely more."

"Yes, but-"

"You aren't returning to that job. All your income will be provided by me. Besides, Maeve's is in the heart of Darragh's territory. Going there isn't safe for you now."

He's right. Maeve literally rents her building from Darragh. There's no way I can go there now. I think about my students and want to cry. I have seven students right now taking private lessons, ranging in ages from six to twelve. I love all of them, even the ones who don't really care about learning violin and are only there because their parents make them go.

I don't want to cry. Not now, not like this. There's something so scarily disarming about Elio holding me like this, and I feel like I'm going to break right open. I finally pull out of his grip, getting to my feet and hiking my panties and pyjama pants back up.

Elio just watches me with those dark predator eyes. As I turn and head for the other bedroom, his voice follows me.

"Get some rest, Songbird. You have school tomorrow."

Chapter 30

Deirdre

When I wake up I still have no reply from Willow. I do, however, have a text and a missed call from Brian. For a split second, I actually consider telling Brian about Elio. Not so Brian can rescue me, but so that he leaves me alone. There's something satisfying about the thought of telling Brian that if he keeps trying to get me back he'll probably end up at the bottom of a lake.

And then my stomach clenches with nausea, because what the hell kind of a thought is that? Having anyone's death on my conscience would destroy me and I know it. And why on earth am I thinking about Elio as my protector in this situation?

I push all of it out of my mind, getting out of bed and heading for the bathroom. Rosa must come in while I'm in the shower, because when I emerge there's a breakfast tray waiting for me and the bed has been stripped and remade. I eat quickly and drink some tea before getting dressed for the day. My hands practically shake as I pull on a pair of jeans and a sweater. I can't believe how excited I am just to go to school. What was once a mundane, everyday occurrence is now a shining beacon of hope and light. It's *something,* something from my old life. Something from the outside world I can hang onto.

After getting dressed I have a second cup of tea, then I start pacing the room. My classes today don't start until 11:30 and it's not even 10am yet. I consider lying about when my classes start just to get out of here now, but then I remember that Elio told me he's memorized my school schedule, so that plan goes out the window.

But I need to do something to pass the time. I have way too much anxious energy to sit around here. My eyes fall on the paper and envelopes Valentina brought me to write to Willow, and suddenly I know what to do. I grab the paper and a pen and start to write letters to each of my students. Saying goodbye, telling them how much I'll miss them, how much potential they have. I have no idea if Valentina will agree to send them, but at least it's something.

By the time I'm finished writing the seven letters, I have to pee desperately. I was on the verge of tears the entire time I was writing, and to stave off a sobbing fit I chugged more and more hot tea. I put down the letters and hurry to the bathroom to do my business, then wash my hands. When I return to the bedroom I nearly jump out of my skin because Elio is standing there.

"Holy... When did you get here?" I ask, gawking at him. Even over the sound of the tap running, I feel like I should have heard him. He's so damn big. He has no right to be as silent as he is.

"You didn't come down, so I came up to get you. Don't want to be late to your first class of the term."

"You... came up to get me?" I echo.

I assumed that maybe Curse, or one of Elio's other men, would drop me off and pick me up. But as I let my gaze drift over Elio, taking in the black leather jacket and the car keys in his hand, I realize I was mistaken.

"Are you my ride or something?" I ask him, trying not to notice that the leather jacket hanging on the bulk of his frame looks way too good.

"Not just your ride," he replies, flipping the keys up and down against the palm of his black glove, the keychain spinning back and forth around his index finger. "Your *chaperone*."

"My..." The word sinks in. "Oh, no. *No way*. You are not attending classes with me! You're not even a student! They won't let you in."

His mouth twitches, twisting on the scarred side, and I don't know if it's the beginning of a smirk or a frown. His tone when he speaks next gives nothing away besides the kind of cool, implacable confidence that comes from killing and kidnapping whoever you want, whenever you want, with absolute impunity.

"They'll let me in."

I shake my head.

"No way. This isn't happening."

"It isn't happening if you don't have a chaperone," he shoots back blithely. "The St George campus may not be in Darragh's territory but I'm still not sending you there alone." His mouth twitches again, and it's definitely a smirk this time. "Besides, I can't have you making a run for it."

I flush hot and cold, completely unnerved by the fact that I hadn't even considered using this as an opportunity to try to escape. *What the hell does that say about me? That I wouldn't even try to run?* I mean, realistically, I have no money and no allies. I could try to go to the police, but my 9-1-1 call from my first night here can tell me how much good that would do. But still, even knowing all this, I should have at least thought about it. Here I was all morning excited about getting to go to school instead of being excited at the chance to cut and run.

Well, there's clearly no chance of that now. Not if Elio insists on being glued to my side.

"Don't you have things to do?" I ask him. "Like, mafia things? You're basically the head of the Titone empire. How do you have time to go to my classes?"

He stops jangling the keys and walks towards me, not stopping until his chest almost brushes mine.

"I know how to delegate," he murmurs, his voice like warm smoke on my spine. His eyes seem to get even darker. "And prioritize."

There's an immediate, instinctive reaction inside me at those words. An undeniable pleasure that surges at being called his priority. Instantly, embarrassment follows. Because how pathetic am I, how little have I been valued, that I would react in such a way to what he just said?

I lean into the embarrassment, escaping from the thrill he just gave me. I don't need to get any deeper into this Stockholm Syndrome, or whatever it is, than I already am.

I can do this. I can be around Elio and not lose myself. I'll prove it, starting right now.

"Alright, fine," I say, brushing past him like he's nobody important instead of the man who's come to dominate so many aspects of my life. "Let's go."

We head down the stairs together, and I am supremely, uncomfortably aware of Elio's physical presence the entire way. Every time I see him out of the corner of my eye or catch a whiff of his deliriously nice cologne, I remember his hands on me last night.

He took his gloves off again...

And not just for a short time, either. He touched me with those huge, scarred hands and left me branded the same way the fire branded him. His touch on me, skin to skin, was incandescent and ruinous.

Ruinous because I want to feel it again. And what can that mean besides the fact that something inside me really is ruined?

I didn't break you, he told me. *I'm just responding to something that was already there.*

At the bottom of the stairs is a guy I recognize. Robbie. I'm pretty sure that's what Elio called him.

"Good morning," I mutter to him as we pass and head towards the front door. I'm not really sure why I say it. Maybe some kind of ingrained people-pleasing politeness, or a survival instinct that's telling me not to make enemies of anyone here. Robbie's eyes bulge at my greeting, and his gaze shifts to Elio as if he's not sure how he should respond.

"Don't be rude," Elio says. "If she speaks to you, I expect you to respond."

I roll my eyes at that, because I'm pretty sure that kidnapping someone and holding them hostage for their father's debt is way worse on the rudeness scale than not saying good morning.

Robbie jerks his head up and down and clears his throat. "Morning."

Elio is still staring at Robbie. "Where's her coat?"

I try not to admire it, but it really is amazing the way Elio commands. One simple question, and this giant tattooed soldier is hustling over to a nearby closet. He pulls out a long, expensive-looking white parka with a creamy fur-trimmed hood and brings it over. He holds it out to me, but Elio is the one who takes it. He dismisses Robbie with a jerk of his chin then turns to me, holding the jacket open so I can slip it on.

"This is for me to wear?" I ask. I've never had a coat like this, but I instantly recognize the brand. It's the most luxurious winterwear brand in Canada. This coat probably costs as much as a year of tuition at school.

"It's for you, period."

"To keep?" I try to clarify. "Am I paying for it, or..."

Elio moves closer with the coat, a wordless command to put it on. There's no point in fighting him. My own coats are at home, and the weather app on my phone told me it's negative twenty-seven degrees Celsius out there today. I slide my arms into the sleek, puffy sleeves. I go to do up the zipper, but Elio is faster and he's already on it. He slides it all the way up to my chin.

"Consider it part of your uniform. No charge," he says, pulling up the hood until the fur tickles the sides of my face. "Don't want you going hypothermic. Can't play violin if all your fingers fall off from frostbite."

I blink at him.

And then I laugh.

Really, truly laugh. I can't even remember the last time I laughed like this. Maybe with Willow, right before everything fell apart. It's probably a sign of my quickly deteriorating mental state, but man, does it ever feel good to just let go and laugh.

Elio stares at me in astonishment as I shake with laughter. Before I can catch my breath, he does something that completely takes it away.

He grasps the back of my neck beneath the hood and slants his mouth over mine.

I freeze, feeling way too hot in this coat now. My mouth had been open, mid-laugh, giving Elio ample space to slide his tongue inside. He strokes along my teeth and tongue, groaning as his other hand rises to cup my jaw. The leather feels exquisite, combining with the ravenous wet heat of his tongue and lips on mine.

He's kissing me.

The thought feels like it comes from very far away. I know I should be doing something, pushing him away or closing my mouth, but I'm completely stunned into stillness. Elio is *kissing* me. Somehow this is far more intimate than his tongue between my legs.

It doesn't feel how things between us usually feel.

It feels like it did when he hugged me.

What finally breaks the spell is realizing that I'm getting aroused from this. I actually have to fight against the urge to kiss him back, stop myself from meeting the bold movements of his tongue with my own. The warm slide of his mouth, the seeking swipe of his tongue, is making my nipples prick and my clit tingle. I jerk and close my mouth. He makes a rough, raw sound in his throat, and I think he's going to pry my jaws open to get back inside. But instead, he glides the tip of his tongue gently over the seam of my lips in between nipping kisses, probing and prodding until I tremble with the control it takes not to open my mouth with a horny, pathetic moan.

When he finally pauses, I try to piece my braincells back together enough to speak.

"What are you doing?" I croak.

"Don't know," he breathes against my lips. "Your mouth just looks so fucking good when you laugh."

I can't come up with a coherent answer to that, so instead I weakly mutter, "I'll be late."

"No." He kisses me one more time and then lets me go. "You won't."

There's a pair of boots for me, too, and mittens, and after putting them on we head outside. I inhale sharply and blink, shocked by the sunlight and the crackling cold air. This is the first time I've been outside in days.

I don't want to think this property is beautiful, but it really is. The bare trees outside look like crystal sculptures, every branch and twig lined with faceted frost. The spruce trees are still dark with greenish-blue needles, casting stark shadows on the glittering snow.

There's no snow on the huge driveway ahead of us except what's been melted by salt. The pavement gleams like ink.

A car emerges from one of the three garage doors at the far side of the house. It's the black Porsche Elio took me to the gala with. It comes to a stop before us and Curse gets out. Even though it's almost thirty degrees Celsius below freezing, he's not wearing a jacket, just a black dress shirt and pants.

"Enzo's at the campus," Curse says. It's the first time I've ever heard him speak in a full sentence. His voice is a lot like Elio's, and I find that slightly jarring. "So far everything looks good."

"Sorry, who's at the campus?" I ask. I swivel to Elio. "I thought it was just you going with me."

The bright sunshine and the snow make Elio's gaze look even darker.

"Enzo is my head of security. He's scoping things out right now."

I thought attending classes with Elio would be bad enough, but now there's a made man skulking around the hallways and classrooms?

"Oh, God. He isn't bothering my professors, is he? Or the other students?"

What if he's interrogating people, or intimidating them? Honestly, even the possibility that he's mildly inconveniencing people because of me makes my chest hum with anxiety. I love going to university, but I like blending into the background as much as possible. I don't even usually go to office hours because I don't want to take up my teachers's time. But now I'm the cause of all this weirdness and upheaval.

"Maybe this was a bad idea," I say with a sigh. I glare at the sun-spangled snow to keep tears from forming. I am so stupid. Why did I think I could just go back to class, go back to that part of my life like nothing had ever happened? Like things were normal?

The fact that nothing will ever be normal again almost knocks me over. Even if I somehow pay my debt to Elio and gain my freedom, my life is beyond shattered. My dad is gone, and I'll still be enemy number one for Darragh if he can't find my dad. Even with the warmth of the parka cocooning me, I shiver. The only reason I'm alive right now, the reason I'm warm and wrapped up in this gorgeous coat, is because of Elio. The man who took me, caged me, lords himself over me like I'm his possession. Fury and fear go to war inside me when I consider the fact that I would be completely lost without him. I have no money to run away and start a new life. I have no close friends except Willow who can't fraternize with me for her own safety.

The sound of the passenger car door opening draws my attention. I swallow hard and look at Elio, holding it open for me like he's guiding me into a dark, enclosed future. A future he created.

And I walk straight to him. Enter through that door and let him close it behind me.

Because as much as I hate to admit it, Elio Titone is all I have left.

Chapter 31

Elio

"Seatbelt," I grunt at Deirdre as I slide into the driver's seat.

"I always wear my seatbelt," she says crisply, sounding annoyed by my command.

"Then why aren't you?"

She looks down at herself, confused, as if she doesn't understand what's happening.

"Oh. I thought I already did it. Lost in thought, I guess."

I watch her buckle up, making sure she does it properly, before starting the engine.

"Penny for your thoughts?" I say, putting the car into drive and heading down the long driveway. The soldier at the gatehouse nods at me through the bulletproof glass and opens the gate the leads out onto the street.

"Only a penny," Deidre says with an ironic sort of laugh. It's nothing like the real, beautiful laugh I heard inside the house. The laugh that turned me sideways and had me kissing her when I haven't kissed anyone like that in years.

"Typical man. You'll pay a fortune for my wet underwear, but only a single coin for what I actually think."

"It's just a saying," I mutter. I keep my left hand on the wheel and use my other to grab a pair of dark sunglasses I keep in the car, sliding them onto my face. I love winter here, love the lung-constricting cold of it, but I cannot fucking stand the flame-like dance of bright sun reflecting on snow.

"Just a saying. So you won't even pay a penny, then?" she replies tartly. Something's got her more pissed off than usual, and I wonder what it is. She didn't seem angry when I was kissing her just moments ago. She seemed disarmed and pliant and quivery in a way that made me want to say *fuck school so you can fuck me instead*.

"One hundred thousand and one. Dollars," I clarify when I feel her questioning frown turn to me. *Merda*, she's cute in that coat with the fluffy hood framing her face. Like some kind of Irish ice princess. "Tell me what you're thinking."

She sighs, turning away to look out the window. I think she's going to reject my offer, but my Songbird is smart and she knows she can't afford to.

"I was thinking about what happens when I pay off my debt. What I'm going to do without..."

She doesn't finish that sentence. Something lurches inside me.

"Without me, you mean."

Her silence is all the confirmation I need.

"Are you worried about that?" I ask.

"I'm worried about the fact I don't have a single friend in the world who can help me when I'm out of here!" she bursts out. "I can't even rely on my own family!" She tips her head back against the headrest. All I can see of her profile from the corner of my eye is her cute freckly nose.

"You don't need friends or family. You have me." *Until the end of fucking time.*

"But what about after? After the debt is paid and you let me go."

"Not gonna happen."

Her voice hardens. "I told you I would pay my debt and get out of here no matter what it takes."

242

We're getting close to downtown now, the buildings crowding together.

"The interest is mounting faster than you're paying it off," I counter. I mean, that's by design. That was the whole fucking point of the deal I made with O'Malley.

"We'll see about that," she whispers. Her voice remains quiet when she suddenly asks, "But what happens if you don't want to deal with me anymore? If I do something to make you angry, or you just want to be done with me?"

"Also not gonna happen." I want to wring her father's neck even more than usual at this moment. He's made her feel like something dispensable, something to abandon.

"You never know. You could get bored with me."

My jaw tightens as I manoeuvre through Toronto's downtown.

"I have watched you and waited for you since you were eighteen years old. You have turned me into a bleeding goddamn heart, or at least a bleeding wallet. I just paid six figures to find out what is going on in that head of yours because I can't stand not knowing a single thing about you. Getting bored is not even in the realm of possibility."

We're outside the building for her first class of the term, a lecture for her *Musical Developments from the Middle Ages to the Renaissance* course. There's nowhere to pull over, so I stop the car in the middle of traffic. Honking bleats from behind me, but I ignore it, focused solely on Deirdre.

"I just need to know where I stand," she says, unbuckling her seatbelt.

I take off my sunglasses and put them down, then grab the bag I arranged for her.

"You will stand where I tell you to," I reply. I get out of the car and walk around it. After opening the passenger door, I grab her hand and pull her to her feet. I hold her hand a second longer than is necessary while traffic piles up behind us, our covered palms sealed together. "You stand right beside me."

Chapter 32

Deirdre

Elio's gaze is so absorbing, dark and expansive, that the sound of angry Toronto drivers behind us is completely wiped out. The sun is bright on the buildings, wet with winter, creating a sparkling, steely backdrop. One of Elio's wayward curls has fallen forward again, and I both want to brush it back into place and tug it further forward to make him look more mussed, more human.

"All clear, Boss."

A voice from directly beside us pulls me out of Elio's void. Elio lets go of my hand, but quickly loops an arm around my waist, drawing me into his side as we turn to face a tall man with short hair and hazel eyes.

Elio hands the keys to him.

"Good. Go park, then keep your eye on things, Enzo."

Enzo nods and gets into the car, putting it into drive and taking off down the street.

"Ready?" Elio asks me. I glance from him to the building behind him. Students are streaming through the doors, carrying normal, everyday things like coffees and laptops and books.

"Not really," I say. "I don't even have my school stuff." I'll just have to pay really close attention since I can't take any notes. *Yeah, pay attention with the most dangerous man in the city breathing down my neck. Sure.*

Elio hoists a bag, holding it up in front of me. I hadn't seen it before, and now that the car is gone it's like he's pulled a rabbit out of a hat. Like the bag came from thin, cold air.

It's a gorgeous bag – a creamy leather backpack the same colour as the fur on the hood of my new coat. I take it from him, opening it to find a brand-new rose gold laptop, along with the books I'll need for the two classes I'm attending today.

"I already have a school laptop," I say with dismay, imagining more money piling on top of my debt. I picture it like a leaning tower of Piza of bills in my head. Like it's about to topple and bury me. I close the bag. "I feel like there should be a rule where if you buy me something I already have, don't need, and didn't ask for, then I shouldn't have to pay for it."

"I highly doubt you still have a laptop," Elio says. "It's pretty likely that Sev's guys took anything of value after your dad left. Or Darragh ransacked the place. Maybe both."

My stomach lurches. I don't know why I assumed the house and my possessions would still be waiting for me after this whole ordeal is over, but I did. *Stupid. I am so stupid.*

"How come you didn't do that? How come you haven't started repossessing all our stuff?"

Elio doesn't speak for a moment. Instead, he takes one of my hands, then the other, lifting each arm and sliding the straps of the backpack up until it hangs on my back. He tightens the straps at the front of my shoulders.

"There was only one single thing of any value to me in that house. Worth more than everything else put together," he finally says. His eyes flick to mine. "And I already got her."

"*Got her.*" I snort. "You mean *took.*"

Elio grins lazily at me, the expression made crooked by his scars.

"Tom-*ay*-to, tom-*ah*-to."

He still hasn't explicitly told me if this bag and laptop is a gift or not, and I give up on trying to figure it out, at least for now. Rather cynically, I wonder, *what's a few thousand more on top of everything now?*

We walk together into the building. It's hard to feel through the coat, but even so it's unmistakeable – the firm, possessive press of Elio's hand on my lower back. The pressure there reignites the curling burn of pleasure from his kiss, and I try to focus on each step I take over the tiled floors instead of his touch and the stupid response my body makes to it.

Luckily, my first class is a lecture of about a hundred people, so Elio's presence doesn't cause any sort of problem. There are too many students in this lecture hall to recognize everyone, so no one really stands out as a stranger, but even so, countless eyes are drawn to Elio as he guides me into the room. He's just so *big*, plus he's older than about 95% of the people here. And he's so commanding. Walking through the aisles and seats like he owns them.

I wonder how he does it. Even though people are looking at him more than me, my cheeks are on fire. This level of attention, just from walking through the room, makes me want to internally combust. But he doesn't seem to feel it at all. There's something magnetic about confidence like that. To go anywhere, be anywhere, and not care what anyone thinks. And it's not like he belongs here – a filthy rich mafia murderer hanging out in a university lecture hall. He is *extremely* out of place. But it just doesn't fucking matter. Because just by being here, he creates his own place. He slices his way through the skin of the world by doing nothing more than walking into a room that shouldn't want him.

The heat bubbling in my veins gets even hotter when I realize that Elio is leading me to a seat in the middle of the front row. The green plastic seat is attached to the desk, but it swivels to allow people in and out. He grabs the back of it and turns it towards me.

"Sit."

"I never sit in the front row," I say, shifting back and forth on my feet. I need to get this freaking coat off. There will probably be steam erupting from me when I do.

"You do now," Elio says. "I won't have you slacking off in the back row."

"Slacking off!" I whisper-hiss at him, all too aware of the fact I'm standing front and centre in the room. "If anything keeps me from giving the prof all my attention it is going to be *you!*"

"Glad to know I'm such a distraction."

"No, not like that. I-"

"Seats, everyone!" calls out a voice from the doorway. Doctor Heaney, a musical historian, tosses her grey hair behind her shoulders as she enters the room. Elio doesn't budge, still holding the chair in its open position for me. Biting my tongue, I plop myself into it, because at this point sitting in the front is preferable to marching to a whole new row after the prof has asked us to sit. Elio crams himself into the seat beside me, and it looks like he's sitting on furniture meant for children.

Luckily, the lecture passes without incident. Somehow, I manage to cobble together a decent set of notes, even with Elio's heavy arm slung across the back of my chair, his eyes endlessly gliding back and forth between what I'm typing and my face in profile.

I'm both relieved and disappointed when the lecture ends. Disappointed because, even with the weirdness of Elio beside me, I can't deny how nice it is to be out of the house and in class again. And relieved because one and a half hours of him doing nothing but sitting quietly beside me with his arm around me watching me take notes made me feel like my spine was melting into my pelvis. Like everything inside me was molten and oozing. I'm almost surprised my legs are still solid and holding my weight when I stand up

There's still one more class to go today, in a room just down the hall from my lecture. This one is a small seminar, and it's the one that's got me stressed. Unlike my morning lecture, this is a very small group of about fifteen students, and it's the same group of students I had a seminar with last term. We all know each other, and the prof knows all our names. Walking in with Elio won't be nearly as unobtrusive as it was last time.

When we get to the room, our professor, a short, grey-haired man with glasses named Doctor Frank is standing in the doorway, handing out the term syllabus to students walking in. I pretty much want to die every time I have to participate in class, but I do it in his seminar because he's such a warm, kind, mentoring sort of person. He smiles when he sees me approach, and I can't help but smile back.

"Deirdre! Hello, hello. Here's your syllabus. Ah." His bushy grey eyebrows furrow when he sees Elio trying to enter the room with me. "I'm sorry. Only students inside."

Doctor Frank isn't a tall guy, and he has to crane his neck back to look at Elio.

"Where she goes, I go," Elio says smoothly. "I'm her emotional support monster."

Doctor Frank's brows furrow further. Which is understandable, considering how fucking insane Elio sounds.

"I don't really know what's going on here," my prof says with a small shake of his head, "but I can't let anyone in here who isn't registered for the course."

By now the students who got here ahead of me are staring from their seats, and I silently beg the floor to swallow me up.

"Let's just go," I whisper to Elio. Maybe I can switch my schedule around to only include lectures this term.

Or maybe I shouldn't have bothered coming here at all.

But Elio acts like he doesn't even hear me. In a quick, controlled movement, he swipes the papers from Doctor Frank's hands.

"Excuse me, Sir!" Doctor Frank blusters, his cheeks turning red. Derek, one of the bigger guys in the class stands, apparently ready to step in even though he wouldn't stand a fucking chance.

Elio ignores everyone, thumbing through the syllabus papers until he gets to a different paper at the end. He pulls it to the front, and I recognize the names there. It's the class's attendance list with the names of the registered students in this seminar. Elio grabs a pen from his jacket, then holds the paper against the wall, scrawling a new name at the bottom of the list. *Elio Titone.*

When Doctor Frank sees the name, he clamps his mouth shut, the red instantly sucked from his cheeks.

"There," Elio says, thrusting the pile of papers back to the prof with the attendance list on top. "Now I'm on the list."

"So you are, Mr. Titone," Doctor Frank says in a mangled rush. "My apologies."

"Feel free to let the rest of the department know," Elio responds. "Since I will be attending every one of Deirdre's classes from here on out."

Doctor Frank nods so rapidly I think his glasses might fly off of his face. God, I don't know what's worse. The scene we've just caused, or the fact that my prof looks like he knows exactly who I'm with. Doctor Frank watches me closely with a pinched look as Elio pulls out a chair for me, no doubt wondering how the hell the quiet violinist in his class has gotten herself mixed up with someone like Elio. If I could talk to him alone, I wonder if he'd try to help me somehow. He cares about his students, and I know instantly he probably would. But that would likely just put him in danger, so the thought wilts before I even let it take root.

Because this class is a seminar, we're all sitting at desks arranged in a circle instead of rows, and I try not to make eye contact with anyone when I sit down. I watch Elio take his seat from the corner of my eye as I open up the laptop. In the lecture hall, Elio had typed in the password for me, as the laptop was already set up with an account for me. But it's locked me out since I closed it up, and I quietly ask him for the password as the last few students filter in.

Instead of saying the password, he spells it out for me, letter by letter, and it's only when I get to the last part that I realize I've just typed in *iloveelio.*

Jesus Christ.

Since it's such a small group, and we all already know each other, Elio's presence is a lot more disruptive than in my previous class. He's like an invasive species, upsetting the balance of the ecosystem. Doctor Frank chooses not to introduce him or acknowledge him when he settles into a nervous, jittery version of his *welcome to the new term* spiel. While I normally try to participate in this class, today I don't say a word. The other students are quieter than normal, too, and I don't need to think too hard about why that might be.

Getting through that seminar is like pulling teeth, and the bit of excitement and relief I felt at attending my earlier lecture is totally gone now. I practically bolt out of there when class is done, barely registering Doctor Frank's comments about next week's assignment.

"Damn, you're fast. You here on a track scholarship?" Elio asks from behind me as I weave through students in the hallway.

"Wouldn't matter if I was," I shoot back. "I'm dropping out."

I shove open the doors and hurl myself out into the bright winter day. In my haste to get out of there, I haven't zipped up my jacket. The bitter cold knifes right through the front of my sweater, but I welcome it. It feels so painfully good that I take the jacket off entirely, breathing in the January air. I know Elio is right behind me before he even speaks.

"You're not dropping out."

"Yes, I am," I snap, whirling on him. He's standing there with the bag, carrying my books like my fucking boyfriend or something. "I can't do this anymore."

"Can't do what? Attend class?"

"Not anymore. Not with you," I tell him.

"Why not? I was quiet, wasn't I? Just sat there like a good boy."

"Oh, *yes*, a very good boy," I huff, clutching the jacket against my front. "You're practically a *saint*."

"Elio, Patron Saint of Songbirds," he drawls. "Has a nice ring to it."

"I can't with you today. We are done here."

The crackle of dark humour in his gaze goes cold, glinting like onyx.

"I decide when things begin and I decide when they end," he growls. "You told me you wanted to go to school. That it's important to you, and to your craft. So, you will go to fucking school. And if I have to get you up and dressed and drag you here myself, I fucking will."

"But I don't belong here anymore!" I stammer, off-balance from the sudden shift in his tone. "And neither do you! When we entered that room, *God*, it was like we poisoned it or something. Everyone was staring at us! My teacher looked like he was on the verge of passing out!"

"My sweet little Songbird, the only one you're capable of poisoning is me. You're in my fucking blood, and I'm pretty sure you've passed the blood-brain barrier, because these days I can barely think around the space you take up inside my head." He raises the arm that's not busy holding the bag, gesturing his thumb backwards over his shoulder towards the doors we just came out of. "And those other dopey fucks in there? They're lucky to even breathe the same air as you. Why do you care what they think? Why would them staring at you keep you from something you want?"

"I don't even know what I want anymore."

"But I do," he says, every word stony with conviction. "And your pretty little ass better be ready for school tomorrow morning, or you'll have to stand at the back of the class because it's going to be too sore to sit on those shitty plastic seats."

A bolt of confused pleasure goes straight to my clit at his clipped commands.

"Well, we'll just see about that," I say with a shiver.

"Yes," Elio says darkly. "We will."

Chapter 33

Deirdre

The next morning I get up and shower, but after that I waffle back and forth about what to do. Should I get ready for class or not? Am I dropping out or staying? I absolutely do not want to repeat yesterday – that was mortifying – but if I go to class there's no way around it. Elio's coming with me. A twisted part of me almost wants to bait Elio. To sit here in my wet towel until he has to come and get me. To see if he really will drag me there. Imagining him storming in here and ripping away my towel makes my insides curl and my thighs squeeze, and it's the rebellion against that arousal that finally has me hurrying to get ready.

I'll go to class, at least today. Going there and suffering humiliation in public is better than submitting to the private humiliation in here. The humiliation that makes me wet. I blow dry my hair, not bothering to style it, and it dries in a frizzy tumble that I tie up in a knot on the top of my head.

The only problem is that I spent so long dithering about what to do that I really might actually be late at this point. My first class is at ten today, and I'm going to be cutting it close. I'm running from the bathroom to the closet, clutching my towel, when Elio strides into the room. He looks the same way he did yesterday – tall and broad in all black, leather jacket and gloves on, keys in hand. He stops short when he sees me.

"You're not ready."

"I am. Almost," I say hurriedly, continuing my way into the closet. He follows me, and my heart starts banging a chaotic rhythm against my ribs.

And my clit.

"I told you what would happen if you weren't ready," he says from behind my back, so softly that it belies the bite of the threat in the words.

"And I told you I'm almost ready," I shoot back.

"Doesn't look that way to me."

I yelp as the towel gets tugged away from me. Before I can cross my arms or try to hide myself, Elio grabs the back of my neck from behind me and shoves my head forward.

"Grab the shelves."

"No," I pant. The feeling of his leather glove on the back of my neck is so fucking hot I can't stand it. I can't let this go any further. Can't let him see what he's doing to me. That's how he wins. Every single time.

Elio keeps his hold on my neck and steps forward, bumping my ass with his thighs until I lose my balance and I'm forced to grasp the edge of the shelf ahead of me. Now I'm doing exactly what he told me to. I'm bent over and bare for him. Even if I tried to stand up, I couldn't, because the weight of his hand on the back of my neck is like an anchor. He isn't even pushing me down, and that's the worst part. The anchor only exists in my head because of how far he's dug his way inside me.

"I told you that you are going to school today and I told you what would happen to this ass if you weren't ready," Elio says from above and behind me. "You know what time your classes are. You know what time you needed to be ready. And you know I don't break my promises." His left hand grazes my hip, and I start, my pussy throbbing. "Don't try to act all innocent and affronted on me now. You're baiting me, waiting for me in only a towel when you're supposed to be dressed and ready."

His hand lifts from my hip, and I tense, waiting in angry, defensive, delirious anticipation of what's to come.

"I told you at the gala that taunting me is not a good idea."

His hand comes down with a tight, sharp movement, searing my flesh. I hold my breath, an instinctive reaction, so that I don't give him the satisfaction of hearing my cry of deranged pleasure. But Elio slides his right hand around the front of my throat, massaging there, until I'm forced to open my mouth and take a breath. With his left hand, he spanks me again, and this time I can't hold back my mangled moan.

"No holding your breath," he orders me huskily. "No shutting down. No silence. I want to hear that pretty fucking song of yours."

It doesn't sound like a song to me. It sounds like panting, pathetic mewling. A reedy, throaty chorus punctured by the staccato beat of Elio's leather glove against my skin. My back is arching, my fingers tight against the shelf, and I can't fucking stop it, because for some reason I need this and I need *more*. After every slap, my ass shoves backward, upward, begging him to keep going.

"I told you, Songbird," Elio rasps. "I told you I could go harder. And look how fucking good you're being. Look how fucking well you take it." He groans, long and low, pausing the spanking to grip my ass cheek and spread it to the side. "Look how fucking well you wear my marks. It's like your skin was made for this."

The unexpected praise mixed with the pain and heat and degradation has me close to coming. I hold onto the shelf for dear life, my thighs trembling, my clit screaming. I can't even feel my own heartbeat now. It's been replaced by the rhythm Elio has created. The stinging slaps that echo through my body even when both of us are still.

Elio's hand eases from my neck, and I hear the unmistakable jingle of a belt being undone and pants hitting the floor. Dread and desire bloom inside me, and I can't move, *I cannot move*, as Elio guides the head of his cock against my pussy.

"Fuck, you're soaked," he groans. "*Cristo santo,* your dripping pussy nestled below that bright red ass is a work of fucking art."

My muscles jump, and I'm at war with myself. My body is frozen under the weight of competing instincts. The instinct to wiggle backwards, to soothe the pulsing emptiness by taking Elio inside me.

And the instinct to run for my life.

"Touch yourself."

When I don't answer or move, another slap makes my nerves spark and sing.

"*Touch yourself.*"

My right arm practically falls from the shelf, like it's dead weight. My fingers find their way between my legs, and I almost fall to my knees at how incredibly sensitive my clit is. I start grinding my clit, already on that breathless edge, as Elio watches and breathes unevenly behind me.

"Good, Songbird," he murmurs, petting the place he's spanked me. That gentle scrape of leather over my burning skin is sensation overload, and I can't get enough. I wonder if Elio's going to press inside me.

I wonder if I'd even be capable of putting together enough coherent sounds to tell him not to if he tried.

His fat tip is right at my slick entrance. I quiver and clench around nothing. One tiny movement, one concise and brutal thrust, and he'd be buried inside me.

His cock jerks, his head nudging slightly harder against my folds, and I strum my clit harder, faster, focusing on my building orgasm so I can't focus on the fact that if he fucks me, I can never come back from it.

With a ragged grunt, his cock pulls away, and I want to strangle the sudden dismay I feel. It's good we're not going that far. I should be relieved. And I am, I swear, I-

"I am going to come all over your ass," Elio growls. He spreads my ass cheek further, opening me. His cock makes contact again, this time thrusting up towards my lower back, the underside of his shaft grinding against me. "And then I am going to rub my come into that skin I've made so pretty and red. And after that, I am going to take you to class so you can sit on it and think about exactly what you've done."

My eyes fly open, and I try to say *no* because I am absolutely not going to class now, not without showering again, at least. But I can't say it, because my throat constricts and all that comes out is a strangled cry. My whole body shakes and then tightens until I'm shattering, *shattered*, completely broken open, the pieces scattered on a dark and undulating sea of molten pleasure. Through the shameful sounds I'm making, I can hear Elio stroking himself, hard and fast and feral, leather sliding over engorged flesh. He grips my hip, holding me still, then lets out a tight, hissed breath. A second later, warmth erupts over my stinging skin, and that sudden sensation makes me shudder and clench and moan all over again.

As promised, Elio rubs the come into my skin, the touch soothing and burning all at once. The evaporating wetness makes my heated skin feel slightly cooler, and I suddenly can't stand that this actually feels good. This smooth, massaging motion, so gentle, almost reverent, when a moment ago that hand was so hard, might even be better than the orgasm. If I ignore the circumstances, it almost feels loving, like he's taking care of me.

But the circumstances blare all around me, like neon signs trying to guide me back to sanity. He's not taking loving care of me. He's rubbing his fucking come into skin he just spanked nearly raw.

"Get dressed," he says, drawing his hand away and pulling up his pants. "I'm going to get new gloves, and then we're leaving."

"No," I whisper. "I'm having another shower."

"Absolutely not," he says. "At this rate you'll only be fifteen minutes late for class. If you have another shower, you'll miss the entire lecture."

I unclench my left hand from the shelf, straightening up shakily and turning around.

"My shower won't take that long. I won't even get my hair wet." I narrow my gaze at him. "I only need to wash something off of *one* part of my body."

"You go in that shower and just see what fucking happens."

I chew on my lip, seething. There's a slight darkness to Elio's cheeks that I've never seen on him before, and I realize with a treacherous flutter in my belly that that flush is there because of me. His breathing hasn't returned to normal yet, either.

"Get dressed," he says again.

And then he turns and walks away.

Chapter 34

Elio

It only takes me about thirty seconds to get new gloves from my room. When I come back into Deirdre's bedroom, I don't hear the shower running, and I'm both satisfied and annoyed that she obeyed. If she'd gone into the shower now, I would have followed her. And then I would have had her up against the shower wall because there's no way I would have been able to stop myself. I barely held myself back from shoving inside her and claiming her when she made that little virgin pussy come so sweetly for me.

Fuck. I'm already going to get hard again. I take my keys out of my pocket and clench them in my fist, focusing on the feeling of blunted metal pressing through my glove.

I can hear fabric rustling in the closet. While I wait for Deirdre to finish getting dressed, I pace the room, pausing in front of her violin and bow. I run a single, gentle finger down the flexible part of the bow that connects with the violin's strings. It's called the bow hair, and it's made from horse hair, one of the many odd, endless facts I've committed to memory in preparation for Deirdre's arrival here.

Something else catches my eye, and I turn my attention to a small stack of envelopes. I pick them up and shuffle through them, wondering who the hell Deirdre might be trying to contact through the mail.

There are seven envelopes, and the mailing address is the same on every one – the address for Maeve's Music School. But the names are all different. Hannah Jankowski, Mingming Li, Hazel Martin, Sam Ford, Leshawn Andrews, Eun-Ji Park, Noah Barber. I use my car key to slide under the seal of the envelope addressed to Noah, open it, and take out the letter.

Dear Noah,

I have had so much fun being your violin teacher! I never want you to forget that. The fact that I'm not your teacher anymore has nothing to do with you, and if I could be there with you right now, I would.

Even though I'm sad I won't get to teach you any longer, I just want you to know how happy I am that I got a chance to get to know you and help you along your music journey, even if just for a little while. You are funny, expressive, and so, <u>so</u> talented.

I know you sometimes get frustrated when the notes don't come out the way you want them to, or when you think the song doesn't sound quite right, but just keep going. Keep trying. Keep practising. Don't ever get discouraged. Remember that the song already exists inside you. The instrument is just our way of letting it out. The violin simply gives voice to what already exists, and Noah, it doesn't just exist in you, it <u>shines</u>. No matter who your teacher is, you have every-thing you'll ever need to excel.

Thank you so much for being my student. Don't ever forget how special your song is,

Love, Miss Dee

"That's private."

Deirdre's voice makes me look up from the paper. I gesture the stack of letters towards the lack of door between her room and mine.

"Right," she says, rolling her eyes. "Nothing's private here."

259

"You don't have stamps. What is this, some writing exercise?" I fold Noah's letter back up and slide it into the envelope.

She stares at me, and I stare back, because fuck she looks good after she comes. Her skin is flushed and glowing. Tiny baby hairs are escaping from her hairstyle, creating an electric orange halo of frizz. My beautiful hellfire angel.

"I was going to see if Valentina would put stamps on them and send them."

"I'm in charge of what comes in and out of this house, not Valentina."

Something unhappy crashes in the blue of her eyes.

"Fine, then," she snaps. "May as well throw them in the fire now because I know you won't let me send them."

Her own reaction to what she just said is almost comical to watch. Like a cartoon character giving life to the phrase "biting my tongue." She tenses, her mouth snapping shut so hard and fast that I think it's probably a good thing I haven't put my dick in there, because that's a hell of a lot of jaw power. I wait without speaking, because I've never been one to find silence awkward, boring a hole into her head with my gaze while hers traces grooves along the wood floorboards.

"Sorry," she finally says, so fucking softly. She uncrosses her arms and starts twining her fingers together in front of her. "That was the wrong choice of words."

She knows.

Not just about the fire, because everybody knows about the fire. My fucking face tells people about the fire.

But she knows it was more than just a fire. She knows what I lost. She knows exactly how I failed.

Fucking Valentina.

The ticking in my head is back, an incessant, uneven thrum that sounds like flames crackling over wood. My hands start tensing, and I have to fight the urge to pulverize the stack of letters in my fist.

"Just throw them away already," Deirdre says.

"I'm not going to throw them away," I say evenly.

"What, going to read them all out loud and then rip them up in front of me?"

"Nope."

She lets out an exasperated breath.

"What, then?"

"I'm going to reseal this one and add it back with the others. Then, I'm going to put stamps on them. And then I am going to send them."

Her ginger eyebrows practically crawl all the way up to her hairline. It seems like she can't stop the question of "Why?" from escaping her mouth. It comes out as a gasp, because what other reaction would an act of humanity in me elicit than pure fucking shock?

I don't have an answer for her. At least not one I want to say out loud. It's something to do with the fact that I know what it's like to lose a woman you love and look up to with no closure and no goodbye when you're a kid.

And it's something to do with the way the image of Deirdre bent over the desk writing such kind, devoted letters makes my chest feel tight.

It isn't just that she's not from this world, like Valentina said. It's that she's too fucking good for it. And if I were a better man, she'd never have ended up here at all.

But then again, if I were a better man, I wouldn't have done the things I've done to have the money I have. I wouldn't have been able to pay her papà and help keep her head above water from the dark and shadowy sidelines. And I wouldn't have been there to take a fucking bullet for her seconds into her twentieth birthday.

"Doesn't matter. Come on," is all I say in reply.

Chapter 35

Deirdre

Other than the fact that we walk into my lecture late and make everyone turn and stare, today goes a lot smoother than yesterday. I'm actually able to somewhat focus, and when Elio notices me squirming to keep weight off tender places, he folds up his leather jacket and shoves it under me like a cushion while giving me a dark look that tells me not to argue or refuse him.

Which is pretty much the last thing I expect him to do. Wasn't he the one who told me if I didn't listen, if I wasn't ready for school, that I'd be too sore to sit on the seats? I assumed that would be part of the punishment, but now here he is turning his own jacket into a pillow for me. Between this and the fact that he sent the letters to my students (I watched him put them in the mailbox myself as we left the property this morning) I can't get my head around who or what he is these days.

A monster. A man. Some scarred, mangled mixture of the two.

And the fact that I seem to crave his touch more and more, the fact that I stayed bent over for him this morning, that I didn't even wash his claim off my skin, means I don't even know who I am, either. From the very first night he took me, there's been this slow, steady, toxic pulse of desire even inside my rage against him. And it only seems to be getting stronger. Faster.

I almost lost my virginity to him this morning. It was only his decision to pull his cock away, and not anything I did, that kept that from happening.

Why didn't he do it?

Did I want him to?

I can't answer that question definitively, which only makes me even more confused. When Brian tried to push himself on me, that fumbling, drunken night in his apartment, I hadn't wanted any part of it. I'd liked him well enough on our dates, but at that moment he became completely repulsive to me, and I couldn't even stomach his beer-scented breath wafting over my skin. My whole body was filled with dread and nausea.

Why don't I feel repulsed by Elio? Elio is ten times worse than an idiot like Brian. He's literally killed people. He's trapped me and punished me and coerced me. But I can't even make myself as afraid of him as I was when Brian was against me, panting, his crotch tented stiffly at the front.

I wonder if my own thoughts somehow conjure him, because when we exit the building after my last lecture of the day, I hear that familiar voice calling my name.

"Deirdre? Deirdre! Hey, Red!"

Elio hears it, too, and his arm descends fast and hard around my shoulders, like the possessive downward sweep of a guillotine. He doesn't stop walking, and neither do I, swept along by his long strides and the other people moving the same direction. God, I hate it, but it actually feels good. It feels good to be with Elio right now. To have his arm so tight around me. Brian's showed up a bunch of times begging for me back, and I'd always been alone.

Not this time.

I don't bother looking back. Elio's got me too tightly pinned against his side. The crowd thins out as we head away from the school building until it's just Elio and me on the sidewalk and a guy running a small poutine cart in the near vicinity.

At least, I thought it was just us. But then I hear the call of "Red!" again, along with the sound of boots hitting the slushy sidewalk in a jog. "Would you just stop and fucking talk to me?"

I'm fully prepared to ignore Brian like I've being doing up until now. I keep on walking, momentum pulling me forward, so that it takes me a second to realize Elio is no longer holding me, no longer walking beside me. I stop and spin just in time to see the black fingers of Elio's right hand close around Brian's throat as he backs him up against the brick wall of a building.

"How about I talk, you listen?" Elio murmurs so softly that goosebumps rise on my skin under my clothes and coat. Once again, Elio's carrying my backpack, and it looks fucking insane, this hulking six-foot-four giant with a woman's book bag on his shoulder and his fist around another man's throat. I have to quell a horrible surge of something that feels icky and dark and wonderful at the sight of Elio towering over Brian the way he does. Brian's not a small guy. He's about six feet tall and I know he works out, but compared to Elio he looks like a gangly kid. And seeing Elio so totally subdue him does something to me. Something bad and wrong that I need to hide from, need to heal from.

If Brian wants to say anything now, he can't. His eyes are wide, and his face is an alarming shade of crimson.

"You will not contact Deirdre. You will not touch her. If you ever see her again, you turn around and walk the other fucking away."

Brian makes a gurgling sound that makes me think Elio has tightened his grip. His boots slip in the slush and he claws at Elio's arm, but it has absolutely no effect. Elio's only holding him with one fucking hand, his other one secured around the strap of the small backpack slung over his injured shoulder. Like he's worried about my books falling into the salt-melted snow. And once again I feel that dark, wrong, lovely feeling. The feeling of being cared for, being protected when my own father couldn't even have been bothered to do it before.

No. This is not a good thing. He's not a good man.

And that not good man is about to murder someone right in front of me.

"Elio," I whisper in alarm. "Please stop. Don't kill him."

I can't witness a murder. I can't watch Brian suffocate like this. I *can't.*

A car pulls up beside us, and how fucked-up am I, how far-gone have I become, that my first instinct is fear that whoever's in the car will get Elio in trouble? My reaction isn't to turn to them for help, to save Brian and maybe even get myself out of Elio's grip entirely. It's alarm on Elio's behalf.

The car is Elio's, though, and Enzo pops out of it, hustling around the hood of the vehicle, his hand inside his jacket in a way that makes my stomach drop and the word *gun* repeat inside my head on an endless loop.

"No, Enzo, wait-"

He ignores me and stops at Elio's side.

"Boss?"

Brian is still conscious, but his movements are getting weaker. Slower.

"Don't kill him!" I whisper-cry in reply to Enzo, even though I know he didn't ask me for direction on what to do next.

Elio doesn't answer Enzo or me. He's still speaking to Brian in that silky-smooth, deceptively calm voice.

"You're lucky my Songbird has such a tender heart, or you'd be nothing but a stain on the sidewalk right about now."

I swallow hard and wonder if Elio knows. If he somehow knows why I ended things with Brian. If he knows what Brian tried to do that night. This reaction seems over the top, even for Elio.

"Make sure he's never on campus at the same time as Deirdre," he mutters to Enzo, finally letting Brian go. Brian sags back against the wall, gasping and clutching his neck before sliding down to sit in the slush.

"Got it," Enzo says instantly. He pulls his hand out of his jacket, sans gun, thank God. My eyes dart up and down the small street. The poutine guy is staring at us. He pulls his tuque further down over his ears. *Hear no evil.*

"Didn't see nothin', Ma'am. Nothin' at all. Hey, you or your man want some poutine? On the house."

I shake my head weakly at him.

My man.

He's not my man. He's my disaster.

Enzo passes Elio the keys and Elio puts his arm around me once again, steering me towards the car.

He doesn't say anything, and neither do I.

But Brian does, because he really is the biggest fucking fool in the world right about now. His voice is weak and croaky, but the words are unmistakeable.

"What the hell, Red? You didn't want to be with me and now you're fucking some forty-year-old psycho?"

Uh oh.

Enzo grabs Brian and instantly hauls him upwards, pinning Brian's back against his front by locking his elbows under Brian's arms.

Elio turns slowly back to Brian, who's now fighting fiercely to get out of Enzo's hold to no avail.

"I'm thirty-four, actually," Elio says. "And her nickname isn't Red, it's Songbird."

When Elio's fist connects with Brian's face, I know his nose breaks, because I *hear* it. A crackling, crunching sound. Like a boot going through too-thin ice.

This time, Brian doesn't say a word as Elio trundles me into the car.

Chapter 36

Elio

I'm still annoyed that all I did was break that fucker's nose as we drive home. I stew on it, replaying the entire interaction, almost wishing Deirdre hadn't been there so I could have ripped that idiot's tongue out the way I'd wanted to. Red? What the hell kind of nickname is that? Reducing her down to something as basic and obvious as her hair colour. No fucking imagination, no art, no homage to the trilling melody of her soul. *Red. Red Red Red Red. Cristo Santo*, I hate it even more than usual now. The only good thing that word's got going for it is that it rhymes with dead which is what that spineless little law student should be right about now. But Deirdre's terrified voice is still there in the back of my head. *Please don't kill him!*

She's too sweet. Too soft. She probably would have blamed his death on herself, and I don't want her wasting a single second of emotion, guilt or grief, on him.

We're nearing the gate to the house when she finally lets out a shaky breath and says, "So, that was a lot."

Not nearly enough.

When I don't reply, she says, "You broke his nose."

"He needed it broken. His face was too symmetrical. Now it'll have some character," I mutter as the gate slides open.

"Is that all?"

"What do you mean?" I ask.

"I just thought... I just wondered, because you were watching me, if you knew. Somehow. If... Never mind."

My fingers tighten involuntarily on the wheel as we pull up the drive to the house. She takes off her seatbelt.

"If I knew what?" I put the car in park and grab Deirdre's wrist, holding her in place so she can't run from my questions. She avoids my gaze while I drill mine into her. "What happened?" I pull her closer and cup her face with my other hand, running my thumb back and forth across her flushed, freckled cheek.

"It's nothing. We broke up, OK?"

"I know that."

She knows I've been watching her. She knows that I know she stopped seeing him weeks ago.

"But why?" I press. "Other than the fact that he's a snivelling, snot-nosed prat who isn't fit to lick your fucking boots. What happened?"

She's doing that thing where she rolls her lips inward between her teeth. She's shutting down. Shutting me out.

"Deirdre," I growl. "If you don't talk, I'll have to go track him down and make *him* talk. And a lot more will be broken than his nose."

"Nothing happened," she cries suddenly, a burst of sound. She says it so firmly, almost fervently, that it sounds like she's trying to convince herself as well as me. "He just... He wanted to, but I didn't want to. He tried to, but... Nothing happened. I got away. I got out of his apartment and ghosted him after that."

I've taken quite a few hits to the head in my time, but I'm able to piece together what she says just fucking fine.

That pulsing tick is back in my brain, but this time it sounds like Brian's voice saying *Red Red Red Red Red Red* over and over again.

It's all I hear. All I see. The car, the streets, the whole city red with the blood of the man I am about to obliterate.

Maybe my eyes have gone completely red even from the outside. Deirdre must see something change in me, because she puts her smooth, cool hands on either side of my jaw. It's the first time she's ever touched me like this. It's both soothing and infuriating, because that one tender, possessive touch makes me want to get down in the slush and the salt and the snow, press my forehead to the ground, and bow. Her hands on my face, on my skin and my scars, solid and unflinching like this, makes me want to fucking beg. Beg her for something but I don't know what. It's both nostalgic and foreign to me, because I haven't begged anyone for anything in decades. Not since I begged God that night in the fire.

"Elio," she says, just a whisper.

And then, for the first time, she kisses me.

It's timid at first. Tentative. Like she's afraid she might be breaking a rule of some kind but she's going to do it anyway. Her lips are so fucking soft, fluttering over mine in timid, exploratory pecks. Last time we kissed, it was all me. I grabbed her and I did it and she stood there and took it like a good fucking girl.

But this time, it's her. *She* is coming to *me*. Before I know it, my eyes are closed. Other than my dick swelling, I don't move a goddamn muscle. I don't want to shatter the spell. I don't want to forget how good it feels to have her hands on my face and her mouth on mine because she's the one who chose to put them there. And maybe it's pure manipulation on her part. Just meant to distract me. But I decide that I don't care. Because right now, I'd crawl over broken glass for her. Walk shoeless through snow and ice for her.

Run back into a burning house for her.

And that kind of devotion is terrible. Terrifying. I haven't prayed at the altar of anything besides death and wrath and money for a long, long time. I want to stay the man I've been for twenty years. The kind of man who doesn't let himself feel anything besides anger and greed and desire.

The kind of man who'd steal a songbird simply because he decided that he wanted her. So that he could trap her, bind her, *own* her.

Not so that he could fucking love her.

When Deirdre's tongue touches my lips, I can't stay still anymore. With a muted groan, I grab her ass and haul her into my lap. Remembering what I did to her ass this morning, the way my come is on her skin right now, makes my cock leap under my jeans. Deirdre gasps against my mouth when she feels that hardening movement against her crotch.

I grind myself up against her, left arm locked around her back while my shoulder pounds, right hand cradling the back of her skull so she can't back up, can't lean away, can't escape. My tongue shoves inside her mouth.

Fuck, kissing her is incredible. It's like an accelerant and an antidote all at once. I'm devouring her, taking everything I can, tasting everywhere.

When she pulls back and whispers, "Don't kill him," all I can do is say, "I won't."

I don't add the next part. She doesn't need to know.

I won't kill him.

I'll just make him wish he was dead.

One hour and forty-eight minutes after getting Deirdre home after her classes, Curse and I have Brian tied up in the trunk of Curse's SUV. We're heading north, back up to one of our warehouses on the outskirts of Thunder Bay. Usually, I'd fly there. But the fifteen-hour drive is good. Gives me all the time in the world to think about exactly what I'm going to do to him. Normally, I don't go this far from Toronto just to make some asshole regret everything he's ever done, but I can't stomach the idea of him in the same city as my Songbird for one second longer.

Curse and I take turns driving. The drive takes longer than fifteen hours because of the snow on the roads. We don't pull up to the desolate, snow-covered warehouse until 7am. It's still pitch black out – no sun. No light at all except for one streetlight illuminating the snowy parking lot we pull into. Besides our vehicle, there's only one other – an old pickup truck. Its owner, Aleksej, is waiting for us, just like I told him to be when we set out from Toronto. Aleksej is one of the only guys working this closely with me who's not a made man. He's not Sicilian, but Serbian, and he's as solid as they fucking come. Works like a dog and, most importantly, he keeps his mouth shut. He and his father ran into problems with the Serbian mafia and relocated here years ago, and Aleksej's worked for me ever since.

Curse and I get out of the vehicle as Aleksej approaches. I head for the back of the car, opening the trunk and hauling Brian out. Curse sedated him, and he's still too out of it to stand or walk. I let him drop to the cold hard ground, then grab the back of his jacket and start dragging him. Aleksej walks ahead and unlocks the metal door of the warehouse, holding it open, his grey eyes looking back out towards the parking lot to make sure no one's followed. Once we're all inside, the metal door closes behind us with a final, brutal clang.

"Strip him down and get him in the chair."

Curse and Aleksej do it, peeling off Brian's jacket and everything else until he's slouched over naked in a plastic chair in the centre of the darkened warehouse. His wrists are tied to the arms of the chair, his ankles tied at the bottom, and at the last moment Curse ties his shoulders to the back of the chair, too. He's barely conscious, and without being tied upright he'd keep flopping over.

Once he's done tying Brian up, Curse cracks his knuckles. I know he's ready to get started, because he always is. He lives for this shit.

"I want him all the way awake before we start," I tell my brother.

"I could break a couple of his fingers. That might wake him up," Curse replies casually.

Aleksej stations himself by the door with his arms crossed,

completely unphased by the conversation we're having. He silently watches with his icy grey gaze, the single bulb overhead casting light down on his ash-blond hair tied back in a ponytail and his closely-cropped beard.

"We wait," I say firmly.

It takes a long time. Hours before the piece of shit in the chair can even lift his head with his weak, wobbly neck. Another thirty minutes after that before he can talk, and the fucker's first words are to beg for water. He's clearly seen a doctor since our earlier run in, because his nose is packed and there's a temporary splint taped on. I walk towards him as his eyes try to focus. I can tell when they do because he balks at the sight of me.

"What the fuck. You again? God, what do you want?"

Just his stupid fucking voice makes me want to slit his throat. *Should have never told her I wouldn't kill him.*

I crouch down before him and slowly, gently, remove the splint from his nose. Then I press my thumb against the smashed bridge and press down. *Hard.*

He's definitely awake now. Pressing on his broken nose lights up a live wire inside him. He snaps his head backwards, but Curse is there, gripping the sides of his skull to keep him in place. So, he starts trying to move other parts. His arms and legs that are bound to the chair, squirming and grunting and hissing in pain.

"The more you fight, the harder I will press," I mutter.

His eyes are wild, and despite the cold and his lack of clothing, he's drenched in sweat. His chest heaves, but he stops moving, hoping I'll let up the pressure. I do, just for a moment, and he lets out a watery breath.

"What do you want?" he asks again, his voice sounding choked-off from his destroyed nasal passages. "Money? I have money, man. I-"

I nod at Curse. My brother releases Brian's head.

Then grasps both his thumbs and twists them from their sockets.

The sweating, quivering man in the chair howls. Curse closes his eyes and breathes out, like he's just taken a hit of his favourite drug.

"Look at me," I say to Brian. He doesn't listen. His face is screwed up with agony and his eyes stay closed. "For fuck's sake. Make him look at me."

Curse returns to his place behind Brian, grabbing his head roughly once more.

"If you wanna keep your eyes in your head, you will open them right now," Curse murmurs. With what looks like a colossal effort, Brian opens them. Tears stream down his face.

"This is about earlier? Shit, I'm sorry!" he babbles, he's blinking hard against the tears, but I can tell he's trying not to. He's trying to look at me like he's supposed to. Pretty fucking wise move, considering Curse really would cut out the guy's eyes if I let him. "I don't know what's going on with you and Deirdre, but it's fine. It's fine! I won't talk to her again."

"No, you won't," I agree. "But this isn't about what you will or won't do. It's about what you've done."

"What I've... What? What are you talking about?"

I stand, and Curse wrenches Brian's head back at the same time, so he's forced to look up at me.

I stare down at his swollen, blotchy face, and pure, unadulterated hatred spews through my body. Hatred and repulsion for this pathetic, stupid, pretty boy with the big straight white horse teeth in a weak jaw that just scream expensive orthodontics. The fact he thought he could even exist in the same room as Deirdre, let alone touch her, is an affront to the natural fucking order of things and I will not stand for it.

"Here's what's going to happen," I tell him, pulling my gun from my jacket.

Every muscle in his chest tightens as he strains against his ties when he sees the weapon. He starts blabbering, like I knew he fucking would, because preppy little rich kids like this can act tough but that's all it ever is – an act.

"No, no, please, wait. I have money. No. God, *no,* please, please, please-"

I give Curse a look, and my brother smashes Brian in the temple with his fist, stunning him into silence.

"As I was saying," I continue, "here is what is going to happen. For some reason my Songbird doesn't want you to die, and for some reason I find I can't refuse her. So, when we are done here, Aleksej is going to take you to a very good, very discreet doctor under my employ who's going to make sure that you don't bleed out."

"Bleed... out..." Brian echoes dazedly.

"After that, you will disappear. You will leave the country. You will not come back. If I hear one fucking whisper about you setting foot back here, my Songbird's misguided mercy won't be enough to save you."

His eyes fixate on my gun as mine roam over his body, deciding where to put the bullets. Kneecaps might be good... Or blow a couple holes through his hands...

"This is insane! You can't do this to me," Brian finally stammers. "Don't you know who I am? Who my father is? I'm on track to make partner at one of the best law firms in Toronto by the time I'm thirty!"

I let out a mirthless bark of a laugh.

"So fucking sue me then."

I put my gun against his dick and pull the trigger.

Chapter 37

Deirdre

After the incident with Brian at school I don't see Elio for three days. I still go to class, accompanied by Enzo now, and I have to admit it's a hell of a lot easier to concentrate without Elio's menacing bulk beside me. I'm still with a gangster, but Enzo keeps his mouth mostly shut. That and the fact he doesn't make me attend class with my tender ass covered in his dry come means going to school with him is practically mundane.

I don't see or hear from Brian either, which is a relief. Getting his nose smashed in must have finally gotten it through his thick head that we're done. Sometimes, at night, when Elio hasn't come back, I replay that punch over and over again. The swift, decisive arc of Elio's fist. The crunching of bone. I want to hate the violence of it. But something in that violence calls to me more than it repels me. It feels good to be stood up for, to be protected, even if the person doing the protecting is the most dangerous one of all.

On the morning of the fourth day, I still haven't seen Elio. There's no class today either, so I have nothing to distract me and nothing to focus on. And I need distraction, today of all days. I've been avoiding thinking about it, avoiding confronting this date the way I do every year. And every year, it still manages to sneak up on me and get its hands around my throat.

The anniversary of Mom's death. The anniversary of the night we crashed.

I do some homework, tapping away on the keyboard of the laptop Elio bought me, as if I can escape into academia. But as the minutes turn to hours, and evening approaches, a sorrow-soaked dread starts closing in on me. Every few words I type get blurred with choking tears, until I'm rising from the small desk and almost blindly stumbling out of the room.

I ignore Robbie, who dutifully follows me from his place at the top of the stairs as I descend. Getting out of the room was good, I decide. I don't feel quite so claustrophobic. Normally, on this day, Willow would come get me out of the house. We'd go see a movie or something. But I still haven't heard from her since that first email she sent, and there's basically zero chance she'll be breaking me out of here tonight.

I swipe at my eyes and wander into the living room that leads into the kitchen. There's floor to ceiling windows here, and heavy, beautiful snowflakes drift down onto the towering pine and spruce trees all around the property. The ground is velvet white, the sky darkening like a bruise.

He still hasn't come back.

I get it. I get that I'm a prisoner here and that he can walk in and out of this house anytime he likes while I cannot. But something about this – about him not being here on this night of all nights – feels worse than usual. I can't hide from the fact that if anyone would understand how I feel right now, it would be Elio. He may never tell me what happened with his mom in his own words, but his wound matches mine in the deepest and most painful of ways.

And right now, it hurts that he's not here. It's terrible and shameful and maybe I'm just insane with grief, but I want him. I fucking miss him, God help me. *God help me.*

I watch the snow falling. As the sky steeps itself in darkness, the snowfall gets heavier, thicker, until I can barely see the trees outside. I probably would stand there all night, numbing myself with the sight of the snow, if the sound of the front door opening and closing didn't make me spin so fast I almost fall over.

Elio.

But it's not Elio. And the resulting disappointment shatters any illusion of numbness. Tears choke me, and I try to swallow and blink them back as Valentina takes off a pair of boots and heads for me.

"Hey! My mom sent me over here to grab something from the kitchen. We're out of the good balsamic, but Rosa has some. Have you heard from Elio, by the way?" Valentina stops in front of me. Her red parka is dusted with rapidly melting snow, as are her long, fluttery lashes. "Are you OK?"

"I'm fine." How many times have I said that?

How many times has it been a lie?

Valentina squints at me for a long moment, and I muster a tight smile. Then she sighs.

"Papà doesn't like when Elio and Curse drop off the map like this. Neither of them are answering our texts or calls. Although..." Her eyes brighten, like she's just gotten a wicked idea. "Maybe if you texted Elio, he'd actually deign to answer."

"Yeah, right. He didn't even tell me he was leaving in the first place. And I don't even have his number," I say, and the words come out much more bitter than anticipated. I wonder if Valentina notices that. If she does, she mercifully doesn't comment on it.

"I can give you his number. I bet if you texted or called him right now, he really would reply."

Honestly, screw that. Yes, I want to see him, but I'm also more and more pissed that he just waltzed out of here and away from me. I'm not pathetic enough to call him after that.

Before I can stop her, Valentina's grabbed my phone out of my back pocket.

"Hey!" I say, stretching my hand for it. But she hustles out of reach.

"Relax. I just want to add Elio's number to your contacts. What's the passcode?"

I clench and unclench my fists, deciding if I should unlock my phone for her or not. I don't need Elio's number in my phone. It's not like I'll ever use it.

But... maybe...

Maybe it might be nice just to know it's there.

"I'll unlock it."

She holds up the phone for me, and I draw the pattern to unlock it. Valentina goes to my contacts and starts typing. Once she's typed in Elio's number, she hands it back, leaving the name field blank. Still annoyed with this whole situation, I name the contact *Monster*.

At the last moment, without even knowing why I do it, I add *My* in front of it.

"I added my number in there as well," Valentina tells me.

I look, and see her number and name, along with a glittery heart and kissing lips emoji at the end.

"Look, I'm not gonna make you call or text Elio, but if you do, and he responds, would you let me know?"

I have absolutely no intention of calling or texting him, but I nod anyway.

"Thanks," she says with a smile.

For a second, I almost ask her to stay. To hang out with me, distract me. But before I know it, she's gotten her bottle of balsamic and has disappeared back out into the snowy night.

I stay in the living room a while longer. There's a massive TV down here, and I turn it on and stare at it blindly. I think it's a cooking show. Or maybe a travel show. I'm so disconnected I don't even know. The entire time, Robbie watches me, and when I can't stand his eyes on me anymore I trudge back up the stairs, heading through Elio's room into mine. My laptop has long since gone to sleep, and the lights are off, making the room dark and still. And empty.

Coming back up here alone was a mistake. Because it's dark just like that night was dark. Dark until headlights shone through our windshield, forcing my mom to crank the wheel and send us careening off the road. I can still hear her yelp of terrified shock, the rapid turning of the steering wheel. I don't remember the impact of the crash itself. Just the breathless moments before. The pure terror of sliding and sliding and not being able to stop. The tires didn't squeal. They made this wet grinding sound across the snow and slush, and it fills my head until I'm desperate to hear anything, anything besides that sound.

I don't even know what the hell I'm doing when I fish my phone shakily out of my pocket. I don't call Valentina. I don't try calling Willow.

I call my monster.

And he answers on the very first ring.

"Songbird," he drawls silkily.

I don't even realize I'm crying until I hear the thick tears in my voice when I reply.

"Elio."

The smooth satisfaction of his voice vanishes. His next words come out sharp and strained.

"What is it?"

What am I supposed to say? *My mom died and I'm sad and lonely and the only fucking person on the planet I'm reaching out to, the only one I want right now, is the monster who locked me up and walked the fuck away.*

Absolutely not. Instead, I retreat into anger.

"Where the hell have you been?" I practically spit.

I expect him to make some joke, to say *Miss me?* in that cruel and knowing tone like he did last time. But maybe it's the tears he hears in my voice. Or maybe things have started to change between us since then. Because he seems serious and sincere when he replies.

"I had to straighten something out up north. Weather's been too bad to fly or drive back the past couple days."

"You... you could have told me that," I whisper, feeling like a fucking idiot. Why did I call him? What did I hope to gain from this?

"Are you telling me you wanted to hear from me while I was gone?"

I want more than to hear from him, and that's what pisses me off the most.

"No," I snap. "Take as long as you need up north. In fact, don't even come back at all if you don't need to."

"But I do need to," he counters instantly, and it sounds weird. Too loud. Like it's coming from behind me, all around me, rather than from my phone. "Because this is where my Songbird is."

I gasp, and my phone falls from my hand as I turn and find him there. My emotions form a cacophony inside me, a chaotic, jumbled song of fear and sorrow and anger and relief.

"You're here," I whisper, taking in the sight of him, wondering if my grief has conjured some kind of hallucination.

"You're crying," he replies softly. He steps into the room, further and further into the darkness with me, like some onyx angel, no, some demon who's not afraid of the shadows. Who's not afraid to go as far or as deep as it takes to reach me. His leather gloves are cold when they graze my neck. He must have just come in from outside and sprinted up the stairs.

His mouth is warm though, warm when it finds the tracks of my tears, kissing the salted liquid from my skin. That warmth seeps into me, turning molten, turning to something that burns all the way down my spine. Scorching need obliterates everything else inside me. Bludgeons the sadness, a cauterizing plug to a bleeding fucking wound. My mouth opens and searches for Elio's blindly as my hands grip the front of his shirt and pull him harder to me.

He claims my mouth and walks, backing me up until the backs of my legs collide with the bed. My stomach flip-flops, because even after everything we've done in these rooms, we've never been in a bed together and I know what it means. I know what it will lead to, and I don't care and can't stop it. Not now, not tonight. Not when this need has eclipsed everything I thought I ever knew.

Elio's hands find the hem of my sweater, tugging it upwards. I stop kissing him (if you can even call it that, because my movements are desperate and messy) and let him pull it off. I didn't bother with a bra beneath the sweater today, and every muscle and nerve jumps to attention when Elio's gloves skim over my nipples.

"You're still crying," Elio murmurs before lowering his head and sucking my right nipple into the demanding heat of his mouth. I cry out, my back arching, and bury my fingers in his hair. He's right. I can feel the warm liquid coursing down my cheeks.

"That's because... tonight..." I breathe, my words halting as plea- surable pangs echo outward from my breast. Elio gives one last, long suck before letting go and pinning me with a dark gaze.

"I know what tonight is." And just like that, he has me. He's got me in his grip, because he knows what tonight is and he knows what I'm feeling and I don't need to say a single word. I don't need to speak or explain because he already knows.

"It's why I drove like a bat out of fucking hell all day to get here when we couldn't fly back," he continues softly, undoing the button and zipper of my pants and sliding them downwards.

He came for me. He came for me because he knew I would be hurting.

He knows what I need, just like he told me. He knows what I need and what I fucking need right now is *him*.

His jacket comes off, then his shirt, then his pants, and then I'm flat on my back beneath him, marvelling at the brutal planes of his body, the heaving of his chest, the frenetic, consuming gleam of his eyes. Some of his hair falls forward into his eyes, and for the first time I don't stop myself from brushing the unruly strands back from his forehead. It's an undeniably tender motion, and I stroke down to his jaw.

"You came for me."

A flicker of agony passes over Elio's face, and he presses his face against my hands. His voice splits the darkness.

"I will always fucking come back for you. Even when you don't want me to. Even when you scream and beg and cry for me to leave, even when you push me away, I won't go. I will come back *every single time*, do you hear me? I will *fucking* be here. *Always*."

The *always* part should alarm me, because always was never part of the plan. I'm not staying here, not with him, not forever.

But right now, I don't want to think about that. I just want to lose myself in the drugging reality that there's somebody who would never abandon me, never lose me, never let me go. He's solid and so fucking warm and God, he's taken his gloves off, his scarred hands running up and down my body, taking possession. One hand settles between my legs, sliding through wetness until I pant and tremble.

The other settles around my throat.

"Right now," Elio whispers against my temple as he works my clit in expert, erotic circles, "you need to feel something other than what you were feeling earlier tonight. You need pleasure. You need oblivion."

I nod, even though it's hard with his fingers closed around my throat, because he's right. He's ripped me open with a few well-placed words and now he's the only one who can put me back together. He gently presses on my throat, and I choke out a moan, my eyes rolling back in my head as my pussy clenches.

"You need *this*, don't you, Deirdre?"

I can't even nod now, let alone speak, because of his grip. But I don't need to, because he knows the answer just like I do. I need this. I need to let go of some control. Let him take away my breath and take away my pain.

He slides a finger inside me, and I try to gasp, but barely get half a breath in my lungs.

"I've strangled men with my bare hands," Elio suddenly rasps, and I must be perverted because my pussy clenches again. "I know how much pressure to exert. I know when to stop." His hand tightens around my throat, and my breathing becomes the barest whistle. "But even so..." He crooks his finger inside me, stroking firmly until I'm shaking, the blood roaring through my body as it searches for oxygen. "Tap my shoulder twice to make me stop."

I'm already on the cusp of coming, about to fall the fuck apart, but Elio stops the movement of his finger.

"Tap my shoulder once, now, to show me that you understand."

My hands feel like they're made of lead, but I raise my right one and tap his shoulder.

He groans. "Good little Songbird."

He starts working his finger again, firm and fast and filling me, adding another while clamping down on my throat until all I can feel is the desperate, breathless writhing inside me. That panicky plea- sure that narrows my focus of feeling to my chest and the place between my legs. I don't even know if my eyes are open or closed – everything is black. The oblivion he promised me is rising, constricting all around me, a pulsing, living darkness that expands inside me until I come.

Just as my insides clamp down on Elio's fingers, he pulls them out. At the same moment, he releases my throat. Instinctively, I suck in a huge, raw breath, the explosion of oxygen only adding to the intensity of the moment. I'm flying and falling at the same time, and only Elio can anchor me. I reach quivering arms around his neck, pull him down to me just as I feel pressure, pressure right *there*. A searching nudge, and then the violent forward motion of a thrust inside.

Pain surges up alongside the pleasure. My mouth falls open in a soundless scream as Elio completely fills me, stretching me, breaking into me. Breaking down the last of the barriers between us. I'm crying again – I can hear the sobs more than I can feel them. Because all I can feel right now is him. The pain of him inside me. The searing juncture of our bodies.

Elio lets out a ragged sound, then thrusts again. My arms are still around him, and I'm squeezing, holding onto him. I could tap his

283

shoulder twice. See if that would make him stop. When he thrusts a third time, harder, I almost do it because it hurts too fucking much.

"Does it hurt, Songbird? Fuck, I can feel you opening for me. Feel you bleeding for me."

Two little taps. That's all it would take.

Elio's moving faster now, and something in the angle has changed, because even though it still hurts there's something new undulating behind that pain. The wetness of my orgasm and the blood of my lost virginity eases the way ever so slightly for Elio's girth until he's grinding even deeper than before, hitting a screaming, shuddering place inside me that makes me feel like everything is loosening and tightening all at once. I'm going to come again. I'm going to come, even while I'm hurting. He's going to make me. It's building so intensely I almost feel like I'm going to pee myself. One of his thumbs starts rubbing hard against my clit, and I know I'm nearly gone now.

"Every time I pull out I can see your blood on me," Elio groans. "You're claiming my cock with your blood the same way I've already stained you with mine. That first night, Songbird, do you remember? When I got shot and bled all over you." He seems to lose his rhythm, his hips snapping chaotically as he breathes. "I would have fucking died for you that night."

The bandages on his shoulder scrape against my wrist as I cling to him. Cling to the man who I should be doing everything I can to run from. But I can't run – not now. Not while my body is reacting like this to his. I moan through the tears as my pussy convulses.

"Yes," Elio hisses between clenched teeth. "My sweet little Songbird. My good fucking girl. Come on my fucking cock *just like that*."

And once again, like so many times before, I cannot help but obey. I scream, muscles clamping down on his so hard I can tell it's affecting his movements. He jams himself further inside as white-hot stars spin out in my pelvis, scattering and shattering. I'm so tight around him, so fused to him, that I feel it happen. Feel the throb of him deep inside as he shunts his hips forward for the final time.

He's coming, shuddering and tensing and coming, coming, coming so hard inside me. As his desire spills into me and mixes with my blood, he lowers his mouth to mine and says directly against my lips. "We are fucking bound together, you and me."

As aftershocks of my orgasm wrack my body, my pussy squeezing him like I can't bear to let him go, I know that he's right.

There's no way to come back from this now. Not for him.

And not for me.

Chapter 38

Elio

I f I could stay inside of Deirdre forever, I would. It's like I was fucking made for this, made for her, like my entire body was designed to have her arms and legs and cunt wrapped around me. It's the closest thing to peace I've felt since childhood.

"I need to go clean up," Deirdre whispers.

"No, you don't," I reply instantly. I want her drenched and staying that way. Stained with my fluids and her own. I don't want to already feel her pulling away from me, which I'm sure she will. Starting with washing this night off of her skin.

Before she can say anything else, a grumbling sound distracts us both. She unwraps her arms from around my neck and places her hands over her face, like she's embarrassed.

"When was the last time you ate?" I ask, pulling one of her hands away. She can't hide herself from me. Not now.

"I ate some breakfast... I think. Rosa brought me lunch and dinner. I just couldn't force myself to eat it."

I understand that. For years, the entire month of August was a fucking shit show for me. Every August from the age of fourteen to well into my twenties, I lost weight no matter what I did.

"Stay here," I say quietly. Slowly, I pull out, and the little mewling sound she emits in return makes me want to plunge right back inside. I force myself not to do it, then get out of the bed, pulling on my pants and gloves. I glance back at her to find her splayed and limp. She's quiet. Not crying now.

"I'll be right back." I say, though she doesn't seem to hear me.

I head for the kitchen, pulling open cupboards and drawers, piling bread and pastries and cookies onto a plate. When that's taken care of, I slide my phone from my back pocket and use voice-to-text in a search engine.

"How do you make tea?"

I've never done it before, and fuck if I know how. In fact, I don't think I've literally ever made anything in the kitchen for anyone. A quick scroll of the results, and I feel like I have my legs under me. I boil water in the kettle, then pour it over a couple of Irish breakfast tea bags in a teapot to let it steep. Grabbing a cup, a pitcher of milk, and a bowl of sugar, I plonk them on the plate and then carry it all up alongside the teapot.

When I return to Deirdre's room, a lamp by the side of the bed is on. It illuminates an empty bed. A flush of the toilet, then running water, tells me where she is. She emerges from the bathroom a moment later in sweatpants and a hoodie. Her hair is tied up in a messy bun on the top of her head. Her eyes are swollen, her nose is wet and red, and I don't think I've ever seen her look more goddamn beautiful.

She sniffs, then sees me with the snacks.

"Sit and eat," I tell her, placing the stuff on a bedside table. For a second, I think she's going to disobey me. My voice hardens, because I'm not going to stand by and watch her pass out. "Eat this yourself or I will feed it to you."

She gives a small nod then climbs up on the bed. I notice how gingerly she sits when she settles herself.

"Are you still bleeding?" I ask.

"Yeah. I'm wearing a pad."

I want to see. Want to strip off her clothes, see the white material marked by the innocent blood I've drawn.

But that's not what she needs right now. So instead, I pour her a cup of tea.

"What do you put in this shit?" I ask her while eyeing the brown liquid with distaste, and holy fucking heavens above, she actually laughs. It's teary, but real, and I stare at her without blinking, memorizing the sound of it and the sight of her in this moment.

"I'll do it," she says, still smiling. She adds milk and sugar. I watch her closely as she takes a sip. She closes her eyes and sighs, and a pinched area of tension between my shoulder blades I didn't even know was there relaxes.

"This is good. Thank you," she says softly before taking another sip. "Never thought I'd see the day when Elio Titone is making me tea."

"Neither did I," I say, sitting beside her on the bed. "Don't tell anyone, alright? Would ruin my reputation in this town."

There it is again. The beautiful laugh that cuts straight through me, just like her music does. Because the laugh, just like the music, is an expression of what's in there, what's inside her. How did Deirdre word it in that letter? *The violin simply gives voice to what already exists.* It's the same with her laughter, her tears, her voice. Everything she does. It's not just her music I've been drawn to, that I've been trying to understand, it's *her*. The essence of her that spills out like goddamn sunshine, bathing me in light when I've spent half my life in the darkness.

She munches on a few of the sweets I've brought, and slowly some colour returns to her cheeks.

"I used to drink this kind of tea with my mom," she says. She reaches over and pours a little more into her cup. "God, she had the most beautiful teapot. A vintage one with the most exquisite rosebud pattern."

The teapot she's holding now is stainless steel. It looks cold and sterile compared to what she's just described.

"Where is it now?"

She sighs, takes another sip, then puts down her cup.

"I broke it. Can you believe that?" She shakes her head. "It was right after her funeral. I was out of my mind with grief. I was alone in the kitchen where we'd always drink tea together and I was so desperate to be close to her again. She would always fill the teapot with warm water while the kettle was boiling, so I did that, too. I tried to, anyway. But I dropped it in the sink and it completely smashed." She stops speaking for a moment, staring at a place on the floor before she continues. "I kept all the pieces in a box in my closet, but it was too far gone for me to try to fix. I've looked for a replacement, but they're really hard to find. Plus, it wouldn't be the same, anyway. It wouldn't be the same teapot. The same one she held, you know?"

I do know. I know because all our mamma's things burned and that fact has fucking haunted me.

"I don't even know why I'm telling you this. I haven't been able to tell anyone about that teapot. Not Willow or *anybody*. I didn't even tell my dad. Can you believe he didn't even notice it was gone?" She wipes her eyes. "But then again, he never wanted to go to her grave with me, either, so maybe I shouldn't be all that surprised."

I slide off the bed, turn, grab her by the waist, and set her on her feet on the floor.

"Get your coat and boots," I tell her, reaching for my shirt and pulling it back on.

Her eyebrows pucker. "Why? Where are we going?"

"We're going to visit your mamma."

Chapter 39

Deirdre

I'm still not entirely sure how I've ended up in Elio's car, heading towards my mother's grave, within an hour of losing my virginity. The place between my legs feels tender and wet and strange. I hunker down in my coat, wrapping my arms around myself. Elio flicks at a button on the dash, and soon I feel gorgeous heat rising from the seat and seeping through my coat and pants. The heat soothes the ache between my legs and eases the muscles in my back. Another uncanny reminder that maybe Elio really does know what I need before I do.

As we pass through the gate and then turn onto the street, Elio calls someone on his phone. It takes a few rings for the other person to answer, and when he does, I can hear a sleepy gruffness to the "Hello?"

"Tony, get out of bed and get down to the store," Elio says without greeting or preamble. I hear the muted response of acquiescence before Elio hangs up. I have no idea who Tony is, or why we need to go to a store right now when it's past midnight, but I don't bother asking. I'm sure I'll find out soon enough.

And I do when we pull up in front of a small shop called *Roset-*

ti's Blooms. A short, balding man is hunched down in a leather bomber-style jacket. When he sees us pull up he nods deferentially and unlocks the front door. Elio opens my car door for me and helps me out, murmuring to watch the ice as he guides me up onto the curb. Lights come on in the shop just as we pass through the door.

It's a flower shop. I stand there, basically dressed in pyjamas under this four-figure-price-tag coat, my face and hair a mess, and I blink like a mole against the bright light. Elio clearly doesn't feel any of my hesitation or confusion. Instead, he sweeps through the shop, taking bunches of flowers from different tables and fridges and peppering Tony with orders. I stand there, still and slow and watching him. He moves with such merciless competence, such dangerous grace, that I can't look anywhere but him. Soon enough, Tony's got a whole array of blooms before him on the counter – red roses and white lilies and delicate little snowdrops – and he gets to work arranging them. When he's finished, he ties the stunning bouquet together with a white silk ribbon.

I don't know why I expect Elio to pay, but of course, he doesn't. He probably owns this shop, or at least controls a good part of it. Even though we've dragged him out of bed, raided his flowers, and haven't paid him, Tony's the one who says, "Thank you," as we leave.

We get back in the car, and I hold tightly to the bouquet as Elio drives us out of downtown. Frankly, I'm shocked that Elio even thought to do this. That he cares about things like flowers for the dead.

"Why'd you do this? The flowers," I ask him as the cemetery comes into sight.

"There's no way I'm going to your mamma's grave empty-handed," he says firmly, keeping his eyes ahead as he pulls up and stops. He pauses, like he's not going to say the next part, but then does it anyway. "Never got the chance to lay flowers at my own mamma's grave."

I shunt the flowers over to one side, then reach out with a free hand, capturing his gloved fingers in mine just as he takes them from the steering wheel. He stares at me in silence for a long moment, then raises my hand, brushing his lips over my knuckles before letting go.

He doesn't let me go for long. Once he opens the door for me he grabs my hand and holds it all the way to Mom's grave.

I know where it is even though I haven't been here in a few years. It's always been hard for me to come here alone, and Dad always got all weird and flighty when I asked him to come with me, so eventually I just kind of stopped. I tried to tell myself that she wasn't here, anyway. She was in other places. The sky, the sunshine, the music she'd once shared with me. And yet, it feels good and bad and right that I'm here now. It hurts, but in a satisfying way. Like I'm doing something I'm supposed to do.

And I'm supposed to do it with him.

It's the strangest feeling. The feeling that I'm where I should be, even though it's Elio beside me. I look down at our interlocked hands, then the striking profile of his face, his expression sombre, and I'm glad he's with me.

The snowfall stopped at some earlier point in the evening, and the sky is clear, a bright moon illuminating the carpet of white between the gravestones. I see Mom's, and my heart lurches in my chest. It's a feeling of pained remembrance. Of homecoming and knowing that my home will never exist again.

We come to a stop before her grave. I clench my teeth and try not to cry, because crying outside in the winter is horrible, and I've already shed enough tears tonight. But I can't hold them back when Elio lets go of my hand, gets down on his knees in the snow, and starts clearing off her grave. I sniff hard, over and over again, watching him meticulously clean snow from every surface, every angle, every letter of the stone slab. When he's done, I assume he'll get up, but he doesn't. Instead, he lays his dark glove against the stone beside my mother's name, Fiona Kathleen O'Malley. Finally, he rises, turns to me, and nods.

I nod back at him, stepping forward with the flowers.

"Hey, Mom," I whisper. It's all I can manage at the moment, and I know she'd probably think that was good enough. I was always good enough for her, even when I didn't feel like it. I bend and lower the bouquet, admiring the silver sheen of moonlight on the blooms, turning them from fresh flowers into what look like crystal carvings.

And then there's a sound. A sound that makes me think of birthdays and blood. The bouquet explodes in my hands, petals ripped and falling like snow.

"Get the fuck down!"

Something solid collides with my back. It's Elio. He crowds over me, shoving me down against the gravestone, before spinning with his gun in his hands. He's so fucking fast I don't even see who he shoots before they fall.

"Elio! What-"

I can't finish my sentence because Elio has turned and aimed somewhere over my head.

He fires, then fires again. A man I can't see screams.

Then hits the ground.

Chapter 40

Elio

Fucking Mad Darragh. These don't look like Sev's guys. They're Irish. At least three of them. I crouch down beside Deirdre, keeping my gun ready in one hand while I pass my other hand over her. They shot the bouquet right out of her hands, and I frantically count every slender finger before I let myself take a breath when I get to ten.

"Are you hurt?" I ask her. She shakes her head, her eyes as big as dinner plates. "Good. Stay here."

I rise, breathing hard, scanning the graveyard.

But I don't see anyone else. At least, not yet. I call Curse, telling him to get Enzo and Robbie down here. Just as I hang up, I hear a groan from behind the grave.

Motherfucker ain't dead yet.

After making sure Deirdre isn't going anywhere and that nobody else is coming for her, I vault over the gravestone. The guy is writhing and choking on his own blood, his gun out of reach. He tries to get it anyway. I press my boot down on his fingers and don't let up until I hear bones crack.

"Did Darragh send you?"

"We weren't gonna kill her," the man wheezes. "Darragh wants her alive. Fuck!"

I press down harder on his hand.

"Just give her up. She's not one of yours. She's Irish. *Ours.*"

The ticking in my head is so loud I swear it makes the grave-stones move.

"She is not fucking yours," I hiss, cocking my gun and aiming it at his head. "She is mine in every conceivable way. And if Darragh wants to take her, then he will be starting a fucking war, because he won't be coming after one of his own, he'll be coming after a *Titone.*"

It's all become so clear. What I need to do. I don't know how I didn't see it before. Parading Deirdre around at the gala and at school wasn't enough.

But this will be. This will make her completely fucking untouch-able, unless Darragh wants to bathe this entire city in blood.

Even though the guy at my feet won't live to pass this message on to his boss, I tell him anyway, because it just feels so fucking good to say it.

"Her name won't be Deirdre O'Malley for long," I say quietly, crouching down. "Because I will fucking *marry* her. And just fucking see what happens when you come after *my wife.* Just see what happens when you try to hurt *Deirdre fucking Titone.*"

The man's eyes bulge. He understood me, I have no doubt. He's the first one to hear my glad tidings, the lucky bastard.

I put a bullet in his head just to fully sanctify that honour.

Chapter 41

Deirdre

I stay huddled in the snow in front of my mother's grave, clutching the ruined flowers. My ears ring, and every breath I take sounds far too loud inside my own head. I think Elio's talking but I can't make out any of the words. Another shot, and then the speaking stops.

Dead.

Once again, Elio's shot someone. Someone who threatened me. He and I are caught in an endless, terrible loop. No matter what I do, I can't claw my way out to something normal. Not while Elio's with me. And not while my father hides from what he's done.

I'm not even afraid now. Just numbed to it all. Emptied out by all the violence, the death, and the destruction. I barely register when Elio scoops me up into his arms and jogs back to the car. Just as he's hauling the door open and helping me inside, another dark vehicle swerves towards us. Curse and Enzo jump out, and Elio bites out orders at them. I only catch some of the words. *Irish. Make sure... No others... Bodies...*

Elio slides into the driver's seat. He starts the car with quick, sharp movements, but doesn't drive until he's fastened my seatbelt.

Thank God he does it, because I'm not sure I have the strength to. My arms, no, my whole body is shaking. Torn and crushed rose petals fall from my hands as the car finally gets into motion.

"We shouldn't have come here," I whisper.

"Yes, we should have. They shouldn't have," Elio bites out.

"They're never going to stop. They're never going to leave me alone," I say dully. I thought being trapped with Elio was bad enough. But knowing that even if I ever get away from him, I'll never be safe, makes me feel like my entire life is getting snuffed out before my very eyes.

"No, they probably won't. Not unless I drag your papà back here and dump him on Darragh's doorstep."

"No," I say instantly.

Muscles go stone-hard in Elio's jaw.

"Even after everything he put you through, you still want to protect him?"

"I just can't have another person around me die!" I cry out. "I can't! I can't handle all this guilt. It's like I'm being buried alive!"

"Darragh's men keep coming for you because they consider you one of theirs," Elio says. "You're Irish. In their minds, you belong to them, not me." He takes a sharp turn, and I flinch at the swerving motion of it. "There's one way to put that thought out of their minds. One way to prove that you're irrevocably mine. Mine in a way that they'd never dare to touch you."

"What? What way?" I thought that was the whole point of me going to the gala on his arm. Clearly, that didn't work.

"You take my ring. You take my name."

"I... What?"

He doesn't look at me as he takes another fast turn, making my insides lurch.

"You marry me."

No. There's no way. I'm sure I've heard him wrong. My blood sloshes in my head. I lean forward and grip my knees, trying to breathe slowly between clenched teeth.

But he says it again. And this time, there's no mistaking the words. There's no mistaking the threat of them. The way they bind me to him more than any debt ever could.

"You marry me, Songbird. Marry me, or I'll tell Darragh exactly where your fucking father is."

Read on for part two of Deirdre and Elio's story in A Vow So Soulless!

I've taken everything from my Songbird. Her freedom. Her innocence.

Even her name. She'll no longer be known as Deirdre O'Malley, but Deirdre Titone. **My wife.** *Whether she wants to be or not.*

It's the only real way to show this city who she belongs to. The only way to tell the world that she's as protected as she is possessed. I'll keep her safe, even if there's no one left to keep her safe from me.

My Songbird made me believe in souls again. And maybe I don't have one. Maybe I never did.

But she does. And I won't stop until I've taken it along with everything else.

Get access to super spicy NSFW character art featuring Deirdre and Elio by subscribing to my newsletter! You'll also receive an exclusive bonus story/deleted scene of Elio going to Deirdre's first violin performance! Subscribe at www.veroheath.com/contact-and-newsletter

TITANS AND TYRANTS
A Debt So Ruthless (Deirdre and Elio part 1)
A Vow So Soulless (Deirdre and Elio part 2)
A Game So Reckless (Valentina and Darragh part 1)
A Trap So Flawless (Valentina and Darragh part 2)

A Vow So Soulless

A Dark Mafia Romance

Content Notes

This is a dark age-gap mafia romance with themes that may disturb some readers. The hero, Elio Titone, is not a good man. Nor is he a particularly reasonable man, especially when it comes to getting what he wants – namely the heroine Deirdre. If you would like content warnings, please visit my website.

Chapter 1

Deirdre

"**I**'m not marrying you."

I say it over and over again in the car on the way back from the cemetery. I say it so much that it becomes a sort of whispered chant, or a prayer, the words eventually rendered meaningless in their repetition.

They must be meaningless to Elio too. Because he doesn't say a single thing in response.

Other than his earlier threat, the threat to marry him or else he'll tell Darragh where my dad is, he hasn't spoken again. He's silent in his fury, his gloved hands hard on the steering wheel, his jaw set. I don't know if I've ever seen his dark eyes so focused. Simultaneously trained on the road ahead and sweeping dangerously from side to side, as if expecting more men with guns to jump out of some shadowy place on the sidelines, like a fucking video game.

Only it's not a video game. It's my life.

Except it doesn't feel like real life. I feel like I'm floating outside of it. Like this is all happening to someone else. I'm shaking, my teeth chattering so badly that my words become a mangled mess, but I barely feel it.

We pull into the long drive and through the gate at Elio's mansion. More men than I've ever seen here before are pacing and standing guard outside, with wary eyes and weapons that I know are there even if I can't see them yet. I look at them, all those men and their guns, and suddenly I can't fucking take it anymore. It's too much. Too much blood pooling at the edges of my life. Eventually, it all starts seeping inside to the centre. Staining. Ruining.

As soon as the car stops and the door is unlocked, my seatbelt is off and I'm running. Running who the hell knows where. I certainly don't. Some part of me is blithely aware that this is a pointless exercise, that I'm a rat in a cage sprinting straight towards the outer edge of the enclosure and that I'll never in a million years be able to scale that brutal wall.

Another part, the mindless, shaking, rat-brain part, keeps on fucking running.

My lungs burn and my hair whips out behind as I head blindly for the trees. Shouts go up around me, and a man from the house is already chasing me. He's almost within reach. His bare, tattooed hand rises at the periphery of my vision, about to clamp down on my arm. Even though I know rationally that this man won't hurt me, not with Elio here, I can't truly believe it. The fear has become a frenzy and I have to get out, get away, get somewhere, *anywhere*. Anywhere but here.

The man slips slightly in the slush, then catches himself. His fingers stab towards me again, disembodied on the periphery, like a severed ghost hand.

But then I hear a voice, not the voice of the man right behind me but *his* voice. The voice that shapes so much of my life these days. A voice that has commanded and cajoled, soothed and seared. It's the first time I've heard his voice since he told me I'd marry him in the car and that suddenly feels painfully long ago.

It's a voice I react to even through the adrenaline-fuelled numbness of my flight, a voice that I want to reach for and run from all at once.

"Don't fucking touch her!" Elio snarls. "Nobody touches her but me."

Nobody touches me but him.

Because I'm his.

His debtor. His Songbird.

His wife.

No.

That was never supposed to be the way this ended. There was always supposed to be a way out for me. Far-off, maybe, and small as a speck of dust on the horizon, but there all the same. Pay the money. Get my life back.

The running makes my blood pound hard. The place between my legs hurts. And I want to cry and laugh at the same time, because who am I to rant about escaping him when I'm the one who wanted him with me tonight? When I'm the one who let him choke me, let him fuck me?

When I'm the one who took his hand in the snow at Mom's grave because I wasn't sure how the hell I would stand up without him?

I can barely stand up now. My knees buckle. I don't cry out, simply suck in a rattled gasp as I go down. But he has me, *he has me*, and I should have fucking known he would.

Because he would never let me fall.

And he would never let me go.

Nobody touches her but me.

The strength goes out of me all at once. I don't scream, I don't fight him. I don't even go back to my muttered prayer of "I won't marry you." I just sag against the roiling wall of his chest, hard and hot as living stone. After my manic, half-assed escape attempt I half-expect him to toss me over his shoulder caveman-style, but he doesn't. He lifts me against his chest, cradling me like I weigh no more than a small child, before turning and taking me back towards the house with powerful, furiously measured strides.

Elio takes me through the front door and absurdly, giddy with the jittery trauma of the night, I think, *Isn't this how a groom carries his bride across the threshold?*

There are soldiers stationed in here too, but with a curt bark of "Out!" from Elio, they disperse in seconds.

And then we're alone.

Elio carries me over to the plush sofa in the living room and sets me down so carefully it's as if I'm made of glass. Maybe something even more delicate than glass. Because it seems like he's worried that, even against the soft cushions, I might shatter.

Without taking his eyes from me, he gathers up a throw blanket and smooths it over my legs, tucking it around my waist so it stays in place. It had always felt so odd to me, that blanket being in this room. Like some bit of décor put out by a professional house staging company, tossed at a stylish angle, not something anybody actually used – certainly not Elio.

But it's finally getting some use now. Warm and tight around me, locking my hands in place on my lap. I don't even bother pulling them out of the bindings of the blanket. What would be the goddamn point?

"Oh," I murmur softly, my gaze snagging on my feet. "My boots are still on. Elio!" My voice hardens with urgency, as if I've just discovered something of life-or-death importance. Something that has to get fixed, and fixed *now*. "My boots. The floor!"

"Fuck the floor," Elio says, apparently not caring one bit about all the salt and slush pooling around my soaking soles. "It'll be fine. And if it's not, I'll rip it all out and put in whatever you want to replace it. Hardwood or ceramic or fucking seventies shag carpet. I don't give a shit. But Deirdre-" He grabs my chin, forcing my gaze up from my feet and into the endless abyss of his eyes. "I am not peeling one single thing off of you until you stop shaking." He pinches my chin gently for good measure, then lets go and straightens, adding, "So just be a good little Songbird and ruin my floor already, would you?"

I hadn't even realized I was still shaking. But now that he's said it, I can't think about anything else besides the stuttered locking of my muscles, the banging of my teeth against each other. I'm trembling so hard it hurts.

The cold has clawed its way in and I don't think I can get it out now.

But Mom always said...

Always said that there was never a cold so deep nor a problem so big that tea couldn't make it better. Or, at least, make a hell of a good start.

"Tea," I whisper. But then I blink in confusion, because I'm saying it to no one. Elio is gone. I hear noises from behind me in the kitchen, most notably a kettle already boiling, which means he started making it before I ever even said the word. Before I even *thought* it.

And my whole world tilts. Forces me to once again acknowledge how my monster knows what I need even when I don't.

But my instincts rebel against that.

He just dangled the threat of my father's death in front of me to force me into marrying him! He doesn't actually care about what I need.

And yet...

He's making me tea all the same.

Elio brings me a large mug with the string of the tea bag still hanging out of it. Fine by me. If ever a night called for strong tea it's tonight. It almost seems impossible how much has happened. The swallowing grief of the date marking my mother's death. Visiting her grave which I haven't done in years, only to be shot at. Having more men die right in front of me.

And losing my virginity.

The man who took it stands before me now, muscled arms crossed over his broad chest. He abandoned his jacket at some point while in the kitchen, but not his gloves of course. As I hold the blissfully hot cup in my hands, I let my gaze track up and down his tall form.

When I get to his shoulder, the place where he was shot last time, I jolt so hard I nearly spill the tea in my lap.

"Are you alright?" I ask, stunned that I never thought to ask before. He could have been bleeding out somewhere on that massive, black-clad body and I wouldn't have known it until he keeled over from blood loss.

If keeling over was even possible for Elio. Frankly, I can't imagine it. The man would probably still be standing on his own two feet the second he goddamn died.

I just...

Don't want that to be tonight.

"Shouldn't I be asking you that?" he replies, his tone giving nothing away.

"I mean, it's pretty obvious that I'm not," I say shakily. "But I'm not bleeding anywhere at least."

But then he cocks his head, and I cringe, because that isn't even true, is it? This night has made me bleed after all. I've got the pad stuck to my panties to prove it.

"I didn't get shot," I clarify flatly. I stare at him as steadily as I can. "Did you?"

"Tonight?"

"Of course, tonight! I know you've been shot other times!"

He pauses, then his gaze grows slightly distant, like he's doing some kind of mental tally. Until this point, he hasn't even paused once to make sure he's alright in the rush to get me back here. God, he was making me fucking tea without even stopping to let the adrenaline wear off enough to see if he was injured!

But then his gaze sharpens with clarity once more, homing in on me like I'm giving off some kind of Elio-attracting beacon.

"I'm good," he says simply. "Or, I will be once you drink your fucking tea."

Relief pours through me, makes my muscles sag. The violent shivering is finally subsiding a bit. I lift the cup and take a sip.

The heat of it is nice, but the taste is not what I'm expecting. I swallow, then cough slightly.

"What is this?" I rasp against the little bit of the tea that went down the wrong tube.

"Some herbal shit."

"Herbal?!"

"The amount of stress hormones that just dumped through your system do not need additional caffeine." He looks thoughtful in a pissed-off sort of way. "If you want something else, I'll get you wine. Or whisky."

"No, no. This is fine. What is it?" I ask, taking another sip. I don't normally drink herbal tea. So often it just feels like a flavourless, watery version of what tea is supposed to be.

Maybe this is how Elio feels about my Irish breakfast compared to his espresso...

He doesn't answer me or move until I take another sip. As if satisfied that I'm actually drinking some of it, he goes back to the kitchen and returns with the box of tea bags and holds it up between us so I can see the name.

"Snoozy Time Tea?" I say, squinting at the curly, cursive font. "What am I, eighty years old?"

"Like I said, no caffeine. It's supposed to be soothing." Elio looks at the box then back at me. "Plus, I like the cat on the front. Reminds me of you."

There actually is a cat on the front. A cartoon one, with ginger fur and giant blue eyes.

"It's wearing pyjamas..."

Elio just shrugs his good shoulder.

"So? You wear pyjamas."

Apparently a snoozy, tea-guzzling cat has got my tongue because I can't come up with a retort to that. I have to hand it to him – he kind of has me there. The blue pyjama set the cat is wearing actually looks a lot like some of the ones I've worn in this very house.

I take another sip of the tea to avoid continuing this absurd conversation. Maybe we've both fucking lost it, talking about a cartoon cat when men have died tonight.

When one of *us* could have died tonight.

I keep on drinking the tea and Elio keeps on watching me, arms stubbornly crossed like some kind of supervisor, the cardboard box of tea bending under the force of his curled fist. There's a tension in his frame. A bristling energy that makes me thing he wants to be doing something else right now – maybe killing somebody, maybe touching me – but he's holding himself back so that he can stand there and watch me drink the tea he made. Like his good little Songbird.

But I don't have the energy to be anything else right now. So I drink my tea, and by the time I'm nearly done the large mug, I actually do think it's helping. I've stopped shaking entirely now, and I feel warm, though very, very tired.

I look around weakly for somewhere to put the empty cup, but Elio is already reaching for it, his huge black hand passing in front of my line of vision and taking the dish from me. He brings it back into the kitchen, and I twist where I'm sitting to follow him with my eyes, staring at him over the back of the couch as he puts the used tea bag in a bin and the cup in the sink.

It's a jarring image, shocking in how unnatural it looks. Elio, moving through the kitchen and doing such mundane tasks like that, throwing away a tea bag and putting a dirty dish in the sink. I remember what Valentina told me once about the Titone men never stepping foot in a kitchen, and here Elio is not only making me tea but also cleaning up after me too.

Even in the massive space, he still looks huge. And honestly, completely out of place. Like some stalking predator has stumbled into a forest cottage and is suddenly doing its best at pretending to be a human who lives there.

Have I domesticated him?

I'm an idiot for even asking myself such a question. If I had any real sort of control over him, he wouldn't be using the threat of exposing my father to get me to marry him.

Marry him...

Where the hell did that even come from, anyway?

I mean, maybe he's right. Maybe it really will get Darragh to back off. But *marriage?* The first time I met Elio, he told me he didn't even fuck redheads, and now he wants to make me his bride?

It doesn't make sense. And surely someone in his position would have a political match lined up, not unlike Valentina with her picked-out fiancé. There has to be some mafia princess promised to him, someone from his world who would be an asset to the Titone empire.

I think of the blonde woman from the gala, think of her possessive hand on Elio's chest, and my stomach lurches in a way I don't want to acknowledge.

Elio hasn't said anything else about marrying him since the car, so maybe he just threw it out there in the heat of the moment. Something he didn't really mean.

But then again, I know him well enough to know that he doesn't say things he doesn't mean.

Well, maybe I imagined it then. Fucking dreamed it, for all the sense it makes.

Maybe I'll wake up tomorrow and realize most of this insane day has been a dream. I'll open my eyes in the morning on the day after the anniversary of Mom's death. Elio will still be up north. And I'll still be a virgin who hasn't visited her mother's grave in years.

But that version of reality doesn't feel comforting either and I'm too tired and shaken up to figure out why.

Elio returns and resumes studying me. Then, as if mostly satisfied with what he sees, he gets down onto his knees and works off one boot, then the other. He holds my ankles and rotates me so that my legs go lengthwise along the couch and my socked feet don't get soaked by the puddles on the floor.

But for some reason, he doesn't let go yet. My muscles tighten and then relax in one big, wave-like movement when he begins to slowly massage the arches of my feet with his thumbs. He's thorough.

Endlessly meticulous. Drawing deep, slow strokes against parts of me that I didn't even know were sore and tired until now.

Whether it's the tea or the massage or the warmth, I'm even more exhausted now. My limbs feel like lead. I sag back against the arm of the couch and watch him. His face is mostly cleared of the pulsing rage I saw from the side in the car. His hard, scarred jaw and dark brows seem to be set in a fairly neutral expression, though I doubt Elio Titone has ever felt truly neutral about anything important in his entire life.

His expression puckers slightly when I flinch. His thumb has pressed into the tender place where my foot was injured from the piece of ceramic from the broken cup. Thanks to his ministrations, the surface skin healed up just fine, but there's still some lingering sensitivity in that spot. Very carefully, he peels off my sock and puts it to the side. He regards the bottom of my bare foot with that same cool look.

And then his eyes fall shut and he presses his mouth to the place that I was hurt. My leg jerks at the unexpected kiss in such a ticklish place, but his hand turns to iron on my ankle, holding me there. When he draws back and opens his eyes, his expressionless façade is still mostly in place. Except for the eyes. They're liquid, molten black. Heat and darkness combined.

Elio places my feet down on the couch, then bends over me, his fingers rising to my throat. I suppress a small whimper, not even knowing if I want him to touch me or not, my skin already anticipating the possessive glide of leather. But instead, he simply grips the collar of my parka and unzips it, letting the coat fall open. He's quick but careful in his movements, pulling one of my arms out of one sleeve, then the other. But just as he's pulling my right sleeve all the way down, he freezes, his gaze stuck on one spot on the sleeve's cuff.

Elio's face goes briefly cataclysmic with rage, and when I look down at the bit of the sleeve he's holding in his hands I can suddenly see why. There's a singed, ripped part on the puffy outside, near the wrist. It takes me a moment to fully realize that a bullet actually grazed me. Or the parka, anyway.

Elio's like a statue, staring at that blackened rip like it's someone he wants to murder.

"It's OK," I say. I know even as the words leave my mouth they're ridiculous. None of this is OK.

But for some reason I just can't stop myself from saying them.

Elio gives me a potent, angry stare, then rips the coat off the rest of the way and hurls it into a heap on the ground. In a second, he's on his knees again, his trousers soaking in the slushy puddles. But he doesn't seem to notice that. He's too preoccupied with a silent, frantic examination of my hands. He holds each of my fingers right up to his face, then scrutinizes the palms, then the backs. Then, he shoves the sleeves of my hoodie up to my elbows, running his ferocious gaze up and down each forearm, then the tender places at my wrists, like he's counting every vein and artery.

"You already did this," I remind him softly. He checked my hands back in the cemetery.

"That was before I knew a bullet actually grazed you," he bites out. "Shut up and let me fucking focus."

"Right," I say, irritated by his command. "Guess I'm no use to you if my fingers get shot off and I can't play violin anymore."

He goes still, his gloved hands locked around my wrists like handcuffs.

Then his gaze rises to mine once more, and the rage has taken on a new depth. This time I can tell it's aimed at me.

"If you weren't on the edge of going into traumatic shock, I would spank your fucking ass for what you just said." Elio lays my hands down in my lap, his movements tightly controlled, then lets me go. "But as it is, I will instead inform you that a thought like that was about as far from my mind as possible."

"I mean, you've said something like that to me before," I remind him, hackles rising further. "Remember? When you gave me mittens

313

and said I wouldn't be able to play for you if all my fingers fall off from frostbite?"

"Yes," he seethes, "and I seem to recall that I was joking when I said it. If I remember correctly, you even laughed." There's anger harsh as iron in his voice. "Look me in the fucking eye and tell me what you just said was a joke."

I avoid his eyes because I can't and he knows it. There was no humour in my comment, just bitterness. Maybe even something mean.

My gaze settles on his gloved hands at his sides, and that bitterness withers in my chest, replaced with guilt. If anyone knows what it's like to go through life with mangled hands, it's him. Is it so hard to believe that he might not want that same fate for me?

I nod.

"You're right. OK," I say quietly after a long, tense pause. I'm not ready to apologize, not to him, not after everything we've been through. But I can accept what he said. That he's acting out of concern for me as a person instead of just worrying that I might not be able to perform like his little Songbird inside the glittering cage he's created.

"OK," he repeats after me, and it looks like he's calmed down ever so slightly. The anger is still there, but it's retreated somewhat, replaced with a nameless rawness in his gaze. "OK," he says once more, a little quieter this time, and I wonder if he's saying it to me this time or to himself.

And then, as if this has been the most normal day in the world, he suddenly holds out his hand to me and casually says, "Let's go to bed."

I stare at his outstretched hand, at the hard, strong shape of it, cloaked in that dull-yet-luminescent black. It's a hand that's hurt me and held me, possessed me and protected me. It's choked the breath from my lungs and left its stinging imprint on my skin.

I don't entirely trust it.

But I rise and take it anyway.

Chapter 2

Deirdre

Elio holds my hand the entire way up the stairs and into my room, and I can tell that if I make one wrong move or even stumble slightly he'll be scooping me up into his arms again. But it feels good to walk on my own, even if my legs are wobbly.

It feels good to hold his hand too. I can't deny it.

We walk through Elio's room into mine. The bed draws me towards it like gravity, but despite how bone-tired I am there's also a buzz of nervous energy in my brain and I don't know if I can sleep right away.

"I'm going to have a bath," I announce. Yes. That would be good. Wash the night off of me.

"Fine," Elio replies. "But no holding your breath this time. Just a normal, relaxing bath, you got it? Put some bubbles or some other shit like that in there."

I nod, because I'm pretty sure if I try to hold my breath for any significant period of time in my current state I'm just going to pass out. I head into the bathroom. It's almost funny, or maybe kind of sad, how my natural impulse to reach out and close the door is

315

entirely gone now. Just like the door itself, I suppose. I peel off my hoodie and let it drop to the floor. Bare and braless, I turn on the light, only to let out a strangled yelp when I see the huge, hulking silhouette in the mirror, standing directly behind me.

"How are you so quiet?" I gasp, spinning to face him and clapping my arms over my chest. "You're like a hundred feet tall! You should make at least some kind of sound when you enter a room. It's got to be against the laws of... I don't know, physics or something!"

I'm babbling. I know it and Elio knows it. But he doesn't try to stop me, just listens quietly.

Or maybe doesn't listen at all, tuning me out as his gaze roams over my exposed skin. I assume it's in a sexual way, but then I see the slight tightening of concern around his eyes, and I realize that he's once again checking my skin for injuries.

This is only confirmed when he takes me by the shoulders and turns me around so that we're both facing the mirror once again. He keeps one hand on my right shoulder, the other skimming between my shoulder blades, slowly tracing the line of my spine until it comes to rest on my left hip.

"All in one piece," I murmur, my eyes on his in the mirror.

"We'll see," he says. He gently squeezes my hip. "Pants off."

"Oh, come on! You know nothing happened to my legs!" I snap. Unlike the sleeve of the coat, there's no ripped fabric or singe marks. Just a few wet spots from the snow.

"Either I check every inch of you here and now, or I do it with you laying sprawled and naked in my bed." His tone is darkly menacing, and once again it doesn't seem as if it's intended to be sexual, just a simple threat. But the words go straight to my tender pussy, because that part of the night is resurging to the forefront of my mind now.

The memory of him slamming into me, claiming every part of me, telling me to come on his cock like a good fucking girl.

Which I did.

And I guess I'm still his stupid good girl, because I hook my thumbs into the waistband of the sweat pants and let them fall without further argument. Elio stands back slightly and then bends to examine my legs, his cool, leather-clad touch sparking sensations that I try and fail to ignore.

"Good," he says. "Now those."

There's nothing left but my panties.

"No way," I say quickly. "What, you think I've got a bullet stuck up there or something?"

"You planning to wear them in the bath?" he counters.

"Obviously not."

"Then off."

My face flames. It's not like I haven't taken off my panties for him before, but I can feel the damp pad against my skin, and there's something extra humiliating about letting him see that.

"*Now*, Deirdre."

Oh, screw it. He's not going to leave me alone until I do it. Letting out a huff of irritated breath, I shove my panties down and then I step out of the whole heap of clothing, keeping my arms crossed tightly over my chest as I do it.

Elio's gaze falls to the bloodied pad, and the muscles go rigid in his jaw. When his eyes lift to mine, I inhale sharply, because his gaze is so fierce and heated it feels like a physical touch. That look claims me with just as much need and force as his cock did earlier, and I hate the way my insides curl needily in response.

Scowling, I stoop and swipe the panties and pad up, hustling over to the garbage can. I'm about to toss it all in when Elio stops me with a word.

"No," he says, his voice thick with something I can't identify. "Not the panties."

I peel the pad off and throw it away, keeping the panties in my hand. I didn't position the pad far enough forward when I put it on earlier, and there's a small area of now-dry blood remaining on the underwear's fabric. A damning splotch of dark red on the white cotton.

Shouldn't have worn white underwear when I'm bleeding. That's just asking for trouble.

"Now to me."

I look over to see Elio with a hand outstretched, eyes hungry.

Of course he wants them. *Of fucking course* he does.

"You have a serious panties fetish," I say, shaking my head.

"Nope," he responds, not appearing even the slightest bit embarrassed by this situation. "Just a Songbird fetish. Now hand them over."

I make a fist, crumpling the fabric possessively in my hand. In Elio's twisted brain, these ones have to be extra special. They're the ones I wore right after he claimed my virginity. They're marked with my blood.

"What are they worth to you?"

Something flashes in his eyes. I can't tell if he's surprised or impressed, but either way he recovers quickly.

"We're back to bargaining, are we?" he asks.

"Yup," I reply. As insane as it is, it feels safe here. Safe in the dangerous place where I still owe him millions. Because money is just money.

But marriage is...

Elio shrugs his good shoulder. Then he turns and takes out a couple of bottles from under the sink, squinting at the pretty fonts with so much focus it's as if they're written in a foreign language. He must have found what he's looking for, though, because he takes one of the bottles – a container of bubble bath – over to the tub and turns on the water. He bends to put in the plug, then unscrews the bottle's cap, dumping some of the bubble bath liquid into the roiling water. Scents of vanilla and lavender bloom in the air.

Elio puts down the bottle then turns back to face me. I'm extremely aware of my nakedness, and I clutch the panties in front of me like some kind of shield. I want to dive into the protection offered by the thick layer of bubbles forming in the tub, but I'm strong enough to at least finish out this conversation first.

"So?" I ask, and I want to freaking applaud at the way my voice doesn't shake. "How much?"

Elio rubs the scarred part of his jaw as he stares at me, his look calculating. I wonder what mental tallies he's conducting in that messed-up head of his. Which sums he's putting up against which others. Blood and money and what it's all worth.

"All of it," he suddenly says as he holds out his hand once again. "The entire sum of your debt. Null and void."

He says it so casually. Like he didn't just make a bomb go off in my brain.

"What?" I breathe the word, sucking it in on a hissing inhale. I narrow my eyes at him, because I know him and I'm certain there has to be a trap in here somewhere.

His face gives nothing away. He takes one huge step towards me, plucks the panties from my hand, then says, "No point in owing millions of dollars to myself. What's yours is mine and all that jazz."

"What the hell are you talking about?"

"Your debt, Songbird. I will take control of it, and since it doesn't make sense to write my own damn self a seven-figure-cheque, I'll wave it all. You can consider the figure paid in full." He leans down, brushing a stray curl behind my ear before adding in a murmur, "When we're married."

Chapter 3

Elio

My words send a physical shock through Deirdre, which is kind of odd, considering I already told her that we're engaged in the car. And I sure as shit know that she didn't forget or mishear me, because she spent the entire ride back here saying that we weren't. And yet, it's like I'm telling her for the very first time based on the way that she reacts.

"We're not getting married," she spits like an angry cat.

She needs more of that bedtime tea. The cat on that box looked chill as fuck.

She swipes her hands like little claws at the panties I'm already holding. As if by taking them back, she can reassert some sort of control over this situation.

Only problem is she never actually had control over this situation in the first place. She can't take it back if I've never relinquished it to her.

I step smoothly out of her reach, tucking the garment of clothing carefully into my pocket.

"We are," I counter. "It's your only option. Being married to me will protect you and you'll be free of your debt all at once. What's not to like about that?"

"What's not to like?" she gasps, disbelief making her words all high and huffy. "How about the fact that I'll be married to *you!*"

She tenses, then clamps her mouth shut, her eyes huge. She's probably afraid that she's just offended me or hurt my feelings or something, but she hasn't. I'm more than aware that I'm not the prize in this relationship.

But I'm also the only one who can give her what she needs now.

I'm the only one who can protect her.

I'm the only one who will own her.

Deirdre Titone.

My wife.

Goddamn, do I ever love the sound of that.

I smirk, and that appears to confuse her, because her fury abates slightly.

"I don't understand," she says, slowly shaking her head. "This makes no sense. You've got to have some actual bride lined up out there somewhere. Why would you marry me just to get Darragh off our backs?"

"I don't believe I've ever made a decision in my entire life for the sole purpose of getting another man 'off my back.'"

Her cute, freckled nose wrinkles with incredulity. "So... You're telling me you actually want this? You just... You just decided you want to marry me?"

"Do I look like the sort of man who does a single fucking thing he doesn't want to do?"

Though to be fair, I never wanted to get married before Deirdre. I know that Uncle Vinny's got some candidates in mind, and that someone like Nat Rizzo would literally claw another girl's eyes out for the chance, but before now I always looked at it as a chore to be put off for as long as possible.

But now...

Hell. I'd marry my Songbird right here, right now. In this sweet-smelling bathroom, my furious, beautiful bride without a single stitch on her.

But she deserves a better ceremony than that.

She deserves a better groom, too, but that part is decidedly non-negotiable.

"Your tub is getting full," I point out blithely when she doesn't answer.

She doesn't move. She's studying me with her pretty mouth pinched and her arms crossed over her breasts, like she's attempting to figure something out. Trying to see a trap from all possible angles.

But there is no angle here. No secret card up my sleeve I'm waiting to play.

I want to marry her and I will fucking do it.

I've already come to possess everything else in her life.

Might as well add her vow to the list.

My fiancée – because that's already how I'm starting to think of her, and *Cristo Santo*, it kind of makes my dick hard – shakes her head again and then walks over to the tub. She turns off the water then carefully gets in. I watch her closely, primed to grab her if I need to because I'm worried those trauma-weakened legs are going to give out like a baby deer's. But my Songbird's made of strong stuff and she gets in just fine on her own.

She refuses to look at me, instead staring mulishly at the foamy bubbles that currently conceal her from her elegant collarbones down. She lifts her wet, soapy arms, tugging at the loose hairstyle on the top of her head until it all comes tumbling down in a wave of liquid fire that makes my heart feel like it's beating both too fast and in the wrong place – in my cock instead of in my chest.

"Alright. I'm in the bath," she tells me. "I'm not going to pass out or hold my breath or anything. You can go now."

I do, but just for a couple of seconds. I leave the bathroom only for as long as it takes to grab the chair from Deirdre's room. Then I carry it into the bathroom and set it down beside the bathtub.

Deirdre had been leaning back against the tub eyes closed, but they pop open at the sound of the chair being set down and my body dropping into it.

"What are you doing? I said you could go!" she snaps.

"See, the thing is, I actually can't," I say. The chair is facing away from the tub. I'm sitting in it backwards, straddling the seat. I rest my forearms along the chair's back and make myself comfortable.

Deirdre gives a bitter laugh.

"You're Elio Titone. Pretty sure you could do anything you set your mind to."

"Almost anything," I correct her. "Leaving you alone tonight isn't on that list. I am physically fucking incapable of that right now."

She rolls her eyes at me, but I'm not exaggerating. I feel like if I walk back out that door, if I put any meaningful distance between us after everything that's happened tonight, then some vitally important blood vessel inside my head is gonna pop for good this time.

I could have lost her tonight.

It's something I've been pushing down, down, down since we got home. A reality I've been stuffing behind softer things like tea and baths because stopping to confront the fact that she could have gotten killed tonight, could have died *right in fucking front of me,* literally makes me think my goddamn heart might give out.

I'm thirty-four years old. I'm way too young to have a heart attack or an aneurysm or whatever the fuck it is I feel like I'm on the verge of when I imagine losing Deirdre.

Darragh doesn't know how lucky he is that his men have garbage fucking aim.

If that bullet had so much as nicked her freckled skin...

Rage, and something else, something that feels far too close to panic, make an ugly mess of my guts. My hands prickle and burn. I grip my elbows, forearms still resting along the back of the chair, and I fucking fuse my gaze to Deirdre, as if the intensity of my eyes alone can create a protective layer around her.

She looks like she's decided to pretend that I'm not here. She doesn't glance at me and she doesn't speak, and that's just fine by me, because I have shit to sort out in my head.

I have to decide what I'm going to do about Darragh. My instincts tell me to gut him like a fish, fill his belly with bricks, and dump him into a frozen fucking lake.

But I also have to be smart about this. Darragh isn't a lowly soldier or some sniveling ex-boyfriend of Deirdre's. He's the head of the Irish mob, protected at all times. Killing him would be astronomically difficult, and even if it were achievable, there's a very good chance I'd take a bullet to the brain in the process.

And then what? Curse steps up to avenge me, Darragh's men step up to avenge him, Toronto's streets run red with blood. And in the Shakespearian-level chaos of the fallout, who the hell is gonna be left to take care of my Songbird?

Fucking nobody, that's who.

Mad Darragh might be a nutcase, but he's not an idiot. Right now, he believes he's taking back something that belongs to him, just like his soldiers said. But I don't think that he would be dumb enough to try to abduct or kill a Titone. His men might not have even realized it was me with her tonight, now that I think about it, because I highly doubt they would have let loose a single shot if they'd been close enough to see who I was. Darragh Gowan chews on grudges like a starving dog with a bone, but I also know that he wants to stay in business and make a shitload of money. Not embroil his entire operation in a feud with the highest levels of *La Cosa Nostra* over a sweet but ultimately worthless little nobody like Deirdre.

Because really, that's what she is to them. Her father was bottom rung mafia. Deirdre is even further removed. She doesn't have money or status or friends.

But she's got me now.

Yeah. I definitely need to think this through. Don't rush.

That's never been a problem for me before. I do what needs to be done – always – but I take my time and I do it with my head screwed on straight.

Only problem is I haven't had my head on straight since that summer day when Deirdre and the sparking music of her soul blew a big fucking hole in the middle of my life.

I look at her while she sits in the tub, so quietly oblivious to everything she's done to me.

Deirdre slides down a little, tipping her head back until her hair is submerged in the water, then comes back up. She looks around, her tresses rust-red and sealed to the glorious curve of her neck meeting her spine. Her gaze seems to snag on something in the shower in the corner of the room, and she sighs and stills.

"What is it?" I ask, leaning forward until my chin comes down on top of my forearms.

"Nothing."

"*Deirdre.*"

"I just wanted to wash my hair, OK? Is that allowed or do I have to ask permission first?"

"It's allowed."

Though I have to say, the idea of her coming to me to ask permission even for the most mundane things is appealing.

Can I take a shower, Elio? Can I go to class today, Elio?

Can I come for you, Elio?

Fuck.

"Whatever. The shampoo's all the way over there. It's fine. I'll wash it tomorrow."

But I'm already up, crossing over to the shower and entering the big glass enclosure of it. I scan the text on the bottles in here, grab the one marked *shampoo*, then figure she might want the others too, so I bring them all. Three in total.

I drop back down in the seat, straddling it once again. I put the other two bottles down on the stone floor but keep the shampoo. Deirdre holds out a wet hand for it, but I make no move to pass it over.

Instead, I peel off one glove, and then the other.

Then I squeeze the shampoo into my bare hands, lathering it up without looking at them. I lean further forward until my chest presses against the back of the chair and my elbows reach the edge of the tub.

"Come here."

"I can wash my own damn hair."

"I didn't ask if you were capable of washing your own hair," I say. "I told you to come here."

Maybe it's the baggage of this night weighing down on her slender shoulders. Or maybe it's the fact that she knows she can't win against me. With an expression of wary resignation furrowing her brows, she slides over to me, then slowly spins on her ass in the tub until her back is to me.

Merda, she's got a gorgeous neck. And shoulders so lovely that they just about convince my agnostic ass that God must actually be real, because somebody had to have sculpted them. Beauty that fucking ethereal doesn't just come out of nowhere. I'm not even entirely sure how someone so beautiful can exist in a world like mine at all.

Fuck me. Even her ears are pretty.

I don't know if she's turned me into that much of a needy fucking fool, or if she really is just that terrifyingly special, but in that moment I feel the truly feral need to stroke myself to climax while staring at her ears. Not her tits. Not her cunt.

Her fucking ears.

Cristo help me.

I ignore the twinge in my dick and instead focus on gathering up all that thick, sodden hair in my fists. But then she makes a small, whimpering sort of sound when I run my soapy fingers along her scalp, and ignoring my arousal becomes a hell of a lot harder.

I want to fuck her again.

And it's not even lust driving me. Not just obsession or physical desire.

There's this deep, unnerving sort of feeling that stirs up when I think about being inside her again. Bizarrely, it almost feels like...

sorrow. Or homesickness. Or some kind of breath-stealing nostalgia. Whatever the fuck it is, it hurts. Hurts to even imagine fucking her again because I want it, want her, so damn bad.

But that's not what she needs tonight.

She needs tea, which I've made her. She needs a bath, which I've drawn her.

She needs her hair washed, which I'm doing for her.

She needs to be tucked all safe and cozy into bed. I'll be the one to do that, too.

Right before I tuck my own scarred body in next to hers.

Chapter 4

Deirdre

"**Y**ou're way too good at this," I mumble. I want to be resentful about it, but the bone-melting pleasure of Elio massaging my scalp makes it impossible.

"I know how to take care of my Songbird."

"Hmm," I say noncommittally. His fingers dig and glide along every point of my head, rubbing slow, firm circles in the lather, making my whole neck tingle. The bubbles in my bath are starting to disintegrate into nothing, putting more of my body on display, but at this point I'm too tired and relaxed from the massage to care. My skin is warm. The place between my legs stings.

Elio works the lather down the lengths of my hair, tugging ever so gently, which makes my scalp prickle pleasantly.

"How the fuck do you have so much hair?" he asks. A question like that would have made me bristle before. Because I used to get comments and questions about my hair when I was younger and they were almost never nice.

And while I can't say that Elio is exactly *nice*, there's not the undertone of icky judgment that usually accompanies a question like that. He sounds like he's genuinely asking, like my hair is some new, confusing thing that needs to be explained to him.

"Um. Genetics?"

"No way. I've seen your papà."

"It was thicker when he was younger," I say, but then bitterness creeps up my throat, and I don't want to talk about my dad anymore. "My mom had a ton of hair. Different colour, though. It was the most beautiful shade of blonde. I used to want blonde hair so badly. Especially after she died."

The fact that it's the anniversary of her death hits me all over again. The events of tonight have distracted me from my grief, but it comes rushing back. So heavy that in normal circumstances it would push my head beneath the water.

But Elio is here. Holding my hair. Anchoring me. Keeping my head above the water.

It occurs to me that it's probably after midnight by now. The anniversary of her death is technically done. There's usually a wooden sort of relief that accompanies the days after the anniversary. A numbness different from the sharper pain. Like I have to slowly claw my way back to living.

Strangely, I don't feel that. At least, not yet.

Maybe it's because this year was different. Maybe it's because I went to see her, even if the night did end in a total shit show. I chew on the inside of my cheek, honestly wondering if, had I known what I know now about how the night unfolded, would I still have wanted to go? I assumed my instant answer would be "no," but I truly don't know. And maybe that makes me a terrible person, because people ended up dead tonight.

But still...

It felt right for me to be there. At least at the beginning.

And it felt right with Elio.

In my state of relaxation, I find myself able to slink around the bad parts of the night and remember what happened before. Remember the heart-achingly beautiful bouquet of blooms Elio picked out just for her. Remember the way he knelt down, more respectful than I've probably ever seen him, painstakingly cleaning the snow from every nook and cranny of her headstone.

Elio is quiet for a while. He twists my hair, squeezing some of the lather out of it, then suddenly says, "Don't ever dye it."

"What, you're in charge of my hair colour now too?"

"Yes."

Isn't that what he said to me on the very first night in this house? *Every flaming hair on your pretty little head. All. Fucking. Mine.*

I almost want to dye it now just to spite him.

Maybe I would. If...

If some twisted part of me didn't feel immense pleasure at the thought of him liking it. Maybe even loving it.

I pull away, needing to rinse and for this to be done.

In response, Elio's fist tightens on the rope of my hair, and for a second I think he's going to snap it back towards him like a leash. But he doesn't. He brushes his knuckles against the tender place at the base of my skull, running them gently down the back of my neck, before he lets go.

Once he's released my hair, I'm off like a shot, as if I've built up some kind of careening momentum being held in place there. I skid along the bottom of the bath to the other side so forcefully that a small tidal wave sloshes up against the white wall of the tub. I clumsily dunk my head backwards, scrubbing viciously at my scalp, trying to get rid of all the good feelings Elio has created there. But I can't. Because it's like his touch has sunk in deep. Past the surface of my skin, into the muscle and bone.

I give up, and once my hair is rinsed decently enough I sit up again.

"Want me to scrub your back now?" he asks, and there's a crooked sort of smirk on his mouth. But there's nothing casual or teasing in his eyes. He looks at me like his gaze can swallow me whole.

"No," I say. "I'm going to get out now."

I'm too tired to do the rest, and if I'm too tired then that means Elio is going to take over and wash every single inch of my body, I just know it. I cannot handle that right now. Soaking in the sudsy water is enough for tonight. At this point I just want to dry off and get into bed.

Elio rises from his chair and grabs a clean, fluffy towel from the nearby rack. He pats his hands dry on it without looking at them, and I can't tell if it's because he's specifically avoiding looking at the scars, or if it's because he's so unwilling to let me out of his sight. Even when he bends to retrieve his gloves, sliding them back on one at a time, he's still watching me.

I wonder if he's going to just stand there and make me get out of the bath to grab my own towel, soaking and vulnerable under his gaze. But, somewhat surprisingly, he instead walks around the bath until he's behind me. He opens up the towel, letting it hang between us, and I cautiously stand up with my back to him.

The towel immediately envelops me, going around my shoulders in a warm, fluffy hug. Only, it's not just the towel hugging me, but Elio. He's got his big arms around me from behind, locking at my front in a tight embrace. He bends down along my right side, the scarred left side of his jaw brushing my cheek as his chin comes to rest on my shoulder. This isn't just hugging now, this is holding. He inhales, his lips moving against the side of my throat, and I'm sure he's about to say something to me.

But he doesn't.

Instead, he just straightens up and starts rubbing the towel along my shoulders and arms. Then, he lifts me easily out of the bath, setting me down on my dripping feet. I let out a shaky sigh, because at some point he's turned on the heated flooring and it feels like pure magic seeping into the soles of my feet. I still find it so surreal, so surprising, when he does those small things solely for my own comfort. He controls me, spanks my ass until it burns, won't let me go anywhere or do anything that he decides isn't allowed...

But he also makes me tea and washes my hair and ensures that my feet are warm.

I could have a whole lifetime beside him and maybe never figure him the fuck out.

"Hold this," he instructs me, thrusting the edges of the towel into my hands. I pull it around myself like a cape while he fetches a second towel and then bends to dry my legs. I go still, shivery heat pulsing through me as he works his way up from my right foot to my calf, my knee, my inner thigh. Blood rushes between my legs so fast it almost hurts when the towel grazes my tender skin there.

But Elio is all business. He whisks the towel away from my sensitive places, moving on to my other leg until the only wet things left on me now are my hair and – I hate to admit it – my pussy.

"Alright," he says, standing and tossing his towel aside. "Let's go."

I don't want to follow him out of the room – I can at least get my pyjamas on my own – so I go ahead of him. But maybe this is even worse, because I can feel him stalking right behind me, his gaze hot on my back.

I flick on the light in my room's walk-in closet while Elio looms in the closet's doorway, leaning his good shoulder against the doorframe, arms crossed. Still keeping my towel fastened around myself, I grab a pair of loose, yellow silk pyjamas. I yank on the pants one-handed, then once they're on let my damp towel drop and quickly pull on the shirt with my back to Elio.

At the last second, I realize I haven't put on any underwear, but I don't seem to be actively bleeding anymore, so fingers crossed it's alright. And if I get blood on these nice silk pants, does it even matter much? It isn't like they're actually mine.

Knowing Elio, he might even like them better that way.

I hang up my towel on an empty hook in the closet, then turn and swiftly head past Elio. He doesn't move aside for me, and he's so broad that I'm forced to turn sideways in the doorway, facing him as I squeeze by. My breasts brush his arm, my nipples tightening instantly. It's like that single brush against him exerts some sort of gravitational pull, because even though I'm more than capable of taking another sideways step out of here, it suddenly becomes a hell of a lot harder. Part of me wants to stay here, trapped between the wood at my back and the man at my front.

Part of me wants him to touch me.

He doesn't, just keeps his arms crossed while gazing darkly down at me. Although, there is a slight tightening in his biceps beneath the black fabric of his shirt. As if he's holding himself back from grabbing me.

"Bed," he reminds me firmly, and I nod, because he's right. I really need to get some sleep.

I finish sidling out of the closet, my breasts dragging along his arm as I free myself. He lets out a soft hiss of breath at the contact, the muscles in his arms flexing again.

Once out of the closet, I hustle over to my bed. I'm about to drop gratefully into it when Elio's words freeze me.

"Not that one."

My stomach does a strange swooping thing, and I can't decide if it's good or bad. I hide my confusion behind irritation. Anger is always easier.

"What do you mean, 'not that one?'" I ask, narrowing my eyes at him.

"I mean that you're not sleeping in that bed tonight. Or any other night. You wanna take a nap or something when I'm not here? Fine, you can use that bed. But from now on you're going to spend your nights in mine."

My blood seems to run hot and cold at the same time.

"Like hell, I will," I snap.

"You will," he echoes. "And if I have to take a hammer to this bedframe the way I did the doors just to take away your other options then I'll do it."

"I'll just sleep on the floor then."

"Then I'll sleep on the floor beside you." There's a smoky tinge of amusement in his voice, but it vanishes when he adds, "You're not getting out of this, Deirdre. You're not getting away from me. And all jokes aside, I'll be fucking damned if I let my wife sleep on the floor."

"I'm not your wife!"

"Not yet. But I wouldn't let my fiancée sleep on the floor, either."

Fuming, and apparently completely tongue-tied by his use of words like *wife* and *fiancée*, I plop down on my bed and cross my arms, glaring mutinously up at him.

He doesn't say a single word. Doesn't even hesitate. He just bends down, fastens his strong hands around my waist, then slings me up against his chest the way he did outside earlier. Before I can even try to wriggle out of his grasp, he's crossed into his dark bedroom. He bends down and then drops me onto the mattress.

Instantly, I'm scrambling out of the bed. And just as instantly, he's in front of me, blocking my way, one of his feet between mine on the floor. He bends his knee and shoves his shin against the bed, turning his leg into a bar that locks me in. I try to stand up anyway, but the press of his leg ruins my balance, and when I halfway straighten up, all it takes is the poke of a single leather finger against my forehead to send me sprawling backwards, arms akimbo.

"You're sleeping here, Songbird. We're not negotiating this."

I lie on my back, breathing hard, watching as the velvet shadow of him starts undoing the buttons on his shirt before shrugging out of it. His hands go to his belt, and my heart leaps rebelliously into my throat when the clink of metal lets me know that he's unfastened it. He lets his clothing fall to the floor and kicks it away. I know without being able to see him well enough in the darkness that he's taken everything off.

Everything except the gloves, I suppose, because when he grabs my wrist beneath the silk sleeve of my pyjama top, it's not his skin on mine.

He pulls my wrist so I'm forced to roll onto my side. Now that I'm out of the way, he pulls back the covers I was on top of with a firmly decisive yank. He forcefully rolls me back into the spot before dropping the covers on top of me.

Then he slides in beneath them on the other side.

I'm so tense beside him that my teeth begin to chatter all over again. I can't help it. I've never shared a bed with him like this. Earlier tonight we were in the other bed together, sure, but we weren't really *in* it. More like... on it. Somehow, having sex on top of the blankets feels way less vulnerable than sleeping with Elio in a literal sense this way.

Elio must feel my trembling, or hear the teeth chattering, because he draws me closer, one of his gloved hands sliding against my lower back.

"Shh," he murmurs against my forehead, and the sound is so soft and gentle it's entirely unnatural and frankly, kind of alarming. "Shh, Songbird. None of that now."

"I can't help it," I stammer. "If you can't sleep beside me then let me go back to the other bed."

His lips skim across my forehead, and I can't tell if it's a feather-light kiss or just a coincidence of motion as he prepares to speak.

"I'd rather stay awake all night beside you," he says, tracing an exquisitely tingly line up and down my spine with his fingertips, "than sleep like a baby in another room without you."

"And what about what I want?" I whisper against his throat.

"I don't think you actually know what that is." He doesn't give me a chance to argue back or get offended. "Think about it," he says. "Think about it fucking properly. Do you really, truly want to go to another room alone tonight? After everything that's happened? Because that wasn't what you seemed to want earlier, and shit has only gotten more intense since then."

I don't answer. Can't answer.

Because I'm afraid that he's absolutely right.

In the silence, I try to slow my breathing. Elio's lips press to my forehead once more, and this time I'm sure it's an intentional kiss, sweet and oddly chaste for somebody like him. Maybe it's some kind of peace offering. A way to tell me that this might actually be alright if I could only let it.

He's so freaking warm. Like a furnace in the shape of a man, and without even meaning to I'm nudging closer to him. My hands are balled into fists against his chest, and I force them to relax. But then I don't know what to do with them, so I clasp them tightly together beneath my chin, the gesture of someone in fervent prayer, or maybe someone begging.

I don't like that either, and with something that feels like a wall inside me breaking, I release my hands from each other and slide them tentatively along his chest, feeling the dark heat of him, the hard muscle, the hair.

The beating of his heart.

It's hammering almost as hard and fast as mine.

"Did you down a bunch of espresso when I was drinking tea or something?" I say, so surprised and confused that I press my hands harder against him, as if I'd somehow felt him wrong.

"Nope."

"Adrenaline really is a hell of a drug," I mutter.

He lets out a chuckle, and I feel the rumble of it under my hands.

"That's not adrenaline," he tells me, shifting slightly closer until I feel the unmistakable nudge of his hard cock against my hip. "That's you, Songbird. You've worked your way in between my fucking ribs, and I can't tell if you're tearing shit apart in there or putting it all back together." He rests his chin against the top of my head and murmurs, "Probably both."

My heart is racing all the faster now, and it's not because of what he's saying but because of the unignorable, undeniable hardness at my hip. He's not moving, not grinding it against me, not doing anything at all to draw attention to it, and yet I can't think about anything else. His cock burns right through the silk of the pyjamas, like it's somehow hotter than the rest of him. And maybe it is. Because I remember the bright sting of that heat inside me earlier. The effervescent stretch of his thick shaft invading my pussy. The way he stroked and stabbed, demanding and giving all at the same time. Jamming himself with hungry expertise against a deep place that made every cell in my body shudder and then explode.

He hasn't cleaned himself off the way I have.

My blood is probably still on him. Dry now, but there all the same.

Why do I feel a sick throb of satisfaction at that thought? The thought that I've made my mark on him somehow. Or maybe it's just because I know he likes it.

You're claiming my cock with your blood the same way I've already stained you with mine. That first night, Songbird, do you remember? When I got shot and bled all over you.

That's what he groaned, harsh and raw, when he broke me open. And then...

I would have fucking died for you that night.

My stomach drops, and my pussy squeezes so hard that it almost feels like a tiny orgasm. I hurt down there, and I can't tell if it's because of what happened tonight...

Or because I feel so strangely empty.

Elio adjusts his position slightly, forcing a thick thigh between mine, his cock jerking away from my hip until its underside is thrust flat against my belly, hooked beneath the pyjama top. Skin to skin.

It's so quiet, barely a whisper, but in the dense stillness of the room there's no mistaking Elio's half-hissed inhale, "*Merda.*"

I'm not sure my heart is located in my chest any longer, because I feel my pulse strongest in my head and in my clit. Elio must be in the same boat. Because his cock keeps doing these tight little throbs against my belly.

But he still doesn't do anything about it. Doesn't grip his shaft to jerk himself or try to make me touch him. He just lies against me, chest heaving with slightly unsteady breaths, cock twitching.

I feel like the tension is going to crack my skull in half. Finally, I blurt out, "You can't possibly mean to sleep like that!"

"Like what?" is his maddening reply.

This man. This fucking man.

"Like... Like this! Like... How you are!"

"You mean so hard I'm on the verge of trying to fuck your goddamn belly button?"

My cheeks flame.

"Well, for lack of a more elegant way to say it, yes!"

"You don't need to worry about that, Deirdre. You need sleep and I plan to let you get it. My blue balls are none of your concern tonight."

There's a certain slant to the word *tonight* that makes me think it is going to be my concern another time, and soon.

"Well, it's not like I can sleep like this either," I huff.

"No? Well, how about this?"

He grabs me and rolls me over so that my back is to him. He seals his molten chest to my spine, searing me through the silk.

Then he shoves his cock between my thighs.

I freeze, barely breathing, but he's not inside me. My pyjama pants are still on, after all. No, he's just thrust himself into the tight place at the apex of my thighs, the smooth tip of him jutting forward between my legs. The pressure against my pounding pussy is crazy, and an involuntary tremor goes through me, tightening the muscles in my legs.

"Oh, fuck," Elio rasps. "Yeah, squeeze down on me like that."

My muscles leap to obey him before my brain can catch up. I squeeze him, and he groans.

"Perfect," he says, voice thick. He grips my hip possessively, buries his face in the crook of my neck, and then impossibly, *insanely*, he mutters, "Now go to sleep."

Chapter 5

Elio

My Songbird is so damn cute when she tries to act tough. She's all stiff and awkward, trying not to give into her body's exhaustion with me behind her, my cock stuffed between her thighs. But I know she's beyond tired, and slowly but oh so fucking surely, her muscles begin to unlock. Her thighs sag, becoming dead weight around my throbbing cock, creating even more pressure there than there was before. My balls feel all hot and tight, and I can tell I'm leaking precum onto her pretty sunshine-coloured PJs. If I want to get any sleep, I'm going to have to pull out and find another position.

But I don't need to sleep quite yet.

For now, I'm just going to indulge in the mind-bending tension of having my cock this fucking hard, this primed to explode between her legs without actually thrusting against her. Or inside her.

I force my breathing into a deep, even rhythm.

I'll stay still like this for as long as I fucking can.

Only, I start to wonder if I'm wrong, if I can't actually stay still at all, because suddenly there's movement down there. Subtle at first, teasing and tentative. But it's there.

It's Deirdre. She's rubbing herself on me.

My blood turns to magma in my veins, and my chest seizes, but I force myself to stay completely still as if I'm actually asleep.

I honestly can't tell if Deirdre is awake or not. She's been quiet for a bit now and I would have guessed she was asleep. Her movements are sleepy, slow, and dreamlike, although getting just a little faster every second. Her breathing is shallow, but she's not making any other noise. She's not doing anything but rocking her sweet little pussy maddeningly against my pulsing length.

I wonder what she's dreaming about. A thread of violence winds through me because if she's dreaming about someone who makes her want to pump her little pussy then she fucking better be dreaming about me.

If she's actually sleeping, I probably shouldn't touch her. I should just stay like this, hard and throbbing and twitching against her while she does her thing. Let her come to dreamy climax while I fight back the feral urge to yank my glove off with my teeth and plunge my hand beneath the waistband of her pants until I find the swollen, needy clit nestled there.

Fuck me, I should never have let her wear PJs to bed tonight. I should have her naked pussy sliding on me now. Feel her fucking wetness.

I think I can, actually, at least a little bit. She's soaking through the thin silk, damp against me as she hitches her hips back and forth in that tiny, gliding arch of motion.

I'm so fucking hard it's like I never even came tonight.

How the hell does she do this to me? With nothing but a sleepy jiggle of her hips, fully dressed in her loose PJs, she's got me on the verge of spewing my goddamn load. My throat goes dry with the need to rip down her pants and jam myself inside her. Make her bleed all over again.

Because she's small and I'm big and I don't think I could be gentle.

Deirdre's movements change a little. She arches her back slightly, angling her hips differently against my pelvis so that she's grinding her clit in a circular motion against my thickness instead of rocking back and forth. But everything she does is still kind of drowsily unintentional, almost innocent, her body moving in a hypnotic haze.

Fuck it. I'm going to touch her. She's mine whether she's awake or she's asleep.

I lift my hand from her hip, ready to rip my glove off with my teeth after all, when she flinches then instantly goes still, like a rabbit under the gaze of the wolf.

I grin, arousal and triumph swirling together low in my belly, a toxic cocktail.

"Caught you, Songbird."

"I didn't know you were awake!" comes her reply, breathless with guilt. She tries to wriggle away from me, but my glove is off and my hand shoved down her pants before she has a chance to run or hide.

"And I didn't know you were such a good actress," I coo viciously against her ear as my fingertips find her clit. Holy Mother of God, is she ever slippery down there. Her clit is taut and swollen, rich with need under my touch. I stroke it and groan, thrusting my hips forward the way I've been holding myself back from doing until now.

I told myself I wouldn't touch her. Told myself I wouldn't fuck her again tonight.

Told myself that wasn't what she needed.

But maybe I was wrong, seeing how my sweet little liar of a Songbird was wide fucking awake while riding my dick through her PJs just now.

She doesn't just need sleep.

She needs release.

With one swift movement, I've tugged her loose pants off of her and flipped her onto her back. I've got my hands on her thighs and my face buried between her legs before she can even take a breath to try to tell me, "no."

She's gearing up to say it now, though, I can tell. Or something

341

similarly argumentative and disobedient. But I cut her off, drive all words out of her head with a hard, greedy suck on her clit.

She bucks and cries out, her quads straining under my fingers as I suck and circle with my tongue. And then I go lower, deeper, tasting her soaked seam. The slight metal tang of blood beneath her sweetness makes my dick pump uselessly against the air. I dip my tongue all the way inside, needing more of everything. More of her wetness, her blood, more of the little moans tearing out of her throat as if against her own will. Her hands find their way to my head, her fingers burying themselves in my hair. But it's like she can't decide whether to push me away or pull me closer, and instead just digs her fingernails hard against my scalp. That zing of slight pain from her nails goes straight to my balls, and suddenly I can't stand not being inside her. I can't wait another minute. Not even another second.

I rise, leaving her on the trembling edge of orgasm, and drag her ankles up with me, keeping them pinned at my shoulders. At the last second, I lean to the side to flick on the bedside lamp. The first time I took her it was quick and hard, a crash of bodies in the darkness.

This time will probably also still be quick and hard.

But I'm going to watch her fall apart on me in the light this time.

Deirdre whimpers and throws her arms over her eyes, like she can't bear to face the brightness, or me, or maybe her own treacherous desires.

She doesn't have to watch if she doesn't want to. I'll watch enough for the both of us.

On my knees, her silken legs against my chest and shoulders, I line my fat, dripping head up to her sopping entrance. My spine is practically vibrating, my balls hot. My heart feels like it's going to burst right out of my dick at the thought of sliding into that tight flesh I've already torn tonight.

Just the thought of it drives my hips forward violently, and I suck in a scorching breath as Deirdre's channel envelops my tip.

Soon as I'm partway inside her she rips her arms away from her face, blue eyes wide and focused entirely on me. I drive myself

deeper, fascinated by the way her face contorts with pain and pleasure at the same time.

I don't necessarily want to hurt her.

But just like everything else – her body, her pleasure, her soul –
her pain belongs to me.

Only me.

I brace, then give one more brutal thrust until I'm seated all the
fucking way inside.

I could literally come like this. Without even moving, my
agonized tip shoved up against her cervix, her wet walls stretching
and convulsing around me.

Deirdre's head is thrown back, her spine straining, her hands
balled into fists around the bedspread. She's still got her yellow silk
sleep shirt on, and I'm too far-fucking-gone to even attempt to undo
all those buttons. I seize each side of the garment and tug sharply
outwards until silk rips and buttons go flying. And then I can see all
of her, bare and beautiful beneath me, skin so creamy and white with
its delicate freckling. Her nipples are flushed and pointed, and I run
my gaze greedily down her form until it collides with the fiery thatch
of hair between her legs.

I draw my hips back, groaning at the sight of my dick sliding out
of her, completely soaked with her wetness. There's an unmistakeable streak of scarlet in the slick, and I couldn't stop myself even if I'd
wanted to from shunting violently back in.

Deirdre cries out, and I splay a soothing hand – the one with the
glove – across her abdomen. My bare hand grips her right breast,
rubbing her sensitive nipple beneath the puckered surface of my
scarred thumb until her pussy gives a mind-numbingly exquisite
contraction around my shaft. She might be hurting, but she's also still
breathlessly close to coming. I can feel it in the swelling of her cunt,
the tightening of her muscles, desperately milking me even as she
bleeds for me.

I don't even realize I'm speaking, let alone that I've slipped into
Italian, until Deirdre's gaze finds mine, glazed with arousal and

confusion. Every thrust grows fiercer, making her breasts shake and her pussy clamp down as words spill out of me in an unstoppable tumble. Words about how fucking good she is, how bad, how beautiful, how sweet. How I'm going to marry her and fuck her again just like this, with her white dress hitched up high around her hips. I tell her how much I want her, how I need her. How I own her.

I think I maybe even tell her that I love her, but at that point I'm too lost to sensation to notice. The words are breaking apart anyway, splintering in the air until they're nothing but senseless, rasping grunts mingling with Deirdre's high moaning.

I drag my hand down from her breast, drumming a demanding rhythm against her clit with my thumb, and I don't even need to watch her or hear her to know that she's coming. I can fucking feel it. Feel the ecstatic flutter and clench of her pussy, drawing me deeper than I would have thought possible. Her hips rise right off the mattress, and her blue eyes are fucking glued to my snapping pelvis. I follow her gaze to the place where my dick disappears into her quaking body. I don't think there's anything more blisteringly erotic or more painfully heart-searing than watching my blood-stained cock claim her over and over and over.

It makes me fucking feral.

I press down even harder on her clit until she shouts and spasms, twisting like a wild thing beneath me. I'm going to come. I can feel tension warming the base of my spine, my balls drawing tight.

Between bouts of thrusting heat, I feel something suddenly sharp inside. It's almost like dismay. Dismay that I'll never be able to fuck this girl out of my system. Every hit of her just drives me deeper, deeper, fucking deeper, until I don't think I'll ever be able to drag myself back out. I'm lost to her in a way that I've never been lost to anyone.

Frankly, it is fucking terrifying.

I crash my mouth down upon hers, because I need to feel her more, need to feel something other than the overwhelm of my own unmooring obsession. She doesn't even try to fight me. Her mouth opens instantly, submissive for fucking once, and it sends me near out of my mind. I surge into her with my tongue at the exact same moment my cock throbs and then explodes inside her. I shove myself deeper even as I spew, like I'm trying to fucking crawl inside her. And in that bleary madness I decide that it doesn't matter if I'm lost to her, if I'm lost to goddamn everything, because the only thing I'll ever need is right fucking here. Moaning and trembling beneath me, wrapping herself around me half-unwillingly, like a part of her doesn't want me but all of her fucking needs me.

And maybe I'm not even lost.

Honestly, how can I be?

How can I be when my home has become a person and that person is in my fucking bed, my arms, our bodies bound by agony and ecstasy and blood?

I said that to her the first time. *We are bound together, you and I.*

I feel it even more acutely now as I fill her pussy for the second time tonight.

Feel that throbbing connection, the blinding truth of it.

And the truth is that Deirdre O'Malley – soon to be Titone, thank you very fucking much – is mine.

Whether she wants to be or not.

Chapter 6

Deirdre

As much as I don't want to admit it, when Elio comes, there's something violently beautiful about it. About him. Every carved muscle straining beneath scarred skin, the tendons in his neck tight, his face flushed in a way that almost makes him look younger, amplified by the messy fall of rogue locks of hair tumbling over his forehead.

But make no mistake, there is nothing innocent or boyish about this man.

Another aftershock of my orgasm rushes through me, sending a stinging flutter over Elio's hardness. I'm so wet down there, and I'm terrified to look and see how much of it is blood.

I can't believe I let him fuck me again.

Did I even let him? Everything is such a hot, chaotic blur in my mind, pain and pleasure and need and shame all intermingled until it's a swirling mess I can't make sense of. One thing I do remember clearly, though, is the stupid way I rocked against his erection when I thought that he was asleep. My cheeks flood with heated colour at the memory of how brazen the act was. So fucking dumb. Because look where it got me – coming and bleeding on his cock again.

I try to focus hard even as Elio gives one more gentle rock inside me that makes stars explode behind my eyes.

I never said no.

How can I honestly tell Elio I don't belong to him, how can I ever extricate myself from the dark pull of him, if in the heat of the moment I can't even do that much?

Hell, my arms are wrapped around him right now! Like I'm the one pulling him closer instead of the other way around.

I can tell him I don't want him but we'll both know that I'm a liar.

But wanting someone isn't the same as accepting them or loving them. I can want things that are ultimately bad for me. Maybe that's just human nature.

Drugs. Booze. Elio.

All addictive.

All toxic.

Elio braces himself on his elbows, his forearms bracketing my head as he lowers himself, pressing his bare chest to mine. The contrasting hardness of his muscles against the curves of my breasts creates a visceral, primal reaction that makes me clench around him again.

He grunts sharply against my throat in response, dick twitching once inside me before he pulls out.

I hate the whimpering sound I make, but I can't stop it. A rush of air hits my wet flesh and the lack of him makes me feel cold. I shiver.

Then I jerk in surprise as I'm lifted right out of the bed. I clutch Elio's neck, suddenly afraid that I'm going to fall even though I know he'd never drop me.

He strides into the bathroom adjoining his bedroom, bumps the light on with his elbow, then plonks me down on the toilet before retreating a couple of steps to stare at me. At some point, I guess right before he picked me up, he put on his underwear, tight and black.

I realize that I've never actually seen him wear another colour before. Except for his white pocket square that night at the gala, that is.

"Pee," he says, a single word of command.

"I can't... I just... What?" I give my head a shake, trying to come up with something more coherent than that. My brain feels like it's made of pudding or something. My body is still floating on the wobbly wave of the orgasm he just coaxed out of me.

Or demanded from me.

"Go pee."

"No, I heard you," I say, scrubbing the palms of my hands over my eyes. "I just need a second to... recalibrate."

Recalibrate. That's a pretty good word. Maybe my brain isn't fully pudding after all.

"Knocked you off balance, did I?" Elio asks, and I snort, because that's one heck of a euphemism for what just happened.

The pudding feeling is back. I can't come up with a retort. So instead I just turn and take some toilet paper from the roll, folding it over and over until it's a tight rectangle. Then I hold it and stare at it, like it's going to help me somehow.

"Go pee, Songbird," Elio says again after a moment of silence.

"I can't pee when you're standing there staring at me!" I snap, hot and cold prickles of embarrassment running all over my body. I know he's right, though, and that somehow makes this situation even more annoying.

I wouldn't have to be sitting here on the toilet, muscles shaking, blinking like a confused mole rat in the brightness if he hadn't fucked me again.

But he probably wouldn't have fucked me again if I didn't let my arousal take over when I rubbed myself on him before. *Caught you, Songbird.* He said it so... devilishly. I heard the grin in his voice, like he was reveling in discovering my need, my wantonness. Humiliation makes me want to melt into the floor, and that makes it even harder to relax and pee.

"Can you go away please?" I grit out, tugging the sides of my pyjama top together so the garment covers me up. I can't do it up properly, though. Most of the buttons have been popped off, and the ones that remain correspond with torn button holes. It's a shame, and it makes me feel oddly bereft. To see this pretty, cozy, silky thing get ruined.

"Thought I already told you that that isn't happening tonight."

"So you're just going to stand there and stare?"

"Yup. Until you pee. Then I'm going to make sure you wash your hands like a good girl. And then I'm taking you back to bed."

"I don't need a supervisor for that. What the hell? I always wash my hands! If anyone needs to wash their hands, it's you!"

He's still got his mismatched one glove on, one glove off thing happening. He raises his bare hand up to his face and distinctly avoids looking at it, keeping his eyes on me while he inhales hard.

When his hand falls away, it reveals a crooked smirk.

"Don't really want to wash them now."

Jesus Christ.

I guess he's mostly joking, though, because he does stroll over to the sink, tug off his remaining glove, then give his hands a scrub. After drying them, he opens a drawer beneath the sink and pulls out a new pair of leather gloves, pulling them on in quick, practiced movements. Before he closes the drawer again I see a veritable sea of leather in there. There have to be dozens of pairs in there.

"Have you always worn gloves?" I ask, gripping my toilet paper tightly. "Since... Since then? When you were a kid?"

Without his shirt, I can literally see the muscles in his back tighten up in response to my question. I chew my lip, wondering if he's going to be pissed or just ignore my question entirely.

But surprisingly, he does neither of those things. He turns around to face me, leaning his hips back against the counter, crossing his arms over his bare chest.

Wearing only underwear and leather gloves, he should look absolutely ridiculous, but somehow he doesn't, and I don't even understand how that's possible, but there it is.

"No. I didn't start wearing them right away," he says. When he speaks, his voice and words are very even, very careful, not even a hint of emotion bleeding through.

"When, then? Why?"

"We came over here in the summer. August." The scarred side of his face twitches on that last word. If they came here right after the fire, then his mom must have died in August. "My skin was too fucked-up, and it was too hot to wear gloves. And then, even in winter, I didn't wear them because my skin was still a mess and having fabric rubbing on them was annoying. And then it was summer again. Honestly, at that point, it never even really occurred to me to cover them up. I just didn't look at them."

I take a shaky breath, willing myself not to let any tears fill my eyes. But it's hard. Because thinking of someone that young – only fourteen – not even able to bear looking at a part of their own body, makes me want to break down. And I know that the last thing Elio would want is my pity. If he sees that, he'll shut down completely, and I really don't want him to. I want to hear the rest of the story. I want to know what's happened to him, what's made him who he is.

"One of Uncle Vinny's contacts in Montreal who helped us get settled ran this fur and leather shop. Coats and wallets and shit like that. It was our second winter here, and my uncle made Curse and me go over to his buddy's shop to help unload a big batch of new inventory. Even after almost twenty years, I still remember how opening all those boxes made my hands hurt like a motherfucker."

He stops, looking lost in thought for a moment, then shakes his head.

"Anyway, I opened this one box, and it was just pair after pair after pair of men's leather gloves. All black. Big seller for the season, I guess. And I don't even know why, but instead of putting them away like I was supposed to, I took out a pair and put them on."

He pauses again, this time for so long I think he's finished speaking. But then, as if waking from a dream, or coming up for air, he breathes in sharply and continues.

"I was able to look at my own hands for the first time in more than a year," he says, and I don't even dare to breathe for fear of interrupting him. There's an instinct inside me that tells me Elio doesn't tell this story to anybody. Ever. That he might not have even told it to me under different circumstances, or on a different night.

"There was no scarring," he said. He stares down at his hands now, flexing them in the air like he's both looking at them in the present moment and remembering looking at them in the past. "No redness, no memory of fire burned into my skin. There was just this smooth, perfect, opalescent black. Fucking flawless. Like my hands were made of fucking iron or something. Like they weren't even mine."

He lets his hands drop.

"Ricky must have seen something on my dopey face and took pity on my sorry ass, because he let me keep them and gave me a bunch of extra pairs too. I've worn leather gloves every day since then. Does that answer your question?"

"Yes," I say quietly.

"Good. Did you pee yet?"

"No." I sigh.

"Well then." He gives a short nod. "You know what to do."

And I suppose I do. Because he's told me.

I cast my eyes down to my feet on the floor, force myself to relax, and finally pee.

"Good girl," he says, never letting his gaze stray from me as I wipe and then flush. I grimace at the red splotch on the toilet paper as it swirls around the bowl and then disappears.

As promised, Elio makes sure I wash my hands, looming behind me and handing me a towel at the precise moment that I need one. He stays close as I fetch new panties and a fresh pad and then slides into bed behind me. He curls a strong arm around me, hoisting my back against his chest and nestling his chin atop my head.

At least there's no erection pressing between my thighs this time, no unbearable, throbbing arousal inside me, but I still don't think I'll ever be able to sleep like this.

Except I'm absolutely wrong. Because sleep comes for me, and it comes quick.

When I dream, I dream of leather.

Chapter 7

Elio

I've never been one for sleeping in. Never really saw the point. Too much shit to do, I'll sleep when I'm dead, yadda yadda. Besides, the more I sleep, the more chance I have of dreaming, and since my dreams often resemble something akin to one of those medieval paintings of Hell, I like to try to avoid that when I can.

But here? With Deirdre in my bed? It's fucking paradise. I don't want to rouse myself. I just snuggle closer, breathing in the sweet scent of her hair, letting the strands tickle my nose. At some point during the night she's rolled over, and I'm no longer spooning her from behind but facing her head-on. Her slender leg is slung over my hips, her crotch pressed against my rapidly hardening cock as she dozes. I crack my eyes open, almost as if to make sure this shit is actually real.

She's so damn pretty. Her expression is all relaxed and innocent in sleep, soft little breaths puffing in and out, her long lashes casting morning shadows on her freckled cheeks. Her hair is dry now, and honestly it dried kind of fucking wacky, all kinky and tangled, spread all over the pillow. I brush a stray strand away from her face and grin at the way her nose wrinkles up in response to my touch.

353

Yup. Paradise.

I've stayed in bed so long that Rosa comes barging into the room with nary a fucking knock, no doubt assuming I'm already gone by now. Because usually, I am.

She stops short, toting her cart behind her laden with cleaning products and a tray of food for Deirdre's breakfast.

"Oh! Signore Titone! You're still here."

That's about as much of an apology as I'm going to get from that stubborn woman, I guess.

"Not so loud," I growl at Rosa, carefully pulling myself out of the blissful little nest I've been cocooned in with my Songbird until now. When I pull away, Deirdre gives a moan of complaint in her sleep that makes my cock and my heart pound in painful tandem.

She wiggles a bit, scooting forward until she's occupying the warm place I left behind. She grabs onto my pillow, hugging it possessively and burying her face in it before giving a soft snore and then falling back into a deeper sleep.

Well. I'm pretty sure that's the cutest fucking thing I've ever seen. It's spooky, goddamn near unnatural, that someone can be that adorable while simultaneously so fucking beautiful it makes me feel like I'm bleeding somewhere inside.

I grab my pants from where I've left them on the floor last night, yanking them up and pulling the belt tight before I speak to Rosa again. She hasn't moved from her spot just inside the doorway. Her eyes are wrinkled, narrowed, as they swing between Deirdre in the bed and me standing beside it.

She's never seen Deirdre in my bed.

She's never seen any woman in my bed because it does not fucking happen.

"This is where Deirdre will be sleeping from now on," I tell Rosa in as hushed a tone as I can manage. My eyes dart down to Deirdre, but she's still fast asleep, hugging my pillow and kind of making me want to die while she does it.

Rosa's grey brows twitch upward in surprise, but she nods in acknowledgement all the same.

"And I expect you and everyone else to call her Ma'am, Mistress, or Mrs. Titone when you address her. Actually, scratch that. Just Mrs. Titone. *Always* Mrs. Titone."

Rosa doesn't recover from her surprise as quickly this time. She openly gawks at me. I hold her gaze steadily, just fucking daring her to say something about it. She's one brave old lady, but even she knows not to put her foot entirely in it, so she swallows whatever questions she so obviously has and simply says, "*Congratulazioni.*"

"*Grazie,*" I tell her. "The wedding hasn't happened yet, but preparations will begin immediately, so get ready for that. I'll get Valentina on board for all the nitty gritty stuff."

Deirdre gives a snort, as if even in her sleep she has to reject the idea.

"You can put her food there. Don't start cleaning until she wakes up," I tell Rosa, jerking my chin towards the bedside table nearest Deirdre as I scoop up yesterday's shirt and put it back on. I'll shower and get properly dressed later. Right now I've got something important I need to do. In fact, if it wasn't so important, I wouldn't be leaving her side for it.

But I do reluctantly, heading past Robbie at his station on the stairs and going to my office on the first floor. I'm not expecting to see anybody there, but Curse is outside the door, and unlike me he looks freshly showered.

"What is it?" I ask as I open the door into my office. He follows and shuts it behind me.

"I texted you."

I don't think I looked at my phone once last night. Too preoccupied with getting my Songbird settled.

And then fucking her.

It's still in my back pocket from yesterday so I pull it out. There are two unread messages from Curse.

"You gonna tell me what they say or do I have to read them in front of you?" I ask, ignoring the text notifications in favour of flipping over to my security camera app so I can see what Deirdre's doing. She's still asleep, and I watch her unmoving form on the screen as Curse responds.

"Last night's message isn't much," he says. "Just letting you know that Enzo and I took the bodies to Darragh's warehouse like you wanted. The one from this morning is more important." He raises his hands, as if to crack his knuckles, a habit of his, but he can't because there's something in his hand. A smooth, white envelope.

"What's that?" I ask, seating myself at the leather chair behind my desk and putting down my phone.

"This is what the second text was about. It came this morning via messenger. They left it at the security booth at the gate. I haven't opened it yet. I brought it straight here. But based on the writing on the front of the envelope I've gotta assume it's from Darragh."

I straighten up, reaching for the envelope which Curse hands over. There's not much on the front of the envelope. It just says, *A chara.*

"What the fuck is a chara?" I ask Curse.

"I looked it up. Apparently, it's Irish for, 'My friend.' It's a common way to start a letter."

Well, if it's Irish, that explains why he thought it came from Darragh, then. Especially if he found the bodies of his soldiers and is sending us back some kind of message. Although the whole "my friend" thing makes about zero sense. I rip open the envelope, scanning the contents of the paper inside.

It doesn't take long. There's only one line of text, and even though it's in English this time, it makes even less sense than the outside of the envelope. I read it out loud so that Curse can hear and maybe provide me some kind of clue about what Darragh might be on about.

"Why can you never iron a shamrock?"

"Uh. Don't know. Never thought about it. It would probably just melt or disintegrate or something," Curse says. He's looking at me kind of oddly, like I'm the insane one instead of dipshit Darragh sending me this mumbo jumbo. Curse eyes my dishevelled hair, my unshaven jaw, the wrinkles in my shirt, and frowns.

"Don't give me that fucking look. That's what the letter says," I explain, flashing the paper at him. He leans over my desk to peer at it with dark, long-lashed eyes. He really did get all of Mamma's good lucks. She had eyes like that too.

"Oh. Huh." He straightens back up, lifting his hands and successfully cracking his tattooed knuckles this time. The motion makes every letter of our mamma's name flex across his skin.

I blink, realizing for the first time that both Deirdre and I had mothers with names that start with F. Fiona and Florencia.

A sign if I ever saw one.

"Sounds like a riddle."

I glance at the paper again and nod, agreeing with him. Then I throw the paper down on my desk in annoyance.

"See, this is why people call him Mad Darragh. Because he's always doing weird fucking shit like this."

Well, that and the fact that he once made another man eat his own severed balls. And not even right after cutting them off, either. It's not like he sliced them off and then told the poor shmuck to open wide, because honestly, I wouldn't be surprised if some of the guys working for me had done some shit like that. It's not out of the realm of normalcy in our fucked-up world. But that's not what Darragh did. He left the guy there bleeding to go cook him a whole-ass meal. Then he brought it back piping hot, letting the guy think he might actually live, like the stew was a kind of olive branch.

Except it was *soupe aux testicules*. Or however the fuck you'd say that in Irish.

Bon appétit.

"Sending another boss a riddle instead of a real man-to-man conversation, or a proper business meeting. The fuck is this shit?" I grumble to myself as I spin my chair over to my computer. I open a search engine and type in the words of the riddle.

Thankfully, the answer pops up right away, which means at least it's a real riddle with a solution out there somewhere instead of some nonsensical bullshit pulled out of the murk of Darragh's brain.

My brother and I both stare at the riddle's answer on the screen.

Because you shouldn't press your luck.

"What do you think it means?" Curse asks.

"Fuck if I know," I reply, rubbing the scarred side of my jaw viciously. I've attended a few university classes recently with Deirdre, but none of them were in literature or philosophy. Or psychology, which is probably more applicable in this situation anyway.

I lean back in my chair, drumming my fingers hard against the arms.

At first glance, an obvious interpretation is that Darragh is telling me not to press my luck. Which is... fucking absurd. I've got more territory than him, more men, more money, more firepower. I'm not the kind of man you send threats to and live.

But then there's that address of *A chara.* My friend. Is that sarcasm? Or some kind of peace offering? Maybe he's calling me his friend and admitting in some roundabout way that he knows he pressed his luck, and plans to back off now? Having three bodies dumped at your door can make you look at your mistakes with fresh eyes, that's for fucking sure.

I give up on trying to figure it out. Having me spin my wheels and stew over this nonsense would probably make Darragh's dick hard if he knew about it, and I'm not going to give him the satisfaction.

Instead, I'm going to bring him a letter of my own.

Hand-fucking-delivered.

"We're gonna send Darragh a message," I tell Curse, and my loyal younger brother doesn't even bat an eye.

"Guns? Bombs? How many men you want?" he asks, already making plans.

"Nope. None of that. Just a letter. Paper. That's it."

His brow furrows.

"What, you want anthrax in it or something?"

"Literally just a letter. No assassination shit."

Curse crosses his arms, nodding slowly, digesting.

"Alright. So what do you want it to say? You gonna send him back another riddle?"

"No," I say, a grin tugging at my mouth. "My engagement announcement."

Chapter 8

Elio

Curse and I find out pretty quick that we're both shit at trying to write this kind of stuff. After squinting and squabbling over examples of engagement announcements online and nearly wearing out the delete key on my keyboard, we give up on trying to get this done by ourselves.

He's a hitman and I'm a mafia underboss. Not exactly prime examples of excellent wedding industry copywriters.

"We need Valentina," I say, and though my brother doesn't show emotion much I swear that he looks relieved.

I grab my phone off my desk and use voice command to call our cousin.

She answers on the first ring.

"Where are you? Where the hell have you been?" her high voice squawks into my ear.

Oh. Right. I disappeared up north to deal with Deirdre's ex Brian and then got stuck there due to the snow. When I came back, I was completely focused on Deirdre and then the chaos that unfolded at her mamma's grave. Meanwhile Valentina had been calling and texting me most of that time, asking me where I'd disappeared to. Uncle Vinny didn't call me, but he didn't need to. I know he doesn't like when Curse and I jet off without telling him what's what and he'll be waiting for an update.

Well, he's going to get one, alright. Soon as we get this announcement out to the media outlets.

But we need to actually write it first.

Since Valentina is one of approximately three females alive on this planet that I actually give a fuck about, and more like a little sister to me than a cousin, I let the rudeness of her greeting slide.

"I'm at home with Curse. Get over here," I tell her.

I hang up and toss the phone down. I know she's going to want to complain or ask questions or argue and I have no patience for that right now.

I also know that if I tell her to come, she'll come.

Curse disappears for a bit to chat with Enzo, my head of security, and update him on what's going on with the letter we received and how we're handling it. While I wait for Valentina, I occupy myself by watching Deirdre sleep. I open the security app on my computer instead of just my phone this time, blowing up the image of her snoozing away on the bigger screen.

It's getting close to 10am now. But after everything that happened to my Songbird last night and the adrenaline that's likely left her rung out like a rag, I wouldn't be surprised if she sleeps well past noon today. Maybe even later.

She's still curled into the place I left behind. I wonder if, at least in sleep, she misses me.

About twenty minutes after I make the phone call, the door bursts open and Valentina sweeps in, followed by Curse. For somebody so damn short, she sure does have presence, our cousin. Must be a Titone thing. While Curse and I got height from our papà's side, Uncle Vinny is our maternal uncle, and like his daughter he isn't necessarily blessed in the height department. But it doesn't matter one iota, because Vincenzo Titone fills a fucking room like you've stuffed a bull into a custom Italian suit and unleashed him on civilized society.

Valentina comes to a moody stop in front of my desk and starts yanking at a ridiculous number of shiny metal fasteners and buttons on a long, army-green coat. Once it's off she tosses it down onto one of the leather armchairs on the other side of my desk, revealing leggings and a bright pink sweater.

"What's going on with your hair?" I ask her. It's wet and clipped messily on the top of her head. I wouldn't normally care, but that's very unusual for Valentina, whose hair is always perfectly coiffed. Going out in public, or even just to my place with kind of fucked-up hair means something's off with her, and I need her on her A game to get this engagement announcement just right.

"You tell me," she says, blowing out a harsh sigh through glossy lips and planting her hands on her hips. "You're the one who dragged me out of the salon before Antonio could start blow-drying it."

"Well, I needed you for something more important than salon shit." I click out of the security all on my computer and re-open the page of engagement announcement examples. The cupcake-sweet fonts swirl in front of my eyes, incomprehensible in their flourishes. "I need you to help me write an engagement announcement."

She tenses, but is quick to relax and not let it show. I see it, though.

"I thought we weren't announcing anything until after my birthday in the summer," she says. "When did that change?"

Oh. Right. Her engagement to that slimeball Dario Fabbri.

"Not your engagement," I clarify. "Mine."

She doesn't try to hide her reaction this time. Her shiny lips part in surprise, her eyes going so wide that I can see white all around the cat-like golden brown of her irises.

"What the fuck?" she breathes. "Papà hasn't mentioned anything! When did this happen?"

"Last night," I reply. "And he didn't mention anything because he doesn't know yet."

An *oh, shit* kind of look comes over her face.

"You're engaged to someone and he doesn't know about it," she repeats, and I can practically hear the panicky grinding of the gears in her head. "Is it at least someone he'd approve of?"

I shrug my good shoulder.

"Unlikely. But I approve and that's all that fucking matters."

She takes out the clip on the top of her head, letting down hair made a much darker blonde by the moisture in it. She shakes her head while finger-combing the wet waves.

"You're so fucking hard-headed, Elio," she says. "You know as well as I do the marriage part means shit and a man like you can have whoever he actually wants outside of that. Just marry somebody Papà approves of and then have your *goomah* on the side. The way God intended," she adds with a sardonic lift of her eyes heavenward.

A fucking *goomah*? She wants me to marry someone proper and then keep Deirdre on the side as my mistress?

Not happening.

There's only one woman who could get me to stand at the end of that aisle and wait for her to walk down it. The thought of marrying someone else and keeping my Songbird as some sidepiece in a house I don't even live in full-time makes my skin crawl and my stomach seize and, honestly, just fuck every possible version of that scenario.

"No." The word comes out of my throat sounding kind of charred. Valentina must be able to see how pissed-the-fuck-off I am, because she immediately backs down.

"It's OK. You don't have to give me that look. I'm going to help you," she says. "At least one of us is going to get to marry who we want, I guess."

I know she doesn't want to marry Dario. I wouldn't either, in her alarmingly high-heeled shoes. But for the first time it occurs to me that there may actually be somebody else she'd had in mind.

"You got a boyfriend?" I ask. Curse cocks his head and peers closely at her from his place by the office door.

"Nope. Just a fiancé," she retorts, rolling her eyes and flashing the garish pink diamond ring on her left hand. "You know Papà never let me date anybody. There's no one else."

I nod. As much as she may not show it with her sailor's mouth, I know that she respects me. She wouldn't lie to me.

"So, how about you, then? Who's the lucky lady?" she asks, seating herself across from me. "Anyone I know?"

"Oh, you know her," I say with a smirk. "Prettiest little Songbird you ever did see."

She collapses against the back of the chair in astonishment, like my words have physically shoved her.

"No fucking way. Deirdre?" she breathes. "You seriously weren't kidding when you said Papà wouldn't approve!"

But Valentina's always been one quick to recover. She sits up straight again, then leans forward.

"She's got nothing, Elio. No money, no alliances, no assets. *Nothing*."

"She won't need any of that shit. She's got me."

"No, no, I know." She raises her hands in a placating sort of gesture. "I'm not saying that in a disparaging way. I actually really like Deirdre and I'd way rather it be her than somebody like Nat Rizzo. I'm just kind of... examining the situation out loud."

She goes quiet for a moment, then says, "Isn't Darragh Gowan still trying to get to her?"

"Yup." I say.

"Some of his soldiers caused a scene last night. We dropped their bodies off to Darragh early this morning," Curse adds from behind her. He leaves his station by the door and sits down in the other chair across from my desk.

"Shit," Valentina whispers. It's hard to tell with the makeup, but I'm pretty sure I can see some of the blood drain out of her face. "I guess she doesn't really have *nothing*, then. Because she's got one hell of an enemy."

I already know what she's thinking. It's the same shit I'm going to hear from Uncle Vinny when he finds out about all this. That

Deirdre isn't worth it, that no amount of tight Irish pussy is worth risking a fucking war with Mad Darragh.

But when Valentina speaks again, her voice firm with conviction, her words surprise me.

And I have to admit, they kind of make me proud, too.

"Good," she says with a decisive nod. "You'll marry her and in doing so can give her the protection of our resources, our name. She'll be a Titone and nobody will wanna fuck with her."

I give her a crooked smile.

"Anybody ever tell you that you're real fucking smart?" I ask her.

She snorts.

"Only Mamma every damn day of my life." She frowns prissily in an imitation of my Zizi, Aunt Carlotta. "'A man doesn't need a wife with a clever mind and a filthy mouth, Valentina! He needs one who knows how to make decent *pasta alla norma!*'"

"*Pasta alla norma* is pretty fucking good," I reply.

"Well, maybe if I ever learn how to make it, I can teach your wife to make it too," she says sourly.

Your wife.

Fuck, does it ever feel good to hear somebody else say it. And now I can't stop picturing Deirdre in my kitchen, lovingly cooking me a meal. Not that she'll ever have to do that if she doesn't want to. I've got Rosa and other people for that.

But I still can't shake the image. My sweet little Songbird stirring a pot, maybe even in an apron or some cute shit like that.

As long as she doesn't put poison in it, we'll be goddamn golden.

"Deal," I tell her. "But first we gotta make everything official. Starting with this." I jab a black finger at my computer screen, gesturing at the various white and pink and red rectangles with their fancy writing. The computer screen looks like Valentine's Day threw up on it, and then I blink, because Valentine's Day is actually really soon, and for the first time in my life I actually might want to do something to mark the day.

Elio Titone celebrating Valentine's Day. Goddamn elementary school shit. It's so fucking saccharine it makes my teeth hurt.

And I don't even care. Because Deirdre is mine in every single way and that means she's my valentine, too.

"Alright," Valentina says. "What kind of announcement are we talking about, anyway? The wording is going to vary depending on if it's something for, like, social media versus an engagement announcement that goes into a newspaper."

I stare at her flatly. Social media? Is she for real?

Not that I don't have accounts, because I do. Anonymous burner accounts I use to keep track of Deirdre's profiles. But she's not very active online, so I don't use them much, anyway.

"Right," my cousin says, reading my look. "So newspaper-style, then?"

"Yes," I confirm. "We'll be sending it out to all our contacts in the media as soon as it's done. Get them to plaster press releases all over their website homepages and get it printed in tomorrow's paper editions."

She nods, all business, then grabs some spare paper and a pen from my desk, beginning to make notes.

"Typically, newspaper announcements like that are from the point of view of the parents," she explains. "Like, *So and So are pleased to announce the engagement of their daughter.* That kind of thing."

"No. Not like that," I say. I don't want Deirdre's papà or mine listed, because neither of them has a name worthy of being printed beside hers. And I doubt my Uncle Vinny and Zizi, who are essentially my adoptive parents, will want to be listed when they don't know this thing is even being written in the first place.

"Make it from my perspective," I tell Valentina. "*Elio Titone is pleased to announce his engagement to Deirdre O'Malley...* Is there a better word than pleased?"

Pleased sounds too... lame. I'm pleased when one of my capos follows my instructions to the letter, or when the car shop does a great job detailing one of my vehicles. There's something too distant and sterile about it to be used in the context of marrying Deirdre.

"Hmm," Valentina says. "How about thrilled? *Elio Titone is thrilled to announce-*"

"No," I cut her off. "That makes me sound fucking giddy."

Valentina purses her lips and taps her pen against her chin.

"Excited? Delighted?"

"Definitely not excited," I groan. If anyone serious in this city reads the words *Elio Titone is excited* in their morning paper they'll probably think I'm on meth or something. "Delighted is a maybe. But it's not quite right, either."

"We could leave out any adjectives entirely," Valentina proposes. "*Elio Titone announces his engagement to Deirdre O'Malley.*"

It feels a little cold, but maybe that's a good thing. I don't need to spill my guts all over the local papers and tell them about the ooey gooey good feelings I seem to have developed for my Songbird.

Yeah, that's probably the best option. I'm about to tell her that when Curse suddenly pipes up from his seat.

"What about honoured?"

Elio Titone is honoured to announce his engagement to Deirdre O'Malley.

Honoured.

Like something sacred has been bestowed upon me and I'm down on my knees with the force of that grace.

"It's fucking perfect. Write that down," I say to Valentina, and she dutifully does so.

I cast my eye over at Curse, who's gone silent again, wondering just when my quiet, violent brother became so eloquent. I guess it's all those books he reads. Though he probably reads about a thousand words for every one he speaks.

"Alright, how do we want to handle the parents thing, then? Do you want anyone else listed on here, or just you and Deirdre?" Valentina asks.

"Our mamas," I say firmly. "I want both their names on there.

But make sure you write Florencia Titone instead of her married name."

Unfortunately, there's not an easy way to do that for Deirdre's side. I could have her mother referred to by her maiden name to avoid associating her with that piece of shit O'Malley, but Deirdre doesn't have another last name to use yet, so the name O'Malley is going to have to be on there anyway.

"Alright," Valentina says. "Careers are usually included. What do you want to be listed as, Mister Boss Man?"

"Just put me down as a purveyor of multiple business interests," I instruct her. "And mention Deirdre's music. And her academic stuff."

"Done. Is there a wedding date?"

"As soon as possible," I answer instantly.

"OK... That's gonna look a bit weird," she says. "Ending off this nice formal notice with *wedding as soon as possible!* It feels kind of frantic. If you don't have a specific date, you can just state the season. Like, winter of next year or something."

"Winter of *this* year."

I hadn't realized Valentina was chewing gum, but she just about chokes on it when I say that.

Coughing and banging on her chest, she stares at me with watery eyes.

"You've got to be fucking kidding me," she rasps. "Miserable Ontario weather aside, there's technically only, like, six weeks left of winter. It's practically February!"

"How about the last day of February? That should give you enough time to prepare," I tell her.

"Too soon," my cousin says stubbornly. "Venues book out a year in advance and-"

"Valentina," I interrupt, and there's an edge of warning in my voice that she recognizes. She instantly stills and listens.

"You will get this done," I tell her, my words very slow, crisp, and even. "This timeline is of paramount importance and I will not accept failure from anyone. I don't care which venue you pick – I'd marry Deirdre in the middle of the fucking dump – but she deserves something nice so you had better *make it nice*. I don't care who the venue has to bump to make room for us, and if they don't wanna play ball then you can kindly remind them that Titones don't play with balls, we play with bullets. You got that?"

"I do," she says succinctly.

"Then it's decided," I say. "Last day of next month. February twenty-eighth"

"It's a leap year this year," Curse says.

"Why the fuck do you even know that?" I ask him, baffled. "You've just got all the answers over there today. What'd we even call Valentina for? You probably could have drafted this entire announcement and planned the whole damn wedding yourself."

He shrugs, and I know I'm not going to get any more out of him, so I turn my attention back to Valentina who's currently putting the finishing touches on the engagement announcement.

February twenty-ninth. Celebrating our anniversary is going to be weird, but I kind of like that we're getting married on a day that doesn't even exist most years. Like the date conjured itself just for us, pulled itself out of thin fucking air. It feels lucky in a distinctly Irish way.

"Is there something special about leap years in Ireland?" I muse out loud, not to anyone in particular, but Valentina picks up her phone to check a search engine.

"Apparently February twenty-ninth is called Bachelor's Day, or Ladies' Privilege," she says, reading from her screen. "I guess it's a day where women ask the men to marry them instead of the other way around."

What kind of dickless wonder waits so fucking long that his woman feels the need to propose?

I snort at what Deirdre is going to think about all this. She probably wouldn't ask me to marry her in a thousand fucking years, but it doesn't really matter at this point. Although it does remind me that I need to get the ring sorted out. I may have bluntly informed her of our impending nuptials instead of actually popping the question, but she's still going to get a ring. And then there's the wedding bands too.

I frown, trying to figure out how the hell I'll wear a ring with my screwed-up hands. I think a ring will probably irritate the scar tissue, plus no one will be able to see it under the gloves anyway. And I fucking hate looking at my bare hands, so wearing an adornment on one of them that will specifically draw my attention feels kind of stupid.

I guess I could just not wear a ring. But I can feel my mouth pulling downwards even further in response to that because I do not fucking like that option.

Hmm.

"What is it?" Valentina asks, no doubt noting my displeased expression. "What part do you want me to change?"

I was so lost in thought that I hadn't even realized she was reading the final engagement announcement out loud.

"I wasn't listening," I tell her with a dismissive wave of my hand. "Start again."

She rolls her eyes but does so, clearing her throat before she reads from the beginning.

"Elio Titone of Toronto, son of Florencia Titone, is honoured to announce his engagement to Deirdre O'Malley of Toronto, daughter of Fiona O'Malley. Mr. Titone is a purveyor of multiple business interests, and Miss O'Malley is an accomplished violinist currently completing her Bachelor of Arts in Music at the University of Toronto, due to graduate with honours next spring. The wedding is set for February twenty-ninth of this year."

"Good," I say. "Now send that out to every one of our media contacts. I want this fucking everywhere. I don't want a single person in this city opening their phone or their newspaper and not seeing this first-fucking-thing."

"Got it," Valentina says, rising. "Can I go up and see Deirdre? If we're going to pull this together by the end of next month we need to get started today."

"No. She's sleeping and she needs her rest," I reply. "And she has school tomorrow. You can come by after her classes to talk about whatever it is you need from her. But don't bug her with too much event-planning stuff. She has classes and music to focus on. You take care of all the details. You're good at that shit."

"Yeah, I'm good at it, but most girls still want a say in their own wedding," Valentina says, giving me an odd look.

"I'm not entirely sure you're going to find that to be the case," I respond dryly, standing up.

A mild way of implying that if Deirdre had her say, there wouldn't be a wedding at all.

"I have so many questions," my cousin says, rising and grabbing her coat. "You know that, right? Alright. Whatever. I'll get this started." She flaps the paper at me, then shoves it under one arm so she can do up the thousand-and-one fasteners on her weird coat.

Curse gets up too, opening the office door for her. Valentina walks through it, already typing furiously on her phone, paper still pinned under her arm.

"I'll be back tomorrow," she calls as she hustles away to the front of the house. A minute later, an email notification pings on my phone and computer at the same time. It's from Valentina and it contains the digital copy of the engagement announcement she just wrote by hand on paper.

I print it off and fold it very carefully so that I don't crease a single word. At the last moment, I take out my wax warmer from a drawer in my desk. It's a small heated plate with a spoon that sits on top that you can melt the wax in. Takes a little longer to set up, but it beats holding an open flame in my hand while dripping wax onto paper.

Once the crimson wax is the right consistency, I pour the glossy, honey-thick liquid onto the paper then stamp it with the Titone seal.

It's the exact same thing I did with the contract I signed with O'Malley a year and a half ago. Feels symbolic.

"Alright. We've got our letter for Darragh," I say to Curse. "Time to go."

Chapter 9

Elio

Curse, Enzo, and I all ride together. Curse drives, Enzo is in the back, and I sit in the passenger seat, idly running the edge of the sealed paper back and forth over my lips. It starts snowing as we wind through Toronto's streets, the sky looking as opaque as grey cotton.

One of Darragh's main meeting spots is the *Briar and Boar* pub. It's in the heart of Darragh's territory, and I keep my eyes focused outside the bullet-proof windows for signs of problems to come. But I don't see any yet. Just legit citizens going about their daily lives, walking down slippery sidewalks and shovelling shop entrances, oblivious to the parallel universe of mob shit happening right on top of them.

For the briefest flicker of a moment, I wonder what it's like to be them. To have your biggest problem be something like, I don't even know, paying your rent on time or something. It always seemed kind of dull. Safer, maybe, but boring as hell. Then I wonder what would have happened if I'd met Deirdre some other way. If I was just a normal dude who saw her walking down the street one day. If I hadn't heard her play in that first moment, would I have even looked at her twice?

See, this is why I don't engage in *what if?* scenarios. They're pointless and they make you feel weird shit. What if Mamma was still alive? What if we'd never left Sicily? What if Uncle Vinny got killed when Curse and I were kids and our family just imploded instead of rising to power the way we have?

What if Deirdre was under Darragh's control even now, abandoned by her father, trapped somewhere on the other side of the city, and I didn't even know about it? Or care?

Shit's enough to turn a man inside fucking out.

I almost crush the paper in my fist and force myself to relax.

Lowering the paper into my lap, I run my thumb over the hardened seal. All those other scenarios don't matter. Every single thing that's happened in my life, both the garbage things and the good ones, have led me to Deirdre and that's what I hold onto now.

"We're here."

Briar and Boar is situated on a fairly narrow one-way side street occupied by big, old brick houses. I know every house and building on this whole street is owned by Darragh and his men. As far as I know, most of them are used for housing, either for Darragh's crew or maybe being rented out to regular folks. The only business on this snowy, tree-lined street is *Briar and Boar*, marked by a big green sign with gold lettering and an image of a boar with a rose in its mouth.

Curse parallel parks in one of the few spots left on the street, just outside the pub, and we all get out. I ignore the city parking metre, but Curse silently slips some coins into it. He's got a much more meticulous and dutiful sort of personality than I do, and I don't bother saying anything to him about it.

At least, not until Enzo starts in on him about how there's an app for that now and you can just pay online.

"Are you two fucking for real? The ins and outs of the Toronto parking situation is not why we are here," I snap.

"Sorry, Boss," Enzo says quickly. "Just trying to be efficient. I just figured we don't need bylaw crawling up our asses when we're trying to get some real shit done."

"Tell me how opening a fucking app and then putting all your credit card info in is more efficient than shoving a coin into a slot?" I ask him. "And tell me exactly which bylaw officer is going to be brave enough or paid enough or dumb enough to come anywhere near my fucking ass?"

Silence.

"That's what I thought. Let's go."

Enzo and Curse fall into step, flanking me as we head to the big, heavy wooden door. I pull it open one-handed, keeping my paper safe in my other hand. Enzo catches the edge of the door from behind me, holding it open so Curse and I can go through before letting it fall closed with a gentle, wooden thud behind him.

I've never been to Dublin, but I imagine this must be at least what some of the places there look like. The floor, tables, and chairs are made of dark wood, the cushions and benches a rich, forest green. Warm golden light pours over the shiny surface of the bar, illuminating countless taps and bottles in front of an exposed brick wall.

Between the bar and the bricks stands a young woman, her black hair tied in a tight bun on top of her head. Her back is to us as she polishes a glass, but even from behind I recognize her instantly as Deirdre's friend Willow Callahan. I've seen them together before, back when I watched my Songbird from the shadows. There are pictures of them online together too. Willow is the much more social media-active of the two of them, posting photos both of Deirdre and herself, but since I took Deirdre Willow's accounts have gone radio silent.

The pub has only just opened and we're the only ones here with Willow. She doesn't turn to look at us but she must hear us come in, because she calls out, "Sit anywhere!"

"We're not here to eat," I reply. "We're here to see Darragh."

She tenses, then turns, a questioning look on her face.

When she sees us, sees *me*, her expression turns to one of shock. Maybe even a little fear. The glass slips from her hands and shatters.

She stares, just for a moment, with her mouth hanging open. Then her green eyes flash with something that looks a hell of a lot like anger. She slams her mouth shut and barrels out from behind the bar at frankly impressive speed, and I wonder if this is who Darragh's got on security now, because it looks like she plans on tackling me.

Curse instantly steps between us. Willow's all of about five-foot-two, but she could have a knife or something on her, and those green eyes tell me she means business.

If she has a weapon beside the rage sparking in that gaze, she never gets to use it. A man comes out from what I assume must be the kitchen area, his eyes huge before he lopes across the pub to grab Willow by both arms, restraining her from behind. I recognize the man too, from a social media post Willow made last year on his birthday. He's her father, Paddy Callahan. The post had included a picture of him blowing out the candles on a cake, and I'd only really stopped to look at the image because Deirdre had been in the background, a smiling smudge surrounded by a halo of orange.

Willow tugs against her papà's hold, staring past Curse and directly at me.

"Where's Deirdre?" she demands, practically spitting. "Is she still at your place? Is she safe?"

Her papà goes so red with rage I think his head is about to explode from his daughter's audacity.

"Shut yer mouth, Willow," he hisses. "My apologies, gents."

"No apology required," I say smoothly, honestly kind of amused by this whole thing. A smirk tugs at one side of my mouth, and I'm already savouring what I'm about to say next. "It's only polite, after all, to enquire about a man's fiancée."

Willow's so startled by that last word that all the fight drains out of her for a second. She pales, then goes slack and still in Paddy's hold.

"Fi... fiancée?!" she echoes.

But then she's back at it with twice the energy, pulling against Paddy's arms and swearing. But her papà has got at least eighty pounds on her. He's got a big gut but also big fucking shoulders and he tilts them, dragging Willow backwards towards the room he first emerged from a minute ago. It's one of those swinging doors, so he just ploughs back-first through it, yanking his daughter along with him until they're out of sight.

But not out of earshot. I can hear them through the door. Paddy's Irish accent gets thick in his fury.

"Question Elio Titone in this feckin' pub? Are ye completely mad, ye eejit? Or just daft? Darragh will have yer empty head if one of the Titones don't blow it clean off yer shoulders first!"

"He's got my best friend! Did you hear him call her his fiancée?! I need to know what the hell is happening!"

"Ye don't need to know nothin'! All ye need to do is pack yer feckin' bags. Ye're going to stay with my sister just like I knew ye should have when all this shite started with the O'Malleys!"

"Oh, *fuck* no! You can't just ship me off to Ireland!"

"I can and I will! And don't even give me that look, lass, because I'm one feckin' hair away from sending you to a bloody convent instead of just to stay with yer cousins and aunt Orla! No, not one more word!"

I'm pretty sure Willow does have another word for him, more than one, in fact, and choice ones too, but I stop listening because someone else has entered from another door at the other end of the pub.

He looks like a fucking Viking, a mountain of a man with a close-cropped ginger beard and thick red hair pulled back into a ponytail. A black T-shirt is stretched to its absolute limits across his barrel of a chest, and his trunk-like arms are criss-crossed with tattoos.

"Darragh sends his greetings," the giant says. "He's currently engaged downstairs, but will be finished shortly. If you'll follow me, he will receive you in his office."

He crosses back to the door he emerged from and yanks it open, revealing a set of stairs going down. I can practically hear Enzo and Curse running scenarios through their heads. Neither of them want to get cornered in a basement shootout or some shit like that. Personally, I don't really give a fuck. I wonder briefly about fire exits, then stride towards the door, Enzo and Curse pulling up the rear.

The Viking leads us downwards. The old wooden stairs creak under the weight of four big men clomping down them. But, somewhat surprisingly, it isn't all dank and dark down here. Wrought-iron lanterns, the kind you'd expect to see outside a building, are nailed to the walls, casting warm light down the stairs. At the bottom there's nothing but a door. I can't quite tell what it's made of. It looks like it could be highly polished wood, but it's onyx-black.

When the big ginger guy opens it, I realize that whatever it's made of, it must be soundproofed, because noise pours out like someone's just switched on a very loud radio.

I know that Darragh runs several clubs and gambling halls, and if his office is also here then I wonder if this one is his main hangout. By what's going on inside this swanky space, you'd have no idea it was only mid-morning up above. It looks like it should be midnight. Men in various forms of dress, all the way from three-piece suits to denim and T-shirts like our bearded escort, are scattered throughout the room, resting on leather chairs or leaning over cards tables, most of them with pints of beer at their elbows. There are women, too, some of them perched in short dresses on the knees of the card-playing men, others weaving to and fro with trays of drinks and snacks balanced on manicured fingers. The sounds are raucous, hearty laughter and insults lobbed back and forth like balls in both English and Irish.

But the men chatting and gambling aren't the main source of the noise in the room. That comes from the furthest corner, opposite from us, where a boxing ring has been set up. There's a bit of a crowd gathered around it, but it's raised off the floor so that over the heads of the on-lookers it's easy to see who's fighting.

I don't recognize one of the men, the one currently taking a pummeling. But I sure do recognize the one doling out punches so fast they almost look frenzied. Because that right there is the head of the Irish mob in Toronto and the current bane of my existence. Darragh fucking Gowan.

"Darragh."

I don't say it loudly, but there's a dangerous hardness in my voice that makes it carry. It slices through the room, silencing men as it goes as surely as if I'd slit their fucking throats. Every speechless head in the room swivels our way until the only one not looking at me is Darragh himself. Even his opponent has cranked his head towards us, which earns him a blow to the temple that topples him. He crumples to the mat, and Darragh finally looks up. From across the room, our gazes lock.

And then the fucker grins at me, waving jauntily like I didn't dump the bodies of three of his men on his doorstep this morning.

He leaps out of the ring with the grace of a cat, prowling through a silent crowd that parts easily for him. He's shirtless, his scarred and tattooed skin shining with sweat. He runs a raw-knuckled hand through tousled hair, the damp locks a dark red colour somewhere between bronze and deep copper.

I've never actually been this close to Darragh. I know who he is, and what he looks like, but as he comes to a stop before me, this is the first time we've actually spoken face to face like this.

He's about as tall as I am, though leaner, his muscles hard, veins and arteries all juiced up and popping along his long-limbed frame. The smooth, clean shave of his face lays bare the hard lines of his jaw and the high, angular cheekbones that jut out beneath a fucking weird pair of eyes.

It takes me a second to pinpoint what's so unnerving about his gaze. It isn't just the relentless, calculating probe of it, because I'm used to that kind of thing. I've been keeping my chin up under hard stares like that since before I entered fucking puberty. No, there's something else disorienting about Darragh's gaze, something that makes me feel like I don't know where I'm supposed to look to maintain eye contact, and I suddenly realize it's because his eyes are two different colours. His right eye is dark brown, his left hazel-green. The lighter coloured greenish one has an inky splotch at the bottom of the iris that makes it look like his pupil is bleeding out into the rest of his eye.

"Greetings, gents," Darragh says, still panting slightly from the exertion of the boxing match, his breath rasping around his slight Irish accent. "Welcome to my humble abode."

And there's that manic fucking grin again. It doesn't reach his lopsided eyes.

I don't return the smile. I don't know what kind of games Darragh's playing and I'm not interested in feigned pleasantries.

"Where's your office? We have business to discuss," I say.

"Straight to business. Don't know why I expected any less from a Titone. Come on, then."

He turns and leads us through the room, past the boxing ring, and through another door. The four of us enter an office, followed by the big bearded guy who closes the door behind us.

The office is a lot simpler and less luxurious than the big gambling room we've just come from. The green leather of the armchairs looks comfortably worn, the wooden desk taking up the centre of the room old and kind of rickety. There's an antique-looking bar cart in the corner of the room, and even the bottles stacked there can't exactly be called new, because most of them are aged whiskey, brandy, or port.

Considering how filthy rich Darragh is, all this old scratched-up shit throws me for a bit of a loop.

But I'm not here to analyze Darragh's interest in moth-eaten furniture. I'm here to tell the bastard to back the fuck off my bride.

Darragh swivels to face us, leaning his hips back against his desk.

"Got your message this morning," he drawls. "Bit dramatic, don't you think?"

I can already tell this conversation is going to be infuriating.

"No more dramatic than sending your men after us with their fucking guns blazing," I reply, keeping my voice even.

"They weren't gonna kill her," Darragh scoffs. "Can't lure her daddy back here with nothing but a body now can I?"

I snort, because I truly didn't think that Darragh was this dumb.

"You think kidnapping O'Malley's kid is gonna bring him back here?" I ask. "He's the one who sold her out to me. He put her up as collateral on his debt then turned tail and ran when I came to collect. He doesn't give a shit about her." My head begins to pound the way it often does these days, a vicious ticking when I think about Deirdre's papà.

"That's because you're too soft with her," Darragh replies coolly. "You're draping her in diamonds and carting her around to galas like she's your new favourite pet." A cold hunger enters his gaze, something mutely hostile and not quite human. "You ever sent a father the severed fingers of his only child?"

The ticking grows, bomb-like and ominous. My blood heats and surges with rage when I remember how frantically I'd checked each and every one of Deirdre's fingers, first at the cemetery and then back at home.

"You so much as try to trim her pinky fucking fingernail," I seethe, "and I will rip your goddamn throat out."

The big guy near the door shifts at the threat. Curse and Enzo both tense, ready for action.

But Darragh just barks a laugh and shakes his head, sending bits of dark copper hair flopping.

"Down, Rowan," he says to the Viking-looking guy. "We're all friends here."

"Friends? That why you addressed that weird-ass fucking riddle the way you did? And just who exactly were you telling not to press their luck?" I ask him.

You know what? I don't even care about the answer. With Darragh, maybe there is no real answer at all. He probably doesn't even fucking know why he wrote that shit. Just trying to get a rise out of me.

"We are not friends," I tell him, my voice cold with purpose. "And if you don't want me as your enemy then you will immediately stop coming after my fiancée."

I punctuate the sentence with a flourish of my hand, brandishing the sealed paper towards Darragh. He snatches it out of the air with animal quickness, pops the seal, and reads, his asymmetrical eyes flying over the words at a ferocious pace.

"You're marrying her," Darragh says, "and throwing the fire-power of your family name behind her, solely to keep her from me?"

"I'm marrying her because she's mine."

Simple as fucking that.

Darragh looks like he doesn't quite believe me, like he's trying to figure out my true motive here, what I might stand to gain. His gaze is narrowed, calculating, before it suddenly widens in astonishment.

"Bugger, you actually *love* her. Elio Titone, the tyrant of Toronto, is in *love*."

I stare him down in silence.

He chuckles. Then he pushes off from his desk, heading for the bar cart and pouring himself a small glass of whiskey, muttering in a slightly sing-song voice, "*Love*. Makes bright the days and sweet the night. And turns men's brains to utter shite."

He holds his glass but doesn't take a sip, staring at the wall for so long I wonder if he's having a silent conversation with the faded wall-paper. But then he suddenly whirls back around to face us, transitioning from eerie stillness to sharp movement so quick it's jarringly unnatural, like the whole motion was some kind of glitch.

"Where is he, then? Your soon-to-be father-in-law?" Darragh asks.

"What makes you think I'd tell you if I knew?"

"Because I demand recompense," he says, slamming down his glass, sloshing alcohol out the sides before he ever even had a drink out of it. "And if I'm not going to get it from the daughter then by the devil, I will get it from her Da!"

Any hint of his mirth from before is gone, like a switch inside him has flipped. The inane fripperies have been yanked aside, revealing the roiling rage beneath.

"Technically, you already got your recompense," I remind him, staying calm where he so clearly isn't. "O'Malley stole from you, yes, but he also paid it all back with Camorra funds. And then he paid the Camorra debt with my money. Between you, Severu, and me, I'm the only one who actually lost any real money here."

"It's not about the money," Darragh says, and I'm actually inclined to agree with him there. It's not about the money for me, either. Because you can't put a price tag on my Songbird.

"It's about the fucking principle of the thing," he continues. "When a man betrays me, he's no longer a man but a rat. And a rat has no right to life or liberty or the protection of whatever fucking hidey-hole he's crawled into."

Once again, I'm inclined to agree. And if it were any other man, in any other situation, I'd just shrug my good shoulder and tell Darragh what he wanted to know. But this is Deirdre's father. And that wasn't the deal I made with her. The deal was that she had to marry me or I would tell Darragh where her father was.

And since she is going to marry me (whether she's accepted that fact or not) then I don't plan on telling Darragh shit.

But I doubt Darragh's going to accept that fact head-on. And I can't just pay him off like I did with Severu Serpico. In many ways, dealing with Sev was smoother than Darragh. Sev's a dangerous man, but he's more easily soothed by cold, hard cash. There was very little emotion tied up in all this for him.

Darragh, on the other hand, is fuelled by rage that has become righteous to him and he won't back down just because I wave a fat cheque in his face. If I want him to accept my terms without simply blowing his head off and instantly getting two hundred and eighty pounds of Rowan stomping my Sicilian ass, I'm going to have to choose another strategy. A smarter one.

"You're a gambling man," I say jerking my chin towards the door we came through, indicating the cards and dice at play beyond. "Why don't we make a little bet? If I win, you relinquish any claim you think you have on my fiancée, and you will not receive any information on her father's whereabouts."

"And if I win?"

"If you win, you will still stay away from Deirdre. But I will tell you where Jack O'Malley is hiding."

"What if I lose, but then I track down O'Malley on my own at a later date? Does this agreement preclude me from doing what I want with him then?" he fires back.

Darragh might be crazy, but he's fucking smart. I don't like the man, but I do have a grudging sort of appreciation for the cunning way he's carving up this offer, making sure it won't fuck him in the ass later.

"The deal only has to do with Deirdre's safety going forward and the information I will or will not give you," I tell him. "If you find O'Malley on your own then you can do whatever the fuck you want with him. Torture him, kill him, I don't give a shit. He is not under my protection. Only Deirdre is."

Darragh picks up his glass, finally taking a swig of the bit of whiskey left in there that didn't slosh out before. When he puts the glass back down, it's empty.

I can see the thoughts whirring behind those mis-matched eyes of his. He's thinking about it, thinking about ways this might go wrong for him. No doubt also thinking that if he doesn't accept, things will likely be even less appealing. At least with the bet he thinks he has a chance at getting info on O'Malley. If he refuses me, then we're back to where we started, except his position is even more tenuous. He still won't know where O'Malley is, and continuing to try to harm Deirdre becomes a hell of a lot dicier for him and his entire operation now that she's going to be my wife.

"What's your poison, then?" he asks, still assessing. "Dice? Cards? Toss of a coin?"

No fucking way. Nothing that can be rigged, nothing he can cheat at.

"I don't leave shit to chance when I can take care of it with my own two hands," I tell him. I undo the top button of my shirt then work my way down until the garment is sagging off me. I shrug out of it, ignoring the stiffness in my still-healing shoulder. The shirt falls, but Enzo catches it before it hits the floor.

I roll my head from side to side, my neck cracking, then flex my fingers inside my gloves before curling them into fists.

Something flashes in Darragh's eyes. Maybe interest, maybe surprise.

Maybe bloodlust.

"What? You're going to fight?"

I nod, already heading for the door that will lead out to the ring, because fuck yes, I'm going to fight.

For her, every goddamn day of my life.

Chapter 10

Deirdre

I feel so heavy that I can't even tell if I'm actually waking up or not. For a long time, I'm caught in some state of half-sleep, aware of the bed beneath me and the blankets on top but unable to move or open my eyes or even think. Just the anticipation of needing to move feels like a monumental effort, so I give up and lie there for a while.

But, little by little, thoughts work their way in, even though I'm not aware of myself actually thinking them. Thoughts in the shape of questions like, *Why does this bed smell different than it usually does? And why does the mattress feel firmer?*

The answers to the questions penetrate the syrup of my mind slowly, and then all at once.

I'm in Elio's bed. The bed he put me into last night.

The bed we shared after I rubbed myself all over him and then he fucked me. Again.

It's as if remembering that fact has a physical echo, because I'm now painfully aware of the tenderness between my legs. I groan, muscles feeling rubbery, and drag myself into a seated position, sagging backwards against the bed's headboard. I stare blankly into

386

the room for a while, taking in this new angle, this arrangement of a place I'm not used to waking up in.

Something tells me I'm about to get used to it.

I don't have my phone with me, but a heavy loll of my head to the side brings a clock on the bedside table into view. It's past noon. I can't believe I slept that long. But I guess after all the insanity of last night, I really needed it.

Apparently Elio didn't, though. The man is nowhere to be found in the bedroom, and without the door on the bathroom I can see that he isn't in there either. I sigh heavily, raking my fingers through tangled hair. When my fingertips graze my scalp, I remember him washing my hair so thoroughly, both tender and possessive.

And now he's just fucking gone.

Lovely.

Not that I expect or even want him hanging around the morning after or anything, but...

But it's hard not to feel abandoned. And I hate that I even feel that at all.

I don't need Elio sitting there staring at me in my sleep waiting for me to wake up so he can say, "Good morning." If anything, I should be grateful for his absence. It will give me some time to fucking think without him unspooling all my senses.

Beside the clock on the bedside table there's also a tray of food. Rosa must have been here. Strange. Usually, she's not very quiet, and she doesn't care if I'm still sleeping when she comes in wielding her vacuum and duster like swords. Things must be different now that I'm sleeping in Elio's bed.

No. Not sleeping. Just... Slept. Once. One night only.

Oh God.

If I'm going to even attempt to work through all the knots of what I'm feeling and thinking, I'm going to need some energy. I eye the tray and select a crusty slice of bread then slather a chocolate spread on top. I don't have much of an appetite, but the food is heavenly, and I eat a hearty portion before pouring myself a cup of tea from the pot. It's gone cold, but I still drink it down appreciatively. I'm more thirsty that I'd realized, so the coolness actually feels quite nice. That combined with the little thrill of caffeine starting to hit my system has me feeling halfway human again as I finish off my chocolate bread.

Once I'm done my breakfast, or brunch, I suppose, considering the time, I ease my feet over the side of the bed and hop down. I suppress a grunt of discomfort when the force of my feet hitting the floor reverberates up to the sore place between my legs.

After such a long sleep and chugging the tea, I have to go pee. Elio's bathroom is much closer, but I eschew it in favour of the one I've been using up until now. It's strange. When I first got here, I was so adamant about not calling that bedroom or bathroom or bed mine. It wasn't my bed or room because it was the one Elio had forced me into.

But now, I call it mine, simply to contrast it with Elio's. Last night I slept in Elio's bed. In Elio's room. Not mine.

So I head for my bathroom now, glancing around just to make fully sure that Elio isn't hiding in some corner I'm not aware of. But nope. It really is just me in here.

Which is fine. Absolutely fine.

I pee, wincing as I gently pat myself dry. I'm not actively bleeding right now, and I consider that a small miracle considering what I put my flesh through last night. What Elio put it through. The pain of plunging right back into the channel he tore.

Still made you come again, though.

I swat away that internal voice, not sure if it's mine or if its Elio's. I wash my hands vigorously, scrubbing my skin like I can scrub away the past twenty-four hours. No, the past freaking month.

When I turn off the tap, I glance up at myself in the mirror and sigh. Not only did I not use any conditioner last night, which is pretty much a requirement for my frizz-prone hair, but all the, erm, activities, then sleeping on it while still damp, has left it completely wonky. The front sections are spiralling away from my face in spastic curls, while the sides and back are all disjointed, crumpled waves that look more like bent pieces of orange paper than human hair.

Oh well. I need to have a shower anyway, after what happened with Elio in his bed last night.

I leave my underwear and pad on the floor, but then think better of it and toss it all in the trash before Elio can do something fucking weird with it. I end up throwing in the torn pyjama shirt too, because with all that ripped silk it looks like a bit of a lost cause now. It makes me a little sad seeing that cheery, pretty yellow fabric shoved down into the trash, like somebody's throwing away sunshine. But I steel myself against those sorts of feelings. Elio's the one who ripped it. If anyone should feel bad, it's him.

And I already know he won't.

Without letting myself dwell on it any longer, I grab the bottles from where Elio left them beside the bathtub and return them to the shower. I turn the tap almost as hot as it will go, gasping at the delicious, punishing sting of heat against my skin. I move my legs apart, letting the scalding water stream between them, and let out a choking sob at the sensation.

For a while, I just stand there with my eyes closed, shivering and soaked under the hot spray. After a while, though, I start to get light-headed, the steam choking the space so much that it's uncomfortable to breathe. And while part of me craves the itchy oblivion of oxygen deprivation, I also want to keep my wits about me right now.

Plus, Elio said I shouldn't do that on my own anymore. Because it isn't safe. And I can't deny the fact that he's probably right.

Not that that matters, I tell myself quickly. *He may be the under-boss of the Titone empire but he is not the boss of me.*

I hate how hollow, how defensive that proclamation feels.

I turn the tap's temperature down a little bit, and the cooler water helps to clear my head a bit. I wash my hair, then work in what feels like an entire fistful of conditioner to help counteract the rough-ing-up my strands went through last night. While the conditioner soaks in, I wash my body, gingerly between my legs and harshly everywhere else. I wash my face too, then rinse everything until I feel, well, not exactly cleansed, but at least a little better.

I wrap a fluffy towel around myself and brush my teeth at the sink. Then, I carefully detangle my hair with a wide tooth comb. But I have to stop, because the pleasant tugs against my scalp keep making me think of Elio last night. The way his fingers dug the most irritatingly gorgeous circles against my scalp. It's actually alarming the way he can both take control of me and take care of me at the exact same fucking time.

Tossing my soaked, half-combed hair over my shoulders, I head for my closet and choose the first comfy outfit in reach – some black leggings and an uber-soft, cream-coloured sweater that I think must be cashmere or something equally luxurious and expensive. The thought of wearing a bulky pad against my clean but stinging pussy is not appealing in the least, so I go with a thin panty-liner in my under-wear then pull on the rest of the outfit.

When I'm all dressed and I emerge into my bedroom once again, Rosa is there with her cart of cleaning supplies.

She doesn't look any happier to see me than she usually does, but she actually says, "Good morning," to me, which is a first.

And for another first?

She follows it up with a moodily deferential, "Signora Titone."

Signora... What?!

"Did... Did you just call me Mrs. Titone?" I ask her as she tugs on cleaning gloves with the competent deftness of a surgeon.

"Sì, sì. Signore Titone tell me."

"But... We're not married!" I squeak, cringing internally at the high register of my voice. But I can't help it. Elio making grand claims of our impending marriage is one thing. It's entirely another to hear other people acknowledging it like it's already truth. Like it's already come to pass and not only did I have no say but I also had no idea. I have to fight the urge to look down at my left hand and make sure there's no mysterious ring perched there, even though I know there isn't.

Rosa doesn't seem impressed by my proclamation about not being married to her boss. In fact, she doesn't acknowledge it at all, she just gets to work stripping the bedding from my bed.

I know it's pointless, but I can't seem to stop myself from hovering beside her as she works, twisting my wet hair anxiously between my fingertips.

"Seriously, Rosa. Just call me Deirdre. I'm not Mrs. Titone. We're not married. And we're not going to get married, either."

Rosa doesn't answer me verbally. Instead, she just holds up the bedding for my inspection. Heat floods my face, and then drains out of it, when I see the unmistakable stains of my blood and Elio's semen.

"That wasn't... That's not..."

Words fail me, and I throw up my hands, wondering why I'm even bothering trying to convince her. She works for Elio. She's loyal to him. It doesn't matter what I say.

I could tell her I'd throw myself off a cliff before I married Elio and she'd probably just nod noncommittally and say, "Si, Signora Titone."

Rosa shoves the soiled bedding into the basket attached to her cart, and I'm so filled with shame I suddenly can't face her. She's seen what we've done. She's seen the blood, the stains. She's going to be the one to clean the bedding, like those marks never even existed in the first place. And then I feel twice as bad, because I realize she's going to find the exact same thing on the bedding in the other room, too.

I have the feral urge to sprint ahead of her into Elio's room, strip the bed myself, and burn the evidence.

But burning anything related to Elio just feels a step too far. I remember what he told me last night, about the relief he felt as a young teenage boy when he covered up his scarred hands with black leather for the first time, and the fight goes right out of me.

But the urge to get away is still there, bubbling beneath the surface. I don't have classes today, so I don't have a pre-authorized excuse to leave the house, but at least I don't have to stay in either of these bedrooms. I start to leave, then at the last moment I grab my violin and bow. The familiar heft of the weighted wood in my hands is comforting, and that's a relief, because I was beginning to worry that violin would never mean what it once had to me. That Elio had ruined it for me forever.

But he hasn't. I won't let him. It's a part of me, and of my mother, and I won't let him take that from me. He can poke me and prod me and humiliate me and make me come, but when I'm alone, my music will still be pure. It will still be mine.

Feeling reinvigorated by that internal decision, or maybe it's a realization, I march out of my bedroom, then through Elio's and out into the hall. One of Elio's soldiers, whom I recognize as a guy named Robbie, is stationed at the top of the stairs. He watches me with eyes that I know have been commanded never to leave me. At least, not until Elio's home.

I do my best to ignore him, but I can't, because when I pass him on the stairs he dips his head and mutters, "Morning, Mrs. Titone."

I nearly fall down the fucking stairs. Robbie lurches forward, but thankfully I manage to find my footing without him grabbing me for support.

"So it's not just Rosa, then?" I say, spinning on the step to look up at him. "You're all going to call me that now?" I blow out an irritated breath, shaking my violin bow in the air, emphasizing each word. "That's not. My. Name!"

"Mr. Titone says that's what we're to call you going forward."

"And because that's what *Mr. Titone* says, that's what goes, huh? Even though that isn't even my real name?"

I almost say "real name yet" and want to smack myself with my own bow. Because there is no yet in this situation!

"Yup."

Unbelievable.

"Well, fine then, if I'm Mrs. Titone then don't I get a say in things? Aren't you supposed to treat me with respect too, as your boss's supposed wife?" I counter. "So don't you have to listen to what I say as well?"

Robbie's thick eyebrows come together over his nose, like I've thrown him off in a way he doesn't expect and doesn't have an Elio-approved answer for. If anything, Elio's probably caused some of this confusion by telling his men they have to respect me or something. But now I'm asking for respect by requesting to be called by a different name and clearly, that does not compute for Robbie over here.

The man looks like his brain is about to melt, so I give up on trying to get an answer out of him and continue on my way down the stairs. I stop in the kitchen, putting down my violin and bow to make myself a fresh cup of tea.

"I can call Rosa for that," Robbie says hurriedly as he follows me into the kitchen. This whole guard following me thing is getting old already. I wonder if one day I'll just be used to it.

No. I can't get used to a life I plan on escaping from. Somehow...

"I can make my own cup of tea," I tell him. "Or am I not even allowed to do that?"

"You're allowed. Boss says you can do just about anything as long as you don't try to leave the house or cause any danger to yourself."

"What about causing danger to others?" I say with false sweetness.

"He... didn't address that specifically."

I snort, shaking my head as I open cupboards, searching for the tea. I find it, rolling my eyes and shoving the sleepy cat tea box out of the way until I locate the bags of Irish breakfast.

"How generous of him," I say as I take down the tea and a cup. I fill the kettle then set it to boil. As the water boils, I stare out the massive wall of windows that look out over Elio's sprawling property. It looks like it's snowed even more since last night, but the sky is brilliantly clear now, the light catching like iridescent fire on all the frozen branches and snow-carpeted ground.

The kettle clicks, steam rising from its spout. I pour the boiling water over my teabag, wait for it to steep a bit, then add some milk before disposing of the teabag in the bin I saw Elio use last night.

With my hot cup of tea, I wander to the windows, staring out at the beautiful world I'm no longer allowed to inhabit. At least, not without him.

"Am I allowed to go outside? If I stay on the property?" I don't turn around to ask Robbie, but I know he's still there because he's been ordered to follow me around.

"Mr. Titone said you're to stay inside when he's not here."

"And he's not here now, is he?"

"No, Mrs. Titone."

I take a scalding sip of tea to keep myself from saying something shitty at once again being called Mrs. Titone. I know the guy is just trying to do his job, and that his boss is possibly the most frightening man alive, but this is already wearing on my nerves.

I take a few more sips, stewing over the fact that Elio's not here. That he can just waltz out the door and leave me here while he gets to traipse around doing who the hell knows what. Meanwhile I'm just stuck here drinking tea and looking out the window and getting more and more annoyed.

Screw it. I'm not going to just stand in this spot looking longingly out at something I can't have right now. I put my tea down on the kitchen island then start to wander the main floor of the house. So far, I've spent most of my time here upstairs in the bedrooms, or down here in the kitchen and living area. But there's got to be a whole lot more to discover considering how freaking huge this place is.

I go through the kitchen to a narrow hallway on the other side I've never walked down before. It branches off in a couple of directions. I choose right and keep walking, aware of Robbie following close behind, monitoring my every movement.

I gasp when the hall suddenly opens into a vast, glittering space. It's so bright in here that I have to squint and shield my eyes for a second. How many lights are on in here?!

But as my eyes adjust to the exquisite luminescence of the space, I realize that there isn't a single light on at all. Instead, almost this entire room is comprised of glass. It's a rectangular prism that juts out from the house, and three out of its four walls, plus the ceiling above, are completely transparent. The sun absolutely drenches the room, and me, and it bounces right back off the floor because it's not a floor at all, but water.

It's an indoor pool. A fucking big one, too. A giant, pristine rectangle of aquamarine blue. Beyond the pool is a smaller circle of water that looks like it has jets and benches built into it. Against the longest glass outer wall, looking like they're backed right up against a drift of snow, is a row of chaises longues with pillows and towels arranged neatly on top of them. The tile of the floor in here is a rich, warm colour that speaks of terracotta, or maybe water-darkened sand. That plus the turquoise of the water and the blinding blue above makes me feel like I've stepped into some Mediterranean paradise. I lick my lips, not realizing how much I'd been craving sun and summer until now. Warm weather is always such a relief after long Ontario winters, especially for me, because that sunshine and heat makes me feel like I've clawed my way out of the cold, dark time surrounding the anniversary of my mother's death. In spring and summer, everything comes back to life. Including me.

I walk along the edge of the pool towards doors on the far side of this glorious room. One door leads into a large closet with what I assume are chemicals for the pool and hot tub, plus extra towels and cushions for the chairs. The other door opens into a huge, luxury change room, the kind you'd see at a massive hotel. There are spa-like showers in there, another closed door for a private toilet, marble sinks, as well as cedar benches and hooks with fluffy white robes hanging on them.

I turn around and shut the door, narrowly avoiding smacking into Robbie's chest.

"You don't need to follow so close behind me," I grumble. "I promise I'm not going to go in the cleaning closet and drink a bunch of bleach."

His face goes a little pale, and then it looks like he's making a mental note, and I realize with a roll of my eyes that the next time I come here I'm pretty sure all the chemicals are going to be locked up somewhere where I can't access them. I already told Elio I had no interest in dying just to escape him, but his men don't know that. And I wouldn't put it past Elio to think that this whole *we're getting married* thing has thrown me over some kind of mental edge I won't be able to pull myself back from.

Which, I mean, it kind of has. He's changed the game on me again, and I'm struggling to find my footing, that's for sure. But things aren't so dire I'm planning to swallow a bunch of toxic pool-cleaning chemicals over it.

I don't bother explaining any of that to the mafia soldier assigned to babysit me. Instead, I just go back the way we came, through the kitchen to the central area of the house. There's another door I haven't gone through and I approach it. Robbie seems to get a little stiff when I reach for the door handle.

"What? Am I not allowed in here?"

"That's Mr. Titone's office," Robbie replies.

"OK. That doesn't actually answer my question."

"Well... He said you're allowed anywhere in the house."

He still seems uncomfortable, though. I eye him closely, then pull back.

"Let me guess," I say. "I'm allowed in here. But you aren't."

His mouth thins into a hard line, and I know I'm right.

"Well, you just stay here, then!" I say, unable to contain my grin. It's probably petty and childish, but I don't care. I yank open the door, practically skip inside, then slam it closed.

One glance tells me there's a security camera in the ceiling here. Since it isn't one of the bedrooms, I know Elio's security team will have access to this feed. Even without Robbie in here with me, I'm still being watched.

Well, it's not like I plan on trashing the place or smashing a window for an escape attempt or something. I'm just exploring.

I survey the office. It's lovely, which I find both interesting and irritating. I know Valentina arranged the gorgeous décor for my bedroom, but everything in here just screams Elio, and I feel like he must have chosen everything himself. The furniture is large, the desk a dark wooden one with clean, masculine lines. There are book-shelves along the walls, a door that leads into a small adjoining bath-room, and a floor-to-ceiling window that looks out on the back of the property. The bright sunlight filtering in makes everything feel bright and warm, like it might actually just be a normal office instead of the workspace belonging to a mob boss.

I wander past the desk with its computer and drawers and scope out the shelves of books. There are a lot of books on law, which I find darkly ironic. *Studying up to best figure out how to circumvent them, Elio?* There are also books on local history, politics, industry, trade. But those end abruptly, turning into something I'm familiar with from the upstairs. Books on violin. Loads of them, stuffed into the shelves.

Just how many books on music and violins did he buy before I came to be here? He was watching me since I was eighteen, so presumably he'd have had more than a year and a half to collect all this stuff, but still. It feels wildly excessive, but then again, what about Elio isn't?

I sigh, moving away from the books. This time, I cross the room behind his desk instead of in front of it. His computer screen is dark, but with a flutter of nerves in my belly I jiggle the mouse until the screen lights up.

It asks for a password, of course. Even a normal person's computer asks for a password, let alone a member of the goddamn mafia.

I don't even know what I'm looking for anyway. In fact, anything I find on there is probably just going to make me angry. I want to learn more about Elio... But is that really what I want when what I will uncover will probably just reveal more and more of the monster he truly is?

Not that I think he cares about hiding anything like that from me. He told me he was a monster my very first night here.

I'm about to turn away from the computer, but there's something niggling in me that doesn't let me. Chewing on the inside of my cheek, I take a wild stab in the dark, typing in the password box.

My mouth falls open when the computer unlocks. I got it right on my first fucking guess.

Songbird. He actually made his password Songbird.

Kind of a low-security password, to be honest. Although it isn't a laptop he could lose, and I can't imagine many people get access to this room to type in their guesses.

Besides me.

My heart hammers. I feel like at any moment someone, maybe even Elio himself, is going to bust down that door and punish me. Imagining Elio being the one to do it makes my clit twinge shamefully.

I ignore thoughts of him coming in here to discover me and take a quick look at the screen.

It looks like it's an email that's been left open. Based on the name in the sender's address, it appears to be an email from Valentina. That alone isn't anything weird or surprising.

But the body of the message certainly fucking is. My eyes get wider and wider as they fly over the letters on the screen.

Elio Titone of Toronto, son of Florencia Titone, is honoured to announce his engagement to Deirdre O'Malley of Toronto, daughter of Fiona O'Malley. Mr. Titone is a purveyor of multiple business interests, and Miss O'Malley is an accomplished violinist currently completing her Bachelor of Arts in Music at the University of Toronto, due to graduate with honours next spring. The wedding is set for February twenty-ninth of this year.

It's an engagement announcement. No fucking doubt about it.

But it's just in an email. It must be a draft version, or something...

Unless...

I check the CC column and gasp when I see other emails listed there. All of them appearing to belong to local news stations and papers.

No longer worried or nervous about doing something wrong, my fingers fly to the mouse and keyboard. I click out of the email and open a search engine, hastily typing in "Elio Titone engagement."

Oh. Oh no.

There it is. Dozens of times over in the search results, displayed digitally by publications from the tiny to the national. My face goes hot while my body goes cold, fury flashing through me.

I told him no. I told him I wouldn't marry him.

And he just told the whole damn world I said yes.

There's a real, virulent urge for me to type a new email and send it to all those news outlets Valentina CCed.

This is Deirdre O'Malley and I would like to make a correction to your recent publications. I am actually not engaged to Elio Titone. In fact, he never even asked me. Technically, I'm some kind of prisoner, or maybe a victim of Stockholm Syndrome, so if you want to write a story featuring my name maybe you should write about that.

I don't type any of that, of course. It's one of those mental exercises where you compile a letter even though you know you'd never send it. I can't even imagine the chaos that would ensue if I went to the media and told them what Elio's done. If they're friends of the family, they probably wouldn't even publish it anyway, but I know there would be hell to pay. For me, and maybe for Elio, too.

I actually play through the scenario in my head. Think about what would happen if even one good journalist got their teeth into this story and helped to push it out there. Even someone like Elio wouldn't be able to wiggle his way out of that one.

He could actually be arrested.

He could go to jail.

Once, that thought might have given me a righteous sort of relief. I would have thought, *Good. So he should. The kidnapping bastard.*

But now...

Now it makes my stomach clench with dread. Which is frankly fucking infuriating. After everything he's done to me, including this engagement announcement cherry on top, I should rejoice about him getting his due.

But I don't. I can't.

A part of me wants to protect him. Even if there's no one left to protect me from him.

I let out a shaky breath, clicking open the first news link from *The Toronto Trumpet*. I re-read the engagement announcement, shaking my head numbly as I do so. That numbness evaporates when I read the final sentence of the announcement again.

The wedding is set for February twenty-ninth of this year.

This year?!

That can't be right. That must be a typo. But a frantic click through of the other news links shows me that they all have the same date listed, and it correlates to the date Valentina had in her original email.

So this is how he's going to play it, then. Force me into this marriage and make it happen so fast that there's no way for me to escape it, no way for me to explore any other options. There's no chance to wait a year or two and see if Darragh cools off, or if he's willing to make some other kind of bargain. Nope, it's just straight to the altar for us, then.

Once again, I can't get over the shocked confusion that Elio is actually going to these lengths to protect me. Or maybe just to own me. Who even knows at this point? But I can't deny the slight twist of toxic pleasure I feel in my belly when I remember what he said last night, when I assumed he couldn't actually want to marry me.

Do I look like the sort of man who does a single fucking thing he doesn't want to do?

Whatever the outcome with Darragh ends up being, Elio does seem to think he wants to marry me. Which is insane, considering we only officially met about a month ago. His stalking behaviour aside, anyway.

I let go of the mouse, noticing the anxiety-sweat handprint I've left behind. I rub my clammy palms on my leggings and then straighten up. I've seen enough in here for now. I yank open the door to find Robbie standing directly on the other side, as if he was trying to use X-Ray vision to peer through the door.

I don't say anything to him. I just walk past him to the kitchen. I pick up the cup of tea I abandoned and take a huge sip.

But the tea's gone cold. And it doesn't do a single thing to help.

Chapter 11

Elio

"I don't love this, Boss," Enzo mutters from below as I haul myself over the ropes and into the ring.

"You sound like an old broad. When was the last time I asked you if you loved a single fucking decision I've ever made?" I toss back at him. Curse stands beside him on the floor. My brother knows better than to question me when I've made up my mind on something. Plus, he knows that I don't fucking plan on losing. He stares at me steadily as I roll my shoulders. Fuck, that stiff shoulder might be a problem. It doesn't hurt too bad right now, but it could be a liability where speed is concerned.

"I'm your head of security," Enzo says with a shrug. "I'm supposed to worry like an old broad does."

Well, I don't need any of that shit right now. Right now, all I need to do is beat this weird-eyed motherfucker in his own damn ring.

"What are the parameters?" I ask Darragh. He's in the ring now, too, bouncing up and down on the balls of his feet so fast he looks like a manic kangaroo or some shit.

"Bare knuckles," he says. "Though those are pretty thin. You can keep 'em on if you want."

He means my leather gloves.

But Darragh isn't wearing anything on his knuckles, not even tape, so I'm not going to be the prissy one covering up my precious, shitty hands. With harsh, quick movements, I tug off the gloves and toss them backwards, knowing that Enzo or Curse will catch them without even having to look.

Darragh's eyes go to my hands as I flex my fingers. He lets out a low whistle.

"No wonder you're always wearing them. You got some real Phantom of the Opera shit going for you there."

I don't know much about Phantom of the Opera except for the whole white mask thing. That and there always seems to be some young, beautiful woman swooning before his monstrous, possessive gaze.

Which... considering the Songbird I've got locked up in my tower, might actually be a fair comparison.

I don't bother responding, just watch him as he bounces around and shakes out his hands. He's actually only a year younger than I am, but there's this frenetic energy burning in him that makes me feel like there's a decade between us.

"First one to land a good, hard blow to the face and draw blood wins," Darragh continues. He swoops his arms in big arcs as he continues to limber up. Which seems kind of unnecessary, since he's probably already warmed up from his last fight, but if he wants to do his weird fucking pre-fight thing then more power to him, I guess. Maybe it'll tire him out a bit before we start.

"Fine. I agree to the terms," I say, giving a tight nod and raising my fists. It's fucking weird to have them this close to my face without the gloves on. But I'm not looking at them anyway. Gotta keep my attention focused on my opponent.

Other than that one nose-crunching punch I gave Brian, it's been a long while since I beat somebody to a pulp in a fight with my fists, but the feeling comes right back as I assume my stance. I'm barely aware of how every person in this place is now gathered around the ring, all of them staring at us as we stare at each other. One of Darragh's men calls the start to the fight, and when Darragh's fist flies at me, jerking back and out of range is as easy as fucking breathing.

But Darragh is fast, I'll give him that. He's not the type to circle his opponent, to learn about them, to slowly try to gain the upper hand. He's the kind who bursts right out of the gate without a single thought of how he'll get to where he's going besides sheer, persistent force. He punches and jabs with astonishing speed, though I have no problem dodging and blocking. For now, anyway.

Unlike Darragh, I don't mind taking my fucking time. Same as I was willing to bide my time and wait to get my hands on Deirdre, I don't rush this, either. I want to get this done, but I won't win if I'm too impatient. So I block, and block, and block again, taking blows against my wrists and forearms and even a couple to the kidney area that take my breath away. But all the while, I'm watching, I'm analyzing. He's got weaknesses. A chink in his armour. Everybody does. It's all about patiently waiting to find out what they are.

So that you can get your thumb inside that crack and push until it bleeds.

At first, his punches are so quick and random that it's hard to discern any kind of pattern. But even a loose cannon like Darragh can't make his movements random and unpredictable forever. A rhythm emerges, a method to his madness, and, strangely, it almost reminds me of the notes of music. Each pumping blow a bright, discordant note that jabs its way into a song I feel like I might actually be able to get a hold of. And predict.

I probably have my Songbird to thank for that. Never gave two shits about music before her. And here I am, turning Darragh's lunging punches into notes so that I can get my head around them. Maybe some of her university lectures have rubbed off on me. Is there a class on turning the physical pain of somebody punching your ribs and your arms into a soundtrack in your head? There should be. Hell, maybe I could teach it. Step one: let some nutcase use you as a punching bag. Step two: do it long enough that the pain turns into art.

And art that you can analyze, not just gawk at like a dumbass. With every moment that passes, I get a better and better sense of Darragh's movements, his patterns, the raging rhythm building in my brain.

So when that rhythm stumbles, when it slows, I know the millisecond it happens.

Maybe it's cliché, but time gets real fucking slow in that instant. The only thing that's fast is my fist, slicing like a shark through water, jabbing straight forward until it connects hard with Darragh's face.

Even with how fast I move, Darragh still manages to bounce to the side slightly, almost avoiding my blow.

But nobody, not even Darragh, is good enough to avoid my fist when it comes down. I may not hit his nose like I'd been aiming for, but my knuckles slam hard against the soft tissue of his mouth, driving his lips and cheek so hard against his teeth I think I might have knocked at least one of them loose.

Darragh stops bouncing and blocking instantly, going utterly still, which is kind of impressive considering the momentum he must have built up. He stares at me with those odd eyes of his, chest heaving but not making a sound. Then, he opens his mouth and spits right there on the mat between us. A big old mouthful of blood and at least one tooth splatter at his feet.

There's no cheering, no laughing, no chatter. The entire room holds its breath. I can practically feel the tension radiating off of Enzo behind me. He, like all of Darragh's guys, is no doubt wondering if I'm about to get knifed in the belly for having the audacity to beat Darragh at his own game and on his own turf.

Darragh doesn't bother wiping his mouth and chin, and blood streams steadily from a very busted lip and some injury inside his mouth that I can't see. Between that and the electric, crazed fucking look he gives me, he looks more like some feral vampire than a man.

Like he just ripped somebody's heart out with his teeth and he's mad that I just stole it from him.

"Fair and square," I tell him when he doesn't say anything to acknowledge my win. My voice is raspy. I'm breathing a lot harder than I realized. Even just blocking his punches was an insane amount of work. He's not only fast as fuck, but he's strong, too. Pain is starting to cut through the fray of adrenaline. Aching in my wrists, and a deep pounding in my side that tells me I might be pissing blood tonight.

"I won. You'll leave Deirdre alone now. That was the deal," I remind him. I reach backwards and get my gloves back from one of my guys without taking my eyes off Darragh. I assumed he'd honour a deal he made, but now I'm not so sure.

Maybe Enzo was right to be worried. Because Darragh looks so intense. Not even specifically angry, just... I don't even know if there's a name for the emotion pouring off of him like poison. It's like anything and everything going on in that head of his is turned up to eleven, every feeling and thought so loud, so explosive, it turns into a big, screaming soup of a mess that's impossible to define as any one single thing.

"Fucking say it, Darragh," I command him as I tug my gloves back into place. "Fucking tell me we have a deal. Or tell me we're about to start a fucking war."

Darragh blinks, and the mute, hostile, writhing thing inside him appears to go completely blank. His expression relaxes, and he finally wipes at his face, smearing blood. He stares down at the blood on his hand for a long moment then says, "I'm done with Deirdre. She's yours, and I won't use her to get to O'Malley." His voice hardens. "I don't go back on my fucking deals, Titone. It's the-"

"Principle of the thing?" I finish for him, echoing his words from earlier about O'Malley.

"Precisely."

He swipes at his face again, shaking drops of blood forcefully off of his fingers. Rowan appears at his side with a clean towel, and Darragh takes it, wiping away both blood and sweat.

"Well, gents," he says, his tone light if slightly slurred by the swelling, his eyes like lasers, "I'd invite you to have a drink with me, but it looks like I'll be making an emergency trip to my dentist today."

"Dentist?" I ask, raising a brow at him.

"Of course," Darragh scoffs. "You just knocked one of my fucking teeth out. Didn't your mammy ever tell you that a man's smile is his calling card in this world?"

"Can't say that she did," I reply blandly, shrugging into the shirt Curse has just passed me through the ropes.

"Ah. Well. Neither did mine," Darragh says with a rueful, disconcertingly bloody grin. "But then again, she and my Da didn't have a single good tooth to count between 'em." He turns, about to leap down over the ropes and out of the ring, when he suddenly twists to look back at me over his hard, bare shoulders.

"Shall we shake hands then, d'ye think?"

"Not necessary," I tell him in response. I don't have much interest in being around this goon any longer than I have to, and knocking his damn tooth loose should be good enough to seal our deal.

"You know what? I like you, Titone," Darragh says, though I don't believe him for a goddamn second. "Fists over handshakes. Blood over ink." He casts a meaningful look down at the crimson splatter with its lone white shard of a tooth.

Then, he finally jumps down out of the ring.

I turn and do the same, landing more heavily than Darragh with his weirdly light-footed animal grace.

"Let's go," I tell Curse and Enzo. "We're done here."

The hushed crowd parts before us, wide-eyed and thin-lipped.

We cross the room to the soundproofed black door, pull it open, then take the stairs upwards, ascending out of Darragh's world and back into our own.

Chapter 12

Elio

When we emerge from *Briar and Boar* onto the street, I swear under my breath, momentarily blinded by the fiery spray of light on snow. In my haste to get over here this morning, I forgot to bring along a pair of sunglasses.

I also didn't put on clean clothes or shower. I'll need to rectify that soon. Can't go to my Songbird all rumpled and out of sorts. I've gotta live up to the standards set out by my impossibly pretty fiancée.

I close my eyes and think of her on the drive home, using the image of her to soothe the ache in my right side and the tight pains in my wrists and hands. I'll be home soon, and I can shower and then slide back into bed beside her. I wonder if she's still asleep, and open my eyes to take a look at the security app on my phone. Looks like she's up. She's in the kitchen drinking something, maybe some tea. Her violin and bow are down there, too, and my chest constricts at the thought she might have been playing music without me there to hear it.

The security app alerts me to something else, too. Uncle Vinny's car at the gate, making its way up the driveway.

Fuck.

I knew I'd have to deal with my uncle eventually, but I was hoping to have at least a little quiet time to myself with Deirdre first. If I ever wanted to hear her play for me, today is one of those fucking days.

But Uncle Vinny isn't the sort of man who likes to wait. And I should know better by now than to expect to just go home and relax whenever the fuck I want to.

No rest for a Titone. Not in this town, anyway.

We're actually pretty close to home, now. We pull up to the security gate on my property and then get to the house just as Uncle Vinny is striding up to the door.

He turns at the sound of the car's tires behind him, scowling into the sunlight as Curse parks and the three of us get out.

Uncle Vinny doesn't waste any time.

"Where the fuck have you been?" he says, jaw working.

"Curse and I had some business to deal with up north," I tell him as we walk up to the door where he's waiting.

That business being Deirdre's scumbag ex, Brian, who now finds himself without a dick as recompense for even dreaming he could touch her.

"What kind of business?" Uncle Vinny says as we head inside. "Since when is your business not my business?"

"Since it involves my fiancée."

"Oh. Yeah, don't think I know about that," my uncle snarls. "Blasting that shit all over every local newspaper's website without even bothering to consult me. What the hell were you thinking?"

"I was thinking about my glad tidings," I say dryly.

"How the fuck did you have time to get that drafted and send that out when you were up north?"

"We got back last night. I did it this morning."

"Where the hell were you coming from just now, then?"

"Had to have a little chat with Darragh."

Uncle Vinny swears loudly in Italian then fixes me with a furious stare.

"Running up north to deal with secret shit you won't tell me about. Making dumb-fuck political moves in the media without running it by me. Now you're antagonizing Mad fucking Darragh. And for what? All for some freckled Irish whore?"

If he were anyone else on this Earth, he'd have gotten a knife through the eye for what he just said. But as he's the man who saved my life and raised me as his own, instead I simply say, "No one is allowed to insult my fiancée in my house." I lean closer, maintaining eye contact. "No one."

Uncle Vinny's eyes narrow.

"I never took you for a fool, Elio. But your behaviour recently is making me rethink things."

"Rethink whatever the fuck you need to," I tell him. "If you want to make Curse your heir then go ahead."

Uncle Vinny freezes, looking momentarily speechless. A damn rare occurrence for him.

"You would give up your inheritance of the empire we have built," he says slowly, like he barely believes the words coming out of his mouth, "turn your back on your family responsibility, just to marry the Irish girl?"

We're still standing in the entry way. Something beyond us catches my gaze. It's Deirdre. She's standing beside the kitchen island, a cup of tea clutched in her hands. When her eyes meet mine, I feel physical heat. An erupting throb of sensation.

I have no doubt she heard my uncle's question.

And I answer loudly enough so that she can hear my answer, too.

"Yes," I say, returning my gaze to my uncle. "I'll move aside for Curse to take over if you want. But I will marry Deirdre. That is non-negotiable." My voice gets lower, my words more pointed. "And no smart man is going to stand in the way of that." My jaw ticks. "Good thing I know you're a smart man, Uncle Vinny."

Our uncle's face is beet-fucking-red. This conversation probably isn't good for his blood pressure.

It's good for mine, though. Every person who admits to my

impending marriage, every person who bends to my will and acknowledges Deirdre as my wife, makes me feel like I'm one step closer to everything being right in my world. Valentina's on board, I got Darragh sorted, now Uncle Vinny. The trickiest person will probably be the bride herself.

But I can handle that.

Uncle Vinny jams his big hands into the pockets of his expensive wool coat.

"*Merda,*" he mutters. "You know as well as I do that I can't turn anything over to Curse if I wanted to cut you out. That boy wouldn't take a fucking shit in the morning if you didn't authorize it."

"He seems to shit just fine without my say so," I reply. I raise my eyebrows at Curse, who's standing right fucking beside us and hearing everything. But he just gazes steadily back and then shrugs, because we both know that, though the wording was exaggerated, Uncle Vinny is right. Ever since we were kids, when I pulled Curse out of that fire with my bare fucking hands – ruining them in the process – he's been loyal to me with the kind of quiet ferocity that no amount of money could ever even hope to buy.

"Well, you do what you need to do, Uncle Vinny. And I'll do what I need to. Starting with marrying Deirdre." I look over my uncle's head to catch a glimpse of her, but she's no longer in the kitchen.

I'm cool. I'm calm. And Uncle Vinny knows he can't fucking win here.

He lets out a rattle of a sigh.

"Well, you were right about one thing. I'm real fucking smart. You're a Titone through and through, and I'm not stupid enough to stand in the way of a Titone when he's got his sights on something that he wants. And I'm also too damn old to start a war with my own flesh and blood, my *own fucking heir*, over where he decides he wants to stick his fucking dick."

He rubs his jaw, studying me with hard, dark eyes.

"Just tell me one thing, Elio. You owe me that much. And it's the one thing I still don't fucking get."

I nod. I don't know if I'll have an answer for whatever he's about to ask, but he's right that I do owe him at least an attempt at a reply. He dragged Curse and me out of the fucking muck and helped make us into men, and that's gotta count for something. Even if I'm willing to blow it all to hell for the girl I plan to marry now.

"So, I parade these Italian girls in front of you," Uncle Vinny says. "Girls from good fucking families. Nice racks, nice asses, and they know when to shut the fuck up. Culture, cooking, upbringing, *everything*. And you don't give a single flying fuck." He shakes his head, like I don't make any sense to him, and maybe I don't these days. "What else could you possibly want in a bitch?" he asks. "What could that Irish girl possibly fucking possess to send you so out of your goddamn mind? To make you give her our fucking name?"

Yeah. He really doesn't get it. And I can forgive him for that, because I wouldn't have gotten it either. Not before her, anyway.

It's got nothing to do with tits or silence, power or pussy. Nothing to do with any of the things we normally value.

It's about something ephemeral and eternal. Ruinous and glorious. The exquisite agony in my chest every time I hear her fucking voice. Every time I see those eyes. Get a glimpse of the music that's inside her.

It's about something I wasn't even sure that I believed in anymore. Until *her*.

"Soul," I tell my uncle, and it feels so pure, so good and true to say it, that the word comes out like a goddamn prayer. "It's about her soul."

Chapter 13

Deirdre

I wasn't prepared for seeing Elio downstairs just now. I wasn't prepared for my own reaction to him. When I was in the kitchen, and he came through the door with the other men, it was like a bolt of lightning straight down my spine. It was all I could do to clutch my teacup and gape. I was just with him last night, I literally slept in the same bed as him, but it was like I hadn't seen him in ages.

The way he fills the space, the way he draws my eye like he exerts some kind of gravity that only affects me is deeply disconcerting. He was with his uncle, whom I'd never seen before, and I didn't even care one bit. I barely even noticed the boss of the Titone family, the legendary man who raised Curse and Elio.

Because I couldn't keep my eyes off of his oldest nephew.

Elio looked a bit rumpled, his clothes wrinkled, shadowy stubble darkening the parts of his jaw that aren't scarred, his hair askew in a way that made my fingers tighten around my teacup with the urge to smooth the rebellious waves.

And yet...

Fuck, I'm an idiot. But I couldn't stop staring at him.

I should have just gone upstairs immediately. Gotten some space to clear my head. But the conversation had been about... Well, me. And I found myself rooted to the spot.

Vincenzo called me a whore.

And Elio's eyes got so fucking dark I was half-afraid he'd kill his own uncle right in front of me.

No one insults my fiancée, he said. *No one.*

And then, the thing that really stole my breath, was when he told Vincenzo he would step aside, relinquish his power within this family, the role he would inherit...

All for me.

Just to marry me.

I hate how much his words affected me. He's always so confident, so certain, so sure. It doesn't matter who he has to confront or convince, whether it's Brian or his own uncle, he never hesitates to stand up for me. To make his connection to me known.

And when he does stuff like that, it makes my belly go tight with twisted pleasure.

I don't even want to marry him. But hearing him say that, that he'd give up everything important in his world, just to have me...

Well, it's making it hard to be as pissed at him as I want to be.

But I'm not that weak. I have to have some kind of resolve here. He still announced our fucking engagement – an engagement I haven't even agreed to! – without even bothering to ask me. Or his uncle, it seems, based on the conversation I overheard down there. I didn't stay until the end. I had to get some space from Elio. And space from all the feelings inside me that, like dynamite he calmly held matches against, were threatening to explode.

I need to focus on something else. So I open my laptop. The one he gave me. I grimace as I type in the password he set up for me – *Iloveelio* – and then open up some school files. I have no idea if it's even safe for me to go to class tomorrow after what happened last night, but I might as well be prepared.

Not that I get much work done. I've only just gotten into my reading for the week when I hear footsteps on the stairs. When the hallway door leading into Elio's room opens, I know there's no one else it could be but him.

I stiffen at my desk, frozen and staring blindly at the screen of my laptop. My throat goes incredibly dry, my chest tightening with nerves and anger and desire and I don't even know what else. I don't hear much movement and I relax slightly, thinking he's still in his own room. But then a low, silken murmur of, "Morning, Songbird," directly behind me makes me leap out of my chair, heart pumping.

I whirl around to find Elio standing right behind my chair. It's not the first time I've thought it, but damn, somebody that big should not be that quiet.

I clear my throat, then lick my lips. Elio's hooded gaze goes to my mouth.

"It's not morning," I say, because I can't think of anything sensible to actually reply with.

"I know," Elio says. He grasps the back of the chair with one hand and lifts it easily aside so that there's nothing between us. "But I didn't get to say it earlier. So, good morning."

Before I can react, before I can even think to move away, he's stepped forward, closing the distance between us. The smooth glide of his leather touch at my jaw as he cups my face makes me shiver. I shiver even harder when his lips press softly, even tenderly, against my forehead.

"And good afternoon," he breathes against my skin. Then he lowers his mouth to mine.

The kiss is so gentle, so nearly chaste, whisper-light against my lips, that I'm shocked into stillness. I don't think he's ever kissed me quite like this. Usually, it's all tongue and taking. Ravishing. Ravaging.

This is like the mist of rain on my skin.

And yet, despite how incredibly soft the pressure against my mouth is, my body reacts like he's kissing my clit instead of my lips. My pulse stutters, my insides going liquid. My knees literally go weak, and if that isn't the definition of pathetic I don't even know what is.

That realization – that I'm literally becoming a weak-kneed damsel in his arms, that he's disarmed me with a single fucking kiss – gives me the strength to pull out of his quietly obliterating embrace.

"We need to talk," I stammer, breathing much harder than I should be.

"Oh?" he says. He starts undoing the buttons on his shirt, and my stomach leaps like a rabbit in response.

I take a prim step back.

"I'm gonna take a shower," Elio says, finishing unbuttoning his shirt and tossing it over the back of the chair he moved aside. The back of *my* chair. The one in here, in *my* room. I stare at the black fabric in my space, and it feels like an invasion. An invasion I don't know how to defend against. A further blending of our boundaries. No longer him and me, but us.

But then again, he's the one who bought me that chair. He's the one who put me in this room, inside his own house.

Was it ever really mine? Was it ever somewhere I could expect to escape from him?

"You're welcome to join me," Elio says with a crooked smirk. "You can come chat my ear off all you like without your clothes on."

"That the only way I'll get you to listen to me?" I ask, bristling.

"No," he says. "In fact, I'll probably be too distracted to listen properly in that scenario. So maybe it can wait."

Oh, hell no. He just left me here, bleeding and sore in his bed, without even telling me he was going anywhere this morning. Now he waltzes back in like everything between us is hunky dory? He doesn't even think he owes me five minutes before his shower to explain himself over the fact that every news outlet in the city, no, the country is proclaiming our engagement to the masses? Our engagement that *doesn't even exist?*

My lungs burn as I prepare to expel all of those angry words.

Except Elio turns to head back into his room, putting his bare back to me, and any fury dissipates, strangled in the cold grip of concern.

"Elio," I gasp, my fingers automatically reaching for him before I close them into a fist and let them drop. "What happened?"

His back doesn't look like it's in great shape at the best of times. Oh, the shape and musculature is akin to a fucking carved statue of a god in a museum, but the skin has seen better days. Various scars, including the burns up at his shoulder and neck, mottle the tissue.

But that isn't what's making the contents of my stomach feel like they're rising up into my throat.

It's the bruising.

It's focused mostly at his sides, around his ribs and below, in the kidney area. It looks like he let somebody very, very angry use him as a punching bag.

Which makes no sense. At all. Because I'm pretty sure he could flatten just about anybody with a single punch to the head.

"Had a meeting with Darragh," he says, turning back to face me. Now that I've noticed those injuries, I can't help but notice others – swelling and bruising along his forearms.

"A meeting?" I ask. My eyes prickle. Seeing Elio all banged up like this is getting to me. It's making me hurt. And if it was with Darragh, then...

It had to be because of me.

"You shouldn't have," I whisper. I blink as fast as I can, but I'm not able to stop a single tear from slipping out from my eye and down my cheek.

Elio comes back and bends, kissing the wetness on my skin.

"Don't cry for me, Songbird," he murmurs before kissing me again. He draws back, running his thumb back and forth against the delicate bone beneath my eye. "I told you before that this body ain't worth shit and that I'd put it between you and a bullet any day of the week. And if I have to put it between you and Darragh Gowan, then I sure as shit will do that, too."

"I don't understand!" I cry. I grab the hand that's caressing my face and lower it a bit. Yup, his forearm is already hot and swollen. When my fingers touch his knuckles through the gloves, he gives a slight hiss of pain.

That sound, barely audible, splinters something inside me. I don't bother asking or waiting for permission. Before he can stop me, I move my grip to the ends of his fingers and pull the glove off.

He tenses instantly, and goes to pull his hand away, but I don't let him, I grasp his hand with both of mine, and he stills.

The scarred skin on his knuckles has torn beneath the leather, and the wound has been bleeding freely into the lining of the glove. It's hard to tell with the reddish scarring all over, but it also looks like the whole back of his hand is slightly swollen and inflamed.

"Darragh's got a hard fucking head," Elio says by way of explanation.

"What the hell happened? What kind of meeting did you two have?" I mutter. I tug him by the hand towards the chair. "Sit down."

"It's fine," Elio says, standing and staring stubbornly down at me.

"I said sit!" I scowl and point to the chair.

Elio raises a sardonic brow.

"I'm not used to being told what to do, you know."

"Well, you're the one who seems so hellbent on getting yourself a wife, so you'd better get used to it!" I snap before I can stop myself. My cheeks go hot when I realize what I just said, that I've referred to myself as his wife, that I've acknowledged this future he's carving out for us, the future I should run from.

Liquid heat churns in Elio's gaze. He doesn't say anything else, but he does actually listen to me and sit down, which I guess is a good thing.

"Stay there," I say. I hurry into my bathroom and grab the first aid kit that Elio once used on me. I wash my hands, then bring it out to him.

I half-expect him to have disappeared when I get back out there, but there he is, looking way too big for the chair. He's bent over my desk, peering at my laptop, as if he's the one who has to do the class reading instead of me. My eyes track over his profile – the hard jaw, the masculine jut of his nose, everything made slightly boyish by the flopping waves of his unruly hair – and I falter, just a little.

Get your act together.

I give my head a shake, then go around in front of him, set the first aid kit down, then open it.

"You doing your homework?" Elio asks.

"Yeah. I was, anyway."

His eyes glitter with satisfaction.

"Good girl."

My insides jolt at his words. I ignore the feeling of ticklish heat building in my belly and star sorting through the first aid kit, taking out some antiseptic spray.

"I can do this myself," Elio says, reaching for the bottle.

"No," I say, barely stopping myself from swatting at his injured hand. He looks faintly amused by the way I've taken charge of this situation, but his expression darkens when I take his hand and gingerly put it palm-down on my desk.

His other hand, the one still wearing the glove, tightens into a fist against his thigh.

"Take that one off too," I tell him. "We might as well do them both at the same time."

"I'll do it myself," he says again, and his voice is steely.

I sigh and plant my hands on my hips.

"What's the big deal? You've taken your gloves off in front of me before."

He shifts in the seat.

"That was different."

"Why?" I ask. "Because you were fucking me?"

"Pretty much."

The only other, non-sexual time Elio has taken them off was when he was treating the wound on my foot and he had to wash his hands. He's never once taken them off in my presence for himself.

Only when it had to do with me. When he wanted to stop my bleeding.

Or he wanted to touch me, skin to skin.

I understand his hands have become a kind of complex for him. I can't blame him after the trauma he's been through. Valentina looked so shocked, aghast when I told her he'd taken the gloves off in front of me at all. *He does not do that*, she'd said.

He's worn them since he was a teenager. Never letting anyone see beyond that smooth and perfect black.

He doesn't want to let me see him now. This is different than him running his bare hands over my body in the darkness. This is sitting still beneath my probing gaze, scars bared in the bright light of day.

"It's OK," I say, gently wrapping my hand around his still-gloved one. "You can be vulnerable in front of me."

Saying words like those to a man like Elio Titone is one hell of a gamble. A muscle twitches in the cheek above the scarred side of his jaw, and I brace for defensive anger.

But it doesn't come. Instead, his mouth twists into a bitter grimace. He pulls his hand out from under mine then bites the glove off with his teeth before releasing the leather and letting it fall to the floor.

"You think this is what makes me vulnerable?" he says, lifting a sardonic brow and stiffly wiggling the fingers of the hand he just degloved. "No, Deirdre. I only have one real vulnerability these days, and it's not some dumbass complex about my scars."

My eyebrows knit together.

"What, then?"

He leans back against the chair, studying me through the glimmering slits of his gaze.

"What do you think it might be?" he says, spinning the question right back at me. "Or better yet, *who* do you think it might be?"

"You don't mean me!"

He snorts.

"Course I do. Do you see me acting as a human shield for anybody else around here?"

"I never asked you to do that!" I exclaim, guilt poisoning me from the inside out.

"You don't have to ask me, Songbird," he says. "I'm gonna protect you whether you want me to or not. Whether you think you're worth it or not. And you are, just for the record, in case there was any doubt in that pretty little head of yours." He leans forward, sliding his injured hand along the desk towards me. I stare down at his torn knuckles and swollen flesh to avoid the piercing thrust of his gaze.

"I would walk through fucking fire for you."

The raw intensity of his voice makes my nerves snap to attention. Goosebumps rise beneath my sleeves.

He's breaking down my walls. Every day, every moment, shoving his way inside, finding cracks I thought I'd sealed. He's digging deeper, deeper, until he brushes up against the broken bits inside me. The bits that cracked when Mom died, and fully shattered when Dad abandoned me.

He would walk through fire for me. Fight for me, burn for me.

He says it and I know it's fucking true.

I can't deal with what that means. Panic is rising, pushing back tooth and claw against the fact that someone might actually think I'm worth enough to fight for.

Throat too hot and tight to speak for a moment, I snatch up the disinfectant spray and unleash the stinging stuff on Elio's knuckles. I watch the muscles jump in his arm.

"*Cristo Santo*, Songbird, you couldn't give a guy a warning?" he grits out.

"Well, you certainly didn't give me a warning this morning," I reply tartly, relieved to get away from the more intense topic of conversation. "I didn't know you were planning that engagement announcement. I had to read it on the freaking news today!"

I can hear the smug grin in his voice as I use clean gauze to dab at the excess antiseptic and dribbling blood on Elio's hand.

421

"It was good, wasn't it? Valentina helped us write it."

"Helped *us*?"

"Yeah, Curse was there too."

"For God's sake," I snap. "It's like you asked everybody else for input instead of me!"

"Why? Was there some wording you would have wanted different? I'll get them to republish a corrected version."

"No! I don't want any version of it published at all because we are not engaged!"

Elio inhales sharply through his nose, but I ignore him. He can be mad about it if he wants. I go to tape some more gauze to his knuckles, but he whips his hand away from my reach. He pinches my chin firmly and forces my eyes up to his.

My breath vanishes from my lungs when his gaze captures mine. It's all-consuming, dark and violently possessive.

"I allow you more leeway than I allow anyone else," he says, every word dropping his tone lower and lower. "And I allow you more disobedience than I allow anyone else."

His grip shifts back. He makes a fist around my hair and tugs sharply, exposing my sensitive throat. My back arches involuntarily. Shaken, my hands shoot out for balance, one grabbing at the desk, the other falling heavily onto his rock-hard thigh. With a grunt, he forces me closer. My legs buckle, and I collapse to my knees between his thighs. He's still got his hand in my hair, tugging my head back with just the right amount of force to twine pleasure alongside pain. My eyes water as I look up at him.

His other hand rises to my throat, a mere echo of pressure before he presses his fingers and thumb into my flesh, massaging the sensitive tissue. I let out a guttural moan, hating the sound and myself for not being able to resist this. Resist him.

"Maybe I've allowed you too much disobedience," he muses darkly. "Maybe I've spoiled you too much. Been so lenient that you've forgotten who you're dealing with. It's my own fault, really. You've made me fucking weak."

Both his hands tighten simultaneously on that word – *weak*. The increase in the pressure changes the angle of my head, and I'm suddenly confronted with the unmistakable shape of his engorged cock beneath his dark pants.

"You see that, Songbird?" he rasps. "You see what you do to me? Even now, while my kidney is bleeding out into my fucking body, I'm that fucking hard for you." His grip on my throat goes briefly vicious, and I see ecstatic stars dance across my eyes before he relaxes his hold.

But he doesn't let go.

"You may be able to affect me in ways nobody else on this planet can, but I want you to hear something right now, and I want you to fucking remember it."

His eyes are black and bright at the same time. How is that even possible? Like flames made out of shadows. Consuming me.

"You are mine," he growls savagely. "You are mine in ways you can't even fucking fathom. You say you're not going to marry me? That's like saying the sun's not going to rise tomorrow. I will drag you down that aisle kicking and screaming if I have to. I will shove a ring on your finger even while you try to claw my fucking eyes out. But make no mistake about it. *You will be my wife.*"

His eyes are searing me. Burning down into my very soul. Something raw, nearly painful, tears through that dark gaze and into me.

"Marrying you is my sunrise, Songbird. It's inevitable. Don't think that you can fight me on this. Because you cannot fucking win."

"It's not about winning," I choke out, my throat catching in the possessive cage of his fingers. "It's about what I want."

"No," he fires back instantly. "It's about what you need. And what you fucking need is *me*."

Chapter 14

Elio

My head hurts. My side hurts. My dick hurts. I'm this fucking close to unzipping my pants and ordering Deirdre to suck. The thought of her gorgeous, stubborn mouth closing over my throbbing head makes my veins feel fucking molten.

God, she looks so good down on her knees like that, her narrow throat trapped beneath my fingers, face flushed, chest heaving with restrained rage and probably at least a little arousal.

My angry little Songbird. Beating so hard against the bars of her cage.

We stare at each other, the silence between us as taut as a flexed muscle. I drink in the sight of her, cock twitching when I see that her nipples are hard and pebbled beneath the buttery-soft fabric of the sweater she's wearing. My hand drifts down from her throat, and it aches like a bastard, but damn does it ever feel good when I press my palm into the braless curve of her breast. Deirdre takes a strangled breath, arching into my touch before she seems to remember herself and starts to pull away.

"Oh, no you don't," I hiss. I've still got one hand in her hair, and I give the strands a firm tug of warning. She stills, then shudders, whimpering when I graze her nipple with my thumb.

"Open your mouth," I whisper, my voice growing rough and urgent. Her eyes flash, and I'm pretty sure she's about to tell me to go fuck myself, but with a resigned, furious sort of submission, her lips part for me.

"Fuck. There's my good little Songbird."

I hook my thumb beneath the edge of her sweater, yanking it upwards and shoving the fabric between her teeth.

"Hold that there," I tell her. She bites down gently, and the sight of her teeth sinking into the plush fabric twists something deep inside me.

She's still down on her knees between my legs, holding up her sweater between her teeth, exposing herself to me so beautifully. Her chest is flushed with the force of her emotions, her nipples rosy and begging to be touched. I lean forward, breathing shakily through the screaming pain in my right side, and suck her left nipple into my mouth.

Deirdre spasms as I latch onto her, sucking hard. I groan, palming her other breast with my bleeding hand. She's so goddamn delicious. She smells so good, like fucking sugar. Her skin is velvet and cream. So sweet it almost seems like she should melt, dissolve like candy. Come apart completely under the wet heat of my mouth. I tongue her nipple, rolling it hard, my eyes fluttering shut in rapture when she moans. Her hands grapple at my shoulders, and I half-expect her to shove me back, but a second later her fingers are burying themselves in my hair. Her touch is an electric fever zinging right up my spine to my scalp. I grunt, suck her harder, graze her flesh with my teeth. I know I'm going too hard. I know I'm going to leave a mark on her.

And maybe that's the fucking point. To give her something she can see in the mirror. Something she can't deny. Truth spelled out in broken blood vessels. A physical sign of who she belongs to.

I don't think I'm hurting her, though. Or if I am, my Songbird must like it. She's trembling and making these little mewing, choking sounds around the fabric in her mouth, burying her fingers forcefully into my hair, dragging me harder against her.

This isn't close enough for me either.

With a quick movement, I hook my hands under her arms and drag her up into my lap. She doesn't weigh that much, but even just doing that makes my right hand throb and my side explode with pain. I breathe it in, drink that agony down, let it hone and sharpen the life-halting ecstasy of Deirdre settling in my lap. She straddles me, her pussy settling against my cock. She cries out at the contact, dropping the sweater from her mouth, cringing away from me and shifting her weight onto her knees.

"That hurts," she says, and it sounds kind of defensive, like she needs an excuse for the sound she just made.

It hurts because I hurt her last night. And made her come. All at the same time.

I lick the fragrant silk of her throat, tasting the rapid pulse there. My injured right hand is at her back. My other slides between her legs – not too far, not to the place it hurts. I circle the front, feeling for her clit through her leggings.

"What hurts?" I rasp against the quivering flesh of her earlobe. "This little virgin pussy you gave to me last night?" I capture that taunting lobe between my teeth. I bite the slip of skin until she gasps, then give a long, soothing suck before I let go. "Want me to kiss it better?"

"You're the one who's seriously hurt," she moans, squirming in my lap. All that wiggling sends delightfully catastrophic friction against my hard-on. My heart hammers wildly, and I distantly hope I'm not actually bleeding too much internally, because my racing pulse is only going to speed up the process if I am.

"Fine," I pant as I drag my mouth from beneath her jaw to her mouth. "You can kiss *me* better, then."

I kiss her, and it's not the innocent little closed-mouth smooch I gave her earlier. This is hard. Punishing. Unforgiving. It demands things from her, from us both, and she must sense it the same way I do, because she opens her mouth against the onslaught of that hunger instantly.

I rub her clit faster. Her leggings are so stretchy and tight it's like they're moulded right to her body. I can feel every detail through the teasingly thin material. I can feel her panties, feel the liner in there. Feel the hot swollen nub of her needy clit. Deirdre's hips hitch against my fingers, seeking the pressure of my touch as my tongue slides through the scorching satin of her mouth.

Deirdre moans into my mouth. Tension prickles along her thighs, making her twitch and flinch in my lap, her hips curling forward. Fuck, she's about to come. I snatch my mouth from hers, planting heated kisses everywhere. Her cheeks, the delicate hollows beneath her eyes, her chin. I want to taste every fucking freckle on her while she reaches climax.

"Oh... Oh..." Little cries tumble from between Deirdre's swollen lips.

It's so fucking cute the way she keeps saying, "Oh." Like she's actually trying to say, "Oh, no," but can't quite manage it under the mind-melting pressure of the orgasm building inside her.

"Oh, *yes*," I supply for her, because as her husband I'm nothing if not helpful as fuck. I crush my mouth to her temple as I work her swollen clit greedily. "Yes, you are going to come. Shh. It's alright. Don't fight it, Songbird. Don't fight me. I already told you, you can't win."

She shudders, making a sobbing sound and clinging to me. Her eyes are scrunched shut, but mine are wide fucking open. There will never be enough of seeing her like this. Seeing her beautiful face crumple in sensual, erotic resignation, submitting to the aching pleasure only I pull out of her.

If I were an artist, I would fucking paint her like this.

Instead, I'll just have to memorize her.

"Ohh," she says again, but this time it's not an adorably worried little hiccup of sound, but rather a drawn-out groan. She's *right fucking there.*

A loud knock at the door that leads into the hallway makes us both freeze. Deirdre's eyes fly open, and she tries to clamber off my lap, but I fuse my arm to her back like a bar of iron.

"Who is it?" I bite out. There aren't many people who'd be brave enough to knock on my bedroom door.

The answer drifts through the door in Italian.

"It's Morelli. Curse says you need me."

Fuck. *Fuck.*

I mean, I probably do need him. But right fucking now?

Deirdre looks mortified, cheeks bright red, eyes huge. That look of petrified humiliation strikes a greedy chord inside me. I start rubbing her clit again in hard, relentless strokes.

"I still expect you to come for me," I whisper.

She yanks a hand from my shoulder, clapping her palm over her mouth to quiet her sounds. She holds herself very, very still, her eyes pleading silently, but I honestly can't tell if they're begging me to stop or to keep going.

I don't think that she knows, either.

"Elio?" Morelli calls through the door.

Deirdre squeaks behind her hand.

"Just a minute, Doc," I call.

"You don't sound right, Elio," Morelli answers through the door. "I'm coming in."

"Not yet," I answer sharply. Morelli's one of the few people close enough to me to call me by my first name, but even he wouldn't ignore my direct command.

Only person I know who'd actually do that is the one shaking violently in my lap and trying not to come.

Her eyes are closed again, like she's trying to block out the pleasure. She pants through her nose, her hand still pressed to her mouth. Where a moment ago she was grinding her hips, now she's got everything locked down tight. As if she can avoid reacting to me by sheer fucking will.

"How long?" Morelli calls impatiently through the door. "Curse said you might have a kidney injury. I need to examine you. And I need a urine sample right away."

Ha. I don't think it's going to take long for Deirdre to come, but the urine sample is another story. I'm so fucking hard I can't even imagine trying to calm down enough to take a piss right now.

"Come on, Songbird," I taunt, kissing her jaw, her throat. "Better keep your hand there, nice and tight. I don't want anybody hearing your song except me."

A suck of breath, then a muffled moan hits her palm. Her eyes open, shimmering with anger, horror, and squeezing arousal as she begins to come. The stillness she'd locked herself into collapses like a building being toppled. It begins with a small tremor. And then, it's violent destruction, everything shaking until her legs give out entirely and she collapses onto the stiff agony of my hard-on.

I groan, still working my fingers against her sensitive clit, holding her fast to my chest. Her face is absolutely crimson, and she's biting down on her own hand now, trying to be quiet and distract herself from the things I make her feel.

"Don't do that," I murmur, finally pulling my hand from between her legs and tugging gently at her wrist. When it comes loose from between her teeth, there's a little red crescent of bite marks on her skin. Jesus, is her pale skin ever reactive. Turns red so fucking easily.

I raise her hand to my mouth, pressing my lips to the marks, then dragging my tongue along the line of them, holding her wild, furious gaze the entire time.

But Morelli is getting more impatient. Another knock sounds, harder than the first.

"You better not be passed out in there!" he calls in Italian.

I mean, I feel like I fucking could. Having Deirdre freshly pleasured and straddling my dick makes my head feel like it's not quite screwed on right. It's like I can't quite get enough air into my lungs. My chest burns with the inescapable fire of wanting her, and my head feels light and heavy at the same time. Pain radiates down my side.

Deirdre scrambles off my lap, and this time I let her go, watching with a darkly amused smirk as she hurries into the bathroom, as if to hide from what we've just done.

"Come in," I call to Morelli.

The tall, grey-haired doctor heads into my room from the hall and looks surprised not to find me there.

"In here."

His head jerks my way, the round lenses of his glasses reflecting light with the movement.

"Why aren't you in bed?" he asks. I've always been so impressed by the way that his round glasses don't make his eyes look owlish and round. If anything, his gaze reminds me of a hawk's. Sharp as any predator's. Doesn't miss a thing. Sometimes I think he almost missed his calling by becoming a doctor. He could have been a big boss if he'd wanted. He's got the brains and the balls. But then again, he's also damn good at what he does, and if I'm gonna to have anybody sewing up my scrapes it's gonna be him.

"Good question," I reply in English, angling my head back towards the bathroom. I can't see Deirdre from here. She must be just out of sight, by the counters and mirrors.

"Lean forward," he tells me brusquely. The crisp white sleeves of his button-down shirt are rolled up.

I lean forward, clenching my teeth at the feverish stab in my right side. Morelli sucks in a breath between his teeth.

"What happened?" he asks, immediately beginning to palpate the injury. Black dots swim before my eyes. I curl my hands into fists on my thighs, which makes my right hand crackle with pain. Well, all this fucking agony will certainly cure my too-hard-to-piss situation, that's for damn sure.

Morelli may mostly speak Italian, but he understands English a lot better than he speaks it. I answer him in English, loud enough so that Deirdre can hear me, because I never actually explained what happened today to her.

"Went to see Darragh Gowan," I grunt. "Let him know in person that his claim on something of mine is null and void."

"His claim on what? The girl?"

"My soon-to-be-wife," I correct him fiercely.

"Saw that in the news this morning. Congratulations," he says absentmindedly, poking and prodding at my left side now. That side doesn't hurt near as bad as the right, but it's still not exactly comfortable.

"Anyway, Darragh didn't exactly want to negotiate on the matter much. So we made a bet. Had a little boxing match. I won."

Morelli tsks.

"What, you won by protecting that pretty mug of yours by offering up your ribs and kidneys instead? What the hell were you thinking?"

"Rules were that the first one to draw blood from the other's face won," I explain. "I let him land a hell of a lot of punches. But I only needed one hit on him to win."

"You could have dealt that blow a little earlier in the match instead taking such a beating first," Morelli says, scowling at me. "I don't think I've seen you take this many risks with your physical health since you were a bone-brained teenager."

"Bone-brained? That's a new one," I say with a grin.

"So much skull there's no room left for brains," he clarifies. "Explains why you're still functioning after all the hits to the head you've taken in your youth."

"Didn't take any hits to the head today, though, did I?" I say with mock sweetness. My grin fades. "Alright, Doc. What's the damage?"

"Your left side is bruised, but it appears to be mostly superficial. There may be some inflammation of the ribs, but nothing seems like it's cracked or broken. The kidney on that side should be alright, but I want to confirm via ultrasound. Your right side, however..." He removes his glasses and polishes them vigorously with a small cloth he pulls from his pocket. He puts them back on and gives me a hard-eyed look. "Your right side is a fucking mess. I think it's likely you have an acute kidney injury. The fact that you're upright and lucid is making me hopeful there's not any detrimental internal bleeding. At this point, I am hopeful that you won't need surgery and that the injury will heal with fluids and rest."

"Good," I reply. "I don't have time for surgery. My wedding is in a month."

Morelli makes a grimly amused noise at the back of this throat.

"I don't think your kidney cares about that, Elio."

"Whatever. You said my left one was fine. Pretty sure I only need one to keep on kicking."

"Certainly, a human can survive with only one kidney. But that's assuming the other one isn't damaged, inflamed, or potentially causing complications like sepsis."

"Those are some big, serious words, Doc."

"Your condition is serious, Elio," he shoots back instantly. I may not always like what he tells me, but he's never been anything but brutally honest with me. "You've only just recovered from a gunshot wound. I hope for your sake that after your wedding things settle down for a while. At this rate that pretty little thing you're so fixated on will be marrying someone more corpse than living man."

I've never been particularly worried about my own mortality. But I am now. Not for my sake, but for the wife I'll leave behind.

His words also remind me I need to draft a new will. I make a mental note to deal with that soon as I hold my hands out for his inspection.

"Superficial bruising," he says crisply, running his competent gaze over my pummelled forearms. "Potentially a fracture of the fifth metacarpal." He rolls his eyes at me. "Called a boxer's fracture."

"Like I told Deirdre, Mad Darragh's got a hard fucking head."

He sighs and sets down my hands on my thighs.

"She the one who started cleaning these contusions and lacerations?" he asks, noticing the bloody gauze and disinfectant on the desk beside us.

"Yup. But you frightened my little bird away with all that loud knocking."

"If she's frightened of something as simple as knocking," he says dryly, "I'm not entirely sure how she's going to survive being married to you."

"She'll be just fucking fine."

"If you say so. You might not be, though. I want to take you downstairs to the med room. Get your urine sample analyzed and do the ultrasound."

He's giving me his best don't-fuck-with-me look. He isn't exactly used to me being the most compliant patient at the best of times. I almost always ignore his recommendations for pain management, and even with my recent bullet wound, I didn't wear the sling he suggested.

But that's not how it's going down today.

"Alright, Doc. You don't need to give me that look. I'll do what you suggest. I don't plan on dying before my wedding day."

There's been only silence from the bathroom this whole time, but what I just said seems to have caught Deirdre's attention. Of course, she doesn't speak Italian, so she hasn't been able to understand all of Morelli's dramatic warnings. She understands what I just said, though.

I hear her intake of breath, then the pitter-patter of hurried footsteps.

"What do you mean, dying?" she demands, coming to a hard stop beside Morelli and me. She plants her hands on her hips.

"Like the sound of that?" I enquire blandly. I heave myself into a standing position. My erection has subsided, but my whole side feels like somebody's stuck a bunch of hot spiky coals in there. "Don't get your hopes up, Songbird. Like I said, I don't plan on actually doing it."

"What?" she gasps, and she looks so fucking affronted by my

comment that I actually think I might have misunderstood her. There's honesty in that kind of outrage. "How *dare* you?" she hisses. "You think I ran out here all excited because you could be dying? I'm not a monster. I'm not like *you*."

Morelli's gaze pings back and forth between my beautiful, furious fiancée and me.

"You told me she got scared of somebody knocking at the door. But she stands up to you like it's nothing," he remarks softly in Italian. He gives a soft chuckle of disbelief. "Never thought I'd live to see the day that a woman spoke to you like that. Fiery, that one." He gives me a long, probing stare. "A fiery woman for Elio Titone. I can't tell if I'm surprised or not."

"What's he saying?" Deirdre asks me in a tight voice. When I don't immediately answer, she turns her attention to Morelli.

"Doctor? Could you please tell me what's going on with Elio?"

"Hey, how come you're so much more polite to him?" I mutter.

"You be quiet," she snaps at me, and if breathing didn't currently feel like somebody ripping a hole in me I would laugh out loud. She's so fucking cute. I can't stand it.

"Please, Doctor," she says to Morelli again. She's got her usual armour of anger wrapped around her, but it cracks a little bit. Literally. I actually hear a crack in her slightly shaky voice.

Holy mother of God.

She's actually worried about me.

My reaction to that is almost as painful as my imploding kidney. It twists a hard knife inside me – in my guts, my chest. It's wrenching something open that I don't know how to deal with. I know how to handle her obstinance, her arousal, even her hate.

Her actually worrying about me? Caring for me like that?

My jaw works as I stare at her freckled profile. I want so many things at once I can't untangle it all. I want to deny the severity of my injuries. I want to exaggerate them, see just how worried she might get. I want to hug her knees like a fucking child and bury my face in her thighs. I want to rip down her leggings, pin her to the

434

bed, show her that nothing can hurt me enough to keep me away from her.

She fears my death. She can hate me and hurl angry words at me all she wants, but ultimately she doesn't want to lose me.

I should tell her that she won't. That there's nothing that could tear me from her now, or her from me. Not Darragh, not death. Hell, somebody could stab me through the heart right now and I know with more certainty than I know my own mamma's name that it would keep on fucking beating just so that I could drag myself back to her.

I don't manage to get any of that up and out of my oddly tight throat. Instead, I just mutter a strangled, "Songbird," while reaching for her with my uninjured hand. She mostly ignores me, pulling her hand away from my reach so she can focus on Morelli. I manage to pinch her butter-soft sleeve between my finger and thumb, though, and I hold onto it, caressing the fabric obsessively while pain slowly poisons my insides.

"Hands, OK," Morelli says to Deirdre in thickly accented English. He see-saws his hand in a so-so gesture. "Kidney, not so much. Needs lots of rest. We go do a scan now."

"Where? The hospital?" she asks.

"No, no. Downstairs."

Deirdre tosses a glance my way. There's no denying the worry in those wells of blue. My finger and thumb tighten on her sleeve.

"But shouldn't he go to a hospital?" she asks.

"Surgery, eh, hopefully don't need it," Morelli replies with a shrug. "Scan first. See what's what."

"OK. Let's go, then."

"You're coming?" I ask, surprised.

"Of course I am! I can't count on you to actually tell me what's happening with your injuries! God, I saw the bruising on your side. I should have never let you..."

Her face flushes, and she looks so guilty and ashamed that I want to soothe her somehow, but she's already on the move, turning and tugging against my hold on her sleeve. When I don't immediately follow, she lets out an impatient breath. Her arm moves, and I think she's going to rip it out of my grasp entirely, and fucking hell that terrifies me, makes me want to fucking beg. Plead for her to let me keep holding onto this tiny little bit of her, let me keep plucking at her sleeve.

Pathetic. What the hell has happened to me?

But she doesn't pull her sleeve from my grasp. She does something about a million times more destructive, though I never would have guessed that something that small, that simple, could ruin me with such tender oblivion.

When she moves her arm, it's not to get away from me. It's not an attempt at escape.

It's to reach back and take my hand.

I've held her hand before. At her mamma's grave. But I made the first move then. This is the first time she's actually reached for me this way. When she laces her fingers through mine, it feels more raw and intimate than fucking. Especially since I'm not wearing gloves this time. And goddamn, does my hand ever look mangled in contrast with that creamy, freckled skin, the elegant fingers. But she doesn't seem to give a single shit. She tightens her hold on me and tugs, leading me forward.

I don't think I've ever followed somebody else in my entire life.

Not the way that I follow Deirdre now.

Chapter 15

Deirdre

We head down to the main floor of the house, and by some miracle we actually make it there in decent time, because Elio is too stubborn to accept my suggestion that maybe we should get a stretcher for him. I swear, his pride will get him killed, and even just thinking about that possibility makes me feel like the floor is about to drop out from beneath my feet.

How the hell could I have let him get me onto his lap like that? Let him tease me, make me come, when he was this badly injured? I mean, I know he made a joke about internal bleeding when I was with him, but I didn't think it could actually be real.

Elio has seemed entirely indestructible to me, for the entire time I've known him, and honestly even before that. His unkillable-ness has reached legend status in this city. The boy who walked through fire and lived. The man who took a bullet for me and barely seemed worse for fucking wear.

But Elio, even with his marvel of a body and his ferocious, finely-honed weapon of a will, is human. He's fallible. He's killable. Even if he doesn't want to admit it.

He might be able to confront such things with a blasé attitude, but I can't. I'm hot and cold all over, my palm sweaty against his. There's a sick, pinching panic in my stomach and my mind won't stop reeling from thought to thought. Thoughts of what could happen to him, then frantic thoughts about how I might prevent it, or fix it, or make it all better. Make *him* better.

And the most shocking part is that this goes far beyond just plain old guilt. There's that, too, especially since he got this injury dealing with Darragh for me. But I don't just feel bad about him getting hurt on my behalf the way I did when he took that bullet the very first night.

I feel really fucking scared.

Scared of what might happen if I lose him. It's such a big, anguished, knot of a thing that I can't look at it head-on. I self-soothe, think my way around the problem. If I can just get him to this scan, get him to do whatever Doctor Morelli says, then he'll be fine.

For now. Until the next mess we find ourselves in. Until the next enemy comes crawling out of the woodwork.

One step at a time. Just focus on what's happening right now.

The med room is a brightly-lit space I haven't come across in my exploring yet. It's well illuminated by the sun streaming in through the windows, though Doctor Morelli immediately pushes a button on the wall to lower blackout-blinds when we're in there. He turns on a much dimmer lamp on a counter by the wall, then I'm pretty sure tells Elio to get onto an examination table, because Elio goes towards it. He doesn't let go of my hand, though, so I stumble along with him.

"You can let go. Let the doctor do what he needs to do," I plead on a whisper, and my voice sounds strangely broken.

Elio's eyes swallow mine in the dim light.

"No," he replies, the word so rough it's like a growl. "He can do whatever he needs to. But I'm not letting go."

"Elio..."

"It's OK," Doctor Morelli pipes up as he wheels over a big machine with a screen. "That's his good hand, eh?"

Elio makes a guttural, possessive sound, holding my hand even tighter. He raises it to his mouth, grazing his lips across the slightly puffy spot where I bit myself earlier. His mouth twitches against my skin when the doctor smears some blue gel against his injured side. Doctor Morelli wastes no time, pressing the ultrasound's wand to Elio's bruises.

It occurs to me now that I've never truly seen Elio acknowledge or show pain before. I mean, I know his shoulder bothers him, and his hands. But he keeps it all so tightly controlled, so casual about it all that I sometimes wonder if he doesn't feel pain like the rest of us.

But when the doctor presses the wand firmly against his side, he reacts like an animal in a cage being prodded with an electric baton. His teeth crash against each other, and every muscle on his massive frame flexes viciously. The tendons along his neck stand out in brutal contrast as he chokes back a groan.

I don't think about what I do next. I react on pure instinct, my heart half surging out of my chest at the sight of Elio locked in this kind of misery.

"Shh," I tell him, stepping closer, right between his thighs. I smooth my free hand over the thick dark waves flopping onto his forehead, finally allowing myself to tuck them back the way I so often want to. Elio's eyes are closed, but he reacts instantly to the contact, groaning and leaning into my touch.

"Shh," I say again, petting his forehead and his hair with tender strokes. He sags forward, pressing his brows to my shoulder, so I start caressing the back of his head and neck. Elio's other hand – his injured one – moves around to my back and fists the part of my sweater than hangs between my shoulder blades.

"Good. Keep him still," the doctor mutters, staring at the images on the screen. I barely hear him, I'm so entirely focused on Elio, the massive monster of a man reduced to clinging to me.

"It's alright. Just hold still and it will all be over soon," I coo quietly, pressing my cheek against the top of his head.

Elio's hand shakes around mine, like it's taking every ounce of will he has not to crush the bones of my fingers in response to the pain.

"It's alright, *mo chroí*, just a little longer. That's it. You're alright now."

His hair is so warm and soft beneath my cheek. I squeeze my eyes shut just as a tear trickles down from my eye, instantly absorbed and lost in the thick strands.

It's getting hard to talk, but I keep going, softly crooning.

"It's alright. I'm here with you now, *a chuisle mo chroí*. I'm here."

Chapter 16

Elio

"All done," Morelli says.

"Not yet," I reply in Italian. Because him stopping the scan means Deirdre's going to let go of me. And I will put myself through any amount of hell, for any length of time, to have her resting her head on mine the way it is now. To hear those gentle words falling from her mouth, brushing over me like fucking feathers from an angel's wing.

"What do you mean, not yet?" Morelli clucks. "I've done enough. I'm not going to keep pressing on the inflamed tissue for no reason. As predicted, your kidney is damaged, but you won't need surgery as long as you rest properly and do what I tell you to. It appears that you have at least one cracked rib on that side as well. There may be more, but the ultrasound isn't perfect at detecting them. Both injuries will take at least four to six weeks to fully heal. The kidney will require bedrest for at least a week, maybe even two."

"What's he saying?" Deirdre whispers with hushed urgency against my hair.

"He's saying I'm going to need lots of tender, loving care," I rasp against her collarbone. She raises her head from mine to give Morelli

441

a questioning glance, and the loss of that contact hurts almost as much as that wand pressing into my freshly butchered internal organ.

Morelli switches to English as he addresses her. "Rest. Bed rest. Two weeks. No alcohol. I give medicine. For the pain. Lower inflammation."

"No," I grunt. Pain reminds me of what's important. Reminds me I'm alive.

"You'll take whatever he tells you to," Deirdre retorts.

"If I'm going to be confined to bed like a Victorian-era invalid I'm at least going to be lucid and not doped out of my mind," I grumble.

"No NSAIDs. Bad for kidneys," Morelli warns.

"I'll take a Tylenol if I get desperate. But I don't think I'll need it." I inhale deeply of Deirdre's scent. "Got my drug of choice right fucking here."

Deirdre makes a huffy sound of annoyance, but I'll be damned if I don't hear a bit of reluctant amusement in it, too.

"At least you're healthy enough to spout total nonsense," she says. Every time she speaks, her shoulder and chest move against me. I don't plan on ever letting go.

"You need to let go," Morelli tells me in Italian.

For fuck's sake.

"You need a splint for your right hand," he continues. "And don't even try to get out of it. Your hands are already damaged enough from the scar tissue and surgeries you've been through. You don't need a poorly-healed fracture on top of that."

"What's he saying now?" Deirdre asks.

"Says I need a splint."

"Good. Yes. You do," she says, nodding enthusiastically and making my head bounce against her shoulder with the movement.

"Whose side are you on, anyway?" I ask, peeling my forehead from her shoulder to narrow my gaze up at her.

"I can't believe I'm saying this," she answers, and my heart twinges when I see the shine of unshed tears in her eyes. "But I'm on yours, Elio. At least in this. Which is why I'm agreeing with everything Doctor Morelli says."

"Least someone is actually smart enough to listen to me around here," Morelli quips. "She could be good for you, Elio. Really fucking good. As long as you stop getting shot and beaten and God knows what else on her behalf."

I send a sweaty, pain-addled grin his way as I slowly release the back of Deirdre's sweater. I don't let go of her hand, though. I rub my thumb back and forth, slowly, across her skin.

"Eh," I say, a nonchalant reply. "Worth it."

Chapter 17

Deirdre

If I thought Elio was demanding at the best of times, it's nothing compared to him now. Because now, he's got the severity of his injuries hanging over both of our heads. Instead of threatening me with a spanking, now he threatens me in other ways. Like when we first get back to his room, and he tells me that if I don't come with him into the shower then who will make sure he doesn't collapse and die in there?

I never should have let him see how scared I was. I never should have let him see me worry. But I don't know how I would have hidden it. The mere mention that he could have died sent me into a tailspin.

And does he ever know it.

"You're supposed to be on bedrest," I tell him stoutly as he limps to the bathroom. "That means, like, a sponge bath or something."

"That's fine then. Long as you're the one holding the sponge," he tosses back. Heat creeps up my neck at the thought of having him lying in bed completely naked as I stroke over him with a damp cloth.

"Fine," I squeak. "A shower. But you have to sit down in there. And you can't have the water too hot. And-"

444

"So many rules," Elio interrupts. "You gonna come in here and make sure I follow them all? Plus, Doc said I shouldn't get the splint wet." He holds up his right hand, which currently has a thick black band around the wrist that connects upward with a protective casing over his pinkie and ring finger. His thumb and other two fingers are exposed.

As much as getting into the shower with Elio Titone sounds like an incredibly dangerous proposition, I actually am a bit worried about leaving him alone for any length of time. And I highly doubt he's going to let anybody else babysit him in the shower.

"Alright. You just... stay there," I say, heading for the closet in my room. Once there, I strip off the cashmere sweater, looking for something to replace it. Something that I can wear in the shower. The leggings I have on should be OK. I tug on a stretchy racerback tank top – the kind you'd wear to work out – then hurry back to Elio's bathroom.

"OK. I'm ready. Get undressed," I say, raising my chin and giving him my best bossy nurse voice.

"You first."

"No," I say, frowning. "I'm wearing this. And don't argue, because you just need to quickly get clean and then rest. You don't need any... *distractions*."

"You'd be a distraction in a fucking potato sac," he grumbles, but at least he doesn't seem to want to press the issue. He's not an idiot. He has to know I'm right. Me with him in a hot, wet, enclosed space wearing no clothes is definitely not a part of his treatment plan.

And maybe it isn't even just that he knows I'm right. There's a sickly grey pallor beneath his naturally tan complexion, and I think that he's probably too tired, and in too much pain, to put up much of a fight. And that makes me nervous. Scared all over again.

I cover it up with huffy efficiency, moving past him to get into the shower and turn it on. I hold my fingers beneath the spray until I'm satisfied with the temperature.

I look up just as Elio, in all his naked glory, steps into the glass enclosure with me.

I can't help the instant reaction that blooms in my belly. It's a hissing frisson of nervous anticipation mingled with near-fearful awe at the sight of him. He's so fucking big as he steps into the stream of water, so close to me that the tips of my breasts brush his chest on my next inhale. He leans his right elbow against the wall, keeping his splinted hand up and out of the water while the rest of him gets doused. His hair is slick with moisture, the thick locks shaping against his skull and causing heavy strands to fall forward. Just like I did downstairs, I don't try to stop myself from reaching for his face. I smooth the soaked hair back, away from his forehead, then let my hands slide down his jaw. I literally feel his jaw go hard as he looks at me, the muscles tensing along the bones beneath my palms.

I don't say anything for a moment, and neither does he. He doesn't even move to touch me with his left hand. Just stands there beneath the water, letting my hands cradle his scarred face.

There's no sound but the water falling around us like rain. I watch the glimmering rivulets the shower creates on his magnificent, broken body, tracking the moisture as it rolls down his neck, flattening the dark hair of his chest, then down, down, down. Down through the carved lines of his abdomen. Down into the thick thatch of black hair at his groin. Even relaxed and soft, he's huge down there. I can't believe he was inside me. My heart patters when I notice the dried, rust-red smears on his shaft, getting wetter now, being rinsed away like old water colour paint. It's my blood.

"You should sit down," I tell him, moving my hands from his face to his shoulders and exerting light pressure. I blink up at him through the mist. I'm not directly under the shower spray, but I can feel the moisture pinging off of him and splattering onto my face and chest. My bare feet are warmed by the water swirling around them before it goes down the drain.

"Not until you tell me something," he says cryptically.

"Fine. What is it?"

He needs to sit down and rest as soon as possible, so I'll tell him whatever it is.

"What did you say to me before? Down in the med room?"

I feel the place between my eyebrows crinkle with confusion.

"I don't know. I said a bunch of stuff. Like, just comforting stuff. Why?"

He shakes his head a little. His eyelashes are so dark and thick. A soaked fringe. He scrubs his left hand down his face, wiping away excess moisture.

"No, you said something else. Like, *muh hree*. Or something." He makes an irritated sound. "I'm butchering it. There was another part, too. *Ah kooshla. Ah kooshla muh hree.*"

He's right – he is butchering it. But my breath catches anyway, because it's close enough for me to hear the real words through the mispronunciations.

"*A chuisle mo chroí.* Is that what you mean?"

He doesn't hesitate.

"Yes."

I swallow, my fingers tightening against his shower-slippery shoulders. I stare at his soaked chest, trying to get my bearings, but it's hard, because I haven't heard that phrase spoken aloud for more than ten years. Not since before my mom died.

But apparently I said it to Elio today. And I didn't even realize I'd done it.

"What does it mean?" he prods me when I don't speak. His left hand drifts to my chin, holding it firmly and lifting my face to his.

"*Mo chroí* means my heart," I whisper, unable to speak at full volume for some reason. "*A chuisle mo chroí* is kind of like darling, I guess, but more meaningful. It translates to 'the pulse of my heart.'"

Some unnamed emotion lurches across his face.

"I like when you speak to me in Irish," he says gruffly.

"I don't actually speak Irish," I admit. "I just know a few phrases here and there. My mom used to say that one to me a lot. When I was sick or afraid."

I still can't believe I said that phrase to Elio. It's a deeply personal term of endearment for me, associated with childhood and innocence and a soul-binding sort of love. I never in a thousand years would have expected myself to be calling this man *a chuisle mo chroí*. But somehow, without even being consciously aware of it, I'd reached down into myself, into my past, into my deepest stores of memory and hallowed feeling and I'd pulled it out. For him.

I've never said that to anyone else before.

"You're supposed to be sitting down," I stammer, trying to distract myself from the strange mix of emotions rising up inside me like a wave. Nostalgia and longing and grief and something stronger than any of those others, something that tightens all around me when Elio's dark gaze pushes forward into mine.

"Only because you asked me to," he finally says. Pain snags along the muscles of his face, twisting them as he slowly lowers himself onto the tiles. I sink down to my knees between his hard thighs, now completely under the spray of the shower and getting more soaked every second. I wish I'd had the forethought to tie back my hair, but it's too late now, so I toss the heavy clumps of it behind my shoulders.

"What else did your mamma do? When you were sick? Or afraid?" he asks.

I glance at him, surprised by the question mid hair-toss. There's a disconcerting, ravenous sort of greed in his eyes. But there's nothing sexual in that gaze, or in the question. It's a hunger I recognize, though. A hunger I've felt myself, a bone-deep emptiness that aches when I see young girls with their mothers, or when I'm sick now and no one gives a damn.

He lost his mother too. I know he has his uncle, his brother, Valentina, and all the other people in his life. But has anyone ever cared for him the way his mother would have, had she lived?

"She would make me tea," I tell him. And then I feel disoriented all over again, like the tiles are shifting under my knees, because someone *has* cared for me that way recently. Someone did make me tea when I was afraid, when I was hurting.

And I'm staring right at him.

"What else?" Elio asks.

"She would sing to me."

His chest rises and falls a little quicker than before.

"Would you sing to me?" he asks.

"God, no," I say with a startled laugh. "Unlike my mom, I don't have a beautiful voice."

"Yes you do."

"No, I really don't," I tell him with a shake of my head. "You've never heard me sing."

"I've heard you speak," he replies insistently. "And I've heard you come. I know your voice is beautiful."

"Well then let's not ruin your impression of it by having me actually sing," I say, giving another awkward laugh that Elio doesn't respond to. There's not even a hint of a smirk on his face. Just arresting, fully-absorbed intensity.

"Fine," he finally says. "Then you'll play for me tonight instead."

"Hey, I never said-"

"Please, Deirdre," he murmurs. Has he ever said please to me before? "It's been too long since I've heard you play."

Nobody's ever asked me to play just for the sheer enjoyment of listening to me. Not since Mom, anyway. Whenever Dad asked me to play, it was usually to impress his friends. My students asked me to play so they could learn something, perfect their own technique. Their parents came to watch me play to reassure themselves that the person teaching their kid actually had a bit of know-how to work with. Willow came to a few of my recitals to support me, but I know she doesn't actually have any patience or appreciation for my music.

But Elio does. He not only appreciates it, he's obsessed with it.

"You really do like hearing me play," I muse out loud.

"Of course I do," he scoffs. "I'm your number one fan."

"Number one fan or number one stalker?" I ask, raising a

sarcastic eyebrow even though there's a little wiggle of pleasure inside me at his words.

"How about number one husband?" he shoots back. "One and only husband since I don't plan on sharing."

A sigh makes my chest buckle. I don't want to argue about the wedding right now, and I definitely don't need to get him all worked up about it. I ignore his last words and grab a cloth and bottle of body wash from the shower shelf. I squirt the body wash onto the cloth, relishing the bright, herbal spice of the fragrance mixing with the steam.

"Here," I say, passing it over to him.

He makes no move to take it. He just watches me in steamy silence, challenge in his eyes. He probably expects me to throw down the cloth and stomp out of here, but I harden against the desire to do just that. I can help wash him. He's hurt because of me. I can stay detached enough, distant enough, to at least do that much.

I crawl forward until I'm between his spread thighs again. We're so close that the shower completely envelops us both in its streaming heat. Steadying myself with a hand on his shoulder, I begin to stroke along his jaw, gentler against the scar tissue. I've never seen him with so much beard regrowth. The stubble is so thick and dark. I run an experimental thumb along the good side of his jaw, a sensation pulling in my belly at the oddly pleasant grit of texture.

"What is it?" Elio asks, his question a humid breath on my cheek.

"Oh. Nothing. I've just always seen you so cleanly shaven."

"Yeah. No hair grows on the scarred side. So it looks kind of weird if I leave it too long. Asymmetrical." His lips tug up on one side. "I could grow a moustache, though, if you're into that shit."

Despite the circumstances, I find myself laughing. Elio's humour always gets inside me and draws out responses I can't control when I least expect it.

"While I'm sure that you could pull it off," I say, drawing the sudsy cloth down to his chest, still chuckling a bit, "I like how you look now just fine."

Elio's pectoral muscles go tight, and I don't know if it's in response to my touch or what I just said. I didn't even mean to say it, to be honest. Elio doesn't exactly have a small ego at the best of times. But it just kind of... slipped out.

Must be because he's so injured, I tell myself, closing my big mouth and focusing on stroking the cloth over Elio's skin. *Makes me extra nice to him or something.*

In the deepest parts of my foolish heart, though, I know that isn't true. I do like Elio's appearance, scars and all. The biting, intractable masculinity of his bone structure. The full lips, the hard nose, the dark brows and eyes like charred embers. The attraction to him is inconveniently ever-present, unmistakable, impossible to shake even if I wanted to.

I rise up higher on my knees to follow the line of Elio's upward extended arm, the one with the splint he's holding against the tile and out of the water. Then I move to his other arm, sliding the cloth down the hard lines of it until I encounter the puffiness of bruising and swelling along his forearm. He doesn't flinch as I gingerly pat at the injured tissue.

"Oh, Elio," I murmur, shaking my head and blinking hard against tears that I pretend are simply drops of water from the shower. "What were you thinking?"

"I was thinking that I'd fucking win. Which I did," he says nonchalantly.

"But was it worth it?" I say on a sigh, my stomach churning when my gaze lands on the poisonous bloom of bruising at his side.

"I'd pay any price for you, Songbird," he says. "You should know that by now." His voice lowers, and his hand rises to caress my lower lip. "I meant what I said, you know. That I would have died for you that night. Or any other night since then."

"You remember saying that?" I ask, surprised. He'd said it when he was buried inside me, right on the edge of coming, and a part of me had wondered if it was something that just came out in the heat of the moment, arousal-induced but ultimately meaningless.

But he did jump between that gun and me. Used his body as a shield without a thought to where the bullet might land.

And he did it again today with Darragh.

He's hurt me, he's confined me, he's stripped me of so much.

But he's also protected me more than anyone else in my life. When I was left for dead, abandoned in the darkness, he was there.

He's always there.

Picking up the jagged pieces of me even if he's the one who broke them.

Before I even know what I'm doing, I've dropped the cloth, both my hands rising and cupping his jaw. Elio gives a shuddery exhale, tipping his head slightly to the side, nuzzling into my touch. But he doesn't close his eyes. He keeps them fixed on me, like he's afraid I'll disappear.

Tentatively, my mouth shaped by the unspoken sound of his name, I press my lips to his.

For a long moment, Elio is utterly still. He doesn't even part his lips to let his tongue touch mine like I expect him to. My mouth moves along the tense seam, softly searching. My fingers thread through the soaked, heavy locks of his hair, black as squid ink beneath the water.

I don't know if I'm apologizing for his pain or thanking him for protecting me or telling him something else, something that I'm probably not even ready to confront yet. Something that feels an awful lot like admitting that I'm his.

No. *No.* I'm not. I can't.

That's not what I'm trying to tell him with this kiss. But I...

I keep kissing him anyway.

When my tongue prods gently at the closed-off wall of his mouth, Elio's locked muscles suddenly jerk into violent motion. He grasps me hard by the shoulder and shoves me back. It's a small movement, very carefully calculated so that I don't lose my balance and fall backwards, but I can feel the brutal force in it all the same.

Elio takes in a strangled-sounding breath, like he was drowning and somebody only just dragged him up for air.

"What the hell are you doing?"

"I'm sorry," I say, pulse quickening with embarrassment and guilt. "I was... I just."

"Fuck, Deirdre. *Fuck*." He presses his hand to his side, just beneath his ribs where the bruising is worst, then fixes me with a wolf-hungry stare. "While I'm recovering from this whole internal bleeding situation," he pants raggedly, "I'd appreciate it if you didn't just casually stop my fucking heart like that."

"I'm sorry," I say again, this time a whisper, choked and thick. "Did I hurt you?"

"Yes," he grits out, "but not in the way you might think. Not physically. And that's the fucking problem." He breathes out harshly and snatches up the cloth, finishing the job I started, scrubbing beneath his arms, between his legs, down to his feet, though he grimaces when he has to bend.

"You," he says, dropping the cloth into a bedraggled heap between us, "are a singularly scorching point of pain for me, Songbird. But it's not like this," he holds up his wet, scarred hand, "or like this," he points to the bruising on his side. "It's here." He plasters his hand against his chest, lets it harden into a fist, then thumps it once, then twice, like a heartbeat.

"If it hurts so much then just let me go," I gasp, a sob building in my throat that I refuse to release.

"Can't," Elio says with a grim smile. "You're the wound and the treatment all at the same time. I can't fucking stop myself. Can't let you go because I always fucking need more. I'm like that guy with the wax who got too close to the sun. What the hell was his name?"

"You mean Icarus?"

"Yeah. That one. You're gonna melt my fucking wings off, Songbird." His gaze turns solemn, but there's still that ever-present, clawing hunger in it. "Maybe that's why I'm so hellbent on clipping yours."

I stare down at the luxurious, expensive tile, water sluicing over it like spilled blood. My thoughts are such a mess that I don't even try to sort through them and come up with a response. Instead, half-blind with shower water and tears, I grab the cloth and squeeze it. I don't know if it's a peace offering or payment or a way to protect myself, but whatever it is, I hold it up between us and say, "Do you want me to keep going?"

"I want... *Merda.*" In a jab-quick movement, he closes his huge hand over mine, squishing the cloth harder between my fingers. "You have no idea how many times I've imagined you in this shower with me. Soaked. Naked. Up against that fucking wall."

Warmth extends tickling tendrils inside me as the image flares in my mind. The place between my legs feels swollen and very wet, and I don't think it's just because my clothes and panty liner are drenched from the shower.

Elio releases my hand just as suddenly as he first grabbed it.

"Go dry off," he says, looking away from me for the first time since we got in here. "Put on something warm and comfy."

"I'm not just going to leave you sitting here alone!" I stammer, annoyed that he'd even suggest it. "You're hurt!"

"*Deirdre.*" The sound of my name is like a physical bite. A fanged warning, a nip that breaks the skin. "If you stay in here any longer I am going to forget every single fucking thing Morelli told me about resting and healing and keeping my blood in the broken parts of my body instead of sending it all to my fucking cock. Go dry off," he orders me again. "For the love of fucking God, save all that pretty disobedience for a moment when I'm more inclined to be able to deal with you properly."

His eyes flash and I can practically feel the swift slap of his leather-gloved hand against my ass. A sick part of me wants to shove back against him simply because I know I'll run up against that sort of punishment eventually. Something wrong inside me wants to push him and push him and push him until he snaps.

But not while he's so hurt. Not like this.

"Fine," I say. "But only because I'm worried about you and not because I'm scared you're going to punish me." I'm no longer on the verge of sobbing and I pin him with a defiant look. "I am not afraid of you, Elio Titone."

"Do you think you should be, Deirdre Titone?"

Confusion at his words, intensified by the unexpected addition of Titone to my name, jars me, makes me pause. I feel like there's a trap inside that question, but I can't tell what it is. Elio's face gives nothing away.

"I... I don't know."

Silence settles, so thick it blunts the sound of the shower hitting the tile. And us.

We stare at each other, so close that we would touch if either one of us moved even slightly. But we don't.

"Go," Elio finally urges me softly.

Shaken by my desire to disobey and a sharp need to stay with him, I rise to my feet and go just like he told me to. But I don't go far. I'm not about to leave him when he's as hurt as he is.

After I've stripped out of my soaked clothes and dressed in dry ones, I walk back into Elio's bedroom and I don't stop until I've reached the doorway the leads to the bathroom.

He's out of the shower now, standing at the sink with a white towel around his hips, running an electric toothbrush along his teeth. He's got a new pair of gloves on already – at least, there's one on his left hand. The right hand may as well be gloved with the thick black splint covering up so much of it. The bandaging at his shoulder is gone now. I can see the deep purple mark signifying the place Dr Morelli yanked out the bullet, the place where he was stitched up on my birthday. Yet another scar to add to all the others. But that one he got for me, and the sadness of that fact crushes down on me so hard that for a moment, I can't breathe.

Elio doesn't seem to notice me watching him from the doorway. The mirror is so fogged up that neither of our faces are reflected back for him to see.

He's leaning heavily on his splinted hand at the counter, but otherwise he seems mostly alright, if you can call it that, for the moment. I'm relieved that no matter what happens – even if he were about to pass out right now – I'd be able to get to him in an instant. It's so darkly ironic that I don't know whether to smile or to scream, but I can't help but be grateful, for the very first time, that there are no doors left in here to lock.

Chapter 18

Deirdre

I'm so used to spending time alone in this house that I expect having Elio here all day is going to be awkward, even suffocating, except it isn't. It's oddly nice to have him here, even though we aren't speaking or really doing anything together at the moment. He's currently dressed in a soft pair of grey sweatpants, shirtless, propped up against a mountain of pillows I insisted on shoving behind him. I'm sitting on his bed, at the foot of it facing him, my laptop balanced on my legs that are crossed at the ankles.

I didn't start out on his bed. I actually started out in my own room, returning to the homework I'd been working on earlier, when I heard Elio make a hissing sound of pain. I rushed back in to find him breathing heavily, trying to get into a comfortable position. Clucking at him like a mother hen, I hurried and hovered, adjusting cushions, tugging blankets, positioning water within reach until I was satisfied that he was as comfortable as possible.

But when I'd gone back to my room, I hadn't been able to focus on the words on my screen at all. My mind kept reaching right on out of my head, reaching for Elio, and I found myself leaning back in my chair to stare through the doorway so often that I eventually just gave up.

So here I am. Doing my homework in Elio Titone's bed.

Luckily, I'm not the only one working. If I had to sit here with Elio staring at me the whole time I'm pretty sure I'd get even less done than I currently am.

But apparently Elio hates lying around doing nothing. About thirty seconds after I got him settled, I heard him call Curse on his phone, asking for some contract or other.

He's got the contract with him now, held in his gloved left hand while his right hand rests in his lap. I thought Elio would be the one watching me, but it's actually the opposite. My eyes keep rising from my screen to look at him. He's so totally absorbed in what he's doing, his dark eyes keen with competence as they move in smooth, quick lines across the papers. I've never really seen this side of him, this utterly cool and controlled tycoon of business. I wonder if he looked like this – so confidently controlled, silent with shark-like purpose – when he signed the papers with my father.

"Whatchya thinking about, Songbird?"

I flinch, surprised that he can tell that I'm looking at him when he's so focused on reading the papers in front of him. I was watching his eyes the whole time – they didn't halt for a fucking second.

But they flick up to mine now.

A small smile touches my lips.

"Last time you asked me that, you paid six figures to get an answer."

He sets down his papers in his lap and regards me coolly.

"Anyone ever tell you you're one hell of a negotiator?" he asks.

"No," I reply honestly. "But I don't think I was before you. I guess I had to become one."

He gives a soft grunt as he suddenly leans to the side, reaching for a drawer on the bedside table closest to him.

"Oh, no! Don't," I cry, tossing my laptop onto the plush bedding and scrambling to reach for the drawer. "I can get it. Just lie still, would you?!"

I'm too slow, though. Elio's already grabbed whatever it was he wanted. I sit back down on the bed beside him as he whips open a chequebook. His eyebrows draw together with concentration as he uses a pen to scrawl with his non-dominant left hand. I watch him fill out the cheque with messy writing.

It's a cheque from Elio Titone to Elio Titone, for the staggering sum of six million dollars.

He signs it with a scratch of ink, then hands it to me.

I frown down at it, unsure what he wants me to do with it.

"Now you give it back to me," he says, his hand outstretched. I do so, my confusion only deepening when he places one edge of the rectangle of paper between his teeth, using that pressure to tear it in half. He takes the ragged-edged pieces, crumples them in his left hand, then throws them onto the bedside table.

"There," he says, as if that explains everything. "Done."

"What's done? You just wrote a cheque from yourself to yourself and then ripped it up. Do I need to go get the doctor?" I eye him with suspicion, wondering if he really did take a blow to the head today that's causing him not to think straight.

Elio rolls his eyes.

"It's symbolic. I already told you that your debt is forgiven. But I thought that maybe you needed to actually witness something to mark the occasion. To show you that our relationship is no longer defined by money or by debt."

"You're the one who made it about money and debt in the first place!" I remind him stubbornly. "Or did you forget that part?"

"I don't forget a fucking thing, Songbird," he murmurs. "Not when it comes to you."

I break eye contact, cheeks hot, then retreat to the safety of my laptop. But after a few seconds of staring blindly at the writing on the screen, I sigh.

"I don't even know why I'm bothering to do this," I grumble. "It's not like I'm going to class tomorrow."

"What do you mean, you're not going to class tomorrow?" Elio asks so sharply I can't stop my head from jerking up to look at him.

"Well I'm obviously not leaving you here like this," I say, flopping my hand towards his bare, bruised torso. "I need to stay here and take care of you."

"Like hell you do," Elio growls. "I told you before that dropping out of school, or even just missing class, is absolutely not an option."

I gawk at him, amazed that he's insisting on something as routine as going to class when he's literally bedbound by his injuries. But then again, that's kind of been his MO this entire time. Do batshit crazy stuff, then try to trick me into thinking that it's just normal, everyday life.

"You're the one who made that comment about needing lots of tender, loving care when we were downstairs!" I sputter, anger rising. "What, you have somebody else around here to provide that while I'm gone?"

Amusement sparks behind Elio's eyes, and it drives my outrage even higher. Damn him, *damn him!*

"Would that make you jealous?"

"What? No! God, you are infuriating!"

My fury seems to entertain him. His mouth stretches into a lazy, lopsided grin.

"The name's Elio, actually. But you can call me God if you want."

Jesus fucking Christ.

"I don't even know why I'm worried about you," I huff. "Clearly, you're fine if you can be such a... a..."

"A what?"

"A freaking arrogant idiot!"

"Great comeback," Elio says with a snort. But then his smile gets crunched, his hand flying to his ribs. "Ah, *fuck.*"

And just like that, my anger, my defensiveness, my irritation with him is gone. Destroyed in less than an instant, shattered by the sight of him in pain.

I close my laptop and toss it aside once more, positioning myself on my knees and leaning over him.

"Are you OK? Do you want the Tylenol now? Or maybe something stronger? I can-"

"Songbird."

He grabs the front of my shirt, holding me in place as he says it a mere breath away from my lips. A shiver runs through my whole body at the exquisite sensation of that not-quite-a-touch.

"Yes?" I gasp shakily.

He fists my shirt harder but doesn't draw me any closer, his words a tantalizing kiss of warm air against my skin.

"I didn't let Mad Darragh use my kidney as a punching bag as part of the bargain to earn your safety in this city simply so that you could skip your fucking classes." His words are falsely gentle, his voice so silken and smooth I could almost miss the warning in them.

Almost.

Not quite.

"So sit down," he continues, each word dripping with dark, syrupy sweetness. "Shut up. And do your homework like the good fucking girl I know you can be."

"Bedbound and you still somehow manage to be a menace," I breathe, a hot spasm of need wracking my core at his proximity.

Elio releases my shirt and gives me a nudge back towards my laptop. He shakes his head, a wry look on his face as he returns his gaze to his papers and mutters, "You ain't seen nothing yet."

Elio and I stay in his room all day. We eat a quiet dinner together that Rosa brought up on a tray, then I head to my bathroom to brush my teeth and wash my face. I know Elio wanted me to play violin for him, so I've got it and my bow in my hands when I return to his room.

461

But even though I was barely gone for ten minutes, by the time I return, he's fast asleep.

I stop short, staring at the colossal monster of a man who looks positively innocent in his sleep. Seriously, how can somebody as big and bad as Elio possibly look like *that*?

He's on his less-injured side, his arm flung over a stray pillow. His hair has dried much curlier than I'm used to seeing it, the rebellious bits looking practically cherubic in contrast to the hard, adult lines of his face.

I've never seen him sleeping like this before. Even when we slept in the bed together last night, my back was to him for a lot of the night. And he was gone before I woke up.

I put down my violin and bow and steal closer, quiet as can be, trying not to wake him up. I should just head back to the other bedroom and let him rest. But that idea leaves me feeling oddly anxious. An achy feeling of tender protectiveness is keeping me here, drawing me ever-closer.

I come to a stop beside him. He's on his left side and facing towards the edge of the bed – towards me. The scars on the left side of his jaw and neck are hidden like this, and a blanket is tugged up just above the ugly bruising around his lower ribs. He looks so peaceful like this. Comfortable. Whole. Like he's never been hurt in his whole damn life.

I watch my hand rise like it belongs to someone else, fascinated to see my own fingers gently stroking his cheekbone, feeling the unfor-giving line of it. I trace the shape of his jaw, stopping to brush a springy lock of hair behind his ear. I must have tickled him a little bit, because a muscle in his cheek twitches, and his nose crinkles as if he might sneeze. It's cute, and I don't want to think about how cute he can be, because that distracts me from the dangers he represents.

But I just can't think of him as dangerous right now. And that might be the most dangerous thing of all.

At this moment, I just can't bring myself to care.

I stroke his cheek again, very gently, as tenderly as I'd touch a baby, this time with the backs of my knuckles. Apart from the little almost-sneeze face he made a second ago, he hasn't moved. His breathing is deep and even.

I'm glad he's getting some rest. I know he needs it. Even someone as strong and wilful as him needs to slow down to heal sometimes. I can tell he hates it, though. Hates not feeling strong as he usually does. A man like Elio wasn't made to stay in bed. He was made to walk through the world like a weapon, bending every corner of it to his will.

Being stuck in bed is probably good for him, I think with a slight roll of my eyes. It will remind him that he's human. And all humans need humbling every now and then.

Even if it isn't easy for them.

I know he's asleep, and that he won't feel it, and maybe that's why I do it in the first place. Silently, I bend down, brushing my nose against the sandpaper grit of his stubble before I place a soft kiss at the corner of his mouth.

He remains in a deep sleep. He doesn't seem to react at all.

Until I straighten up and turn to walk away.

A hand shoots from the bed, colliding with my wrist. I whirl around, heart pumping in surprise. Elio's eyes are still closed, his whole face set in a furious, sleepy sort of frown as he tries to ineffectually close his splinted hand around my arm. With a sleep-gruff sound, he shoves the pillow he was hugging away, snakes his other arm out of the bed, and drags me down into it with him.

"Hey!" I gasp, tamping down the urge to fight my way out of his hold. I don't want a stray elbow hitting one of his injuries. "Elio!" I hiss. "Let me go!"

I was planning on sleeping in the other bed. Elio needs rest, not to have somebody else rolling around and bugging him all night. But he doesn't seem to care about what I have to say. I doubt he even hears me, to be honest. He throws a heavy arm over top of me, buries his face in my air, and promptly lets out a soft, rasping snore.

I stay still, chewing on my lip and trying to figure out what my plan is. I don't know what to do with this sort of closeness. Because it doesn't seem to want anything. There's nothing angry, nothing sexual, nothing violent in his hold on me. It's proximity, apparently, for comfort's sake.

You're the wound and the treatment all at the same time.

I'm a pain point for him. That's what he told me.

But even in sleep he can't stay away.

I breathe in and out until I reach a calming tempo, a rhythm that seems to soothe me. It takes me a moment to realize that this isn't a placid sense of timing I've discovered on my own. I've simply matched up my breathing to Elio's.

Even once I'm aware of it, I can't escape from how I've paired my inhales and exhales to his. His broad chest plastered to my back, we breathe in perfect harmony, as if we share one heart and set of lungs between us. More than once, I try to speed up or slow down my respiration, just to see if I can break away from that connection, but it feels so wrong, so unnatural, that I almost get lightheaded. I relax, sink into it, close my eyes, and breathe with him.

Just for a little while, I tell myself. I'll be gone soon. I know I will.

But not yet.

Not... quite... yet...

Chapter 19

Elio

This is the second morning I've woken up with my fiancée in my arms and it's just as fucking perfect as the first time. There may be a hot poker of death shoved between my ribs that makes every breath an agony, but Deirdre's here with me and that's all that really matters.

A glance at the clock on the bedside table tells me she can't stay here for long, though. Not if she doesn't want to be late for class. Which if she knows what's good for her, she won't.

"Deirdre," I whisper against the thick, sweetly fragrant explosion of hair beneath my chin. "It's time to wake up for class, sweet little Songbird."

Fuck, seeing her all slow and sleepy does something to my insides. And considering the fact that my insides are pretty fucking wrecked right now, that's saying something. She's so pretty, shifting in my arms, rubbing at those big blue eyes of hers.

"I told you I'm not going," she croaks. I've never heard her voice first thing in the morning. There's a grouchy smokiness to it that shouldn't be charming.

But I'm charmed anyway. Go figure.

"And I told you that you are," I remind her firmly. "Enzo's probably already waiting for you downstairs."

Deirdre sighs and scrubs at her face.

"Well, at least you're not insisting on coming with me in your current state," she mutters.

"If you don't get your ass ready quick enough then that could change," I warn her. "You are going to class and you are not going to be late today. And if that means I have to escort you myself to make sure you behave, I will."

Deirdre wriggles free of my hold. I let her go even though I don't really want to. But I can't exactly tell her she's not allowed to be late if me holding her hostage in my bed is what prevents her from being on time in the first place.

I can be reasonable with her.

Sometimes.

If I try real fucking hard.

Deirdre heads into the other bedroom, and probably the bathroom, judging by the sound of running water I hear. The toilet flushes, more water, then I think I hear the shower. But I guess she doesn't wash her hair, because when she comes out all dressed it's dry and tied in a long braid.

I like her hair like that. It makes me want to grab it and, I don't know, dip the end of it into a schoolboy's pot of ink or something. Tug on it until she's forced to turn around and notice me.

That, or wrap it around my fist until she cries out, back arching and throat bared.

"How are you feeling?" Deirdre asks me. Her lips look red and chapped, as if she's been chewing them.

"Just dandy," I grunt.

I'm sitting up in bed now. Just getting into this position took a monumental and frankly embarrassing amount of sweating, swearing, and effort that make me want to get down on my fucking knees in thanks for the fact that Deirdre wasn't in the room to see it. The pain is a lot worse than yesterday, which is irritating in the extreme. I guess enough of the adrenaline has worn off to let me feel the full extent of things.

And the full extent of things is pretty much shit.

I give the clock a meaningful glance, but Deirdre doesn't move. There's real concern in her eyes, her voice, when she says, "I don't really want to leave you."

Not sure I ever expected her to say something like that. I stare at her, dumbfounded, glad to be sitting my ass down so I don't fucking collapse under the blow of what she just said.

"Go to class," I manage to say, fisting the bedding with my good hand. "Get your shit done. And then come back to me."

She watches me for another long moment before sighing and retrieving her school bag and laptop from the other bedroom. She pauses as she reaches the door that leads into the hallway, clutching at the strap of her bag over her shoulder, turning to look back at me.

"Don't do anything stupid while I'm gone," she says, rather tartly, I have to say, like I've stuck a sour sweet under her tongue. But that bitterness doesn't reach her eyes. They're wide and searching.

"Like what?"

"Like dying."

She takes a sudden, quick breath through her nose then slams the door open, disappearing through it before I can say another word.

No, Songbird. I don't plan on dying.

I've got a wedding that I need to survive to see.

Which reminds me...

I grab my phone from the bedside table and activate voice command.

"Call Bruno Lombardo."

The phone rings a couple times before I hear the goldsmith pick up.

"Hello? Mr. Titone? How can I be of service?"

"I need rings," I tell him. "A tray of them."

"Certainly," he says with a slight English lilt to the word. He spent some of his time training in London. "Do you know your size?"

"Not for me," I clarify. "Women's rings. Engagement rings. Maybe some sets with wedding bands, too."

"Ah. Of course. I did see the engagement announcement. *Congratulazioni.* Since it was announced yesterday, I assumed that you'd already procured the engagement ring from one of my other fine colleagues in the business."

"Please," I say, rolling my eyes. "You and I both know you're the best in this city. Stop with the fake-humble, self-effacing bullshit and get over here. Now."

"Ever at your command," he says smoothly before I hang up and toss the phone down.

Bruno's shop isn't too far from here, and it's less than forty minutes before I see his dark-coloured sportscar pull up to the gate on the security app on my phone. I track his progress through the property, watching as Curse opens the case Bruno's lugging, checking it for weapons. Then, Curse leads him up the stairs into the room.

I look up from the security app on my phone, seeing them coming at me head-on from the doorway instead of the birds-eye view I'd had on the screen

"Mr. Titone," Bruno says with a deferential nod.

I nod back. "Let's see what you've got." A strange impatience is poking at me. Maybe it's even excitement. Getting a ring for Deirdre makes this all feel so much more real. I wish I'd had the chance to do this before she left this morning. So that she could have gone out into the world wearing it already.

Bruno comes around to my side of the bed, not saying a word about the fact that I'm shirtless and bedbound. He's a pro and he knows when to keep his fucking mouth shut. I watch him as he sets a large case on the bedside table and opens the clasps.

Bruno isn't what you'd imagine when you think of one of the finest goldsmiths currently alive on the planet. For one thing, he's fucking young for what he's achieved. He's only in his thirties, but he crafts the most exquisite shit that looks like it's got sixty years of experience and training behind it. His shop is frequented by the elite from Toronto and beyond. People fly here from all over to get custom work completed by him. His waitlist runs more than two years long.

Not for me, though.

He's impeccably dressed in a dark navy suit with a crisp white shirt beneath it. His ink-black hair is cut and styled to perfection. Despite his profession, he doesn't wear any jewellery besides a watch, and oddly, in contrast to his designer clothes, it doesn't look particularly fancy or expensive. He opens the case and watches my face with cat-like keenness. His eyes at first glance look brown but are actually an exceptionally dark blue.

There's so much sparkly shit on the velvet tray in the case that I don't even know where to start.

I must look frozen, like a fool, because Bruno mildly asks if I might like some suggestions.

"Fucking obviously. What the hell am I paying you for?" I grunt, trying to ignore a sudden flare of pain in my side that climbs up my ribs like a ladder, burning all the way into my head.

"May I inquire as to Miss O'Malley's tastes and preferences?"

I stare at him, furious at him for asking such a simple fucking question because the answer is, I don't really know.

"She doesn't wear much jewellery," I mutter. That is actually true. Even before I took her from her house, I never saw her wearing much beyond earring studs or maybe a simple pendant at some of her violin performances. I've never seen her wear a ring.

"Something simple, then?" he prods. "Refined. Maybe something subtle?"

"No," I snap. "I don't want subtle. I don't want anybody coming within ten metres of her without seeing my fucking ring on her finger."

Bruno's used to dealing with even more demanding clients than me. He doesn't even bat an eye at my surliness. He just moves onto the next question.

"When is her birthday?"

"January first," I answer instantly. Don't need to hesitate or think about the answer to that one, at least.

"Ah. A garnet birthstone. A red stone," he clarifies.

Of fucking course it is.

Bruno opens a smaller compartment inside the case. He removes a black velvet pouch, then an even smaller plastic bag from within it. Very gently, he spills the contents into an empty, velvet-lined rectangle inside the case.

About a dozen stones in shades varying from blood-red to fire orange send spangles of burning light across the black velvet. It feels like somebody's driving a white-hot spike through the top of my skull. Hitting me over and over again, perfectly in-time to the throbbing at my side and in my right hand.

"Nothing red," I groan.

Instantly, Bruno whisks the precious stones back into their pouch, like they're rat droppings or something, not fit to be viewed.

"Do you have another colour preference? Or does she, perhaps?"

Something the exact opposite of the flame-like colours from a moment ago. Something soft and cool, like water.

Or her eyes.

"Maybe blue," I mutter, suddenly aware of how dry my mouth is. "Or just white. Like a diamond. A big one."

Bruno nods and begins pulling rings from their perches on the tray, putting several of them together in the empty rectangle the garnets had been rattling around in a moment ago. After that, he removes two more pouches with little bags in them, spilling blue and brilliantly white stones among the rings.

"Sapphires and diamonds are both excellent choices for engagement rings," he says. He holds up one ring for my viewing. "They also go very well together, as is the case for this ring, which has both."

It's a big, fat, blue oval surrounded by a sunburst of dazzling diamonds, all perched on a white band. It's alright, I guess, but it's not right for Deirdre.

"Looks like something my Zizi would want to wear," I say with a dismissive shake of my head. "Deirdre's only twenty. No grandma shit."

"Something more youthful or modern, then?"

He sets down the oval sapphire and holds up another ring, this one with a wide yellow-gold band and a rectangular diamond going lengthwise across the front instead of the usual up-and-down sort of setting I'd expected to see.

"This is a flawless emerald-cut diamond. This horizontal style is called an east-west setting. It's very trendy right now."

"Nothing trendy," I tell him. "Deirdre isn't trendy."

"Something classic but fresh, then?"

"Yeah," I say, peering down at the tray again. "That sounds good."

"How about this one? This is an exquisitely-cut pear-shaped diamond in a platinum band."

The stone on the ring he holds up for my perusal doesn't look anything like a fucking pear. It looks like a tear drop. Pretty sure I've made Deirdre cry enough. She doesn't need to be reminded every time she looks down at her fucking hand.

"No pear diamonds. Or anything else named after a fucking fruit," I say irritably. Goddamn, my head is killing. Curse is still near the door, and I call over to him. "Tell Rosa to bring me a coffee."

Curse nods and disappears. Bruno watches him go before turning his attention back to me.

He regards me with those black-blue eyes, his head cocked slightly.

"May I try something?"

"What now?"

"I've never met your fiancée. I have no sense of her spirit, her sensibilities, her taste. I'm working with what you're telling me, and while the process of elimination can be helpful, we haven't yet struck gold, so to speak."

"So what? What do you want me to do about it? You're the one who actually knows about this shit."

471

"But you're the one who knows *her*."

The distinction is clear, as crisp as the sound of an icicle falling from a roof.

"What, then?" I grunt, sitting up a little straighter even though it fucking hurts. I never thought I'd be sweating about women's jewellery like this before. Before Deirdre I probably would have just gotten Valentina to pick something.

But this time it has to be me. It's the engagement ring I'm giving Deirdre for the wedding she doesn't even want.

I have to get it fucking right.

"I want you to close your eyes-"

"Nope," I say instantly. "Start over."

Bruno purses his lips, his professional patience visibly wearing thin for the first time since he's gotten here. We've been clients of Bruno's since he first opened his shop, and even outside of that he knows better than to blow off a Titone. But I guess even he has his limits. Some of the smooth polish has worn away from his voice, replaced with the firm authority of a man who knows his craft and also knows his time isn't to be wasted.

"It's a simple exercise," he says bluntly. "And it will help me make better suggestions for you going forward."

I rub my forehead with my good hand.

"Fine. What the hell is it?"

He watches me for a moment, as if wary I'm going to change my mind and explode on him. I kind of want to. My head feels like it's about to.

"I want you to close your eyes and picture your fiancée. The creature that's captured your heart. The love of your life. I want you to hold the image of her in your mind firmly, like she's physically in front of you now."

I sigh, because if this isn't the stupidest psychotherapy-sounding shit I've ever encountered then I don't know what is. But ultimately, I shut the fuck up and I do it. I close my eyes and let the image of

Deirdre form inside my head, soft and smudgy at first, getting clearer every second that my heart beats.

"Do you see her?" Bruno asks from somewhere outside the vision of Deirdre I've created.

"Yes."

"OK. Now say the first three words that come into your head. No hesitation. No thinking. Go."

"Fire. Freckles. Music"

"Good. Now three more. No thinking. Go."

"Angry. Songbird. Soul."

I'm aware of rustling, like he's rearranging his tray every time I speak. But I don't see it because all I see is her.

"Good. Now what about when she's all dressed up, maybe going to an event with you. What does she look like? What's she wearing? Three more words. Now."

I don't need to imagine her that way. I can remember her. When I took her to the gala the day after her birthday, draped in dark silk, diamonds at her throat.

"Regal. Blue silk. Diamonds."

"What about when she's wearing nothing?"

A growl forms in my throat, but Bruno speaks quickly, placatingly, before I open my eyes and strangle him.

"I'm not asking you to tell me specifically what she looks like. I'm just trying to get at all the variations, to understand the different shades of her. To find something that will suit her whether she's at an exclusive event or doing nothing but sleeping in her own bed. Or, your bed, I suppose. So, what of it? She's naked. She's with you. Three words. Go."

Her blue silk is gone. Her hair is in a wild disarray around her freckled shoulders. Her breasts are full and firm beneath my hands, nipples greedy and needing to be sucked, her cunt wet like a flower blooming under the shivering weight of dew.

"Perfect," I rasp. "Flawless. *Mine.*"

More rustling, more rearranging.

"Alright, Mr. Titone. If you would open your eyes, I have three new options for your consideration."

Only problem is I don't want to open them now. Bruno's not a bad-looking guy or anything, but I'd rather keep staring at the naked Deirdre in my head.

But ultimately, I do want to see what he's come up with. That exercise left me feeling oddly exposed, and I sure as shit didn't go through all that Freudian weirdness not to get a goddamn ring out of it at the end.

When I crack open my eyes, there are only three rings left in the rectangle compartment and no more loose stones at all. All three rings are made with diamonds.

"This," he says, holding up the first one between his finger and thumb, "is another oval-cut stone, like the sapphire ring from before, but as you can see there is no diamond halo around the centre stone, just these two triangle-cut diamonds at the sides."

The big, sparkly oval sits low on a yellow-gold band, accented by two smaller diamonds pointing out sideways, like leaves jutting out from beneath a bloom.

"Much better," I say with a crisp nod. Maybe all that psycho-babble nonsense was actually worthwhile. We're a hell of a lot closer now.

He puts it down and grabs the second ring.

"As you can see, this ring has a yellow-gold band, though I can recreate it with another metal if you so desire. The band is inlaid with pavé-set diamonds, and is crowned with an extraordinary two carat marquis-cut diamond at the centre."

I nod again, reaching out to take a closer look at this one. I hold it between my finger and thumb and bring it close to my face. I like the shape of the centre stone, pointed at both ends. It feels old-fashioned but not in a granny way. Classic but unique.

"Very good," I say, suitably impressed with how much Bruno's refined his suggestions. I pass the ring back and he places it back down. He grasps the third ring and holds it up.

At first glance, it's the most unassuming of the three choices left. The other two have that warm, eye-catching yellow gold, and both the others are adorned with multiple diamonds. This one's band is a bright silver-white in colour, and doesn't have any extra diamonds except a large, round, centre stone.

"Is that one white gold?" I ask.

"Platinum," he replies. "It's more durable than white gold, and more pure as well. Unlike white gold that has other metals present, platinum is a single-element metal. It ages beautifully, whereas white-gold requires rhodium plating to restore its lustre the longer it is worn."

I nod, listening, liking the sound of all that. And I can't help but think the brilliant shine of the cool-coloured metal will suit Deirdre best. But I'm not sure about the overall design. It looks a little too simple.

"The centre stone is a special one," Bruno continues, angling the ring this way and that until it sprays rainbows in every direction. "While it is smaller than some of the others, at exactly one and a half carats, it is one of the finest currently in my collection. This is a brilliant-cut diamond, which I cut myself, and it has been independently appraised as super ideal, which is the highest possible quality of cut available. It is a flawless diamond, which means it has no inclusions visible at a magnification of ten times, and its colour is of the utmost quality – level D."

"That all sounds good," I say, "But I don't think it's big enough. Or flashy enough."

"Wherever possible," Bruno replies, "I advise my clients to go with cut and quality of a stone over size."

"Yeah, well, I want both."

His mouth tightens, like he's trying to hold back an expression of amusement.

"Mr. Titone," he says rather delicately, "When I asked you to list off words that came to you when you thought of your fiancée, never once did you use a word like 'big' or 'flashy.' And, if I may be so bold as to say so, I couldn't help but notice in the engagement announcement it was mentioned that Miss O'Malley is a musician. I think if something is too big, heavy, or obtrusive, it will get in the way of her playing. Although, I suppose she could always take her ring off whenever she wants to play..."

"Absolutely not," I snap, reaching forward and plucking the ring out of his hand. "She will not be taking it off. Ever."

At that moment, Curse returns carrying a small espresso cup which he passes to me. I balance it precariously on the stiff palm of my right hand's splint, the ring still pinched in my left. I lean down, steady the cup against my bottom teeth, then tip it back, swallowing the shot in one go. Curse takes the empty cup from me as I squint at the ring.

It's just so unassuming at first glance, and I think that's what's bugging me. Deirdre deserves the best of the best. The most luxurious jewellery imaginable. No doubt this one is flawlessly crafted, and I believe Bruno that the stone is a special one, but is it enough for my bride?

I'm looking at the round diamond from the top down, and I angle it so I can see it from the side. A jolt goes through me then. Because the diamond isn't held up by simple prongs like the other rings. Instead, exquisite lines of metal taper up and towards each other, touching at the points, the diamond balanced inside the ethereal metal shapes.

They're fucking wings.

The diamond is held in place by four flaring, platinum wings.

I can't think of anything better for my Songbird.

"This is the one," I hear myself say, unable to tear my gaze from the side-view of the ring.

I can hear the satisfaction in Bruno's voice as he replies, "Very good, Mr. Titone. I think she will be thrilled. Are there any modifications you'd like me to make? I see you're very focused on the setting of the ring."

"No. No changes. I like these wings." I run my thumb gingerly along one of them.

"Ah. It's actually called a petal basket setting. They're meant to resemble petals, and-"

My gaze rises to his, and the look I give him is enough to have him backpedalling.

"But, really, wings and petals are so alike in shape, aren't they? Anyway, I'm glad you're happy with the ring."

I shift the ring back and forth, shaking my head at the way something so small can send such a cacophony of colour ricocheting out into the atmosphere.

"What's that called?" I ask. "When it makes all those rainbows shoot out?"

"That is what is known as the diamond's fire. Coincidentally, that was also the first word you used to describe your fiancée when I asked you."

"No shit," I murmur. The more I look at the ring, the more I think it's perfect for Deirdre. Maybe it's not ostentatious, but then again neither is she. And I don't want her to have to take off some big, gaudy thing every time she plays for me.

"Now," Bruno says, "there is the question of the wedding bands."

Thankfully, unlike choosing the engagement ring, I don't have to engage in something one step below a goddamn séance to get it done. Now that we have an engagement ring to set the tone for the look, it's a lot easier to settle on a design for the band. We decide that Bruno will make something custom, perfectly matched to the engagement ring, a platinum band inlaid with diamonds of the same colour and quality as the solitaire ring. He tells me that he'll make it the same size as the engagement ring, unless Deirdre tries that one and it doesn't fit, in which case he can adjust them both to the proper size.

"And I want her wedding band engraved," I say suddenly.

"Oh? Alright." Bruno produces two different, small papers from his case. One is blank.

"Please write the words you want, exactly as you'd like to see them on the ring."

I know the spelling like I know my own name, but I whip out my phone to double check, just in case. I pick up the pen with my uninjured left hand, then hiss in frustration, worried I'm going to fuck something up.

"Curse. Get over here and write this for me."

He obeys instantly, slicing through the room to my bedside. He bends over the bedside table, writing slowly and carefully, glancing at my phone every few letters so that he doesn't make a mistake. Then he hands it to Bruno.

"*An Eala Bhàn,*" Bruno reads slowly, his tongue tangling on the Irish words. "What does it mean?"

"It's the name of a song," I tell him. The first song I ever heard Deirdre play, and apparently her mamma's favourite. "Literally translated, it means *The White Swan.*"

Bruno nods, looking once more at the paper before stowing it carefully in his case.

"Seems fitting," he says. "White swan. And you chose a white-coloured metal ring with a setting that reminds you of wings."

I hadn't thought of that, but now that he's said it, I feel like everything is looping back and connecting. Everything working out exactly the way it's supposed to. Clicking into place.

The other paper Bruno shows me has examples of font that he can use to hand-engrave the band. I choose a simple cursive style, smooth and romantic, but not too curly or flowery.

"And what about your band? We're working with a tight timeline for your wedding date. If you want something custom, we should decide on a style as soon as possible."

I blink at Bruno, completely forgetting about my whole wedding band conundrum. I still haven't figured out what I want to do.

I stare down at my left hand, perfectly smooth and encased in the black leather I've grown so used to. There's that cliché saying, to know something as well as the back of your hand. But I know this leather much more than the mottled skin beneath it.

"I don't know," I say honestly. The espresso hasn't helped my headache, and now that we've got the important stuff for Deirdre out of the way, I'm ready for this to be done. "I wear the gloves all the time. Seems kind of pointless to wear a ring just to hide it. And it might bug the scar tissue."

But even as I say the words, I feel a vicious throb. It feels like loss. I want a fucking ring to match my bride's, goddamnit. If I hadn't already killed my father for what he did – for abandoning us in that fire, letting me destroy my hands to save his younger son – I'd murder him all over again just for making this moment so tinged with fucking bitterness.

I've accepted how fucked-up my hands are now. I've got my gloves, and I don't give them much of a second thought these days. But now, struggling with the fact that I can't just put a ring on like any other brainless shmuck might, I feel an anguished fury expanding in my veins, sending raging ticks of pressure through my throbbing head.

For the first time, I notice there are a few men's wedding bands in Bruno's case. I stare at them like a pathetic, starving dog stares at the butcher's back door. I fucking want one. I want Deirdre to slide it onto my finger during our wedding. I want the whole world to see that I'm hers as much as she is mine.

"Just wear it on top of your glove," Curse suddenly interjects.

My gaze cuts to him. I stare at him, momentarily speechless, because what he just said is so fucking obvious and yet it never occurred to me before.

"You don't think that's gonna be fucking weird?" I ask, even while my mouth waters. I feel literal hunger at the thought of wearing a band matching Deirdre's, prominently displayed on the crisp, buttery black of my hand.

"Wearing leather gloves all day, every day no matter the weather, is already weird," Curse replies. "Who the fuck cares? You want a ring? Then wear a ring."

I shake my head. Between this and all the perfectly-timed, helpful shit with the engagement announcement, I swear Curse has missed his true calling as a fucking wedding planner. Or maybe it's less that he's good at wedding shit, and more that he's exceptionally skilled at solving problems.

A lot of my problems just happen to be wedding-related lately, I guess.

"Alright, then. No sparkly shit for me. Just a plain band. Platinum to match Deirdre's," I tell Bruno. He nods, then deftly measures my left ring finger with my glove on.

"Perfect. No other modifications for your ring? No engravings?"

I mull that over for a second, then nod. "I do want something engraved."

Bruno pulls out another small sheet of paper. I write this one myself. Since it's in English, I'm not worried that my sloppy left-hand writing will confuse Bruno when he's trying to do the engraving the way I thought me writing the Irish with my left hand might. I scrawl the four words then hand it back to him.

Bruno's brows furrow as he reads it.

"*Property of Deirdre Titone.*" He glances at me uncertainly. "And you're sure that's what you want engraved? It's for your ring, remember. Not hers."

"Of course that's what I fucking want engraved," I retort. "It has nothing to do with who owns the ring itself and everything to do with who owns the man wearing it."

Bruno's face clears of confusion, settling into something blankly pleasant and professional.

"Ah. Of course." I think I see an amused glint in those dark blue eyes of his, but I can't quite tell, because he's bent his head and is busily placing the chosen engagement ring in a small black box before snapping shut the case he brought.

"Well, gentlemen, it's been a pleasure." He hands back the

engagement ring in its box to me. "I'll commence work on the two custom bands right away and will be in touch about billing within the week."

"Good. We'll talk then, I grunt. Curse escorts Bruno from the room.

I don't watch them go. I'm too pre-occupied with the little black box in my hand. Even the box looks luxurious, some kind of perfectly carved and polished wood that's been lacquered to obsidian perfection. It's so glossy and uniform that it makes the smooth expanse of my glove look cracked and gritty.

It's so small. And yet, it feels oddly heavy in my hand. Positioning my thumb against the seam of the box, I pop it open.

Inside the lid there's a tiny light that automatically comes on when the box is opened. The light cascades down over the diamond, showing off the gem in all its glory. Shattered bands of colour explode outward, like fireworks, from the white centre.

I sit and stare mutely at the ring for a long, long time.

Entirely fucking mesmerised by its fire.

Chapter 20

Deirdre

I float through my classes in a bit of a daze, unable to focus much on anything that goes on around me. I'm so caught-up in worrying about how Elio's faring at home without me.

Hold on. Did I just say at home? Like... *my* home?

I shake that off and try to redirect my attention to my laptop. But as Doctor Heaney goes on at the front of the class, I find my mind drifting once again. What if Elio's not listening to the doctor's orders? What if he's not resting like he's supposed to? He seemed to hate it last night. There was all this pent-up, burning energy inside him that seemed to make him miserable, especially when paired with how much pain I know he's in.

I hope he's at least taken a Tylenol, the stubborn sod.

I take a few perfunctory notes, already knowing that I'm going to have to borrow some from a classmate for this lecture, because mine are pathetically sparse. Although, that might not turn out to be so easy. Everyone's given me a wide fucking birth ever since we came back from the holiday break and I showed up to the first day of January classes with Elio Titone at my side. I haven't attended a single class unchaperoned since then, and whenever it wasn't Elio, it's Enzo, like today. He may not be as outwardly intimidating as Elio – because let's be real, is anyone? – but he's still very big, very broody, and so very obviously not a man to be fucked around with that it's had every one of my classmates avoiding me like I've got some kind of contagious virus.

There's nobody even sitting in this row with us, even though it's a decently full room. Enzo and I are completely alone here.

Enzo doesn't say anything, and I don't find him nearly as distracting as I do Elio, but it still isn't easy to concentrate beside him. His head is on a constant swivel, casting his fierce hazel gaze at the students behind us, then back to the front of the room, then to the windows, then to the door, before repeating it all over again. He's Elio's head of security, and man, does he ever seem fit for the role. He's like a German Shepherd in the shape of a person.

The lecture ends, and I give a sigh of relief. I still have a seminar right after this, but at least I'm halfway done now.

Never thought I'd see the day where I'm anxious to get out of class so I can go back and check on Elio. The hold that man has managed to wrap around me is insane. I'm so busy imagining all the ways he could make his injuries worse doing something stupid that I almost miss Doctor Heaney's reminder from the front of the room as we all file out.

"Don't forget about your assignment! It's due in March!"

Shoot. I had forgotten about it. There's still lots of time, but that's not what has me worried. What has me worried is that I don't see how I'm supposed to actually complete the assignment within the given parameters. We're supposed to go to a live music event and write up a comparative report outlining the similarities and differences to live music productions in the modern age versus a historical period of our choosing. It actually sounds like a really cool assignment. The prof didn't give us any real restrictions on the type of music. It could be anything from a symphony to a metal concert to a live band in a pub.

But there's no fucking way Elio's going to let me go have a night on the town listening to live music.

I take my studies seriously. I've never been the type to slack off too much or cheat. But for the first time in my uni career I think I might either have to skip this one or really fudge it by making up a fake music event and writing a report on that.

I blow out a sigh. I'll worry about that later, I guess.

Maybe I can use my fucking wedding as the music event, I think with mirthless irony. *I'm sure there will be music there...*

If it even happens. Which it won't.

The seminar goes much the same as the lecture, with me finding it difficult to focus. It gets so bad towards the end of the class that I do something I typically make it a rule to avoid, because it always just feels so disrespectful, especially in a small, intimate seminar versus a lecture.

But I do it anyway. I take out my phone, hiding it behind the open screen of my laptop. I scroll through my contacts until I reach Elio, who's still listed as My Monster.

I choose the text message option, biting hard at my lip as I stare at the blinking cursor in the text box.

What do I even want to say? I've never texted him before, and it's got me feeling unnecessarily anxious. And that makes me so annoyed with myself I start typing out of sheer anger.

Are you following the doctor's orders? Are you in bed?

His reply comes in almost instantly. And I hate, fucking hate, the way the speed of it makes my heart do an odd little dip.

Good afternoon, Songbird. Are you supposed to be texting in class?

My cheeks flame. Oh, for fuck's sake. I scowl at the screen, thumbs flying.

You answer my question first and then I'll answer yours.

Once again, the reply comes in quickly.

Yes. I'm being your good little patient. All tucked in nice and snug. I didn't know being injured would make you so damn bossy.

There's a slight pause, and as I try to figure out what to say to that, another text comes in.

I should get you a cute little nurse's outfit. I'd let you scold me all you wanted if you wore it.

Jesus Mary and Joseph. How this man is finding it in him to flirt while he's laid up in bed with a busted kidney is absolutely beyond me. But it does sound like he's doing alright at least, and there's a pleasurable little rush of relief at that.

You never answered my question, comes another message. *Are you supposed to be texting right now? Or are you supposed to be listening to the teacher?*

Before I can answer, Enzo's phone vibrates. He takes it out and appears to read a message that's just come in. Then, without a word, he snatches my phone out of my hand and shoves it into his pocket.

"Hey!" I whisper-hiss at him. But even though I'm trying to be quiet, my voice carries. This isn't a large lecture hall where you can get away with a quiet conversation in the back row. It's a fifteen-person seminar, and when I look up every set of eyes is on me.

"I'm sorry," I say instantly, wanting to fall through the fucking floor and disappear. My professor Dr Frank, a kind man I've always looked up to, shakes his head rapidly, face probably even more red than mine as his gaze goes to Enzo beside me.

"Not at all, Deirdre. Not at all," he stammers. He's clearly worried about some kind of reprisal from Enzo, or Elio, if he says anything about me disrupting the class.

God, he must have seen the engagement announcement by now. They probably all did. What must they think of me, their normal, boring, quiet classmate engaged to one of the most brutal men to ever walk Toronto's streets?

Now that I think about it, the last time I was on this campus with Elio he broke my ex-boyfriend Brian's nose, right out in the middle of the fucking daylight, not a care in the world for who might have been witness. I wonder if Brian's seen the announcement. He must have. He always kept up to date with news and politics. There's no way he would have missed it, the way it was plastered across every news site big and small.

Most of my classmates have already averted their gazes from me. It's as if, sitting beside a made man, I've become the sun. Distracting, but too hard to look at for long without imminent pain. Everyone tries to appear very focused on what Dr Frank says next. Well, everyone except for one student, a dark-haired girl named Annabelle Choi. I like her, or at least, I did before, back when I had friends and wasn't cut off from the whole damn world even as I tried to make my way back into it.

Annabelle and I worked on a project together as partners last semester, and as someone who tended to take on the majority of group work in school growing up, working with her was a dream. She's whip-smart, detail oriented, a fast talker and an even faster writer. I can feel how keen her gaze is on me as I turn my burning face back to my laptop, her brown eyes brimming with about a million unspoken questions.

A few minutes later, the class ends, and I practically bolt out of it. Enzo and I join the crush of students leaving their classes from adjacent rooms. As we pass by a door into one of the women's bathrooms on this floor, I stop.

"Hold on a second. I'm just gonna pop in here," I tell Enzo, heading for the door. I go through it, expecting Enzo to wait outside, but infuriatingly, he doesn't. He strolls right in after me.

"Hey!" I say, embarrassed and annoyed. "This is the ladies' room. Out you go!"

Enzo doesn't budge.

"There are stalls," he says with a shrug. "Not like I'll be watching you."

Not like at home... Where I don't even have a door at all. Good grief.

"It doesn't matter! You're still not supposed to come in here!" I glare and point furiously at the door.

Enzo doesn't seem impressed. Light brown eyebrows rise over his hazel eyes.

"Look, Mrs. Titone, I have very specific orders that I've been given to follow in Elio's absence. While he's not here with you, I'm not to let you out of my sight."

"I'll already be out of your sight in the stall, so why can't you go outside the room?"

He jerks his chin towards the gap between the bottoms of the stall doors and the floor. I follow his gaze, seeing one set of winter boots in an occupied stall. The other two are empty.

"I'll still be able to see part of you."

"Oh, come on! There are no windows in here. It's not like I can run away or someone can come in without you seeing them at the outside door!"

"It's not happening, Mrs. Titone," he says coolly.

God, I wish he'd stop calling me that.

"And you can glare at me all you want," he adds, "but I'm a lot more afraid of pissing off Elio than I am of you. What was it he said about watching you? Oh, right. 'Protect my fiancé like her life is your own, because it is.'"

"What does that even mean?"

"It means he'll kill me if something happens to you."

I gawk at him, amazed at how casually he says it. He doesn't seem upset in the slightest that his boss has literally threatened to kill him if he fucks up. It's like he's talking about being written up for being late to work.

"You should report him to somebody. To the Ministry of Labour, or something," I mutter sarcastically, giving up on arguing with him and heading into a stall. I really do have to pee, and I don't think I'll make it home at this rate. Might as well just suck it up and go. I feel bad for the other girl in here, though. Must be kind of weird to suddenly hear a man's voice echoing off the bathroom walls when you're not expecting it.

I end up in the stall beside her, whoever she is. I meant to leave a stall between us as a courtesy, but the lock on the other stall at the end was broken, so I don't have much choice. If I have to pee with Elio's head of security in the room, I'm absolutely not going to do it in a stall where I have to lean forward to awkwardly hold the door closed with my hand.

It takes me a second to relax with Enzo out there, but after a couple of seconds I can pee and finally get out of here. As I go to reach for the toilet paper, though, I freeze.

Something's down there, held aloft beneath the barrier cutting my stall off from the one beside me. It's a notebook and a pen.

I suck in a breath, stealing a glance at the closed stall door. Enzo doesn't seem to have reacted as far as I can tell. Our feet are far enough forward that he can see them, but now that I think about it, the paper is held under the part of the stall nearest the back. Enzo wouldn't notice unless he was lying on the floor to look.

Curiosity getting the better of me, I snatch the notebook and pen.

It's open to a lined page with some quickly-scrawled writing on it.

Hey! It's Annabelle! Sorry, this is so weird, but I didn't know if I could text you anymore. I saw that guy take your phone in class. Who is he? Your bodyguard? I also saw the engagement announcement. Are you seriously engaged to Elio Titone?

PS I promise I didn't wipe yet so there's no gross germs on the pen or anything.

I snort at the post script. This may be the weirdest form of conversation I've ever had, but it's really nice to talk to someone other than Elio or one of his men. I like Valentina, but sometimes I just need to converse with someone who isn't a Titone or someone working for their family. And since I haven't heard from Willow in a while, I guess passing notes with Annabelle is all I've got for now.

I fiddle with the pen a little bit, wondering how I should reply. I certainly don't consider myself engaged, but is it a good idea to tell other people that right now?

I take the easy way out, trying to stay away from the messiness of explaining, *Well, Elio decided that we're engaged right after he shot three men for me.*

Instead, I just write,

It's complicated.

PS I also didn't wipe yet. Yay for no germs!

I pass back the notebook and pen, and it's snatched from my hand instantly. A moment later I hear the rustling sound of the book and pen getting shoved into a bag, then more rustling, then a toilet flushing. I finish up and flush as well, exiting the stall at the same time Annabelle does.

Our eyes meet in the mirrors ahead before I break eye contact and turn on the tap at the sink. Enzo is leaning his hips against the counter, arms crossed, his gaze moving constantly between Annabelle, me, and the door.

Even while I focus on washing my hands, just like in the classroom, I can feel Annabelle looking at me, her curiosity like a physical touch on my skin.

"If you want to ask me anything else, you can," I say, somewhat spontaneously. But honestly, at this point, screw it. If Enzo wants to hang around me non-stop then I'm not going to let him get in the way of actually talking to somebody. If he has a problem he can take it up with Elio.

Annabelle's eyes get really big, like she wasn't expecting me to address her in front of Enzo. She finishes washing her hands, wiping them on a brown paper towel.

"So," she says slowly, watching Enzo like he's a tiger about to pounce. "February twenty-ninth, eh? That's pretty soon. And a Titone wedding. That's going to be some event."

"I guess," I say noncommittally, drying my own hands and tossing the paper towels in the trash.

"Need an extra bridesmaid?"

I'm pretty sure she's joking, but Enzo's reply is swift and serious.

"You're not on the guest list."

"How do you know?" she asks him, raising a dark eyebrow. "You don't even know my name."

"Yes I do," he counters. "Your English name is Annabelle. Your full Korean name is Choi Ha-Rin. 21 years old. Third-year English student taking music as an elective."

Annabelle's mouth falls open, but she recovers quickly.

"Why do you know all that?" I ask Enzo.

"It's my job to know all that. Same why I know the names and backgrounds of every other student sharing classes with you this semester."

"Well, that's intense," Annabelle says. She pauses, as if unsure she wants to say the next part, but then appears to decide to just go for it.

"Am I allowed to text you?" When I don't answer immediately, she turns her attention to Enzo. "Can I text her? Are you going to give her phone back later?"

"She can have it back now," Enzo replies with a shrug. He pulls it from his pocket and hands it to me. "Boss didn't want you texting in class but he told me to give it back to you afterwards."

"How kind of him," I reply with mock cheeriness before turning back to Annabelle. "Yes, you can text me. I've still got your number."

"OK," she says with a nod. "Well... I'll do that then. And I'll see you in class next week?"

She asks it like a question, as if she's worried I'm going to disappear off the face of the Earth. Which, considering the kinds of circles I'm running in these days, maybe isn't so unrealistic.

"Yes," I tell her firmly. "You will."

She smiles again, then heads out the door, leaving just Enzo and me in the room.

"Well, we might as well go," I say, surreptitiously checking my phone. There are no more messages from Elio.

"Good," Enzo says. "Let's go. Boss wants to see you."

"Oh? What about?" I ask as we head through the door into the hallway and then outside into the cold afternoon air.

490

"What do you mean?" Enzo asks.

"I don't know. You said it like he has something specific he wants to talk to me about."

"Oh," Enzo says. "No, I think he literally just wants to see you. That's what his most recent message to me said. 'Bring Deirdre home now. I want to see my fiancée.'"

Chapter 21

Elio

Much as I try to ignore it, I feel worse and worse as the day goes on. I think I'm going into Deirdre withdrawal. It makes me feel like my whole fucking body is shutting down.

I use voice-to-text to send Enzo a text message.

"Bring Deirdre home now," I tell him. "I want to see my fiancée."

My voice sounds raspy and dry. My head throbs with every word.

Not long after that, Enzo's reply lights up my phone.

"We're at the vehicle and heading your way."

Feels like fucking forever before I see the car show up on the security cameras. I follow Enzo and Deirdre on my phone's screen until they're mounting the stairs together. Enzo doesn't go any further, but Deirdre does.

The door opens, and in she walks.

I swear the whole room gets brighter with her in it. She looks just as cute as this morning, maybe even more-so, because a few curly wisps of hair have escaped from her braid.

"How was school?" I ask, making an effort to sit up straighter. I've kind of slouched down in the bed as the day's gone on.

"Fine. I guess. I couldn't focus."

I smirk.

"Too much texting?"

She shoots me a harried look as she sets down the school bag I bought for her.

"Technically you sent more text messages than I did," she replies sourly. "And you didn't need to tell Enzo to take away my phone, by the way. I don't even usually text in class."

"You did today. You messaged me first."

"Yeah, because I needed to make sure you hadn't passed out or something without me here to watch you."

It's adorable the way she tries to mask her concern behind irritation. She looks pissed, but even now she can't stop her feet from carrying her towards my bedside. There's a little worried divot between her ginger eyebrows that I want to poke. I would do it, too, if lifting my arm didn't feel like such a pain in the ass right now.

"How are you feeling?" she asks quietly. "You look flushed."

"Probably because my fiancée just walked in."

Her mouth twists.

"Could you be serious for two minutes? Also, I'm not sure how comfortable I feel about you calling me that. I haven't exactly-"

Her words go silent when her eyes settle on my bedside table.

She sees the ring box. I left it open specifically for this moment, the single solitaire diamond luminescent on its wings of platinum.

She stares and stares. And doesn't say a thing.

Nerves prickle along my spine. It's the perfect ring for her. I'm sure of it.

I... think.

Fuck.

I am going to tear Bruno a new one I swear to fucking God.

"If you don't like it," I say without emotion, "we'll exchange it."

She didn't get to pick her groom. I guess I can at least let her pick her ring.

She startles, like I've woken her from a dream.

"Oh, no. It's not that," she whispers quickly. "I definitely don't dislike it."

Satisfaction spreads through me, hot and venomous.

"Try it on."

"Oh, Elio..." She shakes her head. She's shutting down. Trying to put distance between us.

"Deirdre," I throw her name like a grappling hook, trying to pull her back. "I told you before that I would get a ring on your finger even if you were trying to claw my eyes out. Are you going to put a sick and injured man through all that? Or are you going to be good and do what I ask?"

She thins her lips and gives me a flat look.

"Just do it," I grunt, losing patience because I feel like I might be losing even more than that. Like every second she refuses to put on the ring I chose it's like she's getting further and further away from me. Even though I'm sitting up in bed, I'm suddenly thrown wildly off-balance. My left hand shakily reaches for her left wrist and I latch on like she's a lifeboat.

I guess I must look just pathetic enough, because her face softens and she gives a little sigh.

"I'll try it on," she says, emphasizing the temporariness of the act. But I don't care. It's something. I release her wrist and watch her as she carefully takes the ring out of the box. She handles it so delicately, barely touching it, like she's afraid it's going to sting her or stab her or something.

"It's just a ring," I tell her. "It won't bite."

"Oh! No," she says, looking at the ring then back at me. "It's just... It's so nice. I don't want to damage it somehow."

"Because you think we're sending it back?" I probe sharply. What, she wants to keep it in pristine condition because she thinks I'm going to try to get a goddamn refund on it?

"I actually hadn't thought that far ahead," she says, tossing me a frown. "It's just... I don't know. I didn't want to break it." Her eyes look big and deep and dark. "It really is beautiful, Elio."

And suddenly I remember what she told me the night I took her virginity. The story she'd never told anyone else. About how when she was ten years old and all broken up inside from the loss of her mamma, she tried to make a pot of tea in her mamma's beautiful old pot. Seeking comfort in one of the last places left to her. And she broke it. Dropped the teapot and smashed it into pieces. When I picture it, a sad little Deirdre staring at the broken pot, it feels like one of those jagged hunks of ceramic is lodged in my throat.

She's not worried about sending the ring back to Bruno in perfect condition so she can get out of the engagement. She just doesn't want to break something beautiful. Something special. Even if that something came from me.

My chest feels like its cracking, and I don't think it's from the broken ribs.

"You're not going to break it, Deirdre," I tell her softly. "And even if you somehow manage to seriously damage a platinum and diamond ring, I will get it fucking fixed for you. Alright?"

I need her to hear me on this. I need her to understand.

There is nothing in her life that I cannot control, reshape, repair. Nothing I can't fix for her. Protect her from.

That's what a husband's fucking for.

"Alright," she says, and there's a tremulous quality to her voice, a liquid-shimmer sheen in her eyes that makes me think she might be about to cry. And I don't want her to cry, not now, but then again maybe it's a good sign. Don't some girls cry when they're proposed to? But I didn't actually propose. So what the fuck do I know?

I don't get time to dwell on any of those questions because Deirdre is sliding the ring onto her finger and, like a lick of lightning in my head, she burns away all other thought. As I stare at her, I wonder if this is how other people feel when they step into a church.

And not just any church. One of those big, old ones with a saint's bones inside. The kind of place where miracles happen.

Never believed in miracles before.

Not until I had one standing in my bedroom with tears in her eyes and my ring on her finger.

"Fits," she says tightly. Just one word, choked from her throat. Like she can't manage saying anything else without bursting into tears. Her throat works, the muscles constricting, and she suddenly draws her hands together, like she's going to rip the ring off, but once again I capture her wrist in my fingers.

Apparently, I too am only capable of a single fucking word in that moment.

"Don't."

"Elio-"

"*Don't.*"

She opens her mouth, ready to argue with me, but instead she just breathes out and nods.

"Just for a bit," she finally says.

Just for a bit? Try just for-fucking-ever.

But I know when to take my victories when I get them. She's no longer itching to take the ring off, and that's a win in my books.

It's as if all of the energy goes out of her at once. Her knees bend, and she sits down heavily on the edge of the bed beside me. A flickering expression, like the shadow of a smile, is briefly visible on her face before it fades. She leans towards me, brushing hair away from my forehead. She lays her knuckles against my skin, so silken and cool that I groan without meaning to.

"You feel a little warm," she says, her brows drawing together. This time she's close enough to easily reach, and I do poke the little wrinkle that appears between them with the tip of my index finger.

"What are you doing?" she asks with exasperation as I run that finger down her freckled nose.

"Touching you."

"Well, obviously."

Her knuckles glide down across one of my throbbing temples, coming to rest at the top of my cheek.

"You really do feel warm," she says.

"I run hot. It's a Titone thing."

"That's true. You were like a furnace even before you went to see Darragh. But still..."

I poke the dimpled spot between her brows again. Which, ironically, only makes the wrinkle deeper as she gets annoyed and swats away my hand.

"Has the doctor come to check on you today?" she asks, pulling back a little bit, presumably so that I stop poking her face.

"Is this what people talk about when they say they have a nagging wife?" I mumble, letting my hand drop. I always thought I'd hate that kind of thing. But not now. Not with her.

"You're the one who decided you wanted a wife," she reminds me icily. "If you don't like me nagging you about important things like fevers then I don't know what to tell you." There's a bit of bite in her voice, but the caress of her knuckles against my cheek is very gentle. Tender, even. A sweet supplication of her skin on mine. Without even realizing I'm doing it, I close my eyes and tip my head, leaning harder into the touch.

"Nah. I like it just fine."

At my lean, she changes the position of her hand, flipping it so that her palm and fingers are cupping the side of my face. Her left hand rises to do the same on the other side, and it's like those cool hands are holding me together. I sense a change in the weight on the mattress, and realize she's gotten much closer to me when I feel the heated whisper of her breath against my mouth.

"Gonna stop my heart again, Songbird?" I ask, already tipping my face forward to find her mouth.

"No," she says. "I just want to look at you for a minute."

I crack my eyes open, nearly drowning in the gorgeous blue before me. It's not very bright in here, and her pupils are huge, wrapped in a ring of hushed midnight.

"And what is it that you see?" I ask.

Maybe she'll say she sees a monster, a tyrant. She's called me those things before. And she was right.

But somehow, I don't think that's what she'll say. That is, if she means to answer at all. She doesn't look pissed at me, or betrayed, or like she wants to run. She almost looks sad, but that's not quite right. Sombre, maybe. Serious. Searching. There's an anguished gravity in her gaze that draws me in and devastates.

Cristo Santo. Bullets and bruised kidneys are nothing compared to how I ache for her.

I've always been a survivor. Fucking unkillable.

But I don't know if I can survive this. Survive the kind of desire that eats you up from the inside out.

And suddenly I can't stand it. I can't stand her being so close but so far. Having her look at me in stoic silence, not knowing what the hell it is she sees. It would be better if she called me a monster and pushed me away just like she's done so many times before. That, I know how to handle. I spank her, choke her, make her come. Dole out pain and pleasure until she breaks in my hands and I'm the only one who can put her back together.

It was never supposed to be the other way around.

I lurch forward to capture her mouth with mine at the precise moment that two other things happen. One, the door to my bedroom opens and somebody comes in.

And two?

Deirdre turns away.

Like a frightened animal, she bolts, nearly leaping off the bed.

"Valentina!" she cries. "Hi! Um. Hi."

"What the hell are you doing here?" I growl at my cousin. Now that the drug of Deirdre touching me has been ripped away, the agony floods back in. My side flames. My brain pounds like somebody's using it for hammer practice.

Is there even such a thing as hammer practice?

Fuck me, I'm rambling inside my own miserable head.

"I told you I was coming!" Valentina says, giving me an affronted look. "In fact, I'm pretty sure you were the one who told me to come at this time." She clears her throat and deepens her voice in what I'm sure she thinks is a hilariously accurate impression of me. "'She has school tomorrow. Come after her classes.' Word for fucking word!"

"Yeah, well, come back tomorrow," I say, staring daggers at my cousin. "We're busy."

"I'm sorry if I interrupted anything," she says with a roll of her eyes that tells me she isn't sorry at all. "But you are the one who gave me this insane timeline to work with. If we're going to pull off a wedding for the twenty-ninth then we need to get started now."

I can see the effect Valentina's words have on Deirdre, specifically the words "wedding" and "twenty-ninth." Deirdre's face is hidden from this angle, but her reaction is clear as anything even from here. Her back goes ramrod straight, muscles tightening along her spine.

If Valentina notices the tension, she doesn't say anything. She just ploughs right on ahead. She's kind of like Uncle Vinny that way. And maybe a little bit like me.

She strides all the way into the room, grabbing Deirdre's hand and pulling her.

"Come on," she said. "When I told Donata the deadline we're working with she nearly shit a fucking brick."

"Who's Donata?" I snap. "Where are you going? When will you be home? Who's escorting you?"

"Curse is coming with us. And Donata's our favourite dress designer. God, Elio, I must have told you that a hundred times. Mamma and I go see her whenever we need new dresses. She made our gowns for the gala, including Deirdre's. She... You know what? Never mind. I can see you tuning me out already."

I'm not exactly doing it on purpose. It's just that I'm now currently picturing Deirdre at a dressmaker's shop, trying on long white dresses, looking like a bride, *my* bride, and it's short circuiting my fucking brain.

"Ignore him," Valentina says when Deirdre twists to throw me a questioning glance. "Curse has the car ready for us already. Giulia and Lucia will be there too. They cannot wait to meet you! Don't worry, you'll like them."

Giulia and Lucia are alright. They're Morelli's twin girls, and close friends of Valentina's. I guess it's probably good for Deirdre to have a couple other female friends, especially since Willow's getting packed off to Dublin from what I heard at Darragh's.

Which I still haven't told Deirdre, now that I think about it.

Now's not the time, though, because my fiancée is being bodily pulled out the door by the much shorter but also much stronger Valentina.

I don't expect her to look back at me as she goes.

But she does. Her eyes meet mine, a fleeting flash of blue, before she finally disappears.

"Have fun," I call, though it's really more of a weak grunt.

But I guess she hears it. Because she volleys her reply back at me, a loud response from somewhere down the hall.

"Stay in bed! And take a Tylenol!"

I want to chuckle at that, but even thinking about laughing makes my ribs feel like toothpicks somebody's fixing to snap.

I grab my phone and watch Valentina and Deirdre move together through the house, put on coats and boots, and leave. When the front door closes, I call out once again, knowing Robbie is stationed in the hallway near the stairs.

"You heard my fiancée. Somebody get me a goddamn Tylenol."

Chapter 22

Deirdre

Valentina is such a force of nature that I barely even know what's happening until I'm sliding into the creamy leather backseat of a big, black SUV. I don't think I've been in this one before. Just how many luxury vehicles does this family own?

Curse is in the driver's seat and he starts driving as soon as we're buckled in.

"Don't be precious," Valentina tells him, leaning forward in the backseat beside me. "We're already late."

"She'll wait," comes Curse's flat reply.

"I know that she'll wait!" Valentina says. "She's closing the shop to the public and hosting us privately. But some of us prefer to actually build relationships and rely on social fucking civility instead of just throwing the weight of the family name around to make people respect us."

Curse doesn't say anything else, and Valentina rolls her eyes then leans back against the seat and looks at me.

"Donata's amazing. But I don't like wasting the time of a competent businesswoman if I can help it, let alone someone with the kind of artistic genius she's got."

"Valentina..." I say hesitantly. I start fiddling with the solitaire ring, my ring, twirling it nervously. "I don't want to do this. If you don't want to waste her time then we shouldn't even keep this appointment at all."

"Why not?" she asks. "Do you have another designer or dress you already had in mind or something? Trust me, Donata is the fucking best."

We're out of the dense, dark quiet of Elio's palatial property now. Street lights bob past us, sending stripes of light over Valentina's heart-shaped face. Her expression is smooth, almost innocent, like she truly has no idea why I would really want to skip this appointment.

"I don't... I don't plan on actually marrying Elio."

There's no discernable reaction from the front of the vehicle, but when my gaze shoots furtively to Curse, I see his eyes on mine in the rear-view mirror. Feeling oddly embarrassed, I look back at Valentina. But I don't get much relief there, either, because she's looking at me like I just told her I like to drown kittens in my spare time.

"Hon," she says, her big eyes nearly bugging out of her head, "What are you even talking about?"

All my embarrassment fades, replaced with irritation. Why the hell should I have to justify myself in this?

"I don't want to marry him!" I hiss in the hushed interior of the vehicle. "He never even asked me!"

"If he never asked you, then where did that beautiful ring on your finger come from?"

Valentina's question freezes me. My gaze lurches down to the ring I'm swivelling around on my finger. I could have taken it off by now. Put it in my pocket or even thrown it out the damn car window.

But I didn't.

"Did you help him pick it out?" I ask. I force myself to stop touching the ring and curl my fingers together in my lap.

Valentina shakes her head, her long blonde curls rustling against the fur-trimmed hood of her white parka.

"No," she admits. "God, I would have loved to, though. I absolutely love this stuff. I didn't get to pick my ring and it would have been so fun to have helped pick yours. Although..." She leans towards me, straining her seatbelt, capturing my left hand and squinting at the ring. "The stone's not as big as one I probably would have chosen for you. I'm actually a bit surprised he didn't pick something bigger."

I feel suddenly protective of the ring, with what I already consider a pretty big diamond. I pull my hand from hers and frown down at it.

"I wouldn't want anything bigger than this," I tell her. "Something big or heavy would throw off my violin-playing, now that I think about it."

"You know what?" Valentina says, a small smile tugging at her lips. "I bet you Elio took that into consideration."

"Ah, yes. So considerate picking a ring I'd like for a wedding I don't even want."

Valentina's smile goes a little bit hard. Brittle. Like her expression could splinter any second.

"Yeah, well, not all of us get the weddings that we want," she says. Her voice is very calm, very even, but there's a throb of emotion beneath the words. "And, look, I get how fucking shit it is not to choose your own path. But you could do a lot worse, a *hell of a lot fucking worse*, than my cousin."

I purse my lips, remaining quiet for a moment. Valentina has always seemed like an ally, someone in a similar situation to me. Stuck in an engagement she didn't choose. It's easy to forget that Elio is her family. That's where her ultimate loyalty lies.

"I won't make excuses for all his crazy," Valentina continues. "And I know he hasn't exactly been a knight in shining armour for you. At least not in the beginning. The whole taking you for your debt thing..."

I make a humourless snorting sound, and she sighs in response.

"Yeah. It's fucking ugly," she goes on. "It is. I know it is. But..." She turns her head and looks out the window, leaving me to study her profile in the alternating light and dark of winter city driving. "But nice things can grow out of ugliness. Maybe not perfect things. But nice things. Maybe even beautiful ones. Strength can come from scars."

She's quiet for a long moment while I ruminate on her words. Then, without warning, she turns back to me.

"I care about that idiot," she says. "He's the big brother I never had. And I like you, Deirdre. I really do. I sympathize with everything you're going through. But I won't stand for anybody breaking Elio's heart."

"Breaking his heart?" I echo, completely rattled by her assertion. As if such a thing were even possible. "You've got to be kidding me."

"Serious as a goddamn heart attack," she responds dryly.

"So you're saying I should marry him just so that I don't, what? Hurt his feelings?"

"No," she replies. "I'm saying that he is marrying you out of great personal cost, both to himself and to our family. Do you know how many rich princesses, how many daughters of connected families, that my papà had on the list of his potential brides? But instead, he chose you. He's paid millions for you, and now sacrificed a couple ribs and a kidney, too." Her eyes brighten unexpectedly in the darkness, her voice turning emphatic. "He cares more about you than I've ever seen him care about fucking *anything*, Deirdre. Do you know how insane that is? How rare?"

"No, I don't!" I cry. "I've known him for less than two months!"

"Well, I've known him for my whole fucking life," Valentina shoots back, "And let me tell you, without a shadow of a doubt, that man fucking lov-"

"We're almost there," Curse interrupts from the front seat. Valentina shoots the back of his seat a glare that looks like it should melt leather. She closes her eyes briefly, rubbing her forehead, before turning back to me. She seems calmer now.

"Sorry. I get very protective of the people I love," she says. She smiles. "It's a Titone trait you're obviously intimately familiar with. Look. Marrying Elio will keep you safe. Darragh's backed off now. This engagement is the only reason you can step foot outside the house and go to school. Or go to this dress appointment at all. And... Elio... He cares about you. And the wild thing is, I think you care about him too."

I flinch but force myself to continue meeting her gaze.

"I saw you two," she says quietly. "When I came in his bedroom just now, before we left. He wasn't holding onto you, trapping you, pulling you anywhere, or forcing you to be with him. He was just lying there on the bed, all fucking broken. And you were kneeling over him. You were cupping his face. So close to him, and holding him so fucking gently. Like you were going to kiss him. Like... Like you're falling for him."

"I know," I whisper, not even bothering to hide from what she's just said because it's true.

And that's part of the problem.

"What is it you're afraid of?" Valentina asks, and my throat aches with a hundred possible answers.

I'm afraid of being trapped. I'm afraid that I'm too weak and soft and easily guilted into things. I'm afraid that I'm too prickly, too ungrateful, that maybe I'm a fucking bitch.

I'm afraid of losing him. I'm afraid of all the pain he's taken on for me. I'm afraid that I pull away from him as a way to protect myself, protect us *both*, and not because it's what I want.

Because what I want... What I really, truly want...

Well, maybe I'm afraid of that too.

Valentina and I regard each other, everything else fading away at the edges. The silence is so thick between us that it becomes tangible, like it's wrapped us in velvet.

Curse's voice cuts through it like a knife, making both of us in the backseat jump.

"We're here."

Chapter 23

Deirdre

Donata's shop and studio is a temple devoted to the worship of sartorial luxury. Every detail in here is perfectly placed to enhance the glittering atmosphere. From the pale, unobtrusive, yet warm colour of the hardwood floors, to the creamy walls, to the lighting that cascades in cones of champagne gold over mannequins draped in silk and satin and lace.

It's a boutique shop, not very large, and I can tell already that the clientele must be very exclusive. And very, very rich. With my chapped lips, messy braid, and just-come-from-class outfit of jeans and a sweater, I feel uncomfortably out of place.

Valentina isn't, though. She breezes in like she owns the place, her eyelids sparkling and her long lashes casting thick shadows on her cheeks. Her glossy lips part in a beaming smile as she waves at someone coming towards us from the back of the room.

"Donata! Hi! Sorry we're late!"

I don't know why I expected Donata to be older, like a twin of grouchy Rosa, but she isn't. She can't be more than thirty, and she's stunningly beautiful. Large, dark eyes with subtle winged eyeliner stare out from beneath perfectly shaped black eyebrows. Her hair isn't black, though, but rather bleached near-white. The black eyebrows and platinum hair combination should be jarring, but somehow she pulls it off flawlessly, tying the whole look together with crimson lipstick on a wide, full mouth. Her hourglass figure is hugged by a knee-length, cowl-neck sweater dress in a buttery shade of beige that compliments her golden complexion.

"Not at all," Donata says smoothly, embracing Valentina and kissing her on each cheek.

Then she turns her appraising eyes to me.

"And this must be our bride-to-be."

I flush under Donata's gaze, and without realizing it I've already started fiddling with my ring again. She smiles, then suddenly leans forward, kissing both my cheeks like she did to Valentina. Or, rather, she brushes her cheek against each of mine, probably to avoid smearing her lipstick. Her perfume is lovely, not floral but almost spicy. It reminds me of the scent of tea, and that puts me a little more at ease.

"Come," she says as she pulls back, nodding, all business. "Let's get started, shall we? The Morelli girls are already on their second glasses of champagne."

"Morelli?" I ask Valentina as we shrug out of our winter coats. A young woman appears from nowhere, like a very quiet and polite ghost, to take the coats from us.

"I thought I mentioned them," Valentina says, kicking off her winter boots. I do the same, both of us putting our boots on the mat by the door. For a second, I wonder if Curse will ignore that and clomp right in there in his snowy black boots. But surprisingly, he doesn't. Without a word he takes them off, putting them down carefully and very precisely beside ours. Then, he locks the door behind us.

"You mentioned Giulia and Lucia," I say. "I didn't realize they were related to the doctor."

"Oh! Yeah. They're Doctor Morelli's daughters. Identical twins. You'll see."

I don't see anyone from here, at least not yet. But I can hear voices from beyond a wall that juts out towards the back of the shop. Past that wall, there is a big white sectional couch facing a pedestal with three full-length mirrors ahead of it.

As Valentina and I round that wall, two dark shapes on the white couch become blurs of motion. They glom onto Valentina like one entity, enveloping her in a giggly, shrieking hug. It's only after they disentangle themselves from the hug that I can get a look at them.

And, wow, Valentina wasn't kidding. They really are identical.

I knew two other pairs of identical twins in school growing up, but I never found it too difficult to tell them apart. They always had a tell – one would have a slightly more rounded face than the other, for example. But even after staring good and hard at the two women before me, I can't find a single difference between them. They're dressed differently, but their faces are shockingly identical. They have the same olive skin tone, same brown eyes and dark eyebrows, same tumble of thick, black hair down their backs.

"I'm Giulia," says the one on the left, the one in the white T-Shirt.

And then, with a voice so eerily the same I'm surprised to see it come from the other woman's mouth, "I'm Lucia." Lucia is wearing a University of Toronto sweater.

"Hi. I'm Deirdre," I reply. "Deirdre O'Malley."

"Oh, trust me, we know," says Lucia, beaming at me. "We've been dying to meet you."

"Yes! The Irish girl who snagged Elio Titone when he doesn't look twice at anybody else. Seriously. I have so many questions for you!" Giulia says. "Starting with, how the actual fuck?"

"Giulia!" chides Lucia, shaking her head.

"Sorry. It's the champagne. But still!" Giulia says. She flops back down on the white couch, soon joined by her twin and Valentina. Curse stands behind us, a dark and silent sentinel. I stand awkwardly in front of all of them, not sure if I'm supposed to sit down or what.

"I had the biggest crush on Elio when I was a teenager. He's got

509

that whole dark-eyed scarred thing down pat. My God," Giulia says, grabbing a half-empty flute of champagne from a small glass coffee table in front of the couch. "We used to come over and swim and I'd wear the tiniest bikini you could imagine just on the off-chance I might run into him. But no matter what I did, he didn't give a fuck."

I gawk at her, completely at a loss as to what I'm supposed to do with that information. And, with horror, I realize I even feel a little bit of jealousy.

"Giulia," Lucia says again, this time a groan. "Can you not talk about how you used to want to bang her fiancé? Deirdre just met us. She's going to think we're insane."

"Oh! No," Giulia says quickly. "Don't worry. I've long-since moved on. And like I said, he never looked twice at me. Never really seen him look at anyone. It's why I'm so surprised he's engaged, and not to somebody his family arranged." Giulia leans forward, staring at me over the edge of her glass. "Seriously. How did you pull it off?"

"If I knew, I'd tell you," I say with a shaky laugh. I don't know how to handle all the attention being heaped on me right now, but there doesn't seem to be any envy or malevolence in Giulia's gaze. She just looks sincerely curious, like she's been confronted with some kind of phenomenon she'd always believed to be impossible. Like I'm a flying pig or something, and she's simply asking me about the physics involved.

"Well, I bow before you," she finally says, "because getting that man to agree to a wedding is some goddess-level shit." She hoists her glass higher, then gives a mock bow.

"OK. Enough out of you," Lucia says, snatching her twin's champagne and putting it back on the table. I still can't detect any differences in their faces or their expressions, but slowly, some subtly contrasting characteristics are emerging. Lucia seems a little bit quieter, softer, more worried about being polite than her bolder sister. She's almost motherly in the way she seems to reign Giulia in. I wonder if she's the older twin. They look like they're around my age, or maybe a year or two older.

When Lucia smiles at me, it's a little more serene than Giulia's grins.

"Congratulations," she says, and I think she means it sincerely. "Getting married is such a beautiful thing to be celebrated!"

I'm saved from having to reply to that by Donata sweeping into the space with her assistant, both of them carrying what look to be a pile of gowns in their arms. They go to an empty rack and begin to hang the gowns before Donata turns to me.

"A truly custom gown will be near-impossible on this timeline," she says matter-of-factly. "I can do it, of course, but it's going to be tight."

"There's no budget," Valentina pipes up helpfully. My gaze cuts to her, finding her waving a shiny black card in the air with Elio's name on it.

"Oh, please," I stammer. "You don't have to make something custom!"

I can't even imagine how much that would cost. The fact that it's Elio's money doesn't make it any less nauseatingly stressful.

"Well, we'll start you off with some of these off-the-rack options. They're all one of a kind, of course, designed by yours truly. And I can make any adjustments or alterations required. Like, say, if you wanted to add sleeves, since it will be a winter wedding." She looks thoughtful. "Will it be indoors or outdoors?"

"Indoors!" Valentina says from the couch. She's got a glass of champagne now and is sipping it happily.

"Where is it?"

Donata and I ask the question at the exact same time. My face flames as Donata, Lucia, and Giulia all give me an odd look. Yeah. I guess it is pretty odd that I don't even know where my own wedding is being held.

"The Royal Thompson Hotel," Valentina replies with an expression that almost looks a little smug.

"Oh my God!" exclaims Giulia. "Are you for real?" She turns to me, eyes alight. "Your wedding is going to be amazing. The Royal Thompson, are you shitting me!"

I'm almost as surprised as Giulia is. I've never stayed there myself, but I know the location. It's one of Toronto's oldest and most expensive hotels. Events there are hosted by the nation's elite.

And that's where I'm apparently getting married.

None of this seems real. That sense of unreality only intensifies as Donata dresses me in gown after gown. They all begin to blur together, and I barely see myself in the mirror, swathed and swallowed by all that white.

My quietness doesn't seem to bother the onlookers. Valentina and Giulia have more than enough opinions to make up for my tight-lipped numbness.

"Too boring," Valentina says to a silk sheath dress. Giulia, now on her fourth glass of champagne, blows a raspberry and gives a dramatic thumbs-down.

"It's simple. Refined," protests Lucia. "Don't listen to them, Deirdre."

I stare at myself without emotion. This dress is just as good as any of the others I tried on, I suppose. It's jaw-droppingly beautiful and crafted to perfection, there's no question about that. But I don't have any real feelings towards it, either positive or negative.

"What kind of dress do you want?" That question comes from Donata, who's watching my face with a pensive look. "What did you always picture yourself wearing when you were a little girl?"

I laugh, but I think it might only be to stop myself from crying. Because once my mom died, I stopped fantasizing about the big life events that would come afterwards. I never imagined going wedding dress shopping because I knew she wouldn't be there with me.

No one speaks, and it's clear I'm expected to answer.

"I don't know," I say woodenly. I like dresses, and I do wear them, but a cute sundress isn't the same as picking out a wedding gown.

Donata taps her finger against her chin then turns to the rack. Valentina puts down her drink and jumps up off the couch, coming to Donata's side. They mutter quietly to each other, sliding dresses along the rack, the hangers making a metallic scraping sound.

"Ooh," Valentina chirps suddenly. "What about this one?"

Donata pulls a gown off the rack and carries it over. In her arms, it's hard to get a sense of the design. All I can see is cream lace over top of a slightly darker silk, along with the glitter of beading.

In a changeroom beside the couch and mirror area, Donata and her assistant Polly help me take off the sheath dress and step into this new one. There is no mirror in this room, and even if there were, I doubt I'd care to look much anyways.

I hear chatter and laughter as I step out of the changeroom, but it immediately ceases when I move out into view. Giulia, Lucia, and Valentina stare at me, and even though there is only one set of twins, and they're not triplets, they're all wearing identical expressions of stunned shock. During the fitting, Polly brought out a tray of appetizers, and Giulia drops the one she had in her hand onto her lap without even seeming to notice. Curse is the only one who looks completely impassive, standing off to the side with his arms crossed the way he has been this entire time.

My heartrate picks up at the eerie silence and gobsmacked faces of the usually very talkative women in the room. Suddenly nervous, I grab a champagne flute and take a few big swigs of the fizzy liquid before putting it back down and stepping up onto the pedestal. I stare down at the floor as Donata and Polly fuss with the dress, flaring out the train behind me on the floor and clipping excess fabric at my lower back. Donata pulls the hair tie out of my braid, arranging the waves around my shoulders in a loose style. I don't see what it looks like because I'm still staring at a very interesting whorl in the wood on the floorboard just below and ahead of the pedestal.

"Deirdre." At some point, Valentina must have gotten off the couch, because she's speaking from beside me now. "Jesus. Just *look* at you."

I don't know why I'm avoiding the mirror. I've looked at myself in every other dress, blinking blankly at my own reflection, and it hasn't really affected me. This should be no different.

I take a breath and look up.

And immediately, I know I've made a mistake.

Because the dress is perfect. So perfect that it hurts.

I'm so bowled over by the overall effect of what I see that tears instantly rise to my eyes. It takes a minute of blinking and deep breathing before I can even see clearly again.

When I can see my reflection once more, I try to analyze the dress in bits and pieces so that I don't get so overwhelmed again.

It's the first one I've tried on with long sleeves. They're three-quarter-length, the swirling flowers and petals of cream-coloured lace fitting tightly until midway to my wrist. The sleeves lead up to mostly bare shoulders, where they connect to a deep sweet-heart neckline. The bodice of the dress is tightly fitted until it flares out at the hips into a lusciously-shaped skirt, not too narrow and not too full. The beading glitters like dew in shades of pearl and pewter, more densely arranged and sparkly at the bodice then thinning out, like sprays of stars, along the skirt and long train.

My strategy of trying to look at only one bit of the dress at a time completely fails me, though, when Donata comes up behind me and reaches up to secure a veil to the back of my head. The gossamer fabric settles around my shoulders, light as mist, and I can no longer just look at the dress in severed, detached parts. Because that's me in the dress.

And I look like a bride.

My eyes are huge, shining with unshed tears. My thick hair is loose and long, curved into waves from my braid and turned a brilliant golden-red by the soft, warm lights in here. The veil ripples around me with the ephemeral thinness of a butterfly's wings, coming to a silken stop well below my waist.

A tear escapes one of my eyes, quickly followed by another, rolling in hot stripes down my cheeks.

"God," I mutter, sniffing hard. "I don't even know why I'm crying!"

Valentina shakes her head rapidly, pressing her lips together and vigorously fanning her face with both hands before shakily stammering, "I'm crying too. Gah! It's because you're so fucking beautiful!"

"You look like something from a fairy tale," Lucia breathes.

"Like a medieval Irish princess," Giulia agrees from beside her on the couch.

But soon they, like Valentina, are standing at my side, as if they've been drawn inexorably forward. They circle around me, gasping and sighing as they take in all angles of the dress and the veil. And me.

"This is it," Valentina says. "They always say when a dress makes you cry, you know that it's the one."

"Do they say that?" I ask, swiping at my wet cheeks.

"Well, if they don't, they should," Valentina replies with a teary laugh. "This is the one."

I look at myself in the mirror again, and this time I'm not looking at me with my own eyes but Elio's. This is how he will see me walking down the aisle.

And I'm terrified, because I *want* him to see me like this.

That sends me back-pedalling internally, fighting panic. Now I want to rip this dress off of my body and go back to one of the other ones. One of the safer dresses that didn't make me look like a bride and didn't make me cry.

I feel like if I agree to this dress, the dress I actually love, then I'm agreeing to everything.

"I don't know," I stutter, my voice quavering as I run my fingers over the beaded bodice.

"I think you do know," Valentina replies with such conviction that it takes my breath away. "I think you know exactly what you want, and you're just afraid to say yes to it."

I haven't eaten dinner or any of the appetizers brought out. And maybe it's the champagne I drank on an empty stomach hitting my system all at once, but I'm suddenly too exhausted to keep fighting. To keep saying no.

Feeling like I'm probably making a terrible mistake and just not finding it in myself to care, I give one stiff, tight nod to Valentina. Her eyes light up. Giulia gives a cheer and Lucia claps her hands together beneath her chin, beaming.

"Congratulations, Deirdre," Donata says. "While you're still in the dress we'll take some measurements and begin alterations immediately. Of course, a deposit will be required tonight. Fifty percent of the cost of the gown is due now, which works out to twenty-five thousand dollars."

I just about fall off the damn pedestal, but Valentina doesn't even bat a long-lashed eye as she hands over Elio's shiny black card.

"Charge it to this," Valentina says breezily, as if we're simply buying coffees instead of something the price of a nice car. "And do as many alterations as you need to. Elio wants everything to be *perfect*."

Chapter 24

Elio

I didn't realize how damn long it took to pick out a dress. Even I took less time than this with the rings and I didn't have a clue what I was doing. With Valentina there, shit should be a piece of cake. So when a couple hours go by and Deirdre isn't back yet, I start getting restless.

I don't know if it's because the Tylenol hasn't done diddly squat for me and my side and head feel worse than ever, but my mood is fraying as I pick up my phone and use voice command to tell it to call Curse.

He picks up immediately.

I realize I don't really have anything specific to ask him or to say. The girls are at a dress shop. What am I going to do, ask for a play-by-play?

I settled on a grunted, "How's it going?"

"Fine. No security issues. No sign of Darragh's men. He's honouring the agreement."

I nod with satisfaction even though no one can see me. That's good. There would be hell to fucking pay if I was this busted up in bed and Darragh decided to renege on everything. But it really does seem like I've finally managed to make Deirdre safe in this city. Just gotta seal it all up with a kiss. At our wedding.

The phone is on speaker setting, and I stare down at it, unwilling to hang up. I know Curse won't hang up before I dismiss him, and the silence stretches.

Until it's broken by the sound of female voices and laughter. I tense, hearing Deirdre's voice among them but not able to make out what she's saying.

"What's happening now?" I ask sharply.

"They're drinking champagne."

I rub the scarred part of my jaw, remembering that my Songbird didn't eat dinner before she left the house.

"Has she eaten anything?" I ask Curse.

"There's some tray of little snacks. *Antipasti.*"

"OK. Good. Make sure she eats some of it."

I hear rustling, then footsteps as Curse presumably walks across the room. Curse speaks, just barely audibly, to Deirdre instead of me this time.

"He wants to make sure you eat."

"Is that Elio on the phone?" That question comes from Deirdre, clear enough for me to hear it now.

Then another slightly slurred voice. I think it might be Giulia. Or maybe Lucia. Can't tell them apart for shit.

"Elioooo," she calls loudly, "just wait until you see the dress we picked out for your beautiful bride!"

Laughter breaks out again, which is then dulled when Curse sounds like he walks away and presses the phone to the side of his head once more.

"She's chosen a dress?" I hiss, suddenly sweating, my heart giving an unexpectedly painful throb. "What does it look like?"

"I don't know," Curse says. "It's white. It has... sleeves."

"Real helpful," I mutter. Not that I can really blame him. He doesn't have an unnatural, bordering on psychotic Songbird obsession like I do. He doesn't drink down every detail of her appearance like it's water necessary to stay alive.

"Want me to go find it and send a picture?" he asks.

Goddamn, I've got a good brother. Because I know he'll fucking do it. Somehow, the fact he's willing to do shit like this for me feels like even more a mark of his loyalty then all the men he's killed at my behest.

"No," I say, though I think I may regret saying that later. "I'll just wait and be surprised. Did..." I pause, wondering just when I turned into such a fucking sap, "Did Deirdre like it?"

"She cried."

Well, shit.

"What kind of crying?" I press.

"There's more than one kind?"

"Course there is, you dope."

Deirdre in particular has a million shades and versions. Infinite nuances in every single shimmering drop. Fury. Longing. Shame. Grief. Pain. Arousal. Sometimes all at once.

But I didn't call Curse in order to have a philosophical conversation on all the complex types of tears exhibited by my fascinating future wife.

"Make sure she eats," I remind him. "Then bring my fiancée home."

———

Curse seems to follow the second part of the instructions better than the first. Because less than one hour after hanging up, he does indeed bring her home. I'm just a little less sure on whether or not he successfully got her to eat enough. Or maybe she just started drinking too early. Because my Songbird, when she returns, is undeniably tipsy.

She can walk alright, I'll give her that, as she comes back into the room, followed by my brother. But her freckled face is extremely flushed, her eyes glassy. And when she sees me, I shit you not, she fucking *grins*.

"Elio!"

Is this all I had to do to make her happy to see me? Get her drunk first?

Noted.

"Hey, Songbird," I say as she flops down onto her ass beside me on the bed. "Heard you found a dress."

Her cheeks are so red. I want to fucking bite them.

She waves away my words and doesn't answer me, instead fixing me with a distinctly uncentred stare. "Did you stay in bed? And take your Tyle... tylemol?"

"I don't know what the fuck a tylemol is, but I did take a Tylenol." I look at Curse who's standing in the doorway. "How much did she drink?"

"Less than Giulia and Valentina," he responds, "but she didn't start eating until after the first two glasses."

My gaze returns to Deirdre.

"Bit of a lightweight, are you?" I ask her, smirking.

"Pfft!" she folds her arms across her chest. "I won't be for long. I'm gonna need to drink *a lot* to deal with being married to you."

I'm rendered momentarily speechless, not because I'm offended by what she's said. Far from it. But because this is the first time she's admitted that she's marrying me.

Before I can wrap my slow brain around a response to that, she bops up onto her cute little feet and shuffles away into the other bedroom. Soon, I hear water running from the other room's adjoining bathroom.

"Did you fucking hear that?" I croak at Curse. "About marrying me?"

I'm suddenly paranoid that I imagined it. That it was some fucking hallucination.

520

But Curse confirms it with a casual, "Yup." He cracks his knuckles. "Bit of a different tune from what she was singing in the car though."

"Why? What was she saying?"

"Just that she didn't plan on marrying you."

"Yeah, well, what else is new," I grunt back at him. "Been hearing that since I told her we're engaged."

"Not now, though. You know what they say. *In vino veritas.*"

"Booze makes you honest. Yeah. Yeah..."

I break off slowly, pondering what he's said, when he suddenly turns my fucking world upside down with a single fucking sentence.

"She also said she's falling for you."

My gaze turns blade-like, slicing to him.

"What the fuck did you just say?"

"In the car," Curse goes on. "Valentina said something like, 'I think you're falling for him.' And she said, 'I know.'"

I can't believe I'm sitting here gossiping about what the girls said about me in the car, like I'm twelve years old or something. And I don't even care. I'll take any fucking scrap of her I can get, even if it's regurgitated conversation from when I wasn't there.

A sound makes both Curse and I turn our heads at the same moment. Deirdre is back, wearing a set of pink silk pyjamas. She's carrying her violin and bow.

Curse slips silently from the room. The only reason I know he goes is because I hear the door to the hallway click shut behind him.

"What's all this?" I ask, waving my splinted hand in the direction of her instrument.

"I feel like playing tonight," she says. "And I figure that I should, since I promised I would last night, anyway. But you fell asleep."

Maybe she's had a little water, and her buzz is wearing off a tiny bit. Because, though she's still flushed and a little looser in her movements than usual, she's pretty composed as she rests her chin on the violin and raises the bow. As the fingers of her left hand settle in place against the strings, the diamond of her ring catches the light.

She's still wearing it.

I kind of figured she would have taken it off in the bathroom.

But she didn't.

She takes a little breath, shakes a bit of hair out of her face, and then begins to play.

The first notes slug me hard, send me sagging back against the pillows. My breathing quickens in time with the rhythm of the song. I don't recognize it, but it's beautiful, quick and lilting. Deirdre's eyes are closed. Her brows twitch with focus. But her mouth is relaxed. Nearly smiling.

This is it. This is what I've fucking wanted the whole fucking time. Her. Coming home to me. And playing for me without being asked or told or punished. Because she already knows that she belongs to me.

My eyes swing back and forth from her face to the glint of the ring on her fingers. As far as I can tell, it doesn't seem to be bothering her while she plays, and that fills me with satisfaction.

It's been so long since I've heard her play. Even longer since I've seen her play like this. Unafraid and unselfconscious, spilling her soul out onto the strings. It's like she's forgotten that I'm even here.

But I know she hasn't. Because she said she's playing for me.

And I want to do so many things at once. I want to lie here and let those notes keep slicing at me until I fucking bleed. I want to get out of bed, put my fingers round her throat, and crash my mouth to hers. I want to fall asleep to her song. I want to never close my eyes again so that I don't miss a single second of her.

The notes stretch out and slow, and Deirdre seamlessly transitions into a new song. This one is haunting. I don't recognize this tune either, but it sounds like it could be a lullaby.

I try to keep my eyes open. She's so fucking pretty when she plays. But I can't. Now that she's back I can finally relax, and the enormity of my weakness crashes down on me. It feels like my weight suddenly doubles, like something's sucking me down against the mattress and pillows. My eyelids slide, and no amount of effort in the world can hold them open.

But I can still hear her. Hear the sad-sweet melody she's pouring through the air.

Sleep comes for me. And even in that darkness, music follows.

Chapter 25

Deirdre

I t's a couple more songs before I realize Elio's fallen asleep. When I notice, I immediately cease playing, lowering my bow and my violin to my sides. My arms tingle, and there's a lightness in me that isn't just the giddiness of the alcohol. It felt good to play like that. I can't believe it, but it felt good to play for *him*.

I thought he'd ruined violin for me, maybe forever. I thought I'd never get back to the heart of it, never be able to love it again. The one talent I shared with my beautiful mother. I thought he'd ripped it away.

But he hasn't. I actually wanted to play for him tonight. And seeing how relaxed he is, how the slower music helped him fall asleep, makes my chest feel like it's filled with warm honey.

Quietly, I set the violin and bow down. As I do so, I'm surprised to see something sparkling on my left hand. The ring. I never took it off.

I forgot to. How the hell did I forget to? When Elio gave it to me, I told him I'd only wear it for a little bit. And now, it's like it's a part of me. I didn't even notice it was there.

I should go take it off. And head back to my own bed. Elio is sound asleep, his big, bare chest rising and falling with quick, shallow breaths. I won't wake him if I leave.

Which I should.

But...

I don't.

On silent feet I pad over to the bed, turning off the bedside lamps. Before I can stop to think or let logic back in, I lift the blankets and scoot in beside him. I don't get too close – I'm nearest his really bruised side, and I don't want to poke any tender places. So instead, I lie on my side facing him, and I settle for placing my hand flat on his chest. His skin feels very warm, his heart throbbing beneath my fingers. I wonder if he's dreaming, and if he is, what he's dreaming of. Blood. Money.

Me.

I stay like that, my hand on his chest, and eventually I fall asleep. I don't have any dreams. But some time later, I'm woken in the darkness so suddenly that I almost feel like I'm dreaming. The bed feels like it's moving, and it takes me longer than it should to realize that I really am awake.

But no. It's not the bed moving. It's Elio.

I suppress a cry and flinch out of the way just in time to avoid a flailing arm.

"Shit," I whisper, pulse racing. I crawl to the edge of the bed and turn on the lamp before spinning back to see what the hell is going on.

The first thing I notice is the unnatural way Elio is arching, digging his head back into the pillows. The fist the flew by my head a second ago is now wrapped in blankets, and he's pulling, like he's fighting something.

"Elio? Elio!"

His eyes are open, but there's no way that he sees me. His gaze shoots sightlessly around the room, wide and dark and blank. He's panting hard, his skin flushed and sweaty. He groans, but it's kind of choked. Muted. Like in the dream, he's trying to scream.

He's going to hurt himself.

He's moving way too much for someone in his condition.

"Elio," I say, crawling towards him. "Elio, you're dreaming."

"Fire... Get... Out..."

I barely register the words, they're so strangled, so raw.

"Have to *get my Songbird out.*"

"Elio! I'm right here!" Not knowing what else to do, I lean over his contorted face and press my hands to his jaw, trying to wake him, to focus him, to make him see me.

But I instantly draw back, gasping. He's burning up. Like the fire in his dreams are so hot, so real, that the heat is licking its way out of his skin.

"Elio. It's alright. I'll be right back," I stammer, flinging myself off of the bed. I wonder if some part of him recognizes that I'm getting further away, because he suddenly twists and thrashes harder, grunting, like he's trying to fight his way back to me.

I want to go to him. Stay with him. Cradle his head in my arms.

But I leave him there, sprinting into the hallway. Fucking hell! The one time I need somebody, and there's no one in that stupid spot at the top of the stairs!

I run down the hall to the stairs, going them so fast that my footsteps sound like a furious drumbeat on the metal.

"Hello!" I call out frantically. "I need someone!"

Curse and Enzo come instantly into view, both of them crossing from the kitchen towards me with ground-eating strides.

"What is it?" Enzo asks, both of them already mounting the stairs to meet me halfway. I instantly spin and start running back up, not wanting to waste a moment. I've already been away from him to long.

"It's Elio," I pant, my words flying up and out of my throat like something's chasing them. "He's burning up! We need to get Doctor Morelli here or take him to a hospital. Or..."

"Shit," I hear Enzo mutter. In a matter of moments, both men are on the phone barking orders, Curse telling Morelli to get his ass over here now, and Enzo seeming to alert the other soldiers stationed on the property as to what's happening.

The three of us burst into the room at the same time. Enzo turns on more lights while Curse and I both go straight to the bed. Elio's still tense and twitching, the tendons in his neck standing up with brutal contrast, every muscle in his chest and abdomen contracting. The bruising looks so much darker today, his whole side painted with blackened violence.

Curse wears no expression, but his eyes are deadly focused as he whips the blankets away from Elio's heated body. Shit. I should have done that before I left the room.

"I'll get wet cloths," Curse says tightly. "Get his pants off."

I don't bother to acknowledge him. I don't even nod. I just get started, working the soft fabric of the grey sweatpants down over his hips. It's hard, because he keeps twitching and threatening to thrash, but with effort I get them rolled all the way down and whisked away from his ankles. I know he wouldn't like it, but right now I don't give a damn, and I take off his leather glove, too. I consider taking off the splint, but worry in his condition he'll damage his bones even more than they already are, and decide that the small amount of heat he might lose from the skin around that wrist isn't worth worsening the fracture.

I'm just setting the sweatpants and leather glove aside when Curse strides swiftly back into the room from the bathroom, his hands laden with sopping wet cloths. I don't wait for instructions, instantly running to him and taking some of the wet cloths out of his hands. We go to work side by side, me hauling myself up onto the bed between Elio's legs, running the cool cloths along his thighs and abdomen, Curse up higher, near his head.

The instant the wet cloths come into contact with his skin Elio hisses, then moans, writhing as if to get away.

"It's alright, *a chuisle mo chroí*," I whisper. "Just stay still for us now, love."

Curse doesn't say anything, but somewhere in Elio's burning

brain, he must know his younger brother is there. Because his wild eyes suddenly lock on Curse's face.

"Have to get her out," he croaks frantically. With shocking strength, his good hand shoots up and locks onto Curse's shoulder. "Fire. Got... to get her *now*."

"It's alright," Curse says, voice low. "Mamma's not in danger anymore."

"Not Mamma," Elio moans. I've never heard him sound so desperate. "*Deirdre*."

Curse's gaze sears to mine. His voice is clipped, almost like he expects me to argue with him, or run away. "He needs you."

He heard everything I said to Valentina. About how I don't plan on marrying his brother, how I feel trapped by the person he's most loyal to in this world. He thinks I'm going to abandon his brother now, right when Elio needs me most.

Yeah, well. He doesn't know me very well.

I sling myself over one of Elio's taut thighs, straddling it and trying to keep him still with my weight. If it weren't for his injuries, I'd move up further, straddle his waist or even his chest. But this will work for now. I lean forward, run trembling fingers up his chest until I'm cupping his face once more.

"Elio. Elio, I'm here. Everything is going to be alright."

I don't expect him to hear me, but I guess some part of him does. His hand falls away from Curse's shoulder, dead weight thudding to the mattress beside him.

His dark eyes are glazed, but they seize on mine with savage power.

"Songbird," he pants. "You have to go. Have to..."

"I'm alright, Elio. *Mo chroí*. I'm safe. And so are you. The doctor is coming. Just try to be still."

His face twists in agony.

"I *can't*," he whispers, and on the next words, his voice breaks. He looks younger than I've ever seen him. "I can't reach you."

I don't notice I'm crying until hot drips fall onto my own hands.

But strangely, my voice comes out steady when I speak next. "Then I'll just have to reach you instead."

I lean down to him, my hair creating a curtain around us, and I press my mouth to his.

There's nothing controlled about it. The kiss is a messy one. There's terror and tenderness in the searching slide of our mouths. Desperation and desire. Elio's lips part instantly, and he groans into me, his movements weak but frantic, spiked with feverish adrenaline.

But it seems to be working. I think he really knows I'm here now. One by one, I feel his muscles unlock beneath me, until his whole frame is trembling now instead of furiously tense.

I lose all sense of time and space. Lose my awareness of anyone else around us. There's only Elio, the man who needs me so fucking badly, the monster only I can tame. I feel like I'm melting into him, like the borders between our bodies are wavering, turning soft and transparent like liquid.

I would have stayed there longer, locked in that starving and soothing embrace, if not for the stern, accented voice calling into the room, "Everybody back!"

I break the kiss, feeling like I break my heart as I do it. But I have to make room. That voice is Doctor Morelli's.

I pull away from Elio, straightening where I'm sitting on his upper thigh and preparing to scramble off the bed. But at the sudden distance between us, Elio bucks in revolt, making a sound that reminds me of an animal in a cage.

"Don't move," Curse says quietly to me. "If you get off him now he's going to lose his fucking shit."

Doctor Morelli sends everything on Elio's bedside table crashing to the ground so he can slam open his case. He doesn't say anything else, I guess not caring that I'm on Elio's leg so long as he can do what he needs to do. His eyes flash behind his glasses, his face is drawn tight.

"What is it? What's wrong with him?" I ask. I don't want to distract him, but I can't stop the words from spilling out. Doctor

Morelli doesn't answer for a moment. He checks Elio's blood pressure, then his temperature, then curses. His reply, when it comes, is in rapid Italian.

"What's he saying?" I ask Curse, who's moved out of the way for the doctor. As Curse listens long enough to translate I vow that as soon as things settle down I am learning fucking Italian.

"He's only just recovered from the bullet wound, and his body wasn't ready for the ribs and kidney. He's got a secondary kidney infection now."

Curse says it evenly, nearly robotically. There isn't a trace of resentment in his face or voice, despite the fact that these are all injuries Elio's gotten for me.

"Is he going to be alright?" I ask, my voice rising higher and higher.

Morelli speaks rapidly again as he tightens a tourniquet around Elio's arm and starts tapping firmly at his inner elbow. He eases a needle into a vein, then barks a command at Enzo who's waiting by the door. Enzo disappears.

"He needs IV antibiotics," Curse says. "Enzo's going to get the IV stand from the med room." While waiting for Enzo to return, Doctor Morelli holds the bag of liquid aloft after connecting the tube to Elio's arm.

"But is he going to be alright?" I ask again, more forcefully than I think I've ever spoken in my entire life. I nearly shout it, and I don't mean to, but I can't seem to help it. I feel like I might die if somebody doesn't answer me right fucking now.

"Sepsis with multi-organ failure is a possibility," Curse says flatly. He doesn't get loud like I did, but nonetheless the calm delivery of his words hits me like a blow.

I blink away tears and tear my gaze from Curse, looking down at Elio. Elio seems to have slipped back into a deeper sleep. His eyes are closed now, his chest rising and falling rapidly. He probably can't hear me, but I talk to him anyway, forcing myself not to sound as petrified as I am.

"Elio," I say sharply through my tears. I'm going to start sobbing soon. I can feel it, pressure in my throat and eyes and lungs. But I have to say this. I have to get this out. "Elio Titone, I want you to listen to me. Listen closely. Because I have a proposition for you."

I sniff against the tumble of tears threatening to spill. "It's a deal. A good one, too. Alright?"

I rub my hands in quivering circles across his hot chest, not sure if I'm trying to comfort him with my touch or comfort myself with the solid bulk of him beneath my fingers.

"These are the terms," I choke out. "And there's no negotiating. You have to hold up your end of the bargain." My hands curl into fists against his skin. "You have to live, Elio. You have to get through this. Survive, and I'll stop fighting you. Stop denying you. Live, and-"

There's no going back now. But I don't hesitate one bit.

"-I will marry you."

Chapter 26

Deirdre

The next few days pass in a stressful blur. Elio sleeps a lot as the powerful antibiotics and IV fluids work their way through his battered system. Doctor Morelli stays at the house 24/7, and is joined by Lucia, who it turns out is a trained nurse. She tells me she studied it at the University of Toronto, and I remember seeing her U of T sweater at the dress shop. That fitting feels so long ago now. Like it happened to somebody else.

I try to learn everything I can from Doctor Morelli and Lucia. Lucia has the right temperament for a nurse, I think. She's the slightly more reserved and softer-spoken, sweeter twin, but she's also extremely competent and she's thankfully patient enough to teach me. Soon, I know how to interpret all the numbers and screens on the machine that Doctor Morelli has brought up to Elio's room, and I can switch out the bags of IV fluids with ease.

It makes me feel a little less useless while Elio's so damaged in that bed. If I don't have something I can do to help him, I think I might go crazy.

I skip my classes, not able to bear the thought of leaving Elio here like this. What if something happens to him, and I'm not here? What if he needs me? All thoughts of running from this man have suddenly been replaced with how I can best stand by him now. The reversal should be enough to give me whiplash, but I'm too busy taking care of him. Fortunately, it seems like nobody except Elio actually cares if I go to school or not, and while he's incapacitated, no one tries to make me.

I don't even think his men notice me at all, to be honest, except in the context that I'm almost always hovering somewhere in Elio's room. They're too distracted, too on edge, too worried about their boss. The number of soldiers in the house has doubled, and sometimes I hear Vincenzo Titone's gruff, loud voice booming from downstairs. Elio's condition has turned this house into a hornet's nest of stressful, buzzing activity.

But I tune it all out. It's calmer here, at the centre of the storm with Elio. When we're alone, I wipe his face with cool cloths, brush his hair back from his forehead, and talk to him. I remind him of our deal – that he has to live for me to marry him – and I try not to think about the fact we had another deal, once. One that I'd never quite agreed to. The deal that I was supposed to marry him in exchange for my father's safety.

Marry me, he'd said. *Or I'll tell Darragh exactly where your fucking father is.*

I try not to wonder what it means that I was fighting so hard against the marriage when it would save my father. But now, I'm grasping at it with both hands, hoping that it might somehow save Elio.

And hell, maybe it does. Maybe it helps, just a little bit. Because on the morning of the fourth day, Elio opens his eyes, looks at me exhausted, but lucid, and says the first words I've heard him speak in days.

"You're here."

He's too tired to sound actually surprised, but I gather that he is. He stares at me almost uncomprehending. Like he thought I'd vanished, somehow, while his eyes were closed. I lean forward in the chair I'm sitting in at his bedside, running my fingers over his forehead, his cheek, so that he can feel me.

"Of course I'm here," I whisper. I can feel tears biting at me, but I don't let them fall. "Who else was going to make sure you held up your end of the bargain?"

When he doesn't say anything in response to that, I smile softly.

"The wedding, Elio," I explain gently. "I'm not fighting you anymore. I agree to everything. You get well. And we'll get married."

"I..." His voice croaks, and I grab water from beside us and ease it up to his mouth. But he ignores it, never taking his eyes off me, his gaze weak but somehow just as intense and arresting as ever. "I thought I dreamed that."

For some reason that makes something inside me feel like it's cracked. To know that, while he was burning and in pain, my voice actually got through. I put the water back down, taking a moment to steady myself before I respond.

"No," I say, "It was real."

"I thought I dreamed *you*," he says, his voice getting stronger with each word. "All of you. Everything." He raises his hand, lifting it as if trying to reach my face. But it's too heavy. It falls back to the bed. I reach for it myself, grasping it and stroking along his scarred palm.

"You're here," he says again, so softly I almost can't hear.

"I am. Although, I really should go get the doctor..."

I move to rise, but his fingers fasten themselves around mine.

"Don't go," he says. And I want to fucking weep with relief, because there's the Elio I know. He's not begging me to stay.

He's commanding.

I don't weep, but I do beam tearily at him as I ease my hand out of his grip.

"Just because I'll be your wife doesn't mean I plan on giving into your every demand and whim," I tell him. "You just lie here for a minute and I'll be right back with Doctor Morelli."

I rise fully from the chair this time, making sure Elio can't grab any random parts of me to try to haul me back down. He tenses as I move away, his dark eyes eating into me like he's starving for something, like there's an empty ache inside him that food could never even hope to touch.

I feel that soul-hungry gaze, hard as teeth against my skin, even as I leave and close the door behind me.

Chapter 27

Elio

This fucking blows.

Maybe not eloquent, but it's true. I haven't been this busted-up and out of commission since recovering from my burns when I was fourteen. Morelli's got me pumped full of all kinds of shit, fluids and antibiotics and I'm certain there are some painkillers in the mix, because the agony has receded far quicker than it should have just based on my own healing. For more than a week all I do is lie around, and that doesn't even include those first blurred days when my fever was raging at its worst.

But I've avoided having all my organs shut down on me, so at least there's that.

And there's her. My Songbird. *My fiancée.* She flits and flutters and hovers, running cool fingers over my skin, giving me prim, cute little commands about resting and drinking water and yadda yadda yadda. She plays for me every night without being asked, then crawls like a kitten into bed beside me. It takes a lot of cajoling, and the eventual threat of dragging myself out of bed, before I can convince her to start attending her classes again with Enzo and Curse alternating as her chaperones.

By February thirteenth, after more than two weeks of doing absolutely fuck-all, I decide I'm sick of this shit and leave the bedroom after showering and getting dressed in some real clothes. There are no more tubes in me, nothing keeping me stuck here.

"Are you supposed to be up?" Curse asks as soon as I emerge from the bedroom.

"I've got shit to do," I tell him.

"Not quite what I asked."

My brother and I head down the stairs together. I can tell I'm still recovering, but I feel a hell of a lot better than I did. My ribs are still healing, and my kidney isn't back on track yet, but the infection has cleared and I can feel some of my old energy returning.

"What do you need to do?" Curse asks as we reach the main floor. "I can take care of it for you."

"You can come with me. But I have to do it myself."

Deirdre's at school right now, so I figure now is as good a time as any to get this done. Might as well, since she's not here to distract me.

"What is it, then?"

"You remember the lawyer I asked you to look into for me?"

"Course."

"We're heading to his office."

I have another lawyer already, of course. He looks after all our family interests. Which is exactly why I don't want to use him for this particular task. No, this new lawyer Curse has done some research on for me isn't one of our family's trusted contacts. He's not even Sicilian.

His name is Gabriel Hades. And he is going to help me rewrite my will.

The law firm of *Hades, Mason & Gould* is located in the heart of Toronto's financial district, taking up the whole upper half of a glittering glass office building. Despite only having three guys listed in the name, it's a massive operation with more than one hundred attorneys, associates, and paralegals employed here.

Several of them try to stop Curse and I as we stride right past their cubicles and offices, heading for the one with Gabriel Hades written on the door.

"Excuse me!" says a middle-aged blonde woman from a desk outside the sleek door. "Can I help you? Do you have an appointment?"

"No. But I've been in contact with him," I tell her. "He'll be expecting me."

"Can I at least get your name so I can – excuse me! Sir!"

The woman's voice fades to a spluttering chirp as Curse reaches for the office's door handle. He doesn't need to actually press down on it, though, because the door swings inward, opened from the inside.

The first thing I think is that this guy looks younger than someone who's the earned the reputation he has. In Curse's research on him, I've seen him called everything from shark to devil to demon. I guess his last name kind of fits.

"You Hades?" I ask. I want to make sure I haven't gotten a hold of some junior lawyer who doesn't know tits from ass.

The eyes behind his sleek glasses are a very pale, steely grey. They move meaningfully to the name listed on his door.

"If I'm not, then I imagine I'd have some explaining to do as to why I'm alone in this office."

"Mr. Hades," the woman says breathlessly as she hustles over in clicky shoes, her cheeks very red. "I'm so sorry. These men don't have an appointment. And I tried to-"

"It's alright, Margaret," he cuts in. "After our correspondence earlier this month, I expected to see at least one of the young Titones show up here eventually."

"Young?" I ask him. "I doubt you're any older than I am."

"I'm forty," he replies coolly.

"Really? No shit," I say.

Despite her boss's assurances, Margaret looks like she's about to blow a fucking gasket. If her cheeks get any more red I honestly think they might pop, like over-filled water balloons.

"Mr. Hades," she huffs, "Your schedule today is *very* full. Perhaps if these... *gentlemen*... would like to make an appointment, I could-"

"We're not in the habit of making appointments. Or being kept waiting," I say.

"Reschedule *Garrison Oil and Gas*," Hades tells his assistant. She looks like she's about to argue, but he silences her with a single look. It's a look I recognize. A sort of look I've given countless times before. The kind of look I learned from men just like my uncle.

Gabriel Hades may be a swanky lawyer wearing a nice clean suit up here in his big shiny office, but there's something brutal in him. Something that I recognize, that I can sniff out the way a dog goes digging for blood.

I'm not sure if it makes me trust him more...

Or less.

But either way, when he holds the door to his office open, Curse and I both go through it.

I flinch at blinding brightness. The whole far wall of his office is made of glass, and February sunlight, normally kind of sickly and weak this time of year, is blasting right through.

"How the fuck can you work in here?" I croak, holding up my splinted hand to shade my eyes. My head pings with pain as flame-like light glances off of every surface.

But then there's instant relief. With the touch of a button, Hades has activated some kind of shading technology, darkening the windows. It turns the Toronto cityscape into a collection of silhouettes and shadows.

"I have to admit I was surprised to receive your correspondence, Mr. Titone," Hades says. "I figured your family would have an army of lawyers at their beck and call."

"We do," I grunt in confirmation. "That's exactly why I'm here. I don't want any lawyers connected with my uncle touching my will with a ten-foot pole."

"Why?"

I stare at him. Even with the glass tinted the way it is, plenty of light filters in. It gleams on his odd hair, the palest blond I think I've ever seen on a grown man. He's tall, and pretty built for a guy who probably spends most of his time behind a desk.

"It's been a long, long time since I've let a man working for me ask me why I do anything," I say, more bemused than anything.

"We haven't signed an agreement. You're not my client and I don't work for you. Yet."

He removes his glasses, polishing the lenses with a cloth he pulls from... somewhere. I have no clue where he got it. This office is absurdly clean and clutter-free. His desk has nothing on it but a computer monitor, and while there's furniture in here, something tells me it's more for clients than for him.

"Your name was enough to get you in my door without an appointment," he goes on, "which is already a rare feat. But I have protocols and principles in place. To borrow your earlier language, I don't touch any new work with a ten-foot pole, no matter how lucrative or how important to the client it may be, unless I have a full and transparent understanding of the client's needs and motivations. So, I will ask you again, and if you want to work together I expect you to actually answer me. Why are you refusing to work with your current representation to craft your will?"

He puts his glasses back on and gazes relentlessly at me with those gunmetal eyes. I can feel Curse shifting closer to the door, ready to lock it and smash Hades' white-blond head into his desk as soon as I give the signal.

But I don't. For some reason, Hades' cold confidence isn't pissing me off. I don't think there's much arrogance or ego involved. It's just that...

He isn't afraid of me at all.

Usually, I'd say that's a sign of a very stupid man. But I already know that I'm not dealing with a stupid man right now.

A grudging tendril of respect for him takes root, and I decide to answer his question honestly. He's probably smart enough to figure it out on his own anyway, when he sees who I'm leaving everything to.

"Our family's lawyers have been working for our uncle since before I turned eighteen. They were his lawyers first, and when push comes to shove, I can't count on them being loyal to me over him. I need fresh-"

"Blood?" Hades offers.

"I was going to say eyes, but yes. That's the gist of it."

"And do you expect push to come to shove?"

"I don't necessarily expect my uncle to contest my will if I die before him, if that's what you mean," I say, shaking my head. "But I don't want a lawyer connected with him helping to draft it. I don't want some stupid sneaky clause added in that I don't know about, or some not-so-accidental mistake being made that renders the will null and void."

"I see," he responds. "Well, it certainly makes sense for a man of your position, wealth, and, shall we say, liability-laden lifestyle to have a will in place."

I snort, then instantly regret it as pain splinters through my ribs.

"Liability-laden?" I repeat, raising my brows. "That's some real smooth lawyer-talk if I've ever heard it."

Why, no, I'm not part of a violent crime family with enemies everywhere I turn. I just live a liability-laden lifestyle.

Cristo Santo.

"Anyway," I say, "I already do have a will. Due to the aforementioned lifestyle and position and wealth. I own multiple corporations and have significant investments and property in my name. This would be a new will, to supersede the old one."

"I see. And are you adding beneficiaries?"

"Adding one," I confirm, "and removing another. Currently, everything I have is entailed upon my uncle, all of it to be rolled into the family estate. But I want to change that. Everything should now go to Deirdre Elizabeth O'Malley."

"Soon to be Titone, I presume. That is your fiancée, correct? I saw the engagement announcement."

"Yes. After February twenty-ninth, she'll be my wife. I want everything I have to go to her. Every cent. And I want it done in such a way that nobody can touch it. Not even my uncle. If we have to set up trusts, we'll do it. If we have to start funneling money out of the country and set up a safe haven for her in Panama or Switzerland or some shit, we'll do that too."

"I see why you're looking for discretion and some distance from your family's usual representation."

"I figured you would," I reply. "No one ever accused you of being dense, I take it?"

"I doubt you'd be here if they had."

"True." I gesture towards my brother. "Curse will be the executor. He's the only person in my family I fully trust around this issue. If Deirdre needs help managing anything after the event of my death – winding down a corporation, for example, or if she decides she wants to sell some of my property later on – Curse can assist her with that."

"As Accursio also subscribes to the same liability-laden lifestyle that you do, who do you want to manage things in the case of his death?"

I mull on that for a moment. If Valentina weren't Uncle Vinny's daughter, then maybe her, but as it is she's not the right choice.

"There's no one else," I say after a pause. "If Curse is unavailable then you will be the executor and will act as Deirdre's lawyer and advisor. You can take your future pay out of the estate."

He tilts his head slightly, making light gleam on the metal frames of his glasses.

"You should know that I typically bill more than two thousand dollars an hour. Even with your stipulations and investments and corporations, a will like yours wouldn't be overly complex for one of our junior partners to take care of."

"I didn't come here to pass this off onto anybody that has junior in their title," I snap. "I want perfection. And I am willing to pay for it."

As evidenced by the millions I spent on my flawless fucking fiancée...

"Understood," Hades says. "But I'm a corporate lawyer. I don't typically do estate work like this. Why should I take this project on?"

"Double your usual fee. Quadruple it. I don't give a shit. And don't forget," I add, "that having a Titone for a friend is a powerful fucking thing."

"I don't need any friends."

"You might one day," I counter. "There may come a time when you need an ally who has more than just money, one who didn't come from a fancy office like this."

His face is a smooth mask. I can't really tell if my argument is swaying him, and I've already worked out that threats aren't going to get me anywhere.

But then something shifts in those ghost-grey eyes of his.

"Acceptable," Hades suddenly says.

He walks behind the desk he's been standing in front of this whole time. Bending slightly, he activates a button I can't see from here, but it must be for an intercom system, because then he says, "Margaret, bring me a client intake form for Mr. Titone."

He releases the button then turns back to Curse and me.

"Alright, Mr. Titone," he says. "I'll help you draft your will. Not for quadruple, but quintuple the price of my usual fee, and..." His eyes glint. "One future favour."

Chapter 28

Elio

The will stuff takes longer than I thought it would. After hashing out multiple scenarios and untangling every nitty gritty aspect of my estate, my head is a ticking, throbbing mess. Even Curse grows a little agitated being shut up in that office the whole time. Not Hades, though. It's like the guy sucks energy out of this academic, legal shit, his eyes and intellect sharpening the more into the complicated weeds we get. There's something almost predatory about it, like a type of bloodlust that takes over. But it doesn't make him sloppy. If anything, it seems to make him more intensely calculating. By the end of the multi-hour session he seems invigorated, his words coming crisp and quick, while I feel like there's a big, dull bullet making its very slow way through my brain.

But it's done. And that's what counts. There's immediate relief at that. That I'll be able to take care of Deirdre, to protect her, even if I'm gone. Which I don't plan to be. But recent events have put everything into sun-sharp clarity. That fever was not fucking around with me. Shit could have gone south real quick, and then Deirdre would have been left with nothing. We aren't married yet. We aren't even considered common law at this point. She'd have no legal rights or recourse, plus, my uncle doesn't give a fuck about her. If I'm gone, he could turn her out of my house with nothing to her name, and he likely would. I'm pretty sure Curse or Valentina would try to at least make some arrangements to help her out, but with all my money getting tied up in the family estate, there wouldn't be much they could do.

But now, no matter what happens to me, she'll be protected.

After we leave the offices of *Hades, Mason & Gould*, we get into the car and Curse begins to drive. Thank fuck night has fallen and the sun is no longer searing itself into my skull. Because I'm not ready to go home just quite yet.

"One more stop," I tell my brother.

"Where to?"

"O'Malley's place."

It's the house Deirdre used to live in, but I call it O'Malley's because it isn't hers. Not anymore. She will never live there again. She lives where I tell her to, in the house that I own.

"What's the plan?" Curse asks as we head north to Thornhill.

"Not sure," I say honestly. I don't have a specific goal in mind. But I've wanted to check out the house for a while now. See what kind of shape it's in. I doubt O'Malley has returned. Even he isn't stupid enough to do that. "I just want to look around."

We're silent for the rest of the drive, and we don't speak as we pull up to O'Malley's place. It looks alright from the outside. Nobody's torched it or anything. But it's clear nobody's been living here. The driveway hasn't been ploughed in weeks, and there are no recent footprints or tire tracks.

Curse and I approach the door. I had a key for this lock cut more than a year ago, but I've never actually used it before. This door was unlocked on New Year's Eve, probably because of the party. I don't need to use the key now, either. The door is unlocked, which doesn't surprise me, considering the shit storm that accompanied the abandonment of this house. O'Malley knew he was leaving for good. I guess he saw no point in locking the door behind him, even though he'd left the most important fucking thing in the world behind.

The visceral hatred I feel for O'Malley briefly makes pain flare, like fireworks, in my head and side. I'll never forget the sight of him running, running across the snow for his worthless, miserable, putrid life, while that Camorra soldier aimed his gun at Deirdre. It's a scene that came to me more than once in my fever dreams. Sometimes, she was standing in the snow, just like that night. Sometimes fire.

The inside of the house is nowhere near as untouched at the outside looks. The place is absolutely trashed. It's obvious that anything of value has been stripped out of here and the rest was destroyed just for the hell of it. Couches sliced open, glass and dishes shattered on the ground, stains on the walls. Entire appliances have been yanked out of the kitchen. The cupboards hang open and empty, like dead, toothless mouths. Considering how fast I paid off Sev, I doubt this is the Camorra's work. No, this was probably Darragh taking out his rage after O'Malley disappeared and I snatched Deirdre out from under him.

Curse and I move through the wrecked house together. I can sense how alert he is, constantly checking the surroundings for any danger, but there's nothing. No one's here.

We head upstairs. While I've never been up here, I know the general layout of the house. At least, I know where Deirdre's room is, based on where I've seen the balcony outside. I head there first, and even though I don't give a shit about any of this stuff, because it was from her life before me and therefore it means nothing now, it still makes my insides go dark with fury when I see that Darragh smashed his ugly way through Deirdre's room too.

The bed has been sliced open with a big, jagged cut down the middle. Maybe Darragh was looking for money or valuables. Or maybe he was trying to send her a message if she ever dared to come back here. Her closet is open, her clothes torn and trampled. If there was a laptop or other computer in here, it's long gone, along with any other electronics. My shoe crunches on something, and I look down to find myself stepping on the flat glass of a picture frame. I crouch and then open the frame from the back, sliding the photograph out and holding it up to my face. While there's enough moonlight pouring in from the glass doors leading out to the balcony for me to have surveyed the overall state of the room, it's not bright enough to get a good look at the photo.

"Light?" I ask, knowing Curse is close by. I hear him hunt around the room. The only lamp in here has been smashed, but evidently the power hasn't been cut, because when he finds a wall switch, the room comes to vivid life. It makes the violent mess in here look even worse than before, but I ignore it and focus on the photo in my hands.

It's a picture of Deirdre and her mother, Fiona. While Deirdre may have gotten her colouring from her papa, she got all her mamma's beauty. The tanned, smiling face of the blonde woman in the photo has echoes of the freckled face I love so much. It makes me feel like I know this ghost of a woman, even though she died long before I ever even learned her name.

Deirdre can't be more than nine or ten in the picture. I wonder if this was taken the summer before Fiona died. Deirdre's smile is almost as big as her mamma's, both of them beaming, locked in an affectionate embrace in front of a tangle of rainbow arches that I recognize as roller coasters. I think they're at the big amusement park in Vaughn, a little to the northwest of here. Deirdre is holding a stick with a cotton candy puff bigger than her head. Her mamma is holding her.

This photograph makes me feel things I don't know what to do with. I don't have any photos of my mamma, and if I did I'm not sure if I could even stand to look at them. To see her beautiful face again, forever smiling and trapped in a photograph, a static slice of a memory. But at the same time, I have no doubt that if there were photos of my mamma floating around out there to find, I would fucking want them, whether I planned to actually look at them or not. I can even forgive the fact that it was probably O'Malley who took this photograph as I stand and slide it into my pocket. At least he isn't in the photo with them. If he were, I'd have to cut him out.

There isn't much left to look at in here. Curse heads out onto the balcony to look around while I head back towards the closet. There's no jewellery or anything of real value left here, just ruined clothes that she doesn't need because I will buy her new ones. There is a box, though. A carboard box on the floor. It's been ripped open but was ultimately left behind. When I bend over to peer inside, I see why. Because there was nothing in there for Darragh to destroy – the thing inside was already broken.

It isn't even a thing at all. It's a collection of pieces, curving and jagged-edged. Some nearly as large as my hand, others smaller than a baby tooth. The broken material is hard and white, and some pieces are intact enough to see the painted image of blooming roses. When I reach into the box and pull out an intact spout, I know exactly what it is I'm looking at.

It's the teapot. Deirdre's mamma's teapot. The one she broke after the funeral.

It's pretty fucking ruined. I can see why Deirdre didn't even bother trying to piece it back together. But even so, even though I know it's pointless – the thing is shattered and dead and done – I find myself returning the spout to the box, picking the whole thing up, and putting the box beneath my arm.

"What's that?" Curse asks as he steps back into the room from the outside balcony, closing the door behind him.

"Something broken."

His gaze lingers on the box, but he doesn't ask any more questions about it. Which is probably good, considering I don't have any more answers.

We turn off the light and leave Deirdre's old bedroom, heading down the hall to the house's primary bedroom. It's just as topsy turvy as the rest of the house – mattress sliced open and tossed down to the floor, clothes everywhere, anything of value long gone. There's even a safe that's been left open. I don't know if O'Malley emptied it himself or if one of Darragh's guys managed to get it open after the fact, but either way there's no money or gold or anything in there. There are a couple of pieces of paper littering the floor in front of the safe that Darragh must have deemed worthless. There are some random legal documents, Jack and Fiona's marriage license, Fiona's long-expired passport. There's another piece of paper that just looks like a letter, and I turn on the lights in here so I can read it, wondering why it was once hidden away in a safe.

It's addressed to Jack O'Malley. There's very little text in the body of the letter, just one sentence, and the text itself isn't all that unusual.

If the terms of the loan repayment are not met in a timely fashion then I will be forced to engage in other less desirable forms of recourse.

It's signed by some guy named Charlie, no last name included. I don't think I know anyone named Charlie or Charles, but it doesn't surprise me that O'Malley ran up other debts besides the ones I already know about.

No, there's nothing particularly odd about this letter.

Except...

The date.

My eyes snag on it and stay there.

And it's like the rest of the room, the entire fucking world, disappears.

I have devoted almost two years to learning everything I can about my Songbird. I know her birthday. I know her exam schedules.

I sure as fucking shit know the day her mamma fucking died.

And this letter is from the same year. Dated exactly one fucking day before.

My throat works, and I'm very, very still. But not a calm sort of still. The stillness of a bomb about to blow.

O'Malley gets a letter about debt repayment and "less desirable forms of recourse" the day before the car accident that killed his wife?

549

Shit like that does not just happen. That is not a coincidence. Not in the world men like O'Malley and I inhabit.

I fight to control myself, to not obliterate the paper in my hands, but it's fucking hard, and for a long, ugly moment that tastes like metal and smoke I can't even see straight. My mind careens back and forth, picking up pieces like bits of a broken teapot from a box, putting them together until everything suddenly becomes clear.

The car accident that killed Deirdre's mamma wasn't an accident at all.

Somebody planned it. And O'Malley fucking *knew*.

Chapter 29

Deirdre

When I get home from class and head upstairs to find Elio, I stop with a jolt to see that he isn't there. I stare at the empty bed, freshly made by Rosa, panic rising faster than I know what to do with. I set my bag down and spin on my heel, throwing myself right back out of the room to find him.

I almost take out Doctor Morelli as I do so, who's currently walking down the hall. He catches me with a pair of strong, steady hands around the elbow and makes sure I don't fall before letting go.

"Sorry!" I say quickly. "I'm looking for Elio. He's not in bed. Is he OK?"

"OK," the doctor responds with a small smile. "I say he can get up a little bit." His smile grows, turns into a grin. "Strong boy. Eh? Sometimes staying in bed... It's worse than being sick."

"You're telling me," I say on a sigh, relieved. "I can't even believe he stayed in bed like he was told for as long as he did."

"Because of you," the doctor says without hesitation.

"What?" I cock my head at him.

"He wants to marry you. Wants to live. Never listened to me that

551

much before. *Non frega un cazzo*. Eh... Normally, he doesn't give a – *pardoni* – doesn't give a shit."

This body ain't worth shit, Songbird.

"Well, I'm glad he does now," I say quietly. "Do you know when he'll be back?"

"No."

"OK. Actually. I have a favour to ask you. Or not really a favour. I..." My sentence breaks off into embarrassed silence. I cross my arms, face throbbing with warmth. I peek around Doctor Morelli to see a soldier in the usual place at the top of the stairs and I lower my voice. "I want to get on birth control."

I got my period while Elio was sick with his fever, thank God.

Let's just say that I'm pretty invested in making sure that it comes again next month. And it's not like I can just wander out of here anytime I want and make an appointment at a local clinic.

But Doctor Morelli doesn't nod or instantly agree the way I'd expected him to.

He hesitates, runs a hand through his grey hair, then says, "Gotta ask the boss."

"I... hold on. What? Did I just hear you right?" I say, absolutely flabbergasted. "I know Elio is in charge of just about everything around here, but I have to ask his permission to go on fucking birth control?"

"Not you," he says quickly, as if that's comforting. "Me. I must ask the boss before I can give to you."

"That's... That's even worse! You're a doctor! You shouldn't have to ask a person with no medical training for permission before you administer an important drug to someone else!"

"Not just someone else," he replies. "Boss' wife. You see?"

"No! I don't!"

Well, I'm certainly not being quiet now. The soldier at the stairs is craning his neck and frowning at us. His attention is torn away, though, by the sound of the front door opening and then closing again. I can't make out the words, but I catch the rumble of Elio's voice.

A heady combination of relief and rage fill me at his return.

"Don't bother asking him," I tell the doctor, already heading for the top of the stairs. "I'm going to do it myself. *Right now*."

I jog down the stairs. From here, I can see the door and entryway. Curse is striding away, heading for somewhere else in the house. It looks like he's carrying a cardboard box, but I don't get a clear view. Plus, it's his older brother that I'm focused on right now.

It's hard to remain righteous in my rage when I see him. There's an intense, drawn look on his face, and my steps falter a little. I wonder if he's hurting. If he feels worse than before because he went out.

He's so lost in whatever emotion or sensation he's processing that he doesn't even notice me until my foot hits the floor at the bottom of the stairs.

His head cranks up, his eyes lock on mine, and then he's in instant motion, coming straight for me with the singular, relentless drive of a torpedo. He barely even stops when he reaches me and crushes me against his chest. It's only the hard bars of his arms around my back that keep me from falling backwards.

"Songbird," he murmurs against my hair, bending and breathing in deeply. I can feel him making a vicious fist in the back of my shirt with his non-splinted hand.

"What is it?" I ask, my earlier panic returning with twice as much force, bringing with it an acrid taste on my tongue. "Are you feeling worse? Are you in pain?" I shift and pull in his arms, ignoring his growl of complaint and the way he tries to drag me even closer. I manage to get one of my hands up from where it was jammed between us and I slap it, harder than I mean to, against his forehead.

A shuddering sigh escapes me. His skin is blissfully cool, kissed by the winter air outside. No hint of returning fever.

"What is it?" I ask again, because he's still holding me in a way that makes me feel like something's wrong.

"Nothing," he bites out after a long pause. "Just learned some shit today I wish I hadn't."

Before I can ask him more about that, I hear Doctor Morelli addressing Elio in Italian from behind me.

"I'm good," Elio replies in English. "It was good to get out there. Stretch my legs a little. Already feel even better than I did this morning."

"Good," I say, yanking myself out of his arms. "Now that I know you're alright, I can be mad at you."

Elio's brows rise, an expression of dark amusement shaping his mouth.

"Oh?"

"Yes! Why did you tell Doctor Morelli I can't go on birth control?"

His brows fly even higher before crashing down.

"I don't recall specifically telling him that," he says with a frown.

"He said he needs to get your permission before he can give it to me!"

"Yes," Elio says, slowly, as if explaining something to a child. "Everything that happens to you happens by my say-so, Songbird. And Doctor Morelli reports to me, not to you."

My hands curl into fists at my side, as if I can punch some good sense into this man.

"So, what?" I hiss through gritted teeth. "If something happened to me and you weren't here, what then? What if I was on the brink of death? He wouldn't be allowed to even give me a fucking bandage without calling you first? He'd just let me bleed out on the floor, then?"

A look so black and thunderous contorts Elio's face that, for the first time in a long time, I feel a frisson of fear when I look at him.

"Do not," he bites out, "even fucking joke about that, Deirdre."

"Who says that I'm joking?"

Doctor Morelli, clever guy that he is, makes himself suddenly scarce as Elio locks his uninjured hand around my wrist. Elio starts walking, dragging me along with him. "We'll talk about this some-where else."

I expect him to try to pull me up the stairs, but he doesn't. It's as if the bedrooms are too far away and he wants to hash this out right here, right now. Fine by me. He opens the door to his office, shoves me inside, then slams the door behind us.

I stumble, then spin around to face him, already sucking in a huge breath to tell him off. But that breath stutters right out of me when Elio wraps his fingers around my throat and slams his mouth to mine.

Surprise, anger, and desire all melt together until I can't tell them apart. Elio's mouth is hot and urgent on mine, and there's no way I can remain closed to him. My lips part under the onslaught, and he doesn't hesitate even for a moment before shoving his tongue inside. Claiming.

His hand slides down from my throat to my waist, and before I can react I'm being turned towards the desk. The cool leather of Elio's hand finds the back of my neck, exerting a gentle warning of pressure.

"Bend over."

"No," I seethe. But even as I say it, even as furious as I am, there's terrible, wanton warmth blooming between my legs. I try to buck out of his grip, but he's right behind me, his massive body caging me in against the desk. The wood chews into my hipbones and something else hard grinds against my ass. I gasp and moan, then slam my treacherous mouth shut.

"Watch yourself, Songbird," Elio murmurs against the sensitive skin of my ear. "Just because I only have one good hand doesn't mean that I can't punish you exactly the way you need right now. Now bend the fuck over or *I will make you.*"

His fingers massage the base of my skull, exerting tender tension that I know can turn hard and brutal any moment.

He can make me bend over. He can make me do anything he wants to.

Even make me care about him. And that's the most damning part.

Breathing heavily but trying to hide it, I hinge at the hips until my breasts and belly are mashed against the smooth wood of the desk. Needing something to hold onto, I grip the far edge of the desk, my knuckles white with pressure.

"Fuck. Love seeing you wear that ring," Elio groans as he tugs my leggings and panties down to my knees. I raise my eyes, chin hitting wood, to see the sparkle of it against my curled fist. I'm suddenly reminded of my second night with Elio, when he took me to the gala and made me wear a literal collar of diamonds. This is a type of collar too. An even more permanent and meaningful one.

One that, ultimately, I have chosen.

My whole body jolts with painfully needy awareness when the smooth, naked tip of Elio's cock slides against my pussy.

"You're already wet," he breathes heavily from behind me. I hold my breath, scrunching my eyes shut in shameful anticipation. I don't even mean to, but I rise up on the balls of my feet, already trying to angle myself for him to enter me.

"Oh, Songbird," Elio coos darkly, swirling his tip against me, soaking himself with my wetness. "I've been neglecting this pretty, greedy little pussy, haven't I?" Gloveless fingers reach beneath his cock and between my legs from behind, circling my clit until I'm shaking.

"Tell me," he says, his voice going hard and rough, "did you want me while I was stuck in bed? Did you pet this sweet little pussy while imagining my cock sliding into you?"

I can't hold my breath anymore. It whooshes out of me, shaped sloppily around the word *no*.

Elio's hand instantly withdraws from my clit and I want to fucking scream.

It returns to me, though, in the form of a crisp slap against my ass. "Don't lie to me."

I hate that he even knows I'm lying now. Because I did, I fucking did touch myself, angling myself away from the camera in the bathroom while I showered. Or sometimes even right beside him while he slept.

"Tell me what you did."

When I don't answer immediately, another slap rings out and makes my flesh jump. He's never spanked me without his leather glove on. It feels different, oddly intimate, and makes every nerve buzz with stinging arousal.

He follows that up with one more crisp smack, then rubs my throbbing skin.

"Tell. Me."

"I... touched myself," I choke out, not feeling an ounce of relief with the admission, only horror and shame. Elio doesn't seem horrified, though. I can literally feel his cock jerk against my pussy at my words, and his breath hitches.

"Where?" he demands.

"You know where!" I cry. "Between my legs, where else?"

That earns me a quick, smart slap to the ass. Tears fill my eyes, but not because I'm sad or scared. And it isn't even just a physical response to the shock of the spanking, either. It's like something inside me is breaking down. Some lever of control starting to crack and falter. I've been so scared with Elio sick in bed. So worried about maintaining control of the rapidly deteriorating situation. Giving it up now, submitting to Elio who's so strong and healthy and fucking alive, feels like the darkest sort of salvation.

"Did you touch yourself here?" His hand skims from my smarting ass to my clit, thrumming a quick, demanding rhythm that has me convinced I'm already about to come. "Or here?" He slides his fingers back and dips two of them into my quivering pussy.

"Yes," I whisper shakily. I'm gripping the desk so hard it hurts. My nipples ache against the wood. My hips are arching back towards him, seeking more than just his fingers.

He curses softly, withdrawing his hand until I whimper.

"If I hadn't been fucked up in bed for so long," he says raggedly, "if I hadn't been lying there for two fucking weeks wanting you, I would make you wait a little longer. Spank you until you were falling apart and fucking begging for it. But as it is..."

My heart stutters and slams when he suddenly pushes his hard cock into me. A nudge at first, and then a dizzyingly powerful thrust that sends him deep inside.

He never finishes his sentence from before. He just makes a gruff sound.

Meanwhile, I don't make a single sound at all. I'm too overwhelmed by him. There's no bright, bloody pain like the first two times he was inside me. But there's an incredible, searing stretch as he seats himself fully that steals every breath out of my lungs.

Everything inside me tightens around his shaft, like no matter what my brain thinks about it, my body wants to hold onto him, to draw him even deeper somehow. Not that I think that's physically possible at this point. This angle is new, and I feel him in places I didn't even know he could reach.

I don't realize I've started holding my breath again until Elio grabs my braid, wraps it around his fist, and yanks my head back, forcing me to draw a quaking breath.

"None of that now," he chides. He gives another firm tug on my hair, pulling until I'm lifting off of the desk, bending my spine towards him. My fingers uncurl from the far edge of the desk as I move, my hands sliding towards my hips before planting themselves flat.

"You don't stop breathing," Elio adds with a grinding thrust, "unless I tell you to."

He releases my hair, but before I can slump forward his palm slams into place at the front of my throat. His fingers dig into the side of my neck, his thumb pressing possessively into the pulse-point beneath my jaw. At the same moment, he draws his cock all the way out and then slams mercilessly back in.

Scars and skin. Blood and heat. All I'm aware of is him. Inside my body. Around my throat. Going harder, harder, until stars spark in front of my eyes and pleasure coils in my pelvis. My breathing is reduced to a reedy whistle, dizzying, disastrous. My head feels oddly light, like it could float upwards, but ultimately can't, because my whole body is anchored by the possessive plunge of Elio's cock.

The room ahead blurs. I can't tell if it's from tears or reduced oxygen. I let them slide closed, and when I do, every sensation in my body moves down, down to the place Elio is rutting so deep inside. The powerful pulses of his hips send my clit bumping against the wooden edge of the desk. I can't make a sound like this, with that leather cage of fingers at my throat.

In silence I stagger and fall apart. My insides go taut as my mind unspools. Elio groans, giving a throb inside, before loosening his grip on my throat. Oxygen rushes in, flooding my brain until I'm flung over the edge of another orgasm that instantly follows the first. My eyes flare wildly open, my fingers curl and claw at the desk. Elio doesn't give me a moment of reprieve. He maintains a vicious rhythm, his breathing tight.

"*Merda*," he bites out. "I've been waiting to feel this needy pussy come all over my cock again."

I moan, feeling my throat vibrate beneath the solidness of his yet-lingering hand. And then, like I've just been dragged from a dream and thrust into the harsh light of day, I flinch and gasp.

He's not wearing a condom. And we haven't sorted out the birth control situation, either.

I try to pull away from him but there's nowhere to go. The solid wood desk is before me, Elio behind.

"Don't..." I pant raggedly, panic clawing at me. "Don't come."

Elio's thrusting hitches slightly, losing its tempo, before resuming with even more intensity. His fingers twitch at my throat, then move away, returning to my body with a breathtaking smack on my ass. Now that he's not holding me up, I collapse forward onto my elbows, bent over for him at a lurid near-90-degree angle. It's the perfect position for him to spank me again, which he does. Waves of prickling fire undulate across my skin, moving inward, inward, until it feels like he's slapped my clit.

"You don't tell me when to come," he growls, giving me another tight smack. "I tell you when to come." Another collision of his hand on my ass. Another pathetic mewl ripping itself from my throat. "And I want you to do it right-" *smack* "fucking-" *smack* "*now*."

I have to disobey. *I have to*. I've given so much to him that I can at least resist this. Can't I?

The answer comes to me with a quaking in my core. Elio is hitting some deep, delicious, terrible place inside me that makes me feel like I might come or pee or maybe both at the same time. There's no stopping this riptide of pulsating pleasure, so intense and raw that it almost borders on pain.

"I said *now*, Songbird."

The quaking inside ceases, and I clamp down on Elio so hard that I can tell he's affected by it. By *me*.

He slams forward and gives a broken-sounding groan, his hand seizing on my hip to draw me even closer to him, even though my raw, red ass is already right up against his groin. Anxiety spikes, fear that he's going to lose control and come, or maybe come inside me just because he wants to, to send me a message, remind me who I belong to. But that quiver of distress only sends my arousal shamefully higher. Every nerve inside me is splayed and screaming for him, and I hate, *I hate*, that a part of me wants him not to pull out.

But he does, so suddenly that I jerk with the shock of it, almost like I've been hit.

And the emptiness he leaves behind feels just like a bruise.

Chapter 30

Elio

The amount of control it takes to pull out of Deirdre's sweet, pulsing little pussy should earn me the title of a fucking god among men. I wrench my cock out of her, staggering backwards until my legs hit my office chair and I fall heavily into it. My pants are tangled around my ankles, and I kick them off and to the side with a grunt.

Leaning back, I grip the arm of the chair with my unsplinted hand, chest heaving, cock wet and twitching, and I stare at Deirdre's perfect, reddened ass. She's still bent over, nearly boneless, her legs shaking, her pussy glistening. Fuck me, from this angle I can literally see the aftershocks of her orgasm drawing the muscles around her cunt tight, over and over again, like the throb of a heartbeat.

"How does it feel to squeeze around nothing?" I groan. "How does it feel to keep coming like that, without my cock inside you?" I take my shaft in a stiff grip. I'm not sure if I want to stroke it and give into the battering need to come, or if I want to clench my fist around it and gain back some semblance of control.

"I..." she stammers between heavy breaths, "I feel so... *empty.*"

I just about come on the fucking spot.

I hiss through clenched teeth, squeezing myself so hard it hurts and scrunching up my face.

She needs me. She feels empty without me.

I can find another way to fill her.

"Get over here," I grit out, cracking my eyes open to make sure that she obeys.

And she does, but so fucking slowly I want to grab her by the fucking hair again. It's as if her muscles aren't working quite right in the aftermath. She gets her hands under her on the desk, pushing upwards until most of her weight is on her wobbly legs, before she haltingly turns around.

There isn't a lot of space between us. My chair wasn't that far away from the desk. But the distance yawns like a fucking chasm, because she isn't with me yet and if I can't touch her then even one single step is a step too fucking far.

"Closer," I rasp. I use my splinted hand to gesture to the place on the floor between my feet. "On your knees."

She hesitates, that beautiful, damning, arousing disobedience flashing in her big blue eyes.

"Deirdre," I warn, my voice lowering dangerously, "I am going to come inside you. And if it's not inside your cunt then it will be inside your mouth or your ass. Your choice. Now fucking *make it.*"

At my words she shivers so hard I see it happen from here. Her tongue darts out to wet her lips, and I'm this fucking close to shoving her down on that desk again and burying myself in the pulsing paradise of her pussy.

Look. I shot my own father in the fucking head. That doesn't exactly make a man keen on producing his own spawn. I doubt that I'm prime papà material and until today I haven't even thought about bringing a baby into this equation. But the thought of coming inside the wet, fertile channel of Deirdre's body, seeing her get all big and swollen with my baby in her belly, makes me burn so hot with lust that it's like there's fire in my veins, fire that won't ebb or cool or let me go until I literally fuck it out of me.

Cristo Santo. Fuck.

I've literally never felt like this before. So mindless with electric need that I'm prepared to throw all reason out the fucking window. Hell, I haven't even shot my load in another woman without a condom in more than ten goddamn years.

But everything's different with Deirdre. *Everything.*

Including me.

Dio help me, I'm going to take her by the throat, then shove until she's flat on her fucking back on my desk, splayed entirely open for me.

And then I'm going to rut her like a fucking animal in heat.

My legs tense, preparing for me to rise up out of the chair.

But at that exact moment, Deirdre makes her choice and steps forward. The soft press of her hands on my thighs as she lowers herself to her knees is all it fucking takes to freeze me there.

She kneels between my legs, and it's a beautiful fucking sight. Her wide gaze moves from the iron-hard rod of my cock to my face and then back down.

"I don't..."

Jesus fucking *fuck.* I can feel her breath on my damp skin as she speaks.

"I don't know what to... I've never done this before," she admits. I ease my fingers away from my cock and grasp her chin firmly, my thumb pressing against her lower lip.

"Open your mouth."

She swallows, her throat bobbing, and for a second I lose myself imagining what that mouth, that throat, are going to feel like from the inside.

"*Open.*"

She finally does so, parting her lips slightly until I can see the blunt, shiny edges of her teeth.

"Wider, Songbird," I groan. My hips roll without me meaning for them to, the tip of my cock colliding with her lips and smearing precum there. I press my thumb harder at the place above her chin, pushing downwards against the lower half of her jaw until her mouth is forced into a pretty pink O shape. My slick head is right fucking there, and it only takes a miniscule nudge to send it past her lips and teeth and into the wet cavern of her mouth.

"Now suck."

She does so, an experimental tug of tension against the tip of my cock that has me straining in the chair. Her tongue prods delicately at my leaking tip, then lower, stroking its silken surface across my glans. I can tell she doesn't know what the fuck she's doing. She's treating the tip of my dick like a lollipop instead of sucking me down deeper, but for the moment I don't give a flying fuck. My balls get hot and tight, my shaft practically vibrating, needing more and needing her not to stop even for a second all at the same damn time.

I bury my hand in her hair, gripping the back of her head and mussing up her braid, guiding her down at the same time that I thrust up. She gives a muffles squeak of surprise that I feel all the way down to my balls.

But she doesn't let up. Sloppily trying to time herself to my new gyrating rhythm, she bobs her head. Instinctively, she slides a hand further up my thigh until she's got her fist sliding up and down the throbbing length of me.

"You're doing so fucking well," I groan, bucking up into her mouth a little harder than I mean to, making her choke a bit. I slide my fingers out of her hair to the soft place beneath her jaw, then lower, to the front of her throat. Massaging there, I coax her, "Take me deeper."

Her eyes meet mine. Searing, endless, heart-stopping fucking blue. Her face is flushed, her hair a mess, her mouth filled with my cock and she couldn't look any fucking better.

She used to fight me. She used to fight me so fucking hard. But now I've got her on her knees with my dick in her mouth and she isn't even trying to bite it off. And when I nudge myself further inside, she relaxes and she fucking takes me deeper.

"Fuck. Stay like that," I breathe, returning my hand to the back of her head as I fuck her mouth. She's not trying to move on her own or suck now, I'm going too hard for that. All she can do is kneel there and fucking take it, holding her mouth open for me as her eyes slide shut.

I cannot fucking wait to marry this girl.

Maybe I'll have her suck me off right before the wedding, when she looks all pristine with her hair and makeup done, her white dress pooling around her body as she kneels.

A heady moan fills my lungs at that image, and my dick spasms hard in the silken wet of my fiancée's mouth. A jet of come shoots forward, filling her and probably surprising her, because she makes a garbled sound and tries to pull away. My hand turns hard as stone on the back of her head, holding her there, trapping her.

"I said," I grit out between waves of mind-bending pleasure, "that I was going to come inside you. Do not fucking move."

I can't believe she obeys, but she actually does. She stops fighting my hold as I spurt once more into her mouth. Forced to either swallow or choke, she chooses the former. Her throat contracts, and the suction in her mouth increases, making me bite back a gruff moan as my dick grows exquisitely sensitive.

There's a temptation to let my eyes roll back in my head and just enjoy the physical sensations. But I don't. I keep them wide fucking open, fastened on Deirdre's blushing face as she struggles so prettily to swallow everything I've given her.

Eventually, the pressure of her mouth on me turns into a breathless sort of torture. I ease my grip and let her wrench herself off of my cock with a wet-sounding gasp. Her mouth hangs slightly open as she pants, her lips swollen and smeared with saliva and the remnants of me.

It makes me feel like I'm going to get hard again already.

It makes me want to get back inside her pussy.

"Morelli will get you the pill," I grunt, yanking my clothes from the floor and hitching them up over my hips. I tuck my dick back inside and fasten everything into place without standing. I'm not entirely convinced my legs are going to hold me yet.

Deirdre's glazed look morphs into a glare, as if she's suddenly remembered that she was supposed to be pissed at me.

"I shouldn't have to ask your permission for something like that," she says, getting shakily to her feet so that she's looking down at me instead of up. Her face gets even redder when my gaze goes to her bare legs and pussy and she snatches at her clothes, pulling them up violently like she's even more mad at them than at me.

"Don't worry, Songbird. I don't plan on making you into a mamma just yet," I reply. "Want to enjoy you as my wife first. Keep you just for me a little while longer."

"Alright, well... That doesn't cover everything, though. The pill, I mean." She hesitates, and I stare at her unblinking, waiting for her to spit out whatever the fuck it is she's trying to say. She takes a steeling breath then says in a rush, "Have you been tested recently?"

"Tested? Like, *tested* tested?"

She nods.

"I need to know," she says defensively, even though I'm not offended in the slightest. "Since you don't use..."

"Condoms?" I say with a sardonic smirk. "Actually, Songbird, I pretty much always use condoms. Have for more than a decade. And I have been tested recently. Results are all clear on everything. Morelli's a demanding son of a bitch, and I don't always ignore his recommendations."

"You..." Her eyebrows do that cute frowny thing that creates the wrinkle between them that I always want to poke.

Or lick.

"You always use protection? But... with me..."

"Not with you." I rise from the chair, towering over her, forcing her to crane her neck and stare up at me. "Never with you. I told you that we are fucking bound. No barriers."

I palm her neck, then lower my mouth, sucking gently at her ear until she shivers and gasps. Releasing that slip of skin from between my teeth, I murmur hotly, "You have no fucking idea what it feels like to be inside you with nothing between us. To feel how fucking wet you are, gripping me the way you do. Like your pussy can't get enough of me even if that stubborn little mouth won't admit it."

She looks pissed, and almost a little guilty, no doubt because she knows I'm right.

I can't stop myself from sucking her ear into my mouth again, then nipping down along her throat. She shudders, then plants two ineffectual hands against my chest.

"I have homework," she objects. "I need to... to..."

She's losing her train of thought as I lick the sensitive places her heart beats.

But her homework is important, especially since I know that she skipped some of her classes while I was indisposed.

"Go," I say, taking one last, obsessive inhale against her skin, my cock twitching, before I straighten up. "Now. Or else I'll be coming inside you again and this time it won't be your mouth."

She turns and runs like prey.

Chapter 31

Deirdre

I don't see Elio again that night. Apparently he has a business meeting with Valentina's fiancé, Dario Fabbri, as well as Dario's father. Something to do with a financing deal the Titones are offering in relation to a real estate development in Northern Ontario. Other than a quick meeting with Doctor Morelli, when he gives me my first pack of birth control pills to start taking tonight, I don't interact much with anyone.

Alone, I think about sleeping in the other bed, the one I haven't touched in weeks. But I can only imagine what would happen if he came home late at night and found me there. Either he'd slide right in beside me so that I didn't have any distance from him at all.

Or he'd drag me out by the hair and take me back to his bed to punish me. So far, he's been willing not to come inside me. I figure it's better not to push him now.

Besides, I've gotten used to his bed, as crazy as that is. Even though Rosa changes the sheets every day, the bed still smells like him. I curl amongst the pillows and I fall asleep alone.

I'm alone when I wake up in the morning, too.

But clearly, Elio has been here at some point in the night. Because the first thing I see when I open my eyes is a small box on the bedside table that I know for a fact wasn't there last night. Behind the box is a vase exploding with roses, each one of them with petals as rich and uniformly black as Elio's leather gloves.

I sit up in bed, stroking along the edge of one of the black petals. It's so luscious, almost like it would melt at the heat of my touch, like frosting.

"He had to go with black," I say with a slight chuckle, brushing some of my hair out of my face. It's dark and dramatic and so positively Elio. I let my eyes fall from the flowers to the box. I don't move to touch it for a long time, staring at the envelope on top of the perfectly-wrapped shiny silver box.

But ultimately, my curiosity overpowers any reluctance. I take the envelope from the top of the box and open it, pulling out a plain, thick white card.

Songbird,

I hope you enjoy the flowers and the gift. Wear something nice later because I'm taking you out.

Happy Valentine's Day.

Eternally yours,

Your future husband

I stare at the card so long the words all blur together. This cannot be fucking real. Elio Titone wrote me a Valentine's Day card?!

I completely forgot today even was Valentine's Day. With being so worried about him, the days have been slipping by almost completely unnoticed. But even so, even knowing what day it is now, this completely confounds me. Elio does *not* seem like a Valentine sort of guy. He's the kind of guy who'd send somebody a severed hand before he sent them a card.

Was I supposed to get him something? What the hell do you get the horrifically rich man who kidnapped you, used your debt against you, and manipulated you into agreeing to marry him?

The man who's somehow worming his way into your heart no matter what you do to try to stop him?

"No," I say aloud, "I refuse to feel guilty." But even so, I'm already frantically trying to think of last-minute things I could do for the big, murderous idiot as I tear the glossy paper off of the small box.

Inside the box is a large, shiny metal rectangle. I pull it out, peering closely at it, trying to figure out just what it is. It has hinges on the side, like it's meant to open. It's not too large and fits easily into the palm of my hand. It almost reminds me of a case for cigarettes, but I obviously don't need one of those, and with all of Elio's aversions to things fire and smoke-related that doesn't seem likely. I trace my finger along the seam of the rectangle, then over the gorgeous engraving of a violin and bow on the front. It's the exact same colour as my ring, I realize. I guess it must be platinum.

Pondering the mystery of what exactly this gift is supposed to be, I shrug, find a small latch along the side, then open it.

And for a second, I actually think I must be dreaming.

Because inside, the way a tiny photo would be nestled into the heart of a locket, is my favourite photo of my mom and me. I stare at our wide grins and feel oddly off-balance, like I'm staring down a long tunnel and into my own past.

It's not the photo itself that's throwing me off that much. This picture had a prime place on my desk in my old room. I looked at it every fucking day.

It's seeing the photo *here*. It's having it again, seeing her smile again, when I wasn't sure I ever would. Elio told me the house was probably looted by enemies of my father.

But somehow, someway, he must have saved this little piece of my heart. I wonder how long he's had it. The platinum case fits the photo perfectly, and between that and the engraving I have no doubt it's been custom made. But Elio has so much money and power he could probably pay somebody to do a project like that in less than twenty-four hours.

He was gone a long time yesterday...

I never found out where he went.

I fumble for my phone, sniffing hard against tears I didn't even know were there until now. With shaking fingers I call him.

He answers immediately.

"Good morning, Songbird," he purrs into the phone, his voice like smoke and chocolate. "Did you get my gift?"

"Yes," I croak. I clear my throat. "When did you... How..."

He chuckles, and I swear I feel the sound of it between my legs. I press my thighs together.

"Can't a man have any secrets?"

"Not from your wife," I say, rather smartly, I think, considering how my mind is reeling.

He laughs again, softly, the sound pouring into my ear and making my nipples harden.

"I was there yesterday. Stopped by after taking care of a little legal matter."

"How..." I swallow, my throat suddenly dry. "How was it?"

"Trashed," he replies, "just like I thought it would be. Anything of any value was taken and everything else was basically destroyed."

"But this... You found this. And you brought it back for me," I whisper, my eyes filling as I stroke the side of the photograph. I still remember that day so vividly. It was the last birthday I shared with my mom. It was *her* birthday, but she wanted to go to the amusement park because it would be more fun for *me*.

"Of course," he says nonchalantly, "I wasn't going to leave your mamma there in that fucking mess."

"Thank you," I say, but it comes out more like a sob.

Elio is quiet on the other end while I take a moment to collect myself.

"God," I say, swiping at my wet cheeks, "I used to look at this picture every day. But now it's like I'm seeing it for the first time. She was so, so beautiful."

"Like mamma, like daughter," Elio says, and it's gentle, maybe more gentle than I've ever heard him.

I laugh tearily.

"I don't know. I never thought I looked much like her."

"Really?" Elio says, sounding genuinely surprised. "There's different colouring, sure. But when I saw that photo, I thought you both had the exact same smile."

My breath catches. No one has ever told me that before. Anytime anyone ever commented on my appearance growing up, it was always to remark upon the red hair I inherited from my father. But as I stare down at the photograph, I suddenly see that Elio is right. How did he notice that when nobody else did? Not even me?

I wipe at my eyes again, then hug the photo, platinum case and all, to my chest. Now that I know what's inside, the violin and bow engraved on the front are even more meaningful. Because that's something that I shared with her.

"Was there anything else at the house of note?" I ask, trying to move my mind onto more practical questions because otherwise I think my heart might crack right open. "Anything to do with my father?"

I'm curious if there were any signs that he's been back to the house, though I doubt he has been. And after everything that's happened, after it's become crystal clear that he never planned to come back for me after selling me out in the first fucking place, I have no interest in seeing him even if he does come back.

"There was..." Elio pauses for so long I think something's gone wrong with the call.

"Elio?"

"There was nothing else." His voice is suddenly clipped, like he's pissed about something. Maybe he doesn't want to talk about my dad.

Which is fair enough. Because neither do I.

"Alright, well... I guess I'll let you go," I say, but the words are halting, like I don't want to end the call at all. The bed suddenly feels so empty, and before I can reign it in, there's a stab of desire. The desire to have Elio here with me.

"Did you sleep in the bed last night?" I ask abruptly.

"Sure did," he says, and he doesn't sound annoyed anymore. He sounds like a very smug cartoon cat with a bird's wing caught beneath its paw. "You didn't even stir when I got home. Guess I tired you out too much in my office yesterday."

"Where are you now?" I ask, ignoring the lurid implication of his last words.

"Why? Miss me?"

The thing is, I actually do. And that's kind of terrifying.

"Can't a woman have any secrets?" I huff, copying his earlier question and feeling my cheeks warm.

"Not from her husband."

"You're not my husband yet," I counter, trying to control the slightly giddy feeling rising in my chest. I think it's very fucking likely that I am flirting with my fiancé and I really don't want to acknowledge that possibility.

"Not long now," he muses, and I can hear the smile in his voice. "Two weeks and a day."

My stomach flips. That's really, *really* soon.

And for the first time, I'm not filled with utter dread at the prospect.

What is happening to me?

"Valentina's coming over later," Elio says. "She's going to bring you some dresses. Get you all dolled up."

"Where are we going?"

"Out for dinner."

"You realize we're doing this in the complete wrong order, right?" I say, letting out a breathy laugh. "Usually going out for dinner for the first time is something you do *before* you get engaged."

"Yeah, well, most guys don't get shot the first time they meet their fiancée, either. What can I say? We're unconventional."

I snort loudly. I'm not crying anymore. It actually feels good to talk with him like this. Despite what he just said, it feels oddly normal.

I hear a man's voice in the background.

"You still haven't told me where you are," I remind him.

"Downtown," he replies. "We're providing the concrete for a construction project. I'm checking on things."

I have trouble picturing him somewhere as mundane as a construction site.

"Are you wearing a hard hat?" I tease.

A gruffness enters his voice.

"How about we talk about what you're wearing instead?"

"I'm still in bed. If you were here last night then you know what that is."

"Ah. Right. Those grandma jammies that you somehow manage to make look fucking sexy. Still don't know how you do that, by the way."

I hear another voice in the background, along with the beeping sound of a truck. Elio tells me that he has to go.

"I'll see you tonight," he murmurs. "Happy Valentine's Day, Deirdre."

He hangs up before I can say it back.

———

As promised, Valentina shows up later that afternoon. And she doesn't just have dresses for me. She's got a whole rolling case of stuff that, when opened, spills over with fabric samples and stationery and catalogues, all of it distinctly bridal in aesthetic.

"I came a little early," she says, hauling stuff out of the case and dumping it on the island in the kitchen. "I figured we could do some wedding stuff before you got ready. Although... If you don't want to, I can make all the final decisions myself."

She pauses then, swatches of pearly fabric in her fists, and eyes me like she expects me to object the way I did on the way to the wedding dress fitting.

"It's alright," I tell her with a small smile. "I'll help."

She looks surprised for a moment, then grins.

"Resigned yourself to your fate then, eh?" she says cheerily.

Not long ago, that sentence would have made me recoil. But now I just give a disbelieving laugh. "Something like that."

Now that I've agreed to the wedding, it doesn't seem fair to make Valentina take on so much work to plan it on her own. So I throw myself in head-first right alongside her. I don't know anything about event planning, but it that doesn't matter much. Valentina's knowledge makes up for my lack. And it seems like she mostly just wants my input on things, which I've grown to appreciate.

This isn't a wedding I ever could have anticipated. But at least I'm being consulted on things like the flowers and the décor.

We're elbow deep in wedding stuff when Valentina glances at her phone and swears.

"Shit. We have to get you ready!" She leaps off the stool beside the island, and I follow suit. She snatches the garment bags she brought with her and hustles up the stairs with me close behind.

This reminds me so much of that second night here, when Valentina came to help me get ready for the gala. But this time, I'm much more willing to do everything she asks. I try on both dresses quickly without dithering about the camera the way I once did.

I grimace to myself, remembering what she said. About how I'd get used to things here.

And it seems like I have.

We both agree on the second dress I try on. It's a gown of opalescent silk that looks white at first glance, but gleams in the palest shades of lavender and shell-pink at certain angles and in certain light. Something about the design feels Grecian – the silk is draped in flowing swoops at the shoulders, and it's cut not too low in the front but very low in the back. As I reach up to adjust the shoulder of the dress, Valentina smacks her forehead.

"I forgot you don't have any razors. I didn't bring one this time. Quick. Take that off. There's a waxing kit in the bathroom."

I'm not exactly keen on waxing right now, but it seems like the only available option at the moment. And it turns out that Valentina's got a deft hand for the job. She waxes beneath my arms and along my legs with a ruthlessly competent efficiency that makes the stinging not as bad as it probably could have been in other circumstances.

"Want me to do your bush?" she suddenly asks.

I nearly choke on my own spit at the completely unselfconscious way she says it. Coughing, I stare at her with watering eyes.

"Um," I gasp, "I hadn't really thought about it..."

She shrugs.

"No biggie. I just thought, you know, special occasion and all that." She waggles her perfect eyebrows at me and I want to melt into the floor.

I'm about to tell her no, but I'm suddenly seized by the idea of Elio undressing me later, unwrapping me like a present, and finding me smooth and bare down there.

Would he be surprised?

Would he like it?

I can't get the thought out of my mind. Before I can lose my nerve, I nod and squeak out, "OK!"

Turns out waxing down there hurts a hell of a lot more than the other places. But even so, Valentina is still quick and competent. It's almost hard to be embarrassed even spread-eagle for her because she's so casual about the whole thing, like she's used to it.

"How are you so good at this – fucking *ouch!*" I exclaim.

Valentina presses her fingers to the raw place, letting the hot throb cool to a quiet pulse of pain. "I always wanted to own my own business. Guess that runs in the family," she says with a slight roll of her eyes. "For a long time, I thought I'd open a hair salon or a spa. Even though I'd be the one running it, I still wanted to know the ins and outs. Lucia and Giulia used to let me practise stuff like this on them all the time."

She whips another strip of wax away, and I have to wait for the sting to subside before I can ask her, "You don't want to run a salon anymore? What do you want to do now?"

"Honestly? I don't know. Things aren't exactly going the way I imagined they would."

She prepares to yank another strip of wax, and when she moves the light sparkles on the pink diamonds of her rose-gold ring.

It's almost as if she senses my sudden pity, or that I'm going to say something mopey that she doesn't want to hear, because she gives a swift tug and all I can manage is a yelp. We don't talk much after that until the waxing is all done.

"I need a drink," I groan, my whole body feeling like an exposed nerve. "Or an ice bath. Or both."

"No time," Valentina replies, handing me a bottle of some kind of soothing post-wax lotion. "I still need to do your hair and makeup!"

Since we're running late there's no time for any elaborate heat-styling of my hair. Valentina settles on leaving its natural wavy-curly texture as-is. She pins it up, leaving little curls falling around my ears, then frowns at her phone.

"Elio's gonna be here soon and I can guarantee he's gonna be pissed if you're not ready," she says, looking worriedly at my bare face.

"That's alright," I say quickly. Last time Valentina did my makeup the result was stunning but it didn't feel like me. The foundation was so perfectly-applied that every freckle on my face had vanished.

Elio told me once that he liked my freckles.

We settle on some light concealer, mascara, and very dark red lipstick that adds drama to an otherwise softly ethereal look. I forgo a bra with the low back of the dress, and with a surge of erotic defiance I decide not to wear any panties, either. When I put the dress back on, the silk of the clinging skirt brushes the newly-bare skin between my legs. My clit responds instantly, my nipples pebbling. I take a few experimental steps, just to feel the delicious kiss of the silk against my exposed, sensitive places.

"Thanks for all this," I tell her, reddening a little thinking about how much time she spent between my legs helping me get ready. "And for... for the wedding stuff."

I can't believe I'm thanking her, or anyone, for anything to do with that wedding. But here I am.

She grins, brushing long blonde hair away from her face.

"Elio runs one tight fucking ship, I'll tell you that much," she says, but it sounds affectionate. "Only he would demand that I plan a whole wedding in basically one month. And not just some elopement shit either. A big grand affair. 'Deirdre deserves something nice,'" she says in a suddenly deep, growly voice, "'so you had better make it nice.' That's what he told me."

"He said that?"

"Sure did."

"And what about you tonight? Are you doing anything for Valentine's Day with Dario?"

"Ugh, gross," she says. "Definitely not. Some flowers arrived for me this morning and I'm 99% sure his secretary sent them instead of him. Wasn't even a handwritten card or anything."

"Oh." I don't know what else to say to that. Valentina deserves a hell of a lot better. I almost feel guilty now, thinking of the immensely personal and thoughtful gift that Elio gave me.

"Oh, God, please don't look so sorry for me," she groans, shooing me towards the door.

"You and Elio are a lot alike, you know," I tell her as I let her usher me into the hallway and down the stairs.

Valentina laughs. "I don't know if that's supposed to be a compliment or not."

"It is," I say instantly.

Downstairs in the kitchen, Valentina produces a few pairs of shoes from the case she brought. We settle on a pair of blood-red pumps to match the lipstick, as well as diamond-and-ruby studs and a matching pendant. After I'm fully ready to go, she starts putting all the wedding stuff away, but then seems to give up.

"I'm just gonna leave this stuff here," she says. "Now that I know you want to help with the planning, I'll have to come back again anyways."

"Sounds good. I-"

A noise from across the main floor of the house cuts me off. It's the sound of a door opening. I lean around the kitchen island to see Elio striding from his office.

Like I'm drawn by marionette strings, I move out from behind the kitchen island without conscious thought. There's an irresistible pull towards him that I can't ignore or even try to fight.

Elio falters slightly when he sees me. But maybe he feels that pull too, because he starts walking again, faster this time, heading straight for me with hunger in his eyes.

Valentina says a quiet goodbye to me and leaves.

And then it's just Elio and me.

If I thought my whole body felt like a raw nerve after the waxing, it's ten times worse now. The buzz of pain is still present along my skin, but now there's this tight, hot bundling in my belly that only adds to the overwhelm. I feel giddy and nearly nauseous when I look at him, when I take in the black-clad bulk of his body, smell the heady spice of his cologne.

He hasn't said anything yet. He's just staring at me like he can't tell if he wants to hug me or eat me.

"You look nice," I blurt in the silence that throbs between us.

God, what a bland word. *Nice.* There's nothing nice about Elio, not even how he looks right now. He's dark, devastating, beautiful the way a blade is. But I'm not articulate enough, or maybe not brave enough, to say any of that aloud. So 'nice' it is, I guess, even though it doesn't come close to describing the luxurious fit of his all-black suit, the clean shave of his hard jaw, the thick and swept-back hair, the arresting embers of his eyes. I barely even see his scars anymore.

"And you look like a fucking angel," he says so intensely that he nearly sounds angry. The leather of his fingertips glides to my collar-bone. "Are you ready?"

"Yes."

"Good."

He turns to walk towards the door. I catch his unsplinted hand between both of mine. He halts and turns back towards me with a questioning look.

"I just... I just wanted to say thank you. For that gift you left for me."

"You already thanked me on the phone."

"I know," I reply. "But that's not the same. I just... I don't think you know how much that meant to me."

"I know, Songbird."

I squeeze his hand.

"Do you have any photos of your mom?" I ask him.

There's a flicker of emotion behind his eyes that he instantly shuts down.

"No."

I can tell he doesn't want to talk about this anymore. So I just nod and give his hand another squeeze before letting go. Then I put my hands on either side of his jaw and tug him down. I press a very soft kiss to his cheek. Despite how gentle I am, it's like I've electrified him. I feel the muscles and tendons jump in his jaw and neck beneath my fingers.

"I don't have a gift for you," I say as I let him go. "I forgot what day it was today."

Heat jumps from his gaze to my skin.

"I can think of other ways," he drawls darkly, "that you can make it up to me."

I shiver, feeling so exposed under his gaze.

"Well... I guess we should get going," I say. "Do we have a reservation at a certain time?"

"Don't need a reservation when you own the restaurant."

"Oh! Well... Alright then. Oh, crap!"

"What?" Elio says, pulling me against his chest and scanning the room with urgent eyes.

"No, no, nothing serious," I say, pulling away. "I just noticed the lipstick kiss mark I left on your face!" I lick my thumb then reach up to smudge it away, but Elio catches my wrist in an iron grip.

"Don't."

"You want to go out to a nice dinner with my lipstick on your cheek?" I say with a disbelieving laugh.

Elio doesn't laugh. He's utterly serious when he simply says, "Yes," and then pulls me out the door into the night.

Chapter 32

Elio

"This is your restaurant?!" Deirdre cries as we enter the luxurious dining room of *Le Moineau*. "Doesn't it have a Michelin star?"

"Two, actually," I tell her as the maître d' gives us a deferential greeting and leads us through the opulent space. I keep Deirdre close, my hand on her lower back as we walk. Her dark red shoes click along the highly polished wood of the floors as we approach my usual table.

It's secluded from the rest of the restaurant, the table tucked into an intimate corner that's further separated from the other people dining by a wrought iron trellis with plants curling along its shape. Not that there are any other patrons here. I've closed out the entire place for us tonight.

The maître d' pulls out Deirdre's chair for her, but one look from me has him moving swiftly away. I replace him behind her, pushing her chair in for her as she sits. She turns around to thank the maître d', then blushes fiercely when she sees it's me.

"Thanks," she whispers. "Where is everyone?" She cranes her neck to see past the wrought iron trellis with its dark, curling leaves.

"Eating in somebody else's restaurant tonight," I say with a shrug as I sit across from her. I don't really give a fuck where the rest of Toronto's idiotic lovebirds have ended up tonight. I only care about the Songbird sitting on the other side of the table.

The lighting in here is dim and soft. It makes Deirdre's skin glow and her eyes look huge and dark. She looks like a fucking painting sitting there with those eyes and that hair and that dress. A work of fucking art that should be hung up on a wall somewhere and studied.

Only by me, of course.

She casts her eyes down at the menu then looks startled.

"Oh, wow. They don't even put prices on the menu here," she remarks, picking up the menu like she's afraid she'll break it or get it dirty.

"The kind of people who eat here aren't concerned by prices or budgets," I tell her. "You're one of those people now."

She puts down the menu and sighs.

"It's hard to get used to. Not long ago I was in such a massive amount of debt. Now I'm someone who doesn't have to worry about prices?"

"That's what happens when you marry the right man."

I fully expect her to scowl at that remark, but instead she laughs. Just a little one.

Still tears my heart out all the same.

"Noted," she says, her tone teasing. "You're going to have to advise me on what to order, you know. I've never been somewhere like this."

"The menu's not too crazy," I say. "This isn't the kind of place where they're going to feed you sea urchin foam on top of a single pine nut or some shit like that. If you don't know what you want we'll just order it all."

She's got her glass of water at her lips, and she coughs loudly as some of the drink goes down the wrong tube.

"All of it? The whole menu?"

"Yup."

Before she can argue with me, I've already signalled the maître d' and told him to prepare the entire menu for our table. I tell him to bring wine, too, and to keep Deirdre's glass filled. My kidney's healing up, but I decide to forgo the booze tonight, figuring I'd better not push my luck if I want to make it down that aisle in two weeks with no issues. Plus, I drove us here, and I'm not about to get plastered and get behind the wheel with such precious fucking cargo.

My ribs are doing better lately, too, but they still give the occasional twinge. Same with my fractured hand.

Soon enough, the food starts coming, plate after plate of appetizers and entrees that make Deirdre's eyes just about bug out of her head. There are individually seared scallops with garlic mascarpone drizzle, slices of raw steak served with a rosemary balsamic glaze, fall-off-the-bone braised lamb shank, freshly hand-shaped pasta with pear and gorgonzola cream sauce, bowls of lobster bisque, and pristine little salads with jewel-coloured vegetables and fruits.

Every time Deirdre tries something new, she says, "Oh my God, that's my favourite thing." Then she tries something else and says, "No, wait, *that's* my favourite thing!"

It's fucking adorable. I barely eat, I'm so focused on watching her take her cute little bites.

She drinks her wine too, barely noticing the maître d' who comes to replenish it whenever it gets low. Throughout the meal her cheeks get more and more pink, her voice and gestures more animated than usual. I don't know if it's the wine or the present I got her or what, but she seems to be opening up to me more. Chatting away like a bird chirping on a branch. She tells me all about the wedding stuff she's worked on with Valentina, and what's going on at school.

"I have to go to a live music performance," she tells me before popping a bite of the lamb into her mouth. Her eyes flutter closed and she moans quietly, making my dick twitch in my pants. I stare at her mouth as she slowly chews and swallows. Most of her lipstick is gone now, leaving behind a ferociously erotic stain of colour that makes me want to lick her lips.

Or bite them.

"What kind of performance?" I ask her, trying to focus on what she's saying instead of getting distracted remembering what it was like having those lips wrapped around my cock.

"Any kind of live music performance. I have no idea what I'm going to do."

"Did it not occur to you that I could help you with that?"

She blinks slowly at me.

"Really? I didn't think I'd be allowed."

"I let you out for a nice dinner tonight, didn't I?"

"Well, yes. I guess so..." She takes a big swig of wine.

"Now that Darragh's not pissing bullets all over this city trying to mark his territory, you'll have a little bit more freedom, so long as I or one of my men is chaperoning you," I tell her. "We can probably even get the music performance sorted out tonight."

"Really? Why, where would we go tonight?"

"I have a place."

"Alright. That works. I wondered if I'd have to use our wedding for the project, in case there was a live band there." Her liveliness fades slightly. "I can't believe Willow won't be there."

"Willow Callahan?"

"Yeah," she says dully.

"I saw her that day at Darragh's."

She instantly straightens in her chair.

"You did? Why didn't you tell me?" she demands, her eyes-overbright.

"Well, I was a little busy trying not to die of sepsis," I remind her until she looks down at her plate, chastened. "I overheard her papà telling her that he's sending her to stay with family in Ireland."

"You're kidding!" she breathes. "Wow. I knew she had an aunt over there, but I never thought she'd actually have to go there." She tugs at a stray curl, looking pensive and sad at the same time. "I haven't heard from her much since my birthday. Her dad took away her phone. She was able to send me a couple of emails, but it's been total radio silence lately. I wonder if she's already gone..."

"It's been a couple of weeks since then. And her papà didn't exactly sound like he was going to fuck around much. I wouldn't be surprised if he got her on a plane that night."

Deirdre blows out a breath through tight lips that makes me think she's trying not to cry.

"We always promised that we'd be each other's maids of honour," she says quietly.

"You'll have Valentina," I tell her, "and Lucia and Giulia if you want."

"Yeah... I guess..." She gives me a guarded look.

"What is it?"

"If I... If I had another friend I wanted to invite... Could she come to the wedding? Or even be a bridesmaid? There's no way Willow will be there. I know that. But it would be so nice to have somebody else I know there."

"You know me."

"Of course I do. For better or worse," she adds, but she smiles softly while she says it.

"Who did you want to invite?"

"One of the girls I go to school with. Annabelle Choi."

"I'll have Enzo take a harder look at her. If he clears her, then sure."

"Really?"

"Yes, really," I say. "Why are you always so surprised when I allow you shit like that?"

She snorts and takes another sip of wine.

"Do you really want me to answer that?" she asks with a throaty laugh.

Before I can reply, the maître d' and servers start bringing over desserts, sweeping away the other empty plates.

"More food? I can't eat a single bite!" Deirdre exclaims, throwing up her hands in a gesture of surrender.

"Bring her some Amaro," I say to the servers. One of them returns swiftly with the amber liquid in a tulip-shaped crystal glass.

"What's Amaro?" she asks, taking the glass and peering at it suspiciously.

"It is an Italian digestif, Mrs. Titone," the maître d' replies. "It is bitter-sweet and infused with various aromatic herbs. It helps settle the stomach after a large meal."

"Well, I definitely need that," Deirdre laughs. She takes a small sip, then makes a sound of pleasure and takes another, larger one.

"Good?" I ask her.

"Very! It's like port or icewine or something, but not as sweet."

"Glad you like it. Now eat your dessert."

She laughs again, but makes an effort to try everything they've brought out. Bites of goldenberry-topped cheesecake, crème brulée sprinkled with candied orange, and dark chocolate mousse with a shiny apricot syrup glaze.

"OK, now I'm seriously done," she says, collapsing back against her chair. "I feel like I'm about to go into a food coma."

"Don't go comatose on me yet," I tell her, rising from the table and offering her my hand. "We have one more stop tonight."

"Where?" she asks, taking my hand letting me haul her upright. She wobbles a little bit, and I steady her, drawing her against my chest for a scorching moment that makes me want to say fuck the rest of the night, I'm taking her home *now*.

"You'll see," I murmur into her fragrant hair.

She doesn't figure it out, though, until we're walking right up to the doors of the Four Seasons Centre for Performing Arts.

"Hold on... Are we at the ballet?" she gasps. "Oh my God. I used to come here to watch *The Nutcracker* with my mom when I was a kid!" She turns big eyes on me as we approach a black-clad employee checking tickets. "Do we have tickets for tonight?"

"I don't need tickets. I'm their largest donor and as such I have a private balcony they keep empty for my use."

"For your use?" she echoes as we get waved inside. "You come here often?"

"Never," I say. "I just write the cheques."

"The Royal York Ballet, the Art Gallery of Ontario... Who knew that Elio Titone was such a generous supporter of the local arts?" she quips.

"It's good to remind this city that I can give as much as I can take," I tell her, placing my hand firmly on her lower back as I lead her further into the Four Seasons lobby. It's huge, open, and modern in here, with pale wood floors and walls of windows letting in the glittering lights of downtown Toronto at night. Women in nice dresses and men in suits mill around, some of them with glasses of wine or ice cream bars in their hands, procured from the little bar near the doors that lead into the auditorium.

"I suppose it's a good reminder for me, too," she says quietly. "What's the biggest donation you've ever made somewhere?"

"When I paid for the construction of the burn unit in the pediatric ICU of St. Michel's Hospital."

She stops walking to stare at me.

"Don't give me that sappy, doe-eyed look," I grunt. "It was a tax write-off."

"I'm sure it was," she says softly, but she's still staring at me, those eyes burning a big blue hole through my brain. My fingers twitch against her back, my scars itching badly beneath my gloves. She looks like she's going to say something else, something I'm not entirely sure I want to hear, when she's cut off by a chime alerting patrons to head into the auditorium to find their seats. Deirdre closes her pretty mouth and doesn't say anything else until I've led her up all the stairs to the top level.

"Which show are we seeing? I don't know what's playing this season," she asks as an usher greets us and leads us to the door to my private balcony booth.

"Don't know," I reply. "I just knew there would be something on tonight. And live music. You'll have a good view down into the symphony area."

"Tonight's show is *Firebird*," the usher, a young man, tells us as he opens the door to my booth. My Songbird shoots me a look before going through the door, and I give her a grim smile in return, acknowledging the irony.

Firebird.

Of fucking course it is.

The door to the booth closes behind us with a hushed click. There are only two seats up here, side by side, both plush with dove-grey cushions. The modern look of the lobby continues into the vast space of the auditorium, the warm light cascading over curving architectural lines and the light, neutral-coloured floors and seats below us. For some reason I expected it to be all gaudy and musty in here with worn red velvet and brass everywhere, but it's not. It almost feels airy. After making a quick mental map in my head of how I'd get Deirdre out in the case of a fire, I settle myself in one of the seats and watch her.

She doesn't sit yet. She goes to the front of the small balcony, her fingers curling over the pale wood guardrail.

"You're right!" she says, throwing me a thrilled look over her shoulder that makes something low in my belly clench, "I can see right down into the orchestra pit!"

The musicians must be warming up down there. Odd scrapes and jabs of instrumental sound create a rhythmless cloud of notes. I can pick out the string instruments, maybe even the violin from among them, but I feel nothing.

Only Deirdre's playing does something to me. Gets its exquisite hooks into me and fucking *yanks*.

Apparently the chaotic-sounding warm-up is fascinating to my fiancée. She bends over further to get a better look.

"Careful," I warn, frowning at the way she leans so cavalierly over the guardrail. When she doesn't immediately respond, I stand

and grasp her by the shoulder, pulling her upright. "I said be careful."

"I was being careful," she says, already twisting in my grip to try to peer back down again.

"Not careful enough," I reply, dragging my knuckles along the exposed length of her upper back. "You don't actually have wings, you know."

"Well, I'm sure my fiancé will catch me," she tosses out blithely. *Cristo Santo*, the wine must have made her all fucking sassy or something, because she seems to have no idea what she's doing to me, hanging over this break-neck edge and calling me her fiancé like that.

"Go sit in your chair right fucking now," I rasp, grasping at an errant orange curl with my finger and thumb and tugging it.

"Or what? *Ouch!*"

"Oh, Songbird," I groan, thrusting my thickening cock against her ass and tugging on that cute little curl again. "You play a dangerous game when you ask me questions like that."

Another chime rings out, and soon after the lights in the grand, arching auditorium dim. The musicians lapse into silence, and a hush falls over the seated crowd.

"Go sit in your chair," I say between greedy kisses along her throat, "or I will drag you over there myself and make you sit on my lap where I can keep my eye on you. Is that what you want? To sit on my hard fucking cock for the entire performance?" I give a dark, taunting laugh, and she shivers. "I don't think you'll be able to pay much attention sitting like that. I can already imagine how much you'd fucking wiggle."

Her spine arches subtly against my front, because at least a part of her wants it. She wants to sit on my cock in the darkness, to rock herself on top it in panting, straining silence, so high above the sea of oblivious people.

My hand glides down and around to her front until I find her nipple. I tease it into swollen tautness and give her ass one more hard thrust of warning.

"I'll... I'll sit in my chair," she whimpers, though she makes no move to do it. It isn't until I pinch her nipple that she's shocked into action. She scurries away from me, but there isn't far to run. This balcony is small, the two chairs nestled beside each other directly behind us.

She sits down in her seat, chest rising and falling rapidly, like she's trying to slow her breathing and failing. I lower myself into the seat beside her, locking her thigh in the possessive black grip of my hand just as the curtains part.

Chapter 33

Deirdre

At first, it's hard to focus on the music and the dancers because I'm so utterly aware of Elio beside me. My thigh practically vibrates beneath his hand, and it's only embarrassment and a whole lot of willpower that keeps me from parting my legs, just a little bit more, in case he'll move that hand upwards.

God, I shouldn't have had that much wine at dinner, and that delicious spiced Amaro with the dessert. I'm not drunk but I feel looser and less guarded than usual. And I think it's contributing to the slow pound of need between my legs.

This is for school. Pay attention!

I don't know if I'll get another chance to see a live music performance for my paper, so I try to block Elio out as much as I can and just focus on the ballet happening below.

In the horseshoe-shaped auditorium, we're at the highest level, and are at the far right end of the horseshoe. It actually isn't ideal for watching the dance because I'm almost looking at the ballet dancers sideways, but being this close is perfect for glimpses into the orchestra pit. It's too bad I don't have anything to take notes with, but

I think I have the vague semblance of a thesis taking form as I let the music flow through me.

I haven't been to the ballet since Mom died. I didn't realize just how much I missed it. I've never been a coordinated dancer, despite a few wayward lessons in my youth, and I was always entranced by the way the dancers could fit their bodies so elegantly inside the sounds. Sometimes Mom got us tickets near the front, and before the show started I'd stand staring down into the pit, watching the violinists warm up with hushed awe.

Kind of like I did just now. With Elio.

A sudden rush of tears blurs my vision. I blink them away, hoping Elio doesn't notice. I was so excited when we first got here. I didn't think I would be affected like this. Didn't think I'd be suddenly adrift in a cacophony of notes that harbour nostalgia and grief and joy all in equal measure.

I don't know how he does this. Reaching right into me and exposing every hidden, painful place. Cracking every barrier I've built up, some of them years in the making, until I'm trembling and exposed and he shoves me naked out into the light.

It's infinitely painful. And yet, it feels oddly necessary. I thought that Elio had put me into a cage.

Maybe he's pulling me out of a different one.

Maybe it's the wine, or maybe it's the overwhelming beauty of the music and dancers, or maybe it's the grief or the darkness or the heat penetrating the glove on his hand and the skirt on my thigh, but I want to be closer to him. I tip to the side, leaning my head against his shoulder and wrapping both my arms around his. Now he hasn't just got me locked in. Because I've locked him in too.

I feel a tightening of surprise in his muscles, but it melts away immediately. He strokes his fingers against my leg in a movement that's somehow almost more comforting than erotic. I give a shaky sigh, and let the tears flow freely down my cheeks now, all of them silent.

We stay like that for a long time as the dance progresses. The

Royal York Ballet's soloist Katerina Turgeneva flits about the stage in her red tutu like a living flame, whirling and leaping so fast she becomes a glittering, heated blur.

A creeping sort of tension manifests itself in Elio's arm. Leaning against him the way I am, I can tell the way that his breathing quickens, grows uneven. His fingers dig into the flesh of my leg.

"Elio?" I whisper, lifting my head from his shoulder and giving him a puzzled look. He doesn't seem to hear me – maybe because the music has reached a feverish crescendo. Or maybe...

Because he's not really here with me right now.

I've seen him like this before. Where he seems to get unsteady, lost in something beyond what I can see. The fires of his past. I remember his fear, his panic, when he was living out his nightmares during his illness, and my throat closes with pain for him.

"Elio," I say a little louder this time. "It's alright. You're here with me."

Unsure what else to do, I slide out of my seat and clamber into his lap. I place both my hands on his face, feeling the scars and the smoothness, and put my eyes directly before his own.

"You're here with me," I repeat. "We're at the ballet and everything is alright."

His eyes bore into mine, his chest heaving beneath my elbows.

"I know," he says gruffly.

"Show me that you know," I murmur, stroking his skin, like I can draw his pain out of him with the touch of my fingers. "Show me that you're here with me."

I figure that he'll nod and calm down, or maybe hug me or something. So I'm completely unprepared when he wordlessly tips his head forward and fits his mouth hungrily against mine.

The unsplinted hand that was once on my leg is now seared to my spine, a hot leather stamp against the skin exposed by the low back of my dress. Using that hand as support, Elio leans forward in his seat until I'm tipping back, his mouth travelling in a scorching, wet line across my jaw and down my neck. The kisses are rough, messy, greedy. Claiming me with lips and tongue and teeth. Dazedly, undone by the sensations, I wonder if I'm going to have a dark necklace of hickeys on my own wedding day. I gasp when he dips lower, tonguing my nipple through the exquisitely thin silk of the gown.

"Elio!" I force out as white-hot need twists my insides. "Stop! We're in public. We're at the ballet! We-"

"Right," he growls against my breast. "You need to see what's going on for your schoolwork."

It's amazing how strong he is, how easily he can manipulate my body when one of his hands is almost completely out of commission. But before I know it, I'm wrenched upwards and spun around so that I'm facing forward once again. I think he's letting me go, so I lurch forward to get off of his lap and return to my own seat, but his arm locks like a bar of steel around my waist. He hitches my ass backwards until I feel the shape of his hardness.

"Keep your eyes open," he murmurs against the side of my throat. "Don't miss anything. I expect you to write that fucking paper."

His right arm stays tight around my waist while his uninjured left hand drifts upwards to stroke my left nipple through the dress. It tightens into diamond hardness, so sensitive I want to cry. Cry for him to let me go.

Cry for him to give me more.

"Someone will see," I mewl, straining in his hold.

"It's dark."

It is dark, but only up to a point. The lights aimed at the stage give off enough of a glow that I can see the ghostly shapes of people in the audience below. And if I can see them from here, then any one of them could look up and see me too. See me squirming and panting in Elio's lap like the sordid little Songbird he's turned me into.

"Stop moving so much," he grunts as my ass bumps his erection. "Pay attention."

I don't know if he's telling me to pay attention to the music and the ballet or to what he's doing to my body. Maybe both. But it's impossible. My brain isn't big enough to process all of that at once.

The stage fades to a bright blur, the music turning into nonsensical background noise as Elio's touch overpowers everything else. My nerves flare and leap, just like the dancer below.

Elio's touch darts back and forth across my chest, teasing one nipple, then the other, until I'm arching and panting and pathetic, unable to tell him to stop, unable to pull myself out of the wicked hold he has on me. I wonder if something's wrong with me, that his touch can break me down so completely, or if it's just a testament to the kind of power he has over me.

But maybe I have some kind of power over him too, because his breath is rough and ragged, his erection grinding against me as he claims my breast with a possessive, kneading motion.

I cry out, then instantly clap my hands over my mouth. Luckily, the music is loud right now, but it won't be loud forever. I need to get a hold of myself.

I need to tell him to stop.

But I'm terrified that if my hands come away from my mouth now, that the moan that escapes is going to be so lurid and dirty that everyone in this whole fucking place will hear me, from the audience members to the ballerinas right down to the bored employees waiting for intermission in the lobby.

Panic and need rising with equal force inside me, I feel Elio tear his glove off with his teeth.

"Spread your legs," he commands, sliding his now-bare hand beneath my long, flowing silk skirt and over my knee.

I shake my head rapidly, keeping my left hand plastered over my mouth and grasping his forearm with my other one.

"Fine," he hisses, his voice like ripping satin at my throat, "If you won't spread them then I'll make it impossible for you to keep them closed."

His hand glides softly up my thigh, a whisper of a touch that draws my muscles taut as a string on my violin. I'm shaking trying to keep my thighs pressed together. The skirt shifts against my bare pubic area, and I feel so much more sensitive and exposed than before. It heightens everything that Elio does.

Elio draws a brutal-sounding breath when his fingertips reach my naked vulva. My voice skitters up my throat, muffled by my sweating hand.

"Are you fucking kidding me, Songbird?" he seethes quietly. "No fucking panties? And no hair, either." He kneads my skin, as if getting used to the new sensation of me bare beneath his fingers. My clit zings with the need for him to move lower, but he doesn't. Not yet.

"You don't have any razors," he breathes against my ear. "How'd you manage that? Was it wax? Did you get that hot, sticky stuff all over you so that you could make this plump little pussy all smooth for me?"

He splays his whole hand flat against my pubic area, the tip of his middle finger dipping down just far enough that I feel a coaxing pressure right above my clit.

I clench my teeth against a moan.

"You just fucking love taunting me, don't you?" he bites out. "As soon as you part these pretty thighs for me, I know I'm going to find you fucking *dripping*."

My body urges me to do it. To open to his hand. But I don't. I can't.

Because then he'll see that he's right.

"When we get home," he warns softly, "I am going to punish you for this."

I hate how much that excites me, anticipation and arousal slamming through my bloodstream. He nudges his middle finger down a little further until it's pressing directly against my clit. Between his touch and the squeezing of my thighs, I know I'm already on the verge of coming.

Elio's tongue is at my ear, my jaw, my neck, exploring. Demanding. His mouth moves but his hand doesn't. Now that he's got the pad of his middle finger nestled up tight against my clit, he just leaves it there, so infuriatingly still that despite my efforts I find myself rocking subtly against him, seeking more friction.

"Open to me," he commands.

As if my body is more loyal to him than to me, my thighs ease a fraction of an inch apart. It's barely what could even be called wiggle room, but Elio seizes on it like a predator lying in wait.

That small easing of my muscles, that tiny slice of space gives him enough purchase to shove his hand downwards and force my thighs apart. I'm glad my hand is already slapped over my mouth, because I'm sure that the guttural moan that hits my palm would have every head in this place turning towards me if I let it out fully. It would probably cut right through the music. And everyone would hear, would see, what he's done to me.

That thought only makes hateful, blinding pleasure surge. Elio makes a thick, growling sound when his fingers slide down to my soaked entrance.

"Just like I fucking thought. Fucking soaked for me."

The heel of his hand grinds hard against the apex of my thighs while his middle finger slides deep inside me. And now I'm spreading wider for him all on my own. I can't blame him for this – this is all me now. It's my pussy throbbing for him. It's my back arching against him. It's my voice coming in stuttered, sobbing moans against my own hand.

It's my legs spreading as far open as they can go as my hips rock shamelessly against his hand.

But no, it's not shameless, not really. Because if someone were to see me now, I'm pretty sure I would die.

And I'll die if he stops touching me.

"You're close," Elio whispers, a damning remark that I know is fucking true. "*Cristo Santo*, I can feel you getting all quivery and tight inside."

I am. I can feel it too. My core is swelling and tightening, extraordinary physical need rising higher and higher, right alongside the music. A frenetic crescendo that makes every one of my nerves sing, scream, and-

The music suddenly stops, replaced instantly with applause.

And then the lights come on.

No!

My eyes snap open, then immediately scrunch shut against the bright light. The sounds of chatter and rustling from below fill the space. God, if anyone looked up here right now...

I try to scramble out of Elio's lap, but his arm is still around my waist and his hand is still stroking deep inside me.

"Oh, no you don't," he coos darkly. "We aren't going anywhere until you come for me."

He cannot be serious. But as I twist my head and turn my wide eyes onto his, I flinch at the molten resolve I find there. He's not going to let me go unless I come.

At this point, I don't think I could stop myself from coming even if I wanted to.

I slam my legs shut around his hand and turn sideways in his lap, looping my arms around his neck and burying my face in his chest. My core is already starting to pulse, drawing his finger deeper into my body. The hard part of his hand digs into my clit, and fuck, I shouldn't, I don't want to, not here, not under these lights, not like this, I can't, I-

"Come."

I do.

I grind helplessly against him, catching the collar of his shirt between my teeth and biting down to keep from making the kinds of sounds I'm desperate to let out. Elio groans softly, and I feel his cock leap against me through his pants.

That gives me an idea. A way to shift the balance of power. A way to make him feel as vulnerable and fucked-up as I do. I reach blindly down, find his thick shaft, and squeeze.

I'm rewarded, or maybe punished, by Elio instantly pulling his finger out of me and leaving me unbearably empty. He seizes my wrist and lifts it easily away from his cock.

"Nice try," he says, his eyes burning into me, his hold merciless. "But unlike you I'm not a shy little thing. I'll get my cock out for you right here, right now. If you're going to get all rebellious, then I'm going to have you down on your knees so fast you won't be able to take a single breath before I'm fucking the back of your throat. So unless you want everyone to see me using your disobedient mouth under these bright fucking lights, you will behave yourself until we get home."

He would make me do it, too. He's not kidding.

He takes a grating breath, then says, "Did you get enough for your school project from the first half?"

"Yes," I whisper.

"Good. Because we're leaving."

Chapter 34

Deirdre

Elio doesn't waste any time once we're home. As soon as we're back in his bedroom he seizes on the skirt of my dress and yanks it up over my head. The fabric briefly snags at my nose, leaving my body and my mouth exposed but my eyes covered. A bolt of anxious desire goes through me when I think that he might leave me like that, blind to everything but his touch.

Blindfolded by silk, he forces me to walk backwards by stepping forwards and he doesn't stop until I unexpectedly hit the bed and collapse down onto it.

Elio pulls the dress off my head and then higher along my arms, but for some reason he doesn't peel it all the way off. Once the slippery silk is bunched around my wrists, he twists the shoulder straps tight, then loops the whole garment over the iron post of his headboard.

My heart spins out in my chest, and I panic a little, realizing that he's got me strung up like a pig in a butcher's. My wrists are pinned above my head, and a few frantic tugs make it clear that I'm stuck.

Elio stands at the side of the bed, watching me with a look of terrible satisfaction as I struggle against the silk. My arms soon tire, and I sag back against the pillows, breathing hard and glaring up at him.

"You can't leave me like this," I tell him.

"Who said anything about leaving you? I'll be with you the entire time."

My throat goes dry as he begins to undress, shrugging out of his suit jacket then undoing the buttons on his shirt, one by one. He's doing it painstakingly slowly, and he's got to be doing that on purpose, to make me wonder what's coming next. His shirt falls to the floor and he stares at my pussy while he undoes the buckle of his belt.

I've got my legs squeezed closed again, trying to protect myself from the unstoppable, devious drag of his eyes. He's got his bedside lamp on, illuminating my nakedness, the way my body is so stretched and vulnerable to him.

I look down at myself, trying to see what he sees. Because my arms are up over my head, my breasts look higher and plumped. My pussy is so smooth, the skin red, though I don't know if the redness is from the waxing or from his hand before.

When I look back up at him, he's naked except for his splint. Even in this humiliating position, when I should be curling away from him, I can't help but turn more towards him. He looms, huge and aroused, and I can't tell if he's a god or a monster or a man. His cock juts out thick from the dark hair at his groin as he gets onto his hands and knees above me. I stifle a gasp.

Like this, he's all I can see. Like the dark sky between stars, he expands everywhere, covering absolutely everything until there's nowhere I can turn, nowhere I can look where I won't find him.

He braces himself on his right elbow, skimming his left hand up my anxious abdomen until it comes to grip my breast. Bending, he takes my nipple into his mouth.

I moan, unable to stop myself. I held back so much when we

were at the ballet that I seem to have used up all my ability to remain quiet. He sucks me hard, then moves to the other side, nipping and licking until my treacherous legs are already spreading for him without even needing him to ask.

What am I even doing? He just made me come in public. Now he's got me restrained. And I'm opening up for him again?

But there's something inevitable about this. About the dark pull of his body to mine. The shuddering heat that only he can draw out of me.

He releases my breast with a slick sound, kissing down my belly.

"Fucking flawless," he groans when he reaches the place between my legs, using his fingers to spread my folds open for his gaze. "I've wanted to lick this pretty pussy since I put my hand up your skirt and found out just how fucking smooth your skin could be."

I whimper in response, needing him to do it more than I need air.

"But I thought... You said you were going to punish me."

His eyes flick up to mine. He holds my gaze as he extends his tongue and gives my clit a long, circling lick.

"I am going to punish you," he says darkly, his breath fanning over my wet skin until I'm squirming. "But that doesn't mean I'm not going to enjoy myself first."

I can't manage a reply to that, because soon he's feasting on me, sucking hard on my clit before licking down to my wet, pulsing entrance. My whole body comes alive, muscles springing to attention beneath my skin, everything tight and hot and exploding. Elio groans, an expression of raw need carving his features as his eyes fall shut. He hitches my legs up over his big shoulders, angling my hips as he dives inside me with his tongue.

"Oh, please, Elio, I..."

I don't even recognize my own mewling voice. But I can feel myself saying the words.

"I'm going to come!"

He immediately withdraws his tongue.

"Not yet," he growls.

In an instant, he's flipped me onto my belly.

"Ass up."

"What? What are you-"

"Ass. Up."

It's awkward with my hands tied up so high the way they are. I manage to get my knees underneath me, getting into a wobbly position with my ass up in the air, bracing myself against my tied wrists.

A bright light fills my head as Elio's hand connects with my ass.

"That's for coming out with me tonight without panties when you knew exactly what it would do to me."

He spanks me again, and I cry out, my core convulsing. I'm so close, so fucking close, the sting of the slaps bringing me higher and higher, right to that edge.

"And that's for disobeying me when I told you to open your legs for me."

One more. One more. Please, one more.

God, what has become of me?

He gives it to me, a tight, firm smack that has me throwing back my head with twisted pleasure, back arching needily.

"And that's for when you grabbed my cock before. You really thought you did something there, didn't you?"

"No, I-"

Smack!

"Don't lie. I can always tell."

He sees right through me. He knows exactly what I was trying to do when I touched him. Trying to tip the scales. To grab back some of the power for myself.

And look where it's gotten me. Tied by the hands, ass stinging while my insides curl at the very edge of release. Elio massages my smarting flesh, petting me tenderly when I flinch at the feeling of his cock pressing inside me.

My mouth falls open in a soundless moan, my eyes rolling back as he fills me so completely. Just like before, in his office, this angle is so deliciously different. He hits the deepest, shuddering places on his very first thrust.

I clench around him as he exerts a vigorous rhythm, my fingers scrabbling at the headboard, the silk twisting around my wrists as he slides out and back in, over and over again.

"I've only been on the pill for a day," I moan, barely able to get the words out as my climax gathers around me like thick fog. "You can't... come inside..."

"I am going to come inside," he says gruffly. "But I'm not going to do it in your cunt."

Above the sounds of his wet thrusting and my voice, I register the sound of a drawer opening and then a clicking noise. I quiver in surprise as new wetness dribbles onto my ass from above. Elio's thrusts slow as he seems to begin to focus on something else...

Sliding his fingers around my ass.

Instinctively I tighten, and that earns me a soft slap to my ass cheek.

"Relax," he tells me, grinding his hips in such a way that I feel like I'm melting. "That's it."

The pressure of his fingers come back, rubbing at that tight, puckered hole, coaxing the spasming muscles into something slightly looser. He works the tip of one thick finger in, waits a moment, then slides it into the next knuckle.

I cry out, every muscle in my body twitching, including the ones currently clenching around his finger. Between his finger in my ass and his hard cock in my pussy I feel like I am entirely invaded by him.

But this is Elio. And Elio is always looking for more.

After a few minutes of stretching and sliding, he nudges another finger inside.

"It's too much," I say instantly, even though there isn't any pain. Just this obliterating stretch, this fullness everywhere inside. Elio adds a little more lube, but he doesn't give me any relief besides that. And the strangest thing starts to happen as he works those two fingers in and out, in and out, at the same pace of his thrusting cock.

I start to want more.

The promise of the climax that was hovering around me before draws closer, so close I feel like I could kiss it. But then Elio takes out his fingers, and I choke out a cry as if bereft.

Pressure returns, but this time it isn't a finger. It's something deliciously smooth, cold, and coated in lube. Elio presses it inwards and my flesh relents, accepting the bulbous shape of whatever it is. It's bigger than Elio's two fingers were, but my body is getting greedy, and I contract, sucking it deeper inside until it stops because of a wide, flat shape at the end that remains outside my body.

"What is that?" I moan, my ass spasming around the unforgiving hardness of the object.

Elio's thrusts get faster and he gives a strangled groan, like he's too aroused to answer me.

"That's the stamp I used," he finally rasps, "for the wax seal I used on that contract with your father."

Shame and heat rocket through me in equal measure. Tears bite at my eyes, air tearing in and out of my throat.

"You're so perfect, Deirdre," Elio groans. "You have no fucking idea what I'm seeing from this angle. Your pussy filled with my cock. And your ass filled with the very thing that helped me get you in the first place."

There's pressure at the back, as if he's pushing against the flat circle of the stamp, nudging the smooth handle deeper inside.

"You are mine," he grinds out, his thrusts relentless. "Now and for-fucking-ever. Say it, Songbird. Tell me that you're mine."

"I... I..."

I'm going to come.

He stops thrusting and pulls his cock out of me. Then he pulls the stamp slowly but firmly out until I give a shameful whimper of complaint. I'm so fucking empty without him.

But suddenly, there's new pressure against my needy flesh.

Something hard and slick pushing into me from behind, not cold and smooth like the stamp but twitching and hot and alive.

It's Elio's cock, claiming me from the back. The stretch is unreal, so much more than what I experienced from the stamp or his fingers.

He hisses, pausing to let my tight ring adjust to his girth. After a moment that feels breathless for both of us, he thrusts forward, all the way to the hilt.

Slowly, he grinds in and out. His hand is like burning metal on my hip, squeezing the tingling skin as he begins to fuck my ass.

"Say it. Say that you're mine."

I barely hear him. I'm barely aware of anything besides the glorious, lascivious, terrible way that he fills me. He gives a mangled moan, then stutters into faster motion.

"Say it *now*."

"I'm yours!"

I don't just say it. I scream it

It's true. I'm his. Irrevocably.

Just like my mouth admits it, so does my body, erupting in the most bone-shattering orgasm I've ever experienced. It nearly crushes me, wipes every ounce of energy from my cells, until I'm collapsing, the silk ties of the dress the only thing holding my hands in place. Even my legs can't hold me up anymore. My knees slide outwards, and I collapse onto my belly. Elio's still inside me, and I drag him right along with me.

The violent sound of silk ripping fills my ears as Elio fists the dress and tears it away from the post, allowing my chest and head to fall onto the pillows. This position is even more intense, me flat on my belly with Elio driving into me, fucking me down against the mattress, the remnants of that perfect, ruined dress around my wrists like the most beautiful chains.

He's so deep inside me, his elbows braced on either side of my shoulders, his head lowering. He buries his face in my hair, and I know that's the moment that he comes. I feel the hot, explosive throb of him inside that private, spasming place, feel the way he loses his rhythm, overwhelmed just like I am. He fucks his way unsteadily through his orgasm, like he's trying to get deeper with every twitch and spurt.

But there's nowhere deeper for him to reach. Nowhere else for him to touch me.

Because Elio is already everywhere.

Chapter 35

Deirdre

The next two weeks pass in a busy blur. My days are dominated by the usual sorts of things – school and wedding stuff with Valentina. I attend my classes, sometimes with Elio, sometimes with Enzo if Elio has other business going on. And I go to extravagant cake tastings and printer shops and dress fittings with my bridesmaids – Valentina, Lucia, Giulia, and Annabelle. Enzo did a more thorough background check on Annabelle, and Elio allowed me to invite her into the group after all. The days seem to pass faster and faster, like dominoes colliding against each other, picking up speed as they hurtle towards an inevitable destination.

And my nights?

My nights belong to Elio.

Every night, he claims me, burying himself in my mouth or my ass. Even fucking my breasts, dragging his hot, veiny shaft between them until he explodes all over my throat. As soon as it's safe, he starts coming in my pussy again, and in a quiet voice I'm pretty sure he thinks that I don't hear, he says it feels like coming home.

On the twenty-eighth, though, the routine changes. It's the first night in ages that I haven't slept beside Elio. I'm currently ensconced in the jaw-dropping bridal suite of the Royal Thompson Hotel, while Valentina, Lucia, Giulia, and Annabelle try to get me to have another glass of champagne.

"I can't," I laugh, my stomach flip-flopping in rebellion against that idea. I'm so fucking nervous, and the drinks I've already had haven't done a thing to help.

"True. Probably better not to be hungover on the morning of your wedding," Annabelle says, pulling the bottle away from Valentina who was trying to hold the spout over my head and dump the bubbles down my throat.

I shoot Annabelle a grateful glance, and Valentina groans, flopping onto the bed beside me.

"No fun," she says, pouting, looking younger than she normally does with no makeup on and her blonde hair fanning out around her on the bed.

"No one said you had to stop drinking," I say, poking her with my freshly polished toe. This whole day has been a series of treatments at the hotel's spa with the other four – facials and waxing and smoothing of things that I didn't even know needed to be smoothed.

"And you'll get your chance soon enough," Giulia says, grabbing the champagne bottle from where Annabelle put it down on the table beside the gigantic bed Valentina and I are on. "Have you and Dario set a date yet?"

"Ugh! Don't remind me," Valentina grumbles, sitting up. "No, there's no date yet. And whenever there is a date, I don't think I'm going to get any say in it. I'll be informed of it. Same way I was about the engagement itself."

"Well, I certainly know what that's like," I say, poking her with my toes again.

"Yeah, but you're at least marrying somebody who cares about you," Valentina sighs. "That boy is obsessed."

"That man is not a boy," Giulia snorts.

"Amen to that," Annabelle says quietly, and Lucia laughs. An odd feeling of pride makes my belly warm. Pride that Elio is mine.

Never thought I'd see the day.

And tomorrow, I will marry him.

I glance at the clock, startled to see that it's already 1am. Valentina follows my gaze and says, "Well, ladies? What do you think? Gotta let the bride get her beauty sleep."

There's a chorus of agreement, and a slightly tipsy-sounding complaint from Giulia, but ultimately everybody gets up to head to their own rooms.

"You're good?" Annabelle says after the other three head out the door and into the hotel's hallway. Enzo is stationed outside my door, and his gaze meets Annabelle's for a moment before she turns her attention back to me. "You sure you don't want someone to stay in here with you?"

It's a kind offer, trying not to make me feel alone tonight. Maybe it's the champagne or the impending wedding or the empty bed in the room, but loneliness suddenly stabs between my ribs.

Or maybe it's the fact that Willow isn't here when I always thought she would be.

And neither is Mom.

"It's OK," I tell her, proud of the fact that I don't feel tears in my eyes even though there's that familiar ache in my throat. "I'll be alright on my own."

I don't tell her the other thing.

The thing about how I half-expect Elio to buck tradition and come to me tonight. And if he does, I don't want to have to kick one of my sleepy friends out of my bed to make room for him.

Strangely, imagining him coming to this room tonight pulls out the knife of loneliness and patches up the wound. A smile touches my lips, and it's genuine. Annabelle smiles back, gives me a hug, then hurries down the hall to her room. I close my door and the last thing I see before it clicks shut is Enzo watching Annabelle walk away.

I turn around and flatten my back against the door, surveying the very large and now very empty room. It's by far the fanciest hotel I've ever been inside, and from what I understand, this is one of the best rooms, reserved for the bride the night before the wedding, and for the couple to stay together the night after. The bed is huge, piled with pillows and gold-stitched bedding, and there's a massive, spa-like bathtub in the centre of the bedroom, right in front of a crackling fireplace.

I'm exhausted, but I force myself to brush my teeth before I turn off the fire and the lights and crawl into the magnificent bed. I've brought my Valentine's Day gift from Elio, the platinum case with the photo of Mom and me. In the gloom, I open it, holding it close beneath the covers, straining my eyes and wondering if Elio will come.

I fall asleep staring into my own past and dream of my future extending its hand towards me. Coaxing, waiting.

And that hand is gloved in black.

Chapter 36

Elio

Staying away from Deirdre the night before our wedding just might be the hardest thing I've ever done. And I've done some hard fucking shit in my life. I'm only just down the hall from her. I get up three times in the night and snatch the key card to the bridal suite from my bedside table, striding to the door before I stop myself and turn back.

I want her to have this. This is a real wedding, and I want everything done correctly. Including the whole no-fucking-the-bride-the-night-before thing.

Whoever came up with the tradition deserves a boot up their fucking ass.

I miss her. And not just because I'm a ball of loose, lusting ends when it comes to her. I miss her on a cellular fucking level, like there's not quite enough air in the room when she's gone.

I don't sleep much. I'm still babying my kidney, so I didn't get blasted with Curse and my uncle and I can't rely on the sweet embrace of alcohol to make me sleep. I spend most of the night half-hard and wanting her, imagining what she must be doing, what she might be wearing. What kind of magical, mysterious girl shit does a bride-to-be get up to the night before her wedding?

I have no fucking idea.

But I still try to imagine it anyway.

I picture her in white, lacey, wedding-themed lingerie.

I picture her completely naked.

My splint is finally off my dominant hand, and I jerk my cock to thoughts of her, but it isn't fucking enough and I give up with a groan of frustration.

One night. Just one... fucking... night.

I must fall asleep eventually, though, because I wake with a start when someone pounds on the door.

For a single, mind-searing second, I have this terrible fucking thought. This thought that whoever is on the other side of the door is banging that loud because they have something bad to tell me.

I'm out of bed like a shot, tugging on underwear and yanking the door open.

"Where is she?"

"What?" Curse says from the other side. "You mean Deirdre? She's in her room. Enzo was at his post until two, then Robbie took over and he's still there now. She hasn't left the room. Valentina and the other girls are in there now. They're all getting ready."

The throb inside my head eases to a dull ache.

"Good. What is it, then?"

Curse has something slung behind his shoulder. He heaves whatever it is forward. It's two garment bags, dangling from his fingers by hooks.

"Our tuxes." He gives me an appraising look. "I assume you aren't planning to get married like that."

I look down at myself and grunt, opening the door wider so he can come in. Curse settles himself in the room while I head into the bathroom to shower. I've got plenty of time, but I still find myself rushing, eager to get out of there and get the day rolling. I'm experiencing a new sort of paranoia that I do not fucking like. A paranoia that tells me Deirdre could vanish any moment, and that I won't really, truly have her until she's said, "I do."

Thank fuck Valentina planned a morning wedding. The ceremony is scheduled for 10am, then there's some big brunch thing and a dinner thing and a dance thing. I don't care about any of the stuff that comes after.

I just care about making that girl my wife.

When I get out of the shower, it's only 7:48, and I swear, pacing the room as I scrub a towel over my head.

"Don't do that shit. Your hair's gonna be crazy," Curse admonishes me. I blink at him, then hurl the wet towel his way. He catches it easily out of the air then hangs it on the back of the chair at the desk in the room.

"What, you gonna do my hair for me?"

"Yeah. If you shut up for a second and sit the fuck down, I will."

It's then that I see all the shit Curse has on the desk beside that chair. A full shaving kit is splayed open, along with combs and various jars.

"Are you serious?" I ask, more stunned than anything. "Where'd you get all this?"

"Valentina helped me out. She knew you'd be too wound up to have Uncle Vinny's barber working on you this morning."

"She is too fucking smart for her own good," I say, crossing the room and heaving my body into the chair. Curse stands there for a long moment, just studying me.

"Are you gonna just stand there or do something?" I grunt. "I don't wanna be late."

"We have more than two hours."

"Yeah, two hours for you to fuck something up." I eye the straight razor gleaming on the desk. "Deirdre didn't change her mind, did she? Didn't convince you to come in here and cut my throat this morning or something?"

Curse makes a gruff sound in his throat, about the closest he gets to a laugh.

"I'll only cut you if you don't stay still and keep talking shit."

I hold my hands up in a gesture of surrender. I've already got my gloves on. Put them on first thing after getting out of the shower.

Curse doesn't start with the shaving, though. He starts with my hair, muttering something about not letting it dry wrong. He spreads some kind of spicy-smelling pomade between his fingers, working it through the strands before combing everything back. He's surprisingly thorough. Or maybe it isn't that surprising. He's always been methodical and detail-oriented. I just didn't realize that extended to styling another man's hair.

When Curse is satisfied with my hair, he moves onto the dark shadow lining my neck and jaw. He smears shaving cream with firm, efficient strokes, then handles the razor the exact same way.

Despite my joke about him cutting my throat, I don't feel even a hint of anxiety with Curse holding a blade to my jugular. For one thing, the man knows what to do with a knife. He's probably slit more throats than anyone I know. He won't make a mistake.

And for another thing, he's Curse. The boy I pulled from the flames. The man who I know would do anything for me now.

Titone men. We don't talk about our feelings much. So I don't know how to address the odd way this act touches me. It fucking means something, what he's doing right now, helping me with this shit on the morning of my wedding.

When he's done, and he wipes a warm, wet towel over my jaw, I thank him.

"I'll do the same for you on your wedding day," I tell him.

"I won't have a wedding."

I snort.

"Yeah, well, that's what I always said too. And look at me now."

"No," Curse says, quietly emphatic. "I won't have a wedding."

"Why not?"

"You know why."

And I sigh, because he's right. I do know why.

"Still her, huh?"

"Still her."

Neither of us need to name Aurora to know that's who we're talking about. She's the only girl Curse has ever wanted, even though he only met her once, back in Sicily, when we were all dumb little kids.

"You saw the announcement, then," I say, more a confirmation than a question.

Curse's eyes flash with some coiling emotion, maybe anger, maybe not. It's hard to tell with him.

"Yeah. I did."

Like me, Aurora Bianchi has recently gotten herself engaged. Her family lives in Buffalo, and after all the shit that went down with our papà none of them wanted to touch us with a ten-foot pole. Since they're in the States, it never really mattered all that much. We didn't need the Bianchis for money or power or clout, though they've got that shit in spades. Aurora is now engaged to one of the big bosses of New York. Her parents announced it earlier this year, and evidently, Curse and I both saw it.

If there had been a way to get her for my brother, I would have. But after the shit our papà pulled, it was like we had the fucking plague. Her parents never would have agreed to a match with Curse. And unlike me, he's not the type to abduct a woman in the dead of night and force her into it, consequences be damned.

Curse flips the razor open and closed over and over, watching the morning sunlight glance off the blade. I know he doesn't want any more words from me, or any pity either. Neither of us can fucking stand that shit. So instead, I just clap him firmly on the shoulder and tell him, "Come on. Let's get dressed."

Chapter 37

Elio

Only problem is getting dressed doesn't take all that long. There's still more than an hour to go before the ceremony and here I am all ready to go, prowling around the room like a trapped animal. Curse is gone to do a final sweep with Enzo, and now I'm here watching the clock tick down so slowly it feels like it's mocking me.

I need to see her.

I waited all night. I didn't disturb her sacred little bridal suite last night. But I'm not going to wait anymore. Fuck the old adage about bad luck before the wedding.

Titones make their own fucking luck.

I snatch the key card to the from my bedside table and hurl myself out the door. The bridal suit isn't too far away. Just down the hall. I reach it in less than three minutes. Robbie is at his station outside. He straightens up when he sees me. "Boss?"

I ignore him, unlocking the door and slamming it open.

The first person I see is Valentina. See is actually a mild way of putting it. I just about collide with her. She's coming out of the bathroom just as I step into her path.

618

"What the – Elio?!"

"Out," I tell her, looking over her head for my fiancée. But all I see is a wall of dark blue fabric, broken up by the occasional arm or face. Valentina's wearing the same blue, a long strapless gown of it. She slams her hands onto my hips and scowls at me.

"What do you mean, out? If anyone should be getting out, it's you! You're not supposed to see the bride!"

"Out," I say again, then, more loudly, "Everybody. Out right now."

Valentina throws up her hands as Lucia, Giulia, and Deirdre's friend Annabelle all give each other uncomfortable glances.

"Well, you heard the man," Valentina huffs at them. Then, to me, she says, "Don't fuck up her hair or makeup. Or the dress. You know what? Don't even touch her. Just stand across the room and admire her like the piece of art she is, because she's fucking perfect and I want her looking just like that when she walks down the aisle."

I barely restrain myself from rolling my eyes. She doesn't need to tell me what a work of art my fiancée is.

"Out, Valentina. Don't make me say it again."

She waves at the others, gesturing them forward like she's their general or something. They hustle out of the room, closing the door behind them. Once I'm sure they're gone, I turn around again. And finally, I see her.

And it's like the rest of the world falls away.

She looks like something from a fucking fairy tale. Like something from another world, another age. I don't know shit about dresses, and wouldn't know how to describe this one properly if I tried, but even I can see what a masterful garment it is. The top part hugs her breasts and waist, the skirt flaring outward in a dramatic sweep of silk. There are long sleeves, oddly prim and pure, going almost all the way down her arms, but the illusion of modesty is ruined by the gorgeous expanse of skin exposed at her shoulders and collarbones. My throat goes dry when my gaze roves over the luscious curves of the tops of her breasts. The whole dress sparkles, like it got left outside on a cool night and somebody hasn't shaken the dew off of it quite yet.

But it's not just about the dress. Because this dress would just be a dress if it weren't for the bride wearing it. *My* bride.

Deirdre's hair is swept away from her face, the front bits pinned back, the rest of it falling in a glorious, curling tumble of flame down her back. I don't know what kind of makeup she might be wearing, but it looks fairly simple, enhancing the shape and glow of her features instead of shadowing them.

My angel of perfect ruin. My Songbird, my phoenix, my fire.

My wife.

"Say something," she whispers.

"I love you."

She gapes at me, her painted lips parting with shock. She almost looks stricken.

"What?" I ask, finally finding the will to move, crossing to her in an instant. "You're shocked by that? I'm fucking marrying you today."

"But you... You've never said it before," she breathes.

I'm actually fairly certain that's not true. It's just that I'm pretty sure it slipped out when I was delirious with desire, buried deep inside her pussy. And I think it came out in Italian instead of English.

"Well. I'm saying it now." My hand rises to stroke her throat, because I can't stand not to touch her, damn whatever Valentina said about it. "I love you," I tell her again, feeling her pulse jump beneath my glove in response. "If I thought I had a soul I'd say you owned it."

Her next inhale sounds wrecked, all shuddery and shattered.

"You don't need a soul to love someone," she murmurs. "Just a heart."

"Yeah. Well. I'm pretty sure you own that too."

"Oh, Elio..."

"It's alright," I say, but the words feel jagged, like maybe it isn't alright at all. "You don't have to say it back. You already told me that you're mine. And it's enough."

A teary, disbelieving laugh flutters up out of her throat. I feel it under my hand as well as hear it.

"Elio-"

"I said it's alright."

"No!" she nearly shouts. She presses the tips of her index fingers against the inner corners of her eyes, as if she can keep any wayward tears inside. Then she flings her hands back down in a violent slicing motion. She looks like she doesn't know what to do with them now, so she gathers up some of her skirt in her fists and stares me down with such ferocity I feel like I should be on my fucking knees.

"It's not alright," she says fiercely. Her voice shakes, but there's no hesitation in her words. "I love you. And it's not alright. Nothing's been alright since the day you forced your way into my world."

Her eyes are blue fire, and I'll never escape from that blaze.

I don't even want to.

"It's not alright, Elio!" she cries. "But maybe I'm self-destructive, or broken, or just as crazy as you. Because I love you. It's not alright. None of this is alright. But I *fucking love you anyway*."

Need batters its way through my body so hard it leaves me breathless. My fingers tighten on her throat, and I back her up against the table where all the hair and makeup shit has been left behind. Brushes and bottles rattle when her ass collides with the edge, and with one wide sweep of my arm I send all of it crashing to the floor.

The next instant I've got my hands on her waist, lifting her to sit on the table, my fingers diving beneath her skirt. For fucking once she doesn't fight me. Doesn't hide from me. Doesn't deny me anything. She moans, wrapping her arms around my neck and spreading her thighs wide beneath the layers of her dress. I yank her panties roughly to the side, my lungs burning, heart slamming, cock straining. I fumble with the fasteners of my tux, desperately tugging fabric until my hardness is freed.

Fuck, it's so good to have use of both my hands again. I grip her hips, dragging her forward, making her skirt bunch as I line myself up to her entrance. There's no foreplay, no languor, no slowness or stillness. There's only a hard, rough claiming as I jam myself inside her, moaning when I find her already wet.

Deirdre moans, too, her head lolling until it hits the mirror behind her back. She clings to me as I plant my hands on either side of her hips, rutting into her as hard as I fucking can. The whole table slides and shakes from the brutality of my motion, the mirror slamming against the wall over and over again until I half wonder if it might break.

Seeing the bride before the wedding. Broken mirror. Two for fucking two today.

But the mirror doesn't break. And neither does Deirdre. She bucks against me, driving her hips against mine in frantic jerks. She climaxes quick and fucking *hard*, milking me with spastic contractions until I can't think, can't stop, can't do anything but fuck her and fuck her and fuck her before I come with a ragged cry.

Deirdre sags back against the mirror, fogging its surface with her body heat and the fine mist of perspiration on her skin. Still buried in that sweet cunt, still spurting, still spilling everything I have inside her, I taste that sweat for myself. I give the side of her neck an open-mouthed kiss, relishing the velvet of her skin, smelling sex and perfume and Deirdre.

I don't want to pull out. I don't want to leave her, even if it's only for the short while left until she walks down the aisle to me.

"Elio," Deirdre pants, "The time. I'm still not ready. I have to fix my hair. And the veil..."

"I know."

I slide myself out of her slowly, relishing every inch of that wet channel until I'm all the way out. I tuck myself back inside my clothing as Deirdre fixes her panties. She stops, then looks around with dismay.

"What is it?"

"I need a tissue or something. It's so wet."

"Good. I want part of me still on you, still in you, the moment we get married."

I lift her off the desk and set her on her feet, kneeling for a brief moment to lay her skirt nicely before I stand again.

She smooths her slender fingers over the beaded fabric, almost obsessively, as if she's worried someone will see a rogue wrinkle and know what we've just done.

"I can't believe the today is actually here," she remarks into the silence.

"Is it the wedding part you can't believe?" I ask. "Or the groom?"

She looks up at me questioningly.

"What do you mean? Is there a difference?"

"Sure," I reply. "Don't tell me you never imagined getting married before."

"Well, I suppose, but..."

"But not to someone like me."

She doesn't answer, so I go on.

"Probably to some snivelling little prat like Brian. Not that he'd be able to fuck you the way I just did. Considering what I did to him."

Deirdre goes very still. Her freckles look suddenly darker. But they're not. The rest of her has just gotten paler.

"What do you mean?" she asks. "What do you mean, what you did to him?" She presses a hand to her belly and bends over slightly, like she thinks she might be sick. "Did... Did you kill him?"

"No," I tell her, and she relaxes a little, only to tense right back up when I add, "I shot his fucking dick off."

"What?! When?"

"That's what I was doing up north when I was gone. Took him to one of our warehouses up there. You don't have to look at me like that. Alexei took him to a doctor afterwards. I let the little shit live. Just for you."

"You," she croaks, grasping at the edge of the table we just fucked on for support, "you abducted my ex-boyfriend. Disfigured him. Because of me. And then you came back on the anniversary of my mom's death and took my virginity."

"Yes."

She leans over and clutches at the table for another moment, breathing heavily, before she stands up, her spine so straight I could use it as a fucking level. Her voice, when she speaks, is flat and grim.

"There's an old Irish tale, you know. *Deirdre of the Sorrows*. The story goes that Deirdre was kidnapped and forced to marry a tyrant king instead of the man she loved."

"Clearly, I'm the kidnapping tyrant in this tale," I scoff. "But are you telling me there's actually some other man out there you'd rather have?"

"No."

That's good at least. I wasn't exactly imagining hunting down some random guy and smashing his skull in on my wedding day when I got up this morning.

"But that's just the thing," Deirdre continues. "What am I supposed to do when the tyrant and the one I love are one and the same? You even look a bit like Naoise, her lover in the story. He was supposed to be beautiful. With raven-black hair."

Well, I have the black hair going for me, I guess. I don't bother addressing the "beautiful" part because there's only one beautiful thing in this room and it sure as shit isn't my scarred ass.

"What happened to Deirdre?" I ask instead. "In the story."

"She threw herself out of a chariot and killed herself."

The room tilts sickeningly to the side. I feel like I won't be able to remain standing upright if I don't do something and do it right fucking now. It's the same way I felt back when I smashed the doors right off their hinges at home that very first night.

But there are no more doors left in here to rip down. No more men to kill, at least for now. She's got the ring, got the dress.

There's nothing left to do but make her mine in all ways, before my uncle and this city and the eyes of fucking God if He can even stand to look at me.

So I don't do anything. I just stand there with my hands balled into useless, aching fists and say tightly, "Then I suppose it's a good fucking thing we took a bullet-proof limo to the venue instead of a chariot, isn't it?"

She gives a lifeless laugh.

"I already told you, Elio. I don't plan on dying just to get away from you."

"But do you still plan on getting away from me?" I demand, seizing her chin and forcing her to look at me. "After everything, do you honestly still think you can escape?"

After everything, do you really want to leave?

To leave me?

"No, Elio," she says. "Don't you see? You don't need debt to bind me now. You don't need to hold threats about my father over my head. You got me to love you." She raises a trembling hand, stroking her fingers over the scarred part of my jaw. It takes everything I fucking have not to lean into that hand like a touch-starved animal.

"I love you," she whispers. "And that's more powerful than any other cage you could have constructed." Her hand falls down, pressing flat against my chest, right above the place my heart beats.

"I love you," she repeats one final time, and I'm suddenly terrified that I'll never hear her say it again. "And now I can never leave."

Chapter 38

Deirdre

I don't have much time to process what just happened with Elio, because as soon as he leaves the room Valentina and the other bridesmaids storm back in like a cloud of anxious bees.

"Jesus, look at the mess!" Valentina says, stopping short when she sees all the hair and makeup stuff that Elio knocked to the ground.

"Sorry," I say softly, seeing that many of the various jars and bottles are now broken.

"Oh, God, don't be! Elio paid for all this shit," Valentina says. "And I can pretty much guarantee you weren't the one throwing it all down on the floor."

Well, that is true, I suppose. But I was still complicit. He swept it all off the table to get me up on there. So he could fuck me. Because we both needed it so badly. Sticky wetness pools in my panties as I look down at the items in disarray on the expensive floor.

Elio did it. He broke these things.

But he did it with me. *For* me.

Just like what he did to Brian.

I haven't seen him on campus lately. I assumed it was just

because Elio had hit him that other time and told him to stay away from me.

I shot his fucking dick off.

He said it so casually. Like he took Brian out for ice cream.

And the worst part of it all? The thing that really made me want to throw up? It wasn't feeling bad for Brian, who probably would have raped me that night. It was the instant, toxic squeeze of pleasure I felt, learning just how far Elio would go to protect me. If someone tries to hurt me, he will hurt them twice as much.

And then the guilt had crashed in, a sickly green tidal wave, because who the hell thinks like that? Who feels protected and treasured when they find out their fiancé permanently disfigured their ex in one of the most horrific ways?

I didn't want to let Elio turn me into this. Or maybe this is already who I was, and he's just revealed that inner ugliness.

But no matter how many layers Elio has pulled back, no matter which parts of me he's exposed, he's never once turned away.

There's relief in that so palpable that it nearly knocks me over, but also pain, because I have turned away from him. Over and over, I've pushed him away, told him I would run. Even this morning, when he told me about Brian, I compared him to the tyrant king of that old story.

But not now. Not anymore.

"I'm ready."

There's a calm conviction in what I just said. Valentina's fingers stop poking and prodding at my hair.

"Alright," she says. She picks up the veil, the sheer fabric rippling in the air as she secures it above the pins at the back of my head. "There. *Now* you're ready."

I turn to look at myself as the veil settles around my shoulders. I feel at peace. Maybe even happy, if I can let go of all the fear and the guilt and just let myself be.

Two of the event coordinators are waiting outside the room with Robbie when we emerge again. One of them speaks hurriedly into a headset about how she's "got the bride" and I feel like she's treating this like she's escorting the Prime Minister somewhere instead of just me.

But I'm not just me anymore, am I?

I'll be a Titone now.

We all get into an elevator, but even the elevator is spacious, so it doesn't feel cramped with my skirt and the seven other people clustered around me.

Robbie heads out first, casting his gaze critically over the lobby before he nods and the rest of us come out. The two event coordinators arrange us into a line – the bridesmaids first, then Valentina as my maid of honour, then me at the end. People in the lobby stop and stare, their eyes big and their voices hushed as we pass. A little girl with bouncy curls tugs against her mother's hand, crying out, "Princess!" I wave at her, acknowledging that in a way, that little girl is right. Elio is the closest thing this city has to a dark prince.

Once through the massive, beautiful lobby, the coordinators lead us down a large hallway with champagne-coloured walls. Two heavy wooden doors are propped open at the end, and it looks like they lead into a sort of antechamber with another set of doors beyond, those ones closed.

Inside the antechamber are our bouquets. Valentina helps hand them out, the blooms pure, glorious white with accents of blue and greenery springing out at artistic angles. My bouquet is the largest. I expect my hands to shake when I take it, but they don't. I clasp my fingers around the cool stems and watch first Annabelle, then Lucia, then Giulia pass through the doors into whatever lies beyond. I can't see into the room yet.

"Alright, now Valentina!" one of the coordinators says, peering through the slightly ajar door before holding it wider for my maid of honour.

"Holy shit. Ah! OK." She turns around to give me a quick, reassuring smile. "You look so beautiful. See you in there!"

And then, in a flounce of dark blue silk and a click of high heels, she's gone.

And now I'm alone.

I mean, not entirely. Robbie and the coordinators are here, both of them keeping hawk-like gazes on whatever's happening in the room beyond so they'll know when it's my turn. But I feel alone. For the first time, it occurs to me that I don't have anyone to walk me down the aisle.

And that really fucking hurts. My dad should be here.

He should have been a different sort of man.

I haven't thought about him or his betrayal in a while now. It was so easy to get swept up in all things Elio, to feel so overwhelmed by him and his world that I could almost forget about the painful way I was forced out of mine. Tears rush to my eyes, and my throat works, and I will not cry over my father right now, goddamnit!

"OK! The song for the bridesmaids is ending! Time for the bride!"

Both the coordinators turn to me in unison. I sniff and blink, squeezing the stems of the flowers between my fingers to give myself something else to focus on that doesn't include my tears. That doesn't include the great big hole of pain opening up inside me at the thought of walking down that aisle alone.

But the tears come anyway, especially when I hear the song that starts up as soon as I walk through the doors.

It's *An Eala Bhàn*. My mother's favourite song.

I don't think I've ever mentioned that to Elio. How would anyone even know that?

I start walking, letting the tears roll down my cheeks because there's no way for me to stop them. I stare straight ahead and don't get a full view of the wedding hall just yet. After entering from the antechamber, I've come at this larger room from the side. I'm walking behind the last row of seats right now, and I can see a sharp turn in the path ahead that will take me down the main aisle to Elio. I hear wooden benches creaking, and gasps and murmurs, as people begin to turn their heads towards me, but I don't look back at any of them. I just stare at the floor ahead, focusing on putting one sparkly shoe in front of the other as the notes of my late mother's favourite song swirl around me.

I'm almost at the place where I need to turn. But, oddly, the floor here isn't uniform. There's a pair of large feet encased in beautiful black dress shoes at the beginning of the main aisle. I finally start to pull my eyes up from the ground. Up over long legs and a pair of hands hanging loose at the side. Black gloved hands.

My teary gaze snaps right up to his face.

"Elio." I mouth the word instead of truly saying it. I don't think I could force a word out of my throat even if I wanted to right now.

He doesn't reply right away. He just angles his elbow towards me, as if he wants me to take his arm. And I do it, because I'm not sure I can remain standing otherwise.

"Your father already gave you to me a long time ago," he says quietly, his gaze fierce and heavy with meaning. "But that doesn't mean I'm going to let you walk down this aisle alone."

His arm feels so hard and solid linked with mine. His touch tender as he dabs away my tears. Together, we turn towards the front of the room.

For the first time, I actually look up enough to take in the vast space. And it truly takes my breath away.

The walls in here are almost entirely windows, the glass panes arranged in arrow-like shapes that lead the eye upward, creating a cathedral-like effect. That effect is only amplified by the high, arching ceiling, beams of wood adding a slightly rustic flare. The sun has emerged from heavy winter clouds, and it pours through the glass, warming every surface, making everything shimmer in a way that feels almost sacred. The benches are carved from the same wood the beams above are made of, and luscious flowers are draped along their backs, petals scattered everywhere. The wedding guests, none of whom I recognize beyond the wedding party and Elio's aunt and uncle, are standing, watching us, hushed as Elio and I pass them by.

But there isn't silence in the room. *An Eala Bhàn* is still playing, and I notice the live string quartet just off to the side.

"This song," I choke out. "How did you know?"

"Didn't I ever tell you?" Elio says, looking down at me from the side. "This was the song I heard you playing the very first time I saw you. And then I learned that your mamma loved it. So it felt fitting."

I shake my head, a tiny movement so as to not draw much attention from anyone besides my groom. I had no idea. I never remembered or thought to ask what song he heard me playing that summer day outside my father's house.

But Elio remembered.

When we reach the front where the bridesmaids are standing in a row on one side, Valentina comes forward to take my bouquet of flowers from me, leaving both my hands free to be swept up into Elio's. Elio doesn't have four groomsmen to match up with my side – it's just Curse standing up there. Elio and I step up onto the platform, standing facing each other beneath a banner of blooms. A single white petal from over our heads drifts down, fluttering like a feather between us. I watch its floaty trajectory until it hits the ground.

And then my eyes meet Elio's.

There's ferocity in his gaze. Pure, possessive intention. His fingers may be closed around mine, but it's his gaze that truly holds me there.

It's a gaze that tells me, no more running. No more waiting.

I am his.

And it's time to prove it to the world.

Chapter 39

Elio

My impatience from the morning is completely gone. Now, I'm savouring every fucking second that I'm standing here with Deirdre, staring down at her in her veil and her dress, knowing that it's my come soaking her white panties. Every time the wedding officiant – and old man with snow white hair and a deep, resonant voice – asks her if she plans to do something (honour me, cherish me, trust me as her husband) and she answers "I do," it's like I'm fucking reborn.

I keep my eyes locked on hers when I answer the officiant's questions for myself.

I do.

I do.

I do.

Curse comes forward with the rings. I slide Deirdre's on first, admiring the diamond and platinum gleam on her finger and the way the wedding band matches so perfectly with her other ring.

Deirdre takes my wedding band from Curse, and clearly has a moment of hesitation about the glove situation. But then, her brow clearing of confusion like clouds moving out of a bright sky, she slides the ring over top of my glove and onto my ring finger. Just as I'd intended.

We both stare at our hands, contrasting in so many ways – hers small, mine large, hers smooth, mine scarred, hers pale and freckled, mine gloved in dark leather – but now similar in at least one. We've both got the rings.

She and I have been connected for a long time now.

But now the entire city can fucking see it.

When we kiss, I can tell Deirdre's going for something chaste in front of the crowd. She keeps her lips primly closed. I lock my hands on her waist and dip her backwards until she gasps. When her mouth opens, I deepen the kiss, and it's like I'm fucking pouring myself into her. My bride.

My wife.

I don't want to break the kiss. But there's other shit to do. Signing the forms that make this ceremony one-hundred-percent official. I won't have any corners cut. She will be my wife in every fucking way. So we sit and take our time, signing the pages that the officiant whisks away when we are finished.

Once that's done, we stand together, her hand in mine, ready to walk forward into the future as man and wife. And it's gonna be a good fucking future. I can tell just by the way it feels to hold her hand like this, and by how fucking good this moment smells. Like perfume and flowers and gasoline and –

A wall of heat scorches my back. I'm thrown forward at the same moment that glass shatters all around me. Reflexively my fingers clench, but they clench around nothing. Deirdre's hand is gone.

The panic that rises instantly is blunted when my temple collides hard with the side of the wooden bench in the first row. Dazed, I raise a shaking hand to my temple, the leather of my glove sliding through hot blood. There's screaming, footsteps, ringing in my head, and smoke, fucking smoke everywhere, so thick I can barely think let alone breathe.

I have to get to her.

Fighting a wave of nausea, I drag myself up onto my knees, my ribs screaming. Two strong arms go beneath my armpits, hauling me up. I grab at the back of the bench to keep from falling over as Curse swims into blurry view.

"Where is she?" It feels like my mouth is full of sand.

Curse says something to me, but it's a meaningless wallop of noise. I push him away, stumbling past him back towards the place I'd been standing with Deirdre not one moment before.

She isn't fucking there.

The flowers that had arched above us while we said our vows are ruined, singed and smoking, the white and blue petals now black with burning edges. They fall, drifting like ash, to the ground. The wall of glass has been blown to smithereens. The wood beams are burning.

This place is on fucking fire and I cannot fucking find her.

I turn around, feeling off-balance and slow as I do it. My eyes lurch drunkenly around the room. I see my uncle holding up Zizi and barking orders. I see Enzo snatching Annabelle out of the way of a massive falling piece of glass. Valentina is with Lucia and Giulia. Curse is with me.

Who the fuck is with my wife?

"Where is she?" I say again, choking on fumes. My scars blaze beneath my gloves. I stare down at my hands for a moment, wondering if I never woke up at all this morning. If I'm trapped in a nightmare.

It doesn't even fucking matter. Not one iota.

Because whether in reality or in dreams, I will always fucking find her.

Chapter 40

Deirdre

There are moments in life that you can only experience in shattering pieces. The car accident that killed my mom was like that. I don't remember any real linear progression of how that night unfolded. I just remember us driving at night in winter.

Then the flash of headlights through our windshield. My mom's choked sound of fear. Then rolling and smashing and glass and light and dark.

This moment is just like that.

There's an explosion that smashes through the room, and then everything flashes through me in clipped little still frames. Hands at my waist, hauling me out into cold air.

Not Elio's hands.

I cry and flail, but now there are two sets of hands. I scream, but it's only one of what sounds like ten thousand fucking screams. Beams glow with new flame, and the last thing I see is Elio, my husband, being dragged bodily from the ground, as if he can't do it by himself. He's hurt. He's hurt and there's fire and I'm not there to help him.

I scream again, and it is a sound of visceral mourning. I scream and I scream and maybe I scream all the oxygen right out of my body, because consciousness suddenly sputters, like a candle in the dark. Heat pricks at the side of my neck, like an insect biting, and I try to slap it but my hand doesn't move at all.

My muscles are no longer my own. My voice betrays me, silent in my throat. I hold the image of Elio in my head for as long as I fucking can, but it's no time at all. He's already fading, disappearing into darkness that smells like smoke.

Not willing to let him go, I disappear right along with him.

When I regain consciousness, I'm only just barely on the edge of awareness. My head pounds. My tongue feels like it's been sealed to the roof of my mouth. My limbs are floppy and cold. My legs in particular feel extraordinarily heavy, and when I'm finally able to flutter open my eyes I see wet, beaded silk clinging to them. I'm sitting up. I think. In some kind of plush seat. Wind howls. But it doesn't sound right. It's too uniform. More like the din of a machine.

I crack my eyes open once more with monumental effort. Bright light blinds me from right beside my head. When I can finally look into that oval of light, I see clouds. Not above me, but below.

My head hurts so much. Agony just to hold my eyes open.

I could just sleep. Sleep, and then I'll wake up next to Elio. He'll be beside me and I'll tell him about the clouds and he'll give me that crooked smile of his and call me Songbird like he always does.

There's something nudging at the back of my brain, something telling me that that's not right, something's wrong, and when I wake up maybe he won't be there after all.

But it's too late. My thousand-pound eyelids close. I drift out of consciousness, carried away by clouds and the sound of engines.

The next time I awaken, I'm much more alert. My head is still throbbing, and I'm drowsy, but I'm able to hold my eyes open and actually try to take in my surroundings.

Only my surroundings don't make any sense.

The first thing I notice is the heat. There's sun bathing my body, but it's not the week winter Toronto sun. It's bold and brilliant, warming me even as salty water splashes and sprays me. Somewhere above, a bird caws loudly, the sound making me think of the beach. I'm sitting still, but also moving.

The *boat* is moving.

How am I on a boat? *Where* am I on a boat?

It's not very large. A sort of little speedboat. I'm facing the back of the boat, watching the wake foam out behind. I twist weakly to see two men at the front. One steering, the other staring out over the water.

I gasp loudly and begin to struggle, only to find myself strapped into the seat I'm on.

"Ah, there she is."

I freeze as one of the men notices I'm awake and comes towards me.

He's a man that I don't recognize. I don't think I know the other one with him, either.

"No struggling. No funny stuff. Or I'm putting you to sleep again."

They drugged me.

The realization crawls through my addled brain. Whoever these men are, they sabotaged my wedding. They took me. They drugged me. And now they've got me God knows where. My heart feels sluggish in response to the adrenaline trying to flood my system. It makes me feel weak and queasy.

"Our names don't matter," the man says. "You won't know them because you don't know us. But I think that you'll know *him...*"

I follow the man's gaze. We're approaching land. A lush, sun-stained beach, with thick tropical greenery beyond it. The man isn't looking at the beach, though. And he's not looking at the trees.

He's looking at a dock.

And standing on that dock is my father.

Chapter 41

Elio

I t feels like I'm lost in smoke and fire forever without her. Even though, in reality, it only takes a few minutes for the hotel's emergency sprinkler system to activate and drench the few people who are left in here. Sirens wail, and I stagger out of the wedding hall, walking through what used to be a glass wall and out into the snow.

"She's not inside," Curse says. "She had to have come this way."

"Not alone," I rasp, my throat raw from the explosion.

"Who do you think would take her?"

"Who do you fucking think?" I shout, whirling on him. My hand flies to my temple, like I think my brains might start oozing out at any moment. "Fucking Darragh! He loves blowing shit up. He reneged on our deal and now he has her."

Enzo's out here now, and Robbie, jogging over the snow to Curse and me.

"You," I snarl at Enzo, my hand seizing on his tie. "How the fuck did this happen? My goddamn head of security! Tell me why I shouldn't put a bullet in your head right fucking now!"

"I'm sorry, Boss," Enzo says gravely. "It looks like it happened after our last sweep. Apparently one of the hotel staff was given a wrapped gift box and was told it was for the ceremony. She was told that it was from the father of the bride."

My brain halts its frantic spinning.

"The father of the bride?" I echo. At that moment, Curse looks down at his phone and frowns.

"The name Charles Brigham mean anything to you?" my brother asks.

"No. Fuck! Why are you asking me this pointless shit? My wife is fucking out there somewhere!"

Now I'm not so sure it was Darragh, and that's even more terrifying than him having her, because that means I don't have a single fucking lead.

Father of the bride...

What the fuck is going on?

"It's just a hunch," Curse says, "But one of my contacts just told me a private flight is taking off right now, and that it was chartered by someone named Charles Brigham. Its destination is Bermuda."

Bermuda.

Father of the bride.

Charles Brigham...

Charlie.

The name on that letter to O'Malley, all those years ago.

The man who very likely was responsible for her mamma's death.

And now, he has her.

"She's on that plane." As the words come spilling from my mouth, I know they're true. "My wife is on that fucking plane to Bermuda."

"Then I guess we'd better get on ours," Curse replies.

Things happen real quick after that, though everything feels maddeningly fucking slow. Every moment the four of us spend in the car and then getting into our private on-call jet is another moment that my Songbird flies further and further away from me. Our jet is faster than a normal plane, so we make good time to Bermuda, but I spend the entire flight feeling like I want to crawl out of my own skin.

"Who the fuck do we know in Bermuda these days?" I ask Curse tightly as Enzo and Robbie prepare round after round of ammunition.

"Caruso is my main contact," Curse replies. "He retired there about eight years ago."

Cat-Foot Caruso. I remember him. A skinny, wily capo of my uncle's who once got thrown off a balcony but somehow managed to land on his feet. He broke both ankles in the process, but it was better than his spine, and it earned him a nickname that's been stuck to him for more than twenty years now.

"Get him on the phone," I hiss savagely. "Make sure that what-ever we need, he has it fucking ready for us."

Curse gets Caruso on the phone, tells him what went down at the wedding, then mentions the name Charles Brigham.

When Curse puts the phone on speaker, I can hear Caruso whistle.

"Oh, old Charlie boy. Rich British son of a bitch. Pretty nasty loan shark. He's got a private resort on one of the smaller islands. Only accessible by boat."

"Tell me you've got a fucking boat for us," I say. *Cristo Santo.* At this point I'd fucking swim to her if I have to.

"I've got something better," Caruso replies. "I've got a helicopter."

Chapter 42

Deirdre

I sit in the boat staring up at my dad on the dock for so long that the two men are forced to unstrap me and physically pull me out of the seat. They try to lift me out of the boat, but my skirt gets snagged on something. One of the men pulls out a knife, and I cringe away from the blade as he saws through the silk, turning the flawless full-length gown into a garment that ends choppily above my knees. I'm lifted much more easily from the boat this time, held by the waist and then deposited on my ass on the dock, facing towards the boat. I stare down at the beautiful beaded silk, the dress I wore for Elio ruined in the bottom of the boat, and feel a small part of myself die.

"Here, lass, up we go now," my dad says, grabbing my arm and trying to pull me into a standing position.

"Don't touch me!" I surprise all three of them, and myself, with the force of my scream. I rip my arm out of his grip and get shakily to my feet on my own. My muscles feel looser than they should. My whole system slowed by whatever they injected into me.

My dad looks good. And that is like a slap in the fucking face. He's sun-kissed, healthy, wearing shorts and a fine linen shirt that rustles in the warm breeze. His hair is a little longer than when I saw him last, and it looks like he's even lost some weight.

He's been living one good life out here without me.

"What are you doing?" I ask, my throat scraped raw. "Why am I here? Where is Elio?"

"Elio?" My dad looks surprised I've mentioned the man that I've been living with since he abandoned me. "Back in Toronto, I'd imagine. He doesn't know you're here."

"Why the hell am I here?" I don't even know if Elio is alright. It looked like he was hurt badly in that blast. My hands crawl anxiously up to my head, clenching at my hair until it pulls hard at the scalp. "You have to take me back!"

"Back?" My dad gawks at me. "No, Dee. I always meant to get you back eventually. My business partner has finally helped me to do just that."

"Get me back? You're the one who left me there!" I point my finger wildly out over the water, swinging it like it's the arm of a compass that can find Toronto and Elio by some kind of magnetic force. "You signed me away to *La Cosa Nostra* when I was eighteen fucking years old! You ran away like a coward on my birthday when that Camorra soldier was coming at me with a gun! And now you're trying to tell me that it was all part of the plan? That you were going to come back for me eventually? After my life was already completely destroyed?"

My arm drops, heavy and limp to my side. "You want to know who was there when you weren't? Elio. That very first night you ran, he took a bullet to protect me. While you were getting on a plane for this fucking paradise, Elio was getting stitched up from a wound that could have killed him if he hadn't been just a little more lucky than he is."

"See?" my dad says, nearly scoffs, defensiveness clear in his voice and face. "I knew he would be good to you. Take care of you while I was gone. That's why I felt good about making that deal with him."

"That is bullshit and you know it!" I snap. How have I never truly seen this side of my father before? This wriggly, gaslighting person who lies like it's nothing? "Elio Titone is a monster and in many ways he was a monster to me. But he's my monster now. He's my husband. And you have to send me back to him!"

I stop shouting and try to get control of my breathing.

Maybe if I can just find the right angle, the right negotiation tactic, I can swing things around my way.

"I won't tell him it was you," I say quickly, already hating the promise I'm making because I know my husband is going to try to get the information out of me by whatever means necessary. "I won't tell him what happened. I'll make something up. Just get me on a plane. Send me home!"

The open, placating look my father has had on his face for most of this time suddenly cracks, then crumbles completely away, revealing something hard and cold.

"I can't."

"Why not?!"

"Because Mr. Brigham's taken an interest in you."

My head snaps to the side, because it's one of the other men who's spoken now.

"Ah. There it is," I say grimly. "What happened to, 'it was always the plan to get you back'?" I ask my dad. "I'm still a pawn to you. Only problem is I've got a knight behind me now."

Not a bright, chivalrous knight. A dark knight. One clad in black leather instead of white armour.

"He is going to find me," I promise my father, promise all of them. "If you don't send me back, he will come for me."

"He doesn't even know where you are," my father says, but there's a hint of uncertainty I can see working at him now.

"But he knows you're here!" I cry, and my father blanches in response, blood draining from beneath his Bermuda-darkened freckles. "He's known where you are this entire time! When he doesn't find me in Toronto, he will scour the whole world to find me, and he'll probably start-" I point furiously down at the dock between us "-right here!"

"He's welcome to do so."

That's a new voice that I don't recognize, one with a posh-sounding accent, like it was shaped in fancy parts of London. I turn towards the sound to see a tall, lean man standing at the other end of the dock where it connects with the island. Like my father, he's dressed in beautiful, expensive-looking linen, his trousers and his shirt both pristine white. His hair is somewhere between grey and blonde and when he smiles broadly at me I'm confronted with a set of too-large, too-white veneers.

"You... You want him to come here?"

One of the man grabs me violently by the hair, yanking me back until I cry out. My father does nothing but watch as the man hisses, "You don't ask questions of the boss."

The boss in question, presumably Mr. Brigham, raises a tanned, weathered hand and the man instantly lets me go.

"No need to be so rough with our new guest," Mr. Brigham says as he comes down the dock towards us.

When he's close enough I think I can peg him at around fifty-five, or maybe even sixty years old. But he's the kind of man who's aged with health and wealth, like somebody who spends a lot of time on a yacht. His skin has aged from the sun, but overall he still looks strong, muscles cording along the forearms I can see from the way his sleeves are rolled up to his elbows.

I feel that strength for myself when he grabs my chin, turning my face this way and that. I try to pull away, but his goon is still right behind me, and I'm trapped.

"You're even lovelier in person," the tall man says. "Let's get you inside, shall we? Can't have that fine Irish skin getting burned out here."

"Who are you?" I force out of a tight mouth.

"Your father's never mentioned me?" He raises pale eyebrows

with mock surprise. "He and I go way back. Your mother and I go way back, too."

My father turns away, staring out at the water with his hands in his pockets.

"My... You knew my mom?"

"Never met her, of course," he clarifies. "And I really was quite broken up about what happened to her. But that's what happens when you play with fire and you lose." His eyes go to my father. A chill sweeps through me, the beginnings of a suspicion piecing itself together beneath my skin, stealing the heat out of my body even as the sun shines down.

"I didn't expect that you'd survive," he says mildly, like he's talking about the fate of an ant instead of a person.

He didn't expect that I'd survive...

It's like he knew about the crash that killed my mother.

Knew about it *before it even happened.*

"You," I whisper, shock and horror giving way to numbness. It's like there's a pane of glass between me and everything else. "It was you."

I still remember the flash of headlights blasting into our windshield. I always assumed that I'd just seen wrong in the chaos of that moment. Or that maybe somebody else briefly lost control of their vehicle before moving on, and that they somehow didn't see us swerve and crash. Because they never stayed at the scene.

"Not me directly," the man replies. "It's been many millions of dollars since I've had to do any of my own dirty work like that."

Dirty work. Running my mother and me off the road, ending her beautiful life, saddling me with a lifetime of trauma and guilt and regret...

It's just work to him. And dirty work, too.

The pane of glass grows thicker and thicker, blurring everything. When Mr. Brigham speaks again it sounds like it comes from a thousand miles away. "But that's what happens when you don't pay your debts."

My father is still looking out over the water. Like none of this concerns him anymore.

"What debts?" I say, and the words are like ash in my mouth.

"Did you know your father tried to start an illicit import business when you were a child? I was his main creditor," Mr. Brigham says almost cheerily. "But unfortunately, business didn't quite pan out, did it, Jack?"

My father tenses but doesn't turn around.

"He was warned about what would happen. That when I'm not paid I have to resort to distasteful measures."

"Dad?" I can barely say it. This man isn't my dad. He doesn't deserve that title anymore. I've already gotten used to the fact that he sold me out.

But now? Learning this? That he was partially responsible for my mom's death? That he fucking knew it was coming, and did *nothing?*

And I could have died that night too. My father has been playing games with my life since I was ten years old.

"Oh, don't get upset now," Mr. Brigham says with a weary-sounding sigh. "All is well. Your father paid me back quite quickly after that. I believe that's when he started skimming from Darragh. Isn't it, Jack?"

"Yes," he says to the water.

"And now we're good friends," Mr. Brigham says jovially, flashing those big white teeth at me. "Business partners, even. He's been funnelling money to me for a long time now. Helped me build this beautiful place." He gestures behind himself, to a massive, sprawling structure of white stone among the trees. "So when he ran into trouble with Mr. Titone, Mr. Gowan, and Mr. Severu, of course I was happy for him to come and live here. He and Bridget have built a lovely little life on this island."

My knees buckle. No one tries to stop me from falling. I land heavily on my knees and my hands, splinters gouging into the skin until I bleed.

"So what do you want with me?" I ask, watching the red of my blood stain the wood beneath my hands.

"Your father has mentioned bringing you here several times. Once I saw a recent photograph of you, I decided that might not be such a bad idea after all. You'll do very well working for me here."

"Working for you doing what?"

"Anything my guests desire."

My spine ices with dread. I force myself to sit up on my knees, curling my bleeding hands into fists on my skirt.

"Elio will not allow that," I tell him bluntly.

"Then he may come here and negotiate for your release. Ah, I must say, it feels good to take a toy away from someone as powerful as Elio Titone. I imagine that he'll pay a pretty penny to get you back. And if he decides that he doesn't want you, then I'll make good money with you in other ways." He grins, but his blue eyes are flinty and dead-looking. "When my friends finish with you, you'll be so broken that your husband may not even want you back."

"This wasn't the deal," my father says, finally turning around. "That wasn't why I agreed for her to come here."

"Oh? Did you think you were saving her?" Mr. Brigham says mildly, taking a moment to examine his perfectly groomed cuticles. "This is why you're perpetually in debt, Jack. You have no vision. No business acumen. You're constantly two steps behind."

As if deciding that he's done with this conversation, Mr. Brigham turns his back and begins to stroll off the dock towards the shore. The two men haul me up, dragging me between them. My father says nothing and follows silently behind, head bent and face in shadow.

Chapter 43

Elio

at-Foot Caruso's got some nice digs here, but I barely even
notice his big house on the beach. All I care about is
getting on that helicopter and finding Deirdre. My skull
feels like it's splitting open, and I don't know if it's because of the
blow to the temple or because of how many thoughts are gunning
through me now about what might be happening to her without me
there to protect her.

They had a head start, but our jet is fast and the helicopter will
be fast too. With any luck we'll show up and storm the place two
fucking minutes after Deirdre arrives.

"What are we gonna be dealing with?" I ask Caruso as we haul
ass into the helicopter.

"Charlie's rich, and he's involved in some shady shit, but he's not
a real mob boss," Caruso informs us. "He's got some private security
working for him at his place. Don't know how many guys could be
there. He might have some friends staying as guests, but they're
usually just your run of the mill rich assholes looking for drugs and
whores. I doubt they'd be ready for a shootout. Your wife's papà lives
there with his cute little piece of ass, too."

I grunt, taking that all in as we lift off. Caruso has made good use of his retirement, learning new skills, I guess, because he actually knows how to fucking fly this thing.

We lift off over his property, heading for the open water and an island beyond. As we get closer, a big white building comes into view.

"That's Charlie's place," Caruso tells me via a microphone and the protective headphones I've got on. "He's got a landing pad. We won't have the element of surprise if we land there, though."

"Do it," I tell him, palming the pistol at my hip and the automatic strapped to my side. I don't give a fuck about the element of surprise right now. The second they took Deirdre, they should have known I'd follow them. Fuck surprise. I'll kill any man who didn't see this fucking coming.

And I'll kill the rest of them, too.

Caruso banks and begins to descend towards a large helipad on the property, about 500 metres away from the main building. There are already two guards in tan uniforms with guns on their hips waiting for us. Enzo, Robbie, and Curse all wait for my command.

We land, buffeting the uniforms of the two men who've come to meet us. I don't know if they're here to escort us to Charlie or if they're going to pick us off one by one as we get out of the helicopter.

"This is bullet-proof, Boss," Caruso says as we all take off our headphones. "We can sit here a minute and think."

"No." I say instantly. I don't need to fucking think. I already know what to do. "Anyone in this fucking place is complicit in the abduction of my wife. No one," I say savagely, meeting the gaze of every man in this helicopter, one after the other, "will be left alive."

"There may be an easier way than just blasting our way in and hoping we don't get our heads blown off in the process," Caruso says. He gestures at the two guards waiting. "Those men are locals Charlie's hired. They're not loyal to him. They're loyal to the almighty dollar. Pay them off and they'll get us in. And if they say no, well..." He shrugs. "Then we kill them."

"It's a good idea," Enzo says.

"You shut the fuck up," I tell him, my head feeling like it's gonna burst. "If you hadn't shit the bed back at the hotel this wouldn't have happened. I'm still not even convinced you're going to be alive at the end of the day."

Enzo lapses into silence. Curse and Robbie are both too fucking smart, I guess, to offer any more helpful suggestions right now.

But maybe Caruso and Enzo are right. Having two men who know the lay of the land lead us right to their boss, right to Deirdre, will be more efficient than just trying to shoot our way inside. And I can't sacrifice time for violence if I can avoid it. My number one priority is getting to her, not taking out my rage on the people in between.

"This thing got a speaker system?" I grunt at Caruso. He nods, grabbing a walkie-talkie-looking thing and handing it to me before flipping a couple of switches. When I speak, it echoes outside the helicopter and the guards straighten up.

"There are five of us in here and we're well-armed," I say, watching the guards through the window as I address them. "You might get in a shot or two, but you're outgunned and you're both about to die."

The two guards look at each other uneasily.

"But I need access to the building and I am willing to pay. What-ever your annual fee is, triple it. Get us in there with no funny shit, and not only will I let you live but I'll make sure you're fucking paid. Show me you understand and that you agree by laying your weapons on the ground."

The guards are tense and uncertain. They speak quietly to each other, but I can tell that Caruso's right. These guys want to go home to their kids tonight. They're not here to get blown up protecting their foreign boss.

Slowly, they both lay their guns on the ground and straighten up with their hands in the air.

"Time to go," I snap.

We pour out of the helicopter. Caruso is still light-footed as fuck. Even though he's the oldest among us by at least fifteen years, he's fucking flying across the tarmac. He picks up one of the discarded guns and Curse is right behind him to grab the other.

"Anything else on you?" Enzo asks, immediately beginning to pat down one guard, then the other.

"No, Sir," says the guard on the left. The other one nods in agreement.

"Good. We're keeping these," I tell them, hooking my thumb towards the weapons we've confiscated. I can tell that they don't really like that, but I don't give a shit. They'll get paid if they do what I need them to. I don't need them able to shoot me in the back when I'm not paying attention.

"Your boss took something of mine," I say to them. "And I need to get her back."

"The redhead?" says the one on the left. "Saw her coming in off a boat earlier..."

"Not just some redhead," I seethe, ready to punch this guy's nose into the back of his skull. "My fucking *wife*."

The guards share an *oh, shit* kind of look. They must not know who I am. Because if they did they'd be shitting their fucking pants by now, too.

"How many more armed guards are here?" Curse asks.

"The boss has two personal bodyguards. They're the ones who brought the... your wife. Other than that, there are four more armed men patrolling right now."

I rub my forehead viciously. Those aren't bad odds, all things considered.

"Who else is on the property? Any guests with guns?" I ask.

"Not right now. There are a few cooks and maids on site. Otherwise it's just the boss, his partner Mr. O'Malley, and Miss Bridget. Plus your wife," the guard adds hastily.

Fucking O'Malley. What does he fucking think he's trying to

pull, stealing Deirdre back from me after I already paid for her? After I fucking married her?

I should have shot him when I saw him run across the moonlit snow that night. I should have fucking buried him when he abandoned her.

"Alright." Plans are rapidly solidifying now. "Caruso, Enzo, and Robbie, you're gonna take one of our tour guides here and disarm the patrolling guards. I don't care if you have to bribe them or kill them. Just make sure they're not a problem. Go."

They nod and take off at a sprint, following one of the guards as he leads them onward. "Curse, you're with me." My brother nods, and we both turn to the remaining guard. "You're going to take us to see your boss. Although he's not going to be your boss for much longer," I say, my lips curling in disgust, "because he's about to fucking die."

Chapter 44

Deirdre

The two men pull me through a large, sunlit lobby into a pretty sort of sitting room with a huge, glassless window that looks out over the dock and beach. The floors are pale hardwood, and white curtains flutter with the tropical breeze. Gorgeous, vivid flowers bloom in pots in corners and on tables. I stand in this beautiful room with my bleeding hands and knees and my ruined wedding dress and feel like I've stepped into an alternate reality.

That alternate reality feeling only intensifies when I see Bridget reclining on a white couch. The same Bridget who used to clean our house. The Bridget who's been secretly fucking my dad for years.

The Bridget my dad chose to bring here with him instead of me. She sits up when she sees me, tossing her glossy chestnut hair behind her shoulders.

"Deirdre! Hi! Do you remember me?" She gets off the couch, the long skirt of her gauzy sundress rippling with the movement. She's holding some kind of drink served in a coconut. Idly, I wonder what time it is here. She's got to be drunk to be as happy to see me as she is. She's acting like nothing's weird about this at all.

I ignore her, my eyes tracking my father as he goes to stand beside Bridget. Mr. Brigham strides to a large wicker chair and settles himself into it with an audible "ahh" sound that makes my skin crawl.

Bridget and my father sit down on the couch, and Brigham's two men leave the room. I stay standing in the centre of them all, silent and swaying on rubbery legs, wondering what the hell is going to happen now.

I feel like I've been locked into a castle with a moat, and the moat is the literal fucking ocean. Elio might not have even figured out I'm here yet. He could be wasting time fighting people like Darragh, if he's even able to fight at all right now.

My stomach twists. If he isn't alright...

I swallow bile, staring at my father.

"How about you look at me instead of him?"

I tense, slowly turning my gaze to Brigham. He leers at me, his thighs spread, his gaze like the thin blade of a knife.

"Come sit with me. You look lonely in the middle of the room like that. And I imagine that your legs must be feeling very weak after the drugs."

He's right. Right now the only thing keeping me upright is my locked knees and the strength of my bones. My muscles are barely more than jelly right now.

"Come here. Now."

His expression goes cold. Sickeningly merciless. This cannot be happening. I've already gone through so much. And finally, with Elio, I thought... I thought...

I thought that maybe I could one day learn to be happy.

"If I have to come over there and get you then you will lose a finger," Brigham says. "One for every second you keep me waiting."

He's not joking.

It's a silly, childish, self-pitying thought, but suddenly I'm on the verge of sobbing, thinking about not being able to play violin anymore. What will Elio think if his Songbird can't sing?

I won't wait to find out. Forcing my body into mindless, mechanical movement, I walk until I'm standing right in front of Brigham. The leer is back, and my insides liquify with fear when I see unmistakeable thickness at his groin.

"I said sit."

I spin like a ballerina in a box and then fall stiffly onto his knee, sitting as far forward on his leg as possible.

"Not like that."

He locks an arm around my waist and drags me forcefully back until I feel the nauseating press of his erection against my ass. My father looks away, face red. Bridget sips her drink as if this shit happens every day, and I wonder what it normally is that happens in this place for her to look so blasé.

I already know that I don't want to find out.

Brigham makes a horrific noise, something like an exhale of arousal that makes my hairs stand on end despite the warmth in here. He kneads fingers across the beaded bodice of my dress, moving downward, gathering the jagged edges of the skirt into his fists.

"I've had another man's wife before," he breathes against my neck, "but never on the actual wedding day." One of his hands dips beneath the layers of silk to my bare thigh, teasing upward until I'm sweating and gritting my teeth against the intense need to vomit.

Maybe I shouldn't fight the urge. Maybe I should just throw up all over him.

I almost do when a single finger nudges at the edge of my panties.

"Has your husband already had you here? I hope not. I'm rather a deft hand at deflowering virgins. But then again... I am intrigued. Let's see how well your husband trained you, shall we?"

I cry out as I'm suddenly shoved violently from Brigham's lap. I collapse into a clammy heap between his feet, panting, trying to get my bearings.

"You are going to suck me off," Brigham says, so cold and matter of fact that it's like he's reading me the weather report. "And don't even think about biting. The last one who tried that got all her teeth knocked out and I used her blood as lube."

"Elio will come for me," I say shakily. "If you hurt me, he will kill you."

The slap comes so fast and hard that I don't even have a chance to flinch away. Stars explode through my head, and they're so beautiful I want to chase them, to follow them into darkness.

I taste metal. I touch my lips and my fingertips come away slick and red.

"At this rate I'll have your blood as lube anyway." Brigham chuckles. "You can stop bluffing now. Elio Titone's heartlessness and lack of serious female attachments are legendary. He's never done anything for a woman who wasn't his own blood. I highly doubt he hasn't already hurt you himself and I truly do not believe he'll care if someone else does it. If he decides that he wants you back then he can come and pay for you and add a little extra on for all the trouble I've gone to retraining you for him. Now get back up onto your knees and suck."

The commands aren't all that different from ones I've heard before. Elio has forced me into his lap, told me to get down on my knees and suck him. But the experience is so vastly, terribly, inhumanly different from this one. With Elio, there's power and control. But there's also desire. And now, as toxic and twisted as it may be, love.

Here, with this man? In this room, my father turned away with cowardice and shame etched into his features like they've been carved there with a knife?

It's like I've fallen down a hole into Hell.

But I can make my way back out if I play my cards right. I have to survive long enough for Elio to find me.

For him to pull me out of the flames.

Resolve like hot lead in my guts, I straighten up. I place my hands on Brigham's knees, feeling the knobby bones, so different from Elio's thick muscularity. His dick is tenting the white crotch of his pants, and I stop and stare, suddenly unable to keep going. To do what I have to to live.

"I thought I told you," Brigham says, fisting my hair so much harder than Elio ever has until my eyes scrunch shut from pain, "to suck-"

There's a bright, dark, shadow-splitting sound. The grip in my hair goes instantly slack. Bridget lets out a piercing, drunken shriek, and my eyes fly open to discover why.

All I can see is that putrid erection right in front of my face.

I tear my eyes up and away from it to discover that that cock now belongs to a corpse. My breath lurching from my lungs, I rip my hands off of a dead man's knees, scooting backwards away on my ass as blood courses from a bullet-wound in the centre of his forehead.

Everything is happening so fast that I feel like my synapses aren't firing quickly enough to keep up. But then a single word cuts through all the noise, slicing past the storm in my head until everything falls quietly away.

"*Songbird.*"

I turn.

A lone man stands in the doorway to the room. He doesn't seem to fit into the airy warmth of this place. He's dressed in the heavy fabric of formal wear, thick leather gloves covering his hands. He's a looming silhouette of darkness, a blot of broad-shouldered ink, with eyes so lit by blackened rage that they look like dying stars.

I let out a sob and I reach a bleeding hand for my husband as he strides fearlessly into the sunlit depths of Hell.

Chapter 45

Elio

Caruso and Enzo were right. Taking the guards along with us instead of killing them turned out to be the correct move. The guard who came with Curse and me – Leon – not only knew exactly where his boss would be hanging out, but he also distracted the two bodyguards just outside the room. With both of them turned his way, trusting and unsuspicious as Leon called out a greeting, Curse and I moved in behind, slitting the two men's throats at the exact same moment.

Swift. Silent. Not a single sound of warning to be heard.

While Leon and Curse dealt with the bodies, I surged forward into the room.

Only to have my entire world implode at the sight of my wife on her fucking knees, shaking, her dress torn, her hands on another man's thighs.

I assumed I'd keep Brigham alive long enough that Curse could get a crack at him, Interrogate him a little. Torture him a *lot*.

But when I see him with his disgusting fucking fingers buried in the flames of her hair my hand rises like it's been drawn by a string.

Every nerve in my body blazes, every ounce of sensation pouring into my hand as I pull the fucking trigger.

Someone screams, but it's not Deirdre. For the first time I notice the other two in the room. A young woman with long brown hair.

And seated right next to her?

O'Malley.

Holy fuck. That bastard was sitting *right fucking there*. Didn't lift a finger to help his daughter.

Don't know why I expected any better.

I would go right to him, nail him to the fucking wall, if Deirdre's movements hadn't regained my attention. Her hands fly from the legs of the corpse, and she falls backwards onto her ass in her haste to get away from him.

"Songbird."

She tenses, then turns, and then I know I'm going to blow this fucking world apart, because somebody's fucking hit her. I sweep into the room with long, vicious strides, coming to crouch beside her. I tenderly cup her face, checking her head and scalp for injuries, but so far all I see is a very red cheek and a busted lip.

There's a sudden choke of relief in my throat. She's bleeding, but she's in one piece. My gaze flashes to Brigham, dead and slouching in his chair, and my mind goes white with fucking fury. If I had gotten here one minute fucking later...

But he's dead now, and he ain't getting any deader. I focus on my Songbird once more, running my hands down her shuddering shoulders until I reach her hands.

Her *bleeding* hands.

I hiss out a curse.

"Who," I ask, feeling like my heart is trying to batter its way out of my body, "did this to you?"

"I... I fell."

"And what about this?" I prod ever so gently at her bloodied lip. Tears spill from her eyes, and she points miserably over her shoulder, as if she can't stand to look at him again.

I already said that he ain't getting any deader.

Fuck that. He deserves a few more fucking holes.

I stand and aim my gun, letting off a volley of shots into the white-clad corpse. I bust open his belly, his chest, even fire off a few at the wilting shape of his foul fucking dick.

I hear another feminine scream, and turn just in time to see the woman – who I now realize is O'Malley's girlfriend, Bridget – sprint from the room. O'Malley, fucking prize that he is, tries to follow her.

"Not another fucking step, O'Malley."

He freezes, and I can see the way his shoulders are creeping up around his ears.

"Turn the fuck around," I tell him.

He doesn't. He's too afraid.

And that makes me so fucking angry that I cross to him in strides I don't even feel myself taking. I smash my pistol down against his shoulder, forcing him down to his knees. As he howls with pain and clutches his shoulder, I step around in front of him, standing between him and the door.

I stare down at him, gun cocked, and suddenly I'm not looking at O'Malley anymore but my own sack of shit papà. He was on his knees just like this at the end. He apologized over and over. Begged me for forgiveness.

O'Malley doesn't even manage that.

Instead, he throws Deirdre in my face, because she's always been his fucking shield and never the daughter he protects.

"You can't kill me, he whispers, voice shaking. "She'll hate you for it."

As if her hate could help him now.

"I know," I reply, because I have no doubt he's right. "But not as much as she'll hate you."

Maybe she's already started hating me, or gone back to hating me, or maybe she never really, truly stopped, even when she began loving me. Because she's started screaming at me like a banshee, her cry forming a raw shape around the syllables of my name.

She wants me to stop.

But what she wants has never been my priority. If I cared solely about what she wanted I never would have taken her in the first fucking place.

No. I care about what she *needs*.

And what my wife needs is a world without this piece of shit in it any longer.

I don't answer my wife's cries. I speak instead to her father.

"You forfeited your life the moment that you took my wife from me."

O'Malley's face pales so fast he looks like he's already dead.

Deirdre isn't just screaming my name now, but something else. Another word tacked on the end. "Elio, Elio, *don't!*"

"I love you, Songbird," I tell my wife as I press the barrel of my gun against her father's forehead. "And as your husband I will honour you and your wishes to the best of my ability. Starting tomorrow."

I slide my finger against the trigger and it feels so fucking good.

"You might want to close your eyes."

I'm saying it to Deirdre, but pathetic O'Malley is the one who actually does it, scrunching his eyes shut as if I'll disappear if he can't see me. One glance tells me that Deirdre's baby blues are wide fucking open. She's stopped screaming at me, her mouth tight and bloodless, her gaze glued to me, to her father, to the gun. Like she's searing this unholy trinity of violence into her brain. For half a second, I wish I'd taken her out of the room for this.

But I've always been a monster to her. She told me that herself.

Might as well prove her right. Let her see who her husband truly is.

Let her see what happens when anyone tries to take her from me.

And I have to hand it to her – she doesn't look away. Deirdre's eyes are blue fire. I can't tell if she's pleading or condemning.

She doesn't blink.

I'm not sure she even breathes.

But I do. And I speak. One last word for my father-in-law before he dies. And maybe not the one he expects.

"Thank you," I murmur to him, and I mean it, too. Because producing Deirdre was the greatest thing he ever fucking did and then he turned around and brought that treasure straight to my goddamn door. In a twisted way, I got my perfect bride because of him, and that deserves some small acknowledgment.

Even now.

Even if it's not enough to save him.

And so, less than twenty-four hours after I married her, as my wife looks on with those soulful, scorching eyes I love so much, I sweep my finger back against the trigger...

And I send a bullet straight through her father's head.

Chapter 46

Deirdre

As my father collapses to the floor, I know that he's dead. Yet I can't stop the question from bubbling up out of my throat, as if I need more confirmation than what my own eyes just saw.

"Did you... Did you kill him?"

"Yes." Elio steps over my father – my father's *body* – and crouches in front of me once more, tipping my chin up until my gaze is snapped away from the blood pooling beneath my father's head.

"What do you think I usually do to men who steal things from me?"

"I'm not a thing to be stolen," I whisper.

"No," he seethes, eyes flashing. "You're my wife. Which makes what he did infinitely fucking worse. He took you. And then he sat on that fucking couch and he *watched*."

He drags a vicious hand through his hair, revealing a crusted patch of dried blood at his temple. My hand trembles violently as I raise it to the bloodied place. Elio's eyes close, and a look of pain that I don't think is related to his head wound flickers over his features.

"We have to go," he murmurs, catching my fingers in his and opening his eyes. "It's time to go home with me, Songbird."

Home with him. Home with the man who killed my father. Home to a life I don't even know how to inhabit now.

Elio doesn't wait for me to stand up or answer. He scoops me up and carries me from the room. How many times has it been like this for us? Him carrying me through some kind of maelstrom into the dark, hushed safety of his cage beyond?

How many times will it happen again?

Elio gives instructions to someone, but I don't see who it is. I've turned my face into his lapel and my body doesn't know if it wants to vomit or sob, so I just hold myself shaking and silent against his chest.

"I'm going to get Caruso to take us back," Elio says above my hiding face. "You three stay here and clean up this fucking mess. There's a boat and lots of water out there. Go feed the fucking sharks."

"What about that girl," says the other person, and by the voice I think it's Curse. "Bridget. She ran off somewhere."

"I don't give a fuck about what happens to her," Elio snaps. "She can go find some new sugar daddy to leech off of or go starve in the fucking jungle for all I care. Just clean this place the fuck up, pay the staff enough to keep them fucking quiet, then get out."

"Understood."

With my face pressed into Elio's chest the way it is, I barely notice when we pass out of the house and into the sunshine. I feel it on me, but I don't see it. I don't even move when Elio carefully fastens a pair of protective earphones over my ears for a helicopter ride back out over the water. After that, we're in a car, then in a plane, then in a car again.

And then...

We're home.

Elio carries me inside, taking me all the way up the stairs to our bedroom. He spent an obsessive amount of time cleaning the wounds on my hands and knees on the flight back here, hunched over my body, vibrating with tense focus as he pulled little slivers out one by one. My palms and knees are freshly bandaged now, and I had ice pressed to my mouth for most of the drive here.

My skin is going to heal.

It's the rest of me I'm not so sure about.

He sets me down on the edge of the bed, passing into the other bedroom and then reappearing with a fluffy robe that he sets down. He doesn't speak as he bends over me and begins to undo the many minute fasteners on the back of my wedding gown. What's left of it, at least.

He peels the dress away from my back, rubbing the tips of his fingers into the red spots the dress has chafed me. So delicately, like he's handling an injured child, he peels one sleeve down my limp arm, then the other. Hooking one strong arm around my back, he lifts me just enough to slide the skirt out from under my bottom. Once it's off, he lets the whole thing fall to the floor.

I sit there and look at the dress crumpled on the floor, naked apart from my panties, and I begin to weep.

I don't ever remember crying like this. Maybe once, when they told me Mom was gone. Great, sucking sobs that make me feel like I'll never take in a real breath again.

I'm lifted up again, and this time when I'm set back down it's in Elio's lap. He presses the scarred side of his jaw against the top of my head, hushing me quietly, sliding his tender leather touch up and down my bare spine. And it feels so wrong, to crave comfort from him now. Now, when I watched him kill in front of me, for me, yet again.

But this time he wasn't killing some faceless soldier.

He killed my father.

"Did you know?" I choke out between strangled bouts of crying. "Did you know about the debt that killed my mother?"

His hand stills. Only for a moment. Resuming stroking, he quietly says, "Yes."

I cry even harder for a moment, not sure if what he just admitted should make me feel better or not.

"Were you ever going to tell me?"

"I don't know."

My father deserved to die.

But the guilt and the grief have got their vines winding hard around me now, and they're tight, and they're thorny, and I don't know how to pull them loose enough to look at this situation with anything close to closure.

Elio's hand feels so good on my back, but suddenly all I can see is his hand on that gun and the hatred in his eyes as he fires.

The vomit I've been holding back for so much of today suddenly comes rocketing out of me. Some of it gets on me, but I mostly just douse Elio's chest with it.

"I'm so sorry," I stammer, trying to wipe the horrible stuff off of his suit with my bare hands. Instantly, he seizes my wrists.

"Stop, Deirdre. Stop."

Once again he's carrying me, this time to the bathroom. He flicks on the light and the floor-heater with his elbow, then sets me gently on the counter, turning on the tap and tugging my hands beneath the warm stream of water.

"Not me," I whisper. "Elio, you're completely covered."

"I'll live," he says flatly, taking off the bandages he worked so hard on earlier so he can wash my hands anew. He removes his leather gloves, making sure not to lose track of the platinum wedding band, which he sets carefully aside.

"Oh, that reminds me," he says, focused on washing my hands and not looking at me. "I drafted a new will. Everything's yours once I'm gone. So if anything ever happens and you need access to it, you can find a copy with Gabriel Hades at *Hades, Mason & Gould.*"

"Don't say anymore," I beg him as he gingerly dries my hands with a clean towel. "Please. I can't think about you dying right now."

And I can't think about him taking care of me, either. I can't think of him in such sharp contrast to my father, who never did anything but put me in harm's way. First with the car accident, then selling me to Elio, then Bermuda. My father is dead now. I already know there's nothing left for me in his will, if he even has one at all.

And here Elio is, putting his physical health and his body on the line for me over and over again. Taking care of me so fucking dutifully that I'll be alright even once he's gone.

He's still trying to make this world safe for me. Even when he won't be in it.

"I really want to clean you off," I murmur miserably, lifting my hands ineffectually and then letting them drop onto my legs.

"No fucking way. Keep your hands clean. We've both seen the kind of shit a bad infection can do," Elio says. He picks up a cup from the counter and fills it with water. He brings it to my mouth. "Rinse."

I do, my mouth feeling painful and swollen, the water dribbling out messily into the sink as I lean over it.

"Now drink some of it."

"I can't," I moan, trying to push the cup away. But he just brings it right back up to my lips.

"*Drink.*"

My stomach rebels, but it feels good on my throat, and I end up drinking more than I expected I'd be capable of.

Once Elio is satisfied with that, he undresses until he's just in his underwear, depositing everything, including his gloves, into a foul-smelling pile on the floor. He works more soap and water between his hands, scrubbing the suds over his chest and under his arms before rinsing and roughly drying himself. He rinses his face and then leans his whole head down into the sink, letting the water soak through his strands. Some of the water turns dark as it rinses down.

"Your head," I say. I want to reach for him. I almost do it.

"I'll live," he says again as he rises slightly. He stays mostly bent over the sink, letting his hair drip moisture into the bowl of it before scrubbing his head with a towel.

"You need to see Doctor Morelli!"

"So do you," he says tensely. "I want to know exactly what they fucking did to you."

"They didn't... I mean... You got there in time. It was just my hands and my knees and..."

And my hands on his legs and his leer in my brain and his fingers so close to –

"*And?*" he demands, fixing me with a fierce stare.

"And some kind of sedative. I think. I don't remember much of how I got there." I reach up and touch the side of my neck. Elio softly bats my hand away, brushing hair back from my skin and swearing.

"I'm going to get Morelli here right now."

He turns to go, and catastrophic fear tears up my insides.

"Don't go!"

I grasp his arm between my hands.

The same arm that aimed the gun.

I instantly let go, just like he's burned me.

"I'm not going anywhere. I can fucking promise you that. I'm just getting my phone."

He digs around in his pile of clothes, finds it, and makes the call, speaking in Italian before hanging up.

"He'll be here momentarily. He's been busy since the shit that went down at the wedding."

"Oh, God, was anyone badly hurt?" I feel like I'm about to fall right off the counter. But thankfully, Elio shakes his head.

"Sounds like a couple people near the front had some lacerations from broken glass. Little things like that. Nothing serious."

"But you hit your head. That's serious!"

"Yeah, well. Maybe I deserve it after letting this happen to you. *Merda*, Deirdre, when everything was burning, when everything was falling the fuck apart and I realized that your hand wasn't in mine anymore..."

He bites off the end of his sentence, staring at the floor, jaw working.

"But you came for me," I remind him in a weak voice. "You found me."

And you killed my father.

"Yeah. But if I had been five fucking minutes later." His eyes slice to mine, and the rage is back. I can tell that it's burning a hole inside him.

Hounding him. Haunting him.

No infinite number of bullets can soothe a fury like that. He could shoot his way through this whole fucking world and still be angry enough to want to go back and kill the corpses.

I'm saved from thinking of something else to say by a sharp rap on the door.

"That's Morelli," Elio says. After he gingerly wipes my face and mouth with a clean wet cloth, he picks me up and carries me back to our bedroom, wrapping the fluffy robe around me and cinching the belt tight before opening the door.

Doctor Morelli's examination of me is quick, thorough, and surprisingly gentle. He gives me an encouraging smile, and then I remember that he's the father of two daughters around my age.

"Lots of rest," he tells me. "Lots of water. A little slow tomorrow – like a hangover. After that, OK."

"What about Elio?" I ask, barely listening to what he says about my condition. He examines Elio, shining a pen light into his eyes and checking the wound at Elio's temple. He straightens, and when he doesn't look too worried I breathe out heavily.

"Eh. He got a thick skull," Doctor Morelli says. "Mild concussion. Rest for him too."

He turns and says something to Elio in Italian.

"What is it?"

"He says we both need to just stay inside for the next two weeks," Elio mutters.

"That's fine with me," I sigh. I feel like I could sleep for two whole weeks.

In reality, though, I only sleep for about two days. Elio wakes me at intervals to drink some water and have some soup, but otherwise I'm dead to the world.

It's better that way. Easier. I want to burrow down into a warm, dark place and simply stay there.

Elio won't let me, though. On the morning of the third day being home, when I make no move to get out of bed, he picks me up and carries my boneless-feeling body into the shower. He sits me down on the tiles, and it reminds me so much of when I helped him shower after his fight with Darragh. Only, unlike me, he isn't all shy and confused and timid the way I was that day. He's almost domineering the way he hoses me down, lifting arms and legs and even scrubbing behind my ears.

He even dries my hair with the blow dryer after a few minutes of swearing while he tries to figure out the settings. He doesn't have a clue about brushes or styling products, so the result is that my hair looks like a fucking bonfire when he's done.

I don't care how it looks.

I can't even care about how it feels. It should feel nice to have clean, warm, dry hair. Especially when I'm too weak and depressed to make it happen myself.

But it just feels like... nothing.

After that, Elio seems to think it's his job to get me showered and dried and dressed for the day. After four more days of it, I can't handle it any longer, and I force myself to get out of bed and go shower myself. Elio supervises me as I do it, and there's a slight look of victory in his eyes, as if he's pleased that he's finally annoyed me into getting out of bed for myself.

His smugness doesn't last, though. When I emerge from my shower two days later, he grabs me by the arm and forces me to stop walking past him like I was trying to.

"Talk to me."

"About what?" I ask dully, attempting to tug myself out of his grip.

"About the fact that you haven't looked me in the eye in days.

671

About how you lie stiff as a board beside me in bed until you fall asleep." His hold on my arm is firm, but his hand at my jaw is gentle as he turns my gaze up to his. When he sees the tears there, he swears softly.

"I miss you," I say, trying not to cry. I need to have a day, just one fucking day, where I'm not crying.

"I'm right here," he tells me, his eyes searching.

"But you aren't! I can't. I..." I wipe furiously at my eyes, trying to put into words the jumble of contradictory emotions that have been chasing each other through me ever since our wedding.

"It's like... Every time I close my eyes, I see you killing my father," I stammer. "And even though he doesn't deserve it, I can't stop myself from grieving him. And then I feel confused by that, because how fucking pathetic am I to be sad about the man who caused me so much pain?"

Elio listens silently as words spew out of me like tears. I take a ragged breath and keep going, because now that I've started I can't fucking stop.

"I miss you because you're right in front of me and I feel like I can't get back to you! I feel like we'll never get back to how it was before."

Elio's eyes are so dark, so focused on my face. His expression draws tight when I whisper, "I don't know if we can get past this."

He exhales tightly and then lets go of my arm very slowly, like it takes a monumental effort.

"You can go back to hating me if you want to, Songbird. As long as you feel fucking something for me. I can work with that."

"I don't hate you, Elio." I hug myself, wishing he'd hug me and already knowing that I won't know what to do with the touch. "Sometimes I wish that I could hate you. Hating you was always so much easier."

"Good things are never easy, Songbird. Thought you would have learned that by now."

"Is loving you good?" I look up at him, and I'm not just being bitchy saying that. I'm sincerely asking him. Because loving him is the fiercest fucking thing I've ever felt, but I don't think I could ever call it truly good. It's poignant and profound and sometimes even poisonous. It defies morality, defies ethics and boundaries and everything I thought I knew.

It's ugly and messy, this love I have for him. It's hard and heavy and broken.

I think we might be broken too.

When Elio doesn't answer me, I feel a suffocating need to get away. Away from him, from this room, from everything. I hurl myself out into the hallway, running down the stairs, moving quickly and blindly through the house.

I know that he's behind me. He's always there, always watching, waiting to hurt me or love me or save me or drown me.

I don't even know where I'm going until I'm forced to stop because one more step will send me into the deep end of the indoor pool. I stand at the edge of the softly gleaming water, breathing hard, and before I even know what I'm doing I'm peeling off my clothing. I hear Elio enter behind me and swear when he sees what I'm doing. I turn around to see him fiddling with his phone, probably turning off the security feed to this room so none of his men will see me stripping down to nothing.

When I'm fully naked, I jump.

The water closes over me like the most familiar sort of comfort. As soon as my head's below the surface, I exhale, sending gurgling bubbles upward so that my body is heavy enough to sink to the bottom. I used to love doing this is a kid. Sitting at the bottom of a pool, just to see how long I could stand to stay there.

It's morning outside, and sun filters down through the water. Even at the bottom, it's not too dark. I keep my eyes open as my body burns with the lack of oxygen. I'll have to push off from the bottom and go back up soon.

I will. I know he's waiting for me.

But I guess Elio isn't content to wait, I've only counted to eighteen before the dark shape of him comes at me like a torpedo. He swims powerfully downward, grabbing my arms before he reorients himself in the water, getting his feet beneath him. Gripping me hard, he shoves off the bottom of the pool, and together we careen upwards until we break the surface.

He doesn't stop there. Swimming like a lifeguard, he hauls me to the shallow end. Once we've both got our feet underneath us, he backs me up against the side of the pool, caging me in with his body.

"Is loving me good?" he pants. "I don't fucking know. Probably not. But I do know that what we have is fucking real, Deirdre. And maybe real things don't have to be just good or just bad. They just have to be strong."

He holds up the sopping, gloved shape of his left hand. He's still fully clothed. His wedding band catches the light, a ring of bright purity contrasting with the darkness of the leather.

"You and me, Songbird? We are fucking platinum." He grabs my left hand, forcing his fingers between mine and then lifting it so that I'm confronted with my own rings. "We are diamond. We are *bound*. By blood and vows and your fucking soul fused to whatever's left of mine. So don't tell me we can't get past something. If I have to, I'll get past it for the both of us, and then I will fucking drag you right along with me."

The arrogance in that statement is almost laughable. Telling me that he will simply make me get over the way my father died in such confusing, traumatic circumstances.

And yet...

That brutal, unerring confidence makes me feel, for the first time in days, like maybe, just maybe, there could be a tiny little light at the end of this bleak tunnel.

We're not there yet. We probably aren't even close.

But Elio will fucking drag me there if he has to. He promised me he would.

And Elio never breaks his promises. Not the ones he makes to me.

With a cry, I throw my arms around his neck and plaster my wet mouth to his. He responds instantly, desperately, drawing my tongue into his mouth and groaning deeply. A hot, powerful shiver builds along my groin, and I suddenly feel more sensitive than I ever have in my life.

Elio's kisses are like those of a dying man. Like I'm his only oxygen. He bites and sucks along my lips, my cheek, my jaw, all the while tearing ferally at the zipper of his sodden pants. He shudders and I gasp, clutching at him when I feel his thick head press against my exposed flesh. He grips my ass and lifts me. The water makes me float, and I lock my legs around his back as he enters me with one terrible, perfect thrust.

He moves relentlessly within me, and I'm already there, already breathless with the urge to come. Everything is water and power and Elio and the hardness of him holding me up, holding me together. I've needed this, needed him, so fucking badly.

I think I'll always need him.

Elio's gaze pours into mine. Neither of us look away as white hot need builds inside the place our bodies meet.

Neither of us speak, either.

Because what is there left to say?

I love him. And maybe it's not easy.

Maybe it will never truly be alright.

But it is real. And it is so fucking strong.

I caress both sides of his face – the smooth and the scarred – and watch with tender, loving agony as his face buckles under the force of his need for me. He pumps harder and I sense that we're both close. Close to too many things at once. Pain and pleasure and a past we can't escape. This connection between us eviscerates. It burns me up and tears me down, building me into something shaped by him and only him.

A guttural sound flies from my throat. Elio's eyes and cheeks darken at the same time. His frame goes rock hard against mine, and one strained breath later he explodes at the same fraction of an instant that I let go into pulsing oblivion.

We grind frantically against each other, riding each other through our climaxes. I don't think either of us want this moment to end. It's a tiny slice of salvation for us both.

But it can't last forever.

"You're shivering," Elio murmurs against my wet throat. "Come on."

He carries me from the pool and sets me down on my feet near a shelf of towels, wrapping one around my shoulders and then placing another on top of my head like a hood. Once I'm thoroughly covered, he shucks out of his wet stuff, wrapping a towel around his hips and grabbing his phone from the tiles of the floor.

"Want a cup of tea?"

Who ever thought that a question like that would make me want to sob?

Overcome with emotion, I nod, and together we head into the kitchen.

When we get there, we both stop short when we see a large cardboard box on the granite island. After what happened at our wedding, seeing a strange package in an unexpected place is alarming, if not downright terrifying.

"It's OK," Elio says quickly, "All the mail goes to the gatehouse and it doesn't make it in here if it's not something safe." But even so, he approaches it slowly, narrowing his eyes at the writing on the label. His expression instantly relaxes.

"Well, that's good timing for the tea, I guess."

"What is it?" I ask as he grabs a knife and starts cutting the box open.

"This was supposed to be your wedding gift from me," he says, slicing tape and pulling tabs of cardboard. "But I had to send it to a master artisan in Japan. And it took longer than I thought to get it back."

He reaches into the box and pulls out something wrapped in a ton of bubble wrap. I watch, clutching my towels, entranced as the bubble wrap falls away layer by layer, revealing something that feels deeply familiar though I can't quite say why.

Not until the last layer is peeled away.

"It can't be," I whisper.

"It is," Elio says softly, watching me. "It's your mamma's teapot."

And it is. It really fucking is. Unbelievably, it's all in one piece again. The shape is exactly how I remember it – high and elegant with the most beautiful tapered spout. Even the painted flowers are just how they looked before, so tiny and beautiful that it almost hurts to look at them even though I can't make myself stop staring.

The only difference?

Veins of gold run through the entire piece, like living blood vessels. Every jagged piece of the teapot has been painstakingly fitted back against all the others, and they've all been sealed with shimmering metal.

And now I'm crying again, because it's so meaningful that it's shattering my heart and putting it back together again all at the same time. It's a sign that beautiful things can come from broken ones. And that sometimes the cracks are the things that make us what we are.

Nothing's ever perfect

But maybe everything can be mended.

Even us.

There will be scar tissue.

But sometimes it's the scars that truly shape the soul of a thing. Sometimes it's our scars that prove that we're alive.

"Don't cry," Elio says, setting the kettle to boil. "You just sit down like my good little Songbird. And I'll make you some tea."

Epilogue

1.5 years later

I shift in the hard wooden seat, tugging at the collar of my shirt. It's hot in here. There are a lot of bodies crammed into this big old University of Toronto hall. I stare over the heads of the other people in the audience. With her hair, Deirdre is easy to spot among the sea of arts students robed in black graduation gowns beside the stage. I don't like being so far away from her, even though I've got a good seat that's nice and close to the stage. But still. It makes me real fucking antsy.

But we won't be here for much longer. The woman behind the podium has already reached the T section of the alphabet. I keep my gaze glued to my wife as she slowly shuffles along in a line of fellow graduates, getting closer and closer to the stairs leading up to the stage.

Millicent Tan, Grayson Teague, Andrew Thacker, Grace Thornton...

Deirdre mounts the stairs, pausing at the top one as the woman at the podium beams and says, "Deirdre Titone."

Pride flares in my chest, and I clap loud and fucking hard, slamming the leather surface of my gloves together as my wife walks across the stage. She looks a little shy at first under all those lights as she takes her degree certificate and shakes an old man's hand. I've hired a pro photographer, so I don't worry about trying to take photos of my own. I just keep on clapping and watching her, so fucking proud I want to smack the back of the head of the guy next to me and say, *That's my fucking wife.*

I'm such a dopey, excited husband that I actually end up doing it. Not the smacking part. But I do lean over and tell first the guy on my right, then the woman on my left, that that right there, that beautiful little Songbird on the stage right now, is married to me.

She pauses while shaking the man's hand, looking out over the audience for the photo-op the way all the other students have done. Her eyes are darting around. Looking for me.

I stand up so she can see me, not caring whose view I block. Her gaze comes home, right to me, and her smile turns big and brilliant. Her shyness disappears, her chin rising, and it's like it's just me and her in the room. Kind of like when I used to watch her violin concerts.

Only she actually knows I'm in the audience this time.

Eventually the woman at the podium announces the next name, and Deirdre breaks eye contact and moves on, shaking two more sets of wrinkled hands before heading off the stage into a hall beyond for her school graduation photos.

I watch her disappear through that door, knowing Curse is stationed nearby and that she's safe. I sit down again, grinning, still feeling so fucking proud I don't know what to do with myself.

She really knuckled down to get back on track after our wedding and the events that followed. She completed all her spring exams and then worked her cute little ass off in her final year, with some gentle (or sometimes not-so-gentle) encouragement from her husband, of course.

She doesn't know it yet, but as soon as this is done I'm whisking her away to Europe. The honeymoon we never got to have. There's been too much shit to focus on here over the last year and a half, and we both just wanted to stay on home turf for a while.

But what am I waiting around here for now? I'm not going to sit on my ass for another thirty minutes until the lady on the stage reads the very last Z name. I stand once more, ignoring the mumbles of discontent as I slide past the other audience members in my row and head out the door.

It's time for me to go and get my wife.

Thank you so much for reading Deirdre and Elio's duet! This couple is very special to me and I'm so glad to share their story with you. If you want access to spicy Deirdre and Elio character art as well as a free bonus story about their honeymoon, subscribe to my newsletter at www.veroheath.com/contact-and-newsletter

Want more of the Titans and Tyrants series? Get Valentina's story in *A Game So Reckless!*

When the brutal leader of the Irish mob murders my fiancé in front of me, I suck the olive right out of my martini and start to choke. Mad Darragh could have left me there. He's sadistic, cruel, and just crazy enough to enjoy watching me suffocate.

But he doesn't. He hooks his fists beneath my ribs, pressing mercilessly. As I lose consciousness the last thing I hear is his voice:

"Every breath you breathe belongs to me now, pet."

Turns out he wants more than just my breath. He wants my hand in marriage.

And he's willing to break every rule in the book to get it.

Darragh doesn't know who he's up against. He may be a gambling man. He may only play for keeps...

But my name is Valentina Titone. And when I play, I play to win.

TITANS AND TYRANTS

www.ingramcontent.com/pod-product-compliance
Lightning Source LLC
Chambersburg PA
CBHW031018030726
47497CB00004B/902